# A DESPERATE MAN

# A DESPERATE MAN

## Claes G. Ryn

### A Novel

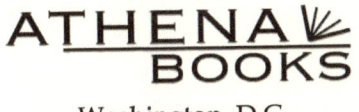
ATHENA BOOKS

Washington, D.C.

ISBN: 978-0-9887508-2-1

Printed in the United States of America

This is a work of fiction. Characters, names, places, and events are imaginary or are used fictitiously. Any resemblance to actual persons is coincidental.

*Men are qualified for civil liberty in exact proportion to their disposition to put moral chains upon their own appetites . . . . Society cannot exist unless a controlling power upon will and appetite be placed somewhere, and the less of it there is within, the more there must be without.*

*— Edmund Burke*

# A DESPERATE MAN

# CHAPTER 1

"Why is Dad so late?" Anne sounded more bored than annoyed.

"That's what I was wondering," her brother said. "First he wanted us to have a late lunch, and now he's late on top of that."

Their mother smiled at them. "Have a little patience," she said. "It's only 1:15. He'll be here any moment."

They were standing, three American tourists, on Champs-Élysées in Paris just a block away from the Arc de Triomphe. Helen Bittenberg, the mother, was an attractive brown-haired woman in her mid forties. She was soaking up the scene. It was a sunny day in early August. The sky was a deep blue and the air fresh, yet pleasantly warm. A downpour in the early morning had dispelled the heat and haze more typical for Paris in August. The city was at its most magnificent. Helen looked admiringly at the imposing Arc de Triomphe. Its architectural strictness and heaviness combined to pleasant aesthetic effect with the softness and color of the large, slowly waving French flag that hung under the arch. She closed her eyes and held her face up to the sun. It was a glorious day.

"One o'clock was late, and now it's twenty minutes past," Anne said and shrugged. She was on the verge of adolescence and prone to sulkiness. Her brother, John, had just turned fifteen. He was examining a map of Paris.

"I know, Sweetie," Helen said. "He's obviously been delayed by something. Paris is so full of tourists. Perhaps he took a cab and got stuck in traffic, or he took the subway and got lost down there."

Anne shot Helen a skeptical look under a lock of blond hair.

"Well," Helen tried again, "he probably left the library with too little time to spare. You know what he's like when he gets caught up in his research."

"You're getting closer now," Anne muttered.

"But he'll be here any second," Helen said. "Let's just enjoy the wait. We're in no hurry."

"Except we haven't had anything to eat since eight o'clock, remember," John said.

"You'll survive, Johnny. Enjoy the weather, enjoy the marvelous view!" She gave her son another smile. Considering his age, he was a patient tourist, she thought. He had been positively interested in some of the sights during the first three days of their European tour, which had been spent in Paris and vicinity. She had seen him clearly curious, even pensive, as when they walked through the halls of the Versailles and visited the Place de la Bastille, at one time the location of a prison for mental defectives, where the French Revolution is said to have started in 1789. Johnny was showing himself more and more his father's son, not merely in looks, she reflected. He had a deepening interest in history, and the sights of Paris fed his imagination. He was fascinated by the fact that these were the actual places mentioned in his books. When John had first seen Champs-Élysées the day before, he had recognized it from an old black-and-white documentary showing the entry of the Allies into Paris during World War II. Anne had also seemed to enjoy herself. She had shown no crankiness. That the children were happy made Helen's delight all the greater.

Helen did not want to admit to herself that she, too, was starting to feel impatient. Richard might have been more careful of the time. They had postponed lunch by an hour to give him the time to do a little research at the old Sorbonne University library. Helen knew well how preoccupied her professor husband could become when dealing with some intriguing bit of research, but now, during the family's vacation, he might have restrained his curiosity. Still, she was not going to show any annoyance at his tardiness. He would be apologetic as it was, and she was determined to make sure that he and the children had a wonderful time in Europe and that she enjoyed herself. This was going to be the perfect vacation. There would be no bad tempers. When they looked at the photographs from this trip they would all be smiling.

Their trip to Europe had started well, and the next ten days should be similar. The weather forecast spoke of no rain and moderate heat. They would not even have to feel rushed. Richard had miraculously agreed to take a full two weeks off. They would spend five days each in Paris and Rome and three on the road in between. Helen had planned the trip carefully to make it leisurely without boring the children. Because Richard had agreed to the trip just a few weeks earlier, it had not been easy to make convenient arrangements. Their choices for travel and accommodations had been more limited than if she had made the reservations six months earlier. The whole world, it seemed, wanted to be in Paris and Rome in the month of August. But all the pieces had finally fallen into place. As Helen envisioned the trip, there would not even be any temporary aggravations or uncertainties.

Helen could hardly believe that she and her family were together in France. How delightful it was and would continue to be for all of them! How relaxing it must be for Richard! She was pleased and cheerful. On a deeper plane she was thankful and happy. Could life be more generous to a person than it had been to her? She had all that she could possibly wish for.

Helen loved Paris. It was her fourth visit, but the children's first. She was curious about their reactions. The sun showed Paris's most famous street to advantage. Only the tourists marred Champs-Élysées for her. There were far too many of them. The hordes dutifully walking up and down the street crowded the wide sidewalks. Those sitting in the outdoor cafés and restaurants faced a wall of gawking passers-by. The Parisians did well to leave their city in August, she thought. What Paris must have been like before the crowds, before Americans in shorts, sneakers and baseball caps and before youngsters in T-shirts and rucksacks! Paris was built for an era of elegance, not for this invasion of misplaced, drifting, ignorant, blank-eyed visitors.

Helen's parents had brought her on various foreign trips when she was growing up, one of them to Paris. Her father had been a rather prominent journalist, a foreign correspondent for five years. Her mother was a translator of fiction in Spanish and Italian for various publishers. When Helen was in elementary school the family lived in Madrid and London. She and her elder sister had gone to American school in Madrid. As a junior at Mount Holyoke College in Massachusetts, Helen had spent a semester in Heidelberg, Germany, and had traveled in Europe and seen Paris for the second time. Her most recent visit to Paris had been a few days with Richard four years ago in connection with his giving a paper at a conference. Her parents had volunteered to look after the children. They stayed with the children in Helen and Richard's home in Washington, D.C., while Helen and Richard were gone. Helen knew German and Spanish rather well, but her French was poor. She had only studied it for two years, and her visits to France had all been brief.

Despite her 47 years, Helen turned male heads. Envious women, too, noticed her lean, well-shaped figure, which was enhanced by a posture that made one think of a dancer. She stood five feet seven. She wore semi-casual but stylish clothes. She had a short red jacket and a white blouse that showed off a beautiful neck, dark jeans-like slacks and moderately high-heeled brown shoes. In Paris you do not dress merely for comfort, she felt.

Her softly rectangular face was intriguing. A beauty expert might have graded her down because the two halves of her face seemed not quite to match. It was as if a skillful plastic surgeon had had to restore one side after an accident but had had difficulty achieving perfect symmetry. Beauty has been said to need a flaw to set it off, and in Helen's case the flaw was surely a part of the secret of her looks. She had striking brown eyes that spoke of a lively intelligence. They sat under thin eyebrows, the one a little higher than the other. Her well-shaped, slightly turned nose had lovely nostrils. Her lips were neither full nor thin, her teeth even.

Helen knew the effect of her smile on both men and women. Because she was friendly but not flirtatious, she used it sparingly with men. She wore light make-up. Her straight dark-brown hair, which reached not quite to the shoulders, was cut with flair and was thrown back at times over one ear. She had a light tan. She was a woman in her best years, perhaps more good-looking and interesting now than in her twenties.

It would have been hard to determine the nationality of her little group without hearing them speak. Helen could have been French, Italian, or even Spanish. Neither of her children wore baseball caps, shorts or sneakers. None of them chewed gum.

"When Dad comes, let's not give him a hard time," Helen said. "He'll be apologetic anyway."

Helen wanted Richard's vacation to be smooth as silk. He needed a period without aggravation. It had been difficult to bring the family's long-planned European trip to fruition. Richard seemed never to be able to find more than a few hours at a time for the family. A professor of history at National University in Washington, D.C., he lived at a pace that seemed to Helen to be distinctly non-scholarly. This pace had only become more hectic in recent years. She found it hard to understand how Richard managed, while handling a number of commitments in addition to his professorship, to do more serious and important scholarly research and writing than most of his colleagues. His field, intellectual history, which in his approach blended with philosophy, political science and other neighboring disciplines, did not even lend itself to easy writing and publication. Though a recognized expert on particular movements of the modern era, he was the opposite of the academic pedant whose articles and books have little theoretical import and are of interest to but a small group of experts. Richard's greatest strength was his ability to discern connections among historical phenomena and to identify important patterns. He was a philosophical historian, well-informed regarding specific historical developments, but primarily interested in how they shed light on the period in question and, by implication, the here and now. His thoughtful, careful scholarship made it all the more paradoxical that he should live as he did. He would fly around the U.S. and the world to give lectures or participate in conferences. Or he would rush around Washington in the morning and early afternoon, meeting people or going to a library or archive, only to arrive home to cloister himself in his study for several hours, sometimes late into the night. In the daytime, he would often leave home at the last moment to teach a class or hold office hours at the university, then return home and plunge himself deeply in reading and writing.

Occasionally Helen would knock on the door to his study in the basement of their Bethesda, Maryland, home and ask, "Richard, have you forgotten your class?" She would find him in the process of throwing together the material he needed for the course. He would leave the house in a rush, too late to have a leisurely drive. Helen never stopped worrying about his having a traffic accident. Only once or twice when she had asked him if he wasn't supposed to be going somewhere that day had she startled him; he had thanked her for the reminder and rushed to keep the appointment. She did not make it a habit to remind him of commitments known to her, because his schedule often changed on short notice. Though frequently running late, he was usually acutely aware of where he was supposed to be. She did not want to be perceived as a busybody. Often when she visited him in his study, which meant that she risked disturbing his concentration, she found him not reading or writing but on the telephone or at the copier and fax machine.

Helen could not understand how Richard found the peace of mind to do the kind of scholarship and writing for which he was known. In the last year she had started worrying about him. Just past fifty, he was and looked vigorous in an almost athletic way, but he had become increasingly rushed and preoccupied. He was supposed to be in decent health, but she worried that he was pushing himself too hard. He was getting wound too tight. Richard was a sometime jogger and tennis player, but his exercise was erratic. Though he was not putting on weight, the hour or two that he devoted to real exercise in a typical week was hardly sufficient. His bad cholesterol count and his blood pressure had been up at his most recent yearly physical. Their lovemaking had become irregular. Previously a sound sleeper, Richard had started waking up in the middle of the night. She sometimes heard him twisting and turning. Occasionally he got up and went downstairs to his study. In the last year she had begun fearing a breakdown of some kind. He tried hard, she knew, to seem relaxed when he was with her and the children, but she sensed that often he felt strong pressure to be elsewhere.

"Mom, it's 1:30. Were we really supposed to meet him here?"

"Of course we were, Annie. We talked about having lunch in one of these restaurants, remember?"

"OK, but he might've gotten mixed up."

The thought had crossed Helen's mind—Richard could be a little absent-minded when preoccupied with his research or writing—but no, they had discussed and settled on this particular spot. In fact, Richard had suggested it. He had wanted to spend a few hours in the library to check some facts for a book he was writing before meeting the family for lunch, and then they would go to the top of l'Arc de Triomphe. When he had left them after breakfast at their small hotel in the Latin Quarter he had said in a jokingly exaggerated American accent, "See you on Chaaamseliiizes." A fifth generation American but one with family connections in Europe and a flair for languages, Richard found the American way of pronouncing French amusing. The diphthongs that pervade especially American English wreaked havoc on the pronunciations of other languages.

"No, he knows exactly where we're supposed to meet." Helen felt a twinge of worry. Her thoughts had started to run in the direction of an accident or illness. She had worried for months about his having a heart attack or a stroke. If he had had one or the other or had been in a traffic accident and had been taken unconscious to a hospital, how would Helen and the children be able to find him?

But her good sense quickly reasserted itself. The most likely explanation for his being late was that he had come across some important material in the library that required a few minutes of extra work. Perhaps he needed to do some copying. Not having to go back to the library for a second day would save the whole family time. Or perhaps he had run into a fellow scholar with whom he just had to talk. He could not call Helen and the children to let them know that he was delayed. They had not bothered to get a cell phone that worked in Europe; in fact, Helen did not want them to have one. She wanted Richard to be out of reach of his ordinary world. They had not even brought a laptop computer. There was only one way for Richard to get in touch with the rest of his family: by leaving a message at their hotel or waiting for them there. Richard had an old friend from Harvard who was now at the American Embassy in Paris, but Richard had not even arranged a meeting with him. "Only if we have some time to spare," he had said.

"Let's just sit down at that nearest restaurant," Helen said to the children. "We can keep a lookout for him and order food. He won't mind."

They wanted a table from which they could see their meeting-spot and so had to wait to be seated. The waiter brought the menus.

"Why's he so late?" Annie tried again. She looked searchingly into Helen's face. John said nothing.

"I don't know, but I'm sure he'll show up any moment. Let's order." Helen was outwardly cheerful and unconcerned, and the children turned their minds to selecting their food.

When they had finished their meals, it was almost three o'clock. While giving the children reassuring possible explanations for Richard's absence, Helen had thought about what they should do next. Richard was not coming—if for no other reason than that he would not expect them to wait for him in this spot any longer. He would have gone to the hotel or left a message for them there. She should call the hotel. Luckily, she had a brochure about the hotel with the telephone number in her handbag.

Helen had never used a French pay phone, and she had no idea how to do it. Probably she had to insert a telephone card of some kind, but where did you buy one? And how did one use it? She dreaded asking to use a phone in the restaurant. In her experience, the French were not very friendly, especially not to outsiders, and they preferred being addressed in their own language. But the restaurant was not as busy as it had been an hour earlier, and she decided to try. She left the children at the table and walked inside. She asked a waiter for a telephone. In response she got that most French and unappealing of all responses, a shrug of unconcern and disinterest. A young woman was standing behind the podium where the restaurant received its indoor guests, and a telephone was next to her. The woman knew English, and Helen asked if she might use the phone for a brief call. The woman informed her that customers could not use this telephone. "I only need it for a minute," Helen pleaded. "My children and I have gotten separated from my husband. I'm trying to reach our hotel here in Paris." But her obvious concern made no difference.

An older woman, perhaps the manager, had overheard the conversation. She smiled at Helen, took the hotel brochure, dialed the number to the hotel, and gave her the receiver. Helen took it gratefully. The younger woman looked offended.

Helen recognized the voice of the man who answered at the hotel. It was the same bald, middle-aged man with a moustache who had registered them when they first arrived. She could see him at his post behind the counter in the small reception area of *Le Vieux Logis*. He knew English, but not well, and it took Helen a while to explain why she was calling. A family friend had recommended the hotel. It was in the Latin Quarter, a few blocks from the old Sorbonne University. It was small but rather charming. The rooms were tiny by American standards, but they had bathrooms and were adequate. They would have been much less comfortable, Helen knew, if the temperature had remained in the eighties, as was often the case in Paris in the middle of the summer. Making a reservation at a hotel without air conditioning had been taking a chance, but the price was half of what it would have been at a four star hotel. Instead Helen had taken two rooms, so that she and Richard could have some privacy. Because of the cool weather, the gamble had turned out well.

"*No, Madame*, I have no message from *Monsieur* Bittenberg."

"OK, then will you please call our room for me, room 38?"

"*Monsieur* not here, Madame."

"Please try anyway."

"*Oui, Madame*."

Helen heard eight rings before the man came on the line again. "*Madame*, no answer."

"Please try the children's room, number 37." Helen thought she heard a sigh at the other end.

"*Oui, Madame*."

There was no answer. For a few seconds Helen said nothing.

"*Merci, Monsieur*. If my husband gets back before we do, please let him know that we are returning to the hotel."

"*Oui, Madame*."

"*Merci*." Helen gave the receiver back to the woman in the restaurant, who had been listening without being obvious about it. "You are very kind," Helen said. The woman, reading the distress on Helen's face, gave her a sympathetic smile.

Back at the table, Helen tried not to seem worried. "Kids, we should get back to the hotel."

"Why?" Annie asked. "Is Dad there?"

"No, he's not back yet, but there's no point waiting for him here after all this time. Let's return to the hotel, have a rest, and wait for him there."

"But we were supposed to climb the Arch and see the view," John protested. "We could do that without Dad."

"Yes, but we can also come back tomorrow. Let's go."

They might have taken the subway to soak up more of the Paris atmosphere and learn how to negotiate the intricacies of the Metro. In the circumstances, the tensions of uncertainty mounting, Helen preferred hailing a cab.

She had to explain the location of their little hotel to the driver. Sitting shoulder to shoulder with her children in the back seat, she was starting to lose control over her imagination. Accident and illness had moved to the forefront of her mind. "Richard, I told you to slow down and to get more exercise!" she said to him silently. Or a car could have hit him.

For most of the ride John was quiet and seemingly unconcerned. Helen wondered if he understood her frame of mind and was supporting her acting for Annie's benefit. But then he looked into her face and asked, "Mom, where do you think he is?"

"I have no idea, Johnny, we'll just have to wait for him to tell us."

"What if Daddy never comes back?" Annie's voice gave blunt expression to what had passed through Helen's mind.

"Annie, dearest, there's nothing wrong with Daddy. He may be at the hotel when we get back, and after we've all had a rest we'll go to Montmartre as we planned. We'll have a good time, and then we'll find a nice restaurant for dinner."

Did they hear the uncertainty and fear in her voice?

# CHAPTER 2

Helen Bittenberg was right: her husband badly needed a vacation. But she did not know the nature and extent of his distress. Richard W. Bittenberg was utterly worn out, though not physically. He was at his wits' end. He was dejected.

He had driven himself hard for a long time. His teaching, writing, and other activities as a professor might by themselves have exhausted him, but it was his additional commitments and a grueling anguish at the bottom of his soul that had robbed him of inner peace. He had lived for a very long time with fears, which had gotten deeper each year, that the leaders of the United States were destroying the country he loved. His misery had been made worse by a feeling that there was little he could do to change America's course. Yet he had not been able to get away from a sense that he had a responsibility to try. But by doing *what*? To be doing *something* he had taken on a range of professional assignments for which he really did not have the time. Only dimly did he realize that he was distracting himself from his fears and generally ragged condition. Then, a year and a half ago, at a time when his sense of powerlessness had begun to take a heavy psychological toll, he had made a radical, momentous decision. Entirely unanticipated, the decision had fundamentally changed his life. It had reduced his frustrations, but had piled large and wearying responsibilities on top of the old ones. It had put him under new strains that were acute and unrelenting.

Helen had, in a way, been aware of what bothered her husband and how important it was to him, but she had not understood how deeply and persistently it assaulted him. He had hidden the big decision from her.

If Helen had been told that at the bottom of her husband's exhaustion was worry about the future of his country, she would have thought about his many expressions of just such a concern over the years, but she would not have regarded these worries as the ultimate explanation for his troubles. When people move toward some kind of personal crisis, she thought, it is not because of something like a concern about the state of their society or the world, but because something is wrong in their own lives.

What Helen did not realize was that to Richard the predicament of the United States and the Western world was a deeply personal, agonizing matter. He had felt progressively guilty about his inaction for a long time. He thought he understood better than most the seriousness of the state of his country, and yet he had not been able to do much to help avert disasters that he regarded as underway or as looming on the horizon.

What Helen thought she saw was a particularly bad case of overwork. Richard's worries about his country did not help, but they were, she assumed, secondary to the heart of his problem, which was that he always demanded too much of himself. This was a serious personal problem, to be sure, and one not easily solved, but the remedy was obvious: Richard had to set more reasonable goals for himself and reduce his stress.

But Richard's main problem was not his workload, oppressive though it sometimes was. He had lived through a prolonged existential crisis touching every dimension of his being. He had finally placed himself in a situation that changed his priorities and redirected his struggles with conscience, but also intensified his personal anguish, though in a new way, just as it increased his preoccupation with matters outside the family sphere in which Helen could observe him. Now the added responsibilities, fears and sometimes excruciating pressures had worn him out. They had left him depleted, even in despair.

Two years before their trip to Europe Richard and Helen had been sitting one Friday night at the kitchen table after dinner in their Washington area home. It was just a few weeks before the seemingly trivial events that would lead to the transformation of Richard's existence. Anne and John had gone to their rooms. Richard had decided that he would not try to escape into his basement study to get more writing done. He felt both physically and mentally tired. He wanted a break. He and Helen had talked noncommittally about seeing a movie in downtown Bethesda, but he lacked the energy and told her so. They remained at the table finishing what was left in their wine glasses.

"Richard, I'm really worried about you," Helen had suddenly said. Nothing in their conversation had introduced the topic, and she could tell that she had his attention. He looked at her, but without saying anything. She added: "You just have to do something to change your life."

"I know." He said the words in a sigh. There was in his manner not a trace of irritability or confrontation. It was as if he had been waiting for her to say what she had said and had been ready for it. His immediate, matter-of-fact reply took her by surprise. She had expected him to defend himself, at least nominally, and to deny that anything was basically wrong.

"You know!? Then why don't you try to find a way to reduce your commitments? You're trying to do the impossible."

"I suppose I should make some more time to relax and be with you and the kids."

"Richard, it would make such a big difference! It would even sharpen you up for the things you most want to do."

"You're probably right."

No resistance, she thought. What had happened?

"Darling Richard, you don't know how glad I am to hear you say that." She got up from her chair and put her arms around his head and neck. "I have been so worried about you." He looked into her face, and he could see from the moisture coming into her eyes the depth of her caring.

"I wish it were as simple as to turn down various requests and invitations."

"What do you mean?"

"Work is not the only trouble. What's really wearing me out is something else."

"What do you mean?" Helen was puzzled.

"Well, you know how worried I am about our country."

"Of course I know."

"But I really mean it, and it's eating at me."

"Oh, Richard, I know about that, but once you have taken some of the pressure off yourself, you will feel differently. You'll see. The problems you're talking about won't go away, I know, but after you've reduced your commitments and gotten into a more relaxed frame of mind, you'll feel better all around. You'll have a different sense of balance and proportion, I know it. The problems you're thinking about won't loom so large. Just you wait and see."

"Helen, you seem to think I'm a little off my rocker from overwork." A touch of irritation had crept into his voice that was modified only by a crooked smile. His words told her that she had strayed into an area where he was touchier than she knew.

"No, of course not, Richard. You're one of the sanest men I know." She did not say that at times she worried that his often hectic pace, his rushed, forced and nervous manner, might show a touch of neurosis. "You just exaggerate a little every once in a while," she continued, "and you work yourself up unnecessarily."

The conversation had ended, leaving Helen with the feeling that she could have handled herself better. But she noticed in the coming months that Richard seemed a little more prone to turn down invitations to write articles or to lecture out of town, but there was no discernible change in his air of preoccupation. She continued to worry, but was at a loss for what to do.

If she had been the manipulative, controlling type, she might have tried to steer his actions by applying psychological-emotional pressure. She could have adopted some version of the role of the martyr, become the long-suffering wife of a workaholic. By various more or less subtle means she might have made her husband feel vaguely miserable whenever he strayed from the course of action she deemed suitable. She could have inflicted on him countless little stings and pointed moods. But she did not want to add to his discomfort. She wanted to help defuse it. She might have to resort to some kind of tough love, she thought, but she realized that female martyrdom, that nagging, self-indulgent power play, was certain to be counterproductive with Richard. It would only make him less inclined to be with her. She would rather have him be preoccupied with his work and be genuinely affectionate when he did spend time with her than blackmail him into giving her more frequent but also grudging, even resentful attention. What man likes to pay his respects to a woman in order to preempt emotional retaliation?

The roots of Richard W. Bittenberg's problem were actually just as he had told her. Even when he was a young man the predominant cultural and social trends in America had made him uncomfortable. He had felt old and staid as compared to his friends because he resisted what they seemed to accept or take in stride. The United States seemed to him to be moving inexorably away from what he most admired about it. Observing the evolution of American popular culture and the changing attitudes of people of supposed sophistication who set the standard for the rest, it looked to him as if America was turning its back on its traditional ways and virtues, the kind that had been both represented and admired by that marvelous breed of people who set America on its course in the eighteenth century. He tried telling himself that he was not sufficiently receptive to what was good about the new America and that it made up for what was being lost, but his disgust with some current trends and his dread about the future always reasserted themselves. After becoming a father he had begun to ask himself just what life in America would be like, concretely, for his children by the time they had reached adulthood and had children of their own. The future looked bleak. He found little to alleviate his fears. With time they merely intensified.

He could never have predicted the sharp turn that his life had eventually taken, but he could see in hindsight that his anxieties and desire to act had driven him almost inevitably towards a fundamental change of course. The change had relieved some of his disquiet and restlessness. It had provided an outlet for his pent-up desire actually to *do* something, but it had given him daunting new obligations as well as new, more severe anxieties and a nervous tension that only got worse. The redirection of his existence had been all the more taxing in that he had had to try to appear to be still the same person as before. Helen had sensed the growing pain of his predicament, but had only a limited, blurry awareness of its origin. A few weeks before the Bittenberg family's departure for France the pressures had brought Richard Bittenberg to the point of collapse.

# CHAPTER 3

Helen and the children were back at hotel *Le Vieux Logis* at 3:30 in the afternoon. Helen walked up to the reception desk with forced calm. The bald middle-aged man with a mustache was still at his post.

"Did my husband return?"

"*Non, Madame.* Not here. The key *ici.*"

"Any message for us?"

"*Non, Madame.*" The man took down the keys to their rooms from the wall behind him and handed them to her. They were of the old-fashioned type and were attached to a heavy, bulky knob. The management wanted the residents of the hotel to leave their keys in the reception when leaving the hotel.

In the tiny elevator she found herself thinking that perhaps there was a second key, that Richard had forgotten to leave it at the hotel, and that he had returned to the hotel when the man at the counter was answering a call of nature or making a delivery. Richard would be waiting in their room. She was being silly, she knew. Besides, Richard disliked filling his pockets. He would never have left the hotel with a key attached to a heavy and unwieldy object. She swallowed.

Their room was empty. Helen followed the children to their room next door.

"Well," she said cheerfully, "we'll just have to wait a little. Why don't you rest for a while and watch some TV. I'll let you know when Dad's back."

"Mom, the TV's no good — look at this small, blurry picture — and even the American shows are in French," Anne said.

"OK, dear, just rest then."

Helen was surprised that they let her go. She returned to her and Richard's room. Having closed the door behind her, she put her back against it as if needing support or as if trying to keep something out. She drew a deep breath. She could no longer hold back the feelings of dread that she had managed to hide in front of the children. A wave of shearing anxiety passed through her. She put her hands across her face. She knew that something was very wrong. If some urgent business had come up and Richard had known that he would be substantially delayed, he would not have waited to leave a message for them at the hotel, their one point of contact.

Helen fought not to give in to emotion. She had to collect herself. She sat down on the bed trying to concentrate, then got up and started pacing in the small available space. She glanced at the telephone. Should she not be making calls? But where? And how did one use the telephone in an old French hotel? How did you get an outside line, how did you find a telephone number? She looked through the room for a telephone book, but did not find one. Perhaps the Paris phone book would take up too much space in a room of this size. How could she get directory assistance?

But where would she call? She was now convinced that Richard had had an accident or fallen ill. The thought terrified her. He might even be dead of a stroke or a heart attack. If he was alive and conscious in some hospital, he would have asked someone to leave a message for his family at the hotel. If he had been taken unconscious to a hospital, it should not take the personnel long to learn who he was by looking in his wallet. His passport was in the hotel safe with those of the rest of the family. Having once had a passport stolen while traveling, Richard wanted to minimize the danger of one of them losing a passport when they did not need to carry one. But he had his driver's license, Triple A card, and credit cards. They should make it obvious to anyone that he was an American. Any phone numbers they might find would be to people in the United States. Had he perhaps written down the telephone number to the hotel? If they found it without any identifying marks, would they try calling? Would it occur to anybody that this American might have a spouse or family waiting for him in Paris? Would he have brought with him a brochure for the hotel? Probably not. He was always trying not to stuff his pockets.

But suppose he had brought the hotel brochure — did it list an email address? Helen looked at the brochure she had and found both an email and an Internet address. She felt a surge of hope. If Richard had been near a computer, perhaps he had found it more convenient to send a message by email than to go in search of a pay telephone a telephone card, or the right coins. No, it was unlikely. When it mattered, he played it safe. He had no way of knowing whether email messages were checked continuously at their old-fashioned little hotel or whether its computer was even on all the time. Helen lifted the telephone receiver and dialed the reception. The same man answered. She was able to make him understand her question about a possible email from her husband.

"*Madame,* for this I have checked when you call first time.

*Un moment, s'il vous plait,* I see again." Helen could not remember a computer screen in the small space behind the counter. The man must be ducking into the room behind the reception. His voice came on the line within seconds.

"*Non, Madame,* nothing for you."

"*Merci,* Monsieur." She replaced the receiver.

She sat looking at the telephone, thinking again that she should start making use of her main contact with the world. But where to call?

"Of, course!" Helen said aloud. When people at a hospital or a police station figured out that Richard was an American, they would call the American Embassy! Would they not let the consular section track down his next of kin?

Helen spent the next several minutes finding out how to make outside telephone calls from her room. She had to consult the man in the reception more than once, and he started to sound a little irritated. Yes, there was a telephone directory in the reception, he told her, and she was welcome to use it, but she could not remove it from its place. She finally managed to get through to directory assistance. The operator spoke little English, but Helen employed her own halting French to get the information she needed. She could finally dial the number to the U.S. Embassy.

As she listened to the signals she realized that she could no longer hide the truth from herself: Something was badly wrong.

By the time Helen got through to the American Embassy it was 4:30 PM. Three hours had passed since Richard failed to meet his family for lunch on Champs-Élysées. She listened through a lengthy telephone menu. None of the choices quite matched her business. A receptionist finally picked up. Helen stated her business succinctly.

"I'll connect you with the consular section," the woman said.

There was another telephone menu and a long wait before another female voice came on the line. Again Helen gave the reason for her call.

"Please hold."

A third woman answered, and Helen repeated her business.

"Let me see if Mr. Warner is still here. Please wait." The line went dead. Helen wondered if she had been put on hold or had been disconnected. Sounds on the telephone were different in France. About two minutes went by. She was resigned to hanging up and calling again when a male voice came on.

"Warner. May I help you?" The man seemed rushed or out of breath. He sounded middle aged or younger.

Helen introduced herself and told her story. Warner asked

for additional information. She could tell that he was taking notes. Helen thought she detected a Boston accent.

"Have you had any calls about my husband?" Helen asked.

"Not that I know," Warner answered. "Let me check." Helen could hear him talking to someone. He was back on the telephone in less than half a minute.

"Mrs. Bittenberg?"

"Yes."

"We have no record of any call to the consular section from or about your husband."

"Could a message have been left in some other section of the embassy?"

"That's unlikely, Mrs. Bittenberg. Any message of this type would have been passed on to us."

"Are you sure?"

"Ma' am, we have procedures for this kind of thing. There's no record of any telephone call or other message."

In one part of herself Helen felt relief. In another part she felt downhearted and lost. The uncertainty was becoming unbearable.

"Mrs. Bittenberg, when did you say you were supposed to meet your husband?"

Helen told him again and gave the reasons why there could not have been any misunderstanding between her and her husband. She repeated that Richard had not contacted their hotel.

"Mrs. Bittenberg, I can understand that you are worried, but you do realize that it's only been a few hours since your husband failed to show up."

"I do realize that, but I'm certain now that something's wrong."

"Let's hope not," Warner said. "Do give this matter some more time. There are plenty of possible harmless explanations for your husband's absence. If somebody should contact the consulate about your husband, we have your telephone number at the hotel. Don't worry, I'll put the information you gave me into our computer system. The embassy and consulate are closing for the weekend now, but there's an emergency number for after hours, and a consular officer is always on call."

Helen had completely forgotten that it was Friday afternoon.

"Thank you, Mr. Warner," she said.

"You're welcome."

They hung up.

Talking to another person, an American, had provided distraction and some relief, a return to normalcy. It had pulled her out of her darkening frame of mind. Warner had been both polite and understanding. He had not tried to brush her off. He had been sensible and considerate. Yes, Warner was right. She really ought to try to stay calm. There were undoubtedly many explanations other than an accident or a health problem for their not having heard from Richard; she just hadn't thought of them yet. What explanations there can be for people who are tardy or do not show up! She and the children might all be laughing at dinner when they talked to Richard about what had happened and how they had misunderstood each other. They would tell him how terribly worried they had been and enjoy themselves all the more for having had such a scare. They would be happy together again.

But Helen believed none of what she was telling herself. In her heart of hearts she was despondent.

# CHAPTER 4

Richard Bittenberg often asked himself why he was so different from many of his fellow Americans. Why was he out of step with the general trends of his country? He had arrived at no definite answer, but was certain that his personal history, especially his family background and life in the community in which he had grown up, had predisposed him to particular beliefs and behaviors at least as much as his systematic reflection on the state of America and the Western world. He did not think that the lives of individuals are determined or fated — he was convinced to the contrary that human beings made their own lives through their choices — but at every juncture, previous events and experiences color a persons sense of reality and incline the person in one direction or the other. Though free in every moment to choose, the person's past, including, most generally, membership in a certain culture, influences the present. When Richard tried to explain to himself why he had come to feel so acutely that his country was headed for disaster and that he had a special obligation to do something about it, he was always drawn back into his own history. The explanation for his anguish regarding the state of America lay in large part, he thought, in attitudes that he had formed in interaction with members of his own family and local community. He was led back to Charleston, South Carolina.

Though now a resident of Washington, D.C., Richard still thought of Charleston as home. Most of his closer relatives, including his mother, brother and sister, lived in Charleston. Some of them had lived in other places in America or outside the United States, but had returned. Richard's paternal grandfather, William, had been a diplomat and lived much abroad. Some of the Bittenbergs had contacts with relatives in Germany. Yet the American Bittenbergs all considered Charleston the family home. They gathered there for the big holidays or for engagements, christenings, weddings, and funerals.

The first Bittenberg in America, Wolfgang, was a young naval architect who settled in Charleston a few years before the outbreak of the Civil War. He had left his home city of Hamburg, Germany, after a family rift. Wolfgang eventually became a partner in a South Carolina shipbuilding business. Having been virtually ruined by the outcome of the Civil War, he became modestly successful not in shipbuilding but in shipping. He married the daughter of a Charleston cotton merchant. One of their sons, Bernhard, was Richard W. Bittenberg's paternal great grandfather. Bernhard, who was an army officer, married a member of the soon to disappear planters class. He was a lieutenant colonel when he was sent to Europe to fight in the Great War.

Most of the American Bittenbergs felt that America had had no business entering the war. This was a European conflict. It seemed to these Bittenbergs that forces that were less national than international were trying to get America into the war. There was much talk among the Bittenbergs about the fact that members of the German branch of the family, the *von* Bittenbergs, members of the lower nobility from northern Germany, were fighting on the other side. One was a general in the cavalry. Bernhard lost much of a leg in the war and almost died. Upon returning to Charleston, he joined an elder brother in the shipping business that their father had started. Called "the colonel" for the rest of his life, his pronounced limp on a prosthesis was a reminder to all of his military past. He achieved a reputation for great rectitude and personal dignity. Richard heard from relatives that "the colonel" had regarded the harsh peace terms imposed on Germany as ungentlemanly and dishonorable and likely soon to spark renewed conflict in Europe.

The Bittenberg shipping business was modestly successful until the Great Depression almost bankrupted it. Bernhard's youngest son, William, would be Richard's paternal grandfather. He studied at the University of Virginia. William married Julie Ashworth, the daughter of a professor of history at the Citadel, Charleston's military academy. They had a daughter and two sons, the younger of whom, Peter, became Richard's father. William's diplomatic career brought his family to several countries as well as Washington, D.C., where he had three tours. The family's connection with Charleston sometimes became tenuous, but he and Julie continued to think of his childhood home on Rutledge Avenue, near Colonial Lake in the southern part of Charleston, as his real home in America. After the death of Bernhard and his wife in the mid 1950s, William and Julie were able, with difficulty, to take over his parents' house by buying out his siblings. Having rented out the house for a decade, William and Julie took up residence in it after his retirement from the Foreign Service.

Peter's older brother was a successful lawyer. His younger sister, Ruth, who briefly considered getting a doctorate in art, married a Charleston banker and devoted much of her free time to promoting the heritage and restoration of the city. Like his siblings, Peter had received much of his schooling in the cities abroad where his father was posted, including Vienna and Rio de Janeiro. In the early 1930s, when his father was stationed at the U.S. State Department in Washington, D.C., Peter spent two years at St. Alban's School for Boys on Mount St. Albans in the shadow of the Washington National Cathedral then under construction. Though signs of the Great Depression were everywhere, the Bittenberg children felt safe and comfortable. The family rented a small house not far from St. Alban's School. Peter understood from conversations between his parents that he overheard that, even with the assistance of the State Department, expenses for the education of the three children were a heavy burden. Peter's brother was at Princeton. Ruth went for a year to the Cathedral School for girls near St. Alban's. Both Peter and Ruth could walk to school. The William Bittenbergs exhausted their modest independent means. As the shipping business of William's father and uncle was struggling in the throes of the Great Depression, his father could offer only modest financial assistance.

During Peter's senior year in high school, his father learned that he would be sent to China. As Peter had formed no definite idea of what kind of future he wanted, his parents urged him to consider going to the Citadel in Charleston, partly so that he could be near relatives. Peter had never seriously considered becoming an officer, but the prospect was not entirely unappealing. The Citadel offered him a generous fellowship, which settled the matter. The William Bittenbergs had previously maintained contact with family in Charleston mostly by attending funerals or weddings and visiting for holidays or in the summer. Though Peter resided at the Citadel during the semesters, he saw much of many of the Bittenbergs. He became close to his grandmother Annabelle, who told him about the days of reconstruction and the ways of the Old South.

Peter was more prone to academics than to the practical side of the military subjects, but was good at both. He was long uncertain of his future but was drawn to medicine. After receiving an Army recruitment brochure he decided to apply to become an Army physician. He thought he might like to be a surgeon. When Americans his age, including some from his graduating class at the Citadel, had started dying in Europe, he was in medical school, much of the time in Charleston.

The Bittenbergs had initially opposed efforts to get America involved in yet another European conflict. They were reminded of "the colonel's" view that the way in which the First World War had been ended set the stage for another war. It seemed to many of the

Bittenbergs that forces behind the scenes were again outmaneuvering strong and widespread opposition to American entry into a foreign conflict. The Japanese attack on Pearl Harbor changed the terms of debate, produced a surge of patriotism, and pushed reservations about American involvement in Europe into the background.

While in medical school Peter Bittenberg met Hannah Chambers, a slender dark-haired woman with strong intellectual interests, whose parents were descended from Charleston aristocracy but had only modest financial means. Her parents had moved to a different part of the state before she got to know Peter. Hanna had become the subject of some social controversy by getting a B.A. "up north," at Radcliff, in Boston of all places, and by taking a job at one of the Charleston newspapers. She was known to harbor "progressive" views on the race issue. Hannah and Peter were engaged three months after their first date and were married two months later, the week after Peter received his M.D. degree. He was about to start the protracted residency that would qualify him to practice medicine independently. Peter and Hannah had every reason to expect that Peter would be shipped to Europe at the first opportunity. She wanted them to be man and wife before his time came. They had a truncated, pared down wartime wedding in Charleston. William and Julie were in attendance but left just days later for Brazil, where William was to take up a new diplomatic post. The honeymoon of the newlyweds was three days in Savannah, Georgia. Four weeks after the wedding Peter was ordered to Norfolk, Virginia and was shipped to France. The Normandy invasion had just taken place. Hannah stayed with her parents in Soth Carolina.

Many years later Peter Bittenberg would tell his son Richard of some of his wartime experiences. He would do so in a subdued almost reluctant manner that conveyed to Richard the pain associated with those memories. A few of his stories would make a deep impression on Richard.

Though an M.D., Peter was far from a licensed surgeon when he arrived in Europe. He was supposed to assist other, more experienced doctors and be directed by them. In France Peter was assigned to field hospitals near the front where working conditions were sometimes very difficult. When a large number of soldiers with life-threatening injuries demanded immediate attention, normal rules and routines simply broke down. Because of frequently chaotic circumstances and a workload that sometimes overwhelmed his superiors, it repeatedly fell to Peter to assume responsibility for badly injured soldiers and to make medical decisions for which he was not really qualified.

Peter's surgical training had placed much emphasis on battlefield injuries, but his intended role was to stabilize patients so that others could attend to them later. Yet some of the soldiers brought to him in connection with battles were so seriously wounded that there was not time to transport them to an operating theatre elsewhere. Death had to be kept at bay here and now. Often the surgeons already had their hands full with equally urgent cases. Having had a dreadfully wounded soldier thrust upon him, Richard felt compelled in the middle of terrible commotion, the screams of the wounded, and an almost deafening din to interrupt his commanding officer, who was dealing with the gaping wounds of two other soldiers at the same time, to ask him what to do. In response he received an angry glance and a barked order:

"You handle it, Bittenberg, can't you see I'm busy?"

"But—"

"Dammit, captain, get on with it!"

God help me, he cried inwardly.

Peter had to attempt very difficult operations on the spot, with poor lighting, insufficient equipment, constant disruptions, and sometimes with only a medical orderly to assist. Hygienic conditions could be appalling. Some of the injuries brought to him defied his theoretical learning and were wholly outside his limited practical experience. He had to make daring guesses and decisions and improvise procedures. His continuing medical training became a learning by doing and too often a learning by his mistakes. In moments when the pressure of work lessened and Peter had some time to reflect on his situation a sharp sense of inadequacy assaulted him. He realized with agonizing clarity that his inexpert actions had cost patients their lives.

Once after a grueling straight ten hours in the large ramshackle tent that was the field hospital, he staggered outside for a breath of fresh air. It was an early morning in late September somewhere in northeastern France. Low sunrays were beginning to find their way through the trees surrounding the tent. The morning air was crisp. The sky peeping through the branches was a deep blue. Though he could hear the rumble of guns in the distance, he felt that he had entered a world wholly different from the chaotic, noisy one that he had left. The intense pressures seemed to lift. The scene outside the tent was almost serene. But the feeling of relief and peace proved transitory. Within moments reflections on his predicament flooded his mind. He was in an impossible situation. The enormity of it hit him with full force.

Thirty yards away he saw his commanding officer, Colonel

Billick, leaning against a tree and smoking a cigarette. Billick was a tall, heavy-set man with a balding head. His white scrubs were stained with blood. Peter knew he had to talk to him. Weeks of agonizing about his own inadequacy burst to the surface, and he walked up to the big, burly physician.

"Colonel, sir! May I have a word?"

Billick turned his head wearily in his direction. His face was drawn and haggard. "Sure, son, what's on your mind?"

All of Peter's distress welled out. "You see, sir, sometimes I'm really out of my depth in that tent. I think I've made some terrible mistakes."

"Don't you think I know that?" Billick's voice was not unkind but had a touch of impatience. "We're in the middle of a war here, captain. This is not Boston General. We do as well as we can in the circumstances. There's no other choice. Besides, we all make mistakes." The colonel drew deeply from his cigarette.

"But I'm not really a surgeon yet, sir."

"Captain Bittenberg, would you rather have the nurses or orderlies try to patch up our wounded? Should we let those poor wretches suffocate in their own blood and vomit or let them bleed to death while we wait for a properly qualified surgeon to take care of them?"

"No, sir."

"Then remember this!" Colonel Billick turned his entire body in Peter's direction. He looked into Peter's eyes and held his gaze as he continued. "The people you treat have at least a chance of surviving. That's more than can be said of the ones we can't get to in time. And the ones you treat who do survive have you to thank for their lives."

"I suppose so, sir."

"Did you hear what I just said?"

"That those who survive have me to thank for their lives."

"But are you *hearing* me, captain?" The colonel had raised his voice.

"Yes, sir, colonel, sir! I think so."

"*You make do with what you've got!* That's all you *can* do!"

"Yes, sir."

"And, son, let me tell you—considering the circumstances, you are doing pretty darn well. You've saved many lives."

"Thank you, sir."

*You do as well as you can with what you've got*—that was how Peter would sum up the colonel's words in years to come. He would teach his children and others the same thing. He thought of the colonel's admonition as "Billick's principle."

The colonel's words had an almost immediate effect on Peter. They took the sting out of his agony. He was actually doing the very best he could in given circumstances, which included his own limited experience as a surgeon. Sometimes nobody was available to take over for him. In the next several days Peter started to feel better. The desperation that had gnawed at him started to fade away. He hated his own shortcomings and could not forget the faces of the poor, suffering youngsters, most of them just a few years younger than he, who died in spite of his best efforts. Could he have done better? In ideal circumstances, yes, but this was real life, this was inexperienced captain Bittenberg, and this was war.

One day during a shelling barrage that was directed against advancing American forces a few miles ahead a stray shell almost ended Peter's life. It exploded just thirty yards from Peter as he moved among wounded soldiers placed outside the hospital tent. He was trying to decide which of them needed help most urgently. Two orderlies and several wounded soldiers nearer the exploding shell were blown to pieces. Two big trees between Peter and the explosion deflected some of the blast, but he was thrown to the ground, and a small piece of shrapnel tore into the side of his left thigh. For a moment he lost consciousness. He bled profusely but no major artery was cut. He could see that his injury was not immediately life threatening. He was able to stem most of the flow of blood himself by pressing just above the wound. He asked for some bandages and used his belt as a tourniquet. He could not rank himself very high on the priority list. The shrapnel was eventually removed by one of the junior doctors, and he was stitched up. He was offered to spend a week behind the front in a proper hospital, but he declined. He spent a day in his own portable bed, sleeping for the better part of 24 hours. After doing light duty with his injured leg up for a couple of days, he returned to regular duty. He received a medal for having been wounded in battle. Later he received another medal and commendations for his service as a doctor.

Toward the end of the war, Peter Bittenberg worked at a military hospital in western Germany. After the many months in the field, the frequent moves, the unpredictability of battle, the sometimes almost unbearable strain of the work, the mud, the stench, the heat or the cold, working in a regular hospital was like being on an extended vacation. The orderliness of hospital routines, the cleanliness, the availability of instruments and medicines, the regularity of shifts, and the time off felt almost unreal.

Just before V-E Day Peter was transferred to a military

hospital specializing in reconstructive surgery located in the city of Wiesbaden in southwestern Germany near the Rhine River. It had been largely untouched by the war. It was like an oasis, an exception to ordinary life, a reminder of a normal existence that he had virtually forgotten. As part of his medical rotation he also served in different departments of a general hospital in the same town that was run by the American occupying forces.

Peter could have requested a transfer back to the United States, but Hannah had written to him before the armistice saying that, if possible, she would like to join him in Europe before he returned home — an unexpected wish that he initially resisted. But she wanted to share with him at least some of what had to have been for him a life-changing experience. She did not want the war to remain for her an abstraction, something in newspapers and newsreels. Having thought about her reasons for coming to Europe, he realized that it showed great affection for him.

In May of 1945 Hannah received special permission to join him. She traveled across the Atlantic and then from Amsterdam through war-ravaged Europe. Nothing had prepared her for the utter devastation in many places. There were beggars on the platforms of the train stations. When Hannah and Peter were finally reunited in the late summer of 1945 they had not seen each other for more than a year. He had written only sparingly, especially during his first several months in Europe. His letters were full of longing for her but also of a suppressed but poorly concealed sadness.

When Hannah first saw Peter from the train at the station in Wiesbaden she did not recognize him. He was in uniform, was gaunt and looked much older than his years. He seemed a middle-aged man. But his smile upon seeing her showed his old self. When they embraced he would not let go. He seemed to shudder. She wondered if he was crying. Their reunion was sweet and tender, but muted because of their long separation and his psychological scars.

They were allowed to live privately in a small apartment near an American military base. His old humor eventually revived, but he had a new seriousness. While thousands around him had died, he had been allowed to live. He wondered why. What was expected of him? He must not waste a life that had been spared.

With Hannah now at his side in Germany he resisted the temptation to return as soon as possible to America. He felt that by staying he was obviating a guilt that he could not quite explain. Why this sense of guilt? He was but a part of the force that had crushed the Germans. What had been done surely had to have been done, yet war was an abomination, a result of the perversity of humanity, not a few evil men. Most of those killed were merely following orders. They knew little about the real reasons for the war, knew mostly the propaganda of their own side. Were those young German soldiers more evil than their American counterparts? He felt, as surviving soldiers often do, guilty of some of the death and destruction and undeserving of having been spared. He had saved the lives of many German soldiers, but still felt that he owed the defeated something.

As he grew up, Richard Bittenberg listened with fascination when his parents spoke about the war and its aftermath. He asked his father many times about battles in which he had been involved, but found him strangely reluctant to speak about the specifics of his service in the field. Richard came to realize that for his father recalling those particular parts of the war was painful. That reluctance taught him more about the suffering and destruction of war than his reading of historical accounts.

Though his father avoided talking about the battlefield, he did tell him about the circumstances of Colonel Billick's advice to him. More than once he would later advise Richard by citing Billick's principle. "You have to do the best you can with what you've got. There's no alternative. There's no use wishing things were different." Richard would make the principle his own. It had a way of cutting through self-indulgent agonizing and exposing indecision caused by a failure to face reality.

Richard's mother and father told him about the utter destruction of parts of Germany and the desperate lives of many Germans in the year just after the war. Some of that desperation, Richard discovered in his historical researches, was the result of a deliberate American policy of starving the defeated Germans. Much of what remained of German industrial plants was dismantled and sent to the victorious powers. Peter had managed to locate a couple of his surviving German relatives. Several von Bittenbergs had died in the war or disappeared into the Soviet Union as prisoners of war. During a week of leave in the spring of 1946 he and Hannah visited a second cousin of his father on his estate outside of Hamburg. Having lost three sons in the war, he was weighed down by sorrows. They also met the man's only surviving son, a young former major in the German army, Klaus von Bittenberg. He had led a handful of survivors of two German army companies from Russia across Poland, catching an occasional ride with retreating German military vehicles but walking much of the way. He and his group had miraculously evaded capture by the Russians, who were advancing on Germany and Berlin. A couple of days after the armistice in the east, he and his group had been able to surrender to Americans west of Berlin. Klaus, who stood six feet two inches, had then weighed 135 pounds. He had been barely able to walk. He had spent two weeks in an American hospital recuperating before being sent on to a camp for processing. When Peter and Hannah met him he still looked emaciated. His eyes still spoke of horrors and great suffering. The Bittenbergs whom Peter met were very grateful for the small gifts of food and other items that Peter and Hannah were able to bring.

Richard's childhood conversations with his father about the horrors of the battlefield and the effects of war on the general population was one of the reasons why he abhorred the knee-jerk hawkishness about military matters that had become so common among his fellow Americans. He realized that sometimes there was no alternative to war, but it seemed to him that any civilized country would go to great lengths to avoid it. He had no tolerance for people who, recognizing the great military might of the United States, wanted to enjoy some of that power by having their military kick some ass.

Richard's older brother, Hubert, was born in Germany just before his parents returned to America. Peter received a permanent staff appointment at the Walter Reed Army Hospital in Washington, D.C. He was by then a fully qualified and certified surgeon and was paid a regular salary. The little Bittenberg family rented a small house in the northern part of the District of Columbia near Rock Creek Park. They lived there for several years, visiting Charleston from time to time. In 1955 Peter received a very flattering offer to become the chief of general surgery at a hospital in Charleston. Hannah was delighted at the prospect of going back to Charleston permanently. She had in fact done what she could to make such a move possible. Peter wanted to return to civilian life. Having reached the military rank of lieutenant colonel, he accepted the Charleston offer and switched to the military reserves.

For the first few years back in Charleston, the Peter Bittenbergs lived in his parents' home on Rutledge Street, which had been rented to outsiders in his parents' absence. Richard's sister, Susan, was born while they lived there. In the late 1950s they bought their own house on Society Street near Meeting Street, and Richard was born about a year after they had moved in. The new Bittenberg home was in a somewhat run down, predominantly black area, but it was spacious and close enough to the more fashionable parts of town. The young surgeon, who had good looks and a reputation as a war hero, was soon regarded as a distinguished member of the medical profession. At forty years of age he already had the standing and respect that might come to a good professional ten or twenty years his senior.

Especially as his wife had deep and aristocratic roots in Charleston, Peter and Hannah Bittenberg soon were a part of Charleston high society. They derived great pleasure from being at home and from living near their extended family.

Growing up, Richard Bittenberg lived nowhere but in Charleston. He had a happy childhood and youth. He loved and admired his parents, and they were devoted to their children and each other. Richard was close to his siblings. His brother, Hubert, was considerably older, but shared some of his interests, though at a different level, and gave him the benefit of his much greater experience. His sister, Susan, doted on him. The Bittenberg children had their rivalries and disagreements but few serious conflicts. Richard liked most of his relatives, liked his city, and had good friends. He almost enjoyed school. He struggled for a while in mathematics, but was all the more attracted to and adept at literature and history. He did not resent having to go to church on most Sundays. He had his growing pains and personal problems, some of which were troubling. As an eleven-year-old he became enthralled with a girl in his elementary school. When she and her family moved to a different part of the United States he had a hard time getting over the separation. He never quite forgot her. As a teen-ager he was inflicted with a particularly severe case of eczema, which embarrassed him for years and made him shyer, especially among girls, than he would otherwise have been. But none of the trying aspects or events of Richard's formative years were chronic or crippling. There was in his childhood and youth no devastating trauma, no deep, pent-up resentment of the kind that might make a person hate and reject his own past. Not even during adolescence did he go through a period of surly rebellion against his own background and his own people.

Richard knew little of the serious though transitory financial strains on the family caused by a financial advisor who made his father invest in a couple of ultimately disastrous business ventures. Richard's years in school were a pretty typical mixture of highs and lows, thrills and tedium. In high school he was particularly good friends with the son of a businessman. They were frequently engrossed in discussion about the meaning of life and other serious subjects and were both avid readers. Richard got high grades without greatly exerting himself. For his own enjoyment he read history and philosophy as well as novels. He was one of the best in school at each of his main sports, football, medium and long-distance running, and tennis.

After his paternal grandfather William retired from the Foreign Service and he and his wife moved into the house on Rutledge

Street where he had grown up, Richard often visited them, especially in his early teens. Both of his paternal grandparents were always pleased to see him. He and his grandfather talked in his grandfather's study. Richard loved listening to him tell about his youth, his long diplomatic career, the various places around the world where he had served, the Second World War, and the lessons life had taught him.

One of Richard's fondest childhood memories was of accompanying his parents and siblings to Europe in the late 1960s before his grandfather William's retirement. Richard was ten or eleven years old. Their ultimate destination was Copenhagen, Denmark, where his grandfather had received his first ambassadorial appointment. It was the longest vacation his father had ever taken. They set out from New York by ship in mid June. They traveled on a marvelous English ship to Portsmouth, England. His parents had said that the era of crossing the Atlantic by sea would soon come to an end. Looking back, Richard realized that they had traveled first class. The passengers wore black tie for dinner. The Bittenbergs were invited to sit at the captain's table. The captain had a finely trimmed beard and looked splendid in his white dress uniform. The ship seemed to Richard opulently luxurious. The service, provided by men and women uniformed according to rank and function, had been quick, discreet, and ubiquitous.

The family took the train to London. Richard could not take his eyes off the scenery outside the train window. He noticed every difference between America and what he now saw. He listened to the English dialects and other languages of the other travelers and observed the differences in dress and manner. He was entranced. London seemed to him in some ways a more imposing version of Charleston, but, ah, it was larger than life, magnificent, so full of grand, impressive buildings, inviting and intriguing stores, and general pomp and circumstance. Richard stood gaping in awe at the Houses of Parliament. Westminster Abbey was like no church he had ever seen. History oozed from every nook and cranny. The changing of the guard at Buckingham Palace had him spellbound. He tried to catch one of the grand, perfectly still, bear-hatted guards outside the gates in an involuntary movement. Richard had started reading about the British Empire, and it seemed to him wholly plausible that this city had been its center.

They took another ship to Denmark. Continental Europe intrigued him with other discoveries. The land between Esbjerg, Denmark, where the ship from London had taken them, and Copenhagen was almost flat, but it was still nothing like the swampy country around Charleston. The fields were all a deep green or had the soft yellow-beige color of grain. Some fields were a sharp, clear yellow. Denmark seemed to be all farms. And how well kept they all were! No old, dilapidated and unpainted barns or outbuildings. The usually white stucco farmhouses and the villages were picture perfect. There were flowers and little well tended gardens everywhere. All young Danes seemed to have light blond, almost white hair.

Richard had started studying German in school. In Denmark he encountered another foreign language. It surprised him that people could actually, *actually* speak a language wholly different from English. The capital of Denmark turned out to be a substantial, rather attractive city with its own distinctive look. They were clearly in a culture different from America's or England's. Richard found it hard to imagine that some twenty-five years earlier, German soldiers had been seen in these same streets. Richard noticed how much the Danes seemed to enjoy the June summer weather. They liked to sit on park-benches or in sidewalk cafés with their heads turned toward the sun. In Charleston at the same time of the year, people who had to be outdoors would look for shade. Most would seek refuge in air-conditioned buildings.

Richard and his sister stayed for a week at the U.S. Ambassador's imposing residence in Copenhagen. Hubert was put on a train to visit German relatives outside of Hamburg, and Richard's parents took a four-day trip on their own to Paris.

Richard was mighty impressed by the empire lorded over by his grandfather and by the great respect with which he was treated. He seemed made for his role. His grandfather was above medium height and had a craggy rather handsome face with gray hair. He dressed meticulously but discreetly. He had a dignity that required no special effort. He had gracious, refined manners. He seemed always to be trying to put others at ease.

"Only people who are unworthy of their positions feel a need to put others down," he told Richard. "Blustery people always have something to prove or hide. They impress or scare only the timid ones."

But he also said, "Statesmanship can be a rough business, m' boy, believe you my words. Sometimes you have no choice but to deal harshly with people, and even if you don't want to use methods like that, your opponents especially have to believe that you might. If they believe that, you may not have to be very rough."

Richard was permitted to accompany his grandfather to the embassy for two mornings of their stay. While the ambassador conducted business with his staff or visitors, Richard would sit on a chair with a book, legs dangling, off to the side in the ambassador's large official office. His grandfather would wink at him. It gave Richard a wonderful sense of security and pride to be in the confidence of such a man. Richard's senses were wide open. He absorbed everything.

Only many years later did Richard learn that his grandfather's diplomatic career had suffered from his getting in the way of one of President Harry Truman's secretaries of State, James F. Byrnes, who served 1945-47. A fellow South Carolinian, Byrnes knew some of the Bittenbergs and might have advanced William's career. But William Bittenberg had made some substantial difficulties for him, and as a result Byrnes had blocked his grandfather's elevation to a post in the State Department to which he had aspired and which would have greatly advanced his career. He had been held back once more by resisting a scheme that powerful international financial interests pushed hard but that seemed to him not to be in America's interest. Richard's grandfather never fully explained either the run-in with Byrnes or the latter episode. He merely said that they had involved matters of conscience. Later William Bittenberg had expressed reservations about the U.S. military involvement in Vietnam.

The unexpected death of his grandfather when Richard was seventeen years old was a frightful blow. Richard had remained very close to him, often listening to him give his views of life or tell about his career. His grandfather would be forever a presence in Richard's life. Richard transferred some of these affections to Hanna, his grandmother. He was fond of his maternal grandparents, too, but they lived far from Charleston, and he got to see them only seldom. His memories of them became more diffuse.

After high school, Richard followed in his father's footsteps and enrolled at the Citadel. He, too, received a fellowship. Richard was not at all certain that he wanted to become an officer, but he had no other idea about a career. He had been influenced by the opinion often heard among the Bittenbergs that the Citadel would be a good start in life for *any* young man, whatever his plans for the future. He liked the school. He did not mind the military discipline, and he excelled in sports and athletics, but what most appealed to him were courses with a high content of history and ideas.

One of Richard's professors strongly suspected that he would not pursue a military career. He was Colonel Stewart Eddington, who taught him history and philosophy. Richard was a sophomore when he took Eddington's course on modern Western civilization. Eddington was one of the more colorful members of the faculty, a large, robust, red-faced man in his mid fifties who walked with a slight limp. He had been an army officer and had been wounded in

Korea before joining the faculty at the Citadel. History seemed to matter deeply to him. He spoke of the past as if it were a part of the present or had a direct bearing on it. He lectured in a narrative manner rather than by imparting historical facts for memorization. He stirred Richard's imagination. Eddington quickly noticed that Richard was more perceptive, incisive, curious, and thoughtful than any of his other students. Richard came to Eddington's office to ask questions and to get suggestions for reading. He took one more of Eddington's courses, then a third, a fourth, and a fifth. Eddington became his mentor, a friend across the generations. Eddington, too, had been a student at the Citadel. As Richard got to know him he learned that one of Eddington's teachers there had won him for the subject. For that teacher, history had been not primarily events and dates and archival research but an exploration of human nature. In history you saw on display the desires, weaknesses, strengths, and foibles of human beings. To understand historically significant events and relationships was ultimately to understand yourself and your own time better. Eddington taught philosophy as well as history.

Richard graduated with a major in history and a sprinkling of philosophy courses. He was near the top of his class and received a couple of awards. Most of his teachers and the president of the Citadel expected him to have an exceptional military career. He would undoubtedly become one of the schools' most distinguished alumni. Eddington, who had never had a better student, hoped and expected that he would give graduate study in history or philosophy a try.

Richard did so, but before having come to a definite conclusion about what he wanted to do with his life. He was different from his brother Hubert who had seemed to know from the start that he wanted to be a lawyer. Hubert went to Yale for his undergraduate studies. He was accepted to its law school and to another law school in the North, but chose to go to the University of Virginia. "A little more like home," he said. Uncertain of his way in life, Richard followed Colonel Eddington's advice and applied to the History Department at the University of South Carolina in Columbia. They offered him a graduate fellowship. He soon caught the attention of the faculty as an unusually promising student. He enjoyed most of his courses, and did not rush his studies. He read widely outside the course assignments and selected to write a Master's thesis.

At the university he made a new friend, Robert Preston, who was, paradoxically, in the law school. Robert somehow managed to find the time to do serious reading on the side in politics, history, and philosophy. Richard guessed that, if Robert had not had a father and grandfather who were lawyers, he, too, might have done graduate work in one of the liberal arts. Many of their discussions lasted late into the night. Because Robert's parents lived in Columbia, Richard met them several times, and he was more generally introduced to life in Columbia. Robert's parents knew some of the state's leading politicians, and Richard met a few of them. Robert's father's law practice was located in the shadow of the State Capitol.

Looking back, Richard recognized that he had been lucky and privileged. He had lacked nothing of a material kind, but more importantly his life had felt meaningful. Even at the time, he was vaguely aware that he was happy. Thinking back to his years in Charleston and his home induced in him warm feelings, even nostalgia. Richard had long known that there was another kind of America, very different from his. It could suddenly intrude, not least through movies and the national news media: it seemed to him to be a new, self-indulgent, irresponsible, self-hating, neurotic, fragmenting America. It did not much affect his early youth, but it acquired ever-increasing strength and forced itself on him more and more brutally. He realized that this other America would consider him and his family and his society oddities, throwbacks to an earlier era, curious aberrations. Unlike so many others his own age, Richard was not in mutiny against everything and everybody in his own past. He did not struggle against the very terms of his social and cultural inheritance.

Thinking about what had made him take the extraordinary step that had transformed his life, Richard usually found himself reflecting on his life in Charleston. He had a love for particular people, affection for particular places, and a related sense of gratitude. He felt he owed these people and places his support and protection. His love for America was an extension of these feelings. So was his resentment of those who were trying to destroy his America.

What ultimately accounted for his allegiance to his own people and society and made him so oppositional to what was undermining traditional America? It was, he thought, that the sense of direction that his people and society had transmitted to him had built meaning into his existence. Despite their many and obvious shortcomings and their occasional perversities his people and society had pointed to and partially embodied a life worth living. There was, Richard thought, some kind of connection between the best of what they represented and what ultimately matters.

Richard was generally religious. He was not a doctrinaire or ostentatious believer, but he went to church regularly. Traditional liturgy and doctrinal discipline seemed to him to be a steadying, centering influence and an antidote to religious sentimentalism. From his youth he had sensed the presence of a great power and mystery above and beyond transitory human arrangements and wishes. It encompasses and holds existence together. Ultimately beyond intellectual definition, this reality induces a sense of awe, wonder, and gratitude. A church service gives special, communal expression to and extends these intuitions. It arms the person for ordinary existence. The core of religion was for Richard the struggle to bring daily life into harmony with this higher power as known in conscience. Richard was forever assessing his own impulses and actions. He judged himself severely for his own moral weaknesses. A few particularly egregious lapses in his past kept bothering him. How could he have behaved in such a way? Original sin was for him not so much a dogma of Christian belief as a sinister force known all too well in personal experience. It puzzled Richard that so many people he knew seemed not to sense any great mystery about human existence or to take good and evil seriously. Life appeared to them pretty simple and straightforward. They seemed to go through life as if its chief purpose was to collect transitory pleasures and reduce elements of discomfort.

As one familiar with the traditions of the religions, Richard knew in his head that human beings must have modest expectations of life. Their existence is in an important sense always precarious, threatening all the time to turn vicious or to fall apart because of greed, desire for power, lust, cruelty, and arbitrariness. No achievements are permanent, and disaster may threaten over the horizon. The human predicament is in a manner of speaking always desperate. But Richard found it morally unhealthy to indulge the streak of self-loathing that was so prominent in the religion of many Christians. To put heavy, unrelenting stress on the need for faith and divine grace seemed to him potentially sickly, an invitation to demand little of self and others. Dwelling too often on the utter fallenness of man served as an excuse for people who could have done better. Richard thought he knew something of the role of sheer evil in human affairs, but he was not a cynic suspecting foul motives behind each and every human action. He did not despair of the possibility of civilized life. Human beings were capable of responsibility, even nobility. Had not his own people and society at their best offered examples of how civilization can tame the lower potentialities of humanity and lift existence to a level of some decency, wisdom, and elegance? And was not his Charleston a microcosm of the admirable qualities of America?

But America's new leaders were abandoning this religious,

moral, cultural, social, and political heritage, sometimes even appearing to hate it. Richard's worries about the future had only deepened as he grew older. He thought he saw ever-new signs of a deep and pervasive crisis. Though the crisis seemed to him to be ultimately moral and spiritual, it had a broad range of manifestations. His country's chronic and worsening political and economic problems were among the most obvious and conspicuous symptoms. As Americans had long assumed that their political and economic systems were easily the best in the world, glaring, seemingly intractable problems with both were to him ominous indicators of crisis.

It had greatly troubled Richard when the United States, once considered an economic powerhouse, finally lost its Standard and Poor's triple A bond rating. That politicians and commentators had minimized the significance of this development had made it all the more disturbing. Then came the desperate but half-hearted attempts to put government and the economy on an even keel, the adoption of the federal value added tax, the VAT. Several American states and numerous counties and municipalities had started defaulting on their bonds and pension obligations, which was followed by bankruptcy proceedings against many of them. The unemployment rate was persistently high as was the inflation rate. There were large riots in American cities, recurring protest demonstrations in Washington, D.C. and around the country, and a general feeling of unrest and uncertainty.

Richard regarded the economic troubles as particularly telling signs of America's precarious condition, not because he considered economic developments to be the most reliable indicator of the state of his country, but because Americans regarded the U.S. economy as their special strength and pride. If the economy was sputtering and the federal, state, and local governments of the United States of America could not live up to their most basic obligations, in what areas could the United States still make a respectable showing?

Some of these developments still lay over the horizon when Richard put his old life behind him. Yet his own past, his worries about ominous trends, and his frustration at being able to do next to nothing to reverse them had predisposed him to seize the seemingly far-fetched opportunity to act that had suddenly and unexpectedly presented itself. He found himself in circumstances that, if somebody had earlier suggested that they might be possible, he would have dismissed as wholly implausible.

# CHAPTER 5

Immediately after the telephone conversation with Mr. Warner at the American consulate Helen sat on the bed in the small hotel room as if paralyzed. His words had comforted her as they were spoken, but their soothing effect faded in mere seconds. The enormity of what had happened assaulted her and made her gasp. She buried her face in her hands and rocked back and forth. What was she to do?

A thought struck her. Perhaps Richard *had* left a message at the hotel after all? What if someone other than the middle-aged man in the reception had taken the message and neglected to take it down properly or had put it in the wrong place. Helen stood up. Richard could have left a message long before Helen called from the restaurant. Another person might have been on duty in the reception.

Helen almost ran down the stairs to the lobby. The same man was sitting behind the counter. He stood up when she approached and smiled solicitously. Helen suspected that her female charms made him friendlier than he might have been after her repeated entreaties, but she was too preoccupied to care. He listened attentively, but it took him a while fully to understand her question. Then, softly shaking his head, he told her that he had been at his post since 9:00 AM that morning. He had never been so far away from the reception that he could not hear the telephone. He had even had his lunch, a meal he had brought from home, in the little room behind the counter. He had smoked a couple of cigarettes during the day on the sidewalk just outside the hotel, but the door to the hotel had been open — what a beautiful day it had been! He had not been more than ten meters from the counter. And, no, he had not misplaced any message. The only one that day had been left by a German for his mother. There had not even been any mail for any of the residents of the hotel.

Helen smiled, half appreciatively, half apologetically. She had probably been pegged as easily excitable. She stepped into the street outside the little reception to breathe some fresh air. The narrow street, just off Boulevard St. Michel, was crowded with cars, and the fumes were heavy. It was rush hour. The sun cast lengthening shadows on the other side of the street.

What would she tell the children?

She took the elevator upstairs. When she stepped out on her floor, she found Anne in the corridor just about to open the door to the children's room. Helen called out, and Anne turned.

"Mom, where *were* you? I knocked on your door forever! Why didn't you tell us you were going somewhere?"

Helen cringed. She and Richard were always telling the children not to behave as she had just done. The children were not allowed to go anywhere, not even to their next-door neighbors, without letting her or Richard know.

Helen hugged Anne. "I'm sorry, dear, I went down to the reception. I should have told you. I plain forgot."

"What about Dad?"

Helen realized that she could no longer feign unconcern and cheerfulness. She had to find a way to talk to the children about Richard's disappearance without revealing the depth of her own fears.

"Anne, please get John so that we can talk in our room."

Helen told them about the call to the consulate. For the next half hour they talked about possible explanations for what had happened and what they would do next. It surprised Helen that John seemed as calm as he did. He was highly intelligent and perceptive. Darling Johnnie, he was helping her make Anne feel better. Hugging Anne again, Helen looked over Anne's shoulder at John. When he looked up at her she gave him a smile. His smile back showed that, yes, he was trying to be brave. Consciously or unconsciously, he was stepping into the role of the male in the family.

Helen told the children that she wanted to spend the evening at the hotel in case Richard returned or called or the consulate or anybody else called. She would try to find out which hospitals would have been likely to receive him if something had happened to him near the Sorbonne or between Sorbonne and the Champs-Élysées. The police would know.

She told the children to try to relax in their own room. She would eventually get some dinner for them, and she would let them know immediately if there was any news. Helen then thought about calling the consulate again. In the rational part of her mind she knew that she would have heard from the consulate in case it had received any kind of message about her husband, but she would leave nothing to chance. She dialed the number. The consulate now being closed for the weekend, the telephone menu had changed. At the very end of it was the option of contacting a consular officer on duty for emergencies. She chose that option. A person named Bennini answered. He was probably in his home with his family,

Helen speculated. To judge by his voice he was youngish, about the same age as Warner. Having waited for five minutes, she learned from Bennini that nobody had called the embassy about an American citizen.

"How do you know?" Helen asked.

"Please, ma'am, I know. Take my word for it. We have our ways. Computers are wonderful things."

"But what if the police or a hospital had left a message at the embassy after it closed."

"The telephone menu would have steered them right. They would have contacted the consular office on duty, as you did."

"I suppose so. Thank you very much, Mr. Bennini."

Helen told the children that she would be away briefly to inquire about the location of the nearest police station. When she came downstairs she saw that a man in his thirties had taken over at the counter. He was dark, tall, and gangly, and wore glasses — seemed an academic type. His English was quite good, and Helen asked if he was connected to the Sorbonne. He turned out to be a doctoral student in anthropology. He would be at the reception through the night. Helen told him her story and found him both kind and understanding. He told her that there was a police station only two blocks away.

Helen returned to the children's room, where John and Anne had been watching a music program. Helen told them about the police station and that she would go there first and get some food on the way back.

"Do you want us to come along?" John said.

"No, thank you, John. You keep Annie company here."

The evening was lovely. It would have been a perfect night for walking around in the Montmartre. At the police station, communication first proved a problem. After some unpromising conversation with a middle-aged policeman at the desk where the public was received, another man in uniform, who was considerably younger but had more stripes, was called in from the back of the station. He was dark haired, of medium height and build. He gave his name and position. His manner did not betray any annoyance at having been disturbed. He even smiled faintly as he asked, in somewhat awkward English, how he could be of service. Helen was able to make him understand why she was there. She realized that he must think her visit to the police station rather premature; Richard had been missing for just a few hours. But to her surprise, the young policeman was not dismissive or irritable. Had he just come back from a training session for promising young police officers on how to deal with the public in the new Europe? Or had her looks been sufficient to soften the heart of a man about ten years her junior? He took down some facts on a notepad and disappeared. Helen sat down on an uncomfortable wooden police bench, got up again out of sheer nervousness and paced the floor. A few minutes later the policeman returned, shaking his head. Ambulances had been called at various times during the day to the relevant areas of Paris, but none of the calls had involved a male of Richard's age. Nothing else in the police records seemed relevant.

Helen's relief was followed immediately by new anguish. What if Richard had had a heart attack or stroke in a place where nobody had seen him? Perhaps he was slumped in the stall of a restroom at the Sorbonne library. A cleaning woman might not get to it until early the next morning. The young policeman agreed to keep Helen's name and telephone number in case he should come across possibly pertinent information. She thanked him with real warmth and left the station.

The traffic was still heavy. The lights would soon be turned on in stores and restaurants. She had earlier seen a McDonald's just a few blocks away and decided to get their evening meal there. In America she only seldom took the children to McDonald's, however much they wanted it. Now that they were in France she would in different circumstances have been even more reluctant to go there. But it seemed just the right thing to do. It might lend an element of normalcy to their dinner. A McDonald's bag in hand, she stepped into a small grocery store for some fruit and tomatoes and a bottle of red wine.

She walked briskly back to the hotel. Why briskly, she asked herself. She didn't think that Richard would have returned or that any message would be waiting for her.

# CHAPTER 6

Richard Bittenberg had a strong, though non-partisan, interest in politics, but his study of history had convinced him that the ideas and attitudes of leading intellectual, cultural, and religious figures were better indicators of what was in store for society, including politics, in the next few generations. Politicians could affect how historical trends work themselves out in particulars, but history's general direction was set, for the most part, outside of politics. He was amused as well as discouraged by all the people who seemed to think that the future would turn on the outcome of the next political election. How many times over the years had he heard political candidates declare that "this is an historic election" or "this is the most important election of our time"?

What sometimes brought Richard to the brink of despair about his country was that a new culture, based on moral and other assumptions radically different from those of traditional Western civilization, was replacing the one with which he identified. The change seemed to him to involve a fading of moral and spiritual seriousness and the crumbling of a sense of propriety and limits. Everywhere he detected an expanding, inordinate desire for transitory satisfactions: for power, wealth, creature comforts, entertainment, sexual pleasure — self-indulgence of every kind. The notion of a higher purpose of life and a common good seemed increasingly anachronistic, though it still showed up in the self-serving rhetoric of politicians. Their actual conduct evinced a sometimes appalling cynicism and ruthlessness. Richard loathed the crassness and crudity of the commercialization of American life and the signs that America's business and financial culture was shedding what remained of traditional standards of honesty and restraint. Stories about greedy and crooked investors, money managers, and CEOs had become so common that they no longer appeared on the front pages of the newspapers. And these published stories, Richard knew, were just the tip of an iceberg. Most of the spreading debauchery remained in the shadows.

The growing immorality, immodesty, garishness, and vulgarity of American life were most glaringly obvious in popular entertainment, whose providers pandered with seemingly boundless cynicism to an ever lower common denominator of popular taste. Richard often wondered what had made the originators and purveyors of this corruption in entertainment into what they were. Whence their sheer perversity? There was money to be made in pandering to and encouraging lewdness and salaciousness—that went without saying—but what predisposed so many people into making money in this particular way? Were they not embarrassed to be selling what society had only recently scorned as contemptible, as incompatible with civilized life and good taste? Had they no sense of shame? Richard thought he could observe a symbiosis between those whose products fed the moral-cultural corruption and those who argued for ever greater tolerance and freedom of expression. But he noticed that these individuals were actually highly selective in their tolerance. They were clearly *in*tolerant of the traditions that they were undermining. They seemed to hate old-fashioned standards of conduct. Why was it, for instance, that film connoisseurs always hailed the Marx Brothers as "classics" of movie comedy? Richard had never liked them. These characters seemed singularly obnoxious and vulgar and lacking in human warmth. Who were usually the butt of their jokes and ridicule? They were people of some refinement and good manners, sometimes clothed in tails or other formal dress to make their supposed phoniness obvious. Whence this desire to ridicule and tear down whatever might be civil, elevated, and admirable? Whence this deep need to show civilized life to be mere appearance and pretense?

Once, when flying to California one afternoon to give a lecture at the University of California at Los Angeles, Richard was upgraded to first class. He was seated next to a dark-haired, balding, bespectacled man in his late forties. The man was browsing through something that Richard guessed was a movie script. After take-off the stewardess asked what they would like to drink, and they both ordered cocktails. To initiate a conversation Richard asked if the man was in fact reading a script and received an affirmative answer. Richard introduced himself, and his neighbor reciprocated. The name sounded somehow familiar, but it took Richard a while to realize that he was sitting next to a prominent Hollywood producer. He actually remembered seeing his name on movie screens. The man did not seem eager to return to his reading, and they started talking. Richard welcomed the opportunity to prod the motives of this man, obviously a major force in Hollywood. He was likely to clash fundamentally with him, but he decided to avoid comments that might make the producer clam up. Without lying Richard would simply let the man believe that he was a typical academic, hence a dedicated believer in freedom of speech who rejected "authoritarian," old-fashioned beliefs. Having emptied his drink rather quickly and ordered another, the producer seemed to enjoy talking to Richard. He told him that he was traveling as he did because his corporate jet was grounded for service and repairs.

Richard learned a great deal about what goes into the production of a Hollywood movie. Although he thought he knew the answer, he wanted to ask why Hollywood was so prone to making movies that attacked traditional mores, values, and tastes. Was there simply no money in respecting them? That appeared not to be the case, because sometimes movies were made that appealed to traditional audiences, even as they included politically correct ingredients. To get the producer's frank opinions Richard tried to seem sympathetic to Hollywood.

"I suppose lingering traditional puritanical views put some restrictions on how far you can go in showing human life," he said.

"Sure, it's always a balancing act, but we always try to push the envelope a little."

"I assume that at the same time you don't want to lose all the more traditional folks."

"No, we produce those feel-good movies that punish the bad guys, you know, reward good behavior and celebrate family values. We've been making more of those in recent years. But we usually make up for the corniness by sending some worthwhile messages at the same time, such as putting groups that used to be denigrated in a better light. And the people who most embody outdated ways usually come across as pretty rigid and unimaginative, right? It's the open-minded, tolerant, modern individuals who come out looking the best."

"What do you say to those who accuse Hollywood of exploiting sex and violence?" Richard asked, giving no hint that he might be one of those critics. The producer was halfway through his second drink and seemed unconcerned.

"That's *such* a hypocritical stance, isn't it?" he said. "We just try to mirror life, for heaven's sake. And we give people what they want. The same people who complain of sex and violence go to see precisely those movies. Besides, why should people who are uptight about these things be able to dictate to all the others? When it comes to sex people are far more accepting of a frank portrayal than they used to be, thank god. We've gotten away from the old taboos and prejudices. Thank god we are living in a more open society."

"Perhaps in large part thanks to Hollywood."

The producer nodded. "We *can* take some of the credit. We

do affect the way people look at things. Take the dramatic change in attitudes in the last several decades on race, sex, homosexuality, and national origin. The movies prepared the way for the necessary social change."

"And what would you say to people who blame you for destroying traditional America?" Richard had started to feel resentment, but he smiled to mask that he identified with the mentioned sentiment.

"Traditional society?" A disdainful look broke through the producer's alcohol-induced euphoria. "Americans are moving on. Sure, the movies break down old taboos and penetrate the nice, hypocritical surface of things. That's because the sophisticated, creative people in the movie industry are quick to pick up on deceit and whatever else's wrong with society. They can show the hypocrisy in vivid colors. They help us to detect injustice and to empathize with groups that have been wronged—blacks and other minorities, women, and so on."

"It seems that movie-makers agree on who the biggest enemy is."

The man looked quizzically but not very attentively at Richard. He was getting to the end of his second drink. He seemed still unaware that he was being scrutinized. He looked a little glassy-eyed at Richard. "What do you mean?"

"Well, you know" — Richard tried to make his comment seem less pointed and serious than it was by looking and acting somewhat jocular—"I'm thinking about that person or persons behind the scenes, the big shots who manipulate others for nefarious ends."

"Yeah, right."

"I'm thinking about the really bad guy behind the scenes. He's usually well spoken, well mannered, well groomed, lives in a tastefully decorated mansion, is very upper class in appearance, may even speak with a faintly British accent, and is driven by a chauffeur in a highly polished limousine. But he's never what he seems, right? You know what I'm talking about." Richard smiled again.

"Of course I do." The producer emptied his drink as if to counter a twinge of pain. "People like that have a lot to answer for — that phony old elite, those smug, pretentious, condescending snobs. They deserve to be kicked off their high horses."

"If they haven't already fallen off all by themselves."

"Perhaps they have, but we movie people certainly have their number." The producer's smile contained malice as well as glee.

Richard, who was finding it increasingly hard to maintain an air of sympathetic interest, said: "I've noticed that the most vicious, callous characters, the contract killers, enforcers, and goons are from the same kind of stock, just lower class."

"What do you mean?"

"You know, they usually have very blond hair and very blue eyes — are Nordic types, sometimes almost look like albinos. They are cutthroat, lower grade versions of those polished, suave characters behind the scenes. Really scary."

This time Richard had let some irony seep into his voice. The producer apparently noticed and gave him a curious if rather diffuse glance.

"So?"

"One might get the impression that Hollywood's trying to turn the audience against people of northern European ancestry — against the kind of people who settled and built this country."

The producer looked at Richard, now paying closer attention to his features, then shrugged his shoulders and said: "I think Hollywood has an excellent record of fighting prejudice."

"With at least one exception, it seems." Richard could no longer deny himself a pointed comment. "There seems to be always open season on one American group, those northern European Christians, the WASPs particularly. Them you can always disparage or ridicule."

"Well, they're hardly blameless, are they? Look at all that puritan intolerance, all they did to the Indians, the blacks, and other groups."

The producer would lose interest in the conversation now, Richard knew. He permitted himself a final comment.

"Aren't we supposed to treat all groups equally? The WASPs are hardly the only group with flaws."

The producer shrugged again and gave Richard a vaguely condescending look: "You sound like some kind of a conspiracy theorist."

He returned demonstratively to his script. Soon he was asleep.

How could America's enormous moral-spiritual and cultural problems be solved through politics? The best that a political movement could hope to achieve in the given historical circumstances, it seemed to Richard, was to help retard America's decline. It might be possible to obstruct particularly pernicious political and economic developments and to mobilize public opinion against what the purveyors and arbiters of culture were propagating. In spite of his limited faith in politics and his recognition that he was a scholar rather than a man of practice, it had crossed his mind to try to collect like-minded and substantial people who might try, though seemingly against all odds, to start a new political movement or party. A deteriorated culture could not be transformed through politics, Richard thought, but perhaps an intelligently conceived and led political organization could help crystallize and inspire opposition and complicate matters for the people promoting perverse ideas and corrupt self-interest.

Yet the rot in American society might be too far-gone and widespread. The chatter about America being a model for the entire world, an "exceptional" country, the very embodiment of the wonders of "democracy," made Richard cringe. The Framers of the U.S. Constitution had actually warned of the *dangers* of democracy, and the new American "democracy" would have elicited their disgust. It seemed to Richard that demagogic, cynical leaders who could manipulate an ill-informed, easily swayed populace had made a mockery of American constitutional government. "Democracy" had become a cover for ruthless power seeking and sheer irresponsibility. The Framers had done what they could to restrain and humanize the will to power, but that will, dressed up as a desire to do good for Americans and all the unfortunate people in the world, was now breaking through what remained of the institutional checks that the Framers had set up. The restraints on power that they had constructed were, Richard thought, collapsing. The decline of American liberties had been far-advanced already before 9/11, and since then ever new reasons had been found to impose a stricter and stricter national-security regime. 9/11 itself and the later acts of terrorism in the United States and Europe had provided the justification for curtailing civil liberties, short-circuiting checks and balances and boosting the police power of the federal government.

The burgeoning American police state had been further boosted by the need to contend with the many riots and violent protests in American cities. Many of the states, desperately short of funds, had appealed to the federal government for help with security and protection. The first and most infamous of the protests and riots, the protracted disorder called "the Chicago summer," had started as a protest against unemployment and cuts in public assistance. It had turned into looting, violence, killing, and wanton destruction. The disorder had lasted for the better part of a month. Many had been killed, hundreds wounded, and several hundred arrested. The media coverage of these and other protests and riots had brought home to the American public the instability of large parts of American society. The first of the big "pension protests," the one in Portland, Oregon, which had been triggered by cuts in public pension benefits, had evolved into a violent confrontation with police. This demonstration had shown that the potential for conflict and turbulence was by no means confined to the inner cities. Later protests had shown the same.

To handle the riots, the police had become progressively militarized, and the National Guard was employed routinely to establish order in especially turbulent trouble spots. The Pentagon might not long be able to resist efforts to employ regular troops within the United States. It was widely argued that security considerations had to take precedence over the old prejudice against domestic use of the federal military. The use of electronic surveillance in public places had grown rapidly. Many police forces routinely employed drones. The protests against the expansion and intrusiveness of the new national security regime had been ineffective.

Richard reflected that the spreading disorder and America's many problems should have resulted in a political earthquake. It seemed to him that, despite much rhetoric about the need for radical change, the general dynamic of America's political and economic system had changed only marginally. The media establishment formed a protective wall around the existing order. Individuals or movements that raised issues potentially dangerous to the powers-that-be were sooner or later co-opted, discredited, or destroyed outright. Before serious challengers could achieve real political momentum, they were brought low by scandal, innuendo, or fear-mongering. Only persons who accepted the reigning moral, political, economic, and cultural order could achieve political influence. The presidency, cabinet positions, the leadership of key government agencies, and the most important positions in the U.S. Congress remained the almost exclusive domain of the permanent power structure. A partly hidden network of people, who exercised much of their power through the media elites, could shape public debate and set the public agenda. They could select and define the issues for debate.

It seemed to Richard that the American people in general, disoriented though they were, had not yet been quite as badly corrupted as most of their leaders. This was a source of some comfort. But he also believed that the power to determine the basic direction of a society never comes from the grass roots. For that reason the common folk could at best be mobilized in support of halting the moral and cultural decline of America.

For Richard the pervasiveness of economic-financial irresponsibility was a particularly revealing symptom of America's decline. A many-sided culture of instant gratification and indebtedness made a high proportion of American families walk close to the brink of financial ruin. The financial system had its usual way of shifting resources from the general population to the big financial houses. Most disturbingly, government itself lived far beyond its means. Opportunistic, pandering politicians at the federal and state levels continued to promise the electorate benefits that they knew the voters would not pay for through taxes. Huge budget deficits were the order of the day, and the national debt was staggering. The U.S. government routinely financed a large part of its expenditures by taking on new debt, shifting the burden of payment to coming generations and eroding the purchasing power of the dollar. Kicking the can down the road was the normal and expected way of handling this worsening problem. America was becoming poorer and poorer in relation to countries that did not increase their debt at the same rate. It was hard to believe, Richard reflected, that not long ago the U.S. dollar had been the reserve currency of the world. Now most countries had shifted their liquid assets away from the dollar to bundles of stronger currencies. America, once known as a very productive, creative society with a currency respected around the world, now had a sputtering, erratic economy starting to resemble that of a banana republic or third-world country. Once upon a time, national unemployment above 5% and inflation above 2-3% had been regarded as unacceptable. Now the country could not get unemployment under 10%, and inflation had reached 10%. "Stagflation" was threatening to become chronic.

Big Finance around the world had looked increasingly to other countries to make safer investments. People feeling little loyalty to the United States had long dominated the American centers of high finance, and they now regarded the United States more and more as an opportunity for sophisticated financial looting. The old American Protestant Ethic of honesty and responsibility had virtually disappeared. The high cost of protecting investments against deceit and recklessness had become one of the major factors discouraging investments in America. Lawyers and elaborate contracts had long played an absurdly large role in the U.S. economy. Now legalism together with forever expanding regulations had become so cumbersome that, all by themselves, they put a damper on business and investment.

After Standard & Poor's took away America's AAA bond rating the ensuing further downgrading of America's creditworthiness and the country's final arrival at an anemic AA rating had not attracted as much attention. Plenty of court economists, government officials, and public commentators had declared that ratings of this kind were "arbitrary," "did not really matter," and "were of little practical interest." The "fundamentals" of the American economy remained sound, they declared. More traditional economists worried that it might have become too late for America to stage an economic comeback. Only draconian measures could now make a difference, and the powers-that-be and their electoral constituents fiercely resisted them. Richard feared that his country might have passed the point of no return and would be spiraling into economic and social chaos.

The federal value added tax had been introduced after a huge political battle. It was now a major source of revenue. It had been sold to the country as merely temporary and as necessary to deal with the huge budget deficits. Its proponents had offered ironclad guarantees within the bill itself that it would expire in five years and that it could not be raised above the original 5% without two-thirds majorities in the houses of Congress. Still, within a year, the VAT had been raised to 9%, not by the previously stipulated two-thirds majorities but by very close votes. The howls of protest from opponents made no difference. The president signed the measure into law, and it was implemented, though not without lawsuits, recalcitrance on the part of several state governments, and other complications. The tax had given the permanent government some breathing room. It somewhat reassured other countries as to the credit-worthiness of the United States — its bond rating improved to AA+ — but, contrary to solemn promises given when the VAT was first adopted, total federal expenditures were never really cut. They had risen, almost as quickly as the new tax revenue. The wars in the Middle East — the most recent a so-called "police action" to support the Saudi royal family against Islamic terrorists — continued to be hugely expensive. The U.S. government kept borrowing on a large scale and could finance the new debt only through rising interest rates, a vicious cycle that kept the country tottering on the brink of insolvency.

Politicians who had the courage to call for drastic policy changes were few and powerless against the entrenched interests. They were dismissed as "cranks," "extremists," and "alarmists," while defenders of the status quo spoke soothingly about giving new policies a chance to work. Wall Street and international finance, which more than ever dominated America's governing structure, had long ago adapted to America's precarious economic condition, developing elaborate, mathematically sophisticated financial instruments to make money even out of the country's progressively risky indebtedness.

American republicanism had so deteriorated, Richard thought, that it simply could not address America's problems. Politicians were more than ever focused on their own reelection. Most of them avoided talking of hard choices that would not appeal to the voters. A culture of evasion, involving a demoralizing interaction between cynical political leaders and a largely docile but complicit electorate, had made responsible political action virtually impossible.

How quickly Americans had adapted to a situation that earlier generations of Americans would have viewed with great alarm! Richard realized that because of an almost complete lack of historical knowledge most Americans had no idea that what they were now experiencing or seeing on the news was historically extraordinary. That an American state might go bankrupt and renege on fundamental promises made to its citizens would have seemed inconceivable to earlier generations. The federal government was in effect doing the same, but could conceal it by using its monopoly on issuing money. The debasing of the currency had been for decades a routine practice of the U.S. government and the Federal Reserve.

Americans were getting used to the riots. Pictures of burning buildings and cars, looting, and clashes between rioters and police and National Guard troops had become a staple of television news. Stories of this kind were as common as news stories about the American wars in the Middle East or recent sports events. The large riots, starting with the "Chicago summer" and continuing with the demonstrations and riots in Los Angeles, Portland, Detroit, Phoenix, and New York City, were followed by repeats in the same cities and lesser eruptions in places like St. Louis, Cleveland, Richmond, and San Francisco. Smaller and less violent disturbances, usually originating in protests against cuts in public benefits, and the frequent strikes of government workers added to a general sense of disorder. The public was learning to take news stories of the most recent disruption in stride. "Today, rioters clashed with police in Baltimore, Maryland. One person was killed and about twenty wounded before order was restored—"

Richard wondered if, for people below forty years of age, the violence of the videogames with which they had grown up helped give a kind of normality to these images on the television screen. The news analyses of the particulars of the various riots blurred: "Wanton plundering by mobs," "angry protests by the unemployed," "protests against cuts in pension benefits," "protests against Wall Street and the bankers," "racial tension," "protests against Washington"—the common theme was unrest and violence. The American public worried about their safety but got used to taking precautions. They took care to stay alert to trouble and to avoid places with acute

problems. Reports of similar disorders in Europe only contributed to
a sense that social disruption and widespread criminality were a part
of ordinary life. Large businesses relied more and more on private
security firms to protect them, as did well-to-do private citizens who
wanted their homes and neighborhoods kept safe. Gated communities
were becoming more and more common.

For Richard, these troubles had not come as any surprise.
They were, it seemed to him, the more or less expected practical
consequences of a moral-spiritual and cultural crisis that had gotten
progressively severe. For most of his life—before America finally
started to break apart, as he thought of what was happening—he
had regarded his country as being in better shape than Europe.
Now he had begun to wonder if distinctively American weaknesses
had made the decline of the United States more or less inevitable.
From his study of history and his travels in Europe, sometimes
to visit relatives, Richard knew that America had never had quite
the sophistication, refinement, and style that once characterized
Europe's upper and upper middle classes, but he felt that Americans
had made up for a certain lack of polish with a kind of moral and
political sturdiness and vitality. Especially when it came to political
life and institutions, Americans seemed to have a superior aptitude
and skill. The U.S. Constitution, though now in an advanced state of
disrepair, had lasted for a long time. Americans seemed to have had
an admirable predisposition to and knack for compromise. He could
not ignore the abominable Civil War, but he preferred to think of it as
the great exception to a general rule.

He used to think that America also had a neighborliness,
friendliness, and cheerfulness that, though they might strike
foreigners as superficial and forced, facilitated human interaction
and made for a folksy, informal kind of refinement. Americans
had their own desire for good manners, though these might strike
some Europeans as spotty and as having a coarse aspect. American
manners were still pretty genuine and helped make day-to-day
existence more pleasant.

Richard could never decide whether, on balance, the
American propensity for informality was a good or a bad thing. He
recognized, on the one hand, that a general laxness and casualness
in human interaction was a sign that no one really took other human
beings or life itself very seriously. A measure of formality and ritual
is symptomatic of treating others with respect, as if they and life
generally really mattered. To live decorously was to understand
and to signal to others that life is no mean, trivial matter. On the
other hand, an elaborate and unyielding formality, the kind of

rigidity that he associated with periods in ancient China, were artificial and destructive of the human bond. Inflexible formalism suggested a preference for form over substance. He liked to think that the manners of the better people in his hometown of Charleston had struck a proper balance. At the same time, he cringed at the pseudo-enthusiastic chumminess and informality of so many of his countrymen.

What he had always liked about his fellow Americans was their can-do energy and creativity. As combined with and restrained by moral seriousness and decent taste, these traits had made them rather admirable in the sphere of practice.

America most certainly did not lack intellectual sophistication, especially not in the natural sciences and technology. In those fields America had taken the place of Germany and had no really serious competition. If America had had few truly great composers, poets, painters, or novelists, it had a large number of such people of the second rank. Some of its symphony orchestras and individual performers were among the best in the world. America's vast entertainment industry had produced numerous excellent achievements. In the first half of the twentieth century American entertainment had begun to set the tone for the entire Western world, and the trend continued. This development made Richard all the more sensitive to the increasingly offensive side of American culture. It offered now a plethora of seemingly unbounded vulgarity, garishness, and noisiness. The sheer size of the entertainment industry and the stupendous rewards bestowed on its leading figures had always suggested to Richard something fundamentally wrong with the American sense of proportion and reality. The Hollywood dream machine and its counterparts in television played a huge role in shaping the American outlook on life, and that role was largely destructive of a traditional view of human existence.

The great prominence of sports and the enormous amounts of money circulating there gave him similar feelings. Was there an element of truth in that snotty European notion that Americans are not quite adults, but loud, overgrown children? But in that case the Europeans showed in their fondness for things American that they had the same propensity.

Though Europe and the rest of the world always formed part of Richard's consciousness as he grew up, he never felt that Americans were generally inferior to their European forebears. The Europeans seemed to be losing the best of their heritage even faster than the Americans, whereas Americans had kept alive and even breathed new life into some of the traditions, religious and moral not least among them, that were fading away in Europe.

Richard had always been proud to be an American, yet as he grew older he had come to the realization that America was losing its claim to being a truly civilized country. For a while a seemingly undiminished commercial and technological ingenuity and vigor had masked precipitous erosion at the moral and cultural core. The old American emphasis on character and personal responsibility as the basis of a good society had yielded either to sheer cynicism and greed or to purely sentimental notions of virtue. To be morally admirable meant not so much to improve yourself and do right by those closest to you, your own family and community, but to put forth sentiments of compassion for people in general, to empathize, to feel the pain of underprivileged groups somewhere in the distance. Richard saw in this sentimental virtue a moral cop-out, a way to avoid shouldering real responsibility for self and others. Doing good was becoming less and less a matter of personal character and action and more and more a task for benevolent-sounding politicians. The new public moralism had a way of lifting the moral burden from particular persons and transferring it to its proponents, which was convenient for those relieved of obligation and perfect rhetorical cover for politicians wanting more power.

The do-gooders were always in favor of some new urgent cause, which they waved in everybody's face. They always assumed that advocating their cause showed great moral stature and a right to universal approbation. That they might not care so much about their own family or local community was supposedly irrelevant. These moralists were in Richard's experience typically rather shady characters, whose benevolent-looking schemes hid a desire for power and sometimes covered up egregious personal failures closer to home.

In Richard's university, the faculty member who seemed most to embody the type was a sociologist who was forever agitating for the downtrodden—in the world, in America, or at National University. Sidney Green was a rather scruffy-looking sixty-year-old associate professor with a ponytail. He was a latecomer to and leftover from the campus radicalism of the late 1960s and early 1970s. His academic career had long been on hold because he did not publish much. But he made it seem that his personal advancement had to take a back seat to helping correct the injustices of the world. He appeared at every faculty gathering and was the spokesman for those oppressed by authority. He was always morally put out by some violation of justice and human rights in the world or in the administration of the university. His speeches were a mixture of moral indignation and unctuousness. Green wanted the world to know that he had a very big heart—he wore it right on his sleeve—and that he was a great fighter for good. Most faculty members resonated to his type of moral sensibility. The more mediocre faculty felt all the more comfortable with him because he did not represent any academic threat to them. Indeed, he made them feel less badly about their own professional shortcomings by showing how much more important it was to be morally noble than to publish. He let them all be morally superior together. Yet they also detected something self-serving and merely pretentious in his moralism.

Not long after Richard joined the National University faculty Green came to see Richard in his office to get him to sign a petition to the university's board of trustees to replace the university's president, Dr. Leslie Gestler, an economist and mainstream academic liberal who was trying to tighten the institution's academic standards. Gestler had been under attack for making tenure and promotion more difficult to obtain at the university and for making it easier to reward the academic performance of outstanding faculty.

"As you know," Green said, his face full of deep caring, "the general faculty here have been suffering for many years from a depressed salary scale—we are far behind comparable universities—and now we are seeing a flagrant violation of justice and fairness. Gestler is penalizing faithful faculty service and throwing the scarce resources available for salary increases in the direction of a few favorites. I hope we can count on your support."

Green always made it sound as if he spoke for hundreds and thousands of mistreated people. At first Richard tried to get rid of him without creating resentment by saying, "Thanks for coming, Sidney, but I don't think I'm entitled to have an opinion on this matter after just a few months at the university. I need to get my feet on the ground first."

But Green would not accept such moral evasiveness. "Oh, but what's going on is plain to see." Without missing a beat he increased the moral pressure: "It's becoming painfully clear that Gestler's treatment of the faculty forms part of a general lack of fairness."

"I take it you don't agree with his plan for improving the university's academic reputation?"

Richard realized as soon as he had formulated the question that it was just the wrong one to ask. The cat was almost out of the bag.

"Surely you recognize that rewarding a few favorites will do nothing to enhance our reputation. Don't you see, Richard, that his talk about raising academic standards is only posturing? Gestler is just trying to build his own power structure, a circle of faculty and administrators beholden to him. There's nothing wrong with our academic reputation. We reject at least as many student applicants as we admit. The real issue here is fairness, which is a moral issue."

"I see. But, as I said, I don't think I know enough yet to take sides in this controversy."

"But surely you recognize that this is ultimately a *moral* issue." Green was employing the argument that he felt ought to make the most recalcitrant professor yield. "The problem with Gestler is elitism coupled with moral callousness, a lack of concern about equality. How typical that Gestler has never shown the slightest interest in the university doing something for the underprivileged in the District of Columbia. He's perfectly content to let this campus be an oasis for the well-to-do in the middle of glaring poverty."

Richard couldn't resist complicating Green's task. "Middle of poverty? Isn't this campus located in a pretty wealthy part of town?"

Green was showing signs of exasperation. If he had expected a satisfying touchy-feely session in which he would have had another opportunity to display his powerful moral conscience, he was sorely disappointed. Richard clearly lacked the proper moral sensitivity.

"Don't be so literal. I'm talking about a wider responsibility for our fellow human beings. I don't need to tell you that over 50% of the population in the District of Columbia is black and that a large portion of that population suffers from poverty and other degradation. We can't ignore such an affront to the principle of justice. It's the same heartlessness that makes the U.S. ignore the Third World, especially Africa."

"I thought that American foreign aid was pretty substantial."

"A mere pittance, considering the wealth of this country."

Richard was getting impatient and said, "You mean that if we oppose Gestler, we would strike a blow for the Third World?"

For a moment Green wondered whether Richard might be somehow ridiculing him, but Richard's face was expressionless. Green shrugged off his unease. Richard was simply a moral dullard, a hard sell, Green decided. He would leave Richard alone, but not without making a morally dignified exit. He got up.

"Do give the petition some thought, Richard. We need your support." He paused briefly to give added emphasis to his parting sentence: "Somebody has to stand up for the weak—speak truth to power."

As Green walked out of the office, his ponytail seemed to give a flick of moral superiority.

Richard wondered how Green could have failed to notice that, in academia, virtually everybody was, in theory at least, a deeply caring champion of the downtrodden. It took no courage whatever to speak in their behalf among university faculty. President Gestler, by contrast, needed guts and will power to press his academic "elitism." But a person like Green could not afford to face the obvious. It would rob him of his sense of uniqueness and moral worth.

Richard bemoaned that the churches, too, had been invaded by this sentimental parody of traditional charity and love of neighbor; indeed, they were themselves sources of the transformation of Christian morality into a demonstrative emotionalism that made the old idea of character as well as specific old principles of morality irrelevant. One of the reasons why his church attendance was somewhat grudging was that he found it hard to take the often sentimental and politically correct tones of the rector of the Episcopal Church in Bethesda to which his family belonged. He wanted to find a more traditional church, not least for the sake of the children, but he had not taken the time seriously to look for one. On the one hand, Richard was sad that people were drifting away from the churches, but, on the other hand, he was not convinced that they would be better off staying in them.

Those who set the general tone in American society were, Richard thought, morally disoriented at best, positively amoral or perverse at worst. The trendsetters were only superficially civilized, having the usual academic degrees. They were often glib and articulate, but it was rare to meet a person in a position of real authority who had obvious moral integrity and some personal gravitas and refinement. The general moral-spiritual decline that Richard thought that he detected seemed to be accompanied by aesthetical decline. Even in America's so-called upper classes — membership in which was determined more and more by wealth alone — very few could be expected to have distinguished tastes or to have anything beyond the most elementary grasp of etiquette or sartorial standards. There was for Richard little comfort in the fact that much the same had become true for Europe. The Americanization of Europe and the rest of the world was in some ways a source of pride, but it bothered him that Europeans and others were so often attracted to what was least admirable about his own country.

The decline of American manners and standards of deportment seemed to Richard to reflect a more general and deeper problem. So did the fact that Americans were becoming ungainly, fat, and otherwise unattractive. They remained rather genial, but only as long as they were not provoked or subjected to pressure. They were, among other things, greatly confused, torn in different directions by a fragmenting culture.

Once, when Richard and the family were traveling by car in Arizona during a vacation, they had stopped at a McDonald's at the children's insistence. As they ate and talked, Richard observed, as he always did, the behavior and demeanor of those around him.

"Do you notice anything in here?" he suddenly asked Helen and the children. John had just become a teenager.

"Now what?" Helen asked. She was used to Richard making disparaging remarks about people and phenomena around him. She did not so much disagree with his observations as regret the effect they had on conversations. His noticing what was unappealing rather than appealing about a particular scene detracted from what could have been a pleasant time together. Helen also did not like to be reminded of her husband's inner sadness. "What's wrong this time?" she said.

"I didn't say anything was wrong. I just wanted you to look around to see if you notice anything out of the ordinary."

Helen gave him a faintly disgruntled look but quickly hid it behind a smile. The children looked about them.

"Did you see anybody we know?" Anne said. "How could you? We are hundreds of miles from home."

"No, it's something different."

"I guess it's something not being right," John said. He had become attuned to his father's moods and predilections.

"Well, in that case, what would that be? Look around you."

"I don't see anything," John said.

"Neither do I," said Anne.

"Richard, we can't be expected to follow the vagaries of your imagination. Different people notice different things," Helen said.

"But I think this is rather striking."

"What do you mean?" John said. "I don't see anything out of the ordinary."

"I don't either," Anne said.

"Well, come to think of it, I suppose you are *right*. There really *is* nothing out of the ordinary about this scene. That's a part of what's so remarkable. You see the same thing everywhere—not just at McDonald's but in stores, homes, schools, movie theatres, etcetera. And you don't even notice."

"What *are* you talking about, Dad?" Anne scanned the restaurant as she spoke.

"Don't you notice—nothing really matters to any of these people. They don't really care very deeply about anything?"

"They don't?" Helen asked. "I would have thought that they are like most people. They think about how much is left of their vacation, they look forward to the Grand Canyon, or they worry about those mounting bills waiting at home or about whether they will make it into their favorite college or about whether the cancer has spread, or they wonder about whether they will get a promotion or whether they might go to the movies tonight."

"Mom, what *are* you talking about?" Anne said.

"I'm talking about these people and saying that they are like most other people—not out of the ordinary. Many of them are just like us, passing through on this highway."

"But look at them," Richard persisted. "Look at their dress. A jump suit, or a part of one, a pair of torn jeans, sneakers, boots, a baseball cap, knit cap, shorts, whatever—without any idea of what might be appropriate for particular circumstances. They just put on what happened to be within reach. Not so much as a hint of taste or personal dignity."

"Richard, that simply isn't true! You're being ridiculously judgmental! Some of those girls thought long and hard about what they would wear."

"Wasted effort then, wasn't it? Their aesthetical sensibilities are so undeveloped that they might just as well have put on whatever lay on top of one of the piles in their messy rooms."

"You know nothing about their rooms. They may be very tidy."

"Why do I doubt it?"

"That's your problem." Helen was resisting her husband mostly for the sake of the children. Richard often engaged in hyperbole and did not expect to be taken literally, but she did not want the grief behind his comments to infect John and Anne.

"Besides, most of them are on vacation," she added.

"Oh! On *vacation*! But that excuses *everything*, doesn't it? Then they should be allowed to look any way they want, *shouldn't* they?"

"Richard," she said pleadingly.

"All right, forget it," he said, forcing a smile to lighten the atmosphere. " I think you've confirmed my hunch. These people are not much different from the rest of the American people, which means that we've become a pretty sorry bunch."

"C'mon, Richard. You shouldn't go by superficial appearances." She smiled, trying to conceal that she was getting annoyed with his sniping.

"Superficial? These supposedly superficial appearances are a manifestation of a state of soul."

"Surely, there is more to these people than meets the eye."

"Of course, but the way of talking, thinking, dressing, and interacting, reflects a general state of being."

"Some really good conversations may be taking place."

"Oh yeah? How could that be? Those youngsters are not far beyond the grunting stage. Can't you hear them? The girl says: 'Like, you know, like, Mr. Jones, was, like, upset, and I was like, like' — get it?' And the boy says: 'Sure, he's like, so, like — yeah, . . . . You know. Benny thinks that, like, you know, like I said, ah, and he's like — you know?'"

"And why do you assume it's as bad as all that?"

"Because I've heard them talking and because these poor souls have been left in the lurch by people who should have taught them better — parents, teachers, preachers, entertainers, intellectuals, political leaders. There are no proper models for young people. In fact, nobody's opinion is supposed to be superior to anybody else's — except that you're supposed to disdain all old models. These poor youngsters get their standards from mixed-up, drugged-up, odd sports figures and actors and performers. That's how their pitiful little imaginations work."

"Now stop it, Richard!" Helen exclaimed in a sharp but half-joking manner. "Can we enjoy our vacation?"

"I'm going too far, am I? But these people have only the foggiest idea of what might be a proper way to live. The only reason they aren't in mad houses is that the older American traditions haven't quite died out yet and are giving some structure to their sorry lives."

"Can't you hear how you sound? Let's talk about something else!"

"OK. Let me just nail down this point. America doesn't have a leading class any longer with sound standards and the influence to transmit their moral and cultural values down the line. The people who dominate this country today are trying to destroy whatever remains of traditional norms of conduct and deportment."

Anne had lost interest in what seemed to her an increasingly weird and abstract conversation and concentrated on her French fries. John feigned a similar disinterest, but kept listening.

"I'm willing to concede," Richard continued, "that many of these people are really pretty decent, and they are in a way not to blame for their predicament. Nobody's teaching them anything better, offering them a better example. But because of that lack of direction and the state of our popular culture they're floundering."

"You're exaggerating, as usual."

"So I'll admit that I'm exaggerating a little to make my point. These people may not all be morons, but they sure look and act the way you would expect morons to look and act."

John said, "Can we get back to the car now?"

Richard was for some reason particularly dismayed by the looks and demeanor of certain middle-class, middle-aged women. Their hefty, square, frumpy, sex-less bodies, and matching dowdy clothes suggested that they had no sense of elegance or erotic flair. They would arrive in clumps of twos or threes at a restaurant for a girls' night out, their stocky frames topped by non-descript, indistinguishable heads, all adorned by short graying hair worn a little longer up top—cut, presumably, for convenience. They seemed to be proper, decent, and responsible and had done their best to "dress up" for dinner at a restaurant, but what was this strange absence of taste and style, of anything extra? Was it not ultimately discomfort with their sex? Richard reflected that their husbands seemed not to notice or care. They were the male counterparts of this barely female race, though, on average, heftier than the women. These men and women seemed to put up with each other, Richard thought, even get along rather well together, but how was this possible? They seemed to be only slightly different versions of the same middle class unisex. Were they decently content with their lot because happily unaware of anything else? Or did they, under that plain exterior, all entertain wild, rebellious daydreams that gave some perverse lift to their lives? No, if they had daydreams, as was surely the case, even their sexuality had to be dowdy and lackluster. Was this what it meant to be "solidly" middle class? It was a bland and flabby solidity.

Richard realized that in ruminations of this kind he tended to seize upon the more discouraging aspects of phenomena. He did not consider himself at heart a pessimist or killjoy, and others did not regard him as glum, but he simply could not get away from the fact that the trends that he observed in his country formed an ominous pattern.

What Richard knew most about was American academic life. In the leading universities, whose intellectual trends Richard assumed to foreshadow what is to come in general society a generation later, he found a spreading moral nihilism and a desire to pull down remaining traditional intellectual and social structures. His fears about the future of his country had intensified while he worked on his Ph.D. in history at Harvard. Among the professors in his department and in other departments and among his fellow students he had encountered beliefs that he found not just difficult to reconcile with traditional Western civilization, specifically American culture and constitutionalism, but also positively virulent in their likely effect on what he admired. He realized that ideas proliferating among the Harvard faculty and on faculties of similar reputation would eventually shape American public opinion and the broader culture. After the Second World War moral and cultural relativism often tinged with socialism had had the intellectual initiative at leading academic institutions. During Richard's years at Harvard those currents had been challenged by a radicalism that was even more thoroughgoing and that exuded a spirit of cultural revolution.

He had had reason to believe that his professors and fellow graduate students assumed that he had backward, unsophisticated ideas. As soon as he opened his mouth his southern accent gave him away. His was an educated inflection, but in the ears of others it was fraught with terrible racial, religious, political, and sexual overtones. He could have developed a different way of speaking, but he was not ashamed of his South Carolina origins.

Partly to understand better what he would be up against in years to come, he took a course in English literature with a professor famous for his "deconstructionist" views. Richard was one of a dozen students. The professor brilliantly exposed what he considered the more or less blatant, sometimes tyrannical biases that particular literary works foisted on readers. These, the professor claimed, were subtle schemes of dominance, of controlling the reader's outlook. The professor showed that novels and poems contained no universal, interpersonal, enduring meaning, no truth about "the human condition," but were mere texts that different readers would understand very differently. The work was what the particular reader made of it. Traditional literary canons were arbitrary and deserved no special respect. Perhaps to show that he was above old-fashioned assumptions and expectations, the professor usually wore jeans with a T-shirt or an unpressed sports shirt or a torn sweater. His hair was longish and seemed not to have known a comb or brush. Richard kept a rather low profile in the course, which was made up largely of aspiring so-called literary "theorists," who hung on the lips of the famous man. But occasionally Richard cautiously challenged the professor, feeling each time that his fellow students regarded him with condescension, perhaps to prove their allegiance to the professor. About midway through the course Richard asked:

"As an historian I'm used to thinking that there are no objective historical facts sitting out there waiting to be collected, as many historians used to think. There's no single *meaning* of history. Historians and others necessarily bring their own perspectives to whatever historical evidence they study—which seems to be similar to what you are saying about reading literary texts. But why would the personal, idiosyncratic element in study or reading have to preclude shared human meaning? Couldn't we be historically situated beings and nevertheless manage to transcend our own biases, at least to some extent?"

The professor smiled. "*T-r-a-n-s-c-e-n-d*," he said deliberately and with emphasis. "Now there's an old-fashioned word." Richard knew that having asked the question in a southern accent had made his intellectual provincialism all the more obvious to those in the room. The other students looked at each other smiling, and, in a couple of cases, giggling.

"Using a word like that shows how tied we still are to old linguistic habits," continued the professor. "Here's a word that refers to a postulated extra-historical essence. What I've been trying to show is that literary conventions, including the belief that there's something universal beyond historicity, something *transcendent*, something beyond our merely personal perspectives, are arbitrary and ultimately part of an attempt to foist perspectives on others to exercise power over them."

"So, there's no transcending the outlook of the individual?" Richard asked. "We're all alone in the universe, stuck within our own idiosyncrasy?"

"Well put, Bittenberg. You've caught my meaning."

"*Your* meaning, professor? Yours only?"

The professor was temporarily put off-stride. Some of the students looked anxiously at each other.

The professor was finally ready with his answer and said in an authoritative manner: "We have to face that we're ensnared in domineering, repressive linguistic conventions, and that we have to free ourselves from illusory notions like 'transcendence.'"

The professor's arrogance annoyed Richard, and his rejoinder became more pointed than he intended: "But why should we give up older apparent meanings that seem to have the support of many generations and adopt an opinion that is, if you're correct, only yours?"

The professor looked flummoxed and a little irritated, but concealed his discomfort behind a tolerant smile.

"Do you want to live under pretentious, tyrannical illusions, Bittenberg?"

"No, but you seem to be saying that there are no meanings, period, only texts, only perspectives."

"What of it?"

"Then what are we doing here? Why are we taking courses,

why do we aspire to publishing books and articles? Why are you trying to persuade others—if there's no such thing as shared meaning?"

The other students looked incredulous and disoriented, and the professor was showing growing irritation. Richard knew that he had gone too far. He would have to make amends later to have a chance for a good grade. In his comments in class and especially in his remaining paper for the course he should dwell on what he could accept in the professor's teaching. In his writing he had better quote liberally from the professor's published work.

Having caught his breath and collected his thoughts, the professor spoke in magisterial tones that ruled out contradiction: "What we are doing here is unmasking thousands of years of oppression—of women, the poor, people of color, and so on—trying to set the individual free to be what she wants." Richard wanted to ask why the professor's point of view was not just another example of the imposition of arbitrary belief on gullible people, but he kept the thought to himself. He reflected that, while the professor's scruffy appearance and disdain for literary canons supposedly expressed his independence from intellectual convention, he did not seem to want to give up the traditional authority of a professor.

When the students filed out at the end of the class, a male student Richard didn't know passed him and said almost in a whisper, "Way-to-go, Bittenberg. I agree with you."

Were there others who agreed with him, Richard wondered. If so, they had been silent. They had reluctantly gone along with the professor—just as some of his acquaintances ground their teeth about social and political trends, but did little or nothing to oppose them.

In his ensuing academic career Richard ran into many varieties of radical or revolutionary thought. Most of them made no secret of their hatred of traditional Western society, but some actually masked that animus as a defense of "American values"— this in order to sneak radicalism up on naïve traditionalists. The trick was to redefine "American values" as having been inherently radical from the beginning: America had liberated people from the bad old days of Europe.

A supposed expert on classical Greek political thought in National University's political science department, who also wrote columns for the smaller of the Washington newspapers, kept urging Richard to attend campus events that he arranged. One was a public lecture by a media celebrity that Richard dutifully attended. The speaker's main point was that America is an "exceptional nation" and is called to help bring democracy to the rest of the world. After the lecture the political theorist was flushed with pleasure. "Wasn't that great?" he asked Richard. "Isn't he such a good speaker?"

"He doesn't seem to know much about the founders of this country."

"What do you mean?"

"Well, he seemed to assume that the founders believed in democracy and wanted America to spread it abroad."

"So?"

"Well, I thought it was pretty well known that the framers of the Constitution spoke rather disparagingly of democracy. What they wanted was a constitutional, representative republic and a central government of limited powers. They also wanted to keep their noses out of the business of other countries. They were afraid of foreign entanglements, remember?"

"Ah, well, yes, perhaps, but in today's world they would certainly have wanted to spread American values and fight Islamofacism."

Richard thought of making a dismissive remark and walking away, but he said, "We should be careful not to read too much of our own preferences into the minds of people from the past. We don't want to commit the fallacy of anachronism." Because he could not resist a dig against what he knew to be one of the political theorist's favorite ideas, he added: "How would you, an expert in classical political thought, like it if some ideologue asserted that Plato was not really a proponent of elitism and a fierce critic of democracy but actually *preferred* democracy?"

The political theorist glanced suspiciously at Richard, who kept a straight face, and then stuttered, "Well, but—that's, ah, actually not so far from the truth as you might think."

At that comment, Richard bid the political theorist good night. He already knew that the political theorist and other representatives of the same "school" of political thought interpreted Plato, the archenemy of democracy, as a democrat in disguise.

"Boy-Scouts," he thought to himself. "But up to no good."

The super-patriotic advocates of global democracy were just another self-serving group speaking in the name of America. They were actually tearing at the traditional American body politic in their own way. Richard knew several such self-proclaimed patriots. They had intellectual pretensions and were arrogant and cocky. They derived their sense of self-importance from the constant propagandizing and reinforcement available within their own large network. But if pushed even minimally outside of their accustomed ideas and formulas, they became flustered and hid behind attitudes of superiority and condescension. They were intellectual activists rather than scholars and philosophers. Most of them merely parroted the ideas of others who also manipulated them. Although these patriots gave the impression of despising moral nihilism and defending high principle, Richard knew most of them to speak with forked tongue. In practice they seemed to be little more than narrow-minded, nasty, two-bit Machiavellians, jockeying for advantage for themselves or their group. These were supposed to be brave, noble defenders of America?

It deeply worried Richard that public debate in America and the other western democracies had sunk to the level of simplistic sloganeering and demagoguery. Issues that should have been the subject of broad and intense discussion—such as the large role played by shadowy, unaccountable figures behind the scenes, not least in high finance—could not even be raised in the major media. Perhaps most disconcerting of all was that a veritable avalanche of self-applause accompanied America's precipitous descent. America was better than all other countries, America was exceptional, America was called to create a better world. America . . . America . . . America . . . .

A week after his encounter with the Plato expert, Richard ran into him again on campus, and the political theorist wanted to talk.

"I didn't want to give you the wrong impression the other day. I realize of course that America and the world have changed a lot since the Founding. But surely, today the principles of the founders require that America be a strong proponent of freedom and democracy in the world."

"You think so? You don't think the framers would be more concerned about making emergency repairs here in America? Look at what's happened to the moral virtue they considered necessary to sustain constitutionalism? Traditional American values are retreating all the time. And it causes a wide range of severe problems. We have reasons to be deeply worried about our own country, don't we? This is hardly the time to impose our 'values'" — Richard made the quotation sign with his fingers — "on other peoples? Sorry, Nathan, I've got to go."

The notion that America should try to become the uncontested global hegemon appeared to Richard a sign that American leaders were simply loosing touch with reality. America's severe domestic problems demanded attention and resources. And who were Americans to assume that they are superior to all other peoples? At the height of their time of empire the Brits had at least had a highly educated, polished ruling class. How could a bunch of ignorant, gum-chewing, obese yahoos in shorts, sneakers, and baseball caps man an empire — the notion was preposterous. Such people made up for their lack of sophistication by being all the more loud, pushy, and belligerent. He thought of them as "let's kick-some butt-nationalists." Schemers behind the scenes easily and routinely manipulated these simpletons.

Richard had never been a political partisan. He found both of the major parties guilty of shortsightedness and irresponsibility. Their leadership formed part of America's permanent power structure. It seemed obvious that traditional America with its political institutions could not endure these trends. With the disappearance of old-fashioned American moral responsibility and self-restraint, the craving for power was becoming ever more insistent and blatant. That politicians and others want power is only to be expected and by itself not disturbing, but more and more the desire for power was casting off the checks imposed internally by moral conscience and externally by the Constitution. The will to power was turning into an all-consuming end in itself.

Among those wielding the greatest political influence, Richard had found, the pursuit of power had become virtually indistinguishable from the pursuit of riches. Behind the politicians, in a kind of symbiosis with them, were the large financial interests, which had largely shed traditional moral and institutional restraints. As an historian Richard knew well that Big Finance and Big Business always play big roles in the making of government policy, but now these interests had achieved unprecedented power, and they had become progressively greedy, cynical, and brutal. The national institutions that might have checked their power were for these interests obstacles to be overcome. Under their sustained attack, national sovereignty was dissolving. Richard noted with frustration and disgust how powerful people both exacerbated and took advantage of a deteriorating culture to advance a hidden agenda.

Thus, it seemed to Richard, proceeded a general, far-reaching erosion of American society. The progressive destruction of America's constitutional tradition was just one of the more obvious manifestations of a crisis that he regarded as, at bottom, moral and spiritual. The growing opportunism and cynicism of politicians and other leaders and the growing fickleness and superficiality of the general public reminded him of other historical periods of great decline. The parallels to imperial Rome seemed to him obvious.

The powers-that-be that Richard saw as ruining traditional America were so entrenched and effective at crushing or defusing challenges that opposition seemed virtually pointless. For that reason he sometimes wondered if he should simply turn his back on the decline and corruption, which robbed him of peace of mind. As he could do little or nothing to stop America's self-destruction, should he not try to create for himself and those closest to him a separate existence that shielded him and them to the greatest extent possible from what was happening? But every time he contemplated withdrawal from what alarmed him, another, stronger part of him protested. This perverse, wicked assault on civilized life had to be resisted. But how?

# CHAPTER 7

Helen had hoped that the food from McDonald's would give the children a sense that the world was still the same, but it seemed to make them think more about what was wrong.

"Dad would have loved this," Anne said.

It was true. Richard loved a hamburger with fries. The only reason he did not have them often was that he tried to maintain a healthy diet.

They ate in her and Richard's room in case Richard were to contact them. At least two other individuals might telephone, the consular officer on duty at the American Embassy or that nice French police officer or some colleague of his.

There was no longer any holding back the children's worries and questions. Helen could only try to signal to them that she did not expect any really bad news. The truth was that, though the wine was now taking some of the edge off her anxiety, she was starting to despair.

At the same time she felt a need to act. She wanted to be by the telephone, but she also wanted to look for Richard. She wanted to go to the Sorbonne to make inquiries at the library, but if she left the hotel she would not be able to act immediately on any messages they might receive.

She went downstairs to ask the doctoral student at the reception if he might know where in the Sorbonne library Richard would have been likely to go for his research that morning. She knew in general the subject of his most recent scholarly efforts, the role of international networks in the shaping of American thinking prior to America's entry into the Second World War. Presumably, he was looking for French involvement.

The anthropology student was rather confident that a person in Richard's field would have gone to a certain part of the main Sorbonne library and gave Helen directions. She thanked him and asked him to ring her room at any time of the day or night if somebody tried to reach her.

Helen was again of a mind to visit the library right away, but she realized that if she went now she probably would not find any staffers there who might have assisted Richard in the morning. She decided to stay at the hotel for the evening to be with the children and be close to the telephone. Immediately after breakfast the following day she would go the Sorbonne library, much as Richard had done.

"I would appreciate it, Johnnie, if you would stay at the hotel to watch the telephone while Anne and I go to the Sorbonne."

"Sure, Mom."

For the rest of the evening they discussed what might have happened to Richard and what they might do to find him. She did her best to seem optimistic, but waves of apprehension came and went.

Finally, after 9:00 PM, Helen suggested that John and Anne should go to their room to get ready for the night. She really wanted the children to stay with her for the night, but she feared that asking them to do so would worry them more than following routine.

She was surprised that Anne did not protest. Helen brought them to their room. Having tucked them in and hugged them she did not linger. As she was leaving, smiling and saying "good night," she caught a dark glance in Annie's eye. Helen had to leave the room quickly not to let them see her blinking back tears.

She knew that Mr. Bennini would be annoyed if she called the consulate again. If he had had anything to report, he would have called her. But she couldn't stop herself. What if he had called while she put the children to bed? She reached for the telephone. When she got through to the consular officer on duty this time he sounded sleepy and confused rather than irritated. As it was just before 10:00 PM, perhaps Bennini had fallen asleep in front of the television set, she reflected. Or perhaps he and his wife had gone to bed early.

Helen apologized. "I know you said you would let me know if you received any news about my husband, but I'm beyond myself, Mr. Bennini. There has been no word from my husband or anybody else. He's been missing for nine hours. Would you please see if you might have any further information?"

"Mrs. Bittenberg, I understand that you're worried, but I have no new information. The consulate is closed, and any emergency calls to the consular section would be routed to me. Still, I will check again. Let me call you back."

After ten minutes, during which Helen paced nervously, Bennini called.

"Mrs. Bittenberg, as I suspected, we've not been contacted in any way about anything that might concern your husband. I talked just now to the consular officer who was the last to leave the consulate this evening, I even talked to security, and I did some more computer checking. There's no information that might relate to your husband's disappearance."

"Thank you Mr. Bennini. I shouldn't have bothered you. Sorry to be such a pest."

"Don't worry about it. I would be just as upset as you are. And please believe me when I say that we will contact you if we should learn anything at all that may relate to your husband. We do have your number at the hotel."

"Thank you."

Helen thought to herself that if she ever got Richard back, she would call the American ambassador to let him know about the kindness of young Mr. Bennini.

She thought of calling her parents in Washington. It would be very early morning where they were. Her father might soon wake up on his own. But what would such a call accomplish? It might make her feel better to share her misery with someone, and it might help steady her nerves to get the perspective of someone not immediately involved. But she would not call. If she did, her parents would expect good news. She would only upset them, and they would be able to do nothing to help.

Could she call anyone else? What was the name of the man at the embassy whom Richard knew and had gotten to know at Harvard? He was not a close friend, like Robert Preston from South Carolina, but Richard had talked about looking him up in Paris if they had some time to spare. Helen had met the man a couple of years ago at a Georgetown reception for a foreign dignitary in whose country he had served at the American Embassy. What was his name? Donaldson? Robertson?

Exhausted but fully alert, Helen finally got ready for bed. She watched television, looking for local news. She realized how foolish she was to do so, and there was no mention of any accidents or disruptions that might explain Richard's disappearance. She speculated endlessly about what might have happened to him. Some of the thoughts that rushed through her mind were far-fetched, even preposterous. In some moments she tried to convince herself that all would be well in the end. She tried to rein in her raging imagination and to be more practical. She ran through various plausible contingencies for the near future and made plans for the next day. If Richard had not returned or been found in a day or two, they would obviously have to cancel their European trip. She would have to send the children home. Her parents would have to take them for as long as she remained in Paris.

She turned out the lights but simply could not settle down.

She prayed. Though in ordinary circumstances she did not pray regularly, she did it often enough for the act to be familiar and natural. It gave her some peace, but it did not last long. Her spirit was squirming in pain. After midnight, she turned the light on again. Over the next twenty minutes she drank the rest of the wine, over half a bottle. Unused to drinking more than a glass with dinner, or perhaps two at a dinner party, she finally passed out.

Helen woke up with a start. It was four o'clock in the morning. She did not wake up *from* a nightmare but *to* a nightmare. She could not fight it off. She gasped for air and felt a little queasy — the wine, she thought. But she had to check if there was any news. She sat up.

She called the front desk. She had told the young man to put through a call at any time of the night, but she had to make sure he had not forgotten or that someone else had not replaced him. When the man answered he sounded groggy. He must have been sleeping in the little room behind the reception. Helen detected a note of irritation when he confirmed that no one had called.

There was no point in even trying to get back to sleep, she decided. She was wide-awake, and she felt her stomach churning. She went to the bathroom to no avail and then lay down on the bed again. Her nausea was worsening. It was as if her whole being rebelled against the reality she had to face. She finally had to run back to the bathroom. She threw up. Drained and miserable, she collapsed on the bed. She closed her eyes. Suddenly she was asleep again.

# CHAPTER 8

Several months before his talk with Helen about his ragged state, Richard had had a long discussion about politics with his oldest and closest friend, Robert Preston, that had deeply upset him. The friendship had formed when Richard was a graduate student in history at the University of South Carolina. What had brought the two together was a similar outlook on the world, together with a desire to prod behind the surface of life. They had spent long hours in conversation trying out ideas on each other. They were rather unusual university students. While others partied, they talked. When Richard completed his Master's degree and returned to Charleston and later when he went to Harvard to get a doctorate in history, he and Robert stayed in touch and met whenever they could. Robert followed in his father's footsteps and became a successful lawyer in Columbia. He then became a state senator, and finally a U.S. Representative. By that time Richard had gotten his position at National University, and the two could meet more frequently, now in Washington. Richard was delighted that a person like Robert could be elected to the U.S. Congress. He admired him, and his views were almost identical to his own. Robert was his best friend.

Robert was more than Richard the typical southerner. His South Carolina inflection was more pronounced than Richard's, and he spoke more slowly and in a more ornate manner. Richard sometimes got impatient with his friend's more deliberate, roundabout rhetorical style. As tall as Richard, Robert was more portly. The hair on his pleasant head was thinning.

Robert, his wife, and their two children rented a small boxy colonial in an old Bethesda neighborhood just west of the District of Columbia line off Massachusetts Avenue. The Preston house was not far from the C & O Canal, which runs parallel to the Potomac River and is a favorite spot for bikers and walkers. Robert noted that their Washington house was smaller than the one they owned in Columbia but would be almost twice as expensive to buy. Richard and his family also lived in Bethesda, but in a more affluent neighborhood about a mile away, further into Maryland. Though Richard and Robert had difficulty finding the time—Preston wanted to be back in his district at least two weekends a month and Richard was always swamped with work—the two families socialized fairly regularly. Richard and Robert met rather often for breakfast in a little restaurant in downtown Bethesda that offered Louisiana food. They sometimes did not leave until lunchtime. The discussion that so unsettled Richard took place in Robert's home. They were alone for the conversation, sitting on the screened-in back porch on a pleasant fall Sunday afternoon. They had discussed the growing role of political opportunism and that it had become rare for politicians to say what they really believed. Richard had turned the conversation in the direction of a bill before the House of Representatives, opposed by the secretary of defense, to keep a number of military bases and facilities open that the Pentagon had scheduled for closing. Richard had seen a story in the *Washington Post* about congressmen maneuvering to keep money flowing to their states and districts. As was common between them, Richard and Preston found themselves in agreement on the general political issue: The "military-industrial complex," in President Eisenhower's term, had to be reined in. Too much money was being frivolously spent. But Richard noticed that Robert was uneasy talking about the subject. It finally dawned on Richard that his friend was planning to vote against his own convictions.

"Do I understand this correctly, Bob? You are going to vote for this bill that we both agree is not only misguided but very costly to the American taxpayers?"

"You understand correctly."

"Then there must be something I don't understand, something you haven't told me."

"I'm a politician, Dick."

"You don't need to tell me that."

"But you may not know that a politician has to balance a lot of considerations. He cannot always insist on having his own way. You have to compromise."

"I understand that, but you're not going to compromise away your fundamental beliefs, are you?"

"Dick, what use am I, if I don't get reelected? If I vote against this bill, which directly affects South Carolina, including your hometown of Charleston, the other party will field a strong candidate against me. I might even have opposition in my own party primary. I may well lose my seat. My margin of victory when I first got elected was just a couple of thousand votes. The last time the margin was just three times that. The guy who replaces me is likely to be a lot worse than I am."

"You mean you're never going to be willing to risk your

reelection?"

"Dick, this bill is going to pass whether I vote for or against it. Why should I risk my reelection for the sake of some grandstanding?"

"Grandstanding!? Didn't we just agree that this is a really bad bill? Don't you have the responsibility of telling your constituents what you think of it?"

"I'm sure the vast majority in my district disagree with me."

"But if you don't speak out and try to change their minds, who will prepare the way for a better policy? If winning reelection is always more important than enlightening your constituents and the American people, the majority is always going to win, however foolish and irresponsible it is. Then you serve no useful purpose. You become just a rubberstamp for what others want."

"You are simplifying too much, Dick."

"Am I? If nobody is ever going to risk losing the next election, who is going to warn the people? And if keeping your seat is all that matters, who's going to stand up to the president when he is pressuring everybody to support a really bad policy?"

"You have to pick your fights, Dick."

"Granted, but if you're not going to stand your ground on a really important issue, when is it going to be?"

"This bill is important, but, on balance, it's not all that significant."

"No? It will waste millions and millions of dollars."

"Dick, it's easy for you to throw stones at people like me. You don't have to take the heat. You don't know what it is like to stand up to the pressures around this town."

"But, if you are not going to do it, Bob" — Richard's voice was rising — "who will?"

The main reason why this conversation put a pall over Richard's thinking for a long time was not really disappointment with his old friend. A part of him agreed with Robert Preston. He was certain that Robert had a good deal more integrity than most of his congressional colleagues. He probably showed more courage as a congressman than he had let on. In his conversation with Richard he had probably spoken out of exasperation as much as anything else, perhaps out of a bad conscience for giving in too easily at times. Some of what he had said had probably been hyperbole, born of frustration with the relentless pressures to conform and with how difficult it was to change existing ways. He had probably spoken more in sorrow than out of conviction.

What so bothered Richard about this conversation was that

it brought home in a concrete, incontrovertible way what he thought he already knew about a broad decline of American traditional values and institutions. That the new system could have this effect on a person whom he liked and admired told him that the moral weakening and corruption was in fact ubiquitous and virtually inexorable.

Richard was appalled by the opportunism and cynicism evident among America's political leaders. The national or common good was for most of them a mere word, behind which hid a rapacious desire for more or continued power. Their irresponsibility was sometimes mind-boggling. Letting future generations pay for today's overspending was considered normal. And some of these politicians thought nothing of sending young men and women to die in wars that served, not the national interest, but their own personal interest or a special interest to which they had to defer for the sake of political survival.

The sometimes belligerent, sometimes rash, and often crudely nationalistic use of American military power deeply troubled Richard. The ease with which the president could bypass or overwhelm the U.S. Congress in foreign policy was to him an egregious example of the crumbling of the constitutional restraints and priorities that the American Framers had established. Although he had never seen war up close, he felt that he knew something of its horrors. He had been a student at the Citadel, the military academy in Charleston, and he was an historian with an imagination and a capacity for empathy. He had talked extensively with his father, Peter, who had been a battlefield surgeon in Europe during the Second World War. His father had seen the most gruesome aspects of military conflict and had more generally observed the devastation and protracted suffering of war, not least as inflicted on civilian populations. His mother, who had received permission to join his father in Europe just after the war, had also seen up close the utter destruction, desperate poverty, and numbing grief suffered by the survivors of war. It amazed and infuriated Richard how cavalierly certain American politicians and pundits contemplated military action.

The same wanton attitudes were evident in the willingness of politicians to spend money they did not have. Their habit of saddling children and grandchildren with debt was despicable. Richard saw the same shortsightedness and recklessness behind tolerating the large-scale legal and illegal immigration into the United States. This development was, he thought, one of the reasons why traditional America's distinctive values and liberties were being replaced by something much different. It upset Richard particularly that the dissolution of traditional American culture did not merely result from haphazard evolution. Many of the political, intellectual, and cultural trendsetters and those who supported them financially were *deliberately* destroying his America.

Feelings bordering on despair sometimes overcame him. The riots around the country, triggered most immediately by America's economic condition, showed that not even basic physical security could be taken for granted. Sooner or later the financial house of cards would collapse, which might fundamentally unsettle American society. American leaders might drag the world into some horrendous military conflict. The prospect of U.S. leaders resorting to nuclear weapons to save money or to deal with frustrating opposition was terrifying.

Paradoxically, Richard was not a natural brooder. Despite his sad or biting comments about his fellow Americans, not even Helen regarded him as gloomy. He did not walk around under a cloud. His temperament was rather balanced. He had a cheerful streak and a good sense of humor. He typically remedied moodiness with action, such as getting on with the writing of a book or a conference paper. His professional activities were a source of satisfaction. He believed in what he was doing and knew that he was good at it. Most of his peers respected him as a scholar. A growing number of students wanted him to direct their doctoral dissertations. He was the main reason why in his department the field of intellectual history had become nationally recognized, much to the consternation of colleagues who thought this field and Richard's particular interests out of date.

His family was a source of happiness and gratitude. He thought himself very fortunate to be married to Helen. She was smart, had values similar to his, was interested in what was happening in the world around her, was beautiful, feminine, considerate, and very good with John and Anne. He sometimes wondered whether he deserved her and his two healthy, intelligent, well-behaved children. He was surely not always easy to live with. He usually kept a hectic pace, was preoccupied, and did not spend nearly enough time with the family. When at home, he typically isolated himself in his basement study, reading or writing. His chronic worries about America and his acerbic comments about persons and developments put somewhat of a damper on their family life. He could be a better husband and father. He knew that he didn't sufficiently show his gratitude and appreciation. That an inheritance from his father had made it possible not to worry greatly about family finances only underscored how fortunate he was. Although Helen did not work outside the home, they were able to afford a rather spacious, desirable home beyond the reach of the average academic family.

Really to tell Helen about the depth and scope of his worries would upset her too much, so he expressed his concerns in muted ways. But his unhappy comments had probably become more frequent. This had made her more and more uncomfortable and oppositional. It was not so much that she disagreed with him, he realized. She just did not see the point of dwelling on what was going wrong.

"Dick, why do you keep harping on the subject? It's not your fault things are the way they are, and you can't do anything about them."

"I suppose I'm looking for some reassurance and support." He smiled and made a funny face to make his words seem less serious.

"OK, so I agree you have a point. Am I supposed to say 'amen' every time you make one of your observations and then have a gloom and doom session with you?"

"I guess not."

"Then, what is it you would like me to do?"

"How about a kiss?"

"Maybe later. Right now you need to remember that you have a family and that everything you say affects John and Anne."

"What do you mean?"

"Dick, really, how do you think it makes them feel to be told all the time that the world is coming to an end?"

"*'All the time'*!? I seldom discuss issues like that in their presence."

"Oh yes? You have said quite enough for them to believe that it may be all over by tomorrow." Helen's voice had acquired an edge that made Richard watch his words.

"You don't think that's a little exaggerated?"

"It's *not!*" Having put a great deal of stress on the "not," Helen tried to sound a little more affectionate when she added:

"Dick, you have two very intelligent children, and they adore you. They admire you. Johnnie hears *everything* you say, and he thinks about it, believe me. He's not a little kid."

"I know he's not."

"Then, understand that you do not have to say much for his young mind to get very busy. He is fourteen, you know, and he is very receptive. Do you know what he is reading now?"

"No, I've been so busy these last couple of weeks."

"That's another problem, Dick, you don't take the time to find out what he's thinking."

"I suppose I have to plead guilty. Now, what's Johnnie been

reading?"

"Gibbon. The rise and fall of the Roman empire and all that."

"I get your point."

Richard met others who shared at least some of his worries, but it discouraged him that they were not sufficiently upset to wish to do more than complain in private conversation. Their attitudes were in a way understandable. Politically correct opinions and rituals were so dominant in American public debate that one who spoke frankly about America's problems risked losing his reputation, if he could gain access to any of the major channels of communication in the first place. The existing order was quick to spot potential troublemakers. Dissenters who voiced marginal criticisms and posed little real threat to the existing power structure could speak, but persons who raised serious doubts about the system and were getting through to the general public were quickly silenced. The powers-that-be could count on fear and greed to effect the desirable self-censure. People did not want to jeopardize their careers and income, and there was a great deal of money and other advantages to be had by individuals of ability who were willing to support or not challenge the existing order. What most bothered Richard was the dearth of people of courage and integrity who might do and say what they thought right although it would cost them something.

The reign of anti-traditional orthodoxy in the universities was painfully familiar to Richard. Especially in the best-known universities, brilliant professors expended great energy in attacking what remained of an older Western view of man and society. At the same time that Richard bemoaned the destructive influence of these trend-setting academics, he was bored with the intellectual predictability and sluggishness of their epigones, the general type that dominated the faculties of American universities and colleges. In theory and in his or her own estimation, that person was a most tolerant and intellectually independent freethinker, a principled champion of academic freedom. In practice the person was a conformist and panderer to academic authority. Richard thought of one of his colleagues at National University as the embodiment of the type. He was Stanley Carnack, the chairman of the Department of Sociology. Richard and Carnack had served together on a couple of university committees. Richard thought of Carnack as the intellectual and moral cousin of his older faculty colleague Sidney Green, the anthropologist who was also the reigning moral conscience of National University. Carnack was in a kind of competition with Green, but he was less of an anti-administration campus activist in order not to give university administrators the idea that he was a troublemaker unsuitable for administrative advancement. Carnack's record of scholarship was undistinguished, as is typical of aspiring administrators, but he frequented and often spoke at general faculty meetings that the more active scholars tended to avoid to have more time for their research and writing. Carnack spoke earnestly of the need to defend academic freedom, but Richard knew that the only freedom he cared about had the automatic support of fellow academics, who were anxious to prove *their* devotion to the same noble cause: the freedom to dissent from traditional conceptions of scholarship. To stand up for this freedom thus took no courage, was merely self-applauding posturing. "Dissenters" of this type actually dominated university faculties. That it was scholars of a more traditional kind who could use some academic freedom was not the concern of Carnack and his ilk. He had been a radical in his youth, but even then of a cautious, calculating type with an eye to what might advance his career. A picture of Che Guevara had long adorned his website, a signal to all that in his heart of hearts he was not some standard establishment academic but a *revolutionary*. Needless to say, he was a revolutionary only in his own imagination. He was an integral part of what was now conventional American academia. He was a medium-sized fish in a not very large pond. In theory, Carnack was an admirer of Nietzsche and disdainful of mass man, but he was the quintessential academic conformist, whose flirtation with unorthodox ideas could not be more abstract, half-hearted, and cautious. Deep down Carnack was an opportunist with an eye to the main chance. He played different roles with different people, trying to give each person the impression that he agreed with him or her.

Carnack, Green, and most of Richard's other colleagues exemplified another problem with American academia: that it was full of people uncertain of their social status. That uncertainty was not unrelated to America's widespread anti-intellectualism, but it had as much to do with the modest social origins of much of the American professoriate. In the United States more than in most Western countries it had long been possible for people to reach positions that had been far beyond the reach of their parents. It was not uncommon for persons who were the first in their family to go to college to become academics. More typically, faculty members were the sons and daughters of schoolteachers or other people of middle or lower middle class background. This pattern contrasted sharply with that of old Europe and, to a lesser extent, old America, where the traditional Western elite prejudice against utilitarian, "professional" activities blended almost imperceptibly with respect for more nondescript and contemplative pursuits. Academics in the older Western world were drawn predominantly from the upper classes. All this had changed, especially in America, with the spread of egalitarian attitudes and the fading of the traditional Western belief that utilitarian, wealth-producing work ranked below contemplative work. The intellectual life had been slowly but surely demoted. In America particularly, it had become rather firmly established that a truly accomplished, admirable person was financially successful. Young people from the upper classes who could went into finance or banking or aspired to the upper echelons of the professions. Teaching and scholarship was for those who couldn't quite make it in competition with the really smart people. The transformation of the professoriate was assisted by the fact that the WASP establishment, the upholders of the old American and Western standards, had lost their moral and cultural vitality and abdicated their position in the leading universities as well as in finance and the professions. They had been replaced by intellectually gifted, energetic, and assertive persons of predominantly humble social origins, who pushed ahead, battling, as they assumed, old obstacles to the advancement of "the unwashed" and inferior. It seemed to Richard that many in the new professoriate exhibited a psychology of social inferiority and resentment. This was often true, he thought, of descendants of the late arrivals in America, the so-called "ethnics," but was particularly pronounced among those who felt culturally most like outsiders in America. A psychology of social discomfort and inferiority was the breedingground for radical ideology. Even when such individuals made their way in academia and achieved an apparent equality with people of higher social origins, they remained aware of the old pecking order and felt resentful when reminded of the continued existence of upper class WASPs. It intensified their resentment that people who had much less education than they made far more money and moved in more elevated social circles. Richard saw in the lax general demeanor and dress of so many faculty members a more or less conscious declaration of indifference to or disdain for traditional standards: They would not even *try* to measure up to obviously outdated, artificial, and pretentious norms!

Most of Richard's colleagues, including the brightest and most productive, had separated themselves from the kind of holistic and morally anchored view of life that he associated with traditional Western civilization. Either they pursued some narrow, out-of-the-way specialty, or they preferred methods that disconnected areas of study from concrete, actual human life. Economists, political scientists, and the like, who might have been expected to take an interest in the real world, often seemed deliberately to distance themselves from that world by imitating mathematicians and natural scientists or by adopting abstract ideologies. It was for Richard a very bad sign for the future that even people in the supposedly most humane subjects, such as literature and philosophy, seemed to prefer unhistorical theorizing to the substance of life. And then there were the avant-garde circles that ridiculously exaggerated or twisted partial truths and hid from criticism behind undisciplined, chaotic verbiage.

It was because of America's precarious moral, intellectual, and cultural condition that Richard did not place much hope in political action. Politics ultimately acquired its direction from those now badly polluted sources. A political movement sufficiently broad and well grounded to be able to reverse present political trends presupposed a major reorientation of thought, imagination, and moral sensibility, which would require generations. It was highly unlikely that political figures would appear whose beliefs and desires would deviate sharply from those of the present system. Even if such politicians were miraculously to gain a foothold they would have great difficulty increasing their influence.

Yet *something* had to be done! Richard had never had any political ambitions. He had little interest in party politics. He had come to despise the political establishment's self-indulgence, cowardice, and escape from reality. But if the needed change could not be effected through politics, why was he so concerned about the lack of leaders who might challenge the present system? Did he actually hold out some hope for salutary political action? Did he in a part of himself concede the possibility that he was exaggerating the depth and scope of America's problems? If the situation was not quite as desperate as he normally assumed, society might benefit from some kind of political emergency treatment, a jump-start that shocked it awake. Appearances to the contrary, might some tough, dedicated politicians with the integrity and smarts of his friend Robert Preston break the political monopoly and point Americans away from the abyss?

Richard was the opposite of a political agitator, but he found it more and more difficult to maintain his scholarly detachment. Did he not have a duty to step in where others failed to act? He had indirectly alerted others to trouble through his writing, but his books and articles were not about contemporary society, only its forerunners, and they were written primarily for scholars and well-informed general readers. They were carefully balanced and rather subtle in their conclusions. This was because the complexity of the historical record seemed to him to preclude clear-cut, categorical conclusions, but also because Richard did not want too many of his peers to dismiss him. If he were to spell out his innermost beliefs, those peers would become leery of him. There was already discomfort with him in some scholarly quarters. Did not his writings implicitly question some of the most basic premises of political correctness? If he were to start writing about the America of his own day and speak his mind, many historians who had spoken well of him would be quick to disassociate themselves from him, notwithstanding their frequently stated support for academic freedom. Would any of them publicly endorse his basic beliefs?

In recent years he had become a little more outspoken in his courses, especially at the graduate level, but even there he exercised caution. He had to admit that he was doing something similar to what he blamed the better politicians and opinion molders for doing. His defense was that if he became too outspoken, he would undermine his own influence. But, then, who was he to have criticized his friend Robert Preston for not having taken a principled stand on those base closings?

Richard's life was becoming untenable. He was only vaguely conscious that taking on commitments was a way of distracting himself from the depth of his anxiety about America. He had a strong intuition that he could not long postpone a radical choice: either he had to put aside his worries and learn to appreciate what life still had to offer him and his family, or he had to engage the great problems of his society in a more direct way. He had a growing sense that withdrawing into scholarship and family life would be incompatible with maintaining his personal integrity. He would have even greater difficulty living with himself than now. Something had to change.

Richard repeatedly found himself asking what his father would have done. He felt that if he retreated into the merely personal sphere, he would, among other things, be letting his father down. He had wondered why that was so. His late father, a prominent surgeon in Charleston, had been very intelligent and thoughtful, but he had not been one to assert strong opinions or to insist that his two sons or his daughter should measure up to some particular standard. A man of considerable willpower, he was not an authoritarian. He had dignity, but was modest, courteous, and considerate. The boys knew less of where their father stood from his stated views than from his personal example. He did not so much argue as embody a set of values. He had been a strong presence in their lives. Richard felt more and more indebted to him. He realized that his father had come to represent what an American should aspire to be. He owed it to his father to defend what he had stood for. He had been a civilized American, a pillar of a kind of society that deserved to continue to exist, however much it drew the antipathy of the new American powers-that-be. His father, his larger family, and the society in which he had grown up needed him to be their advocate and defender. The change he made had to make some tangible difference for them and the America he loved.

But should he break out of his self-imposed censorship and speak and write with greater frankness and urgency? As a tenured full professor, he probably would not lose his main source of income, just the support of his dean and colleagues. He might have to forego salary merit increases. What he would most jeopardize was his reputation and — this did hold him back — the comfort and security of his family. Helen would be properly concerned about his becoming involved in controversies that would give him a "bad reputation," which would affect Anne and John. He often thought about how he would change his intellectual agenda to speak more freely and get wider attention for his views. But he had not found his way.

It was when failure to reach a conclusion regarding the way forward was beginning to wear him out that he got to know Mr. Herbert M. Vandenhorst.

Vandenhorst had at first seemed just another well-educated, well-mannered, intellectually curious person. It happened fairly often that people from outside the academy who had become interested in Richard's writing approached him. Some would strike up a conversation with him after his giving a public lecture. Others would write, email or telephone him to express their appreciation for a book or article. Some asked if they might meet him. Richard did not have the time to see every such "history buff," but he acceded to a few of these requests.

One person he had gotten to know was the managing partner in a large law firm; one was a just-retired admiral; one was the wife of a Supreme Court justice; one was the director of one of the Washington museums; one was some kind of top figure at the FBI. They were all familiar with his writing, were more than superficially interested in history, highly intelligent and pleasant. A few of these individuals had tried to stay in touch with him, and he had met several of them more than once. The admiral and his wife had invited him and Helen to a dinner party at their home. Richard found that he had more in common with this man than an interest in his field of history. A comment by Richard about American public debate minimizing America's problem had started a discussion about the sad state of the country. They became increasingly frank with each other and discovered deep agreement about the need for far-reaching change. Richard had felt sufficient rapport with and confidence in the admiral to broach the subject of whether "shock treatment" was now the only way to save America from disaster. In response the admiral had started talking about societies whose deterioration had led to political "takeovers." At yet another meeting with the admiral Richard had found himself discussing whether such a fate might befall the United States and what form a takeover might take.

He had lunch with the man at the FBI in a restaurant on Pennsylvania Avenue just across from the FBI building in downtown Washington. They discussed Richard's writings but also the role of hidden networks, including agents and spies of other countries, in the governing of the United States. Richard knew more than most about such networks in history — it was one of his areas of academic expertise — but he was startled by some of the information about ongoing hidden or clandestine activities in the United States that the FBI executive imparted. Richard realized that this man, who was obviously a person of considerable influence, trusted him with confidential, perhaps classified information. Was that not rather careless? This conversation too turned to whether rule according to the Constitution had become impossible. To Richard's surprise, the man from the FBI strongly implied that the time might have come to plan for extraordinary political action.

"The Constitution has in effect already been scrapped," the FBI man said. "We're getting further and further away from what the framers intended. You have to wonder if people who care about our constitutional heritage don't have to get organized to get the impostors out of the way."

"Get them out of the way? How?"

"By whatever means."

As Richard didn't really know the man, he didn't want to pursue this line of conversation. Was the FBI man provoking him into making some compromising statement? Or was he just indulging in tough talk, exaggeration, and extravagant speculation, as many men like to do? Thinking back on the conversation, Richard assumed that the FBI man had just let off some steam. From time to time Richard talked to people who complained of the worsening condition of the United States and employed extreme-sounding rhetoric, but he had never gotten the impression that one of them really meant what he said.

Mr. Herbert Vandenhorst, a gray-haired gentleman of retirement age, had seemed to be just another enthusiast for the study of history. That interest was clearly genuine, but Vandenhorst had proven to be a great deal more than a student of the past. After he and Richard had gotten to know each other better, he had invited Richard to take a drastic step. He had opened the door to a world with which Richard had previously been familiar only as an historian. That world lay very far from the peacefulness and leisure of scholarship. Richard had walked through that door knowing that it meant a break with his earlier life. His old existence would be placed on hold, perhaps abandoned forever. Though he had understood that he would have to face a new, uncompromising reality, he had had but a vague premonition of what awaited him. The actual, concrete circumstances of his new life had been permanently tension-filled, sometimes harsh and terrifying. He had subjected himself to pressures for which his past had barely prepared him. He had had to find his way in a world that could not be managed in the usual way. From then on, a sense of danger that sometimes turned into dread had never left him. He had had to live with constant unpredictability. He had had to marshal all the toughness and resilience that he possessed. His new circumstances had precluded all real repose.

On the surface, little seemed different about him after he had taken that step. Not even those who knew him best could tell that the ground had shifted under his feet and was weaving and twisting. In his outward demeanor the only hint that something was different was that sometimes a veil seemed to come down over his eyes, indicating that his mind was elsewhere. Perhaps there was also a new edge to the signals that he had always emitted that he was very busy and had no time to waste. But not even Helen suspected that the basic terms of his existence had changed.

Though his new predicament was in a sense wholly unexpected and strange, it was not because it was inherently implausible or hard to fathom. His earlier agony over the state of his country and his inability to make a difference could be seen as the natural prelude to his new life. As an historian Richard knew of many individuals who had suddenly found themselves in dramatically changed circumstances and who had to make decisions of a new kind that would directly affect the lives of thousands of human beings. What he still found difficult to believe was that he, Richard W. Bittenberg, thoughtful scholar, respected professor of intellectual history, husband of Helen and father of John and Anne, had been thrust, or, more precisely, had thrust himself, into this situation.

If he had had a presentiment that getting to know Mr. Herbert Vandenhorst might place him in just these circumstances, would he have declined to meet him?

Richard could see that in some ways his entire earlier life had pointed him in just this direction. That he might have to play a more than intellectual role had often occupied his thoughts in recent years. At times some such involvement as had now materialized had crossed his mind, but it had never become more than a fleeting idea, a game in his imagination. What would have been the point of seriously contemplating something that seemed not to lie in the realm of possibility? But it was now reality — of the most concrete and intrusive sort — though not of the kind that he had imagined.

# CHAPTER 9

When Helen woke up sharp daylight was coming through the drapes. It was almost seven o'clock. She had a headache. She remembered the wine she had consumed the previous night. But she had to get up. This was the morning when she would try to retrace Richard's steps at the Sorbonne. She called the children's room. She wanted to have breakfast with them at 7:30 so that they would be repeating the routine of the day before. She wanted to walk to the Sorbonne at 8:00 as Richard had done. Although it was a Saturday, she would try to find some librarian or other library employee who had worked the previous morning and who might have seen Richard.

After breakfast in the tiny breakfast room facing the street, they set out. As agreed the day before, Anne came with Helen while John waited at the hotel. They would be back in three hours. John would read or watch TV. He would be allowed to go downstairs as long as he stayed near the hotel reception.

They were at the main Sorbonne library in ten minutes. Though the library was open—major academic libraries rarely close except for a few hours in the middle of the night; the scholarly mind cannot wait—not many people could be seen. Helen asked library personnel she could find where Richard would have been most likely to go, and she concluded that the doctoral student in the hotel reception had known what he was talking about. Helen had brought Richard's passport, and could show his picture to persons she talked to. Nobody remembered seeing him. She had to wait until 10:00 for the main librarian in the most likely section of the building to arrive. Luckily, that person had been on duty the day before.

The librarian, a middle-aged woman, confirmed that this was indeed the part of the library to which one with her husband's research interests would have been most likely to come. But when Helen showed her Richard's photo she shook her head. She had been at her post in the morning the previous day, but nobody resembling Richard had been there. She showed Helen the ledger where each visitor to the research collections had signed in. Richard's signature was not there. Was there any other place in the library where he might have wanted to go to do the same kind of research, Helen asked.

The librarian pointed out that most research projects have an almost infinite number of possible angles. Her husband could have been in almost any part of the library. Helen sighed. Feeling hopelessness well up within her again, she told herself that she must not give up. She would try other sections of the library.

A short line of people had formed behind her. She was just about to walk away when a young mousy-looking woman with glasses immediately behind her said:

"May I see that picture?" The voice was obviously that of an American.

Helen let her see the passport photo.

"I may have seen him yesterday."

"You *did*!?" Helen pulled the young woman out of the line to talk to her. She could see that Anne was looking intently at the girl.

"Well, I can't be sure. You know what the pictures in passports and on driver's licenses are like. I may just have seen somebody similar. About fifty? Graying blond hair? Some kind of shirt, brownish maybe?"

Helen could not hide her excitement. Richard had been wearing a thin light brown summer jacket, and the rest of the description matched Richard.

"When did you see him?"

"Not here."

"Not *here*? Then where?"

"In the cafeteria. Two buildings from here."

"When was that?"

"I'm not sure. Maybe eight thirty. I was having breakfast."

What would Richard have been doing in the cafeteria before nine in the morning? He had just had breakfast and plenty of coffee at the hotel. Helen wondered if the young student was mistaken about the time.

"I wouldn't have noticed them except I could hear they were Americans, and I thought they looked a little out of place."

"*They*!?"

"Yes, there were two of them. They were sitting a couple of tables away from me in a corner. They talked quietly, but I could hear they were Americans."

Helen took the arms of the woman.

"Please tell me everything you saw." Helen introduced herself, and explained why she was so eager for information. The young woman gave her a sympathetic look and then gave her own name, Susan Kavanaugh. She was a junior from the University of Wisconsin, an exchange student in French who would soon start courses at the Sorbonne.

"Well, they were sitting in the corner away from the window. The other man had a suit and tie on—in the middle of August—which I thought was kind of strange, definitely out of place. Nothing like the people who work here or use the library."

"What else did he look like?"

"I don't really remember. I think he was about the same age as the other man. Darker hair. I think he wore glasses."

"Can you take me to the cafeteria?"

"Sure, if you'd like."

The cafeteria was located in an ugly modern all-purpose building. The cafeteria was large and impersonal.

"They were sitting over there." The girl pointed to an out-of-the-way corner. "I was at the table right there, so they were sort of behind me."

"Could you hear anything they said?"

"Not really. I wasn't listening, just wondered who they might be. There was a lot of regular noise, people talking, plates and silverware clanking, and so on."

"Did they leave before you?"

"Well, they were here when I got here. I don't think I saw them leaving. I was reading. I just noticed they were gone."

Helen gave the young woman her telephone number at the hotel and asked for her address and telephone number and thanked her.

"Good luck," said the American student. "I do hope you find him."

Helen located the manager of the cafeteria to find out whether the waitress who had handled the table in question would be on duty. She would be, but not until eleven o'clock because it was Saturday. While Helen and Anne waited they went back to the library. They walked around the building asking library employees and others if they had seen Richard. No one remembered him.

They were back at the cafeteria before 11:00. The waitress they wanted to talk to had arrived and started to serve customers. She was in her mid twenties, irritable and not very attractive. Had she slept badly the previous night? Had she just broken up with her boyfriend? But her English was good. Helen complimented her on it and learned that she had been an au pair girl in America for a few months. She was now a graduate student.

Helen explained the reason for wishing to talk to her, which made her less prickly. Helen then asked whether the waitress remembered two men sitting at the table in the corner, probably before nine o'clock the morning before.

"I worked from 7:30 to 2:00 in the afternoon, and I served a lot of people. I can't be sure, but, yes, I think there were two older men at table fourteen or thirteen some time in the morning. It could have been around nine. Americans. I could tell when they ordered. I think they only wanted coffee."

Helen showed the waitress Richard's passport photo. The waitress's face did not register immediate recognition, but neither did she shake her head. She continued looking.

"Yes, this may have been one of them, but I just can't be sure. Is this photo old?"

"A few years."

"Well, I'm thinking about the hair color of the one who could be this person."

"What about it?"

"I think it may have been grayer than in the photo. But he was rather cute for his age." She smiled at Helen.

Helen was becoming convinced that the waitress had seen Richard. "Do you remember anything they said or anything else about them, such as their clothes?"

"Well—the one had darker hair than the cute one. He was much more formally dressed, looked as if he was going to an important meeting. He could have worn a white shirt. The other one's clothes were more unremarkable."

"How do you mean?"

"Well, he was more informally dressed, looked more like some of the people who come here."

"What was the color of his clothes?"

"I think he wore some kind of jacket, beige perhaps, nothing striking."

Again, Helen did not doubt that the waitress had actually seen Richard. "Anything else?"

"No, and I really have to get back to work."

"I understand."

Helen managed to get the woman to give Helen her name and telephone number and even to accept the telephone number to the hotel. "In case you think of anything else. Thank you very much."

Helen and Anne walked away. It suddenly occurred to Helen that they were late. They would not make it back to the hotel within the three-hour limit they had set.

As they were about to leave the cafeteria, they heard a voice behind them. "Madame!" Helen looked around. The waitress had followed them and was motioning to them. Helen went back.

"I just remembered," the waitress said, "they may have been upset or were talking about something serious. They didn't like it when I asked them if they wanted more coffee, so I stayed away."

"Did you see them leave?"

"Yes, I wanted to pick up my tip and clear the table."

"What did you see?"

"Only that they seemed about the same height. Rather tall."

"Anything else?"

"No."

"Thank you very much."

"Don't mention it." The French waitress seemed pleased to know the American phrase.

They rushed back to the hotel.

# CHAPTER 10

Once during his graduate school days at the University of South Carolina when Richard was back in Charleston and his parents gave a party he met the editor-in-chief of the *Charleston Observer*, Andrew Harrington, a tall handsome man who immediately impressed him very favorably. He seemed to be not only civilized, a southern gentleman in the best sense, but a highly intelligent and literate individual with well-thought-out views of life and politics. Richard was happy to know that such journalists still existed. They talked about Richard's studies and their respective views of America and the world.

A week later when Richard was back in Columbia working to complete his Master's thesis he received a call from Mr. Harrington.

"I would like to offer you a job, Richard."

"A job? What kind of job, sir?"

"I need somebody in whom I can have confidence to help write editorials and edit the commentary section of the *Observer*. I have two assistants, but they have more specific tasks than what I have in mind for you. I need someone with depth and breadth who can see the larger picture, understand what's really happening on the national scene, and help decide what we should write about."

"But I have no newspaper experience, sir."

"For what I have in mind that's not very important. You're an intelligent young man. You'll learn quickly what you need to know about journalism. The reason I'm interested in you is that you have a mind. For a person your age, you have a mature, coherent view of the world — one that's amazingly similar to mine." Mr. Harrington chuckled.

"But I don't even follow politics very closely."

"You've got something better, Richard, a thoughtful vantage point from which you can assess the events of the day. Many of the journalists on our staff can throw a story together pretty quickly, but I sometimes wonder if they know what's going on in the world."

"But I have never so much as written a letter to the editor of a newspaper."

"Don't you worry about that. I called that professor you like so much, Clive Winslow — I happen to know him rather well — and he's pretty high on you, not least your writing ability. He thinks you should become a professor, but he had to agree with me that you would be a darn good editorial writer. Do come to see me at the paper, Richard. Let's discuss it."

Richard was flattered by Mr. Harrington's offer. Harrington was a prominent Charleston figure, and he had asked Richard to influence the opinions of the people in his hometown and environs. Richard had much on his mind that he would like others to consider.

Richard had thought very seriously about getting a Ph.D. in history and had obtained information about doctoral programs at various universities. He had been getting ready to send out a few applications. A career in teaching and scholarship would afford him the opportunity to pursue intellectual interests that had been with him since his youth. They demanded further attention. But Richard was still not certain about what kind of career he wanted. He had an activist side. He worried much about America losing its direction. Its moral and cultural foundations were getting shaky. He wanted to win others for insights he thought he had and help change America's course.

Richard met Mr. Harrington at the *Charleston Observer* and shortly thereafter accepted his offer. He would start after completing all the requirements for his degree. The salary for the first year would be modest, but he would get a substantial increase in the second year provided his employment turned out to be mutually satisfactory. Only days after finishing up at the University of South Carolina he reported at the editorial offices. He would spend the next three years of his life there. He quickly learned the routines of the editorial department, and he was given more and more responsibility. In the second year he received a 30% salary increase as well as the title of assistant to the editor. Because of fellowships and the financial support of his parents he had virtually no student loans. He was now rather comfortable.

Richard got more and more writing assignments. He did not like sometimes having to write under acute time pressure, and he always found it hard to express a worthwhile opinion in a limited space. One of the reasons why he was increasingly disappointed in the mass media was that they were less and less receptive to reasoned, fully supported points of view. Short, snappy comments with more entertainment value than substance were the order of the day. But he learned to make the necessary compromises, and, especially in the first two years at the *Observer*, he felt that he was doing some good. Under Mr. Harrington's benevolent supervision, he became more and more often the author of the main editorial, the voice of the paper. Occasionally he was allowed a signed op-ed article. Mr. Harrington complimented Richard by saying that one day he might become a syndicated columnist.

Richard took an apartment near the intersection of King and Calhoun Street on the outskirts of downtown Charleston. In his free time he continued reading history and philosophy, now with a heavier emphasis on politics. His social circle expanded. He became a member of a Charleston historical society. He played more tennis. He traveled, taking two vacation trips to Europe. He visited some of the places where his father and mother had spent time during and after the war.

At the end of his second year at the paper he was given wider responsibilities and a new title, assistant editor. Mr. Harrington told him that he could soon expect to advance further. Richard made new acquaintances among the influential people in Charleston and the state capital. Despite his youth, he was offered membership in a new Rotary Club. He suspected that Mr. Harrington had pulled some strings.

But he had deepening doubts that he belonged in journalism. He might one day get full control of the opinion section of his newspaper and eventually gain even more influence as a syndicated writer, but newspaper articles were rather quickly forgotten and did not lend themselves to the kind of in-depth writing on large topics for which he longed. He might be able to do some serious writing on the side, but the pressures of daily work would steal his best energy. An important side of his personality would be thwarted. That part of him demanded more attention. His reading kept pulling him back in the direction of scholarship. Only as a university professor, he thought, would he be able to write in the sustained, systematic manner that he preferred and spend much of his time on the large questions of life.

Just a few months into his new position at the *Charleston Observer* Richard finally came to the realization that he should be in academia.

Richard recognized that as a professor he would have a more modest standard of living than professionals with an education as protracted as his, a physician, for instance. But, he told himself, as a somewhat successful academic he would at least be economically on par with a successful military officer. And he would have a great privilege not enjoyed by anyone else, except an independently wealthy person: a great deal of control over his weekly schedule and more time to think, read, and write.

Richard might have gone back to the University of South Carolina for a Ph.D. in history, but the professor there whom he most admired strongly encouraged him to go elsewhere. The professors at a place like Harvard would not necessarily be superior to the better ones at supposedly lesser universities, but, for the foreseeable future, a person with a Ph.D. from a "name" university would be more competitive when seeking a faculty position.

Richard sent applications to four universities. Three of his former professors wrote glowing letters of recommendation. Not so much as a single "B" blemished his graduate transcripts. His score on a graduate aptitude test was almost perfect. Each of the four universities accepted him and offered fellowships.

Mr. Harrington, who had become something of a second father and whom Richard had told about a possible return to academia, also wrote a strong letter of recommendation, deeply saddened though he was by the prospect of Richard's leaving.

"You know, Dick, I'd hoped that in a couple of years, when I'll be seventy, I would be able to recommend you to the board as my successor. You would take over this whole paper. But I recognize that you're a pretty unusual fellow. You could manage this newspaper and teach the people of Charleston a few things, but I suspect you have bigger fish to fry."

Richard accepted Harvard's offer. He was sad to leave Mr. Harrington and his colleagues, his family, and Charleston. He knew that everywhere else in the world he would be away from home.

He rented a small efficiency apartment in Cambridge within walking distance of the Harvard campus. He quickly settled into the routines of doctoral work. He made friends among his fellow students, but found some of them rather strange, smart in a way but neurotic and flaky. Some were very radical. His professors did not appreciably change his basic view of history and life, though not for lack of trying. He could confirm what his main advisor at South Carolina had told him: that sometimes scholars of no particular intellectual distinction but with high energy and trendy opinions become Harvard professors. He also learned that brilliance and productivity is no guarantee of wisdom and balance. Richard was partly appalled, partly amused by the sheer intellectual frivolity of a couple of the more voguish Harvard faculty. He was amazed at the mind-numbing and compulsive pedantry of one of the more well-published history professors, a "rigorous" scholar of modern British history. He churned out tomes almost as full of elaborate footnotes as of regular text. Richard was careful, for the most part, not directly to challenge those of his professors whose view of the world was quite different from his own, which was virtually all of them. He knew that his South Carolina accent had by itself put him on intellectual probation. But Richard was intellectually stimulated by several of his professors, including one who seemed to him on the verge of mental breakdown. One, a leftover from a bygone era, reminded him of Eddington.

It offended Richard that, to judge by their general deportment and dress, many of the Harvard faculty felt no particular regard for their profession or surroundings. They seemed to show some kind of contempt for the university and even for themselves. Some undoubtedly thought that they were striking a romantic pose, perhaps that of identifying with the working class, but what was the romance in a professor looking like a person dressed for a job of plumbing?

Richard received a couple of B's from ideologically intense professors to whose intellectual prejudices he simply could not bring himself to pander, but all his other Harvard grades were 'A's. His reputation in the department was high. He was offered an opportunity to teach his own undergraduate course at the university and showed himself a good teacher. It was assumed that he would have a distinguished academic career. The members of his dissertation advisory committee were pleased to work with him and happy to recommend him for academic positions.

He made one especially good friend at Harvard, Donald Kiefer, a former student in the law school who had switched to the doctoral program in history. Kiefer was from New York City. He specialized in intellectual history. He was especially fond of the ancient Greek city-states and their culture and philosophy. He and Richard had overlapping interests in the study of the formation of elites. Donald, a genial, plump redhead, was one of the smartest people Richard had ever met. He had almost photographic memory, a very sure, quick intuition, and a prodigious capacity for logical induction and deduction. He was the son of a Wall Street investment banker. Once over beers in Richard's small apartment, he told Richard that he was escaping from his family and the entire world in which he had grown up. He launched into a tirade.

"Dick, you have no idea what the financial world has become. You don't *want* to know. There are still some big boys who have standards and moral scruples and who grumble about the wrong kind of people taking over, but those old fogies are dying out. Some of the new big boys have some superficial polish and speak about social responsibility, but the only thing they really care about is making money and manipulating others. Do you suppose they refuse to deal with the really bad guys, like big investors who finance the drug trade behind the scenes? Not if dealing with them promises a great return and they can claim ignorance of who their shadowpartners really are. The young go-getters who come up in their firms are getting more and more shady. They run ragged, cut corners, cheat, and take terrible risks, usually with their investors' money, to say nothing of the employees of affected companies. Insider trading is one of their stocks-in-trade. You scratch my back, and I'll scratch yours. They are very good at taking advantage of people with the old kind of moral scruples, the poor naïve bastards. The new types, who're just taking their signals from the big bosses, are poisoning the atmosphere, but they're getting away with it, and sometimes they make huge amounts of money. Most of them are positively repulsive cocky and arrogant bullies. Some are hollow, pill-taking wrecks. Few have intact families. Some don't bother to get married. Pitiful. But scary too. If this is capitalism, you can have it."

"Isn't this just the financial side of what's happening all over society, in politics, for example?" Richard asked.

"Of course it is. It's all the same in the end."

"What do you mean?"

"Dick, I saw it all in Skull & Bones at Yale, the fraternity for the offspring of the rich and powerful and other promising young men"

"What did you see?"

"The spread of that same nasty desire to get rich and to control everything. Skull & Bones was always a place where the future rulers of America and the world formed friendships and alliances for a lifetime. That fraternity was always intertwined with the rulers of the British Empire. The imperial set-up is still in place, but, shall we say, under new management. It used to be that the bluebloods in the leadership class had some concern for the good of America and the world. Nowadays all the talk about a better world for mankind is little but a cover for acquiring more power and making more money. Those who dominate the empire today probably laugh their heads off at the has-beens who have some of the old intentions. No, by now they've stopped laughing. These days they probably only feel disdain for the bluebloods."

"You don't think you're exaggerating just a little bit?"

Donald slammed down his bottle so hard that he spilt some of his beer on the table. Donald was not drunk, just somewhat under the influence, and Richard realized that the subject was painful to him. Donald's face was reddening and he stared at Richard as he said:

"Let me tell you something. These types couldn't care less about the people they dominate. Ordinary people are either just potential foot soldiers for their schemes, or obstacles in their way. I tell you, Dick, they don't live in the same world as the rest. They live, eat, and breathe in their own sphere. They pay attention to the world of ordinary people only to the extent that it affects their own designs and because they have to manipulate others to get their way. I would go as far as to say that they are largely above governments. On issues that really matter to them they are able to control the policies of the United States. Republicans or Democrats—it doesn't matter. While the parties bicker and compete in elections, the big boys in finance are able to slant the entire society in their favor. In one way or another, they always get what they want."

"Don, are you a Marxist?"

"Hell no, but I am not blind, and I sure as hell am not stupid!"

Richard visited Donald in his parents' home on Manhattan. The size and the appointments of the Kiefer house, a large brownstone on the Lower East Side of Manhattan, indicated to Richard that Donald's father must be a rather significant figure on Wall Street. The paintings on the wall suggested unlimited financial resources. Did Donald consider his own father a part of the growing nastiness of high finance, or was his father of the more reputable sort, resisting the spreading corruption and cynicism? Was his father the source for what Donald had told Richard about the financial hot shots? Had the father advised him to have nothing to do with his own business? Richard never asked, and Donald never brought up the subject. Mr. Kiefer seemed pleasant enough, as did Donald's mother. Richard could tell that Donald's having left the law for intellectual history was a sore subject in the family.

Richard had always been interested in the role of economic forces in the formation of social and political structures, but as a result of his conversations with Donald Kiefer he started to give more attention to the role of investment banking. He became more alert to the difference between the attitudes of merchant bankers and owners of businesses, on the one side, and those of high finance, on the other. The latter tended to operate independently of local loyalties and attachments, sometimes in callous disregard for how big economic decisions would affect employees and communities. Some of the really big financiers could manipulate entire countries and engineer economic opportunities that looked more like looting than banking.

At Harvard Richard also got to know one of Donald Kiefer's old friends, Stephen Ferguson, a gangly, preppy-looking man in a bow tie. His father had been a U.S. ambassador and an assistant secretary of State before becoming a top executive in a large American company. Donald had met Stephen when the two of them were undergraduates at Yale. They had been fellow members of Skull & Bones. Ferguson was now a few years into a diplomatic career but had been given five months off to take courses in a special area studies program at Harvard.

"Clearly an up-and-coming fellow," Donald said. "They don't offer that sort of opportunity to the run-of-the-mill Foreign Service officer."

The three of them had beers together from time to time. They shared a sadness about the disappearance of the old America, including the ethos of the old WASP establishment. Unlike most of their fellow students and Harvard faculty, they were critical of present-day America not because they hated America on principle, but because America was abandoning its better traditions.

Though Richard liked Ferguson, he found him a little dry and unimaginative. After Ferguson returned to the State Department and was posted abroad again, Richard made no special effort to stay in touch, but they met a few times, once when Richard visited Donald at his parents' home and many years later in Washington when Richard had just taken up his position at National University. They had lunch together during one of Ferguson's visits to the State Department. Then, a couple of years later, Richard introduced him to Helen at a diplomatic reception in Washington.

All in all, Richard's years at Harvard passed rather pleasantly and uneventfully. He left more learned than he had arrived, but his basic view of life and society had not changed significantly, only become more subtle and sophisticated. Though a few of his professors had deepened his understanding of particular historical developments and relationships, such new insights as he had gained were largely the result of his independent reading and reflection. His years at Harvard confirmed his long-held view that his country was abandoning its moral, political, and cultural heritage. He could see it in the many Harvard professors who had made a sharp break with the old American traditions. Christianity was scorned or simply ignored by most of them. Traditional verities were slighted or ridiculed. As the thinking of the Harvard faculty would spread into society through their students and the readers of their books, the destructive trends could only grow stronger.

Had Richard not had deeply rooted beliefs when he arrived at Harvard and had he not known in general what to expect, his time at Harvard might have produced disillusionment, perhaps an intellectual and moral crisis. As it was, he was able to treat the more disturbing features of his intellectual milieu as facts of life to be simply endured and overcome, and he felt that he learned something even from the professors he considered intellectually perverse. Understanding how they thought and what ultimately motivated them enhanced his grasp of America's predicament. He saw his Harvard days as having been primarily an opportunity to give himself an education.

# CHAPTER 11

Back from the Sorbonne, Helen and Anne found the middle-aged man with the moustache back in the hotel reception. There had been no telephone calls or messages for Helen.

It clearly bothered John to have been left alone for so long. He was glad to see them.

"I was just beginning to wonder if the two of you had disappeared."

"Johnnie, dearest, I'm sorry."

"You were gone much more than three hours."

"I know, John, we had to wait for a person."

"Over three hours is a pretty long time when you're sitting alone in a hotel room somewhere in France."

"Of course, Johnnie. I'm sorry. We should have taken you along, but I wanted you to be here to take any phone calls."

John sighed. "I know, Mom. Forget it. Did you find out anything?"

She related all they had done and heard.

"Is that good or bad news?"

"Good, I suppose. It probably puts the accident theory way down the list of possibilities. His meeting that man was probably the reason we lost touch with him." The children nodded. "So my guess now is that something really important came up, but we never got word of the change of plans. We'll just have to wait to hear from him."

Helen had to exert herself to make her facial expression match her fairly cheerful words. She actually had an as-yet-amorphous but excruciating intuition that what they had learned was bad news. She looked at John to see whether her words had reassured him, but could not read his expression.

Helen decided to call the American Embassy. It was Saturday, and the consulate was probably closed, but perhaps it would be open for a couple of hours. She wanted to make sure that no information had been received during the night or morning. She also wanted help identifying the person at the embassy whom Richard knew. She had met him briefly long ago, but she could not remember his name. He was bound to have considerable seniority by now and should be able to help initiate a search for Richard.

She was glad to discover that Bennini was still on call. He assured Helen that there was no news, and she told him briefly what she had learned.

"At least that gives us something to go on," Bennini said.

The "us" gave Helen a boost.

"Of course, there is little we can do right now. In the absence of special circumstances, 72 hours of waiting is our rule of thumb. If your husband has not returned by Monday, we will get involved."

"But Mr. Bennini, please understand, my husband and I are happily married. There have been no strains in our marriage" — she bent the truth more than a little — "and we're on vacation in Europe together with our children. Richard would never, never leave us like this intentionally." Helen glanced at John and Anne, who were listening closely and observing her. She wished that she had asked them to go to their room.

"I think I understand, Mrs. Bittenberg, but, as I said before, there are a number of fairly innocuous scenarios that would explain your husband's disappearance. Sometimes people seem to have disappeared, but really haven't. They actually think they have informed those who are now worried. That's quite possible in this case. You may hear from your husband at any time, and he may be amazed to learn that you had no idea what happened."

If Mr. Bennini had been in the room she would have embraced him. He was right. She had thought more than once that Richard might have felt it necessary to take care of some urgent and important business but that his message to the family had somehow gotten sidetracked. Perhaps he had asked somebody else to contact Helen and the family, but that person had failed to do so, for whatever reason.

"You're very kind, Mr. Bennini."

"Thank you, but I'm just trying to do my job."

"Would you do me a favor?"

"Let's hear."

"My husband has a friend at the embassy. He got to know him many years ago at Harvard. I have met him, too. He's supposed to have a rather high position. The trouble is that I cannot remember his name. My husband is much closer to him than I am."

"There are a large number of people at the embassy. They're not even all in the same place. And people come and go all the time. I've only been here for six months."

"But suppose you mentioned the names of some of the top

people, other than the ambassador."

"I don't even know all of their names. The deputy chief of mission is a man by the name of Higgins."

"That's not it. More like Donaldson, or —"

"I don't even know the names of those with the rank of counselor. My own section, the consular section, is separate from the rest of the embassy. We are not even located in the main embassy building. Let me see, there's Tutweiler, Berger, Ferguson, Nichols —"

"*Ferguson!* Yes, that's it."

"Stephen Ferguson?"

"That's him!"

"I have seen him, but that's about all," Bennini said. "He's the counselor for political affairs. That's a really important job."

"Mr. Bennini. Be an angel and give me his telephone number."

"Mrs. Bittenberg, it's Saturday. The embassy is closed."

"I mean his home telephone number."

"Really, Mrs. Bittenberg, I can't bother a senior embassy official during the weekend with a matter like this."

"You wouldn't bother him. I would. He won't even think that I'm bothering him. He's an old friend of my husband. And if he were to ask how I got the telephone number, I wouldn't tell him. Come to think of it, he knows my husband so well he would assume I got it from him."

"Mrs. Bittenberg, I'm not even sure that I can find a list of the home numbers for all embassy personnel."

"Please, Mr. Bennini, Ferguson knows my husband very well. They have known each other for years and years."

"I'm afraid I can't be of any help."

"Please!"

"I'm sorry. Good-bye." He hung up.

Helen could not possibly wait until Monday to start searching for Richard. She needed help right now, from someone with clout, somebody who could activate the French police.

"Mom, what's the problem?" Anne asked.

"It's just that this man at the consulate won't give me the telephone number of a friend of Dad's at the embassy. He wants us to wait until Monday when the embassy reopens. They have no report of any kind about Dad, and their rules are not to take any action regarding a missing person until after three days."

"That's weird. They should start looking for Dad right away."

"Of course, dear," Helen said, "but since they don't have any evidence of foul play, they won't do anything. I suppose it makes some sense from their point of view. We haven't learned anything that indicates anything is really wrong."

"Except that Dad's gone!" Anne exclaimed.

"Are we going to have lunch soon?" John's question thankfully broke the train of conversation.

The telephone rang. Helen, who was standing up, was so startled that she felt faint. She had to steady herself. John and Anne stared at her. She took a deep breath. All of the hopes and fears of the last many hours rushed through her as she reached for the telephone receiver. She carefully lifted it from its cradle.

"Yes."

"Mrs. Bittenberg?" The voice sounded familiar.

"Yes."

"This is Daniel Bennini." Helen steeled herself. The embassy finally had some news about Richard. She sat down on the bed.

"I'm calling from my personal cell phone," Bennini continued. "I shouldn't be doing this, but I have the number you wanted."

Helen relaxed, only to feel a rush of excitement and gratitude. She reached for a pen.

Bennini gave her the number.

"And the address is—" He gave it to her.

"Mr. Bennini."

"Yes?"

"You are a professional, but you're a human being first of all. Thank you very much!"

"Good-bye."

Helen told the children what had happened. She wanted to call Ferguson right away but held back. She needed to think through what she would tell him and what she hoped for him to do. The children also needed lunch. John, in particular, needed to get away from the hotel. She would put the search for Richard on hold for an hour or two.

Helen carefully explained to the man in the reception that her husband was still missing. She and the children would go to a near-by restaurant for lunch. Risking irritating the Frenchman with her persistence and repetition, she asked him to be certain to keep track of any phone call or other message to the Bittenbergs, including email messages to the hotel. She tried smoothing over any annoyance on his part by giving him a protracted smile.

They found a little restaurant in the same block. As they looked at the menus, Helen momentarily forgot their real situation.

They were just three tourists in Paris in the middle of one of the most enjoyable events of the day. She realized that the reason why she had been able to lapse into mindless euphoria was that she was suddenly a little more hopeful about their situation. They would soon have the help of an influential diplomat. They would soon be through this nightmare. The hard, tight knot in her stomach would begin to dissolve.

Back at the hotel, Helen asked the children to go to their rooms for a while. Anne protested, but Helen insisted. She did not want them present when she called Stephen Ferguson.

Ferguson was not at home. The woman who answered the phone spoke poor English. She was probably a housekeeper of some kind. Helen asked when Mr. Ferguson would return and was told it might not be until the evening. She asked for Mrs. Ferguson and was told that there was no such person. Helen's next step might have been to ask whether there was any way of getting in touch with Mr. Ferguson, but she could no longer use the argument that she was a close friend. So she said:

"Mademoiselle, I'm calling on a matter of great urgency. It involves my husband who is an old and close friend of Mr. Ferguson. I know that Mr. Ferguson would want to know without delay what I have to tell him. Can he be reached by cell phone?"

"*Je ne sais pas.*"

"Can you ask someone?"

"I the *seul* person here."

"Please, Mademoiselle, this is really important. A man's life may be at stake." Helen knew that she was developing a streak of ruthlessness.

The French woman eventually gave her a cell phone number, and Helen dialed it.

"Steve Ferguson."

Helen was surprised by how quickly Ferguson understood who she was. Richard's name obviously had not been tucked away in some obscure corner of his mind. He also said he remembered Helen well.

She told him briefly why she was calling and asked if she might see him in person.

"Helen, I'm very sorry to hear this. You must be worried sick. I will try to help in any way I can. Unfortunately, I'm not in Paris, and I'm right in the middle of something pressing. When I get back to Paris this evening I have to go directly to an important diplomatic reception."

"When could I see you? I would like to tell you what little I know and ask your advice."

"And I would like to see you. I could make myself free tomorrow morning. Would you like to join me for brunch?"

"That's very kind of you," Helen said, "but I have to look after our children, Anne and John."

"Just bring them."

"In that case, I would be very happy to join you for brunch."

"Splendid, I'll see you at ten o'clock. Then you can give me more details and we can think about what might be done. Do you have a pencil handy? Let me give you my address."

Helen wrote down an address on Avenue Foch.

"I'm in an apartment just east of Place de l'Étoile."

Helen got out her map of Paris. She knew the general area. Avenue Foch was a parade street as broad as Champs-Élysées. On both sides it had smaller parallel streets that were separated from the main roadway by a strip of grass, bushes, and trees. It had large, exclusive apartment houses that seemed to be from the nineteenth century or older. The area exuded wealth. Those who lived there were probably Arab sheiks, members of the international jet set, financiers, pop stars, and other millionaires. She had always wondered what those apartments might look like on the inside. They probably had very high ceilings, parquet floors, hanging chandeliers, and mirrors. Perhaps the U.S. State Department had shown foresight in the previous century and bought some of those apartments for top American diplomats. They had to be prohibitively expensive to rent.

It troubled her that Ferguson had not offered to take action immediately. Why no sense of urgency? He might have offered to contact the French police. She told herself that she was too directly involved to see that, like the people at the consulate, Ferguson had good reasons for holding back. In any case, she could not jeopardize his friendliness by pressuring him. Helen left Ferguson the name of their hotel and her telephone number, and they hung up.

It was good that the children were not there to see her disappointment. She resolved that, whenever possible, she would not speak to anyone about Richard's disappearance within John and Anne's hearing. The scope of her agony and dread might become obvious to them. For the time being, her attitude would be that their ignorance of Richard's whereabouts was due to some silly misunderstanding. Somebody had failed to deliver a message. Their father would return very soon or call to check on them. This hypothesis was not wholly implausible, but she had no faith in it. Why would Richard not have come by the hotel to pick up some overnight things? That meeting over coffee at the Sorbonne had indicated no need to rush. She had to remind herself that the meeting would not have had to have anything to do with his disappearance. It could have been a chance meeting, unrelated even to his research. His disappearance also did not have to be connected to his research. A thought that had crossed her mind a few times acquired more prominence. What if Richard's visit to the Sorbonne had had nothing to do with the book on which he was working? He could have gone there to meet somebody. But why would he have kept that from her?

She could not sit by herself speculating. She had to cheer up the children, get their minds off what might have happened. She should try to act as if she were not deeply worried.

A plan had formed in her mind. If Richard had not returned or been heard from by midday the next day, which was Sunday, she would call her parents and let them know what had happened. It would make them terribly upset, but they needed to be prepared in case Helen had to cancel the rest of their trip and send the children home. She would want her parents to look after the children. The children were very fond of them. Luckily, both of her parents were in good health. If Richard was still missing in two or three days, Anne and John should go back to Washington, if it could be arranged. Helen should call the airline to explore possibilities for travel. She did not know exactly what she would be doing in France, but she could not put the children through a possibly protracted search.

She went to the children's room.

"OK, kids. What would you like to do?"

She got blank stares.

"Well, we can't sit cooped up here all day, can we? We might as well see something of Paris. We'll leave a message for Dad and make sure the man at the reception is on the job, and then we go out for a while. I'll find out how to use a French payphone so we can call back here at intervals. I would like to go past that police station nearby, but then we might go on to Montparnasse, what do you say? We can take the subway a part of the way and then walk up to the squares around Sacre Coeur, that famous white church. There's much to see. The artists love that area. The view of Paris from up there is magnificent. Shall we go?"

The proposal was received with shrugs, but John and Anne got ready. Before they left the hotel the man in the reception taught Helen how to use a pay telephone. He could even sell her the kind of telephone card that has to be inserted into most such phones.

Helen walked into the police station with the children in tow. The young officer of the day before was not there, but, using his name and her female charms, she got to talk to a policeman in civilian clothes, a large dark-haired middle-aged man. As she told the story of Richard's disappearance the man looked at the children with obvious empathy — perhaps he was a father with an imagination whose job had not yet numbed him to human misery. He agreed to do some checking, even acceding to Helen's request that he expand the geographical range of the inquiry by a few miles. He was gone for ten minutes before returning with a computer printout. A few accidents and criminal cases had involved men of Richard's age, but none of the people involved were unknown. Again, Helen left her name, address, and telephone number.

Helen prodded the children to walk with her to Montparnasse. She wanted them to get exercise so that they would have an easier time falling asleep and staying asleep. It was another sunny day, but the sky was no longer as clear, and the temperature had passed the eighty-degree mark. The air in their hotel rooms would be a good deal stuffier that evening. They lingered near the Seine, taking in the scenery. They walked past the Moulin Rouge theatre with its large windmill wings and then up the steep streets to that most painted of all Paris city squares and to Sacre Coeur behind it at the top of the hill.

They stopped at a pay phone. There were no messages for her at the hotel. She merely shook her head to John and Anne. They strolled among the painters who worked or sold their pictures near the church. Tourists filled up almost every space. They saw the panoramic view of Paris from the front steps of the church. It might have been a very enjoyable afternoon at one of the famous Paris landmarks, but they were all subdued. Helen's few attempts at levity were forced and awkward.

"Mom, can we go back?" Anne finally said.

"What do you think, John?" Helen said.

"Yes, let's go back to the hotel."

# CHAPTER 12

Women had always found Richard attractive. He was never pretty, not even as a child, and in his teenage years his looks were marred by eczema. Still, it was obvious at an early age that he was destined to have virile good looks. His intellectual leanings and general seriousness, which were apparent when he was quite young, did not appeal to some girls, but not even in early adolescence was he a taciturn loner. He was rather sociable. He could be charming and funny in a quiet, understated way. He would never outgrow a slight shyness and reticence, but most women found these qualities endearing. The more perceptive were fascinated by something difficult to-define at the center of his personality. It was as if he knew something that others did not and as if a sense of purpose was connected to it. Richard did feel a sense of direction, an obligation of some sort, but it was strangely diffuse, yet to be discovered. Was he destined to accomplish something? Was he supposed to become a leader of some kind? Richard was conventional, safe and pleasant but also intriguingly different. You didn't quite know who he might be.

He could have made many conquests among the girls. His sexual urges were the same as those of other healthy young men, but he tried keeping them in check. At a rather young age he had formed a notion of what kind of human being he wanted to be. It accorded with traditional views of sex. He often had to struggle to contain the erotic impulse, but, given the opportunities available to him, he stuck to his course with remarkable, if imperfect, consistency. It helped strengthen his resolve that his skin problems made him a little uncertain about his appeal to the girls. The possibility of making a sexual conquest did seize his imagination from time to time, and had his plan for life been less deeply rooted, his will weaker, and his skin problem less prominent, the desires of the moment might have turned him into something quite different from what he wanted to be.

For two years before graduating from high school Richard went steady with one girl, Frances Woodbridge, from his own school, which was a private, vaguely Episcopalian academy. In appearance she was the all-American girl, a tall, healthy-looking blonde with a perfect smile. All the boys wanted her, but only the most self-confident dared to approach her. She selected Richard. She was the most admired member of the football cheering squad, but she was also intelligent, liked to act, sing, and dance, and had a serious side. Richard thought they might marry one day. They had good times, liked to talk about life, school, and the future. They kissed a lot, and their petting sometimes got steamy, but, in spite of intense desire, Richard went no further. Of the two of them Frances was the sexually more daring. It somehow hurt and offended her that she did not have to defend her virginity. Richard explained as best he could why he was holding back, but she could not help thinking that he did not find her sufficiently desirable. If he truly loved her, surely other considerations would be secondary. One time she cried over it. If they would eventually be engaged, she said, why would he not want to go all the way?

The boys at the school didn't quite know what to make of Richard. He never participated, except in the most perfunctory way, in the usual boy's talk about the opposite sex. He knew that most of those sessions were little more than adolescent boasting, but they made him uncomfortable. He thought they demeaned the girls as well as the sexual act the boys claimed to like so much. Although he never told those other boys that he detested their lewdness, crassness and vulgarity, they sensed it and censored themselves in his presence. Because his reluctance seemed to imply disapproval, he bothered them. Richard was uncomfortable around boys who seemed to think of little except how to seduce girls. Always to be chasing girls and trying to bed them seemed to Richard primitive and loutish. Only an inordinately vain person or one very unsure of himself would look for the kind of self-gratification and validation that might come from seducing ever new women. Did these other boys not care at all, he wondered, that one day the girls they seduced would want to get married? Who would want to marry a girl who had been with several like them? What would they think of boys who behaved as they did towards their own sisters? Some of the other boys thought Richard a little odd. He seemed to be some kind of prude, and yet he was obviously interested in girls. He was not even offensively studious. Though he was one of the best students at the school, he did not seem to exert himself. There were rumors that he read a lot in his free time, but he was also a regular guy. He was on the football team and was one of the stars in track and field. He certainly wasn't a geek. He was well liked by most.

For the 1970s, he was an anachronism, even for Charleston.

Richard had a more active moral conscience than most boys his age—some might have called it hyperactive—and he was highly prone to self-scrutiny, even self-recrimination. He was always thinking about questions of right and propriety. His constant examination of his own desires and actions, his detachment from the moment, put a distance between him and the other boys, though more of them probably sympathized with him than appeared from how they talked. Others felt that he was different, that he somehow stood on his own. They found it hard to understand the reserve and seriousness behind his general gregariousness.

There was no single reason why Richard and Frances eventually drifted apart. They both realized—Richard sooner than Frances—that their relationship would never lead to marriage. When she left Charleston for college in Atlanta, Georgia, they remained friends, but they made no special effort to stay in touch.

By the time Richard entered the Citadel his eczema had been more effectively treated and had started to fade. Looking back, he wondered if that was a part of the reason why he would then have his erotically most intense relationship with a young woman. It started during his second semester. She was a student at the College of Charleston who came from the northern part of the state. She was his own age. Her name was Beverly Shaw. She was dark and very pretty in an exotic way. She was physically well endowed as well as intelligent and quick to smile. He met her at a dance hosted by the corps of cadets at the Citadel. She knew that the best way to get a man to take an interest in a woman is for the woman to notice the man in an obvious way, but she did not have to expend any effort to attract his attention. She stood out. It was obvious that he would approach her. He asked her to dance.

Richard was soon smitten by her, and she was taken with him. No wonder—he was handsome, bright, and charming. He had an intelligent face with regular features and a strong but not conspicuous jaw. He had blue eyes that seemed darker than they were because they were a little deeply set. His nose was slightly angular. He would have looked even better had not his slightly wavy medium blond hair been cut off at the Citadel. He was over six feet tall. His slender body had become somewhat muscular because of high school sports and physical training at the Citadel. He was pensive and somewhat formal in manner, but he was not awkward around girls. He had a light touch as well as a capacity for serious conversation. He had a good sense of humor, and his eyes often twinkled with amusement. His smile, which showed even white teeth, could, when directed to women, be a trifle flirtatious. Many girls pined for him, and some of the prettiest tried catching him. Beverly wanted him for herself.

Richard invited her to dinner at a restaurant. The dress she had selected was not demonstrative but showed off her full but slender figure. She had done her hair in a way that suited her perfectly. Richard was stunned. They talked and laughed throughout dinner. They were increasingly aware of their mutual attraction. He took her hand. They strolled around the southern tip of Charleston, the Battery, looking out toward the ocean and north along the Ashley River and then walked in the direction of her campus. Being the southern gentleman and a Citadel cadet, he let her place her arm on his. Was it the uneven sidewalks and her sometimes losing her balance that made the arm in which she held him brush up against the side of her breast? He could barely stop himself from seizing her and pressing her to him. But they kept walking, finally reaching the campus. It was pitch dark, and trees and buildings provided greater privacy. He wanted to kiss her goodnight, but he also wanted to be the gentleman, especially on the first date. Outside her dorm, he finally did kiss her, but what he had tried to make an almost chaste touching of her lips she transformed into a prolonged, passionate kiss. Richard was able to stop only with difficulty. He looked around to see whether they had been observed.

On their second date they drove in Richard's old banged-up Ford to Kiawah Island on the ocean about half an hour away, where they walked on the beach. It was April and the air was getting warm. On the way back to the car they stopped among some trees. Richard pulled her to himself and kissed her. She responded with unexpected fervor and pressed herself tightly against him. Richard felt a powerful stirring in his groin. She loosened her grip, took half a step back and started to unbutton her blouse. She placed one of his hands inside the blouse. Feeling the rounded softness that swelled over the rim of her bra, he was ready to throw his qualms about sexual relations to the wind. His conscience shrieked in protest, and he stepped back, thinking about what to do and say, but in the next moment Beverly had removed her blouse and let her bra drop to the ground. What he saw mesmerized him. She moved up to him and made him touch her. The cool heaviness of her breasts and her hand on his swelling groin broke through his last defenses.

In the next several weeks the passion of young adulthood asserted itself with full force. They could not get enough of each other. Richard's pangs of conscience were overpowered by pent-up, raging desire. He and Beverly sometimes took risks that kept them in constant fear of pregnancy. Later in life Richard shook his head every time he remembered their behavior. His guardian angel must have kept watch over him, he thought—assuming that the angel had not turned away in disgust.

Several times Richard came close to violating curfew at the Citadel. Once he did and got caught. Only the mercy of his immediate commanding officer, who was a distant relative, kept his punishment to a minimum.

His and Beverly's passion lasted a little longer than it might have because their opportunities for meeting in private were limited. When, a few months into their relationship, the passion started to fade, he had become increasingly aware of traits in her that did not appeal to him and that he had previously not noticed or ignored. She was constantly looking for new entertainment. Her interest in intellectual and cultural matters turned out to be more nominal than real. She seemed almost unaware of what was going on in the world. She was bright in her way, but he sometimes found it hard to talk to her. Their interests diverged. He discovered that she was more cynical and calculating than he was, a little jaded even. In response to his question, she told him that she had not been to bed with any other man. He wanted to believe her, but did not. They saw each other most weekends for the better part of a year, sometimes during the week as well. A couple of times he had her meet his parents, who were polite but not friendly. Eventually their meetings became more erratic. They started quarrelling. Often Richard's lack of interest in partying and his preference for quiet times annoyed her. They stopped calling each other regularly, sometimes letting a week or more go by without talking. There was never any need to break off the relationship. It petered out. After a quarrel in which some truths were frankly spoken they simply didn't call each other again. A few weeks later, Richard heard that she had been seen with another young man.

Richard was not proud of this episode in his life. He realized that his relationship with Beverly had been based almost purely on sexual attraction. His attempt to justify their erotic adventures as a possible preamble to an engagement had been persuasive only in the first few weeks. Richard knew that he had broken his own rules regarding women. The fact that Beverly had seduced him rather than the other way around did not excuse him. She had taken advantage of him, but so had he taken advantage of her, and the male was supposed to be protective of the female.

He had to concede that he was a good deal weaker than he had thought. But he also considered the possibility that he had set impossibly stringent, unrealistic standards for his conduct. Some of his male acquaintances were trying all the time to avail themselves of what, according to his own principles, he was supposed to deny himself. Should he not cut himself a little slack?

But Richard never really changed. By the emerging standards of his time and society, he remained a prude. Nobody had ever tried to make him one, at least not in words. His parents had generally traditional views but were not puritanical. Like most Bittenbergs they were Episcopalians. Wolfgang, the founding father of the American Bittenbergs, had been a Lutheran from Northern Germany, and his American wife had joined his denomination, but Richard's great grandfather, Bernhard, had followed his wife into the Episcopal Church. Other Bittenbergs had gravitated in the same direction, although by the mid-twentieth century the larger family also included Lutherans, Presbyterians and Methodists. Richard's sister, Susan, was a solitary Baptist, having joined the denomination of her husband, who seemed to the Bittenbergs an anomaly, a Baptist bank president.

Richard's parents were rather faithful in their church attendance but were not outwardly devout. They seldom spoke of overtly religious subjects at home. Grace was said at meals only on special occasions. Their code of honesty and integrity was mostly implicit. They could speak disparagingly of what they considered egregious violations of moral norms, but they were at the same time tolerant of the weaknesses and foibles of human beings. They conveyed what they believed to be proper personal behavior more by example than by words.

Charleston as a whole was, though in many respects socially conservative, also rather tolerant. For a small American city, it was quite cosmopolitan and in some ways liberal. Richard, the historian, knew that while well into the nineteenth century many of the American states required of candidates for public office that they be Christians, sometimes of a particular denomination, South Carolina accepted not only Christians but also Jews. Going all the way back to colonial times, Jews had been a part of Charleston society, though with some restrictions. In the 1960s some members of the Charleston "aristocracy," including Richard's parents, had been quite liberal for South Carolina on the issue of segregation.

Richard realized that his immediate and extended family, their friends, and the general society in which he had grown up had communicated to him in countless unspoken ways a sense of what was proper and improper. Whether his intuitions of what was right had been influenced by persons close to him or the traditions into which he had been assimilated, he felt his sense of moral direction to be his own, not something externally imposed. His moral intuition derived its authority from something deep within him, and he could not separate his own innermost sense of right from what appeared to him incumbent on any decent person in a similar situation. Thinking back on his liaison with Beverly Shaw, what disturbed Richard was that it was a violation of what he most admired, which was letting your actions be governed by your own highest standards, your innermost conscience. He had let his desires of the moment sweep aside his higher intentions. The fact that those desires had been powerful indeed only underlined the need for character.

For the rest of his time at the Citadel Richard dated a couple of other girls, but he did not get close to any of them. When he left to go to graduate school at the University of South Carolina in Columbia there was no painful farewell to be said. In Columbia he dated a pleasant, pretty, intelligent law student from Virginia, an acquaintance of the person who became his closest friend, Robert Preston. But his relationship with her was intermittent, and their intimacies were few, tentative, and awkward. The relationship ended naturally when Richard completed his M.A. in history and returned to Charleston to take up his post at the *Charleston Observer*.

During his three years at the *Observer* a number of women showed strong interest in him. He dated two of them, both attractive and intelligent. The one, a brown-haired divorcée who was about his age, owned a boutique on King Street. He was suspicious of the fact that she had been divorced at such a young age, but she was lively, amusing, and sexy, and he decided to believe that she had simply been unlucky and ended up with a bad apple of a husband. After a month of increasingly affectionate but largely non-intimate dating it seemed to him that her little quirks and fits of temperament, which he had originally found rather charming, were becoming more prominent. He realized that she was a neurotic. Spending time with her eventually became a burden, and he broke with her. His mother let him know that he had done the right thing.

The second woman he dated for an extended period was a newly minted dentist who, though from Pennsylvania, had taken her first job in a Charleston practice. She looked a little like Frances Woodbridge, was bright, cultured, came from a good family, and was very solicitous of him. He withdrew when one of her friends confirmed his growing suspicion that she was determined to catch a husband. She liked Richard, but he was to her first of all a highly eligible male. By the time Richard left for Cambridge, Massachusetts, he had started to wonder if he might die an old bachelor. His mother had dropped hints that he ought to be looking for the right woman to marry.

In Cambridge, Richard became close to a blond Italian doctoral student in anthropology with some blue blood in her veins. After a month Richard was beginning to think that he was falling in love with her. That was when he discovered by talking to a visiting Italian friend of hers that she was engaged to be married to a fellow Italian, a young professor in Florence. Richard confronted her. He actually believed her assurances that she had been getting ready to break off the engagement, but the fact that she had kept it from him and had seen him behind the back of her fiancé made him pull away. Her tears almost made him change his mind.

When he reached the dissertation stage of his doctoral work Richard saw no woman in particular, only met some in the company of others. He spent more time talking with his best male friend at the university, Donald Kiefer. Richard missed female company, but he got more and more absorbed into the work on his dissertation. He spent five months in Paris buried in research collections related to his subject, the interaction of ideology and economic interests in the French Revolution. How long would this celibacy last? He thought quite a lot about women, but would not strike up an intimate relationship that he knew would be merely transitory. Moral qualms combined with the pressure of work on the dissertation to turn him into a kind of scholarly monk.

# CHAPTER 13

Helen, John, and Anne made their way to Stephen Ferguson's apartment by Metro and by walking a few blocks. The sky was cloudy, and it was windy. The fresh air did Helen good. She had slept only two or three hours and felt tired and dazed. They were admitted to Ferguson's apartment building by a concierge in uniform who was seated in the center of a large reception hall with high ceilings, marbled floor, and mirrored walls. The concierge called up to Ferguson's apartment and told them that they were expected. They were to take the elevator to the fourth floor.

Stephen Ferguson waited for them at the elevator, the door to his apartment standing open behind him. He was tall and thin. He had a full head of brown hair that looked darker than it was because combed back with the aid of hair lotion. His rectangular face was rather pale; his eyes had an indeterminate faintly brown color. His ears seemed too large. He was dressed in a brown sports jacket and a black turtleneck sweater. He greeted Helen and the children with a smile and escorted them into the apartment. At the door an unremarkable plump woman in her forties offered to hang up any clothes. Helen assumed she was the woman she had spoken to on the telephone.

"This is Yvonne," Ferguson said. "She's my housekeeper."

They walked into the dining room. Helen was glad to see that Ferguson was casting furtive, appreciative glances in her direction. He did his best to conceal his reaction, but she recognized the symptoms of male interest.

What Helen could see of the apartment matched her expectations. The rooms were large and had very high ceilings and windows. In the dining room, where a table was set, a big chandelier did indeed hang from the ceiling. The furnishings were handsome, if not particularly elegant.

"I live alone," Ferguson said. "My wife died five years ago. I have only five rooms and a kitchen, but it is quite enough to make the minister at the embassy nervous about the cost. I could manage with less except that my duties at the embassy require my receiving guests in style at my home. I have two daughters, but one is at college in New England, one at a boarding school in Switzerland."

Yvonne brought a tray with glasses of juice and mimosa. Helen had the mimosa.

"I'm very sorry that you should be visiting me in these circumstances," Ferguson said. Again Helen detected partly concealed admiration in his gaze. "You must tell me everything, so that we can see just how I can be of help."

Helen was sorry that the children were present. That meant that she had to give Ferguson a rather bland, dispassionate account of what had happened. She would have to hide her strong emotions, which might give him the idea that she was much less upset than she was.

They seated themselves at the table a quarter of an hour later. The brunch was quite elaborate and well prepared. If Helen had had a normal appetite, she would have been tempted to overeat. The meal became awkward. The excellent food and the appealing surroundings contrasted too sharply with Helen and the children's frame of mind.

By the end of the meal Ferguson had the whole picture of Richard's disappearance and what Helen had done to try to find him. Helen appreciated that in front of the children Ferguson asked questions and made comments in a matter-of-fact tone of voice. He expressed sympathy for their worries and his belief that Richard would eventually turn up.

"I think Bennini has a good point. Richard may well believe that you know why he took off and that you know where he is. But we're not going to take any chances, are we? First thing in the morning, I'm going to talk to the person at the embassy who can best handle a case like this. Richard will have been missing for almost three days then, so we should be able to activate the French police. We may approach the French foreign office at the ministerial level, and they will, in turn, contact the French ministry of the interior. That should light a fire under the police."

Helen was disappointed. Could nothing be done right away? Ferguson had seemed to assume that Richard would be missing the following day. Then why could he not try to get the French police started immediately? But she decided that she had better not bully him. It might antagonize him. Presumably he knew what he was doing. Don't look a gift-horse in the mouth, she told herself.

But she had difficulty containing herself. Ferguson seemed to have read her mind, for he said: "In fact, I'm going to call the embassy this afternoon to talk to the officer on call this weekend to alert him to what's happened. Bennini is in the consular section, which is separate from the rest of the embassy. They are the first line of defense in a case like this, but we have additional resources."

Ferguson's attitude puzzled Helen. It was as if he were the victim of mixed emotions, at once hot and cold. Did they include a curious, almost nervous interest in her as a woman?

"I am really grateful to you," Helen said.

"No gratitude is called for. I'm a friend of yours and Richard's. I'm a fellow American charged with representing American interests abroad. Of course I'll do what I can."

Ferguson promised to be in touch with them at the hotel the moment he had any significant news. She might hear from him by midmorning the following day. He asked Helen to call immediately if she should come across any useful information. Should he not also have asked her to call if Richard turned up?

When they said their goodbyes Ferguson showed that he regarded her as more than an acquaintance by kissing her on the cheek in the French way. She thought the touch of his lips might have lasted a split second too long.

They left Ferguson's apartment at 12:30. On a Sunday not many people would be at the Sorbonne, but Helen wanted to return to the university library to see if anybody on duty might remember Richard. She also wanted to call the airlines to see what her options were regarding the children and for cancelling the flights for the remainder of their vacation. Calling hotels on their itinerary could wait. Then she would call her parents. If she called the United States about 7:00 PM, which would be 1:00 PM in Washington, the chances of catching both her parents at home would be good. They typically went to a nine o'clock church service. Often they stayed for the education hour before getting early lunch at a restaurant. Then her father liked to take a nap at home. For each of these calls she wanted to be alone.

Helen decided that they would take a cab back to the hotel, partly for comfort but primarily so that the children would have more of a feeling of seeing something of Paris. But they seemed not to care. They sat silently in the taxi.

"Is there anything you would like to do later today?" Helen asked.

"Not really," Anne said. "I would be thinking about Dad anyway."

"If you want to go back to the Sorbonne, we'll come along," John said. "Right Annie?"

"Sure."

"OK, that's what we'll do, but first we'll stop at the hotel and relax a little. I could use a nap. And on the way to the Sorbonne we may stop at that police station again. When we're done at the Sorbonne and get hungry we can have dinner. You may be hungry sooner than you think. I noticed that you didn't eat very much of the brunch."

"Neither did you," said Anne.

Helen thought that some kind of message, however trivial, might wait for them at the hotel. They had been away for several hours. Or — imagine — Richard might have just gotten back. He would be distraught to learn that Helen and the children had not known where he was. They would have a wonderful reunion, and then they would celebrate and laugh about the misunderstanding. They would continue their vacation. They would be closer as a family than they had ever been.

But nothing waited for them. In the reception there was now a short, hefty, black-haired, middle-aged woman whom they had not seen before. She would be on duty until relieved by the bald man with the moustache the next morning. Her English was adequate. She seemed genial. When Helen started to explain her situation to the woman, she smiled and said, "*Je sais, Je sais*, Michelle told me all about it. Poor Madame, poor family! Tell me if I can help in any way. I will take messages for you and wake you up at any time if anybody calls."

They went upstairs, the children to their room, Helen to hers.

Helen lay down on the bed. She felt tired and even sleepy, partly because of the mimosa at lunch, she thought. But she was certain that there was no point in trying to sleep. She was too wired-up. Thoughts were racing through her mind. She closed her eyes. Within moments she was asleep.

Helen was awoken by a knock on the door. Confused and rattled, she flew out of bed and tore the door open. It was Anne.

"Mom, its 2:30. We thought you'd never come to get us."

"My goodness, I didn't think I would be able to sleep at all. I've slept for an hour and a half?"

"Looks like it."

They left for the Sorbonne. They went past the police station. None of the policemen she had talked to before was there, but again she managed to get an officer to do the kind of checking that she wanted. Nothing. Strange to say, she was starting to have warm feelings for the French police. She realized that they might not present a uniform attitude to the public, and that female beauty might go even further in France than in other countries.

The Sorbonne library was open, but almost deserted. Helen again worked her way through the various departments, including an annex, showing Richard's passport photo. She proceeded deliberately not to miss anything. She asked questions not only of library staff but also of students. In the late afternoon John and Anne started to look bored and tired. They went over to the cafeteria. The waitress she had talked to before was not on duty, and none of the other waitresses had worked on Friday morning. Neither had the manager on duty.

As they were leaving the cafeteria and were in the corridor that led outside Helen saw a black man with a broom and a bucket of water, who was sweeping the stairs near the exit from the building. She walked up to him smiling. He knew virtually no English. He was probably from North Africa or one of the other former French or Belgian colonies. He looked confused by her questions. She resorted to her own halting French. She had forgotten the French word for Friday, but a student passerby solved that problem, and she was able to ask whether the man had worked on Friday morning. He nodded. She managed to ask about "two men" in the cafeteria and showed Richard's photo. The black man shrugged. Helen went on to ask another question, but the black man looked at her uncomprehendingly. Helen finally stopped a young man who looked like a student and asked if he knew English. He nodded. Helen quickly told him her business and asked him if he might translate a couple of questions. He nodded. She was able to ascertain that the black man had not worked in the cafeteria. He had been washing windows outside. Had he seen two men, one well dressed? The black man shook his head. "*Deux hommes Américaines,*" Helen blurted out in French. "Two American men." A light seemed to turn on in his eyes, and he said something Helen did not catch. The student translated: "He says he saw a big car." Helen asked the man to repeat what he had seen.

"*Une voiture noir. Américaine.*"

A black American car. Helen asked for details. The car had been standing in the street outside the building in a no-parking zone. The man walked with Helen to the door and pointed to a spot some sixty yards away where he had seen it. It was on a narrow side street, more a university access road than a city street. The man had admired the high gloss of the car's black paint. The driver had been sitting in it or standing near it.

"When on Friday was it?"

The black man was not certain. Some time in the morning.

Had he seen two men? No, just an American car.

What brand was it? "*Je ne sais pas. Une Ford, peut-être. Nouvelle.*"

Perhaps a Ford, and new.

"If it was big," said John, who had been listening carefully, "perhaps it was a Crown Victoria. Or a Mercury. Or a Lincoln."

The student tried translating the suggestion, but the black man shrugged his shoulders yet again.

He looked tired of the conversation. Still, with the assistance of the student and the help of a few smiles, Helen was able to get the man's name and telephone number. She thanked him and the student, and they left the building.

"Mom, do you suppose the car was waiting for the man who talked to Dad?" Anne asked.

" — or waiting for both of them?" John said.

It was already after 6:00 PM. Where had all the time gone, and how could the children have been so patient? Their only distraction had been some ice cream from a street stand.

"Before we have dinner we should get back to the hotel. I should make at least a couple of quick telephone calls."

"Sure Mom," John said. Anne did not protest.

"Where will you call?" John asked.

"First of all, I need to call grandma and grandpa in Washington."

The short woman was still at the hotel reception. There were no messages. The woman again offered to be of service.

"Thank you," Helen said. "I would like to make a couple of telephone calls to the United States from the room, and I may need your help to do it. I'll call you."

Helen asked the children to take care of themselves in their room. They looked at each other, and then dutifully left.

Helen collected her thoughts and called the reception to find out how to call the United States. She learned how to get an international line and how she could even use their family calling card. Richard had made such a call each to his mother and to Helen's parents just after their arrival in Paris.

Helen's mother, Diana, answered on the second ring. She sounded pleased. She obviously expected a sunny report from happy vacationers.

"I was hoping it might be you, but I thought it could be another few days before we heard from you again. How's Paris?"

"Paris is wonderful, mother, but I have something to talk to you about. Is Dad at home?"

"Yes, dear, we were just going to watch something on TV."

"Would you ask him to pick up the other telephone so that all three of us can talk?"

"Just a minute." Helen heard her mother give her father instructions.

"What's up, Helen?" her father said cheerfully.

"I'm sorry to say that what's up will distress you. Let me give it to you straight. Richard's disappeared."

"Disappeared!?" Helen's parents exclaimed in unison.

For the next ten minutes Helen gave a detailed account of the last two days and answered her parents' questions. Helen's mother repeatedly expressed empathy for Helen and the children. Helen told her parents what she expected to do next and what she would like to do about the children, if Richard had not returned by the next day. Would they be able to meet them at Dulles Airport and look after them in Washington for a while, either at the Bittenberg home or at their own house?

"Of course, Helen." Her mother's voice was emphatic. "We"ll do anything you want."

"Helen, would you like for me to fly over?" her father said. "You need help."

"Thank you, Dad, you are sweet to offer it, but I don't think there's anything you can do. I already have the help of the U.S. Embassy. Ferguson has a pretty high post, and I'm sure he will do what he can. So will the consulate. If I need your advice, I can always call you."

"But you'll be so alone. You need company."

"I'll manage, Dad."

"Have you told Richard's mother or his sister and brother?"

"Not yet. Hannah's gotten older, and I'm afraid she would be terribly, terribly upset. I thought I would wait. I would like to be able to tell her that the embassy and the French police are on the job. If Richard's not back, that is. But I'm planning to call Hubert right now."

"That makes sense."

Helen gave her parents the telephone number to the hotel and assured them that she would stay in close contact with them. She looked up Hubert and Dorothy's number in her little telephone book. Sitting on he bed, she called Charleston.

Richard's sister-in-law answered. She was pleasantly surprised to hear from Helen. She and Helen got along well. A jovial redhead from southern Virginia, Dorothy taught biology half time in a private high school. Helen envied the family scene that she imagined at the other end. Dorothy and Hubert and their four children would be gathered somewhere in or near the family room and kitchen area of their house. Helen heard voices and the sounds of a television set. Their home was located on Murray Boulevard and overlooked the Ashley River. Like all the tourists who walked by that particular stretch of Charleston stately homes, Helen admired what she saw but wondered what would happen to these houses when the next hurricane hit the city. She thought of the people who lived there as real Charlestonians, defiant in the face of the elements. Hubert was certainly a pillar of the old Charleston. He was a lawyerly version of Richard, brainy, energetic, and efficient but also thoughtful, interested in culture, and alert to what was happening in the larger society. She could see him reading a novel or a book of history or politics in the sitting room just off the family room. He was about the same size as Richard but was grayer and bulkier. He was temperamentally somewhat less intense.

Hubert came on the line. "Helen, darling, you're the very last person I expected to hear from. Aren't you vacationing in Europe?"

"I'm calling from Paris."

"How very nice of you to call. I hope you're having a good time." Hubert was known for his disarming pleasant manner. He treated all courteously, putting them at ease.

"Not really, Hubert. That's the reason I'm calling. Richard disappeared two days ago."

"What!? He disappeared? Did I hear you right?"

"You did." Helen told the story. Hubert asked a number of questions. Behind his gregarious, courtly southern manner hid a razor-sharp mind. It had made him one of the leading lawyers in Charleston, indeed, in all of South Carolina. He had argued a couple of cases before the U.S. Supreme Court.

"Hubert, we're completely befuddled. I've no idea what may have happened. Richard would never do anything like this deliberately. Never. Suppose he'd left us some kind of message. He would still have been in touch with us by telephone by now."

"Yes, something's wrong."

"I expect the French police and the American Embassy will start looking for him tomorrow. I'm going crazy waiting for that to happen."

"Helen, it's really not surprising that they would wait for a day or two. They see a lot of weird stuff. Missing persons reports are filed every day that turn out to be plain erroneous. The person isn't really missing. He's just mad at the wife, he's gone on a drinking binge, or he's shacked up with some woman."

"Hubert!" Helen's voice was indignant. "That's got *nothing* to do with us!"

"Of course not, darling. I'm talking about the perspective of the French police and the consulate. They have no way of knowing that Dick's disappearance could not be explained in some such way."

"But I have *told* them!"

"Nevertheless, they have their rules and protocols."

"Damn their silly rules!"

"Calm down, Helen. Things are happening. You seem to have set things in motion and to have found some pretty good clues."

"I have to look for Richard, but I have no idea what to do next."

"The police are the pros, Helen. Leave it to them. The embassy will put some pressure on them. Give them a chance."

"But I can't just sit here twiddling my thumbs."

"I understand. One way you can help is to try to think of anything that happened recently that may give us some clue to why he disappeared, something he did or said, in Paris or back home."

"I have already asked myself that question a thousand times. All I can say is that Richard has been working very hard, and that he's been more preoccupied than ever with his various activities. I was very surprised a few weeks ago when he agreed to go on this trip."

They continued weighing various possibilities. Hubert said: "I'm sorry, Helen, but my gut feeling is that we have to take the possibility of foul play seriously. If he'd had a heart attack, wouldn't you know by now? The hospital would have called the U.S. Embassy. The odds against his collapsing where nobody would notice him are very high. He was in the middle of Paris. Another possibility is that he suddenly had to run away from something very dangerous and that he couldn't risk contacting you for fear of exposing you to danger. He may have been involved in something sinister that we know nothing about. Or he may have been kidnapped. Hard to imagine, I know. Kidnapped by whom and why? And why in Paris of all places? If he had been kidnapped for ransom, you or somebody would have heard from the kidnappers by now. Do you know of any connection between Richard and Paris?"

"Only that he was going to do some research at the Sorbonne library. He said he would spend a few hours there on Friday morning. And he did research here many years ago when he was working on his dissertation. He gave a paper at a conference here a few years ago. I came with him on that trip. Otherwise I can't think of any connection between him and Paris." She paused. "Except the old Harvard friend I told you about, Ferguson, at the embassy."

"Perhaps Dick's come across some material that is dangerous

to someone over there. That someone may have been tipped off and taken action. Or suppose Dick interviewed a person who recognized that Dick had uncovered very dangerous information. Of course, his disappearance may be wholly unrelated to his research. Isn't he mostly interested in rather old stuff?"

"He's been moving closer to our own time, but, as far as I know, he's far from contemporary subjects."

"If there's foul play, perhaps the source of the problem is not in Paris at all, but in the United States. Helen, you have to see if you can remember anything out of the ordinary in the last few months."

"I've already told you, I'm at a complete loss."

"If the source of the problem is in France, the French police are in the best position to help, but if the source is here in the United States, it becomes the FBI's problem. If we can give them evidence of foul play."

Their conversation meandered. Hubert finally said, "I will tell Dottie and Susan about all this, but for now I won't tell Mother. She has not been feeling well, as you know. I'll think about the whole situation and call you back. You let me know if you hear or think of anything. I'm in the middle of an important trial, but it should be over in a day or two. I may have to come to Paris, but if you can give me any anything to go on I can start doing some checking here. Let me give you an example. There's something I have been thinking about during this entire phone call, though I can't see how it might relate to what's happened. I remember Dick once saying something unexpected to me that put a bug in my ear."

"What was that?"

"You remember, over a year ago when Dottie and I stayed with you. It was around the time of the Washington Cherry Blossom Festival? I was to argue a case before the Federal Trade Commission."

"Of course, I remember."

"Well, Dick and I went for a walk in your neighborhood. I remember that the wind had blown the cherry blossoms right off the trees. The ground looked as if there had been a snowfall in pinkish white. Richard and I talked, as we often did, about this country going to hell."

"Oh, that." Helen sighed.

"Yes, Dick carries around a lot of heartache about the old U.S. of A. He worries too much. Not that I really disagree with him, but, hell, life's got to go on. I could tell his worrying was getting to him. It was wearing him out. So I was trying to get him to loosen up a little. I said something like, 'Dick, this worrying business is taking a lot out of you, and what good does it do? You have to live a little. You are one of the really lucky guys. You have Helen and the kids. You have your writing and teaching. Your fretting about America is not going to change anything. All this talk will get you nowhere.' That's when he stopped and looked at me. I remember it well. He looked so serious. His eyes seemed particularly blue against those lovely trees and pink flowers. Then Dick said in a strange, low voice: 'No, Hubert, it's not just talk any more.' I asked him what he meant, and his answer stayed with me. He said, 'If I told you, you wouldn't believe me. And it's best that you don't know anyway.' Of course that made me really curious, and I told him he had to explain. He said, 'I shouldn't be telling you this, but something is happening, and it's big.' Now he *really* had my attention, and I asked him to spit it out. But he wouldn't. He shook his head and fell silent. For a moment he smiled a little. I couldn't tell whether he was pleased with himself or whether it was a sad, melancholy smile. Or perhaps he wanted to make light of what he'd just told me. Then he looked at me and said, 'Hubbie, you're my brother, and I love you, and I would trust you with my life, but I shouldn't have said what I just said. I just couldn't keep it in.' 'What in the world are you trying to say?' I said. I was getting a bit unnerved. But he clammed up and made me promise not to tell another soul what he'd said."

Helen was silent.

"Helen, are you there?"

"Yes."

"Do you have any idea what he was talking about?"

"Hubert, I'm scared."

"You mean you know what he meant?"

"No, I have no idea."

"Then why did you say you were scared?"

"Because what you just told me might be connected to something I've been wondering about. I thought Richard had gotten himself into a vicious cycle of some kind. I could see that he was under greater and greater stress. I think it started over a year ago. Others probably didn't even notice, but I did. I just couldn't put my finger on what was causing the change in him. I assumed he found himself in an unusually bad bind because of too many commitments. He was rushing out all the time, to meet people, to give talks, to go to the library. He worked in his study until late at night. He traveled a lot. He was not quite like himself. He seemed more preoccupied than ever. I was getting really worried about him, and I told him so. I asked if anything was wrong, but all he said was that he had a lot to do and that he hoped to be back to a more normal pace before too long — normal pace, you know. For him that's a constant trot that threatens all the time to break into a sprint. Now, Hubert, you tell me that he may have been involved in something big, something that he hadn't even told me about! That's so unlike him. Now he's gone, and I have no idea why! I'm completely confused. And I'm scared. Something's very, very wrong."

She started sobbing.

"Helen, darling!"

"Yes." She spoke through tears.

"Everything will turn out all right."

"It doesn't look that way right now."

"Helen, do give it some time. Have you had anything to eat recently?"

"Have I had anything to *eat*?! What's eating got to do with anything?"

"Helen, you have to look after yourself. Regular meals. An apple. Sleep. Some wine with dinner."

"I know. I'm trying. But if the kids weren't here I don't know if I would have given any thought to food. Speaking of the kids, if Richard hasn't shown up by tomorrow, I'm putting them on a plane to D.C. as soon as possible. My parents will look after them."

"Good. Knowing that the kids are safe and sound will help your mood, I'm sure."

"It's not good for them to be here and to see me in this state. Poor dears. I try to be cheerful in front of them, but I think they see right through me."

"Helen, you also need to be doing something not to worry yourself sick. See what clues you can dig out of that memory of yours. The more I think about this whole thing, the more I believe the search for Richard may have to start in D.C."

"You may be right."

"What's the name of Dick's assistant, the one he's always raving about? I suppose he's a doctoral student."

"Yes, you mean Ron Turello. Richard's directing his dissertation now."

"Do you have his telephone number?"

"No, and Richard always has his telephone book on him."

"Never, mind, I can easily track him down."

Helen and Hubert talked through various practical matters and finished the call. It had lasted for almost an hour.

Helen was exhausted. She threw her head on the pillow. Conflicting emotions, all upsetting, rushed over her. The knot in her stomach was tighter than ever. She was supposed to call the airlines, but she wanted to see Anne and John. She wanted to hold them. She went to the bathroom to adjust her hair and touch up her make-up. She put on a fresh blouse.

As she was about to leave the room Helen was startled to hear the telephone ring. She assumed that Hubert was calling back. She lifted the receiver.

"Hello."

"Hi, it's Wendy."

"Who?"

"Wendy Kavanaugh, remember, the student from Wisconsin. I recognized your husband."

"Oh, yes, of course, Wendy, I remember."

"How are you?"

"Not so good, I'm afraid. My husband's still missing."

"How awful."

"It's not getting any easier."

"Well, I thought I should call, because I have been thinking about what I saw in the cafeteria, and I think I remember something. Nothing important, I'm sure, but I thought I should tell you anyway."

"What is it?"

"That other man, the dark-haired one —"

"Yes," Helen said impatiently.

"He was wearing a bow tie."

"A bow tie?"

"Yes, how out of place was that! I think it was a part of the reason why I thought the two of them didn't quite belong in the cafeteria. I don't know why I didn't think of it before."

"Thank you, Wendy, I really appreciate your calling. Do you remember anything else that you haven't told me?"

"Not really. There's another thing, but it's so vague that I may be totally wrong. I probably shouldn't even mention it."

"What is it?"

"When I think of the two men, for some reason it makes me think of another man."

"A *third* man?"

"Yes, but I am not sure if he belongs. He may not have been connected to the other two. I just don't know. I think the reason I'm connecting him with the other two is that he, too, had a suit — something dark."

"Where did you see him?"

"I don't know. It's all very vague. It's as if he only passed through the cafeteria."

"How do you mean?"

"I don't know. I'm sorry. It was as if he just said something to the other two, dropped something off, or something like that."

"Do you have any idea what he looked like?"

"No, he was nobody."

"Is that all?"

"Yes, I shouldn't even have mentioned that third man. He may have had nothing whatever to do with the other two."

"Wendy, I understand. I'll keep that in mind."

"Good. I wish you luck though. Good-bye."

"Thank you."

Within seconds Helen had found the number to the waitress at the Sorbonne cafeteria, and she dialed it. There was no answer.

A knock on the door made her jump. She asked who was there, and heard John's voice. John and Anne were standing outside.

"Mom, you're taking forever," Anne said. "You said we would have some dinner."

"Yes, I'm sorry. I just had to make these calls, and one thing led to the other. But I'm ready. We can go now."

She struggled not to look downcast. As they looked for a place to eat she noticed that when John and Anne thought she was not paying attention they were studying her expression.

# CHAPTER 14

It was toward the end of Richard's fourth year at Harvard, at which time he was far along in the writing of his doctoral dissertation, that his monkish scholarly existence was finally challenged in earnest. He had received an invitation from a well-known woman professor of history at a large midwestern university to give a series of lectures on "Principles of the Study of History" at a summer continuing education program for heads of departments of history from high schools around the country. The conference would be held at one of the many colleges in the Boston area and be attended by 100 teachers. The National Endowment for the Humanities provided the funding. Richard would offer three mornings of lectures three days in a row in June, giving two presentations each time separated by a break. One of his professors had recommended him. The conference organizer had actually approached that professor about being the speaker, but he had declined. The organizer had expected to turn to some other well-known academic, but the professor had persuaded her that if she wanted good substance rather than fame she might do as well to invite Richard Bittenberg, a star among the history department's doctoral candidates who had a special interest in the proposed subject. He also had some advanced journalistic and teaching experience and was a little older than most of his fellow students.

Richard was absorbed in his research and writing and did not want to be distracted, but he was flattered to receive the invitation, and he needed the money. The $1,500 honorarium, a princely sum at the time, was a powerful inducement to take the time off from the dissertation. Having given a lecture series at an NEH-sponsored conference would also look good on his academic résumé. In addition, he told himself, the lectures might form the basis for a book on historiography. He felt a little awkward knowing that he would be younger than most of the conference participants; a few of them might even have a doctorate. But he had thought and read much on the subject of the proposed lectures, and he would like to think that as a Harvard man he had the intellectual edge over the typical head of a high school history department. He also had already published a couple of articles in leading journals that had made a mark among scholars in the field. He was not worried that he would not acquit himself well as a lecturer. He had gotten good reviews from the students for a course he taught at Harvard, and he had given well-received talks to student organizations on campus and at conferences. He devoted the better part of two weeks to preparing the lectures, writing out some sections and making elaborate notes for others.

On the day of the first lecture session he drove early to the college hosting the conference. It had one of those lovely wooded campuses with architecturally fairly uniform stone buildings. He met the conference director for breakfast in a building near the conference facility. She was a genial, overweight woman in her fifties named Gladys Herman. She seemed not to care very much about her appearance. They had already discussed the practical details of his lectures by telephone. The weeklong conference was now in its third day. It would end in the evening on the day of Richard's last lecture. The organizer walked with him to the lecture hall before the appointed time to let him acquaint himself with the podium and the room. It was a typical college auditorium twice the size of what was needed. The audience would sit in rows rising towards the back.

As the conference participants started to arrive Richard felt a nervous twinge in the pit of his stomach. Teaching young, immature, ignorant students was one thing, lecturing to well-informed, pedagogically experienced adults supersensitive to flaws in teaching technique was something quite different. He was distracted from his peptic state when he noticed a brown-haired woman in a light beige suit near the doors about twenty yards away. As he fiddled with his lecture notes and made perfunctory conversation with the organizer he noticed that the woman greeted several of the conference participants as they entered. She had apparently made many friends. It was easy to see why the men would be drawn to her. She had strikingly good looks and posture. She was out of the ordinary, almost exotic. She might have been from southern Europe or Latin America. She appeared to be in her mid to late twenties, which meant that she was considerably younger than most of the other people in the room. She was above medium height. She had a quick, engaging smile. His eyes discreetly followed her, making him forget his nervousness. He observed her gestures and the way she moved. She was beautiful, certainly, but she also had a certain easy elegance. Her clothes were businesslike but tastefully feminine. When the conference organizer, a hefty female who wore no make-up, moved to the podium to give some general information to the participants, the woman seated herself several rows back to the side, near one of the doors. She exerted a magnetic pull, and Richard had to force himself not to stare in her direction.

He heard his name mentioned. The organizer was introducing him. His nerves reasserted themselves. He noticed that he was made to sound rather impressive. The professor who had recommended him must have been generous in his comments. When the audience applauded at the end of the introduction, Richard walked to the podium. He felt awkward. His plan was to tell what he thought a really good joke about history before turning to his lecture notes, but he delivered it poorly and almost ruined the punch line. He had hoped for a burst of hilarity and a tide of appreciation and benevolence, but he received only polite, muted laughter. He tensed up. The young woman would not have gotten a favorable first impression. He turned to the more formal introduction that he had written out and practiced, and he started to feel more comfortable. The nervousness began to subside. His mind was beginning to concentrate on the subject, which he loved. He soon hit his stride. And when he started to speak from notes rather than a prepared text, his sentences formed easily.

While lecturing he wanted to look at the brown-haired woman again and again. At the same time he did not want to give himself away, and so paid a disproportionate amount of attention to teachers in other parts of the lecture hall. Her eyes — what color were they? he wanted to know — seemed, even from a distance, to sparkle with intelligence and charm.

During the coffee break midway through his morning session he wanted to talk to her, but it would have been a little too obvious for him to walk up to the clearly most beautiful and remarkable person in the room. He forced himself to remain in the front of the lecture hall, talking particularly with the organizer. He noticed that the brown-haired woman had disappeared. Was she a smoker perhaps who had gone outside? What if she had left the conference for good? But when Richard started lecturing again, she was back in her seat. He was intensely aware of her presence. He found himself speaking to her while looking at others. When the time came for questions twenty minutes before the end of the session, many raised their hands, but she did not. The applause for the speaker at the end was more than polite.

The organizer invited him to stay for lunch. He had completed his assignment for the day and could return to his dissertation, but he happily accepted. But the brown-haired woman was nowhere to be seen. The afternoon session of the conference would start at 2:00 PM, but it would have looked strange for him to linger until then. He said good-bye to the organizer, but postponed his departure by talking to a couple of the teachers. He then walked slowly, slowly out of the building, scanning the premises. It was when he got to his car that he saw her again. She was at the other end of the parking lot. She had just gotten out of a car and was carrying a heap of papers. She seemed to be doing even that with flair. Her hair moved in a special, breezy way. He wanted to catch up with her and see those eyes up close. They had to be brown. But running across the parking lot to catch up with her might even scare her. It would be much too sudden and forward. He swore to himself. He would have to try to approach her the next morning.

Back in his little efficiency apartment Richard had difficulty concentrating on any work. One reason was that he was wound up from the morning's lectures. He was not terrified of public speaking, but being in front of an audience is tiring. It is to be subjected to close scrutiny. No audience is more likely to find fault with you than an academic one. But the main reason for his being distracted was the brown-haired woman. His thoughts kept returning to her. She had really gotten to him—by doing nothing at all. His state of mind was purely his own doing. He scolded himself for reacting so immaturely. He knew nothing about this woman, had not so much as talked to her. His head protested. This was pure, irrational infatuation. With what? A mere image in his head. Besides, this beautiful, perhaps 30-year-old woman was likely to be married—he intensely disliked the thought.

His watching a sports program on television made no difference. When he sat down to do some work on the dissertation, he found himself merely sitting in front of his books and papers. He finally gave up and left the apartment. It was now six o'clock in the evening, and he ducked into a bar for a beer. The TV was tuned to a baseball game. He started talking with a man his own age at the bar who had long, thinning hair. He was a doctoral student in English, and Richard tried to start a conversation about the moral dimension of Shakespeare. But his fellow doctoral student turned out to know virtually nothing about "the Bard." He was more interested in Marxist and feminist literary theory. Richard found more common ground discussing beer and baseball with him.

Back home, Richard made himself a simple meal and tried to work on his lectures for the next day. Again he had difficulty concentrating. That woman had such poise. She probably had an elegant voice, too, he said to himself. She seemed to have long, shapely legs. Her breasts? He hadn't even looked carefully. He was too taken with the whole of her.

Richard finally sat himself in front of the television set with a glass of wine. He watched some news and then the second half of a black and white war movie from the nineteen fifties. John Wayne played himself. Richard finally went to bed and finished a Hemingway novel. Why was it that he never really liked the novelists you were supposed to like? Hemingway wrote very well—but what about the underlying vision of life? He was not able to doze off until long after midnight.

When he woke up after what felt like a fitful few hours of sleep, he realized that he had neglected to set his alarm clock and that it was late. What was the matter with him!? He would have to rush to get to the college in time. He shaved and showered in record time. Instead of taking some extra care getting dressed, as he had intended, he had to cut corners. He did not have the time to iron his one clean shirt and hoped that it would not be obvious to the audience. He swallowed a glass of juice for breakfast, threw his notes and a few books into a briefcase, grabbed his coat and a tie, and ran down the stairs. He tied the tie in the car waiting at a red light. He wished that the air conditioner of his Chevy had worked. On this June morning he was already uncomfortable. The traffic complicated his drive. Once at the college he had difficulty finding a parking place. He half ran into the conference building. He arrived in the lecture hall with less than ten minutes to spare and anything but collected and concentrated. He tried to breathe slowly. Under his jacket he felt sweat breaking through the back of his shirt. He was probably red-faced, he thought. He had probably given the conference director a bit of a scare, he guessed, but he tried to act unrushed, made it appear that he had been on the premises for a good while collecting his thoughts and postponing going to the lecture hall.

This morning she had moved up a row, but she still sat to the side. She now wore a gray skirt and a white blouse. Her hair looked a little different. He had decided that during the coffee break he would ever so unobtrusively, accidentally stroll up to her and strike up a conversation.

His first lecture for the morning went well. He noticed that he had no difficulty holding the attention of the audience. He could relax, even enjoy himself. He started departing from his notes. As before, he tried not to look too often in the direction of the woman.

When it was time for the coffee break he saw out of the corner of his eye that she got up. Perhaps she went to the rest room, he thought. Richard made conversation with a few of the teachers and paid a courtesy visit to the organizer, who complimented him on how the sessions were going. Suddenly the brown-haired woman was standing right next to him. With her came a faint whiff of perfume.

His heart skipped a beat. She had come to *him*! He remembered that he was wearing an unironed shirt and had forgotten to put on aftershave lotion. The woman was obviously waiting for him to finish what he was saying before speaking to him. He stopped and turned in her direction. But she addressed not him but the organizer.

"All's set for the excursion, Professor Herman. The buses will be here at 2:00. I'll make an announcement after Mr. Bittenberg's session."

"Excellent. Thank you, Helen!"

Richard was disappointed, but had the presence of mind quickly to introduce himself.

"Hello, I'm Richard Bittenberg, I think I recognize you from the audience."

She held out her hand. "Yes, I've been listening. I'm Helen Davenport."

"And where do you teach?"

"I'm not a teacher." She smiled. Wonderful teeth. Lovely brown eyes with tiny specks of yellow. Humor wrinkles at the corners. "I'm not really a part of the conference, just assisting Professor Herman. I work for a company in Washington, D.C., that helps organize and run conferences."

"Ah, I did think you looked a little young to be the head of a high school history department. But you seem interested in the subject of the conference."

"I am. Your lectures are not unrelated to my own graduate work. In my free time I'm working on a Master's degree in English at Georgetown. In a course I just finished we examined the influence of conceptions of history on Victorian novelists — the Whig interpretation of history and the like."

Richard suspected that Professor Herman was acutely aware of the attractiveness of her assistant and resented the attention that her speaker was paying to her. If Herman seemed to make a point out of not caring about appearances, it might be because in that respect she considered herself a lost cause. If so, the presence of Helen Davenport must have driven the point painfully home. Richard tried to involve Herman in the conversation. At his suggestion the three of them went to get coffee in the hallway next to the lecture hall. As Helen reached for a cup and saucer he tried to see if she had any ring on the relevant finger, but at that moment another person obstructed his view. But had the finger not been bare? Merely wishful thinking?

Richard sipped his coffee sparingly. He did not want to add any anxiety to the rest of the session by creating a need to visit the bathroom. He had noticed that being in front of an audience was a diuretic in itself. He remembered that he had not had the time to visit a bathroom before starting his first lecture of the day, and now he could not break away. He had to make the most of this opportunity to speak to Helen Davenport. Suddenly, after mere moments, Professor Herman put her cup down, said it was time to get started again, and returned to the lecture hall. She moved to the podium and asked the conference participants to take their seats. It was time for Richard to resume lecturing.

"I hope we can talk some more," he said to Helen Davenport.

"Nice meeting you," she answered noncommittally, but she added a smile that he wanted to interpret as encouragement.

Richard thought that the fourth lecture went better than any of the others. At the end of his formal remarks there was a lively period of questions and answers. He left the podium to the warm applause of the audience. He was startled to see Helen Davenport walking towards him. She was smiling. Was she about to embrace him? But she simply went past him and took his place at the podium. Of course, he remembered, she had some information for the audience. As she spoke about the afternoon excursion Richard was enthralled. She seemed self-confident, articulate, and efficient, and she was pleasant, funny and at ease—perfect for her job. What a woman!

She had no objection when Richard asked if he might join her for lunch. They went to the cafeteria where they were supposed to sit in a part of the dining hall that had been sectioned off for the conference. In the food line as her left hand rested on her tray, he got a good look at it. The ring finger was indeed empty. Amazing, he thought. What might explain that fact? They sat down at an empty table and had just settled in when a couple of female teachers in their early forties asked if they might join them. Richard felt irritation, but he also realized that their company would help to mask his intense interest in one woman.

Helen was a little younger than Richard, but he was struck by her sophistication. Behind her friendliness and charm lay a quiet, unobtrusive dignity. She was rather cerebral, but there was nothing ethereal or delicate about her. He intuited that her polished ways might hide a little Latin temperament. She was a full-blooded female, perhaps a little unpredictable, even a little dangerous.

Richard was overwhelmed. It was a testament to his self-discipline and acting ability that he managed to converse with her and the two teachers without obvious awkwardness. His southern manners kicked in and made each of the three women feel comfortable.

Luckily, the two teachers left the table to go outside for a smoke. Richard wanted to look long and deeply into Helen Davenport's eyes—the brown had streaks of gold—but it would have made his reaction to her too obvious. He must not make a fool of himself.

Suddenly she explained that she had practical matters to attend to and had to go. Richard asked, almost in desperation, whether she would be at the conference the following day. She would be, and he asked if he might have lunch with her then.

"It would be after my final lecture," he said.

"I would have enjoyed that," she said, "but I'm afraid I will only have a few minutes then. I have to help prepare for the final conference sessions." She hesitated. "Besides, it would not look good for me to sit with you again. I'm a staffer here. But thanks for your company. See you tomorrow." She stood up. Richard rose, too, and watched her walk away.

Again he took his time leaving the college, hoping that she would reappear. She did not. He drove back to his apartment in an odd state of mind, feelings of exultation, frustration, and despair taking their turn.

Back in Cambridge he could not settle down. The apartment made him feel claustrophobic. For a couple of hours he strolled aimlessly along the Charles River and on the Radcliff campus west of the river, thinking about Helen Davenport and worrying that he might never have an opportunity to get to know her. During the evening he barely looked at his notes for the final sessions.

The following day he arrived at the conference with plenty of time to spare. He had had difficulty sleeping, but this time he had set the alarm clock. He was neatly dressed in carefully ironed clothes and wore plenty of aftershave. He had even polished his shoes. But Helen did not attend either of his two morning lectures, which unnerved him. But he finished his lectures in good form. The conference participants were especially active in the final Q and A session. Professor Herman had to cut discussion off in overtime—a sign that his remarks had had the intended effect. Herman thanked him effusively, and the audience applauded generously. Several in the audience came up to him to say how much they had enjoyed and learned from his lectures. He was very pleased, felt great relief, and tried to be courteous to those who spoke to him, but his mind was on Helen. She was nowhere to be seen. Professor Herman came up to him to thank him in private.

"I shall let Professor Baker know what a good recommendation he gave me. And when you start looking for an academic post, be sure to let me know. And feel free to use me as a reference."

For whatever reason, Herman did not say anything about his staying for lunch. He felt desperate. Would he have to ask her or one of the conference participants where he could find Helen Davenport? He might have to go look for her in the dining hall. Only as he left the lecture hall and lingered, conversing with a couple of teachers, did he see her coming through the main entrance from the parking lot. She looked rushed and carried a large binder and some papers. She was wearing the beige suit again, this time with a light brown blouse. It matched her hair very nicely. He walked up to her.

"Sorry I couldn't attend your lectures this morning," she said. "We've had some practical problems."

He asked whether she would be at the conference the following day, a Friday, and she said she would. This would be the last day of the conference. It would conclude with a dinner. She would leave for Washington on Saturday morning after loading her car with leftover conference materials.

Richard had a deep-seated diffidence and formality, but he knew that he had to act.

"I wish you would have breakfast or brunch with me on Saturday before you leave. In fact, I would love to give you a quick tour of Harvard and Cambridge. I could pick you up here and then take you back to your car."

He could tell that she hesitated. He was getting ready to persuade her, when she said, "That's very nice of you. I should be ready by 9:00."

"Great! I'll pick you up then."

"I should still be able to get back to Washington at a decent hour."

He was disappointed in the implication that she would allocate just a couple of hours to being with him. The effective driving time to D.C. was about eight hours. To be back in D.C. at a "decent" hour, she needed to leave Boston no later than noon.

"A few acquaintances of mine went to Harvard," she said, "but I've never been to Cambridge, although I spent four years at Mount Holyoke, just an hour and a half to the west."

She excused herself and went in search of Professor Herman. As she disappeared down the corridor Richard looked admiringly after her. Yes, her legs were rather long and shapely. They would look even longer in high heels. She had a very nicely female figure, slender rather than curvy or busty.

As he drove home Richard was exhilarated. He had a solid, if brief, date with a woman who had affected him more deeply than any woman he had ever met. He was in awe of Helen Davenport.

Powerful sexual yearning had fueled his attraction to Beverly Shaw. What he felt for Helen seemed by comparison almost chaste. Her erotic appeal was obvious, but the reason he wanted to be with her was to admire and serve her.

Thoughts of Helen superseded his delight at having ended his teaching assignment and executed it well. The exhaustion he also felt was due not merely to being scrutinized for three days by Professor Herman and her teachers but to Helen's diverting his attention.

It was in this warm afterglow that his mind slowly returned to his academic endeavors. The professor who had recommended him to Professor Herman would get a favorable report. His prospects for getting a good teaching position had been enhanced. In a part of himself he was tired, but he also felt inspired to return to the dissertation. He would get back to it for a couple of hours that same afternoon. He liked his subject, knew that he was doing a good job, and could see the end of the project. In the evening, for the first time in many months, he would treat himself to a meal in a good restaurant. It would mean blowing just a tiny part of the lovely $1,500 check that would soon arrive.

On Saturday morning Richard left early to pick up Helen. It was a sunny day promising more summer heat. He had thought of bringing her flowers, but had nixed the idea because it might look overeager, too forward. One step at a time, he cautioned himself.

She was waiting for him at the entrance to the building where he had given his lectures. She was wearing a light brown skirt and a white blouse. She now wore brown high heels. She was as beautiful as he remembered her, had perhaps put on a little more make-up than when he had seen her before. She had a lovely neck. She smiled spontaneously when she saw him, and he decided that he could kiss her cheek. He took her hand as he did, feeling for the first time her skin against his.

"I'm finished here," she said. "My car's all packed."

Richard apologized for the air-conditioning in his car not working.

"Poor graduate student, you know. Even if I could afford it, would it make sense to spend that kind of money on an old car?"

He was driving the same Chevrolet Impala that he had bought used after starting his job at the *Charleston Observer*. He had taken good care of it, but now had to be very careful about his expenses. When he left for Harvard he had had about $6,000 in savings, but, despite his rather generous Harvard Fellowship, that money was gone. He wanted to use his student loan only for necessities. His father would have given him money or a loan, he knew, but, short of an emergency, he did not want to ask.

From the beginning they found it easy to talk to each other. As he showed her around Harvard Yard and environs, they talked less about points of interest than about themselves. When they sat down in a restaurant near Harvard Square for brunch, Richard was painfully aware that his time with Helen was slipping through his fingers. He furtively looked at his watch. 11:00 AM. He did not want her to leave.

Over eggs Benedict they summarized their lives. Richard learned that she lived with another young woman in an apartment in a Virginia suburb of Washington. Her father, a journalist, was originally from western Maryland and her mother from Charlottesville, Virginia. Growing up, she had spent much time abroad with her parents. In college she had been uncertain of her way, and she still did not know where she might fit professionally. She had taken her present job to make money while exploring whether teaching might be for her. By taking one or two courses per term and one in the summer while working, she had almost completed a Master's degree. She was thinking now about getting a Ph.D. in English.

"I really like literature," she said. "But it seems the young Turks in the discipline are less interested in what a novel or poem has to say than in critical theory. I wouldn't want a doctorate from a department like that."

Richard told her about the doctoral student in English ignorant about Shakespeare whom he had talked to in a bar the other night. "Unfortunately, what's 'in' in the English department here at Harvard soon becomes 'in' in the rest of the discipline."

"That's what I'm afraid of."

Richard hinted that he had not had a girlfriend in a long time. She indicated that she was not seeing anybody either, but seemed reluctant to speak about the subject. Was she holding something back? But he would not prod.

After they had finished the meal and refills of the coffee she looked at her watch and said that she ought to be starting back to D.C. It was 12:30. When he asked her to stay just a little longer, she did not protest too much. They walked slowly around Cambridge. They went into an ice cream parlor. All the time they talked about themselves and about life. When Richard finally delivered her to her car back at the college, it was almost four in the afternoon.

"I simply won't drive as far today as I had planned," she said. "Will probably stay overnight near New York City."

"Be safe!"

He told her how glad he was that she had agreed to see him

and said that he wanted to see her again. He would contact her. He had a strong intuition, amounting to virtual certainty, that if he tried kissing her good-bye, as he ached to do, she would not resist. He decided not to, but as she was about to get into her car, he took her hand, pulled her to him and embraced her. He could feel her embracing him back. When she had sat down and closed the door, she rolled down the window to say good-bye. The engine was in gear, and she would be gone in seconds. Her smile as she looked at him sent a sharp pain through him just as it filled him with joy. She had let her arm rest on the door, and as the car moved slowly forward he grasped her hand and squeezed it. She turned her head and reciprocated the long glance he gave her. She waved as she pulled away.

Richard was certain that this was the woman he would like to marry.

# CHAPTER 15

Helen's dread threatened to engulf and paralyze her. She struggled to fight it off by shutting down her mercilessly rampaging imagination. She did so by trying to focus on what was near and concrete, such as making plans for the next couple of days. On the Sunday evening after Richard's disappearance she and the children had ended up at McDonald's for dinner, the second time they had eaten that kind of food in Paris, but not even the sundaes could create an illusion of normalcy. After dinner they had shopped for fruit and snacks, and Helen had bought another bottle of wine.

Back at the hotel Helen called their airline about possibilities for cancelling flights and rebooking John and Anne. She discovered that for the coming week all flights to Washington on their airline were fully booked in coach. She got to speak to a supervisor and told her story. Could any special arrangements be made? Might there be seats in business class? She was told to contact the airline again on Monday morning.

Helen tried to telephone the waitress who had probably served Richard and his companion at the Sorbonne cafeteria. When finally she reached her at 10:00 PM, the waitress was not unfriendly, but when Helen asked if one of the two men had worn a bow tie, all she could say was *"peut-être,"* perhaps. Had she seen a third man in a dark suit? She could not remember. Had she seen a big black car outside? No, she had been busy in the cafeteria. But, said the waitress, she had been thinking about the two Americans. She might have remembered something.

Helen sat upright on the bed.

"I'm not certain, but I think when they left one of the two men put a cigar in his mouth."

Helen knew it was not Richard; he had never smoked anything. So the man with the cigar would have been the one in a bow tie.

"Why do you think so? Why would you remember that?"

"I'm not sure. I think it was one of those rather big, fat things. It seemed unusual. For one thing you're not supposed to smoke in the cafeteria. The man must have been eager to light up. I think I thought that smoking a cigar didn't go with being so well dressed. I suppose

I'd connected cigars with more rumpled, informal people. If the man had put a cigarette in his mouth I might not have remembered it. That's what you expect people to smoke."

"I am glad you thought of it."

"But keep in mind that I may be mistaken."

Helen spent another restless night. She tried to divert herself by drinking wine and watching television. She fell asleep after midnight with the television on. She did not sink into oblivion but remained in a semiconscious state like an animal alert to dangers. She woke up at two o'clock in the morning, tired and instantly aware of her predicament. She got up, turned off the television, and went to the bathroom. She sat down on the bed staring at the wall. She poured herself another glass of wine, which she tried to drink as quickly as possible. She did not want another bout of nausea, but she had to lessen the pain. She lay down on the bed. After half an hour she dozed off, but just an hour and a half later she woke up with a start. The first daylight was seeping in behind the curtain. She knew she would not be able to get back to sleep. How long, she wondered, would she be able to function on so little sleep? She decided to wash some clothes and to wash her hair.

At 7:00 she knocked on the door to the children's room. They were awake but in their nightclothes. The TV was on. Helen told them that this morning she would arrange for their return to the United States. She wanted to put them on a flight as early as the following day. Anne's first reaction was dismay. She started crying.

"I don't want to leave. I'm so afraid."

Helen put her arms around her. "I understand, Annie," she said, "but grandma and grandpa will look after you, and I will call you all the time."

"But you'll be all by yourself here in Paris," John said. "Won't you feel lonely?"

"Don't you worry about that. I'll be getting help from Mr. Ferguson and the embassy, and the French police will soon start looking for Dad. I've also talked to Uncle Hubert in Charleston, and he'll fly over if he's needed."

Their questions and comments kept coming. It was obvious that John especially had been thinking a great deal about what could have happened to Richard.

"Mom, it couldn't be just a coincidence that he talked to an American and that a big American car was standing outside the cafeteria."

"No, I agree."

"So, isn't there a good chance that Dad disappeared because

of something having to do with the United States?"

"It's possible. That's what your Uncle Hubert suspects."

"Well, I've been thinking about something that happened a couple of months before we left for our trip."

"What kind of thing?"

"Well, I was looking for my old baseball glove in the storage room in the basement, and while I was down there I could hear Dad talking on the telephone. The door to his study was open just a crack. I wouldn't have paid any attention, except he seemed upset. He said something like, "you'll just have to manage without me." I heard him mention the name Herbert. I remember because of Uncle Hubert."

"How long did you listen?"

"Less than half a minute. I found the old glove. But I wondered why he was upset. I guess I assumed he'd been talking about some trouble at the university. When I saw him at dinner he didn't look upset, so I didn't want to ask him. I didn't want him to think I'd been eavesdropping. I thought last night about what I heard because I've been wondering about things that could help explain what's happened."

Pride and love swelled within Helen. She hugged her son. He was not really a kid anymore. "Thank you, John. That could be important. I'll remember that name, Herbert. Uncle Hubert will want to know."

"I think *I* heard Dad talk about Herbert once," Anne said quietly.

"You *did*!" Helen exclaimed.

"Yes, I'd gone down to his study to see if he could help me with my math homework, and he was on the phone. He was talking on that weird, funny-looking phone he's got. He waved to me to come in, and he said to the person on the phone that he would call him back after talking to Herbert. I remembered it too because it sounded almost like Hubert."

"When was that?" Helen asked.

"A few months ago, I guess. We'd started on that new math."

Had she heard that name? Yes, it was vaguely familiar. Richard told her a good deal about his colleagues, students and other acquaintances, but if both Anne and John had heard him use the name Herbert that person must have been on his mind quite a bit. Why then would she have difficulty recalling it? She would call Hubert.

She told the children that after breakfast she would call the airline. They were also likely to hear from the embassy. When they went downstairs to the breakfast room the man with the moustache solicitously inquired about new developments. Helen told him that the situation was unchanged and asked him to be as diligent as before about messages.

Helen expected both Bennini and Ferguson to act when they got to the embassy without her prodding them. She would give them a couple of hours to contact the French authorities and to call her. In the meantime she would try to make the travel arrangements for John and Anne. She wanted for the three of them to go to the embassy or consulate sometime during the day. She wanted to meet Bennini and wanted him and any others dealing with Richard's case to meet her family, so that they would not be mere names in a report.

Back in the room she talked to the manager of the Paris office of their airline, who turned out to be an American. He listened with sympathy to Helen's story and told her that he would do his best to find a way to send the children back to Washington at no extra cost. Just a few minutes later he called to say that the children could fly to Dulles airport in Washington midmorning the next day by Air France rather than his own airline. Helen could trade in her and her husband's current tickets for tickets with an open departure date. Helen would need to bring all the old tickets to the reservation office on Champs-Élysées. She could pick up the new tickets for John and Anne at the Air France office just a block away. Helen knew that the American consulate was within walking distance of these offices and decided to combine the excursions.

Helen kept their tickets, together with travel itineraries and a couple of vouchers, in a small bundle with a rubber band around it. She had half-hidden the bundle in an inside pocket of a blue summer sports jacket that Richard had hung in their closet. She put her hand in one of the inside breast pockets, realizing immediately that it was the wrong one. It contained only a single folded piece of paper. Something made her take it out, and she unfolded it. It was a regular sheet of typing paper with well-worn creases. It had obviously been handled many times. What little was written on the paper was in Richard's handwriting. The text made no sense.

G. 44
V. 10
B. 67
S. 395
D. 72
P1 515
P2 24

R. 14
O. 195

It looked like some kind of code. She would have to reflect on it and ask others what it might mean. She took out the bundle of tickets from the other inside pocket.

The telephone rang. She tore the phone off its cradle.

"Hello"

"Good morning, Helen. This is Stephen Ferguson. I just wanted to let you know that we've alerted the French authorities. I can't predict just how they will handle the matter, but I expect you'll hear from the police soon."

"Thank you, Stephen. That's such a relief. Can anything else be done?"

"For the moment I think letting the police handle things is the best we can do. Let's give them a chance. Is there anything new that I should know about?"

Helen told Ferguson that Richard may have had coffee with an American cigar smoker at the Sorbonne, that a black car had been parked nearby, that the children thought they had heard Richard refer at home to a person named Herbert, and that the children would be returning to America the next day.

"How reliable is your information about the second man and the car?" Ferguson asked. She explained how she had gotten her information and said that she might be a little more confident about the car than the second man. She remembered the just-found slip of paper and told Ferguson about it. He asked her to read the contents.

"That doesn't mean anything to me," Ferguson said, "but it might mean something to one of our people here at the embassy."

"I was planning to go to the consulate anyway," Helen said. "I can bring the paper to you. Will you be at the embassy this morning?"

"The sooner you can come, the better."

"If you can see us at 11:00, we can first pick up some airline tickets on the Champs-Élysées."

"I'll be waiting for you."

"A problem is that I don't want to be away from the hotel. I don't want to miss the police."

"Don't worry about that, Helen. You're not likely to hear from them until this afternoon. The French just heard from us. They have their bureaucratic procedures and have to refer the case to the right place. It will be a while before investigators are assigned. And if you should miss the police, they'll be back. Don't worry."

"I suppose you're right. I'll leave a message for the police at the hotel in case they come early."

"Good. I'll see you at 11:00."

Before getting the children, Helen decided to change into a blue summer dress that showed off her figure and bared some of her chest, however discreetly. She put on red shoes with medium high heels. "I could pass for a Frenchwoman," she thought. She added a little to her eye make-up and put on a more lipstick than she ordinarily would. In the hotel lobby, she noticed that her effort had the intended effect. A middle-aged man who was leaving the breakfast room gave her an admiring glance, and the man with a moustache behind the counter beamed when he saw her. She asked for all of their passports from the hotel safe. She told him that she expected a visit from the police later that day. She and the children would visit the American Embassy in the morning, but would be back at the hotel in a couple of hours. The man assured her that he would be careful about any messages. As they left the reception, Helen felt his eyes upon her back.

Standing with the children in the street looking for a cab, Helen remembered that she had forgotten to tell Ferguson about the second man possibly wearing a bow tie. Not very important, she thought. She would tell him later.

In the taxi Helen showed the children the piece of paper from Richard's pocket.

"Weird," Anne said. "Why would he carry that around?"

"It has to be shorthand of some sort," John said

"Perhaps," Helen said, "but for what?"

"'H' for Herbert," said Anne.

"You don't think that would be a little too much of a coincidence?" Helen smiled at Anne. "And what would the numbers mean?"

Having picked up the plane tickets, Helen and the children walked the few blocks down Champs-Élysées to the American Embassy. Some of the morning freshness lingered in the air, but the typical summer heat was returning to Paris. Helen thought what a delight it would have been to have Richard with them. But that would have been in a different life. What could be more distant than the present from Helen's dream of the perfect vacation? Would she ever see Richard again?

# CHAPTER 16

The day after his time with Helen in Cambridge Richard called in the evening to make sure that she had returned safely to Washington. He told her that he had plans to go Washington for a brief vacation. Would she be able to see him if he came for an extended weekend? They agreed on a time in early August. In the intervening weeks they talked a few times on the telephone.

Richard worked very hard on his dissertation. He tried to make up for the time he had devoted to the teachers' conference, and he wanted to make up in advance for the time he would spend in Washington. He did not have to force himself. The more he explored his dissertation topic the more it engaged him. He was convinced that he had something new to say that would add significantly to the understanding of modern history. The Marxists saw property arrangements as conditioning everything else, including politics and culture. Richard did not believe that human life is determined. Persons are not the mere products of material conditions. What is distinctively human cannot be reduced to a mere expression of the need for economic production. Richard gave considerable weight to economic factors, not least the power of the big investment bankers to move governments. But in any decently civilized society the influence of economic interests was, he thought, more or less circumscribed. Moral restraints, sound thought, and culture more generally affected the scope and direction of economic-financial political power. But in his studies he had become more and more alert to adverse historical circumstances creating opportunities for ruthless financial operators prepared to take advantage of them. Richard's notion of "spontaneous conspiracy" explained how small and hidden but influential networks could accomplish goals greatly at odds with the interests of the larger society. Persons who might not initially conspire in a deliberate way nevertheless found and supported each other and were able to create potent synergies. How the moral, intellectual, and general cultural forces of the French Revolution interacted with the big financial interests seemed to Richard a compelling illustration of his thesis.

Writing had a painful aspect: nothing was more difficult or required a greater effort of concentration than arranging thoughts and pieces of information in a manner simultaneously coherent, lucid and graceful. Richard went through periods of utter frustration as he struggled to present complex material, but he found great pleasure in finally succeeding in expressing well what he wanted to say. His kind of writing was hard work, but he did not quite consider it oppressive. Because he found such satisfaction in articulating difficult material, he would sometimes wake up early in the morning eager to return to his writing. Inspiration gave him energy. Some mornings he almost postponed shaving and showering to get back sooner to his work. His dissertation was coming together. All the really hard work had been done. He was now at the state of a writing project that he thought the most pleasurable, tightening the manuscript and generally putting the final touches to it.

His original plan had been to work right through the summer, taking breaks just to play some tennis, see a movie, attend a concert, have a beer with a friend, or go jogging. He had felt no strong need for anything else. Now his imagination often drifted. He had met a wonderful woman. He thought back to their meeting and ahead to their reunion.

He put his car in the shop for long-postponed service and repairs. He even had the air-conditioner brought back to life. As a native of South Carolina he would have been able to handle the Washington heat and humidity without it, but Helen would be quite uncomfortable. In different circumstances the cost of the work on the Chevy would have caused him major pain, but the income from the lecture series had even made it possible to pay off the balance on his credit card. What were these expenses compared to the wonder of seeing Helen again.

He reserved a room for three nights in the least expensive hotel he could find in a decent part of Washington. This was another big expense, but, for now, he had the money, and he had not had any vacation for a long time. He deserved a break. He would not even visit the Library of Congress. Helen would take a day of vacation, extending her weekend. They would have three days together.

They agreed to meet at a restaurant in Georgetown for dinner in the evening of his arrival. Richard started his long drive in the wee hours of the morning. The trip was as exciting as it was tedious. As he approached Washington imagining what it would be like to see Helen again mixed with nervousness and fretting. He found his Washington hotel, which was located about ten blocks away from the restaurant. He parked his car, got his room and tried to take a nap. He soon decided that he was too agitated to fall asleep. He got up, shaved, showered, and took some care about his dress for the evening. He chose a blue sports jacket, gray slacks, black loafers, and a crisp white shirt, but no tie—he did not want to look too formal. Although he had the time, he decided against walking to the restaurant. He must not arrive sweaty because of the steamy August air. A little too early he took a cab. When he arrived at the restaurant the sun had dipped behind buildings, but it was too hot and humid to eat outside. He checked on his reservation and went back outside to see her arrive.

The streets were full of tourists. All who visit the American capital come to Georgetown, where you can eat and shop and walk around where so many of the rich, famous and powerful live.

A cab pulled up at the curb. Reflections in the car windows made it hard to see who was inside. What he saw first as the passenger tried to get out of the back seat was a red high-healed shoe and a tan and bare female leg. He knew immediately that it was Helen. He could offer her his hand for support. She looked up and gave him a smile of recognition that made his heart jump. She was at least as beautiful as he remembered her. She had that same indefinable exotic look, that same very female demeanor. She appeared a little taller because of her shoes. She was dressed now for an evening out. She wore a red summer cocktail dress. It followed her figure and was revealing without being daring. The front of her dress let him see the soft upper curves of what appeared to be a full but not large bosom. Her brown shoulder-length hair was shiny and brushed to one side. Her make-up might be a touch heavier than he had seen it before. She was incredible. He wanted to kiss her on the lips, but he took her other hand too and pulled her lightly towards himself for a kiss on the cheek that became a little more than just courteous. Had she expected more? Was he being too formal, even stiff?

As they were taken to their table he felt jittery but elated. He was hardly able to control his feelings and was afraid of behaving foolishly. His heart was beating hard. He calmed a little as they settled down at their table. The waiter showed up almost instantaneously, and the typical restaurant routine regarding drinks relaxed him. She wanted red wine, and he ordered a bottle of what she wanted. Soon the small talk flowed more easily. He could not stop looking into those eyes, and she responded by smiling. Had he ever felt better? He could hardly believe what was happening.

They talked endlessly and almost did not notice the rumblings of a thunderstorm outside. Everything new that Richard learned about Helen seemed to him to confirm that Helen was the woman for whom he had always been searching. She also seemed comfortable—happy even?—in his presence. Apart from the erotic attraction that he tried to contain, he found her interesting. They seemed to understand each other. They had similar outlooks on life and had partly over-lapping intellectual and cultural interests. Although the depth of Richard's worries about America surprised Helen, she felt no need to contradict him. She was un-ideological and largely un-political. There were parallels in their family histories. They both had roots in the South and affinities for and connections to Europe. Against all odds, she had even grown up in the Episcopal Church, once prominent as the church of the American elite but now one of the small denominations. She appeared more spontaneous and temperamental than he. She had some Italian blood on her mother's side. Though serious at the core, she could be playful and lighthearted, which balanced his formality and caution.

For the weekend Helen was staying at her parents' home, which was in Georgetown some six blocks away. Her parents were on the Atlantic coast in Delaware. Helen had promised to water their plants and would stay there rather than in her apartment across the Potomac River in northern Virginia.

At 11:00 they were among the last to leave the restaurant. The thunderstorm had gotten some of the humidity out of the air and lowered the temperature. He wanted to escort Helen home and asked if she would like to walk. He wanted to be with her as long as possible. She mentioned her high heels but accepted his suggestion. They walked slowly along M street, which has the most shops and restaurants, and veered north into the pleasant residential streets of Georgetown with their Georgian-style and Victorian houses and large trees. Trying to extend the evening, Richard stopped from time to time, discussing a subject or commenting on the neighborhood. Their only physical contact was when Richard put an arm behind her back to steady her on the uneven brick pavement or to steer her in a particular direction. He badly wanted to kiss her and hold her. Although he expected that she would not resist, he hesitated.

Then, suddenly, he stumbled on a protruding brick in the sidewalk. Helen grabbed his arm and pulled him back to steady him. As he regained his footing he found himself close up against her.

"Here in Georgetown you have to walk carefully," she said, smiling.

Before he knew it he had put his arms around her. When he kissed her she did not try to pull away but put her arms around him and kissed him back. Their first kiss was tender. The second one, after a few more steps, was more passionate. Richard realized that they were in her old neighborhood and that it might make her uncomfortable even in the dark to know that she could be seen from one of the houses. He did not try to kiss her a third time, only kept his arm around her as they walked the short distance remaining to her parent's house. It was located on a quiet side street away from the main residential streets frequented by the tourists. After confirming where to meet the next day, he reluctantly bid her goodnight. He gave her another kiss that he did not want to end.

On the second day they had a leisurely breakfast in a coffee shop closer to Richard's hotel in Northwest Washington. They walked to the National Cathedral, the large gothic Episcopal Cathedral that stands on the highest point in Washington, D.C. Richard had not seen it for many years and Helen showed him around. They walked down Massachusetts Avenue past the vice president's home at the National Observatory, the British Embassy and various other embassies. They crossed back to Georgetown and had lunch there. They returned to the home of Helen's parents, a townhouse of average to small size for Georgetown. It sat on a typical Georgetown street with large trees. Helen showed him the house. It was a well kept, tastefully decorated three-storey colonial that was narrow but extended all the more deeply toward the back. Behind the house was a small yard, most of which consisted of a brick patio. The house had a lived-in look. There were some old paintings and oriental rugs and real antiques but no signs of opulence. There were lots of bookshelves, some of them ingeniously placed to take advantage of small unused spaces. The owners had managed to make the house not look crowded or dark. An inside wall had been taken down, and in the back there was a small addition, a family room with large windows facing the brick patio. An inviting and welcoming home, Richard thought.

But his mind and his eyes were almost constantly on Helen. He wanted to embrace her and kiss her and more, but he did not want to be so forward, especially not in her parents' home. For the moment he had to be the considerate and well-behaved visitor.

"My parents bought the house before we went abroad," Helen said. "They rented it out while we lived in Europe. After we returned they had it refurbished and built the addition. They could do it because house-prices had gone up so much and they could take out a new mortgage at a good interest rate. I love it here. I wish I could afford a house like it for myself. But no way. I need a rich husband for that." She smiled at Richard. Then, for some reason, she winced.

She watered the plants inside and outside. In the little backyard Richard felt as if he were back in Charleston—the same kind of heat, heavy foliage above and around the patio and flowers that needed constant watering.

They strolled through Georgetown down to the Potomac River. It was hot, but the previous night's thunderstorm had cleared the air and clouds and haze blocked the sun. They admired the view. The Potomac River was slow and deliberate at this point of its progress towards the sea, having expended the energy gained in the mountains of West Virginia. Here the river was ready to merge into the sounds of the Chesapeake Bay a few miles to the southeast. Roosevelt Island, low in the water and richly overgrown with trees, looked as if it were drifting slowly down the river toward the Kennedy Center, which could have been a great white ship docked at the river's edge. Diagonally across the Potomac was the skyline of Arlington, Va., whose office buildings were higher than those in the nation's capital. In Washington regulations prohibited construction above a certain height.

They sat down at a restaurant at a table outside with a parasol. They ordered a light lunch and enjoyed the view. They conversed about the architecture and layout of Washington, D.C. Richard commented that he liked that National Cathedral, which is so majestically situated on Mount St. Alban, was by far the highest point in the city of Washington.

"Yes, the location is unbeatable," Helen said.

"I like the symbolism of it—a huge religious building that has the Washington of politics, lobbying, lawyering and business literally at its feet."

"But only symbolically," she said, smiling at him.

"Don't I know it. This town is about money and power, not divine guidance. Whatever we hear in ceremonial, pretentious speeches, the hearts and minds of the rulers of this country have little room for what the Cathedral represents. And yet, there it sits, on top of that large, commanding hill, as conspicuous as it could be, as if it waited for a different era."

"Did you know that there's another equally imposing church building across town?"

"I've heard of a Roman Catholic structure, but I've never seen it."

Helen pointed eastward. "It's located a mile or two north of the Capitol. It's called The Shrine of the Immaculate Conception. It's very big—about the same size as National Cathedral—but built in a very different, quasi-Byzantine style. It was finished before National Cathedral. I'll take you to see it. It, too, is on fairly high ground, considerably higher than the Capitol. I suppose you would say that it's another conspicuous reminder to the rich and powerful that politics and economics isn't the whole story."

"They do need reminding," Richard said. The subject had made him more melancholy. "Something in me likes that National Cathedral is a part of the religious denomination in which I grew up. I can feel at home there. But I'm also very much aware that the American elite who belonged to the Episcopal Church, came up with the idea for this Cathedral, and paid for it abdicated a long time ago. National Cathedral is a monument to something that doesn't really exist any more. One could almost see it as a kind of gravestone."

Helen looked inquiringly at him.

"That's how I feel in my darker moments," he said. "But today is not one of them." He smiled and kissed her lightly. "This is one of my best days ever." They sat silently looking out over the Potomac River.

How paradoxical and yet reassuring and even hopeful, Richard thought, that those two large church buildings had been constructed and completed in the twentieth century, at the very time when religion in the traditional sense was being driven out of America's public institutions, centers of culture, and intellectual life. The elites that now shaped the future were doing their best to expel an older religious sensibility. America's national culture — its trend-setting universities, its movie and entertainment industry, its big media — regarded Christianity with disdain or hostility. As much as half of the American people still attended church with some regularity, but much of popular religion seemed to Richard spiritually decadent. It was sentimental and immature or was little more than a ritual of sociability. And yet, though Washington's most imposing churches might be memorials to a passing era, they would, barring a nuclear disaster, be reminders for a very long time of a different way of looking at the world.

"I'm perhaps not the most devout church goer," Richard said suddenly. "But I'm a fairly regular one. And I think quite a bit about religious and moral issues. It's even a part of my professional study of history. I wonder all the time about what my own religion really is. I have an easier time believing the claims of Christianity symbolically than literally. When the creed is said in church I always put in little qualifiers and additions and reservations. I'm more comfortable with the 'We believe' than the 'I believe' version of the creed. At the same time, I doubt a person can be properly religious outside of all liturgical and theological structures. That's much too subject to personal idiosyncracy, too conceited. Beliefs and practices that have evolved over many centuries must surely have more to recommend them than what happens to be your own flavor of the moment."

"I haven't thought very much about all this," Helen said. "I just go to church most Sundays, and I like it."

"It seems to me that the Episcopal Church is pandering to the spirit of the times. To gain credibility among the trendsetters it's become little more than a kind of baptized political correctness. Episcopalianism seems to be petering out, like the old American elite whose church it was. It seems to be self-destructing more quickly than most denominations, but there are still some decent parishes. I grew up an Episcopalian, and I expect I'll die as one."

"I can't imagine belonging to another church."

"I'm from the Deep South, but I find it hard to put up with some of those evangelical true believers. Their simplistic fundamentalism and literalism and sentimentalism are so obviously a way of covering up doubt and ignorance. Those people can be awfully narrow-minded and intolerant. Their self-righteousness gets to me. Knowledge and intelligence are supposed to be unnecessary as long as you have unquestioning faith! But faith in what? Without some critical intelligence and theological and historical understanding, how could a person know whether he's praying to God or some projection of his own sordid, self-serving imagination. You can understand why simple, spiritually starved people are swept up in the emotional frenzy of those mega-churches, but what does it have to do with religion? Besides, those evangelicals don't even practice what they claim to believe. Abortions and divorces are about as common among them as in other groups."

"A poor choice we have, isn't it," Helen said. "Either hot, dogmatic, emotional literalism or cool, diffuse, and trendy Episcopalianism. But I like the church here in Georgetown where my parents and I have gone over the years."

They watched boaters docking in front of a riverfront restaurant. There were several cruisers and smaller boats on the river. They left the restaurant and strolled slowly and aimlessly along the river.

The conversation about religion had been genuine, but another, very different subject had been much on Richard's mind since he first met Helen in Boston. Whatever else they talked about, it had increasingly demanded its due. He had told Helen in general about the women he had dated and that he had been wholly unattached for over a year. It had surprised him that she did not ask many questions about what he told her. Also, she had not taken the opportunity to tell him about her own experience with the opposite sex. Was she deliberately avoiding the subject? The question kept nagging at him. He realized that many men must have pursued a woman of her beauty and general appeal. That she was not already married must have some special explanation. At best, she simply had not been able to find the right man. She had been waiting for him, Richard. But her reluctance to talk about the subject suggested some more painful, perhaps embarrassing, explanation. A disturbing thought had occurred to him: Had she been married? No, she would have had to tell him.

"What about the men in your life?" he blurted out. He regretted his words as soon as they had left his lips. How abrupt, how prying, how confrontational!

She stopped. A shadow passed over her face. The question kept hanging between them. At first it seemed as if she were not going to speak. Richard wondered if he had broached a subject that would jeopardize their relationship. After a silence that got deeper the longer it lasted, she faced him, looked at him and then looked away.

# CHAPTER 17

Helen and the children arrived at the embassy with time to spare before their 11:00 AM appointment. They walked around outside the embassy compound on the corner of Champs-Élysées and Avenue Gabriel. Beyond the trees of the Champs-Élysées was the wide expanse of the Place de la Concorde with its traffic carousel. The embassy appealed more to Helen than other U.S. embassies she had seen, because it was not a nondescript modern building in glass and concrete. The four-story building that formed the core of the chancery looked more like an exclusive hotel or large, aristocratic mansion-type residence. It matched the architectural styles of other buildings in the area. Trees also surrounded the embassy compound. But the view from the street was quite different from what she remembered from her youth. There was now an unsightly security perimeter blocking vehicles, and access by foot was strictly controlled.

There was a small line of visitors waiting to enter through a gate in the high iron fence. A marine guard in dress uniform asked their business, checked their passports and waved them on. They had to pass through a metal detector to enter the building. In the busy lobby they left word with a receptionist that they were there to meet Mr. Ferguson. They were asked to wait for someone to come to get them.

The American voices, the furniture and the pictures on the wall reminded them that they were back on American territory. Anne commented that it felt good to be there.

"I don't think I like France," she said.

An American woman in her fifties dressed in a strict professional gray suit and a blue blouse came down the stairway. She walked up to Helen.

"Mrs. Bittenberg?"

"Yes."

"I'm Sandra Jones. I'm Mr. Ferguson's secretary. Welcome to the American Embassy." She smiled at John and Anne. "Let me take you to Mr. Ferguson's office." She motioned them in the direction of an elevator. It was probably considered polite, Helen thought, to bring guests upstairs by elevator whatever their destination.

The secretary escorted them straight into Fergusons's office. It was a large, impressive corner office on the second floor, signaling that its occupant was a person of importance. Ferguson rose with a smile behind a large shiny wooden desk, which stood facing those who entered. There were two visitor's chairs in front of it. Each of the outside walls had a window. Through the larger of the two you could see Place de la Concorde behind trees. A sofa, a couple of armchairs and a table stood in a corner. The secretary asked if any of them would like anything to drink. Nobody answered in the affirmative, and after a slight nod from Ferguson she discreetly withdrew, closing the door behind her.

Helen had seen something that astonished her. When Ferguson came closer to greet her with a kiss on the cheek she could hardly move. Her feet felt nailed to the floor. She could make no sense of what she had seen. Ferguson was dressed in a dark, well-pressed suit, looking very much the man of influence. A silly question flashed through her mind. Was he the very picture of the senior diplomat, or had American informality invaded even this preserve of traditional standards? Ferguson seemed perfect. Just the right amount of properly folded white handkerchief was showing in his breast pocket, and his black English shoes had a high gloss. But what had startled her and made it hard for her to move or speak was a mere detail. Ferguson's starched sparkling white shirt with French cuffs set off the small piece of clothing that seemed to her to stand out—a dark-blue bow tie.

Still smiling, Ferguson shook hands with Anne and John. He pointed the three of them in the direction of the sitting group. Helen did not think that he had noticed her reaction. While Ferguson was bending down to say something to Ann John gave Helen a glance that asked: did you see what I saw?

In the very next moment, Helen knew her reaction to have been nothing less than irrational. So wrapped up was she in her own little hell that she had difficulty remembering that the rest of the world knew nothing whatever about her concerns. The lives of millions and millions of people continued as before. Although a few of those lives might overlap with hers in some way, they were not defined by that connection. Her reaction to Ferguson's bow tie showed just how distraught she was. She was tired and sleep-deprived, and she was losing her sense of balance and proportion. Yes, she had a touch of insanity. Hundreds, perhaps thousands of people in the U.S. Foreign Service probably wore bow ties with some regularity. The proportion of people with that predilection might be higher there than in any other American institution, although it was no longer the stronghold it had once been for the old American East Coast establishment. Not even among Americans in general was this sartorial practice unknown. Besides, she told herself, it was no more than *possible* that the second man in the Sorbonne cafeteria had worn a bow tie. She should not even assume that Richard had been in the cafeteria. She had to keep her emotions under control, maintain some critical detachment.

Ferguson again expressed his empathy. He asked Helen to repeat what she had found out since they met at his apartment. Helen had thought she would tell him what the waitress had said about a bow tie, but now she would not, partly because she was afraid that she would create an awkward scene and betray some of her earlier feelings.

"Did you bring that sheet of paper?"

Helen gave it to Ferguson.

He studied it closely. "This means nothing to me," he said. "Does it mean anything to you?"

"Nothing."

"We have a couple of people here at the embassy who specialize in stuff like this. If you don't mind, I would like to consult them?"

"Please do."

"I'm also thinking about anything else I might do to help you find Richard. For now our best hope is the French police. They're the best equipped to track a missing person here in France. We have our own resources, but they can't be employed in a case that has no obvious national security dimension."

They talked for another few minutes about Helen's plans, and she reiterated that the children would be returning to America the following day. She then said that she wanted to get back to the hotel as soon as possible but that they would first visit the consulate. Ferguson explained that it was located a few blocks away, in the Talleyrand Building, the former residence of the French statesman by that name. He gave her directions.

When Helen rose to leave Ferguson said: "I have a long long-scheduled important luncheon appointment, or I would have liked to buy the three of you lunch somewhere."

"Thank you Stephen. That's a very nice thought, but we should be moving along."

"I understand. I hope you will let me invite you to lunch tomorrow or the next day—" She noticed a strange glint in his eye that she could not define. Had he picked up some of her irrational reaction? No, it was not a look of puzzlement or curiosity? He seemed not to want to let go of her gaze. He finally added " — if Richard has not returned — But then, come to think of it, I would love to see the two of you."

"Thank you."

"I will accompany you downstairs. I haven't had a cigarette this whole morning. The building is of course a smoke free zone. I will accompany you into the front yard." He put his arm lightly around Helen's back.

They took the elevator to the ground floor. Helen again noticed Ferguson's eyes upon her. As they came out of the elevator he pulled out a pack of cigarettes. They had barely left the building when he struck a match and lit a cigarette. Helen reflected that he had not even waited to light up until he had said good-bye to them. He must have been awfully eager for a smoke.

With the cigarette in his left hand Ferguson wished the children a good trip back to America and shook their hands. He then embraced Helen — was it not a little too tightly? — and told her to call him if she had any news or there was anything that he could do. He pointed them in the direction of the consular section. Helen thanked him and said good-bye.

The three Bittenberg's were heading for the street when another well-dressed man of about Ferguson's age came through the gate on his way to the embassy. Passing them and seeing Ferguson, he said in a cheerful, bantering manner:

"Time for a smoke, Steve? But I thought you were a cigar man."

Helen almost stopped. She had a strong impulse to turn around to watch Ferguson's expression, but she forced herself to walk on as if nothing had happened. When the man spoke Helen and the children had already walked a few steps toward the street. As he was also facing the other way, Ferguson might well think that they had not heard his comment. She had not reacted in any visible way, and neither had John or Anne. They disappeared among the pedestrians outside the fence.

"Mom," John said in a low voice. "Did you *hear* that?"

"I did, John."

"Can you believe it?"

"Let's not jump to conclusions, shall we."

"Mom, what are the odds against something like that?"

"I don't know."

"What are you and Johnnie talking about?" Anne said.

"That man we met when we left the embassy said that Mr. Ferguson is a cigar-smoker."

"I didn't hear anything? What does it mean?"

"John and I were thinking about that second man in the cafeteria at the Sorbonne. He was supposed to be well-dressed, wear a bow tie and smoke cigars."

"You mean it was *Mr. Ferguson*!?"

"No, dear, we're just speculating."

"Mom," John said, "there was something else."

"What?"

"When you were saying good-bye to Mr. Ferguson I was looking around, and I saw something."

"What, John—*what*?"

"A car drove out from the side of the building and left through another gate."

"So?"

"It was a black Crown Victoria or a Mercury, I'm not sure which."

Helen stopped. Emotions crashed in on her from every side. The ground under her feet felt shaky. If this was the type of car that was used at the embassy for official business, Ferguson would have access to one. Had he gone to the Sorbonne on Friday in such a car to meet Richard? Then his not having told Helen about meeting Richard meant that he had not been on a social visit but was somehow involved in Richard's disappearance. That would mean that Richard's disappearance fit into a context beyond her comprehension. Had the U.S. government whisked Richard away or abducted him? But why would Stephen Ferguson be a part of that kind of scheme? He was one of Richard's friends! Had the government made use of him to entrap Richard? Helen's imagination was spinning out of control. She had to grab a hold of herself. Was she coming apart?

"And there is one more thing," John said.

"Yes."

"I could see the driver. He looked like one of those limousine drivers. He was wearing black."

Yet another coincidence. There were too many of them. The three of them looked at each other.

"Mom, what does it *mean*?" Anne said. She looked at Helen with a mixture of befuddlement and dark fear. Helen was beyond herself observing the agony of her daughter. She was just thirteen years old. She should not have to endure an ordeal like this. Helen bent down and hugged her. Anne cried quietly.

"I don't know what it means, dear. But everything will be all right in the end, I promise. Dad will be back soon." Even as she said it, she knew that she should have promised no such thing. But she had to reassure her daughter. Anne had to have hope.

John said, "Mom, wouldn't Dad have to be involved in something really big for the embassy to hide him or snatch him."

"Perhaps they are protecting him from some danger and can't tell us because it would jeopardize our safety or his," Helen said, giving voice to a flash of wishful thinking.

"What would they be protecting him from?"

"I have no idea, John. I'm as confused as you are."

"There is something very strange going on."

"OK, but we can't assume that there's a connection between Dad's disappearance and the embassy. We don't know that Mr. Ferguson had something to do with it, but even if he did, it might have nothing to do with the U.S. government. We just have to wait and see what the French police can find out. I may tell them about our suspicions, but I have to get a sense of what kind of people they are." What would the French police do with their suspicion, Helen wondered. They couldn't very well interrogate as a suspect the American diplomat who had initiated the contact with the French authorities. Would that not even violate the tradition of diplomatic immunity?

That the U.S. government—the CIA perhaps—might be involved in Richard's disappearance boggled her mind. Richard would have to be a part of something about which she knew absolutely nothing. That Ferguson as a private individual might have had a hand in his disappearance was no more comprehensible.

Did, then, Ferguson know what had happened, whether Richard was dead or alive, and, if alive, where he was? If so, Ferguson was one cool customer. Was that what she thought she had seen in his eyes? He would have had the answer to her questions already at the brunch at his apartment. His behavior would have been all a charade. How could he leave her in such agony and suspense? What cold-blooded deception! Helen quashed an impulse to return to the embassy to confront Ferguson. She had to think. She had to talk to Hubert.

If Helen had not forgotten to tell Ferguson about the bow tie, he might have received the Bittenbergs at the embassy wearing a regular tie. She had told him enough about what Wendy, the waitress, and the cleaner had seen to make him see that, unless he was careful, Helen might suspect his involvement. Because Helen had told him that the second man in the cafeteria might have been a cigar smoker, he wanted to go on record in a memorable way as a cigarette smoker. But why reveal anything at all about his smoking habits? Perhaps to dispel suspicion even before speculation about him could get started.

Had it been obvious to Ferguson that Helen and the children had heard his colleague's comment about his being a cigar-smoker? Probably not, Helen thought. They had been walking away and were near the gate, and there was traffic noise and other distractions. Ferguson had every reason to think that by the time the comment was made, the Bittenbergs had transferred their attention elsewhere. Even if they had overheard the comment, they had no reason to connect him of all people with Richard's disappearance? Tens of thousands of Americans smoke cigars, and many smokers switch among cigars, cigarettes, and pipes. Ferguson did not know about Wendy seeing the bow tie.

Helen's mind was in turmoil. She remembered that she had not asked Ferguson for a copy of the sheet of paper. How could she have forgotten? She had to find some unobtrusive way to ask for a copy or the original back.

The walk to the Talleyrand building took only a couple of minutes. This annex to the embassy struck them more as an impressive aristocratic residence than an official building. They stood in line to pass through security just before noon. In the entrance hall there was a passageway to one side, above which a sign read "Passports and Visas." The passage ended in a large room where there were small lines of people in front of several reception windows. A dozen people were sitting down waiting to be called. Helen walked up to a young woman behind a window that was not open for business and said that she was there to see Mr. Daniel Bennini on urgent business. The woman wondered if she had an appointment. Helen admitted that, no, she did not have a fixed time, but that Mr. Bennini wanted to see her as soon as she could make it to the consulate. The woman gave her an uncertain look and seemed to toy with some kind of bureaucratic response such as "you need an appointment," but she told Helen to have a seat and disappeared.

Only moments later a side door opened and a man of medium height in his late twenties or early thirties with thinning black hair came out. He wore a light, beige summer suit. He looked to Helen like a junior version of Silvio Berlusconi, the former Italian prime minister. He saw Helen and the two children, guessed who they were and walked up to them.

"Mrs. Bittenberg?"

"Yes."

"I'm pleased to meet you. I'd been wondering how you were getting along. I left a message for you at the hotel this morning."

A message, Helen thought—did the embassy now have some

information about Richard?

"Is there anything new about Richard?"

"I'm afraid not, but I wanted to let you know that the French police have been alerted."

"Thank you, I already know. Mr. Ferguson told me. We just saw him."

"Good."

Bennini greeted the children, speaking individually to them, and then asked the three of them to follow him to his office. What is the secret of the Italian-Americans, Helen thought. How do they almost always manage to seem so pleasant? Bennini's solicitousness was not effusive, but she sensed that his concern about these three fellow Americans was genuine. He was perhaps too young not to have become jaded or not to have settled into a detached, bureaucratic frame of mind? Whatever the reason, Helen was glad of his caring. She had to remind herself that the U.S. government might have something to do with Richard's disappearance, but she simply could not believe that this young man was trying to deceive her.

Bennini led them to a sparse, merely functional office whose only window looked out on a courtyard and the back of another building. On a shelf next to the desk Helen saw a framed photo of a young smiling blond woman with a baby on her arm who was holding the hand of a girl who seemed about two years old. It had to be Bennini's wife and children. On the wall there were two university diplomas, one from St. John's University in New York City, and one from Georgetown. There was also a picture of Thomas Jefferson and one of the Manhattan skyline. Bennini offered Helen a seat and excused himself to look for two more visitor's chair.

When they were all seated, Bennini asked her to fill out and sign a form about Richard's disappearance. While she did he took a copy of Richard's passport. He repeated that the French police had been contacted and told Helen what to expect. He listened attentively as Helen told him what she thought she had learned since talking to him on the telephone. She left out all speculation about Ferguson. Bennini made some notes and asked a few questions. She mentioned that she and the children had had brunch at Ferguson's apartment and that they had just met him at the embassy. She did not mention the paper she had found in Richard's pocket.

Bennini said that he was glad that they had a personal relationship with one of the top diplomats at the embassy. That could only be helpful.

"Mr. Ferguson called here this morning," Bennini said, "to let us know that he is aware of Richard's disappearance and would like to be kept informed."

"Had he already contacted the French?"

"Well, no, he hadn't. I was actually a little surprised that he expected us to contact the police, follow our normal practice. I had thought that, as he knows Professor Bittenberg, he might have approached the French at the ministerial level. That would be a clear sign to the French that the embassy attaches great importance to Professor Bittenberg's disappearance. But I suppose he had his reasons for thinking that the case was best handled through normal channels."

Helen felt cold. Ferguson had let her believe that he had personally intervened with the French and was doing everything he could.

"What are the normal channels?"

"We contact a particular office in the French State Department, and they contact the local police in the area where there has been trouble."

"What did you tell the French?"

"I gave them a summary of what you had told me up to that point and told them where you can be contacted."

"How much will they do?"

"They will conduct a serious search, I'm sure, but just how far they will go I just don't know." Bennini smiled to himself and looked at Helen. "I did try to convey to them that we here at the embassy are very concerned and that we will pay close attention to what happens. State Department types are very sensitive to nuances of language. In fact, I took the liberty of mentioning that our political counselor is following the case closely. They know what that means. Mr. Ferguson didn't explicitly ask me to say that, but I thought it might give the French the idea that a little special energy is called for."

"Mr. Bennini, one day, when I have Richard back, I will see to it that you get some kind of reward."

Bennini smiled a warm, Italian smile. "Mrs. Bittenberg, there is no reason. I've been thinking about what it might be like to be in your shoes, and I don't envy you. Of course I will do what I can. It's also my job."

Helen rose to leave. "Is that your wife and children?" She pointed to the framed picture."

"Yes, but the picture is a couple of years old. We just had our third child, another boy."

"Congratulations!"

Bennini beamed.

"We would like to get back to the hotel as soon as possible in case the police try to contact us," Helen said, "but I wonder if Mr. Warner might be in. He was the first one I talked to at the embassy."

"If he's not at lunch, he should be here."

"May I say hello to him?"

"I don't see why not? Let's see if he's here." In the corridor outside his office Bennini turned a corner and led them towards an office whose door stood open. Mr. Warner was there, and Bennini made the introductions. Warner was several years older than Bennini. He was taller and had medium-blond hair. He wore a dark suit and a white shirt and a tie. Helen assumed from his age, the size and appointments of his office, and Bennini's respectful attitude that he was Bennini's superior. Warner remembered talking to Helen on the telephone and listened with interest when Bennini summarized where the Bittenberg case stood.

"I'm very sorry to hear about your troubles," Warner said. "I want you to know that we will assist you in any way we can. We will stay in touch with you, and I know that you will stay in touch with us."

"I'm very grateful." Helen was pleased to notice that Warner seemed not unaffected by her female attributes. Helen gave him a smile into which she put a dose of helplessness.

Helen said good-bye to Warner, and Bennini escorted her and the children out into the reception area.

"Good luck to you Mrs. Bittenberg," he said.

"Please call me Helen," she said and startled him by giving him a hug.

She scooped up the children and walked quickly towards the exit. Bennini stood looking after them.

# CHAPTER 18

Richard's question to Helen about men in her life had seemed to sadden her and put her on edge. She looked out over the Potomac, still without saying anything, then looked straight at him.

"I should've told you sooner," she said.

Her words cut and worried him. He did not want any bad news. He wanted to embrace her unreservedly. He wanted to hear that she had been waiting for him her entire life, that there had been no men worth mentioning. The notion was ridiculous, he knew—a woman like Helen! —and yet he was reluctant to give up the romantic picture.

"Until six months ago, I had a particular boy-friend whom I had seen for a very long time," she said. Richard flinched. This was the very opposite of what he wanted to hear.

"We met one summer here in the Washington area. I still had my senior year to go at Mount Holyoke. We sat at the same table at the wedding reception of a girl friend of mine. The man I am talking about was a few years older than I. He was in business for himself, was a developer working with a partner. His name is Burton Standish. He's called 'Stan.' He is actually Burton Standish, III. His parents are old-line types—Episcopalians even—and wealthy. They live on an estate in Middleburg, Va., in horse country—or should I say hunt country?—about an hour and a half away. Very upper class. Lots of rich and famous friends. Parties. Fox hunts, complete with red and black jackets. As if they were British gentry."

"I know. And all this more than two centuries after the War of Independence."

Richard and Helen stood in the shade of a tree looking out on the river. He did not want to hear the rest, but he knew that he had to.

"We started dating while I was finishing up at Holyoke. I had thought about going to graduate school, but, partly because of my new boyfriend, I postponed a decision and took a job in a Washington lobbying firm. I was admitted to Georgetown and started taking graduate courses in English part-time. Stan pulled me into the horsy set. I met some nice people, as well as some odd ones. I liked them well enough, but began to feel that many of them did not quite live in the real world. I don't mean that they don't have the financial worries of ordinary people, but that they are playing at something and can get away with it only because of their money."

"I'm familiar with the kind. They pretend to be old-line aristocracy, but a very different kind of elite—much tougher and rougher—has already supplanted them where the real decisions are made." Richard meant what he said, but he realized that his voice had an acerbic touch because of his resentment of a particular young man.

"I wouldn't know," Helen said. "But less than half a year after I had returned to Washington and become a part of this world Stan started to drop hints that we might get married. I liked him, but something held me back. We kept seeing each other, and I think his parents grew rather fond of me. I'm sure they encouraged him to get engaged to me. The trouble was that I was not very receptive, certainly didn't encourage him."

Good, Richard thought. Get rid of him.

"But I didn't break with him either. We just continued seeing each other. The weeks and months went by. People got used to Stan and Helen showing up together. I'm sure many started wondering what was holding us up."

"Do you know what it was?" Richard's question made her look away.

"A mixture of things. One was that I was unsure of my own way—in life, I mean. I had a wonderful professor at Holyoke, a rather famous man. He was of retirement age but kept teaching. He was formally in the history department, but he was just as interested in literature and poetry. In fact, he was a recognized poet, even won some big prize. At the end of the fall semester of my senior year, after he had read a term paper of mine on Dostoyevsky, he strongly encouraged me to get a Ph.D. I was very flattered. If a man of his distinction thought so highly of my ability, I probably had what it took."

OK, Richard thought, but when are you going to dump Stan?

"But by that time I had started dating Stan—he had come to visit me at Holyoke—and I was not sure what kind of future I wanted. Partly because of Stan I didn't get my act together regarding graduate school. I thought I might take a year or two to think things over as some of my friends were going to do. Did I really want to teach in a college or university? I returned home to D.C., got that lobbying job, and kept dating Stan."

Get rid of him, Helen, Richard thought. What are you waiting for?

"Looking back, I can only say that I was postponing making a decision about anything serious. I did what I did by default, as it were. The lobbying firm soon promoted me, but I didn't much care for the job. I cultivated congressional staffers and congressmen and senators, arranged receptions, little conferences, and the like—all of this for firms and associations that hired our firm. One of the things I got rather good at was turning down propositions without angering anybody. The months went by. I had known Stan for over two years when I finally agreed to think about marriage."

Oh, no, Richard said to himself. You should be breaking with him.

"It was so unfair to keep stringing him along. He's a nice person, really, and he was good to me. And he was becoming more and more successful building things. He was joining up with big financiers, including his father, to do large projects."

"He must have been rather busy," Richard said, fishing for a negative comment about Stan. They sat down in the grass where they could find some shade.

"He was, but he's a very good manager, and he was very considerate of me. He almost never called at the last moment to say that he had to cancel or delay a date. He really treated me well."

Did he not have *any* bad traits, Richard wondered.

"I started to feel more and more indebted to him. And so I let him think that we were headed for an engagement."

Richard shrieked inwardly.

"There's a socially prominent church in Upperville, Virginia, to which he and his parents belong. When we went there for a service or happened to pass by he would talk about what a glorious wedding one could have there. I could see it. Then one day he forced the issue and popped the question. He did it in style. He offered me an expensive, beautiful ring. How could I turn him down?"

Easy, just do it, Richard shouted—without making a sound.

"I accepted him". Richard felt a palpable pain in his gut.

"But wouldn't you know it? —I didn't want to set a definite date for the wedding. Whenever I think about it I'm ashamed of myself. The announcement was made, though, and people congratulated us. More time went by. Still no wedding date. His parents started to make barely veiled, barbed comments. My parents, too, were wondering what was going on. My mother told me not to forget that organizing a typical wedding would take a lot of time. My father never said so, but I think he knew what the real trouble was. He liked Stan, but he did not think he was quite right for me. Stan was too—too—what?—*uninteresting*—for someone like me. That's it! My mother thought Stan was a catch and a good person besides. What more could any woman want? He was rich and handsome, a Princeton graduate, socially prominent, honest and probably very safe. She thought I was being very selfish keeping him waiting—and she was right. It all became very awkward, and it was all my fault. Why did I have to be such an ambivalent, weak-willed twit!? Would you believe that before this self-made mess I had always thought of myself as rather strong-willed, decisive, tough and resourceful? When I was growing up Dad used to call me "Miss Ironpants."

Where was Miss Ironpants when we needed her, Richard wondered.

They steered up into the central part of Georgetown, walking slowly, finding shade where they could and concentrating on the conversation.

"How did it all end?"

"Stan finally talked me into setting a date. It would be in six months to make possible a big wedding, to print and send out invitations, etc., etc. It was when my parents were starting to make the practical arrangements and we were putting together the list of people to invite that I finally, belatedly, came to my senses. I came to the realization that Stan does not quite live in the same world as I do. I don't mean that we're socially far apart. Our family social circles actually overlapped a little with his. My parents aren't rich, just comfortable, but my father especially has friends whom you might call socially prominent. As a journalist he got to know various political figures as well as some well-known writers, journalists and media people. But our family is more intellectual than the Standishes. We read a lot. The lack of deeper connection between Stan and me lay somewhere in that direction."

"You mean you didn't have much to talk about?"

"Yes and no. Stan's bright and he's civilized, but he seems not to realize that human existence is pretty mysterious, a cause for wonder and reflection. He lives from day to day, somehow, unaware that there are big issues to face. He simply fits in. It never struck him that his social set might have a pretty superficial, narrow idea of life. They can read, and some of them are very smart, like the couple of fabulously wealthy computer geeks I got to know. Sharp, yes, but could they think their way through anything really serious? Outside of their own little field of expertise they seemed never to have an original, unexpected idea. They had all the usual advanced, 'sophisticated' views, including some of the typical PC opinions." Helen took a deep breath. "They were somewhat conservative or moderately liberal in politics. They wanted to keep their money."

Richard was settling down. It upset him that Helen, this woman of his dreams, had been so close to another man for so long, but what could he expect? He realized that his initial reactions to Stan had been too emotional. Helen was extraordinary, an unbelievable find! It was his own very good luck that she was not married.

"I know what that type of rich person is like," he said, now in a fairly dispassionate frame of mind. "Most of the self-made rich haven't had much time to think. They have been so busy making their money. But when they've made it they want to be more than just simple-minded entrepreneurs, so they parrot the enlightened views that you're expected to have. Or they champion capitalism. Count on every self-made multi-millionaire to have a hobbyhorse and to assume that his ability to make money proves his knowing just what society needs. The old money types are more suave and less ready with opinions. They have the resources and independence to ignore the PC crap, but, without even knowing it, they drift with the prevalent cultural trends and provide little opposition to the foolishness."

"My God, they were all so predictable, so unoriginal, well, so — *predictable*! What they talked about most was the last or next big party, the last or next trip to Europe, the last or next hunt, the last or next improvement to the estate, the last or next Range Rover, the last or next threat to their bucolic setting from nasty developers, and so on. There's nothing wrong with any of these subjects, but together they don't amount to much. The depth dimension somehow isn't there. If they bother with Church, it's mostly as a part of the social scene. Sad or bad things that happen are only unpleasant disruptions of the flow. I met plenty of neurotics and drunks and kids on pot, but they seemed not to cause anybody to think that there might be anything fundamentally wrong with the general set-up. We all know about country club Republicans — about the kind of life that is true to form but not quite lived. This was a better-funded, more elaborate version of the same thing, and Stan could see nothing wrong with it. How else would you want to live, he thought. Wasn't this what all people want and always want more of? Stan isn't exactly uninterested in music, movies, the theatre, literature, philosophy and religion. He would go with me to the opera, and he could discuss the arts and literature rather intelligently with me. In college he actually took some history. He has no objection to going to church. But he has no deeper need for any of these things. It was I who kept bringing them up. His conversations with his male friends were always about the same thing, business and finance, and, of course, sports, sports, and cars and horses, then more sports. Politics came up, but usually in relation to how it affected taxes and business opportunities. Stan's a good guy, but I asked myself: how could I have children and spend the next fifty years or so with a man who doesn't quite know what kind of a world this is—a kind of sleepwalker?"

The heat had made Richard sweat, and he suggested that they go inside the up-scale shopping center that hides behind a couple of traditional-looking city blocks in central Georgetown. Helen merely nodded and continued her story.

"No, I am being unfair," she said. "Stan's not as unsophisticated as I am making him out to be."

"I think you have drawn a picture of a pretty decent representative of *homo sapiens*, American species," Richard commented, saying what he really thought. "Stan didn't live up to your highest hopes, but how many men could do that, go contrary to the general flattening out of our culture, the withdrawal from areas where you have to face the ultimate questions? It's not easy to separate yourself from the general trend within your society and civilization. You said that Stan was not all there, but sooner or later most people go with this flow. I guess you were disappointed in Stan because he comes from a good, cultivated family and had the wherewithal to break the mold. He might have struck a blow for what you care about. But before cultural decline sweeps through a people, it affects the privileged classes, only in a subtler, more advanced form. A fish starts rotting from the head. It's in the elite, first of all the intellectual and cultural elite, that decline usually originates. The elite become confused and superficial and, above all, week-kneed. *They* avoid confronting the ultimate issues, escape into various distractions, and the rest eventually follow. In a period of general decline the elite just have marginally better manners and taste, more sophistication. And as they decline more ruthless and energetic people who know what they want take their place."

Helen did not comment. They walked aimlessly in the air-conditioned shopping center. Many tourists seemed to be looking for cool air in the same place.

"So what finally happened?"

She gave him a nervous, hesitant look. She took her time before answering. She almost seemed to have difficulty speaking.

"One day—my parents were just about to sign a fat advance check to a hotel—I simply broke the engagement. I gave him that nice ring back. I said I thought he was a good guy, told him that I had treated him very badly, and that I was very sorry. I simply didn't think we were right for each other. He protested, but I did not budge."

"How did he take it?"

"Quite badly, I think, but I don't really know. He seemed pretty attached to me, and I had become a large part of his life, but I never understood what made him tick deep down. Was there a deep down? He tried twice to persuade me to change my mind, but now I was back to being Miss Ironpants. I was kind to him but firm. He finally understood that it was over between us. He gave up. I felt terrible, all the more so because he didn't chew me out. If he had said some horrible things, I might have had an easier time justifying the break. I really blame myself for stealing a couple of years of his life."

"Hey, wait a minute. Stan didn't exactly hate his years with you, and you never promised him anything until you got engaged. He could have left you when you kept avoiding the subject of marriage, but he didn't, so he must have gotten something out of your relationship. The whole experience may have taught him something."

"Perhaps so, but I had my reservations almost from the beginning. And then, imagine, breaking the engagement after I had had all that time to think about whether I should become engaged to Stan in the first place! Think of all the embarrassment for him, his parents, and my parents. I shudder when I think about it. Surely, I could have broken with him sooner. I don't quite know what attracted me to Stan in the first place. He was bright and handsome, yes — very tall and very blond — very attentive to me, kind, polite, well educated, well dressed, and well to do. I was attracted to the idea of him, I think. All the pieces were there, but somehow they hadn't been put together right." She paused and made an exasperated face. "Listen to me! Who am I to pass judgment!? I'm the one who's not assembled right."

They exited the shopping center and strolled back towards the river. They were silent, both thinking about the impact of the story.

Richard noticed that the worst pain was subsiding. He could examine what he had heard without incapacitating emotion. He could understand why Helen had acted as she did, empathize with her. He had learned much about her. He was surprised that his feelings of jealousy were not stronger.

Helen was deeply conflicted. On the one hand, she was greatly relieved. This was the first time she had told her story to anyone. With her parents she had been oblique, saying simply, "Stan and I were not right for each other." Yet the relief from having spoken frankly about this most touchy of all subjects could not obviate her fear about Richard's reaction. His view of her must have changed. He had to regard her as an immature, indecisive, self-indulgent woman who was also "experienced."

Richard did not comment. He just chatted intermittently with her about what they happened to see. She imagined that he must be rearranging everything that he knew about her. He was embarrassed and didn't know what to do or say.

Returning to the river they sat down on some stairs where trees protected them from the setting sun.

"It's not hard to understand what happened," he suddenly said, as if there had been no interruption in their previous conversation. "Fate handed you a young man who seemed almost too good to be true. How could you not be attracted to him? If nothing else, your reason had to tell you that you were lucky to have met somebody like him. Your mother was clearly impressed, which must have affected you. How could you give up somebody like that? If you had not had that long time with him, you might not have figured out what was missing and how important it was to you. You might have married him, thinking that your relationship would deepen over the years. But most people do not change all that much. You would have become more and more acutely aware of the part of your marriage that never materialized, and, being who you are, you might have become miserable. The important thing is that you realized your mistake before it was too late."

"But I hurt Stan badly."

"Somehow I doubt it. From what you've told me, he does not seem to be the type that falls into despair when things go against him. It's more likely that after a painful couple of weeks he adapted and got on with his life. I wouldn't be surprised if he's got another serious girlfriend. Perhaps he's engaged, even married."

"I think he's engaged."

"Many women must have had their eyes on him."

"Except that the best ones his age would have been snatched up while I was monopolizing him." Helen shook her head.

"And all the social embarrassment I caused!," she exclaimed. "It must have been very uncomfortable for him and his parents. It was bad enough for me, but I deserved it."

"Now there is one thing, Helen, that you may be able to take some pride in." He noticed that he was starting to dwell on the positive.

"Take *pride* in!?"

"Yes, think about your whole situation. You knew that if you broke the engagement people would say that you were selfish, frivolous, and even ruthless. Some would even think you were stupid. After all, Stan was the ultimate 'catch.' With him you would have had security and social standing. He's even a good person. You had also kept him and the two families waiting for a long time. The momentum running in favor of marrying Stan was as strong as it could be. The wedding preparations were far along. The pressure on you could not have been more intense. That's when you announced that you would not marry Stan."

Helen hid her face between her hands.

"I have two comments about that," Richard continued. "First, what you did shows that at least you are not mercenary or a social climber. Marriage means more to you than money and status."

"But it took me a very long time to figure that out and to work up the courage of my convictions. Because of my procrastination and ambivalence I hurt people. I was just plain selfish."

"You're being very hard on yourself. Some decisions are just very big and hard, and you shouldn't make them before you've answered some of the really difficult questions, such as" — he smiled — "*the-purpose-of-life*. Deciding what to do about Stan was obviously all the harder because it was all entangled in your effort to decide what your life ought to be. Unfortunately, our mixed-up, messy society is not much help on questions like that, which puts quite a burden on the individual."

"You're making excuses for me."

"Not really. In any case, what strikes me most about what you did is something else. Given all the circumstances, most women would have persuaded themselves to go ahead. They would have told themselves that they would be crazy to turn down an opportunity like that and that their reservations were just the usual pre-marriage jitters. In the end, you didn't try to fool yourself. You reached a conclusion and you stuck to it. The pressure was on—it really was on—both psychologically and socially. But you didn't cave in. Helen, it took some guts and some strength of will to do what you did."

"I suppose so, but I don't take any pride in it."

"So you don't, but it's all in the past now. It's over. What could be more pointless than to keep going over what you might have done differently? You learn from your mistakes—that's all they are good for—and you put them behind you."

They were plunged deep in their own thoughts. Richard could not hide from himself the sting of knowing that Helen had been so close to another man for so long. He would need time to get used to the idea and revise his romantic image of her. But he already sensed that he could live with what he had learned. It would fade, look insignificant in time. He recognized that in his comments to her he had intended to be comforting. He felt protective of her. He had been in an increasingly tolerant, generous mood. Yet he had meant what he said. Yes, her self-criticism was partly justified. She should have been more decisive. But who was Richard Bittenberg to be critical of indecision? He should have gone for the doctorate directly, but he didn't quite know who he was. And he had not been successful in his choice of women. Besides, he was thankful that Helen had procrastinated. Otherwise she would not have been with him now.

He turned to face her. She felt his gaze upon her and looked up anxiously. He took her hand and said, "In any case, I'm very glad you did what you did. At least the man who gets to marry you can be pretty certain that you have no serious reservations." He smiled. Then, with a straight face, he said, "Or perhaps the next time you're engaged you'll suppress all reservations to be forgiven for your past mistake."

They laughed. He held on to her hand, and she put her head on his shoulder. They sat for a long time in the late Washington afternoon. A hazy, golden orange glow lay over the river, the Kennedy center and Roosevelt Island.

Helen had dreaded telling the story. Now that her relationship with Stan was out in the open she felt immeasurably better. She had not even given Richard a redacted version of the facts. She had made no effort to mask or excuse her own conduct. He must have been very disappointed, but he had not recoiled from her. He was adapting to her past, would be able to live with it. Her story would not hang like a dark cloud over the rest of their time in Washington. She realized how much his reactions mattered to her and how deeply she cared for him.

He proposed a before-dinner drink, and they took a table at one of the riverfront restaurants. Their conversation turned to their respective plans for the future. She would like to finish her Georgetown Master's degree. He would make the final revisions to his dissertation and defend it in the coming fall semester. Harvard would give him a one-year postdoctoral fellowship during which he would turn his dissertation into a book and start looking for an academic position. He wanted to start teaching in the fall of the following year, preferably somewhere on the East Coast.

He learned that Helen was attached to the Washington area. She liked its cosmopolitan ambiance, the cultural offerings, and the general lay of the land. She was also close to her parents. "I think I would like to live somewhere around here when I grow up," she said.

He commented that she had not listed living and working near the politically powerful as one of the city's attractions.

"The politics of the city does add a spice to life here," she said, "but I have lived and worked here long enough not to be star-struck. Listening to my father and family friends and working for that lobbying firm I have also learned that appearances are very often deceiving. Some of the major actors are not nearly so glamorous as they might seem in the media. Many of them are pretty ruthless and think only about their own power. Some of them are truly despicable. A few of them are not much better than criminals. In my book they *are* criminals. They just haven't gotten caught. There are some good people on the Hill—don't get me wrong—but most of them are rank opportunists and careerists. They think all the time about reelection, getting a high appointment in the executive branch, or landing a lucrative job with a lobbying firm or a big business. Some things that happen around here are so abominable that you wouldn't want to know. This is what *I* observed, and I've just gotten a few peeps behind the scenes."

Her words gave Richard an excuse to offer his jaundiced assessment of American national politics, which he related to his view that America's culture was in precipitous decline. She listened with interest and some surprise. She did not quite disagree with him, but she was not used to thinking of politics the way Richard did, as a manifestation of larger social trends in ideas, morality, religion, and culture generally. He had obviously thought a great deal more than she about the subject. She was also struck by the darkness and pessimism of his view of the state of America. It puzzled her that a man who did not seem particularly gloomy, but rather cheerful and positive, would have such opinions.

During the rest of Richard's visit to Washington Helen showed him the main sights. She took him to the neighborhood where Richard's parents had made their first American home and where Richard had been born. Richard had not seen the house since he was nine years old and his parents had taken the family to Washington.

Long before the end of their Washington weekend Richard and Helen realized that they were deeply in love. They had kissed often but had not shared a bed. The night before Richard was to drive back to Cambridge and she was to return to work it seemed to both of them inevitable, self-evident, that they would sleep together for the first time. Richard's sentry-like, prudish self protested in vain and not very strongly. This was the woman he would marry.

# CHAPTER 19

Helen and the children had efficiently accomplished their objectives for the morning, but it was after 1:00 PM when they walked into the hotel lobby. In the taxi from the consulate Helen had worried that Ferguson might have been wrong about the French police not contacting them until the afternoon. She did not want to miss their visit. She was also eager to call Hubert.

"*Madame*, three messages for you," the man with the moustache announced as soon as he saw them.

Helen felt her chest tighten. She had expected one message, from Bennini. Had Richard called? Only through an act of will was she able to maintain her composure. She held on to the counter when the clerk took out the three slips of paper.

Picking up the first message, the man said in his heavily accented English: "There was call from the American consulate at 9:45. Mr. Bennini has said French police informed. They will come see you. His telephone number—*ici*."

"We saw Mr. Bennini this morning," Helen said. "What are the other messages?"

The man seemed not to want to rush to be able to take full credit for being the bearer of news.

"Then police come. Ask for you."

"They *did*!? When was that?"

"They come 11:15. Two men. Left card for you."

The man handed Helen a business card. The name on it was Henri Duparc, and his title was chief inspector. A telephone number had been written on the card above the printed one, probably a cell phone number, Helen thought. She knew nothing about French police titles, but "chief inspector" suggested a detective of some seniority.

Why had Ferguson assumed that the French police would contact her considerably later? The French State Department and police seemed not to have lost any time.

*The sheet of paper*! Ferguson had told her not to expect the police anytime soon so that she would be willing to leave the hotel and bring him the paper. She did not have the time to think through that possibility. She wanted the third message.

"*Monsieur*, what was the third message?"

"A man called 11:30."

"Who was it? What did he say?"

"He asked for you, *Madame*, and I said you were at *l'ambassade*."

"What was the message?"

"No message."

"What was the man's name?"

"He not say."

"Strange." Not leaving a name was obviously deliberate. "I suppose he didn't leave a telephone number either."

"*Non*, Madame."

"What language did he speak?"

"English, Madame."

"Did the call seem local or long distance, or international?"

"Cannot know."

All the people Helen could imagine having called — somebody from the police, the embassy, or the airline, Hubert, her father — would have left a name. This person did not want to be identified. Could it have been Richard? Had he finally called to let them know that he was all right? Was he taking care of some urgent business? Or was he hiding somewhere and concerned not to reveal himself to anybody else? Or had somebody called in his behalf?

The children wanted lunch, but they agreed to wait in their room until she had called the police. She tried the phone number that had been hand-written on chief inspector Duparc's business card, and he picked up after just two rings. She told him that she was now at the hotel. He introduced himself and confirmed that he would be investigating the disappearance of Richard Bittenberg. She was glad to hear that he spoke good, articulate English. He told her that he and another detective would be back at the hotel in an hour and a half. Helen wanted to call Hubert immediately so that she would be certain to catch him before his court appearance, but the children were hungry, and she collected them. To save time they ate at McDonald's. They talked about the events of the morning and the possibility that Ferguson might know what had happened to Richard.

When they returned to the hotel Helen immediately went to her room and dialed Hubert's home telephone number. Dorothy answered and told her that Hubert had left early for the office. Helen then tried Hubert's cell-phone, and after several rings he picked up.

"Darling, I just walked into my office. I have to be in court in less than two hours. Anything new?"

Helen gave him the most recent information, including the

grounds for suspecting that Ferguson might be involved in Richard's disappearance. She told him about the paper with the code-like text and about the name Herbert. She gave Hubert her impression of Bennini and told him that she was just about to talk to the French police.

"Hubert, am I getting carried away by suspicions?"

"Well, those coincidences may turn out to be actual coincidences in the end or to have some harmless explanation, but the more I think about this whole business, the more I think that Dick's gotten mixed up in something with a government angle — God knows what. I would be very surprised if Ferguson is on the up-and-up. The U.S. government must be involved somehow, but I haven't the foggiest idea how. The CIA or some such agency could be behind the disappearance, and for some strange reason the lid has to be kept on very tight. You would think that Ferguson would be able to tell you if the government is hiding Richard, say, to protect him. Ferguson knows that you are beyond yourself with worry, and still he has said absolutely nothing to reassure you. It crossed my mind that it might advance the government's purpose for you to be distraught, and the best way to accomplish that is to keep you in the dark. But, heavens, that kind of callousness would be extraordinary. Whatever's going on, we have to think practically, decide how to act. I think we have to assume that Ferguson is deceiving you. The question is whether he is doing it for Richard's sake or for the sake of some government operation."

Helen had been listening without interrupting.

"That's what I think, too. But should I let the French police know everything that I suspect?"

"That Bennini guy at the consulate does sound all-right. Let's assume that he was telling you the truth and that the consulate contacted the French police through normal channels. That probably means that the police you will be dealing with are not part of some conspiracy. As far as they are concerned, they are on routine business. It sounds as if Ferguson made sure that this case would not receive any special attention from the French police. He could have approached the French at the highest possible level and done it sooner. He may be surprised to learn that the French have assigned a chief inspector. You may have Bennini to thank for that."

"So, should I tell the French about my suspicions?"

"The French police may be your best allies right now. If you get a reasonably favorable impression of them, I guess you should be open with them."

"I suppose I will."

"There's one danger."

"What?"

"If you tell them that you suspect Ferguson, they may conclude that the U.S. government is involved in Richard's disappearance. That will make them want to check with their superiors, and those superiors will perhaps be in touch with the Americans to make sure that the French police won't blunder into some sensitive operation, involving NATO, for example, that has the blessing of the French government. Word may get back to Ferguson that way. On the other hand, unless Dick's disappearance is part of some joint French and American operation, I don't think the French would like the idea of the Americans abducting a person on French soil."

"I'll follow my intuition, Hubert."

"Do that, darling. Hey, are you getting any sleep?"

"Some."

"Remember what I told you. And have some wine. Got to run. I have a judge waiting. But I'm on Richard's case. I called the best private investigator here in Charleston this morning. He's got a contact in D.C., and we will soon have some help trying to find out what Richard's been up to."

# CHAPTER 20

In the three months following his visit to Washington, Richard and Helen spoke almost daily on the telephone. Though it jeopardized his deadline for submitting the final copy of the dissertation for the defense, he came back to Washington twice during the fall term. He met Helen's parents at their home in Georgetown. In November when he was to defend the dissertation she took the train to Boston to be with him to celebrate the successful completion of the requirements for the Ph.D. At the May commencement he would be able to don his doctoral garb and walk in the academic procession. Richard would invite his parents and siblings and some relatives and friends as well as Helen's parents to that celebration. The members of his dissertation committee were highly complimentary about his work and his defense of it. They all assumed that in time a major academic publisher would accept the dissertation as a book. His postdoctoral fellowship would ensure that outcome.

Richard invited Helen to visit him and his parents in Charleston for a few days after Christmas. She had never been in the city before, and she took to it immediately. She loved its southern charm and grace and that it could retain a small-town atmosphere in spite of its size.

"Spring must be just lovely here," she said, "with the flowers and trees in bloom."

When she and Richard went shopping in the downtown area she exclaimed: "I can't believe it! King Street has almost as much good shopping as Fifth Avenue in New York City, and this city is so much nicer. Who would want to live in New York?"

On the second day of her stay Richard's mother took him aside.

"Richard, you marry this girl, y'hear."

Richard introduced Helen to his grandmother Annabelle, who was almost ninety years old, his brother, sister and their families. Aunt Ruth gave a well-attended tea for Richard, the Harvard Ph.D., and his girlfriend, drawing a good crowd of relatives and family friends. At the New Year's Ball of the St. Andrew's Society, Charleston society got to inspect Helen. Frances Halloway, née Woodbridge, Richard's first serious girlfriend, was there with her husband. As the old European etiquette was observed at the ball, Richard had to dance with many different women. He asked Frances. She was now the mother of two. Her husband was the president of a local insurance agency. Richard found her quite changed but very good-looking. He complimented her.

"You are clearly the most beautiful mother here."

"Thank you, Dick," she said, "but the most gorgeous woman at this ball is your Helen. You will marry her, won't you?"

"The possibility has crossed my mind."

He danced the last dance with Helen. As they left the ball she asked: "Who's that stunning blond you danced with?"

"She used to be Frances Woodbridge. She was my high school sweetheart. She's married now and has two children. It was almost fifteen years ago that I discovered that she's not my type. But she thinks you're a stunner, and I agree." He kissed her. They walked home from the party, holding each other tightly, enjoying the coolness and pitch darkness of the Charleston night.

In mid-winter of the new year, Richard was offered a position as assistant professor of history at Cornell University, to start in September. He and Helen announced their engagement. In May, just a week before the Harvard commencement, Richard and his parents joined Helen and her parents for the celebration of her Master's degree from Georgetown University. The two families meshed nicely. There was an immediate rapport between the two mothers, Hannah Bittenberg bringing out the old Virginia side of Lucy Davenport.

The wedding took place on a sweltering day in early August in the Georgetown church that the Davenports had long attended. Her parents had complained that there had not been quite enough time to make the arrangements for the wedding, but Helen had spent all her free time on them while Richard, up in Cambridge, readied his dissertation for submission to a publisher and made preparations for his first year of full-time teaching. The wedding reception was held at a hotel in Georgetown. The number of invited guests had been kept down to 150 only with great difficulty. The list had required the ultimate in diplomatic tact, especially on Richard's side, where a large extended, virtually boundless family might expect some consideration. Helen and Richard spent a brief honeymoon in the Greek Mediterranean.

They rented an apartment near the beautiful Cornell campus, which is situated on a mountain with a sweeping view in the winter half of the year of the surrounding up-state New York countryside. Helen took a part-time position with the University Public Affairs office. She was admitted to the Cornell doctoral program in English and started taking two courses per semester. A year into Richard's Cornell appointment Stanford University Press brought out his book. He had worked to complete several articles derived from papers he had written in graduate school, and two of them, dealing with the ideas and the political role of the Freemasons at the time of the Framing of the U.S. Constitution, were published in leading academic journals soon after the appearance of the book. Like the book, they were widely and favorably noticed. Laudatory reviews of the book, on the interaction of ideas and economic interests in the French revolution, were published not only in several academic journals but also in a few newspapers, including the *New York Times* and the *Washington Post*. Richard was praised for the book's conception, the care and thoroughness of his research and the originality of his interpretation. He had included at the end of the book some reflections on the relevance of his finding of "spontaneous conspiracy" for the present, which hinted that similar patterns might be discernible in other societies and might even help explain developments in the America of today. A few reviewers picked up on these brief and cautiously expressed comments and a couple of them pronounced themselves uneasy with them. Was not "conspiracy thinking," even in this subtler, modified form slightly disreputable? Was there in today's America anything like a "spontaneous conspiracy" of intellectual and economic forces working to dislodge traditional elites? If so, just what did the author have in mind? Such grumblings notwithstanding, Richard had made a name for himself. He was a rising academic star.

At the end of the first year at Cornell John was born at the University Hospital. With the help of Richard's parents they bought a town house further away from the campus.

Early the next year Richard was dealt a hard, almost crippling blow. His father died of a massive stroke without any forewarning. He was in his early sixties and had seemed healthy and vigorous.

Although Richard had been geographically separated from his father for most of the last five years, Richard had remained personally close to him. They had talked often on the telephone, and during Richard's visits to Charleston they had conversed about everything under the sun, especially about what was happening to the United States and why. His father had high intelligence and discerning judgment, wisdom even. He usually offered his views in a low-key manner and was disinclined to sweeping, categorical statements. Peter Bittenberg was a first-class professional, but he seemed to Richard to be first of all an unusually fine human being, a man of dignity and integrity—a civilized man. The principles that others might profess in terms of theory Dr. Peter Bittenberg embodied. They were the kind of principles that an older America admired. Without thinking about it, Richard viewed him as a model. He knew that in Charleston he, Richard, owed much of his own good reputation to being his father's son. Richard loved his father, and Helen, too, had become very fond of him.

The funeral service, held at St. Phillip's on Church Street, filled the spacious church to overflowing. Some could not get inside, but stood in the narthex or just outside awaiting the end of the service and the funeral procession. So many had asked to make remarks at the service that the family had decided not to allow any testimonials, a decision that the rector considered the only theologically appropriate one.

Richard's mother was devastated. It was several months before she managed to adapt to her new life and then only with the support of her children and relatives. Although she had her children Hubert and Susan in Charleston, it was as if she had a particular need to be near Richard. He returned to Charleston twice in the two months after the funeral. Richard then invited her to stay with his family in Ithaca. She came in the early spring. Richard took her willingness to travel as a sign that she was finally ready to start her new life. They talked much about Richard's father.

"Richard, he loved you so much," his mother said. "He followed everything you did, and he was so proud of you. He read your book at least twice. He kept telling me that you would make a difference."

"Make a difference?"

"He never quite explained what he meant. I'm not sure *he* knew. I don't think he was just talking about you as a professor. He believed you would accomplish something, something out of the ordinary."

"I've no idea what he might have meant. I guess I'll be able to write another few books, and, if I'm lucky, one of them will become some sort of modern classic."

"Well, if he didn't know, I couldn't tell you."

The grief hung heavy over Richard for a long time. A thought kept coming to him: that he had been given a new assignment in life, to be worthy of his father. He had to forward his legacy. But just what was that legacy, other than being a decent human being? What would that entail in Richard's profession and in how he related to society? It would surely include helping to reverse America's decline. But just how could he best advance that goal?

In the fourth year at Cornell when Helen was pregnant with Anne, Richard received a telephone call from the chairman of the department of history at National University in Washington, Harry Bowles. Richard had met Bowles, a man in his late fifties, a couple of times at conferences and liked him. He was a traditional historian specializing in the classical Greco-Roman world. In a long conversation, Bowles told Richard that he had followed his writing with admiration and would like to have him appointed as associate professor in his department. There would be a strong presumption in favor of his receiving tenure within a year of his arrival at the University.

"Dick, of all the young historians out there you are just about the best one I know of. I'm getting tired of all those bright boys with trendy theories of this, that and the other thing but no real knowledge of history."

"You must have some of them on your faculty, and I doubt they would like hiring one like me."

"We're actually in decent shape, and I have several strong allies, the older generation, you know. They are as fed up as I am by what's happening to our discipline."

Bowles told Richard that in the next few years he would also like to hire a couple of assistant professors with approaches and interests similar to Richard's.

"Dick, we would be developing a new strength in the department, and you would be able to shape that field. The dean's even promised to appropriate some research money and a couple of research assistantships for this area of the discipline. This dean actually knows what he's doing. He's a Shakespeare scholar, if you can believe it. He likes your interdisciplinary emphasis. Shows you're educated. He's given me a green light on trying to snatch you away from Cornell. The salary will be competitive."

"I'm surprised there are still people like you and that dean."

"I don't know how long we'll last, but for as long as I'm in this job I would like to strike a blow for history—know what I mean?"

"Harry, I'm flattered. I'll think this over and talk to Helen. They have treated me pretty well up here, but nobody's gone out of his way to make me feel welcome either. Perhaps they're starting to figure that I'm a kind of throwback to another area."

"You understand we'll have to advertise our position, have a search and consider other candidates in order to satisfy affirmative action requirements and all that nonsense, but I consider it virtually a foregone conclusion that, if you apply, we'd be able to offer the position to you. I think I'll have the votes lined up. Who in the world would be able to match your qualifications in your area of the discipline?"

Richard had published additional articles and had gotten the impression that his department at Cornell would soon want to promote him. He would be in a good position to receive tenure a couple of years later, but he had liked what Harry Bowles had told him.

Helen was delighted at the prospect of living in the Washington area again. She liked the city and that they would be near her parents. Moving closer to the South appealed to Richard. Academically he liked that National University put rather heavy emphasis on graduate studies. It was not rated one of the top twenty American universities in any of those self-perpetuating rankings, but it was highly regarded in many fields and had a growing reputation in history. Washington, D.C., also had much to offer the historical researcher, especially the Library of Congress and the National Archives, but also several university libraries. The city had many cultural assets. Richard also liked that thousands of well-educated foreigners connected with international organizations, embassies, and journalism added a cosmopolitan flavor. Unlike most of his acquaintances, he was not fascinated by being near the seat of the American federal government. What he saw when walking around Capitol Hill and the buildings of the federal government was an emphatic indication that the old American republic with its virtues of modesty and frugality was long gone. The proliferation of huge, munificent buildings housing federal office holders and their staffs spoke of a federal government out of control and, most especially, of American imperial power. Everywhere, it seemed, Washington signaled its power and desire to impose its will.

After interviewing at National University Richard received a formal offer, and after some negotiating of terms he accepted. He, Helen and the baby went down to Washington to look for a house. According to his father's will, half of his estate had passed directly to Richard, his sister and brother. As a result Richard and Helen could afford to buy a four bedroom colonial in the lovely, settled subdivision of Kenwood in Bethesda, Maryland, just ten blocks or so outside of the District of Columbia. It would take Richard no more than fifteen minutes to drive to National University.

They came to Washington in April for settlement. They drove into their new neighborhood on a warm, sunny Friday afternoon. They were met by an explosion of cherry blossoms. Every tree in the neighborhood seemed to be a large, sprawling cherry tree. When they got out of their car a neighbor told them that this was the neighborhood's cherry blossom weekend. The next day people from all over the D.C. area would walk around taking in the splendor of it all. Richard knew that he had found a corner of the South.

National University proved a good academic berth. Harry Bowles did all he could to make Richard feel welcome. The Department did in time expand in the direction Bowles had indicated. Two new assistant professors were hired in areas adjacent to Richard's, at least one of whom Richard found intellectually very congenial. Two research assistants were assigned to support these three faculty members. Richard here saw the outlines for a research center for which he might request foundation support. These plans were realized with the aid of the University, and Richard found himself the director of a small institute that helped promote his scholarly interests and attract good graduate students. By the time Bowles and the supportive dean retired from their posts Richard's field of study had been institutionalized. This would remain the case as long as he was able to raise the money for the institute's budget. Richard enjoyed teaching, especially at the graduate level. Students began to apply to the University to study with Richard, and he soon had several gifted doctoral students. Some faculty members, begrudged him his success, but he was left alone, and he went about his academic business with dedication and energy. He became one of the handful of scholars with which the outside world associated National University.

Five years after his arrival at the University, Richard was promoted to full professor. He had published more important articles and, above all, another book, a study of the ideas and political role of "hidden" networks like the Freemasons in shaping America's national institutions in the quarter century after the War of Independence. His notion of "spontaneous conspiracy" had become a widely discussed, if somewhat controversial, subject. Despite having spent three years at the *Charleston Observer* and having made no effort to expedite his studies, Richard had reached the highest academic rank at a considerably younger age than most faculty members.

Richard's life seemed in every respect enviable. He was a success in his chosen profession. He could devote himself to work in which he believed and at which he was very good. He was married to a beautiful woman he loved and admired, and he had two bright, healthy children. He had no physical ailments. He was a vigorous, handsome male in the best years of his life. His family owned a comfortable home in a lovely neighborhood. They lived in the nation's capital with its great cultural and other assets. They were financially secure.

And yet Richard Bittenberg was chronically dissatisfied, not with any of these circumstances but with himself. A feeling that somehow he was not living up to his responsibilities kept bothering him. The feeling intensified rather than weakened with time. That he had so much for which to be grateful only deepened a sense that he was not giving enough in return. His work as a professor and scholar and his role as husband and father seemed insufficient to reduce his indebtedness. A real sacrifice seemed called for. He was becoming more and more convinced that it was his responsibility to help alleviate the fraught condition of his country. But by doing what exactly? What could a single individual accomplish? He had a diffuse but growing intuition that what was required of him might place in jeopardy the personal life that he had come to regard as perhaps too great a privilege.

There were few persons with whom Richard could speak openly about his worries. Why startle or offend friends and acquaintances who seemed to him barely sentient. It was to Richard a source of great frustration that so many highly intelligent and well-educated persons — fellow professors, physicians, lawyers, businessmen, and others — were so muted in their reactions to the state of their country. They did in a way see the same things as Richard — the glaring economic and political irresponsibility, the debasement of culture, the demonstrations and the social unrest, etc. — but they showed no signs of despondency, no inclination to take action. They grumbled over this or that, but they largely accepted official views or media assessments of America's condition. Could they not see through this deceptive surface? Could they not connect the dots? It seemed not. They just went on with their lives.

Richard could be entirely open with his friend Donald Kiefer, his closest friend from his Harvard days, who was, if anything, more disheartened than Richard. But after their leaving Harvard — Donald to teach the Greek and Roman classics at a small Midwestern college — their contacts were infrequent. They met at a couple of weddings and saw each other during visits with each other either in New York City, where Donald's parents still lived, Ithaca, New York, where Cornell is located, or, later, in Washington. They spoke occasionally on the telephone. What Donald kept saying about the world of investment banking and its relation to the Federal Reserve, the U.S. Treasury Department, the U.S. Congress, and the International Monetary Fund suggested that ruthless financial interests were engaged in virtual looting in the American and international markets. Donald was the one person Richard knew who made him wonder if he did not take a sufficiently dim view of the condition of the United States.

He asked himself whether Donald's apparent cynicism was due to some purely personal experience that might have embittered him against big finance.

When Donald visited Richard and Helen in Ithaca for John's christening they were by themselves one afternoon in the basement family room in the Bittenberg's townhouse drinking beers and waiting for a football game to begin on television. After another tirade from Donald about Wall Street shenanigans Richard finally asked him point blank, though humorously to be able to retreat if Donald reacted badly, if his perspective was not that of one rebelling against his father. As Donald's father was an investment banker, the question was not far-fetched. After some joking repartee between the two friends, Donald turned serious and pensive, sinking back in a sofa and letting his pudgy frame assume a comfortable position.

"I know what you're thinking. Why would the son of a successful Wall Street banker be teaching college in the middle of nowhere? He should be making his own millions in the same business as the father, right? Since I'm doing the opposite, I must be rejecting my father, right? There's actually some truth in that supposition, but not the way you may think."

Donald drank of his beer before continuing. He was taking his time, looking as if he were trying to explain himself to himself, not just to Richard. He said:

"If I don't want to be like my father, it's not because he's a bad guy and that I can't stand him. He's actually pretty decent. He's got a conscience. I like him. We get along rather well. Believe it or not, he and mother seem to like each other too. But he's spent his life in a very tough, all-absorbing line of work. He's had to do business with or fight people who are quite different from him, some of them terrible human beings. He's been damaged by it—that's about the size of it. Time and time again he's experienced or observed how people with scruples, like him, have had to yield to people *without* scruples. The wrong kind has muscled in. If you detect any bitterness in my descriptions of high finance, it may have come from him. But, whatever the case, I couldn't spend my life as father did. Not with those people. I'm hiding from that world, I know. What's a person to do? I can't do a thing to change this appalling situation. I would rather teach bright kids about the high points of Greek and Roman civilization than make a lot of money among slimy, ruthless profit-seekers."

Once when Donald visited the Bittenbergs in Washington and the two of them were sitting outside at a coffee shop in Bethesda they discussed an announcement by the chairman of the Federal Reserve.

When Donald offered a sinister interpretation Richard protested.

"Donald, are you really qualified to make these comments?" he said half-humorously. "You don't have a Ph.D. in economics or even an M.B.A. in finance."

Donald burst out laughing, and laughed for a long time.

"Yeah, right!" he finally said. "That would really qualify me! We've got more economics Ph.D.s and M.B.A.s than at any time in human history, and our economic system has never been shoddier or more messed up. Most of those Ph.D.s are narrow-minded theoreticians or technicians, pitiful suckers, just little cogs in the machine. They're stuck in various abstract conceptions. They never question their own assumptions. I've got something far better than a doctorate in finance. I've got a mind, Dick, and I'm not a sucker, and I know what to look for. I've been doing it since I was a kid."

"You were never in high finance."

"I was close enough, and I talked a lot with father. He never pressured me into going into the firm, but he may have expected me to. He taught me a great deal about how big finance operates. The older I got, the more he told me about the more baleful stuff that he despises. And there were often big shots at the house for drinks or dinner, sometimes politicians and high government officials. I listened pretty carefully. Father told me about tough, difficult situations he'd had to face and about how the ethos of high finance had changed since the days of his father, who started the firm. I read quite a bit of economics and economic history in high school and college, most of it on my own. And I have a pretty good, realistic imagination. To make a long story short I know a hell of a lot more than those naïve, narrow-minded, cocky Ph.D.s."

Richard and Donald agreed that only some catastrophe — a devastating plague, perhaps, or an economic depression like the Great Depression — might bring Americans to their senses. So confused, superficial, and corrupt had Americans become that their society might be beyond saving. America could go under quicker than Rome.

At one time just months before Richard's life changed he met Donald in New York City at his parents brownstone in Manhattan. It was winter, and they sat in front of a fire in the library. Richard was more distraught than ever and explained to Donald the depth of his worry, disgust and anxiety.

Donald seemed at first not to have any reaction. Then he looked with empathy at his friend and said:

"And yet you don't know what I know about the really big boys and their financial manipulations — how they operate above national boundaries and governments and have the Fed and the international monetary institutions at their beck and call. They couldn't care less about any particular nation or people — except one maybe. But I don't see that anything could be done about it, Dick. It's gone too far. These marauders could advance because Christian culture and the Christian elites are rotting. The old elites can't any longer enforce any standards of decency and honesty and don't even want to. The WASPs are so weak and decadent that they don't even have the desire to survive." Donald took a gulp of his third glass of whiskey and added: "I say, let's shoot the bastards — but that's like saying, let's all commit suicide."

It made Richard feel a little better to know that a person as brilliant, perceptive, and well-informed as Donald could be even more discouraged than he was, but Donald's attitude of turning his back was disheartening.

"Donald, the big question is, what must be done about all of this?"

"That's where we disagree, Dick. You seem to think that it might be possible to save the day. I don't. We're going down, buddy. All we can do is try to make the disaster as painless as possible. I'm angry as hell, but there's no point in making a fuss. I gave up long ago. Why do you think I'm teaching Plato and Aristotle in the middle of nowhere? I've thought seriously of moving to some out of the way place in Europe — money was never a problem — but the Europeans have the same problems, and I think in some ways I would be more miserable there because of all the old European physical monuments to a superior culture. Having them around me all the time would only deepen my sadness and frustration. In my little American corner of the world the contrast between the past and the present is not quite so stark. My life's not so bad. The college is decent, and I've some good friends. Forget the rest of the world!"

Richard sometimes felt a desire to forget the troubles, but it never stayed long. He might have escaped into his research, but he had never been the kind of scholar who buried himself in a specialty distant from ordinary life. His research and writing concerned past events, but as connected to large, enduring questions of human nature and society that were relevant to the present. If he tried to retreat into a circle of family and friends, the concerns about his country would still invade that sphere. Because he thought that he understood better than others what was happening in America, he felt a greater responsibility than they to try to effect change.

The only other person with whom he could have frank conversations was Robert Preston, his friend from the University of

South Carolina. Robert's life as a U.S. Congressman did not give him much free time, but Richard and Robert saw a good deal of each other. They saved their most outspoken conversations for private meetings over drinks in their respective homes. Then Richard held back very little. He even broached the issue of whether the situation in America had become so desperate that some kind of drastic therapy was necessary. Could a political coup be justified? The question was for Richard purely theoretical. He couldn't see how a narrowly political change, a change in government, could address the moral and cultural problems that were the ultimate source of America's problems. Besides, how could a coup with any chance of success possibly be organized? The present system was too elaborate and deeply entrenched. While Robert did not express dismay at the abstract idea of a coup, he showed no inclination to explore it. Richard interpreted his reluctance as partly the caution of an experienced politician who cannot speak with perfect frankness about any sensitive topic even with his closest friend. Also, it was one of Robert's recurring themes that a politician must always approach his craft as the art of the possible. There was little point in discussing ideas that might look intriguing to an academic, but that had no practical relevance.

"That formula about the art of the possible can easily turn into a prohibition against rocking the boat," Richard said.

"You know that's not what I mean. I'm all in favor of trying to change the parameters of what's possible, so that something new can be attempted, but you should not expend any energy on goals that are simply out of reach."

"But you never quite know what is and what is not out of reach," Richard said.

"True, but you must always ask whether some contemplated goal lies in the realm of the possible."

"Of course you do, but if you always put that question first, you may forget that there's something to be said for audacity – for trying to change things through courageous, dramatic action?"

"Again, you have to work within the limitations of the world in which you live."

Billick's principle, Richard thought. *You have to make do with what you've got.* That principle, formulated by the surgeon who had been his father's commanding officer during his most difficult time during the Second World War, was never far from Richard's mind. It removed that most common excuse for not taking difficult, painful action: that the circumstances or resources or information were not quite what they should be. If you have to wait for everything to be just right before taking any serious action, you will be forever inactive, paralyzed, because the circumstances are never quite right. You must get used to acting in an imperfect world. At the same time, Billick's principle required that you do nothing rash, thay you assess possibilities and resources realistically.

"Bob, we don't disagree about the need for realism. If we disagree, it's about what the situation demands and what can be realistically expected to come out of particular circumstances. What I'm saying is that to make the most of available means and make something new possible it may be necessary to take unexpected and daring action. You don't really *know* what might be accomplished until you've tried. I think I may be more ready than you are to take a big risk. Do you remember Fortuna, Machiavelli's goddess of fate? She rewards daring."

"That sounds rather literary, Dick—more romantic than realistic."

"No, I think Machiavelli had a point."

# CHAPTER 21

Helen was touching up her make-up, waiting for the French detectives, when the telephone rang. The police were in the lobby. She asked that they should be sent up to her room. She called the children to tell them about the police and to ask them to be ready to join her. Before she had hung up there was a knock on the door.

After opening it, Helen's first reaction on seeing the two men standing in the hallway was great relief. Having to wait for organized, expert help had been utterly frustrating. Here, finally, were two real human beings, professionals, with resources behind them. The French police were on the case. The search for Richard was underway in earnest. The knot in her stomach loosened for a moment. She felt a stirring of hope.

The older of the two extended an identity card and introduced himself as Chief Inspector Henri Duparc. He was of medium height and build. He seemed to be about 45 years old. He was slightly overweight. His full dark but graying hair was parted on the side. He was neither tall nor short. He had no unusual features. He wore a light blue sports coat and a tie, beige slacks and black, rubber-soled shoes. He looked neat but not conspicuously so. In fact, nothing about Duparc stood out. It occurred to Helen that, if someone were asked to give a description of him after seeing him in passing, that person would have difficulty. Duparc looked ordinary, was Mr. Everyman. But in his eyes Helen thought she saw an intensity not noticeable elsewhere.

Duparc introduced his colleague, Pierre Léger. The latter was taller and thinner and seemed about ten years younger. He wore a light-colored, rumpled summer jacket and a blue shirt open in the neck and jeans. He had blond hair and sharp bird-like features. His neck seemed unusually long.

Helen offered the two policemen the two chairs in the room

and sat down on the bed. She was careful to seat herself so as not to show too much leg. She explained that the children were in the room next door and that she would prefer for them to remain there for the time being.

Duparc nodded. He started by reading back to her from a notebook the information about Richard and his disappearance that had been provided to him. She was surprised to notice that Duparc's English had a slight British accent. It also surprised her that his notes were all accurate. Bennini, she thought. Duparc went on to tell her that a preliminary computer check for the entire city of Paris for the preceding Friday had revealed no cases of emergency hospitalization, killings, or suspicious deaths that might be relevant to Richard Bittenberg's disappearance. Further checking would be done when more information was available. Duparc asked if Helen had Richard's passport. He would like to copy the photo of Richard and circulate the picture. She retrieved the passport from her handbag.

Duparc asked Helen to give a full account of what had happened. For the next half hour Helen related all of what she could remember, including the results of her own investigations. She provided the names and telephone numbers of the persons at the Sorbonne who had helped her. She mentioned Ferguson but not her suspicions. Léger wrote in his notebook. He and Duparc frequently asked for clarifications and raised questions. They explored the possibility of a misunderstanding between the spouses and of Richard having disappeared deliberately.

Duparc said, "Madame, did you and your husband have any quarrel recently?"

"No, Monsieur Duparc, there was no quarrel. My husband and I also love each other. I've complained in the last couple of years about his working too hard, but he knows I've done it because I care about him. Everything's fine between us. Besides, think about the children. Even if he had been very angry with me, he would never subject his son and daughter to this kind of ordeal just to punish me. Never!"

"In our work you see many strange things, Madame."

"I can imagine, but my husband simply is not that kind of person. We're here in Paris on vacation. We were all enjoying ourselves and looking forward to the rest of our trip."

"Don't be upset, Madame. I believe you. Theses are questions we simply have to ask."

Helen's narrative and the questioning continued. Duparc looked closely at her when she spoke. She covered every issue in detail, going perhaps further at times than the two policemen would have preferred. She did not mention the speculation that Richard's disappearance might be related to his having been involved in something back in the United States.

Duparc stood up to stretch his legs and moved slightly in the small space available.

"Madame, this is a strange case. I can't remember one quite like it." He went on to discuss a couple of possible explanations for Richard's disappearance, each of which Helen had already considered in some form. "We will check further with hospitals and other police districts using your husband's picture. We will follow up your leads, which are very helpful, and we will pursue our own investigation, but before we start this work there's something I have to ask you." Duparc stood still. He watched Helen's face for a moment before speaking.

"Is there anything you haven't told me that might help us find your husband? Anything you might be holding back?"

Helen blinked and looked down, avoiding his gaze. In that same instant she realized that she had given herself away. Duparc had guessed that she had not told him everything, and now he knew. If she didn't reveal what was on her mind, she risked losing his trust and good will. She desperately wanted to share her speculations and suspicions with someone she thought would help and whom she could trust, but what did she know about these two men? Almost nothing. She had formed a generally favorable impression, but that meant little. They might be part of a conspiracy. They could be simply trying to learn how much she knew. The two men had behaved in a businesslike, neutral manner, giving the impression that this was for them routine. But she thought she had detected in both of them, especially Duparc, a touch of empathy. Léger did not wear a wedding ring, but Duparc did. There was a good chance that Duparc had not only a wife but also children. Even if made world-weary by long experience, he would be able to imagine himself in Helen's circumstances. Behind his policeman's professional demeanor she perceived a personal interest. She hoped that it was not merely a Frenchman's interest in an attractive female.

She did not decide to do what she did next on the basis of careful deliberation. She did it on the spur of the moment, because she was desperate and because she was tired, dead tired. She had to confide in and trust these two policemen. She had to believe that they actually wanted to find Richard.

"Yes, I have held something back." Duparc and Léger looked at each other. "It's not because I wanted to deceive you but because what I haven't told you is so very speculative. I didn't want to prejudice or sidetrack your investigation."

"Madame Bittenberg, you should let us be the judge of what is relevant."

"You're right. I'm sorry."

Duparc sat down again. Helen went on to give them the missing pieces of her story. This time she connected what she had discovered at the Sorbonne to Ferguson. She mentioned the paper with the apparent code and that Ferguson now had it. She even mentioned the possibility that Richard's disappearance might be related to his being involved in something important back in the United States. She related, though in a vague way, what Hubert had told her about Richard. She mentioned the name Herbert. Léger wrote furiously in his notebook and a few times asked Helen for help with the spelling. Duparc asked questions about the sheet of paper and the possible American connection.

She had told Duparc everything she knew. Confiding in him had been therapeutic. It had lessened the terrible frustration she had felt in the last two days. Her burden was being shared. Two professional detectives, who were supposed to spend all of their time looking for Richard, now had all the information she could provide. At the same time, going over all that had happened and all that she had thought about had put her face to face with her situation again. She was overcome by the misery of it. She drew a deep breath.

"Inspector Duparc, I've held nothing back, but you must remember that what I've said about Ferguson is speculation, nothing more. Something tells me that he is somehow connected to Richard's disappearance, but it's the intuition of a woman whose husband is missing—whose husband may be dead. I can hardly see straight. I'm worn out, Monsieur Duparc. I'm frantic. I don't know what to do." Helen slumped on the bed. She put her hands in front of her face. Sobs rocked her body. "Please help me," she said in a weak, trembling voice.

She felt a hand on her shoulder. It had to be Duparc's. "We will do our best," he said.

Helen looked up, her eyes glistening. "I'll be very grateful."

"Regarding Ferguson," Duparc said, "it's in a way good that you brought him that paper with the letters and the numbers. That gives us a good excuse to pay him a visit."

"Will you have to go through your government to talk to an American diplomat?" She had found a handkerchief in her handbag.

"I don't see why. That would be only if he should refuse to see us, which I don't expect. That would be a pretty clear sign that he's got something to hide. I think he'll agree to see us. If he doesn't, the likelihood of the U.S. government being involved is pretty high. I doubt he would dare to hide behind diplomatic immunity for any other reason."

"Suppose the U.S. government is involved."

"Then we may run into real difficulties. For now, we'll go on the assumption that, if Ferguson is involved, it's in his private capacity, as an acquaintance of Professor Bittenberg. You said he's the only person at the American Embassy who knows your husband. If the U.S. government had anything to do with your husband's disappearance, it would have to be on an issue of American national security or international crime, or the like, and then we are likely to find out before too long."

He closed his notebook. "Thank you, Mrs. Bittenberg," Duparc said, and as he rose, so did Léger.

She rose too. "You speak very good English," Helen said, extending her hand to Duparc. He took it.

"I studied English in school. Then I spent a summer in England with relatives as a teenager. A few years after completing the French police academy I was selected to spend three months at the London police academy. I took courses with police officers from all over the world who were interested in working with Interpol. Then the growth of the EU gave me various assignments requiring proficiency in English. I handle cases with an international dimension."

It pleased Helen that he would speak so personally about himself. She saw it as a sign that he was taking a more than professional interest in the Bittenberg case.

"Mrs. Bittenberg, there is one more thing."

"Yes."

"We would like to talk briefly with the children," Duparc said.

"Of course. I'll get them."

"If you don't mind, we would like to talk to them alone."

"I don't mind. I'll take you to them. Please give me a moment to straighten out my face." Duparc nodded.

Before they left the room Helen told the two Frenchmen that John and Anne would be returning to the United States the next morning, but that she would be at the hotel for the foreseeable future. Helen knocked at the door to the children's room, and John opened after the agreed-upon question and answer. As the three adults walked in Anne looked wide-eyed at the two Frenchmen and then at Helen. Had she seen in Helen's face that she had cried?

Helen introduced the detectives and told the children that

they would like to talk to them for a few minutes in private. Would that be all right? Helen said it would be fine with her. As John and Anne looked at the detectives Helen said, "I've told Mr. Duparc and Mr. Léger everything, including our suspicions regarding Mr. Ferguson. You should tell them anything that's on your minds."

John and Anne nodded. "OK, then, I'll be in the other room. Just let me know if there's anything you want." As she left she glanced at Duparc, who was setting himself down on the bed facing the children. He was smiling. He does have children, Helen thought.

Less than ten minutes later there was a knock on Helen's door. Duparc and Léger were standing outside.

"Thank you, Mrs. Bittenberg," Duparc said. "We have everything we need from you, and we have plenty to go on. We will be in touch with you as soon as we have anything of importance to tell you."

"Thank you."

Duparc turned to leave, but stopped and looked back in Helen's direction. "You have wonderful children, Mrs. Bittenberg." He smiled.

As he and Léger walked toward the stairs, tears again filled Helen's eyes. She rushed back into her room to dab and dry her face and improve her make-up before rejoining the children.

# CHAPTER 22

Herbert Vandenhorst first contacted Richard when he had just published his third book, *Path to War*, a study of the role of hidden interests and corresponding ideas in moving America into the First World War. The book had been favorably reviewed but had also gotten him into some hot water in that the conclusion hinted more openly than his earlier work that patterns of "spontaneous conspiracy" might be discernible in present-day America.

Vandenhorst had left a telephone message for Richard in a modulated, cultivated voice. He expressed great interest in talking to the author of *Path to War*. Would Richard be kind enough to call at his convenience?

Richard called, but before doing so he did a quick Internet search on Herbert Vandenhorst. The name had sounded familiar. Vandenhorst was a man of some distinction with considerable political experience. He had advanced as high as undersecretary of State in a Republican administration and as an assistant secretary of Defense in a Democratic administration. He had served as deputy national security advisor under a Democratic president. He had also held a high post in the Treasury Department. He had begun his professional career as a naval officer. A graduate of the Naval Academy in Annapolis, he had left the navy at the rank of lieutenant commander to work in the State Department. He then joined a government agency in Washington of which Richard had never heard but that involved foreign affairs. Richard wondered if it might have been a cover for the CIA or another U.S. intelligence service. Vandenhorst had earned a Master's degree in history at Georgetown University. He seemed to have had no strong party affiliation and to have advanced to more and more influential positions on the strength of experience, expertise and reputation. After retiring from government he had worked for a large American multinational manufacturing company. He still sat on three corporate boards and the advisory boards of a couple of think tanks concerned with national security and international affairs. He was a member of the board of regents of the Smithsonian Institution and a consultant to the Ford Foundation. When Richard finally met him, he looked,

Richard thought, like a representative of a by-gone area, a pillar of that old America that was no longer in charge of the government of the United States. Getting to know Mr. Vandenhorst, Richard could find in him none of the disturbing traits and views that he had come to expect of people manning America's ruling system.

Their first conversation took place on the telephone and lasted longer than Richard had expected or intended. He found Mr. Vandenhorst not only pleasant and well informed but also perceptive and interesting. He spoke in an articulate, balanced, and nuanced manner. He was obviously highly intelligent and circumspect.

"I should mention to you, Professor Bittenberg, that I knew your grandfather, William."

"You did!?" Richard's surprise was complete.

"Yes, I was in the Foreign Service, in a manner of speaking, for about ten years, and we happened to overlap in Washington for a year in 1964. He was my boss in an indirect way."

"How well did you know him?"

"Oh, I was just a young punk, and he was an elder statesman. I saw him every once in a while as part of my regular work and then at various State Department gatherings and receptions. He was a kind of model for some of us. He had quite a reputation, had stood his ground against some of those ignorant, grasping politicians and special interests. Some of his memos were legendary. We thought of him as one of the real, old school diplomats. He belonged with the likes of George F. Kennan."

"That's very high praise, Mr. Vandenhorst. I'm very glad to hear it. I liked and admired my grandfather very much. Of course, I thought of him as a relative rather than as a professional, but I'll never forget visiting him in Copenhagen when he was ambassador to Denmark."

"If it hadn't been for his integrity, he would have become an ambassador much sooner and ended his career in some very prominent post. It was common knowledge that he'd damaged his career by doing what we assumed was the right thing rather than the expedient thing."

"He never told me what it was, only that it was a matter of conscience," Richard said.

"I'm not surprised. He had unusual integrity. Perhaps it runs in the family."

The flattery embarrassed Richard, and he returned the conversation to history. Richard learned that Vandenhorst had long been interested in the general subject of Richard's book but chiefly with regard to more recent times. Vandenhorst asked if

Richard was familiar with various sources relating to more recent examples of "spontaneous conspiracy." Richard answered that he had not yet concentrated on contemporary America, but had started to form hypotheses. Mr. Vandenhorst offered to share some of his information with Richard. Would Richard like to meet him for lunch at the Metropolitan Club?

Richard was intrigued and curious and accepted the invitation. Their meeting took place more than a year and a half before the Bittenberg family trip to Europe. It was in December, but the temperature was in the low fifties. It was sunny. Richard took the subway from the university to the Farragut North Metro station three blocks north of the White House. He intended to walk over to the Metropolitan Club just one block northwest of the White House, but could not take the most direct route. In Farragut Square a loud demonstration had spilled into the adjoining streets. Signs and banners indicated that teachers from the District of Columbia were protesting the refusal of the D.C. government to increase salaries for the coming year. A large number of policemen were doing their best to contain the crowd. Richard assumed that the protestors had been banned from Lafayette Park, the park just north of the White House, which used to be a favorite location for demonstrators. So frequent and large had protests of one kind or another become, that the Secret Service had kept widening the security perimeter around the White House, forcing demonstrators to look for other venues in the vicinity. Richard could get to the Metropolitan Club only by a circuitous route, avoiding the crowd and the police barricades. In every direction he looked cars were backed up in a giant traffic snarl. On a small side street he noticed a contingent of perhaps thirty riot police with see-through shields and heavy gear standing by in case the demonstration should get out of hand. Richard arrived at his destination five minutes late.

The Metropolitan Club has its own spacious building on the corner of a typical city block. A four-storey building in light reddish-beige stone, its nineteenth-century style sets it off from the modern office buildings in the same general area. A landmark among Washingtonian insiders, the club makes no fuss about its own presence. It is an American version of an old London gentlemen's club. The members like to think that it is a gathering place for some of the most influential people in America. Richard had visited the club before. Having looked at the photographs of former club presidents in the downstairs reading and waiting room, he knew that this had been a stronghold for the American elite that started abdicating about a century ago. In this club members might imagine

that they were still in charge. In the surrounding society the spirit of
the gentleman was virtually extinct, but here some of the members
affected a faintly British or European gentlemanly style. Richard liked
their dress and manners, but there was also, he thought, something
pathetic about them. In spite of superficial appearances, they no
longer set the standards for their society. He strongly suspected that,
for most of the members, the old world look and demeanor was little
but an affectation, window dressing; they no longer subscribed to
the values that gave rise to the type. Richard liked what the Club had
represented, and it saddened him that its old standards had little to
do with the new America.

Mr. Vandenhorst greeted Richard inside the entrance to
the club, where men in chairs were reading papers or talking in
front of a fire waiting for their luncheon companions to arrive. Mr.
Vandenhorst was of medium height and build. He was dressed in a
gray herringbone sports jacket, a white shirt, and a red, striped tie,
dark slacks, and English-style black shoes. His general appearance
and the handkerchief showing in the breast pocket of his jacket
revealed that he knew something about dressing. He had short gray
hair, neatly trimmed and carefully combed, and a lined, rectangular,
distinguished-looking face. He had a well-formed narrow and
angular nose, a small but somewhat protruding chin that seemed to
suggest willpower and energy. His gray eyes squinted from a half-
smile. He seemed to be about seventy years old. He looked, Richard
thought, like one of the presidents of the Metropolitan Club from the
1950s. Vandenhorst reminded Richard of someone, but he could not
think of who it was.

Richard apologized for arriving late because of the
demonstration in Farragut Square. Vandenhorst said not to worry.

"Remarkable, isn't it," Vandenhorst said, "how often
demonstrations are disrupting normal life and tie up city traffic,
right here in the nation's capital? At least here in D.C. disorder is not
allowed to spread. The various police forces have been beefed up, to
say nothing of the Secret Service."

They walked upstairs for lunch. It was obvious from the
attitude of the maître'd and the waiters that Mr. Vandenhorst was
a member of stature. He asked for a quiet table in the large dining
room, and they were seated against the wall in a corner. On the way
to the table Richard noticed two former cabinet members, a current
U.S. Senator and a prominent journalist, two of whom greeted
Vandenhorst briefly. Vandenhorst introduced his guest, effortlessly
putting everybody at ease. His manners were impeccable.

After consulting Richard about his preferences Vandenhorst

ordered their food by following club practice, filling out a small order form that he gave to the waiter. Richard asked how Vandenhorst had come to take such an interest in history, and Vandenhorst wondered how Richard liked being at National University. But even before their plates were brought they were deep in discussion of Richard's notion of "spontaneous conspiracy," an idea that Vandenhorst seemed to endorse. Vandenhorst called Richard's attention to research materials not yet familiar to him that pointed to "spontaneous conspiracy" in today's America. Key people of great influence in the financial world, politics, academia, journalism, the culture, and entertainment were drawn by a partly inarticulate but strong affinity for each other into a powerful synergy hard for others to resist.

One of Vandenhorst's comments made Richard express some his worries about the general development of the United States. He found Vandenhorst very receptive, and the conversation turned more and more to America's troubled state. They revealed to each other, at first cautiously and indirectly and then more forthrightly, their respective views on the subject, which coincided remarkably. When one of them pointed to a particular disturbing event or development, the other would supplement the account with another example. At dessert, Mr. Vandenhorst leaned back from his pecan pie and coffee, folded his hands, and said:

"Professor Bittenberg, you're an historian, but you're very alert to what's happening around you. One of the reasons you're able to see more than most is that you have an historical and philosophical vantage point. I think another reason is your family. Your grandfather was very perceptive. He understood a lot, but kept much to himself." Vandenhorst smiled. "You're the same."

As they finished lunch Vandenhorst said, "It's good to be able to talk to someone like you. Understanding that something is badly wrong with your country is all the more painful because there are so few people who understand how dreadful the situation is. It can be very lonely, don't you think?"

Richard had become tired of grousing about America that remained just talk and answered rather pointedly: "That so few people seem aware of the depth of our problems is bad enough, but what disturbs me even more is that those who recognize the urgent need for change seem not prepared to *act* to try to avert disaster."

"I know what you mean." Mr. Vandenhorst emptied his coffee cup before continuing.

"Professor Bittenberg, I have seen up-close the kind of machinations that you write about in *Path to War*, and worse. I've been in the middle of political and economic events that would

have utterly disillusioned a naïve young idealist. For some reason
I never was one. I was never a cynic either for that matter. I simply
never had very high expectations of human beings. I have the kind
of view of human nature I think the founders of our country took for
granted. The founders were realists. They believed in the possibility
of rule by decent people, by gentlemen, to use an archaic word, but
they also feared the darker side of human nature and tried to protect
against it. Don't give people too much power. Try to block the
blatant opportunists, the greedy types, and other self-seekers. The
Constitution did a pretty good job of encouraging the gentlemen and
keeping the opposite kind down. But their Constitution could work
only as long as their ethos was widespread in leading American
circles and the larger society."

Richard commented: "You probably know the story about
the woman in Philadelphia who asked Benjamin Franklin what the
Constitutional Convention had produced. He's reputed to have
answered, 'A republic—if you can keep it.' The story is probably
apocryphal, but he might well have said something like that. Without
the right kind of people, who act in the spirit of the Constitution, it
could not possibly survive."

"Of course not, and people of that kind are in mighty short
supply these days. What I've seen with my own eyes in government
and business has done more than confirm my view of human nature.
I've also observed a precipitous decline in the quality of leadership
that has saddened and disgusted me. The ruthlessness and greed
of some big actors have boggled my mind. You think that you have
seen the worst, and then someone tops it. You wish it were possible
to apprehend and jail some of these individuals, but they operate in
the shadows. Little of what they do ever triggers any FBI or police
investigations or is brought to light in the media. The media are
forever preoccupied with mischief that is easier for average people
to understand. It seems something snapped in the American soul.
The floodgates opened for people who used to attempt their dirty
business under the cover of darkness. The vicious, unscrupulous
individuals who once had difficulty advancing in society because
of civilized pressures and institutional checks can now move all
the way to the top. Some very callous persons and networks are
operating, not at the periphery but right where the big decisions are
made. These persons and networks can be in competition or conflict,
which creates a kind of checking and balancing among the bad
guys, but the overlap among these special interests makes for a very
strong momentum in the wrong direction. It used to be that no self-
respecting investor, banker, or businessman would dream of making

money on things like drugs, porn, gambling, and prostitution, to say nothing of dirty, deceptive financial dealings. The shady side of life was the monopoly of the crooks. But in the last half-century the bad people have been able to invade general society, infecting everything they touch. The already weakened old social structures have not been able to withstand the assault. The old-fashioned American elites, the gentlemen — sorry, there's that corny old word again — have been pretty much driven from the scene. They just weren't tough enough to stand up to the shady types, the crooks and the bullies."

"And now they're licking their wounds in this club, perhaps." Richard realized in the moment he said these words that as the guest of a member of the club he was being impolite. He was about to apologize, but Vandenhorst's reaction was immediate, and it showed no trace of his having been offended.

"You might say that, although no more than a few of the people in the club are more than marginally important when it comes to setting the direction of the United States. Some members would like to think of themselves as the upper crust of the D.C. establishment, but even in this town they have been superseded. In the country as a whole the real, ultimate power is no longer in the hands of the descendants of the old Anglo-European elites. You have to be oblivious of developments in the society in which you live — that is, be a typical American — not to see that America has a new and different leadership class and power structure, what you, professor, might call "a spontaneous conspiracy." Mr. Vandenhorst smiled. "That power structure is becoming more well-defined and well-established every day. At the top it is less and less spontaneous and more and more deliberate and cohesive. This new establishment is all the more effective because it has long experience wielding hidden influence."

"I suppose you're thinking about the more unscrupulous leaders of what used to be the British imperial and financial order," Richard said, "the power structure that in the last hundred years reconstituted itself as the leaders of the new world order, under nominally American leadership."

Vandenhorst smiled again. "Of course, professor, that's what I mean — a morally and financially corrupt ruling class above national borders but with great influence over the U.S. and other countries. It's great power has to do with the fact that it extends far beyond investment, business, and government. It operates in a kind of symbiosis with leading circles in the universities, the entertainment industry and the arts, which means that American culture is generally in tune with the intentions of the key decision makers. These rulers take advantage of and *promote* a rotting moral, intellectual, and aesthetical culture, which helps break down the lingering resistance of more traditional elites. The worst of it is that with the progressive deterioration of Western civilization some really bad guys, who would have been headed off at the pass in the older society, can now make it into the most influential circles. In a spreading climate of self-indulgence, short-sightedness, and greed they can more easily manipulate other groups and interests."

Richard was amazed. This man had clearly been influenced by Richard's writings, but his way of speaking of complex relationships showed that he was not merely repeating what he had read. He had made Richard's ideas his own or had acquired them independently. Richard was impressed by the discernment and breadth of this man, who was not an academic but a—well, what was he?—a former high official, of an old-fashioned, now probably extinct, type. He was wise to the ways of the world, but was very thoughtful and had considerable learning.

"What you've concluded about times past on the basis of a documentary record," Vandenhorst continued, "is the case today, too, in an especially disturbing form. This country is in very deep trouble. I say that partly because of what I have experienced personally. There are people in key positions who care not at all about America except as it relates to their own interests, but they are bright and hard-driving. They couldn't care less about that older America that you and I would like to see survive. In fact, they despise and resent it. It's stood in the way of the advancement of people of their ilk. The more they can weaken or destroy what remains of traditional America, the stronger they become. They seem to thrive on this kind of destruction. Only one thing holds them back. The more sophisticated among them are concerned, for purely selfish reasons, about how shaky the American economy has become. The financial and political dishonesty and irresponsibility jeopardizes their own schemes. They also worry that the riots around America might get out of hand and lead to calls for strong-arm measures to restore law and order. In circumstances of general chaos they can't be certain of controlling the outcome."

"I've been thinking," Richard said, "that our rulers may use the rioting, on top of the usual fear of terrorism, to stop pretending that their way of governing is constitutional. The time may be coming when they put all of that aside and resort to a frankly dictatorial exercise of power, obviously in the name of protecting Americans and democracy."

"It could certainly happen. I wonder at times if it's too late for America to come to its senses. Great nations come and go. Every educated person knows that. You, professor, seem to have a pretty realistic picture of the condition of the United States, but the situation could be even worse than you think."

Even worse? Mr. Vandenhorst paused to finish his pecan pie, and Richard interjected, "I have none of your experience of high-level politics, but it seems that our country is being ruined and taken over without a fight. The remaining old Americans seem to have lost their willingness to fight, even the basic wish to survive. The end is fast approaching."

"But let's hope, Professor Bittenberg, that good people will put up some resistance."

Richard winced. He was tired of hearing bromides of that kind.

The conversation turned into small talk, and they rose. Richard thanked Vandenhorst and they left the restaurant.

Richard liked Vandenhorst. He was personable as well as knowledgeable, experienced, and insightful. He was clearly very able. He had substance. He seemed a decent man in addition, was perhaps even a good one. Behind Vandenhorst's integrity Richard detected a toughness that he liked. He was the kind of person you would want in a high government position. An impressive man.

Richard reflected that Vandenhorst, the older of the two and a man of some distinction, had not suggested that they address each other by first names. That suggested that he had some of that old-fashioned formality that signals respect for the other person. He also might not take it for granted that he, although the older of the two, was the one to propose less formality. He was perhaps conveying that he regarded Richard as an equal. Richard for his part, regarded Vandenhorst as an elder statesman worthy of deference.

But how typical that Vandenhorst was retired or at least semi-retired! Because no longer in mid career, he would be more inclined to frankness, but for the same reason he also could not be expected to want to take action to change America's direction. In his retirement years Vandenhorst would undoubtedly have many good, well-informed, perversely enjoyable discussions with like-minded people who bemoaned the state of their country. But he and they would remain passive.

"Professor Bittenberg, I would really enjoy meeting you again. There's something practical that I would like to discuss with you."

"What kind of thing?"

"If you don't mind, I would like to wait to tell you. Please bear with me."

Richard was ambivalent. Much as he had enjoyed Vandenhorst's company, he was always trying to conserve his time. He was not really interested in protracted conversations about the sad shape of America. On the other hand, a person of Vandenhorst's background might be helpful in some way to his university institute. He might have contacts with persons who might facilitate some of Richard's research or donate to the institute. He might have access to sources of research. That might in fact be what Vandenhorst had in mind.

"I would be very pleased to see you again," Richard said. "Would you like to join me at the faculty club at the university some time?"

"I would be delighted. Let me call you in a few days so that we can set a day and a time."

It suddenly occurred to Richard whom Vandenhorst resembled. He looked like General Douglas MacArthur, without the comb-over.

They walked downstairs to the cloakroom. Vandenhorst retrieved a dark, attractive Stetson hat and a dark dress coat—echoes, Richard thought, of the age of dignity and decorum that had passed. He reflected that he played a similar role at his university. He was careful not to stick out too much, but he was a kind of academic Don Quixote, resisting the trend towards extreme sartorial informality.

Vandenhorst and Richard left the building together. Outside, as they shook hands, Vandenhorst said:

"You know, professor, something will have to be done about all this."

Before Richard could ask him to explain, Vandenhorst had turned away. He walked down the street—out of place, Richard thought, among the sterile, anonymous office buildings that dominated H Street. In the distance he heard the sound of a bullhorn, the shouts of demonstrators, and the sirens of police cars or ambulances.

# CHAPTER 23

For Helen to put Anne and John on the flight to Washington out of Charles de Gaulle Airport was heart-wrenching. She had been given special permission to accompany her children through security to the gate and to wait for the departure of the flight. She could barely stop herself from breaking down. When the children had to board the Air France flight, Anne would not let go of her. Only after John had coaxed her and a smiling stewardess had taken her hand did she finally agree to walk away. As she turned in Helen's direction a final time before disappearing down the sky bridge Helen saw tears streaming down her face. Helen waved and smiled, then turned around. She walked a few steps and threw her hands in front of her face. Sobs that she could no longer contain shook her body. People noticing her looked at her with sympathy, not knowing whether to offer aid or to respect her privacy. A female airline employee softly inquired if she might be of some help. Helen shook her head.

"I just need to be alone." She sat down behind a pillar at the now empty gate. Fifteen minutes later she watched as the jumbo jet destined for Dulles Airport in Washington, D.C., was pulled from the gate and then moved away by its own power. When the tail had disappeared from view, Helen walked slowly back towards the main terminal.

She was alone in Paris. What would she do? In Paris she did not have a single trusted friend to talk to and ask for advice. What could she hope to accomplish? All she knew was that she had to be as close as possible to Richard. If he was still alive, surely he was somewhere in Paris or vicinity.

She couldn't sit in their hotel room waiting to hear from the French police, the embassy, or Richard's brother. She had to *do* something, be actively involved in the search. She had to form a definite plan, try to organize her days. She had to stay in close touch with the police without annoying them. She had to talk regularly with Hubert on the telephone. Even though she didn't know where to begin, she felt rushed. Richard's fate might depend on her doing all she could. What should she be doing? In America Hubert and everybody else were still sleeping.

As she headed for the airport shuttle to Paris she noticed that it was almost 10:00 AM. She had been out of bed before 5:00 AM after just a few hours of irregular, restless sleep. Considering her early start, it would soon be lunchtime for her, but she was not hungry. She felt slightly queasy. She suddenly remembered that the day before at the American Embassy Stephen Ferguson had said that he would like to take her to lunch the following day or soon thereafter. Why not take him up on the invitation? Especially if he was involved in Richard's disappearance, she had a reason to seek his company. If she could control her emotions and give him the impression that she trusted him, he might inadvertently spill helpful information. If he was not involved, being close to one of the top diplomats at the American Embassy could only help.

She found a pay phone in the arrival hall and dialed the embassy. She reached Ferguson's secretary, who explained that he was in a meeting.

"Miss Jones, do you remember me?" Helen said. "I and my children saw Mr. Ferguson at the embassy yesterday."

"Of course I remember you, Mrs. Bittenberg."

"Please, Miss Jones, could you interrupt Mr. Ferguson for just a moment. Is the meeting in his office?"

"Yes, but—"

"Please, Miss Jones, Stephen is a close friend of my husband, and he has disappeared."

"I know."

"Please, Stephen would want to know what I have to tell him."

"All right, Mrs. Bittenberg, I'll see. Please wait."

Ferguson came on the line.

"Helen?"

"Stephen. Thank you so much for taking my call. I just saw the children off at the airport, and I'm so down. You're my only friend in Paris. Yesterday you said you would like to take me to lunch. Does the offer still stand?"

"Of course it does."

"How about today?"

The line went silent for a moment. "I don't know, Helen. I didn't know that you would be free today. I made appointments."

"Can you juggle them a little? I really need to talk to you. I need a friend, and"—she searched for something to say that would perk Ferguson's interest—"I think I have an idea of what may be behind Richard's disappearance."

"You *do*?"

"I may be wrong, but, yes, I have an idea," she lied.

"OK, Helen, I'll try to get away, but I couldn't make it before 1:00. Could you meet me here at the embassy? We can go from here to a restaurant."

"I'll be there."

"See you then."

"Oh, Stephen, one more thing."

"Yes."

"Please bring a copy of that sheet of paper with those strange numbers that I brought you yesterday. Thank you, Stephen." She hung up before he had had a chance to respond.

She decided to take a taxi to Paris instead of the airport bus, which would leave her far from the hotel. It was an expensive luxury that she would never have permitted herself in normal circumstances. She hoped to take a short nap at the hotel before getting ready for the lunch.

What kind of role would she play with Ferguson? Would she be the distraught woman needing a shoulder to cry on or the intensely involved wife asking for more help from the embassy? Whatever role she adopted, she would play upon his interest in her as a woman. She was well aware of her attraction to the opposite sex, and now she would take full advantage of it. She would use whatever means at her disposal. She would prod for and exploit Ferguson's weakest point. She felt ruthless. She would make herself as appealing to him as she could. To make him lower his guard, she might try to make him believe that she was starting to regard him as something more than a helpful friend. But she had to be subtle and careful. Any overacting would make him suspicious. He was the very opposite of a fool.

Waiting in the taxi line, she noticed that the temperature and the humidity were higher than they had been in the last few days. The sun shone behind a light haze.

No message waited for her at the hotel, which both pleased and bothered her. At least no news meant no bad news. She decided against waking her parents up just to tell them that John and Anne were on their way to Washington as planned. She would have plenty of time to call later. She set an alarm clock and tried to sleep for twenty minutes. After ten minutes she gave up and started to dress for the lunch.

She walked into the lobby of the U.S. Embassy shortly after 1:00 PM and let Ferguson's office know that she was there. She had decided to wear discreet and only modestly eye-catching clothes. She had put on a white short-sleeved blouse, leaving two buttons unbuttoned, a dark-blue skirt that ended just above the knee, and dark blue shoes with heels of medium height that she had brought with her to Europe for semi-formal occasions. She carried a light beige summer jacket and her handbag. She thought that her clothes were right for her purpose. They revealed her slender, moderately curvy figure and showed a good bit of her tanned legs, but were not provocative. She had not put on heavy make-up and had made no special effort to style her hair. Still, waiting for Ferguson in the reception area, she noticed appreciative looks in her direction.

When Ferguson came down the stairs and saw her he smiled broadly. If he was nervous about meeting her, he did not show it. He walked up to her with both hands stretched out before him. He took hers, bent forward and gave her a peck on the cheek. His dress was similar to that of the previous day. He wore a dark suit, black shoes, a white shirt, and a bow tie, this time a red one with a pattern.

"Very good to see you," he said. "How are you? You must feel terrible about having to send the children back to the U.S."

"I do, Stephen, I do. I tell myself I had no choice."

"I think you did the right thing."

He motioned her towards the exit. "Let's have some lunch and talk all this over, shall we?"

He had soon hailed a cab. No limousine with a driver had been waiting for them, Helen reflected. Ferguson told the taxi driver to take them to *Le Carousel*. The driver just nodded. It had to be a well-known restaurant.

Within a few minutes they were seated at the restaurant. It was situated on the "left bank" of the Seine just a block from the National Assembly, which looks out on Place de la Concorde. The restaurant was large and somewhat formal, but it had cubbyholes and rooms off the main dining room. It was almost full, but some of the lunch guests had gotten to the coffee or were making ready to leave. Helen and Ferguson were shown to an alcove away from the main dining room.

"This is one of my favorite restaurants in Paris," Ferguson said as they looked at the menu. "Very French. When the Assembly is in session, you see many of the members here. But I come here mostly for the food."

"Please order for me," Helen said, "I love French food."

"May I recommend a good red wine?" he said.

Helen's first impulse was to decline the wine. She wanted her mind and her senses to be as sharp as possible. When she hesitated, Ferguson said: "Some wine will do you good, Helen. You've had a rough time. You need to relax." How considerate he was.

She forced herself to smile at him. "You may be right. Please order for me." While Ferguson instructed the waiter, Helen observed him closely. He could not have looked calmer or more comfortable. His hands or fingers did not shake, his eyes were not shifty, his voice was not tense. He spoke to the waiter in a friendly but businesslike manner. This might well be the manner of a real friend who was uninvolved in Richard's disappearance, she thought. But it could also be the manner of a hardened conspirator, a seasoned diplomat used to high-pressure situations.

Having completed the order, Ferguson turned to Helen. He looked her in the eye, showing not the slightest tendency to avert his gaze. He seemed to hesitate, then reached over and lightly took her right hand, which was resting on the small table. She almost pulled it back but resisted the impulse. He squeezed her fingers as he said, "You did the right thing to send the children home."

His voice was full of empathy. Helen wanted to believe that this apparent warmth was genuine and that what he had said was true. She could not be certain what was truly best for the children. Deciding to send them back to America had been terribly hard, and parting with them at the airport had been harrowing. She could not get Annie's face on the sky bridge out of her mind.

"Thank you, Stephen. I am glad you think so."

"You really had no choice."

"You're probably right."

"And you are not quite alone in Paris. You can count on me."

"Thank you." He let go of her hand.

How perfect he is, she thought—everything just right, from the crisp French cuffs of his heavily starched white cotton shirt to his carefully combed hair and his sure sense of just what strings to pluck in the soul of this distraught mother and wife. Who could be trustworthier? Her next thought was that she might be profoundly unfair to a truly caring person, the only friend she had in Paris.

# CHAPTER 24

Richard and Vandenhorst met at the National University faculty club three weeks after their lunch at the Metropolitan Club. Most academics having little sense of style and most universities spending little money on the decorative, this university establishment was less aesthetically appealing than functional, but their lunch was pleasant enough. Richard and Vandenhorst behaved this time more like people who knew each other. Vandenhorst being his senior, Richard asked him to address him by his first name. They were soon comfortably Richard and Herbert.

Their conversation initially was similar to what it had been at their first meeting, but Richard noticed a new emphasis in Vandenhorst's talk. Vandenhorst was feeling Richard out about what kind of action might change America. Richard had thought a great deal about this question and had answers, which he gave in a low voice. He was confident that Vandenhorst would never betray his trust and revealed some of his innermost thoughts, including his belief that the American system of government and related structures of finance and media were simply too broken to be fixed. He spoke with unusual frankness, letting some of his despair show. Vandenhorst was not taken aback, and Richard finally spoke of the possible need for some kind of drastic practical action.

"Drastic action?"

"I haven't really come to a conclusion as to what I really mean," Richard said. He had in fact toyed with a definite conclusion in recent months, but he considered it far-fetched and abstract and hesitated to reveal it to a man of Herbert Vandenhorst's practical temperament.

As they finished their meal Richard asked if Vandenhorst would like to take a stroll around the university and then visit Richard's office. The campus, located in the northwest section of the District of Columbia not far from the National Zoo, was a jumble of old and new, mostly undistinguished buildings with some parkland between them. It was not particularly attractive. But it was a sunny, dry, rather warm winter day, and Vandenhorst accepted the offer of a tour. They started walking, continuing their conversation

"One thing seems clear," Vandenhorst said. "This bad situation is not going to resolve itself in the normal course of events. We'll soon be too far gone, if we aren't already. It's necessary to head off disaster. The financial and political debauchery was bad enough. Now the riots show that not even basic social order can be taken for granted."

"Head off disaster? How?" The touch of activism in Vandenhorst's comment made Richard wonder if this man might be more than just talk after all.

"Well, what do *you* think, Richard?" Vandenhorst stopped and waited for Richard to do the same. They looked at each other. Richard hesitated, but then a sudden feeling of calm came over him. Vandenhorst was an honorable man. He would not betray an obvious confidence. Richard decided to say just what was on his mind.

"OK, Herbert. Here's a summary of what I think. Some angry and unsophisticated hotheads might think that the way to save the situation is to roll some tanks into D.C., take over a few key institutions, buildings and television and radio stations — to make a Latin-America-style coup. It wouldn't work. It couldn't work. First of all, organizing a coup would be a daunting task — probably quite impossible — in the first place. The American military is too ensnared in the present system and too dispersed. It's spread out across the country and the world. Even if a coup were to be attempted, the leaders of it could not count on the loyalty or even the passive acceptance of the rest of the military, to say nothing of the general population. And the government in general is so vast and complex — geographically spread out as well — that it couldn't be controlled from some central point. Even if a junta were to occupy the Hill, take control of key departments, a few radio and television stations and newspapers, even the Pentagon, there are many other concentrations of government, and important military installations, and television and radio stations and newspapers, to say nothing of foreign media. In short, the resources for opposing the coup would be plentiful around the country, indeed overwhelming. Defeating the junta wouldn't even require something like a civil war. My guess is that the coup would fizzle in a day or two. The current system has a much greater capacity for protecting itself than some poor junta member might think. Only people who don't understand the great range, strength, and complexity of the present power structure — that is, only not very perceptive people — would be so foolish as to attempt a coup in the first place. The leaders of the coup would soon be isolated and then paralyzed. The impossibility of final success would soon be obvious. I would guess that within forty-eight hours, the leaders would shoot themselves or be taken in hand-cuffs out of the White House or the Pentagon or wherever they were holed up." Richard stopped.

Vandenhorst first did not say anything. A small smile played on his lips.

"Very good, Richard. I'm not surprised to hear you say this." Richard thought that they would now get back to talking about how bad the situation was and that nothing of any consequence could be done. They came to a park bench that happened to be in the sun, and they sat down.

Spring was still far away, but a Washington winter could range all the way from bitter cold to summer-like heat. One unusually warm and sunny Christmas some northern Europeans visiting Richard and Helen had gotten it into their heads to climb the fence around their neighborhood swim club to swim in the leaf-filled pool. There could be huge snowfalls, especially in late February or early March, but most winters there were no great amounts of snow and ice. Sometimes trees started budding too early and were surprised by a return of freezing temperatures. During Richard and Vandenhorst's meeting on the National University campus a foretaste of spring was in the air.

Richard continued, "A coup attempt would give the powers-that-be the scare of their life, but in the end the failed assault would allow them to retrench, to expand, and add to all of the worst features of the existing system. In the wake of a coup attempt we would never hear the end of the constant threat to democracy — with a capital D, you know — which would be on top of the perpetual, great, special threat of terrorism, with a capital T. The riots would provide yet other excuses for emergency measures. We would get an even more elaborate and intrusive National Security Superstate. Civil liberties would be more restricted than ever. The Constitution would be no more. The president would direct the U.S. government. We would have a Caesaristic arrangement, as in declining, imperial Rome. Even the Senate would cower before the executive. That's to say, we would have what we have now, only in a more acute form."

"I agree."

"So what I think is this," Richard continued. "Given the nature of the present system and its capacity for defending itself, partly by inertia and incompetence, no kind of drastic action has any chance of succeeding. The deterioration of American society and government has gone too far, and the ruling system is too deeply entrenched, too extensive, too rambling. What might turn our society around, though at a terribly high price, would be some horrible nationwide disaster, perhaps a deep depression or some frightful epidemic, that scared Americans to death and unsettled the way we do business. Another but very distant possibility is some kind of religious-moral-cultural renaissance, but a genuine spiritual reawakening would act slowly on people, and it would be years before we could hope to see tangible salutary effects in politics. I have seen no signs of that kind of development. We would be more likely to get some pseudo-religious revival—perhaps along the lines of what some of those televangelists are offering—a mixture of sentimental mush and belligerent nationalism. It's as if we were determined to destroy traditional American society."

"And as if some people were working to achieve just that goal for reasons of their own," Vandenhorst injected.

"Here is what's so damned frustrating!" Richard exclaimed. "Although little can be done, no morally responsible person who understands what's happening can just stand aside and let the horrendous future-in-the-making happen. Current trends are already destroying people's lives on a large scale. People are drawn in growing numbers into a polluted, neurotic, corrupt, perverse existence. They're able to hold despair at bay only by pointless consumption and pleasure seeking and, of course, drugs. And look at the rioters. Many of them are hoodlums and riffraff that are taking advantage of disorder, but what kind of society produces hooligans in such numbers? Some of the rioters are spoilt, grasping people who insist on keeping all of their privileges and benefits despite the financial emergency, but many, many are justifiably angry with people in authority. They are suffering the consequences of irresponsibility at the highest political and financial levels. Even greater disasters—economic, political, military, medical— threaten in the future, both internationally and domestically. Terrible people have gained control over America's military might, and it could put millions and millions of lives at stake around the world, including American lives."

Richard turned to face Vandenhorst on the bench. "So, it seems to me that a responsible person who thinks that only drastic action in some form might avert disaster would have to work toward such action in spite of the unfavorable odds. But he must start by dismissing the idea of a military junta taking over the government and setting things right by military decree. It's a stupid idea. Any kind of meaningful drastic challenge to the existing order would have to be much more complex, have much wider scope. It would require a large network of people who have broad, sophisticated views and who recognize the enormity of the obstacles to be overcome. I'm talking about a large number of dedicated, experienced, courageous, highly intelligent, and *already highly influential* individuals. Here I'm just talking about the ones who would be needed in leadership positions. Thousands of others would have to be willing to implement their decisions. The preparations for this drastic move would have to be very intricate and careful, would probably take years. And—so that you will understand how far-fetched I think this whole idea is—all of this would have to be kept secret from watchful, even paranoid representatives of the system."

Richard let out a deep breath in an audible sigh. Vandenhorst just sat in the sun, saying nothing.

"Well, Herbert, now you know why my life has become such a strain. I'm almost paralyzed by the fact that I feel that I must, just *must*, do what I can to help save my country, and at the same time I worry that we've passed the point of no return. One of the reasons why I've worked harder than most professors is that I wanted my books, articles, and lectures to make a difference by placing new ideas in circulation. But I'm just one little voice, and I know well that my ideas do not have any obvious practical implications. They can exert influence only indirectly. Even in the most favorable circumstances, which we do not have, new ideas can change practice only in the long run. As far as I can see, in our historical situation the only thing that might ward off catastrophe is shock treatment. *But* successful drastic action presupposes a large number of people who do not exist, a complicated, meticulously organized super-secret organization, which is impossible, and time that's not available. Checkmate."

Richard fell silent, and Vandenhorst still did not comment. They sat quietly on the bench until the sun disappeared behind a cloud. They got up and walked slowly in the direction of the building in which Richard's office was housed.

Vandenhorst broke the silence. "Anything else?"

"Yes, and it's very important. No kind of drastic action could succeed unless it were perceived by the American public as legitimate. The move would have to be seen as defending society against an acute and very dangerous threat and as being clearly for the common good—to save the Constitution, the American way of life. The people who rule us now have twisted the Constitution into unrecognizable shape. It's become just a mantra to go along with the most recent attempt to do whatever they want to do. But that very practice, brazenly dishonest though it is, is keeping alive a memory that this country is supposed to be governed according to the Constitution. The people taking drastic action would have to stress the need to *save* the Constitution. The leadership would have to consist of people of obvious, recognized credibility, so that the least dishonest and corrupt parts of the upper echelons of the bureaucracy and the military would be reassured. A large propaganda and disinformation campaign would have to accompany the move against the existing government and other institutions, and that campaign would have to be kept going for a good while."

Vandenhorst nodded almost imperceptibly.

"I see you're nodding," Richard said, "but you realize that to list these requirements for successful drastic action is to list the reasons why it couldn't happen. The resources just aren't there. The requisite action cannot be organized. Checkmate. Or perhaps it's stalemate, or Catch-22."

Vandenhorst was again silent, and Richard did not break the quiet. When Vandenhorst finally spoke his voice had changed. It was slower and deeper. "I wonder, Richard, if you're giving your fellow Americans sufficient credit. Think about it. Why would you be the only person of any significance in America to recognize the need for what you call 'shock-treatment'? And why should you be the only one willing to do more than just talk?" Richard was struck by the new seriousness in Vandenhorst's voice.

"Because I simply have not met any people who are ready to do more than rattle on about how bad things are."

"But didn't you just say, Richard, how important it would be for people planning drastic action to keep their planning absolutely secret?"

Richard stopped. He looked in amazement at Vandenhorst. He felt as if he had been hit in the solar plexus. The implications of Vandenhorst's comment were overwhelming. Was it possible? Could an effort to attempt drastic change be already underway? He could not believe it. Vandenhorst was just speculating and enjoying being secretive. He might be referring to some people who were upset and liked to vent and talk tough among themselves, but who did not have any intention of acting on their enjoyably constructed plans.

Richard glanced inquiringly at Vandenhorst, but the latter said nothing. He again smiled vaguely in Richard's direction, and Richard thought he saw a humorous twinkle in his eyes. They had come to the main entrance of the four-storey stone building, one of the oldest on the National University campus, where Richard had his office. Vandenhorst accepted Richard's invitation to visit for a moment, and they walked up the stairs to the second floor. In the corridor they met a slightly overweight, bespectacled young man of medium height and dark hair, who greeted Richard cheerfully. Richard stopped to introduce the young man to Vandenhorst.

"This is Ronald Turello, my research assistant. Ron, this is Herbert Vandenhorst. Mr. Vandenhorst is a retired government official with a strong interest in history." Turello probably assumed, Richard guessed, that Vandenhorst was a potential supporter of the institute.

The two shook hands and exchanged pleasantries. Turello was in his late twenties and dressed in a sports jacket, shirt, and tie, which was rather formal for a modern American doctoral student. Turello was polite and deferential but also humorous.

"I'll see you in my office later this afternoon," Richard said to Turello.

Richard's office was light and spacious, had high ceilings and two tall windows. A tan wall-to-wall carpet nicely matched softly beige-green walls, which were set off by white window frames and moldings. Bookshelves competed for wall space with tasteful prints and a few photographs. There was a large plant. A couple of armchairs for visitors and a low table with a lamp stood opposite Richard's large desk, which had a sideboard with a computer. It was obviously a working desk, but it was not cluttered. Papers, books, and manuscripts were laid out neatly on two side tables. It was a pleasant, even inviting room, far from the messy, ugly appearance of many faculty offices. Richard offered Vandenhorst one of the chairs and sat down in the other. They talked for a few minutes about Richard's teaching and academic routines, but Richard wanted to get back to the subject of their previous conversation. He wanted Vandenhorst to elaborate on his cryptic comment about secret planning. Just what did Vandenhorst himself mean by drastic action? Richard finally asked Vandenhorst point-blank. But Vandenhorst raised his hands in a defensive gesture, smiled, and rose.

"Richard, I would be happy to answer all your questions, but just now I have an important appointment. Let's continue our conversation very soon. I have some friends who think as you and I do."

Vandenhorst's evasiveness irritated and frustrated Richard, but as he collected himself the full force of what Vandenhorst had said began to dawn on him. Vandenhorst had said that he and Richard agreed and that others of his acquaintance were of similar mind.

"The people I'm talking about are substantial, intelligent, and influential," Vandenhorst continued. "We meet for discussion of what needs to be done. We're all pretty thoughtful, but we're intent on action. Would you like to join us?"

Richard did not want to become part of a discussion club devoted to griping, but he had been wearing himself out with questions about his practical responsibilities to his country. He liked and trusted Vandenhorst and had a strong intuition that Vandenhorst would bring him into contact with people worth knowing. Meeting with this group might help Richard figure out what course of action was appropriate for him. He had nothing to lose except time, and he might have a great deal to gain.

"Yes, I'm interested."

"I thought you would be," Vandenhorst said. "We'll meet at my home next Friday evening. We'll have some dessert and then get down to business. Vandenhorst gave him the address and the time.

"You'll recognize one or two in our group."

"Really?"

Instead of responding to Richard's implied question Vandenhorst said, "I would appreciate it if you kept this meeting strictly to yourself."

"Of course."

Vandenhorst shook Richard's hand warmly and said goodbye.

The same night Richard told Helen that he had to go to a professional meeting the next Friday evening. When she commented on the strange time and asked what kind of meeting it was, he told her another half-truth, saying that he was hoping that the gathering would produce some financial assistance for his institute. She made no difficulties, said only that they could have family night on Saturday instead.

In the week before the meeting Richard worked on a scholarly article that was nearing completion and took care of administrative work related to his institute. He taught his classes, advised doctoral students, directed his graduate assistant, and attended to the routine duties of a professor. He tried, though as usual with limited success, to spend time after hours with Helen and the children. But his awareness of the upcoming meeting affected his frame of mind. He had a premonition that it might bring some kind of change in his existence. That it would be a turning point in his life did not cross his mind.

# CHAPTER 25

By the time the waiter at *Le Carousel* brought the wine that Ferguson had ordered, the luncheon crowd had started to thin out. Observing a group of well-dressed people moving towards the exit, Helen almost did not notice that their waiter returned and uncorked a wine-bottle. Only when he poured a little in Ferguson's glass for his approval did she react.

"Oh, Stephen, a whole bottle — that's very good of you, but I couldn't possibly — "

"Of course you can," he said motioning the waiter to fill her glass. "This is Paris, France. Here wine is what you drink with food." As soon as the waiter had poured wine into his glass he lifted it and said, "To Richard's quick return!"

She smiled uneasily and took a sip.

"I'm glad to know that the French police are now on the case," he said. "Chief inspector Duparc and his associate visited me first thing this morning. I'm glad that I was at the embassy. They seemed very competent. They came because you'd told them that Richard and I are old friends. They wanted to see if I could shed any light on his disappearance. I told them all I know."

Would Ferguson mention the paper with the code-like notations, Helen wondered. Duparc had said that he would ask Ferguson about it.

"I took the opportunity to impress upon them that we're following their work closely at the embassy."

"Did they ask you anything unexpected or of special interest?"

"What kind of thing do you mean?"

She was thinking about the paper, but said, "Oh, I was wondering if anything they asked might tell us what they've discovered about Richard's disappearance."

"No, nothing like that, but they haven't had much time."

"I suppose not."

He asked about her immediate plans. She was a little vague, partly because her plans were unformed, partly because she didn't want him to know exactly what she planned to do. She only told him that she intended to remain in her hotel, for now.

The waiter placed plates of pâté in front of them. Helen was not hungry. Her stomach was in the usual knot. But having put a piece of food in her mouth, she found that she could eat.

"This is delicious," she said, trying to seem at ease.

"Isn't it? This restaurant must be one of the best in Paris. Try the wine with the pâté." He raised his glass. She took another sip, making it seem as if she were swallowing a real gulp.

"Now tell me," Ferguson said, "what's this theory you have about what might have happened to Richard."

There it was! Helen had expected him to raise the issue if she didn't. She had not had much time to invent a story to back up her claim to Ferguson on the telephone. She had said what she then said on the spur of the moment, to make him more likely to take her to lunch. In one part of herself the fact that he had actually rearranged his day to see her had deepened her suspicion. Another part was open to the possibility that his willingness to see her was a sign of real concern for her and Richard. Whatever the case, he should be interested in her explanation for Richard's disappearance.

She had decided that she would lie in such a way that Ferguson could relax but also so that his interest in her as a woman would increase.

"Oh, Stephen, it's not really a theory, only a hunch I have that has only gotten stronger. I may be wrong, but nothing else makes any sense." She took another little sip of the wine.

"What's your hunch?"

"I'm embarrassed to tell you."

"Don't you worry about that! I'm your friend, and, if you want, anything you tell me stays between us."

The waiter arrived with the main course. It turned out to be crispy quail in an orange wine sauce with potatoes and sautéed mushrooms. Helen's mouth did not water, but this she could eat. To boost her courage to tell Ferguson her story she took a full swallow of the wine. The wine was rich and heavy. It would have been an especially fine selection for dinner. She reminded herself not to consume more than a single glass.

"Stephen, Richard's and my marriage has been under a great deal of strain for a long time, especially in the last year. Things have gotten worse, not better."

"I'm very sorry to hear that."

"We'd hoped to patch things up for the sake of the children. The trip to Europe was part of an effort to put our lives back together."

"I see. I don't want to prod, but did anything in particular precipitate your problems?"

"Not really. Our case is probably not very different from that of other couples who drift apart and start to get on each other's nerves. A marriage counselor might call our situation routine, but it's pretty bad for those involved."

How had Ferguson reacted? He had not seemed tense or uncomfortable before, and there was no apparent change in him now. The part of Helen that was willing to consider Ferguson a real friend cringed. How embarrassing, she thought, and how unfair to Richard to give one of his friends the impression that his marriage was in deep trouble. She realized that telling this lie was an indication of what she really believed: that Ferguson was no friend.

"So what happened?"

"The day before we left on our trip, Richard and I had a huge quarrel. A lot of things were said. We really had everything out. I said some things I shouldn't have said. The children didn't hear us, because my parents had taken them out for ice cream and some last minute shopping. At first Richard wanted to cancel the trip, but in the end we decided that this would just devastate John and Anne. They had looked forward to it so much. So we covered everything up. I think Richard's mother picked up some of the vibrations when she and Dad delivered the children, and Johnnie gave us some strange looks, but we managed to behave civilly, and we got ourselves together and over to France without the children suspecting the depth of our rift."

"You must be good actors."

"I guess so."

"Then, in the evening the day before Richard disappeared, the bubble burst in the worst possible way. It happened at the hotel. We'd just had dinner with the children. We'd left them in their room. Some comments were made. I didn't handle the situation well at all. Richard got furious and let it rip. The children heard us through the wall. Soon they were banging on the door to our room. I told Richard to control himself, and I let them in. What else could I do? But Richard was beyond himself. I think the children perceived him as threatening me, and they became defensive, standing with me and screaming at him. Suddenly he just grabbed his jacket and left, slamming the door hard. It must have been about 9:30. He didn't get back until well after midnight. By then I'd finally gotten the children to go back to their room. I'd told them not to worry. I said what you might expect: All parents have quarrels, and they really don't amount to very much. All would be fine the next day. I felt very badly about my part in the disaster, and when Richard got back I tried some kind of apology, but he wouldn't talk to me. I slept very little that night, and I don't think he slept much either. Next morning he was supposed to spend some time at the Sorbonne doing research and then meet us for a late lunch. But he would not speak to me then either. At breakfast in front of the children he was not uncivil, but curt and quiet. He gave them the impression that, although he may have been angry or hurt, he had calmed down and might regret his behavior of last night. Then he told us he was going to the library and just left the hotel. That's the last time we saw him." Helen shook her head and reached for the wine glass.

"So what's your theory?"

"I think he wanted to punish us. No, he wanted to punish *me,* and perhaps the children for having sided with me that previous night."

"But that sounds pretty heartless. Is he like that?"

"I didn't think so. If you go by his past, this kind of behavior is out of character. But I provoked him. I went much too far. I was *so* angry with him. I was really unfair and biting."

"So, you think he'll return soon?"

"I thought he would, but I don't know any longer. I thought he wanted really to put me through the wringer for a while, let me suffer the consequences of my behavior. Perhaps he wanted to show the children how hurt he was. At the same time he had to realize that the longer he stayed away, the smaller the likelihood that we would ever be able to patch things up. What I really don't understand is how he could be so cruel to the children. That's the trouble, Stephen. I have difficulty believing that he's really like that. He's never done anything like this before. Even if you intend to leave your family, you don't do it this way. Not in a foreign country. To think that Richard would leave us alone here in France where we are by ourselves and especially vulnerable!"

How easy it was to lie, Helen thought. She had concocted a story, which, however untrue, would not seem implausible to an outsider. She was not worried about seeming credible, because real anxiety, worry, and confusion had been her permanent companions for the last few days. Why exactly was she telling this rather far-fetched story? She wasn't quite sure. She wanted to put Ferguson at ease by giving him the idea that she had a plausible explanation for Richard's disappearance that did not involve anybody else, and she wanted him to think of her as a potentially available woman. But who was Ferguson?

"He must have been terribly upset to behave that way,"

Ferguson said. "But if your hunch is right, why did he come back that first night when he had left you and the children at the hotel?"

"I don't know. Perhaps he wanted to pick up the papers he needed for his research at the Sorbonne. Perhaps he needed some money or to bring some personal things with him. I didn't see what he threw together or put in his pockets. The curious thing is that he didn't take his electric razor or an overnight bag or any of his other clothes. He may have intended to be gone for just that day." Good thinking, she thought. By mixing in pieces of truth, she only made her story more believable.

She added, "Or perhaps he didn't want me to understand that he was leaving for good. The uncertainty would punish me by making me more miserable. But I don't think that's what happened. He didn't take his passport."

Ferguson said nothing.

"What I'm thinking now," Helen said, "is that he probably did want to punish me. He was angry. He felt badly treated. He may have decided to leave me for good, but now he wanted to give me something to think about that I would never forget. He went off somewhere. He took a hotel room. He wanted to stew and to lick his wounds. He probably didn't have any plan, except that, when he came back in a day or two, he wanted to find me softened up and apologetic. But then something wholly unexpected happened. Richard doesn't drink very much, but perhaps this time he did, and then he did something else that he would never have done in other circumstances, got into bad company perhaps. He could have been robbed and knocked unconscious. Perhaps he was killed and thrown into the Seine. Oh, Stephen, I go crazy thinking about the possibilities."

Ferguson once more reached for her hand and squeezed it.

"You must not let your imagination run away with you."

"I know, but that's easier said than done." Helen took another sip of wine and then continued: "Another possibility that I'm finding more persuasive now is that after leaving us on Friday morning he decided to leave Paris for a while, to get away from his troubles, clear his mind, and think things over. He rented a car and drove out of Paris, or he took a bus or a train. But he could have gotten ill or had an accident. This would explain why no trace has been found of him in the Paris metropolitan area. The big question is why, if there was some kind of misadventure, nobody has thought to contact the American consulate. The only reason I can think of is that he has been unconscious in some hospital and had no wallet, perhaps because it had been stolen or misplaced. But wouldn't the labels in his clothes suggest that he's an American?"

"Not necessarily. We live in the era of globalization. The labels were probably from multinational corporations. They may say 'Yves Saint Laurent,' which is French' or 'made in China.' What's a French policeman to make of that?"

"Yes, I've thought of that."

Helen had barely touched her main course, and Ferguson encouraged her. She ate dutifully. Ferguson tried to top up her glass, but she put a hand over it. He served himself some more.

Helen was sure that she had sounded believable, for these were scenarios that had been running through her mind for a long time in whole or in part. She was less certain about the plausibility of her explanation for why Richard had disappeared in the first place. She had suggested that he would be capable of a kind of callousness that had no counterpart in his actual personality. Richard could be angry, hurt, and irritated, but he had never done anything remotely like what she had described. He would never deliberately hurt the children. Their marriage bore little or no resemblance to the picture she had drawn. The problems between them related mostly to her concerns about Richard's welfare and the welfare of the children and the family. The tension was due to his inability or unwillingness to break out of that vicious circle of overcommitment. In spite of her worries and frustration, they were happily married, were they not? Richard's agreeing to the family's European trip had greatly raised her spirits. It had been to her a sign that he might finally be turning a corner. Oh, Richard, where are you? Come back to us!

She might have started sobbing, had not the waiter distracted her by bringing the dessert. Ferguson had ordered the restaurant's set menu. The waiter set a small dish of crème caramel before her and served pitch-black coffee out of a shining pot.

Had she perhaps drawn so stark a picture of their marriage and her husband that Ferguson would find it hard to believe? Would he suspect her of being a shrew?

"There's one major problem with my theory," she said. "I keep returning to it."

"What's that?"

"Richard has a temper, and he can get really angry when I hit him in certain sore spots, but he's normally protective of the children. Something must have snapped."

"And you cannot think of any *other* explanation for his disappearing?"

"No, this is my only 'theory.' Can you think of another explanation?"

"As I don't know anything about your marriage except what you told me and haven't been really close to Richard, I just can't say. Considering what you have told me, I suppose your hypothesis is plausible — for lack of a better one. The police have found no trace of him. If the reason for his disappearance had been an accident or his falling ill somewhere around Paris, you would think it would have come to light by now."

She nodded. They ate of the desert in silence. Why, she wondered, did Ferguson not ask whether Richard might have been involved in some secret or quasi-secret activity, such as work for the CIA? Even if he did not want to draw her mind to such possibilities, would it not arouse her suspicion for him not to mention them?

"Before I forget," she said, "did you bring that sheet of paper?"

At first he looked confused, as if he didn't understand what she meant. Then he said apologetically, "I'm sorry, Helen! I meant to bring it, and I tried to get it from the person at the embassy, but he wasn't there."

What could be more believable? Ferguson really knew how to exude credibility and normality. She didn't believe him. The part of herself that suspected him of involvement in Richard's disappearance took charge. She could barely stop herself from letting him feel all of her bottled-up anger.

"OK," she said. "Please, have it for me the next time we see each other." Intense anger threatened to break through her air of unconcern.

"I will," Ferguson said. "Do you have any reason to think that the paper might be important?"

"Not really," she said. "But right now I'm grasping at straws." A good comeback, she thought. If Ferguson was prodding to see if she suspected him of anything, she had probably reassured him.

They talked about the restaurant and the food. Then Ferguson said, "There is one thing that crossed my mind. Perhaps I shouldn't even mention it, because it seems so far-fetched."

"What is it?"

"Well, in my job, you see many strange things that people never hear about except in movies and novels."

"What do you mean?"

"Did Richard have any contacts that might have gotten him into some kind of difficulty? Did he perhaps do work for some intelligence agency? Could he have had an undercover assignment here in France?"

There it was, she thought. He had to get it out, not to make her wonder why he had not done so.

"It crossed my mind," she said. "But then Richard must have been extraordinarily good at keeping secrets. He certainly never *told* me of any connections of that kind. He's a professor and a scholar. He writes and does research all the time. He's got a small research institute. He travels, giving lectures. He's much too busy to have room for that sort of thing."

"Doesn't he belong to any organizations?"

"A few, but they're academic. He's a member of the American Historical Association and one or two others. He's even a reluctant member, feels out of step. He doesn't enjoy going to the meetings. Richard's not antisocial, but he's not the networking type. If he's been working on something secret, all I can say is that he's kept it mighty secret."

"I understand. Just thought I'd mention it."

If Ferguson was involved in Richard's disappearance, he must now have concluded, she thought, that she did not suspect any kind of government involvement. To give him the impression that she saw no reason to dwell on this subject she switched the topic. "A delicious meal," she said. "I would have enjoyed it even more if the circumstances had been different. Thank you, Stephen. I appreciate your kindness so much."

"You're welcome. Remember that you can always call me. Let's stay in touch. Keep me informed of anything that happens, or if you think that I could be helpful. I will continue to follow this matter closely."

"What would I do without you?" she forced herself to say.

Ferguson started to look for something in his inside pocket, but had difficulty getting it out. He pulled out a pack of cigarettes and placed it on the table. He then found a box of matches in one of his trouser pockets and put it on top of the pack of cigarettes. While performing this little ritual he said nothing, which only drew more attention to it. Helen tensed. He was getting ready to smoke an after-lunch cigarette when they had left the restaurant. He was putting on a performance for her, but was doing it a little awkwardly. His movements did not have the spontaneity of long-standing habit. And don't most cigarette smokers carry lighters? Ferguson's actions confirmed all of her suspicions.

"Would you like me to drop you off anywhere?"

"Thank you, yes, I would like to return to the hotel."

"Nothing would be simpler. That couldn't be more than six or seven blocks from here."

In the street, Ferguson hailed a cab, and as they got into it

Ferguson said to the driver, "*Le Vieux Logis, s'il vous plait.*" When the cabbie said he didn't know the location of the hotel, Ferguson added, "Just off *Boul'Mich.*" He turned to Helen to ask for the street address. She gave it to the driver in her halting French.

At the hotel Ferguson got out of the taxi with her. He embraced her, tightly she felt, and gave her a more than perfunctory kiss on the cheek before getting back into the car. She looked after the taxi as it disappeared down the small street.

Yes, she had given Ferguson the name and telephone number of their hotel a couple of days ago, and she had mentioned that it was in the Latin Quarter. But that section of Paris is quite large. Yet, although not even the taxi driver had known the location of the hotel, he had known it. Ferguson had only needed to ask her for the exact street address. Had he perhaps done so only because he had caught himself revealing that he knew too much?

# CHAPTER 26

Vandenhorst's home was located in Spring Valley, a pleasant neighborhood of medium-sized, traditional houses and large trees in the westernmost, residential part of the District of Columbia. The area is located just off Massachusetts Avenue, also known as Embassy Row, where that street heads for the Maryland line. The Vandenhorst house was a fairly modest, white-painted brick colonial with green shutters. It was getting dark outside when Richard arrived, but he could see that the yard and the house were meticulously kept. The door was opened by a thin, rather attractive and pleasant-looking woman of medium height, whose dark hair was bound tightly in a knot in the back. She appeared to be about 65 years old but was obviously in good physical shape. Richard assumed that she was Mrs. Vandenhorst.

"I'm Richard Bittenberg," he said.

"Dr. Bittenberg, do come in. I'm so pleased to meet you. I'm Celeste. Herbert has told me everything about you." She spoke in a precise and yet gracious manner. She hung up his coat. He could hear voices from the back of the house. As they walked in that direction he could see that here lived people of good, if not remarkable, taste, who knew how to coordinate antiques, modern furniture, paintings and decorations. In the family room, which had been expanded into the backyard, Herbert Vandenhorst was conversing with two other men. All three turned in Richard's direction. He immediately recognized a large, balding man. It was the retired admiral, Gordon Bunker, who had shown interest in his writing and invited him and Helen to his home.

"I believe you know each other," Vandenhorst said, as Bunker extended his hand broadly smiling.

"Delighted to see you," Bunker said, giving Richard an iron handshake. "I was hoping you would join us."

The second person had to be several years older than Vandenhorst. He was above medium height and size and had wavy, thinning white hair worn rather long in the back. Richard thought he looked familiar.

"This is Senator Lester Pickett," Vandenhorst said. "Lester, let me introduce Professor Bittenberg."

"Richard, it's good to meet you," Pickett said. Richard shook his hand.

"Lester used to be the senior senator from Georgia," Vandenhorst said, "He was chairman of the Senate Intelligence Committee for a couple of years." Of course, Richard thought, Pickett had been a prominent member of the U.S. Senate until a few years ago.

"I retired because I'd had enough," Pickett said, "but also because I wanted to do some other things, *this* being one of them."

This? What did the former senator mean?

"We'll have coffee and desert a little later," Vandenhorst said, "but we're having drinks now. What would you like?"

As Vandenhorst fetched Richard a scotch and water, Bunker said to him: "You must've been surprised to see me here. Herb and I go back many years. He was in the State Department, sort of, when I got my first star, and we met in a group charged with coordinating some military and diplomatic efforts. We became close friends."

Two ill-matched men arrived. One was a short, intense-looking, wiry, dark-haired man with sharply chiseled facial features. The other was larger and bulkier and had a round face and light, graying and thinning hair. Richard recognized the smaller of the two. It was Douglas Pellegrini, another of the individuals who had contacted him, perhaps a year ago, regarding his writing. They had met in a restaurant across the street from the FBI national headquarters. Pellegrini had spoken rather provocatively about the need to move the present rulers of America out of the way.

What was going on? It was obviously no coincidence that both Bunker and Pellegrini were present. Vandenhorst had gotten to know Richard even better. They must have subjected him to some kind of screening. Membership in this particular group apparently had strict prerequisites. While it gave Richard a feeling of unease to have been closely scrutinized by three individuals of high intelligence and high-level experience, it flattered him to know that he must have passed their test, whatever it was.

Returning with Richard's drink, Vandenhorst said, "You already know Doug. He's the number three man at the National Security Agency. You know that super-secret government listening post up at Fort Meade near Baltimore."

"Oh, you've moved," Richard said to Pellegrini. "You used to be with the FBI."

"No, sorry, Richard, I was never with the FBI. That's just what I told you. Many people at NSA do what they can to confuse people who may be trying to establish our identity. If truth be known, I don't really exist at all. In my business, deception has to be the order of the day."

"In mine too, I'm afraid," said the bulkier man, "though I actually exist. I'm Randy Gates. I'm the deputy director of operations at the CIA. I'm afraid that the Russians and Chinese know pretty well who I am."

Richard had been right about Vandenhorst. He would put Richard in touch with people of substance. But these individuals were not only bright and interesting; they also belonged to the upper echelons of the U.S. government, or were very well connected in those echelons. Professionally, Richard was the odd man out. He was not a man of practice—a rather prominent academic but a person with no clout in government or politics.

If Vandenhorst was to be believed, these men were agreed on the sad plight of the United States and the need for change. It delighted Richard to learn that individuals of this influence might share his views. But he was also surprised. Were they actually the kind of people whom he had told himself he wanted to find but had had no success in finding? And would they, too, turn out to be mostly hot air? If they meant business, why would they select a bookish professor for inclusion in their group? It was not that Richard felt inferior to them. He was at least their equal with regard to what he could contribute to the welfare of America. He probably understood a few things of importance a good deal better than any of them, even had some knowledge essential to political practice. But he was used to American politicians, businessmen, and professionals regarding professors as somehow irrelevant to the major practical issues of life. Did these men want Richard to provide some intellectual spice, a quaint, if intriguing, change of pace, a break from discussions of what really mattered? Would he make a nice scholarly resource?

Richard noticed a younger man in the dining room who showed no signs of joining the others. He eventually disappeared into the basement. A son of the Vandenhorst's, he speculated.

"We're just waiting for two more," Vandenhorst said. "Let's get our drinks and get organized."

As they seated themselves in the family room the sixth person arrived. It was a woman. She seemed to be about sixty years old and had graying dark hair cut rather short. She was rather heavy but had a light gait and seemed almost athletic. If it hadn't been for her age, she could have been a female discus thrower, Richard thought. She wore a suit that seemed too small. She had a roundish but almost pretty face and brown eyes. Her frameless glasses enhanced an appearance of intelligence and acuity. Vandenhorst and Richard rose.

"Lisa, let me introduce Richard Bittenberg. Richard, this is Lisa DeLeon, *Dr.* DeLeon. In fact, you have doctorates from the same institution."

"That old academic degree is hardly relevant, Herbert. Professor Bittenberg, I'm pleased to meet you. I've heard much about you, and I'm very pleased that you have joined us."

"Please call me Richard."

"If you'll call me Lisa."

"Lisa is one of the highest ranking civil servants over at the Federal Reserve. She runs the department that tracks the movement of money in America and the world. She knows everything worth knowing about the U.S. dollar and central banking and the people making the big decisions."

Vandenhorst went to fetch Lisa DeLeon a glass of Campari and soda. She and Richard were soon engaged in conversation about Harvard and what they might have in common, which turned out to be not very much. Their disciplines and interests had been very different, and they were over a decade apart in age. When Vandenhorst returned with DeLeon's drink Mrs. Vandenhorst brought in the last guest, a tall, dark-haired man.

"I'm sorry to be late," he said. "Another damned strike. The subway workers. And it'd started raining. It was almost impossible to get a cab."

"Richard, this is Robert Bates," Vandenhorst said. "And, Bob, let me introduce Professor Richard Bittenberg." They shook hands.

"Bob's the chief political advisor to the minority leader of the House of Representatives," Vandenhorst explained. Bates seemed to be about fifty-five years old. He was at least as tall as Richard and had a pale elongated face. His hair was combed back tightly with the aid of pomade. He wore strong glasses that made it difficult to distinguish his dark eyes. The others simply waved to Bates or said "hi." Bates nodded unceremoniously. It was obvious that all the others knew each other well. Richard was the only outsider.

Vandenhorst welcomed the seven to his house and addressed Richard: "We all owe you an apology, I in particular. I've not been aboveboard with you, as you have already realized, but I think you'll understand that I had no choice. The members of this group talk about and plan things that are so sensitive that nobody could be asked to join it without thorough scrutiny. In fact, we know even more about you than you might think. Douglas, Gordon, and I have gotten to know you personally—by the way, our interest in history is genuine—but information about you was gathered in several ways.

You're well known to all of us on paper by now. In some respects, we may know more about you than you do yourself."

Richard felt another pang of discomfort. For a considerable time people who really knew what they were doing had been observing him closely. Professionals had been digging into his past and present. They had probably scrutinized his immediate and extended family. They probably knew everything about Helen, too, and her parents, and his brother, and sister and —

"You must feel that your privacy has been invaded and that you've been deceived, but I assure you it was necessary. I know you'll accept and approve what's been done when you hear more about this group."

"What could possibly be so important about this group?" Richard said with a weak smile.

The others laughed politely. Vandenhorst continued. "That will soon be clear. Suffice it to say for now that the members of this group need to have complete confidence and trust in each other. One mistake, one act of disloyalty could ruin what the group exists to accomplish."

"And that is —?"

"I think you know already, but you'll hear more very soon. Let me just say that each person here shares your view of the state of this country. Our leaders are destroying our country. They are acting for their own partisan interests. Irresponsibility, greed, and corruption are organized and epidemic. The situation may be even worse than you think, Richard. The system is beyond reforming. We believe action has to be taken to save the country we love."

"What kind of action?"

"Well, that's the subject we are here to discuss. We're far advanced making plans. What was that phrase you used when we talked? 'Drastic action.' This is no mere discussion group. We talk to be able to act more efficiently."

"But why am I here? I'm a professor and an author. I'm not an activist, certainly not a politician."

"We know, but you have historical insight, a better sense than perhaps any of us of where we really are. From talking to you and studying you closely we know that you are also really tired of mere talk about the need for change. You're ready for action. If you could only find some good, strong allies, you would join them in an effort to save this country."

"But I have little of the kind of practical experience that would be needed."

"We have plenty of that already. You have something that's

just as necessary, Richard. You have an historically informed, keen awareness of the overall situation in which we find ourselves. You can relate particular issues to the larger picture, and you're a realist about what's in the realm of the possible. Let me tell you, Richard, I was very impressed by what you said in our conversation the other week about what will and will not work. On your own, you had reached a conclusion that had taken the rest of us a long time. You had understood with ease, as if it were self-evident, what some of us had realized only after extensive discussions."

"What I said was nothing exceptional."

"Not to you, Richard. But that's my point. You understand some things better than the rest of us."

"All right, but reflecting on life and acting to change it are two different things."

"But the first requirement of effective action is to understand the situation in which you have to act. You can be a great help as advisor to those of us who will have the primary responsibility for practical action — in the military, politics, media, business, and the police, for example. People without long views and a command of history can make terrible mistakes. There are some pretty knowledgeable and thoughtful people in our group. Most of us have high IQs and lots of relevant experience. Many of us read seriously and are interested in history and ideas, but we have spent most of our lives in practical action. You, Richard, can be a doer by providing something indispensable: an historical perspective, a better sense of what we're up against and how we can deal with the obstacles we face."

A few of the others nodded.

"I think you may have an exaggerated opinion of my capacity."

"We don't think so. You may not realize it, but you have admirers, not just among students and fellow professors. You have a reputation among people who think as we do. You've already had an influence. You have also been smart to hide from most people just how bad you think things are and that you think drastic action is needed. There's something else that's unusual and reassuring about you. You're a pretty straight arrow. It runs in your family. Personal integrity and an ability to understand what's happening in the world is a combination hard to beat. I've often asked myself if it's possible to have real understanding without character. The human capacity for self-deception and wishful thinking seems unlimited. Only people who are really honest with themselves will face facts that contradict what they want in the first place."

"I don't think there are any straight arrows."

"Very modest of you to say so, Richard, but you and I know that some people are reliable and realistic and others not."

Mrs. Vandenhorst appeared in the doorway and announced that dessert and coffee had been set out in the dining room. Vandenhorst asked the group to help themselves. "Let's resume our discussions in a quarter of an hour."

Those who had not yet spoken to Richard made it a point to talk to him and welcome him. They were obviously trying to make him feel at ease. He found it at once disturbing and satisfying that they assumed that he had joined them for good. He already had knowledge that could be dangerous to them.

As Vandenhorst had suggested, Richard did think he knew in general what the group existed to do. He just didn't know how far advanced they were in their planning and what their specific objectives were. He was astounded that people of such influence would be involved. They were obviously taking great risks. At the same time their involvement seemed a guarantee that, whatever they were doing or planning, it would be rather well thought out. But how could any plans of this kind possibly succeed in practice? Through their positions and connections they could make things happen. These were seasoned, highly sophisticated professionals or politicians. At least some of them had considerable intellectual acumen. Much as it cheered him that men of such caliber and power shared his concerns, he found it difficult to believe. He had persuaded himself that he wanted action rather than complaints, but he had to get used to the idea that these people had already gotten down to business and that he might now be doing the same. Did he actually want that drastic action as much as he had told himself?

Vandenhorst's remarks about Richard personally had put Richard on guard. Flattery would not pull him into anything that he did not truly believe in. But what had been said about the need for an historical and philosophical perspective was true. Men of practice tend to lack critical distance to the events of the day. It was a good sign that these conspirators did not worship at the shrine of the American can-do mentality that so often produced shortsighted, self-destructive action. The widespread American suspicion of ideas without obvious connection to practice was one of the reasons for the sad state of the country. Whatever the specifics of what the members of this group were planning, they would not behave like bulls in a china shop.

When the meeting started up again, each of the persons present spoke with surprising frankness and detail about their professional roles and what kind of actions they were authorized to take or could take in addition. Richard realized that the conspirators were rehearsing matters that must already be well known to each of them. They were doing it for his benefit. He was particularly surprised by the outspokenness of Pellegrini and Gates. They were obviously confident that nothing they said would reach the wrong ears. Pickett and Bates spoke of their wide contacts in the House and Senate, the White House, throughout the government and among top Washington lobbyists. Bunker and Vandenhorst gave summaries of their former military and governmental experience and of what kind of current connections they had. They were already people of stature by virtue of their former or current positions, but they grew in Richard's eyes as a result of their presentations. The others seemed to look to Vandenhorst as particularly authoritative. He appeared to have the widest experience and range of contacts. He was only nominally retired, was working full time and more.

Richard could see that if this group were to pull in a single direction it could wield great influence. Though each person who spoke was vague about just how he or she would coordinate with the others to enact existing plans, Richard noticed patterns of overlap that indicated the group's special strengths and general purpose. The areas of convergence were intelligence, the military, the Secret Service, the FBI, the police, political and economic affairs, and media. The intended action could be both pointed and daring and broad in scope.

It startled Richard to hear some of what the members of the group said about particular powerful individuals in the top echelons of America's political, financial, and media circles. They referred to blatantly corrupt practices, illegal or just immoral, as if they were known to everyone and required no comment. A picture emerged of the exercise of power at the highest levels that was not incompatible with what Richard had observed or suspected, but it suggested an egregiousness that made him think about Donald Kiefer's comments about high finance. Donald's father, the Wall Street investment banker, had been damaged by his association with unscrupulous people. The people in this room had operated in the vicinity of a similar ruthlessness, callousness, and deceit. How had they been affected? Their disgust had not discouraged them to the point of demoralization. They had endured, apparently without becoming tainted themselves. What appeared to have brought them together was indignation—no, something more, a cold, controlled fury that had become so habitual that it did not have to be voiced. They seemed to feel no need to make disparaging comments about the leading persons they discussed. They were more likely to note the aberration of powerful people who showed common decency.

Richard was reminded of St. Augustine, one of the theological founders of Christianity, who expected only the worst in politics. Because of original sin, Augustine believed, the government of states did not differ much in moral quality from the leadership of a band of robbers. Appearances sometimes to the contrary, sin was pervasive. Augustine's view had strongly influenced Christian political thought and not least the traditional American political mind. It was largely because of a fear of human sinfulness that the framers of the Constitution had been so intent on limiting and checking power. But Richard had always thought that those who most strongly emphasized the inherent depravity of human nature were too ready to disparage the human capacity for decency and nobility. By badmouthing human nature they pardoned their own shortcomings and excused themselves from the painful effort of improving their own characters. Western civilization at its best had, Richard thought, actually put a damper on the potential for evil and made it possible for human beings to show their better side. American constitutionalism and the traditional culture that backed it up had limited greed and the lust for dominance and increased the chances that admirable people would exercise influence. But those ennobling political and societal structures had been deteriorating for a long time. The worst people, most of whom the older society and its institutions would have been able to block or discourage, found it easier and easier to advance to the top. Their motives and actions poisoned what they touched and brought other people like them closer to the top.

As the conspirators talked about the general power structure that was destroying America they kept using a particular term, "the System." They meant a rather prolix configuration involving key figures in the executive, the Congress and the bureaucracy, but also on Wall Street and in the media. "The System" was deconstructing what remained of traditional America. Richard's only reservation was that the conspirators focused on the most obvious and tangible manifestations of a morally and financially corrupt power structure, the phenomena most directly relevant to the need for corrective emergency action. They did not discuss the ultimate moral-spiritual and cultural sources of the corruption. They seemed only partially alert to the central role played by the universities, the arts, the entertainment industry in the broadest sense, "Hollywood" in particular, and the music and publishing industry. It was largely from these quarters that the self-indulgent worldview had spread that both fostered "the System" and made people accepting of its perversities. Not emphasizing this influence might be excusable in the present context, Richard reflected, in that cultural and intellectual damage inflicted by generations could not be undone or remedied through practical emergency action.

"There are three other members of this committee," Gordon Bunker said after he had been the last to describe his experience, operational reach and current activities. "Two are active military, one is Secret Service. You'll meet them soon, Richard."

When Vandenhorst asked Richard for some of his impressions of what he had heard Richard felt no particular reluctance to speak. The frankness to which he had been exposed encouraged him to be forthright.

"I've learned a few things about some of the rulers of my country that I didn't know," he said. All the more reason to try to make a change. The resources of this group also impress me. It could generate some significant countermeasures. You've done extensive planning, and I think I can see in what general direction you are headed. What I would like to know is how these assets relate to a single, central plan? What is the ultimate objective and just how do you expect to achieve it?" Richard spoke with a trace of impatience.

"Richard," said Gordon Bunker in his rather loud military voice, "I'm not surprised that you would get right to the heart of the matter. I picked up that trait in you from the beginning. Of course you want to know the concrete specifics of our plans. But, please, be a little patient. In some respects the plans are sill evolving. In fact, there is more than one general plan. We have to be ready for different circumstances. And we have some areas of fruitful disagreement. Before we can know what we may hope to accomplish, we have to take a more complete inventory of resources that may be at our disposal and determine just what synergies are possible. A number of people must still be cautiously approached, recruited, and influenced. Our preparations are far advanced, but much remains to be done."

*Far advanced*, Richard thought. Was it possible? Bunker, the admiral with an interest in history, must first have contacted him a year ago. Presumably, the group had already existed then in some form. For how long?

Senator Pickett spoke. He still had some of the voice and manner of a senator on the floor of the Senate or in a committee hearing. He spoke slowly in a southern drawl. "Again, what we can do must await some additional recruitment and a more complete assessment of what is possible. We must not allow any wishful thinking. And we have to proceed very carefully not to jeopardize our plans."

Randy Gates, the man from CIA, broke in: "There are those of us who think that caution and care can be taken too far and become an excuse for undue delay and inaction. Planning, planning, planning—yes, we do need it, but long experience tells me that you can't possibly avoid complications even after thinking everything through in detail. Any military officer will tell you the same thing. I used to be one. I served in Vietnam. There are going to be bad surprises, and you have to be prepared to deal with them as they arise—not by hand-wringing, but by decisive action."

"We know, Randy, we know," Vandenhorst said with a smile.

Pellegrini spoke in a thin, articulate voice: "The preparations are so difficult because they can't be made in the same way that you organize, say, an election campaign. You must work without seeming to be doing anything at all. Look at this group. It doesn't exist. Only we who sit here now and three other people know about its composition. By the way, Richard, the other three know that you're here tonight and are pleased about it. Perhaps fifty other people know about the existence of this group and know that it is calling the shots or is near the center of decision-making, but those other people typically know the names of just one or two of the members. Yet others know about the overall general organizational structure, but interact with us only through intermediaries they trust."

Vandenhorst said, "Today's presentations were supposed to fill you in, Richard, and to let you get to know us better."

"I suppose I should be flattered that you have that much confidence in me and trust me as much as that."

"We do. Let me prove it to you. There are a number of other groups that also do not exist but that are working away at aspects of our total effort. Some of them have weighty responsibilities. One deals with business and the economy. Lisa, our woman at the Fed, is in continuous contact with them. One deals with military matters. Guess who is our main contact with them?" Gordon Bunker smiled. "One deals with foreign affairs," Vandenhorst continued. "I'm in touch with them. One coordinates our efforts in the intelligence agencies. Randy Gates is on top of that, gets some help from Doug Pellegrini. Our man at the Secret Service, who's not here, also oversees our contacts with the FBI. Doug assists Robert Bates with overseeing the group dealing with media and communications. We don't have a person representing that field in the central group. We're just now forming two other groups, one covering academia and one covering infrastructure. And there are other groups below the ones I just mentioned. The network of people who are more or less clued in forms a kind of pyramid of partly overlapping responsibilities. You get the picture. None of these groups are very large—a couple of them have only three or four members. The core membership in the pyramid are at present no more than just over a hundred, but we can expect many others to be useful to us. Those others are more tangentially connected to those who are fully committed to our cause, but they will, without knowing precisely what they are doing, be carrying out the instructions of our people. You would probably be rather impressed if you knew the identities of those in the pyramid at various levels. When the time comes, all of these people, acting in concert, will be able to make a big difference. We don't circulate the names of people throughout the pyramid. Usually only one person in each subgroup, the one in whom we have the greatest confidence, knows who the contact person is in the group that spawned it—this one or one below it. Each person in this room has some responsibility for one or two of the subgroups."

"And how do you know that this group is not a creature of some other, more august group?"

There was general laughter.

"Well?"

"You'll just have to take our word for it," Lisa DeLeon said to more laughter. She continued in a calm and authoritative voice. "As you start working with us you'll soon have the whole picture."

"But how can I work with you without knowing exactly what we're trying to accomplish?"

Gates responded, "For the safety of all involved and not to tip off our enemies, we have to operate on a need to know basis. As a member of this group you'll soon know all there is to know, but for the time being we ask you not to press too hard. There's a lot to learn. One thing at a time. Nothing will be held back in the end."

Pellegrini spoke up again. "It was proposed that you should be recruited for another group, the one that coordinates efforts related to think tanks and universities. You would have been the coordinator of that group and the contact between that group and this one. You would be a natural leader for the more intellectual types, but Herbert argued, and we think he was right, that you would be wasted in that role . . . Sorry, that didn't come out right." Pellegrini made an apologetic gesture and quickly continued, "You belong with us. We need you here for the reasons already stated. But you should supervise the group of academics and intellectuals."

"Who are the other three members of this group?"

Bates, the aide to the minority leader of the House, spoke for the first time. His strong glasses made it hard to read his expression.

He seemed eager to reassure Richard. "You'll meet all three in due time. You'll find that they are at least as accomplished and influential as the people you've met. They have to be very careful about how they conduct themselves."

"You can say that again," Vandenhorst said. " The same is true for everybody here."

"And who's the leader of this whole effort?" Richard blurted out.

"Really, Richard, you want to know everything right away, don't you?" said Bunker in a jocular manner.

Vandenhorst said: "Believe it or not, Richard, we've been able to act collegially, by consensus."

"That must mean that you haven't yet gotten to the really difficult issues, the really tough choices." Richard was again surprised by his own bluntness. He continued: "If you're going to deal with something as big and complex and demanding as what you're contemplating, you're bound to encounter strong disagreements. In tense, difficult circumstances, there's no way to please or accommodate everybody. You can't always take the time to call everybody together and let the majority decide. It's just not practical. Besides, you can't expect the majority to know best. People have different levels of experience and knowledge and judgment. In high-pressure situations, somebody's got to call the shots."

The room fell silent. Except for Lisa DeLeon, who threw a furtive glance at Vandenhorst, nobody looked at anybody else.

Then Vandenhorst spoke again. "This group did not form at random. The very opposite. We see eye to eye. We are agreed on the general course that has to be pursued."

"I understand," Richard said, "but when the going gets rough I would think that somebody's going to have to decide for the rest." In the corner of his eye Richard noticed that Gordon Bunker and Randy Gates nodded.

"We know, Richard," Bunker said.

"You seem to assume that we may face rough times," said Pellegrini, a smile playing on his lips.

"Something tells me that what's being planned will not be a cakewalk."

Richard noticed that Vandenhorst was smiling slightly and looking rather pleased. The others wore more unreadable expressions.

Suddenly Gates spoke. "You're right of course. We have to be prepared for some tough sledding. Everything's not going to fall neatly into place. We have to have plans for handling disasters.

And yes, we have to have an agreement on who will call the shots in emergencies." The others said nothing.

"Well, Lisa and gentlemen," said Vandenhorst, "this seems to be a good time to adjourn. The next meeting will be announced in the usual way." The gathering was suddenly at an end.

As they left, each member of the group made a point of saying good-bye to Richard. "Good to have you with us." "Glad you've joined us." "See you next time."

Richard lingered to be able to speak privately with Vandenhorst, which the latter seemed to expect. Waiting for the others to leave Richard noticed that the house was quieter than before. During the discussions he had heard a distant humming sound that continued even when the fan of the house's heating unit switched off. He had wondered if Mrs. Vandenhorst might be using some kind of electrical appliance working at a household project. Now the humming had stopped. In the dining room the young man he had seen earlier in the evening was bending over something that looked like a large car battery and gathering up a black cord.

"Herbert, everybody here seems to assume that I'm now a member of this group, but I need to know more."

"Of course you do, and you'll get all the details. By the time the group meets next time, you'll have a good sense of just what's being planned."

"You seem pretty certain that I'll be at the next meeting."

"Yes, I am. I may know you better than you think. You do not want another discussion club, am I right? You've long been looking for sophisticated, forceful action that might save this country. And you know that's what this group is about."

Richard nodded. "I'm encouraged. It's not just the people involved and the breadth of your approach, it's also how you're organized. I'd thought myself that something like this structure would be the way to proceed."

"Why am I not surprised to hear you say that?"

"You must have been organizing and planning for a long time."

"Yes, a few in this circle are starting to get impatient. They want to act very soon. They're concerned that the longer we wait, the greater the danger of detection. There are other considerations as well."

"And how long have you been at this?"

"Depends on what you mean. A few of us started to collect like-minded, reliable people a couple of years ago. We've proceeded very carefully and deliberately. As for the details of our plans, our thinking has changed somewhat as we have assessed what resources will be available and as we have gone through different plausible schemes. In recent months we've been thinking along three basic lines. One centers on what you might call the ideal scenario."

"Can you be a little more precise?"

"Richard, please don't press me. We shouldn't be talking any longer. Security reasons. Give it some time. I think your own guesses will be rather close to the mark. You understand more than you're letting on. When we give you the specifics, I wouldn't be surprised if you've reached similar conclusions."

"Perhaps so."

They said goodnight.

Walking to his car Richard felt as if he were leaving his old life behind and would never be able to return to it. Whether he stayed in the group or left it, everything he did would be colored by what he had just learned. He had long been fretting about his failure to *do* something. His conscience had been nagging him mercilessly to find some avenue for doing his duty, but he had been unable to decide what it was. The path that had suggested itself to him more and more simply did not lie in the realm of the possible.

All had changed. He found himself in the middle of a serious, far-advanced, well-organized effort involving some very influential and sophisticated people. If he were to disagree with what they were contemplating, he could not assume that his was the superior judgment.

His earlier assessment to the contrary, and to his complete surprise, the prerequisites for potentially successful drastic action might actually be present. Now that he knew about this group, his choice seemed clear-cut: either stop his grousing and complaining and retreat into the woodwork, or commit himself fully to the work of the group. He no longer had any excuse for procrastinating. But to choose the latter course would be to forego the pleasure, security, and predictability of his earlier life — to risk it all. Life would be wholly different. Dark emotions descended on him when he thought of his family: Helen, John, and Anne. He loved them. He would pull them with him into uncertainty and danger. He had a strong intuition that he could not let them, not even Helen, know what he was about to do. He would in effect volunteer them without their consent. But he had no choice.

His home was a mere ten minutes away by car. He drove slowly. It was almost midnight. The traffic lights had turned to the blinking mode.

Risk all? Was he ready? Those other men and Lisa seemed to

be. Others were too.

When he returned home he was glad to find Helen asleep. As he slipped into bed, she mumbled, "How was the meeting?"

"Oh, nothing special." He kissed her cheek. "Sleep well."

# CHAPTER 27

Back at the hotel after her lunch with Ferguson, Helen dialed her parents. It was 3:00 PM in Paris and 9:00 AM in Washington. Her father picked up immediately. She told him that the children should arrive at Dulles according to schedule.

"We'll be at the airport in plenty of time. How are you, Helen?"

"It was hard to let them go. Annie was really upset. At least now they can get back to some kind of normal life."

"Don't you worry about them. We'll take good care of them."

"I'll call often."

"There's something else. Hubert called from Charleston. He's hired a private detective up here, and he asked us to let him into your house to look for clues to Richard's disappearance. Do you have any objections? Hubert seems to have a lot of confidence in this detective."

"I've no objection. Do let him in."

"Anything else?"

"Not at the moment. We'll call you when the kids have arrived."

"I will be by the phone here at the hotel. Thanks, Dad. I should run."

"Mom sends her love. Take *care*, Helen!"

She hung up. Her father's mentioning the private detective made her think again about the danger that someone might be listening in on her telephone conversations. Hubert had mentioned the same possibility. If Richard had managed to escape from people who posed a danger to him and had gone into hiding, those looking for him would be very interested in any phone call he might make to his wife. Or people who had abducted him might want to know what the police were doing. There were yet other angles. She had to be careful. Would the hotel let her use another telephone? If they did, how could she trust the management to keep that information to themselves? For calls that might involve sensitive information she should probably use a pay phone in the vicinity of the hotel. From movies and novels she had gotten the impression that pay phones were the least vulnerable to intrusion. To be even safer, she might use different pay phones. If she was under surveillance, the more unpredictable she was, the better.

Was she being irrationally cautious and suspicious? But too much was at stake to take any unnecessary risks. Using pay phones would be inconvenient and might be a complete waste of time and effort, but she had no other demands on her time. She would tell those who called her about potentially sensitive matters that she would call them back shortly. One drawback was that if the caller's telephone number was unknown to her, she would have to ask for it, and then any listener would know the number also. Another problem was that a listener would eventually realize that she did not call people back from her hotel phone. Surveillance could then be expanded. She should perhaps call her parents and Hubert from a pay phone at set times. She would let them know to confine conversations with her at the hotel to non-sensitive matters. They could agree on a code to alert the other of a need to talk more privately. Did she need to worry about telephone taps back in the United States as well?

If she was truly under observation by someone with great resources—the CIA?—she probably could not protect against eavesdropping. Movies and novels had given her the idea that someone determined to listen in on another's conversation had other means than the old-fashioned telephone tap. If Richard's disappearance was in some way connected with American national security, the CIA or some other agency would probably have more sophisticated technology. How many times in movies had she not seen people in a van parked in the street keeping tabs on someone in a nearby building? Whenever she left the hotel she would look for suspicious-looking vehicles or persons. She had the impression that not even calls between cell phones were exempt from invasion.

She would make any sensitive calls to Hubert from a pay phone. She decided to take an inventory of such phones in the area around *Le Vieux Logis*. She strolled with no apparent purpose through the neighborhood to locate a couple of more or less usable and convenient pay telephones within easy walking distance, which took some time. The spread of cell phones had reduced the need for public telephones. She found one in a post office and one telephone booth in the street. They were old enough to require coins rather than cards. She would have to get a large supply of coins for international calls. She might use a credit card, but she guessed that it would increase the risk of detection. To minimize the difficulty of paying for calls she could ask the person in America to dial her back at the number of the telephone she was using. She started to make small purchases and ask for change. Then, inside a rather large hotel, *La Michelle,* which was located two blocks from her own, she discovered three old-fashioned telephone booths next to each other just off the main lobby that also could not be seen from the lobby. They were located on the way to the restrooms. She decided to make these booths her primary location for sensitive calls. They would probably be accessible at any time, and she would be much less visible there than elsewhere. The hotel even had three different entrances. She could vary her route and pick a different booth each time. She thought of moving to *La Michelle,* but she had left her telephone number at *Le Vieux Logis* with several people. Most importantly, Richard would try to reach her there. Also, any surveillance team would soon discover the change. She might just as well stay where she was. It would be considerably cheaper.

She had to call Hubert. In one of the hotel telephone booths she took out all her Euro coins. She read the instructions on the telephone and then put a large number of coins into the slot and dialed the international access code, the country code and Hubert's cell phone. A blurred recorded French voice announced that she had done something wrong. She groaned in frustration and hung up. Money rattled into the little container at the bottom of the telephone, and some coins spilled on to the floor of the tiny booth. It made her think of slot machines in a casino. She had to get out of the booth and get down on her knees to retrieve the coins. She thought she might have gotten one of the digits in a long string wrong and tried dialing again. The result was the same. This time she caught the disgorged coins. She felt like banging the phone. She tried to calm down and sat silently concentrating. Why were instructions always, always confusing and somehow not quite applicable to the actual situation? She finally decided to omit one of the digits. She finally got a connection. She heard the familiar, American sound of a telephone ringing at the other end. Hubert picked up almost immediately.

"Darling! I was hoping you'd call. How *are* you?"

"Not too well, I'm afraid. The children are on the way to D.C., and there is no news about Richard."

"Dottie and I are so worried about you. We are pretty agitated ourselves, but at least we have each other. You're all alone in Paris. You must be having a terrible time. I'm still thinking that I should come over. We finally told mother last night, felt we had to — what if she heard something from somebody else? She was very upset. She's still not quite over her illness. But she's OK."

Helen told him about her decision to make calls about

sensitive matters from a pay phone. They agreed on a code for announcing when such matters needed to be discussed. Either party would mention a fictional name, taken from the Bible, in some invented but routine-sounding context: "Did Elizabeth call about the Georgetown Garden Tour?" "Gabriel should be able to help with the car," or the like. Or they would relay some information that would sound meaningful to an outsider but mean nothing to those on the telephone. To conceal that secret communication was taking place they should occasionally speak about the search for Richard. Hubert would find a secretive way of letting Helen's parents and the children know about the new method of communicating. Helen would try to make it a habit to call Hubert at certain times.

"Darling, you make it sound as if you're going to be doing this for weeks. We have to be more optimistic than *that*!"

"You think so?"

"Of course I do."

"We should talk about that private eye and other things. But before we do, would you mind calling me back on this pay phone. My coins will run out."

"Of course, darling, give me the number." She did and they hung up.

A minute went by, then two, then three. Hubert was obviously having trouble. Why did everything have to be so difficult? Perhaps he could not call internationally to a pay phone, she thought. Then, when she was beginning to think that she had better call Hubert back, the telephone rang. It worked!

"Sorry," Hubert said. "I had to look up the country code for France, had to find a telephone book. And then I got mixed up on the international access code."

Helen summarized what had happened in the search since their previous conversation. She gave Hubert her initial rather favorable impression of the French detectives. She described her lunch with Ferguson and explained why she was more suspicious of him than ever.

"You obviously can't trust him," Hubert said. "But why in the world would a top American diplomat be involved in Richard's disappearance? It has to mean that there's some major national security aspect. What's so darn mystifying is that you, his wife, are being kept in the dark. I'm hoping that the private eye I hired will get us some answers. The private detective I use here in South Carolina, who's first rate, says he's a good deal more than your average gumshoe. He once worked for the FBI and has investigated pretty complicated and challenging cases. He's got at least one person helping him. I've told him to give the case everything he's got. He will give me his first report tomorrow."

"Have you thought any more about that 'big thing' that Richard may have gotten involved in?"

"Unless we get some other clues, I'll go on the assumption that there is a connection between the big thing and what's happened in Paris. I didn't tell the private eye yet about that conversation I had with Dick, but I said that Dick may have been more than a professor teaching and writing books and *may* have been involved in something secret."

"Be sure to let me know immediately what the detective finds out."

"Of course, darling. By the way, the detective will talk to Dick's assistant — Don Turelli, isn't that his name?"

"Ronald Turello."

"He and Dick are pretty close, aren't they?"

"They are. Richard really likes and respects him. Turello must have been at National University for three or four years. He got his M.A. with Richard, and Richard is now directing his doctoral dissertation. He's been Richard's helper or assistant for at least two years. But, Hubert, you think Richard can tell Ron about some secret business that he wouldn't even tell me about?"

"Probably not, but Turello may know things you wouldn't have heard about, meetings Richard attended, people he met, and so on. He may have overheard telephone conversations and the like."

Helen told Hubert that she would call the French police to get the latest information.

"Keep me informed, darling, and do let me know if I could do some good over there."

"For now, let's just stay in contact as we decided." They hung up.

What would she do next? She was anxious to know what Duparc might have discovered. She took out the business card he had given her. She thought of moving to one of the other booths but realized that she was being irrationally cautious. She sighed, put two of her few remaining coins in the slot, and dialed the number.

Duparc answered after several rings.

"Duparc."

"This is Helen Bittenberg. Sorry to bother you. Is there anything new about my husband?"

"Mrs. Bittenberg. I don't think we should be talking on the telephone."

"I'm calling from a pay phone," she said quickly.

Duparc did not answer immediately.

"Still, it's better to speak in person. I'm also in the middle of something at the moment." His voice gave no indication of how their work was going. His French accent seemed more pronounced on the telephone.

"Then can I meet you somewhere?" Helen said.

"Yes, but let's wait until tomorrow morning. That will give us some more time to follow up a couple of leads."

"*Leads!*? You're making *progress*? You have some idea of what happened to my husband?" She realized that she sounded more like an excitable child than a middle-aged woman.

"Please, Mrs. Bittenberg, we'll talk tomorrow. We could come to your hotel. Or would you like to come to my office? It's on Îls de la Cité, not very far from your hotel. You may know the island in the Seine. Notre Dame is on the same island." Helen said she knew the island. He gave her the address.

"I'll come to your office."

"We'll see each other at 10:00. Just ask for me in the reception. Good-bye."

If Duparc had discovered anything of great importance, surely he would have been willing to talk to her right away. But his setting up a meeting had to mean movement of some sort. It tormented her to recognize that what he told her the next morning could just as well be very bad as good.

She collected her things and stumbled out of the little phone booth, feeling a need for fresh air. She felt hot, and when she passed a mirror in the corridor outside she noticed that her cheeks were flushed. She also realized that she desperately needed to go to the bathroom. There were restrooms just a few steps beyond the telephone booths, so she did not have to attract attention by asking for directions. Physically relieved but emotionally tense and tired, she left the hotel through one of the side exits. She took deep breaths only to realize that she was not filling her lungs with fresh air. It was hot and rather humid, and rush hour was again filling Paris with noxious fumes.

What to do next? She had no plans for the rest of the day and evening except to be at the hotel by the time the children had cleared immigration and customs at Dulles airport. She still had a considerable wait.

Helen told herself that she had to do something about her eating. She needed strength. She was permanently nervous. Sometimes adrenaline was pumping out of control, which must accelerate her metabolism and increase her need for calories. Yet in the last few days she had eaten less than was normal for her. She was used to eating small portions to keep her figure, but now she had certainly lost weight. How to restore some of her peace of mind, relax her taut nerves? She would try to have a glass of wine or even two before dinner in the hope that the alcohol would take the edge off her anxiety and help her appetite. And then she wanted to sleep, sleep, sleep. Wouldn't sheer exhaustion finally knock her out and grant her a full, restful night?

Taking a roundabout route back to the hotel she came upon a square about the size of a small city block with some trees and brushes. The square was not quite an oasis — the ground was more sandy than grassy — but she sat down on a bench in the shade. The heat and humidity were nowhere close to what they were in Washington in the summer. It was really a lovely late afternoon, she realized, only she could not enjoy it. A dog and its middle-aged male owner strolled past. He was a good citizen carrying a plastic bag to be able to pick up any droppings. A mother holding two small children by their hands came in the other direction. She had probably just picked them up at a daycare center on her way home, Helen speculated. Not all Parisians could be on vacation in August. Hospitals, police stations, the Metro, and so on had to be open. Restaurants, museums, hotels, etc., had to serve the hordes of tourists. A young man in a dark suit, white shirt, and tie walked through the park seemingly on autopilot, a briefcase dangling from one hand — a banker perhaps who had volunteered to work in August. He might have come from the Metro or a bus. Or perhaps he was one of the lucky few who could walk to his place of work. An elderly woman walked slowly past with a baguette under her arm. What Helen was seeing, she reflected, was everyday Paris routine. Life was normal. Some of these people were tired and a little grumpy. They had their frustrations and sorrows, but most of them were looking forward to dinner and being with loved ones. It was an almost idyllic scene in the large city. But did these people appreciate the great gift of ordinary life?

As Helen looked around this park, where the city tried to breathe, she noticed to her right a small church tucked in among the houses. She got up and walked towards it. She had not been to a church for almost two weeks. Why did church so often have to yield when normal family patterns were disrupted, as by travel? Was the need to be there any lesser then? Was everything else suddenly more significant? Was it more important to see the Eiffel Tower? How easy it was to come up with excuses! For example, in France virtually all the churches were Roman Catholic, and she was not an RC. Pitiful! She could attend a service anyway. She could pray, and she could confess her sins. One of her acquaintances, who had very Protestant attitudes, would even take communion in Roman Catholic churches. Who were the RCs, he said, to reserve the sacrament for their own people? The gall!

She entered the church and felt the familiar cool somewhat musty air. Candles were burning in a few places. Several people were kneeling in the pews. Some of them might have been there for morning mass, too, she thought. The only daylight came through stained glass windows above the entrance in the back and behind the altar. There were no other windows. The church stood tight up against other buildings on both sides. It was not particularly attractive. The architecture was mediocre to poor, and the decorations were no better. She was often disappointed when she took a peek inside French churches. Were not the odds better in England or Germany that random churches would convey some of the divine mystery? Did English and German church architects have better taste? Did that mean that they had a deeper religious sensibility? Or was the aesthetics of a house of worship a secondary, tertiary concern? Beauty in architecture and liturgy might be desirable — it had to be — but a church was a church. It was sacred ground, a house of God, even if it happened to offend aesthetic sensibilities. In the same way, a mediocre, less than virtuous priest was still a priest. On the other hand, was not an ugly church much like bad television reception or interference on a telephone line — obstacles to communication and understanding?

Helen seated herself in a pew a few rows from the altar. She put down her things and knelt. She looked up at the undistinguished crucifix and the pedestrian decorations behind the altar. She told herself that what mattered was the intention behind these works of art, not the execution. She tried to shut out the turmoil and anxiety of her life as well as the great city that pulsated and made noise outside. Peace reigned inside these walls. She stayed for a long time.

# CHAPTER 28

A few days after the gathering at his house, Herbert Vandenhorst called Richard to arrange a meeting. They decided to have lunch together, and they met at the student union building on the National University campus. It had been snowing since the early morning. Richard had expected that they would eat at the university faculty club, but Vandenhorst suggested that they drive to a restaurant a few blocks away.

"Not a good day for driving," Richard said. The climate in Washington, D.C., usually made driving on snow days more hazardous than in most cities,

"Not to worry. I've lived in Washington for many years." Lowering his voice, Vandenhorst added: "To tell you the truth, I also try to be a little unpredictable in my movements."

"You think you're being followed?"

"No, but better safe than sorry."

They walked to the large campus garage, where Vandenhorst's car, an uninteresting Ford Taurus, was parked.

Vandenhorst had the car radio on. The announcers were dramatizing the snowy weather in the usual manner. The atmosphere on days like this was always the same in the Washington area. The possibility of school closings and other cancellations created excitement among school children, university students, teachers and others. The disruption of normal life and the relaxation of expectations made for cheerfulness and camaraderie.

Vandenhorst drove just a few blocks east to Connecticut Avenue, where he pulled into a side street, and found a parking place. They walked out to Connecticut Avenue and went into a restaurant near the Uptown movie theater. It was almost empty. The snow was keeping lunch-eaters away. Vandenhorst asked for a table out of the way.

After the waiter had left with their orders for drinks Vandenhorst said in a low voice, "Any thoughts about the meeting the other night?"

"Quite a few. Where do you want me to start?"

"Are you with us for good?"

Richard was surprised by the abruptness of the question. He sat quietly for a moment.

"There was never any real doubt in my mind. Yes, Herbert, I'm with you for good."

"I knew you would say that."

"How could you be so certain?"

"I know how upset you are about the state of our country. What was said in the meeting of our group probably didn't lessen your concern. Some terrible people are running the country. And I know you are sick of just thinking and talking about how bad things are. You were probably impressed with the people you met. You could see that we know what we're doing and that we have the wherewithal to do it credibly."

"I was glad to learn that people with that kind of influence and experience think as we do. Apparently there aren't very many of them, but they make up in quality for what they lack in numbers."

"You may be surprised to learn who some of the rest are. A few are at least as prominent as the ones you met."

"I was very surprised to see Pellegrini and Bunker at the meeting, let me tell you. I wonder who else I know will turn out to have been keeping tabs on me."

"I hope you're not too offended."

"It bothered me that you had checked me out so thoroughly — who wants to have his privacy invaded? — but it was also reassuring. It shows you're leaving little to chance. Not to have taken a close look before trying to recruit me would have been reckless."

"We cannot afford any mistakes."

"I still wonder why you approached me of all people and risked bringing me right into the center of things? I would have fitted well into the group for academics and think tank people."

"We do need someone like you right at the center to advise us, someone who hasn't spent his life buried in practical affairs. I and a couple of the others have been looking for someone like you for a good while. I proposed your name because of what I knew about you and your family. Doug Pellegrini, Gordon Bunker, and I had the assignment of sizing you up. You were a remarkably good fit, though not exactly the way we'd expected. You are less interested in practical politics than the person we thought we had in mind, but you are more cognizant of the situation and the need for drastic action than we could have anticipated. You'd even thought about what kind of drastic action might work. So we wouldn't have to spend a lot of time breaking you in. In fact, from the beginning we could learn something from you. The only question was whether you would join us. After our conversation at the Metropolitan Club I never doubted it. It was not so much what you expressly said, although it confirmed my hunch, as your general demeanor in combination with what I know about your family and especially your grandfather. Even in the unlikely event that you would turn us down, you would not betray us."

"So you were right. Now tell me, who's the real leader of this effort?"

"For now, let me just say that, although we've been able to work on a consensual basis in the steering group, one person has been the first among equals at this planning stage. We also have a kind of informal executive committee of four. At the acute operational stage, a particular person will have to be in charge for a while."

"You're evading my question."

"Be a little patient."

The waiter returned with their drinks, and they gave him their food order. Vandenhorst sat silently with his hands resting on the table and his fingers around his glass of beer. He looked searchingly at Richard.

"There's something else you haven't asked me yet," Vandenhorst said.

"Yes, I know, the big question: What exactly is the plan?"

"What do you think it is?"

Richard said nothing for a few seconds. Then he leaned forward, putting his face closer to Vandenhorst's. Turning his voice almost into a whisper, he said:

"You'll try to take over the government, but the question is how? The plan probably includes removing the president and the vice president and several other leading figures, probably killing the first two. You intend to move on key government and media institutions and put into effect an elaborate disinformation and propaganda campaign. You'll probably blame the killings on Islamic terrorists and justify the coup as necessary to protect America from further attacks."

"Very good, very good. I knew you would get directly to the heart of the matter."

"What I wonder about is just how you plan to accomplish this feat and how the coup will be organized."

"There's no single plan. There are several, and you'll now be able to influence our thinking. We're preparing for different possible circumstances. I'm hoping that we will be able to use what we call 'Plan A.' It would produce the least disruption and would be by far the best from the point of view of giving the new government legitimacy in the eyes of the public. Some in our group think that Plan A is too optimistic, a luxury agenda, as it were, too dependent on all circumstances being right. That's not the real world, they say. We have to be ready for a less subtle, more confrontational, more violent approach. If Plan A can't be executed because the time and the circumstances aren't right, we can't wait around indefinitely for an ideal scenario to become possible."

"Are there tensions within the group on this issue?"

"None of them serious. Virtually everybody prefers Plan A, but it means waiting for a rather long time and that much has to go just right. Most disagreements are about the amount of force and number of deaths that we must be willing to accept. Some insist that we must be prepared to use the maximum force available."

"So what's plan A?"

"I'll fill you in completely very soon. Let me just say that it involves an associate member of our group, if that's the right term. You may not meet him for a long time. We're very concerned to keep the connection to him under wraps. So is he. He does not participate in our meetings, but he's very close to our efforts, works every day with one of our members. He has to be extremely careful." Although there was nobody near them in the restaurant Vandenhorst was keeping his voice very low.

"One of the reasons I'm hoping that plan A can be executed is that I agree with you, Richard, that achieving an appearance of legitimacy is crucial to our success. We must do everything in our power to persuade Americans that when we take over we are safeguarding America, trying to preserve the Constitution even."

"Otherwise we would have to rely entirely on force and fear," Richard said, "and that would be very risky without having full control of the military—something I doubt is even remotely possible. We must present the American people with a *fait accompli*, or with what *looks* like an accomplished fact, and firmly establish its legitimacy in the mind of the public. Potential opponents must get an overwhelming sense that there would be no point in even trying to undo what's happened."

"Precisely, and at the same time we have to be ready to put down opposition."

"I would like more operational specifics, but I guess I'll have to wait."

"Don't be impatient. We have yet to reach agreement about all the details. A consensus is emerging, and you, Richard, can affect it."

The waiter brought their food. They turned to their own

personal circumstances. Richard told Vandenhorst about his other commitments and about the need now to keep up appearances in his academic surroundings and at home. He did not want Helen or the children to know anything. Not to tell her would require a great deal of deception, which made him uncomfortable. Vandenhorst nodded to himself. "My own wife, Celeste, knows, but she's been my close confidante in all my professional activities for forty years. She's really sharp, a good advisor, and a good woman."

"It didn't take me long to realize that the only thing of any importance that made me hesitate about joining your group was worries about how my involvement would affect Helen and the children. Even if I don't tell her what I'm up to, they're directly affected and put at risk. I'm thinking that by being silent I'll give them at least *some* protection. But I won't like going behind Helen's back — won't like it one bit.

"Do you think your wife would oppose your involvement?"

"I've asked myself that, and I think she would. It's not that we disagree fundamentally about the state of America, but I expect she would not want me to take such a risk and expose the family to danger."

"Do you think she would be flabbergasted if she knew," Vandenhorst asked.

"Not if she has listened to me all this time we've been married. But I don't think she quite realizes how worried I've been about the U.S. and how much I have fretted over my inability to do anything about what's going wrong. She might also be surprised that there are people besides me, substantial people like you and the others, who think like me and are ready to act. I was very surprised myself. I think Helen has always assumed that I'm one of very few people, a little of a crank perhaps, although one with all of his faculties basically intact."

Vandenhorst brought the conversation around to Richard's role in the group. He envisioned him being like a minister without a portfolio, a roving advisor. He would also be the contact person for the individual chairing the subgroup of academics and other intellectuals.

"Academics and intellectuals are often unpredictable," Vandenhorst said. "They're sometimes impractical or afraid of action. God knows, nowadays there aren't all that many of them who can even tell up from down. And of the few who might understand, only a very small number can be expected to be reliably on our side. It took us a long time to assemble the group that's now operating."

"Who is the coordinator of that group?"

"You have no idea?"

Richard shook his head.

"A president of one of the Washington area universities."

"You must be kidding."

"No, it's Charlton Stephens at Federal University."

"Stephens?" Richard's surprise was complete. "That I would never have guessed."

"Good. Charlton is very cautious, plays things very close to his vest. But I can assure you he's with us all the way. And he's got excellent contacts."

"Extraordinary. I've met him a couple of times—he used to be a pretty decent professor of philosophy—and I remember discussing the state of U.S. academia with him. He seemed receptive to my point of view, but he spoke in broad generalities and gave me some platitude about there being room for improvement."

"Well, he didn't know you very well, did he?"

"No, but I would never have expected him to be one of us."

"You'll probably have more such surprises. Many of our people have had the good sense to keep their deepest convictions hidden. I'll let Charlton know that he can expect a call from you. And if you think that he, a university president, may be offended by having to report to a mere professor, forget it. He's a team player. A couple of the members of our group have known him for a long time, and we've checked him out and tested him very carefully."

"Do these other groups know just what's being planned?"

"Yes and no. The key figures do, but the further you get from the center, the more diffuse the outlines of the plan have to be, partly for security reasons."

"Creating groups for the media and journalism must have been a priority. You'll need a large number of people in key positions who are prepared to do, write, and say the right things at the right moment. But the media and journalism are dominated by people who help generate and justify the present order of things."

"This has been one of our greatest challenges," Vandenhorst said. "People who want a career in those fields have to give proof of allegiance to the reigning mind-set, at least not be dissenters in any serious way. But, believe it or not, even in the networks, big cable channels, and newspapers there are people, a few in pretty high positions, who are disgusted. Most of them have hidden their real views, but they've gotten angrier and angrier. We've been collecting people of this kind."

"What about the military?"

"We're in fairly good shape there. One of the problems is that nowadays much of the brass is made up of careerists and technocrats with graduate degrees. That's what the system wants and produces. It doesn't want independent-minded officers, potential troublemakers. The system doesn't want Douglas MacArthurs. 'Yes, sir,' is more like it. That's one of the reasons why the issue of legitimacy is so important. The brass must feel after a coup that they are receiving orders from a proper authority that is also friendly to their interests. A few generals and admirals, several on active duty, are already firmly in our corner, but only a couple of them are likely to be able to provide actual military assets. We cannot assume that generals and admirals as a group will back us—too many of them are a part of the system, though many joined it kicking and screaming. One big source of sympathy for our cause will be that the brass have seen too many American kids sent out to fight and die for what the brass know are not really American interests. Gordon Bunker is a hero to some of them, not just because he was a brilliant soldier, but also because he stood up to cocky desk warriors whom the special interests had installed at the top of the Pentagon. Gordon is of course our contact person for the military group. If we're really lucky, one of our people might become a member of the Joint Chiefs of Staff, but we aren't counting on it."

"I'll bet you've had a hard time finding good people with real clout in the world of finance and business."

"No more so than in other areas."

"Really? I have the impression that the big money and big business people are even more exclusively about money and greed than they used to be. The old lions and the families with some pretensions to *noblesse oblige* and being above the general grubbiness have been replaced, and the new leading figures are singularly focused on moneymaking. When it comes to everything outside of their business, they are pitifully predictable. Look at the charitable activities of that pathetic Bill Gates. When it comes to those things and value questions I don't think he's ever had an original idea— it's the usual PC all the way. Needless to say, some of the really big money people on Wall Street are at the very core of America's power structure. They helped construct it and are maintaining it."

"You're being a little unfair, Richard. Some of the big money people create smoke screens not to be excluded from the counsels of the powers-that-be. But this is a big country. There are many people with big resources, and there are many exceptions to the general rule."

"Meaning?"

"That several big money people are with us. They've been

as carefully screened as everybody else. I know a few of them well. And, I tell you again, you'll recognize a name or two, and you may be surprised."

"In my experience, rich people, especially the newly rich, tend to be rather conceited. They assume that, since they have been so successful, they must be very smart and understand everything better than everybody else. But when it comes to understanding what lies outside of their accustomed pursuits, they can be awfully dumb, or just terribly naive."

"Isn't that as true of professors?"

Richard gave a little laugh. "*Touché!*"

"Gordon Bunker, too, has some good contacts in big business. He was a pretty big deal in the navy. He got three stars before he retired, and then he was snatched up by industry. He's worked for a while for the Military-Industrial Complex, but even there you find people like us. Not everybody has sold out to the system."

"I'm glad to hear it, but forgive me for being skeptical."

"The situation in business and finance looks worse than it is because so many of the top people have to appear to be in tune with the system not to be completely shut out of business opportunities. That's crony capitalism for you. But some are grinding their teeth, believe me."

"I would love to believe you."

"Let me tell you about one of our business people. He's a fabulously successful entrepreneur, a computer geek who's actually also a human being. His company is headquartered in Silicon Valley, but he's got an office in Washington and a home in Warrenton, Virginia. His company has serviced some of the big banks and financial institutions. He's been very helpful to us. One of our problems is to get money into the right hands without the feds noticing anything out of the ordinary. In the name of following drug or terrorist money the federal government has created banking reporting requirements and computer systems to track amounts over a certain size. But this whiz has come up with an ingenious system to move relatively large amounts or to withdraw lots of cash without attracting any attention."

"And the police?"

"There are lots of police forces in the Washington area, but partly because of where we have the best contacts, we've concentrated our efforts on the Capitol Police, the Washington Metropolitan Police and the FBI. We have some assets also in the Fairfax County police in Northern Virginia and even in Montgomery County, Maryland. We have just a few people in any of those police forces, but they are in rather high positions and can order others around. In connection with the coup attempt, when everything's confused and scary, a few people acting in concert can accomplish a good deal. We also have a very good man who is very well placed in the Secret Service. He's on the steering committee. You'll meet him soon."

"What about foreign governments? For example, some intelligence services are very active in this country. The survival of a new regime in America will depend in part on whether other countries will give it diplomatic recognition. I can imagine many governments sitting on the sidelines until the smoke clears, which could be dangerous."

Again, Vandenhorst seemed pleased by one of Richard's questions.

"You are right, of course. You've thought quite a bit about the challenges we face. Unfortunately, our ability to affect the attitudes of other governments will be very limited. We're hoping that our disinformation campaign and propaganda offensive will make them recognize the new regime quickly. We're in a position to send reassuring signals to foreign intelligence operatives. We have some people in the CIA, the State Department, and among American diplomats abroad. We even have a few well-placed foreign nationals working with us who are close to key figures in our operation. They're very upset about what's happened to the United States. They think that America's present course is badly damaging the rest of the world. But staying in touch with the people abroad presents especially tricky security problems."

As they finished their meal, Richard pondered what he had heard. Vandenhorst finally asked him for his general impressions, and Richard said:

"What's reassuring about these plans is also what'll make them very hard to execute—their scope and complexity. And yet I can't see any alternative to acting in this general way. As I mentioned to you once before, I could imagine some stupid tough superpatriots or blood-and-guts military types attempting a Latin American-style coup, relying chiefly on military force. Even if they could marshal some serious military strength and blast their way into the White House and other places where they need to be, they would eventually be defeated by the forces they were not smart enough to recognize, including opposition in the rest of the military, in the bureaucracy, the media, and so on. This country and its government are simply too big and too decentralized. Sheer brute force cannot achieve the objective."

Vandenhorst nodded. "We also have to confront a huge

paradox. For our plans to succeed we have to cover a lot of bases and do it with extreme caution, but the longer we prepare and the longer we wait for the right moment, the greater the danger that the organization will begin to fall apart or that we're found out. The feds are not exactly asleep."

They sat quietly for a while. The waiter brought them more coffee.

"Considering how involved the project is and how far advanced it is, you must have started thinking about it and strategizing a pretty long time ago," Richard said.

"As an idea it was conceived about five years ago. Three individuals did most of the early thinking. Was it even possible to do what we envisioned? We finally decided we had to go ahead. It then took a long time to build up a core of committed individuals. It involved lots of scouting and investigating and lots of meetings with individuals and small groups. We had to approach people very carefully, starting with ones who were already known to us as excellent prospects. Nothing could be rushed. We found really deep, pent-up resentment and anger among the kind of people we most needed, but it took a couple of years to identify and assemble a group of about twenty-five like-minded people of substance who were sufficiently smart, dedicated, and dependable to be entrusted with the task of recruiting others. Much time went into the proper sequencing. The most committed, capable, and influential formed a kind of steering committee. The more systematic organizing of people into subgroups with particular objectives and the drawing up of specific, concrete, and detailed plans started about two years ago. Recruitment has gotten a little easier with time. More and more people recognize how rotten and deceitful the people are who are now ruling us. Discontent is turning into indignation and hatred."

"And you've been able to keep the loyalty of all who joined your effort?"

"Because we proceeded very cautiously, the closer a person now is to the core, the greater that person's commitment. Two key figures had to withdraw because of poor health. One died. We were able to replace them. A few who came on board and then drifted away had never gotten close to the center. The reason they retreated was not disillusionment with the project, but complications in their own lives—family difficulties, business problems, and the like. The ones who fell away had never gotten the outline of the entire project. For them, we created the impression that the original plans had fizzled and that the plans had been chiefly word play, a way to let off steam."

"What I can't quite understand is how you've been able to keep all these groups and individuals focused. It sounds as if you've collected people of real ability and influence, and such people have strong wills and ideas of their own. They won't simply do as they're told. They'll want to tell others what to do."

"In selecting people this has been one of the important considerations. We've had to exclude individuals who might be too hard to control."

"But *all* people out of the ordinary, the kind you need, are potential primadonnas, want things done their way."

"Which is why diplomatic tact and skill at persuasion and negotiation have been required. Toughness, too."

"A rather intricate balancing act."

Vandenhorst sighed. "That's life. That's certainly politics. Rarely can you have it simply your own way. Here's an example. One of our operational principles has been that, except for the contact person in a subgroup, members of that same group should not know who any of the people in the group at the higher level are. But, as you said, some people are not used to subordinating themselves. They want to know firsthand what's happening. So we've had to make some exceptions to our rather rigorous layering and sectioning. In the case of a few particularly valuable individuals, we've had to set up a direct, informal channel to the core group."

"The intricacies of the enterprise boggle my mind."

"It's sometimes hard to keep everything together and moving in the same direction, but let's not exaggerate. There are'nt all that many people in the core structure. Just about a hundred people have a clear idea of what's being planned and are actively moving the project forward. They have authority over many others, though, who know little or nothing of our plans and will be largely unwitting participants when the time comes. Among the more or less unwitting we have tried to cultivate persons in especially influential positions who can be expected to follow the instructions of the ones in-the-know when the action starts. They, in turn, will pull others with them. In this way the conspiracy can probably move a few thousand people — at least in the crucial first few days. That does not count any of the troops that our people should be able to command."

"For how long will you be able to hold all this together?"

"Long enough." Vandenhorst spoke with a self-confidence that Richard found hard to understand. If his manner was partly an act, there was no outward sign of it.

"And when do you expect everything to be ready?"

"We should have everything in place in a year or so, but

several variables will affect what we do. As I told you, one particular scenario that we have discussed at great length would be by far the best, but we cannot depend on it, and so we have alternative plans. How the next election to the House of Representatives turns out may decide how we proceed. If things go against us on that front, we have a plan B, and a plan C. Whatever plan is going to be implemented, a great deal of preparation remains in a broad range of areas."

"Security must be a huge problem," Richard said. "For example, wasn't it dangerous for the people at your house to meet as they did the other night?"

"It could have been, but we'd taken special precautions for that gathering, not least against eavesdropping. Did you notice the strange background noise in the house? That was from an electronic device protecting us against electronic intruders. And we have our routines for how to avoid creating suspicious patterns. It helps in a way that our base is Washington, D.C. Almost every night there are hundreds of receptions and dinner parties around town where prominent people congregate. Lots of such people are on the move all the time. Why should anybody pay special attention to individuals going to a particular place? We try to come by varied and circuitous routes and park away from the location for the meeting. We try to meet in different combinations and in all kinds of places. Everybody involved is aware of the need to stay alert."

"Herbert, I need to learn more about how to stay in touch with the group and how to avoid drawing attention to my involvement."

"Funny that you should bring up that subject," Vandenhorst said, again smiling. "You need a full security briefing on the do's and don'ts of your participation in our work. That briefing will take some time, at least half a day altogether. You need to know how to contact particular individuals, what to watch out for, how to avoid drawing attention to yourself, what to do in an emergency, and many other things. Do you have any time today?"

"Today? I was intending to spend some time on institute business and work on an article at home, but both things could wait."

"Good, then perhaps you could spend three hours right away."

"Right away? As in *now*?"

"Yes."

"*You* are going to give me a security briefing right here, in the restaurant?"

"No, you'll get that briefing from 'Hick' Garvey. 'Hick' is his nickname. He wears it with pride."

"'Hick' Garvey? Who's that?"

"He's one of the young men who look after me. He's very smart and very good at what he does. He'll break you in after we leave the restaurant."

"What do you mean when you say he looks after you?"

"He scouts, makes sure that I'm not followed, looks for things out of the ordinary, that sort of thing. He doesn't literally work for me. He and the two other men who have been detailed to me are employed by one of the best security companies in the U.S. The owner is one of our stalwarts, and he's handpicked these particular individuals."

"*Three* people are looking after you?"

"Not at the same time and not full time."

"You never brought any shadow with you when you met me."

"I'm glad to hear you think that."

"You *did* bring one!?" I didn't notice."

"So much the better."

A thought occurred to Richard, and he looked around the restaurant.

"He's sitting over by the door at the window," Vandenhorst said.

A man in a suit with a crew cut who appeared to be about thirty years old was drinking coffee and reading a newspaper. Outside, the snow kept falling.

"I recognize him," Richard said. "Wasn't he at your house the other night?"

"Yes, he was. He had the security duty."

# CHAPTER 29

The call from Helen's parents came almost exactly when she had expected. Their joy at having the children with them was obvious. She got to talk to Anne and John, who seemed to be in surprisingly good spirits, though they were tired after the long flight. They asked immediately about their father. Anne sighed audibly when she heard that there was no news, but she did not cry or make some emotional comment. Helen even thought she detected a note of cheerfulness. They loved her parents, she knew. Their having left Paris, whose atmosphere must have appeared ominous to them, and returning to their accustomed environment had probably helped assuage their fears and distract them from what was so terribly wrong. Their improved mood made Helen feel better at the same time that it intensified her loneliness.

It was clear from what her mother and father said and did not say that Hubert had contacted them. Nothing of a sensitive nature came up. Her parents spoke almost exclusively about the welfare of their grandchildren. Helen promised to call the following day.

Knowing that the children were back in their normal surroundings and that they were safe and lovingly cared for had a marked effect on Helen. The tension and anxiety that she had felt in recent days dissipated somewhat. She wondered if she might be able to consume a real meal. Since her lunch with Ferguson she had dutifully eaten just a few grapes. Was that an appetite that she felt coming on? She might not have to douse herself with alcohol to be able to eat.

She decided to postpone dinner a while longer to be able to go to bed soon after eating. She did not want to wake up in the middle of the night because she had gone to bed too early. She put on comfortable shoes and went for a walk. It could only help her appetite, she thought. The air was pleasantly warm. She walked towards the Seine, trying not to think of Richard or her own situation. She had to find ways of dispelling the dread that had mercilessly beset her. She had to relax, eat, and sleep, or she would not be able to function effectively. She realized that exhaustion had begun to incapacitate her.

She walked along the Seine. Daylight was fading. The river, now dark and glimmering, reflected the last orange glow of the sky and the city lights now turned on. Even in her depressed condition she recognized the beauty of the evening and the city. Lots of people, most of them looking like tourists, were in motion. Their only concern, she reflected, was how to spend the last moments of the day most pleasantly. Remaining on the left bank she passed the island in the middle of the river where she would visit Duparc the next day. Except for Notre Dame, which was now lit up against the evening sky, the island seemed to consist mostly of gray, heavy, official-looking buildings in nineteenth century style. She rejected the idea of having dinner in a restaurant near the Seine. She wanted to eat near the hotel so that the walk back would not invigorate her and make it more difficult to sleep.

Having forced herself to walk around for an hour, she went into a restaurant near the hotel that looked a little more expensive than most of the restaurants around *Boul'Mich*. She hoped that it would have particularly good food. It was a regular weekday night and a little late for dinner even for Paris. There were just a few diners left in the restaurant. A couple sat at the bar. She ordered snails in a garlic sauce, a small salad and veal in a cream herb sauce together with a half carafe of red wine. She noticed that, while waiting for the food, she ate pieces of baguette smeared with butter and sipping wine. She must have an appetite. A well-dressed, rather good-looking man her own age two tables away tried to flirt with her and even held his glass up to toast her. He was finishing coffee and a cognac. Frenchmen, she thought. She ignored him. The man conceded defeat and left. When Helen finished her meal she was alone in the dining room. She had eaten almost all her food and forced herself to empty the carafe. Except for that hellish night, she had never had so much to drink in a short time. On the way back to the hotel she felt a little uncertain of her step. She was almost glad that the man in the reception, now the gangly doctoral student from the Sorbonne, had no messages for her.

Back in her room she got ready for the night in a slight daze, slipped under the covers, turned out the light and buried her head in the pillow. She was asleep in less than a minute.

Helen awoke at 7:30 the next morning. Though the shades were drawn, the room was filling with daylight. She had slept deeply without interruption. For a moment she did not even know where she was. When reality finally assaulted her, her first thought was that she had overslept. She was supposed to be somewhere and was in a hurry. She remembered that she had nothing planned before 10:00

AM. Duparc. She had plenty of time. Her next thought was of the children. No need to worry about them either. They were safe. They were sleeping soundly in their own beds. She would call later in the day. Richard? She had to stop torturing herself with speculation. What good did it do? Still woozy with sleep, she felt as if she could sleep even longer, but she struggled to her feet. How long had she slept? It had to have been over nine hours. Thank God, she said to herself.

Îl de la Cité had little of the charm of other parts of Paris. It contained mostly large, impersonal, gray official buildings, if not in any twentieth century style. There were few restaurants and stores to enliven the streets. Helen crossed over a bridge to the island fifteen minutes before her appointment with Duparc. She soon found the street location. It was near the huge *Palais de Justice*. Duparc's building looked anonymous in an imposing way. No signs outside the building gave any hint of what institution it housed. Neither did the reception area just inside, which had a marble floor and a high ceiling. Helen gave her name to a man in uniform and asked to be announced to Chief Inspector Duparc. She was told to take an elevator to the third floor. She stepped out into another reception area and gave her name to another receptionist. She was asked to have a seat. Here, too, the space and the walls of stone produced an appearance of heavy officialdom. Duparc appeared through a big door secured by a coded lock. This time he wore an undistinguished gray suit, a blue shirt, and a tie. His dark hair looked more combed than last time she saw him. He walked up to her, smiling slightly in recognition. He wore an undecipherable expression. She extended her hand, and he shook it in the light French way. He invited her to follow him to his office.

Helen had dressed in low-key fashion. She wanted to derive whatever advantage she could from her looks, but she had avoided any conspicuous touches either in dress, make-up, or hairdo. She had washed and dried her hair but had attempted no special styling.

The corridor and rooms through which they walked bore no resemblance to the police station near the hotel. Neither did it look like any American police station Helen had seen in real life or in the movies. There were no scruffy-looking detectives or arrested criminals. The surroundings had a rather tidy bureaucratic, official look. Here and there office doors were open, and light came in through windows framed by discreet, tasteful curtains. Duparc's office was near the end of the corridor, where a large window let you see between two other buildings to the Seine, the Paris cityscape and, in the distance, the Eiffel Tower. Duparc showed Helen into his office and closed the door. The office seemed bigger than it was because it had a high ceiling and a high window, through which came plenty of midmorning light. The furniture was mostly modern, the kind you find in Scandinavian furniture stores. Not a bad work place, Helen thought. Duparc offered Helen a seat next to his desk, which faced the wall. A fat computer monitor dominated his desk. On the desk Helen noticed a picture of what she guessed was a wife and two sons about the same ages as her own children.

"How are you?" he asked.

"A little better than when I saw you last. I actually just slept through the night, for the first time since Richard disappeared. I sent the children back to America yesterday morning, and they're now with my parents in our Washington home. Both things have lifted my spirits just a little. But do you have anything new to tell me about Richard?"

Duparc ignored her question. "You probably wonder what kind of police station this is," Duparc said, as if he had read her earlier thoughts about the physical surroundings. "It's not a police station in the ordinary sense. This is a unit of the French police that deals with cases with a prominent EU or international dimension. We routinely work with Interpol and cooperate with the police forces of other countries. Whenever we need it, we ask the regular French police for help. Routine cases involving foreign nationals usually don't end up here. Your husband's disappearance was assigned to us because it was reported to the French authorities from the American Embassy and in a way that would get us involved."

"What way was that?"

"The person at the U.S. Embassy must have made it seem that the embassy attached special importance to this case."

Darling Bennini, Helen thought. One day I will thank you appropriately.

"Do you have any news about my husband?"

"We haven't had much time. But we're making some progress."

Helen sat up straight in her chair. "What kind of progress?"

"Don't get your hopes up, Mrs. Bittenberg. Most of the progress is in finding out what probably did *not* happen to him. For example, using the photo you provided and everything else we know about your husband we have pretty much ruled out the possibility that he was in any accident known to the police and taken to a hospital."

"You mean here in Paris?"

"Within a 150 kilometer radius of the city. We have cast a

wide net, using available police channels and computer programs. We have our well-developed routines for this kind of thing. We had to check out a couple of mystery cases that might have been relevant, but they had nothing to do with our inquiry. It's of course still possible that your husband fell ill or had an accident without anybody knowing it."

"What about the other leads?"

"We are following some of them up. Let me compliment you, Mrs. Bittenberg. You had done a very good job of finding witnesses at the Sorbonne. You've been a good detective." He smiled half appreciatively, half humorously. "Even your writing down telephone numbers saved us a lot of work. We have been able pretty much to confirm what you discovered on your own."

"Did you talk to each of the persons on my list?"

"Yes, and we have come up with a lead or two in addition."

"You *have*! Please tell me!"

"I'm not sure that I should, for reasons having to do with the integrity of our continued investigation, but I will tell you, provided you do not tell anybody else."

"You mean Stephen Ferguson?"

"I mean anybody."

"Can't I even tell Richard's brother, Hubert? I trust him as I would a brother, if I had one. He's a prominent lawyer in Charleston, South Carolina. He's trying to find any clues to Richard's disappearance back in Washington." Helen wondered whether she should tell Duparc about Hubert's speculations that Richard might have been involved in "something big." She postponed a decision.

"Mrs. Bittenberg, I understand your feeling the need for a friend who can help you, but it wouldn't be good for the police and the family to get in each others' way. If we should find that your husband's disappearance has been due to—what do you say in America?—'foul play'?—and if we suspect that there's an American connection, we will request the assistance of the FBI. But we have to have a good reason."

"Are you saying that the family should just sit back and wait?"

"I can't say that. For the time being we're going on the assumption that the reason for your husband's disappearance lies here in France. How could I tell people in another country what they can or cannot do? I'm only saying I hope you won't do anything that might complicate our work here."

Helen nodded. But could she leave the search for Richard entirely in the hands of this French detective and his colleague?

Besides, how would she know which of her actions might hamper his investigations?

"Have you been in touch with Ferguson since we talked the last time?" Duparc said.

"I have, and I trust him less than ever." She told Duparc about her lunch with Ferguson and her lies about Richard and their marriage. "I misled him because I'd lured him to lunch by telling him that I had a theory about Richard's disappearance, and I wanted him to think that my thoughts were running in a very different direction from suspecting him of involvement. I'm hoping that he will lower his guard and inadvertently say something that can help us find Richard. I'm also trying to take advantage of the fact that he seems a little taken with me."

"Mrs. Bittenberg—"

"Please call me Helen." Duparc was momentarily flustered.

"Helen—You need to remember that when you start lying and dissembling, you very easily trip yourself up, and then Mr. Ferguson will really know you're suspecting him. Also, is it not possible that he's genuinely concerned about you and your husband?"

"The vibrations are all wrong."

"It doesn't hurt to be suspicious. Which brings me to our visit with Mr. Ferguson at the embassy." Helen tensed. "He was quite willing to see us, did not seem nervous, and was not uncommunicative. Did you know that your husband called him from America a couple of weeks ago?"

Helen was startled. "No, Richard never mentioned it."

"According to Mr. Ferguson, he called to say hello and to say that he would be coming to Paris."

"Why wouldn't Richard have told me? I knew that he had this friend at the embassy, but Richard showed no particular interest in meeting him. Only if we had some extra time, he said. I couldn't even remember Ferguson's name when I had reason to contact him."

"Mr. Ferguson said he thought the call meant that Richard would contact him while in Paris. But when he disappeared he had not yet been in touch."

"But Ferguson never mentioned any call to me!" Helen exclaimed.

"Perhaps he assumed you knew about it. Otherwise, Mr. Ferguson confirmed what you told us about him and Richard. He said that they're friends, but not really close."

"What about that paper with the strange codes?"

"We did ask him to see it, but he said that he'd given it to someone at the embassy and that this person was not there at the time."

"When did you see Ferguson?"

"First thing in the morning. About nine."

"I called him later that morning to ask him to take me to lunch, and I asked him to bring the paper. Then during lunch I asked him for it. He told me that the person at the embassy who had it had not been available. Did you ask for the name of that person?"

"We did," Duparc said and pulled out a notebook. "He said he could not reveal the name 'for diplomatic reasons.' I asked him to specify, but he smiled — very regretfully and politely — and said that being a diplomat sometimes imposes 'awkward restrictions' on a person. I suppose he was trying to tell me that some kind of intelligence functionary had been consulted, though we all know that allies do not keep any kind of spies in each other's countries."

"But why would Ferguson think that something from one of Richard's pockets would make any sense to an intelligence operative? It's as if he connected Richard's disappearance with the world of espionage, isn't it?

Duparc smiled. "You would have made a good detective, Mrs. Bitt — eh, Helen." He put down his notebook.

"But, if he's involved because of some national security angle, wouldn't it be foolish to make you think in precisely those terms?"

"In a way, yes, but if he didn't want to give up that paper, he would need a good excuse, and what he came up with was pretty good. He knew that we would challenge him and go above his head to the ambassador only if we had strong evidence of illegal conduct on his part."

"Won't he have to give up the paper sooner or later, anyway?"

"He might find some other excuse."

"But wouldn't you then start really suspecting him?"

"True, but our suspicion would be too vague to risk a diplomatic incident. As of now, we have no hard evidence of 'foul play.' He may have been telling the simple truth."

They looked at each other.

"Did you learn anything more from your interview with Ferguson?"

"No, but Léger, my associate, was able to find out a few things about the use of cars at the embassy. A number of Frenchmen work on that side of things. Through these sources we learned, unofficially" — Duparc gave a crooked smile — "that Ferguson always has a chauffeur on call and uses an embassy car quite often."

"But not when he took me to lunch yesterday, just as he didn't smoke a cigar but a cigarette after lunch."

"They try always to give him the same car and driver, a Lincoln, but if the regular car and driver are not available on short notice, he can get one from a driving pool for diplomats above a certain diplomatic rank and for others who put in special requests. Drivers always wear a black uniform."

"Isn't it pretty obvious that Ferguson was the one Richard met at the Sorbonne?"

"It's very likely. The reason I say so is that we found another witness, a groundkeeper at the Sorbonne." Helen's eyes widened. She was again on high alert, listening to Duparc's every word.

"This man, too, saw the black car that was parked on the side road where that maintenance man you found noticed it. The groundkeeper was gardening in the area. He had a wagon with dirt, seed, and tools with him, and the car was in his way. He asked the driver to move it. Parking was not even allowed in that spot. The driver was sitting in the driver's seat reading a newspaper. He was dressed in a white shirt and a black tie. The groundkeeper saw a black coat on the passenger's seat. The driver responded in French. He simply agreed to move the car a few meters, said he didn't think he would be there much longer."

Helen was excited and showed it in her movements.

"So, what we thought we'd found out was correct."

"You did a remarkably good job of detection. And there's one more thing to tell you about the black car. It had diplomatic plates. The groundkeeper was certain of it. He remembered being annoyed when thinking that drivers of diplomatic cars were probably used to stopping in no-parking zones."

"Have you identified the chauffeur?"

"We're trying. Here we're moving in a gray area. We probably shouldn't be talking to people working at an embassy without checking with their diplomatic superiors. But we'd like to save time, and if we can identify the driver we hope he will be willing to talk to us. We're hoping he's a local French employee and not some kind of bodyguard doubling as a driver. Especially if he's an American, he may be unwilling to talk to us."

"If Ferguson wanted to abduct Richard, why would he have done it so out in the open? The driver of the embassy car would've had to be in on the abduction. Wouldn't he have had to be some kind of agent rather than a chauffeur?"

"We can't conclude from Ferguson seeing Mr. Bittenberg that he abducted him. All we have reason to suspect is that Mr. Ferguson is hiding something. What that might be — a national security secret or something else — we have no idea. Perhaps the reason he is so tight-lipped is that your husband swore him to secrecy about meeting him. In any case, we may have to confront him with our suspicions and see how he reacts. But first we need to see if we can find and talk to the driver. And we have to pursue another lead further."

"Another *lead*!?" Helen cried.

"Yes, another person may have talked to your husband that Friday morning. We found another witness."

Helen's right hand shot out spontaneously in Duparc's direction. It landed on and squeezed his arm. She had completed the whole movement before she became aware of what she had done. At the same time she had filled her lungs with air. She was holding her breath.

# CHAPTER 30

Richard completed his security training in the week after his lunch with Herbert Vandenhorst. In the following months he got to know the conspirators better and better. Vandenhorst gave him assignments of growing importance that integrated him fully into the work of the steering committee. In a meeting with Vandenhorst, Gordon Bunker, and Douglas Pellegrini — the three who had personally screened him for membership in the committee — Richard finally got the details of Plan A. It was on a cold night in February. They had left a meeting of seven of the conspirators in a small restaurant on Capitol Hill. The others had come to the meeting by subway or taxi. It had been decided beforehand that Pellegrini would drive the three of them to their respective homes, although it would add over an hour to his driving time. His own home in Olney, a Maryland town in the proximity of Fort Meade, the location of NSA, was twenty miles north of Capitol Hill. Bunker's home was to the west, in McLean, Virginia, across the Potomac River, Vandenhorst's on the western outskirts of the District of Columbia, and Richard's a couple of miles further west in Maryland. Delivering these passengers would provide a good opportunity for sensitive conversation.

"This is my private car," Pellegrini said to his three passengers in his usual clipped manner of speech. "It was just swept and prepared by Stripling. That means we can talk pretty openly. To make talking even safer I'll turn on the radio." Pellegrini punched the button for an all-news station. "Annoying, I know, but better safe than sorry."

"Stripling is one of our security guys," Vandenhorst said to Richard, who was sitting next to him in the back seat. Bunker sat up front.

Pellegrini drove a comfortable Lincoln town car. Rush hour had ended, but there was snow and ice on the streets. Pellegrini humorously announced that he was a very careful driver. He would drive slowly to give them more time.

In the next hour Pellegrini also made a number of unnecessary turns and detours. He stopped a few times, partly to make sure that they were not being followed, but mostly to extend the time for conversation.

Their main subject was plan A. Bunker and Pellegrini did most of the talking, and Richard asked most of the questions. He learned that under Plan A Robert Bates's employer, the minority leader of the U.S. House of Representatives, John Peck of Iowa, would play a central role.

"John's about fifty-eight years old," Bunker said turning his great bulk to face Vandenhorst and Richard and putting an arm over the back of his seat. "He's an old political hand. He started his career as a small-town mayor and a state representative. He was elected to the U.S. Congress in 1988. His district just reelected him with a big majority. He's managed to get to where he is in spite of the fact that he is a very reluctant part of the system. It's quite remarkable. It's as if he's stayed because of a sense that one day he might be able to do something to set the country right. I first got to know Peck because he was chairman of a defense subcommittee in the House. I often represented the Pentagon in discussions up on the Hill. John and I hit it off, came to trust each other. It didn't take me long to figure out that privately he was often very uncomfortable with what he had to go along with in order to remain on the inside of the power structure. John's pro defense, but he also knows the behind-the-scenes workings of the military-industrial complex—that's Dwight Eisenhower's term, by the way—and how it fosters all this unnecessary spending, partly by always getting us into war, creating conflict and warning of new enemies."

Richard commented, "Did you know that in the speech in which Eisenhower used that famous phrase he actually intended to say 'military-industrial-*congressional*' complex? But his advisors told him to remove the last part so that he wouldn't step on too many toes at the same time."

"I didn't know that," Bunker said, "but I can see why they made the change. Seems the system was striking back even before Eisenhower had a chance to open his mouth. In any case, John Peck is really fed up with that whole game and a host of other things. We had some pretty blunt conversations. He didn't leave the Congress as so many do who are fed up. God knows why he stayed. It's as if he actually bided his time, waiting for something. If he'd had hopes of running for president he should have tried to become governor of his state or at least a U.S. senator."

"Did he have strong allies in the House or the Senate?" Richard asked.

"Sure, in both parties. Lester Pickett in the Senate became his close friend. But he never pressed his case publicly, never tried to organize firebrands and backbenchers who wanted to challenge the system. Some of them probably saw him as selling out to the dominant interests."

"And didn't he?" Richard said. "Why, if he felt so strongly about the system being perverse, didn't he become a leader in opposition to it?"

"He did what he could without ruining himself with the powers-that-be. He thought he would go along within limits until he had a more secure platform, had a chance really to effect some changes."

"How could you make a difference without building an alternative political structure?"

"Richard, don't ask me to explain how he thinks. God knows how those people on the Hill can stand business as usual. All I can tell you is that he's gotten increasingly angry and frustrated. It was a few years ago that I broached the Big Topic, ever so carefully at first. I also got to know his main political advisor, Robert Bates, who is, if anything, even more upset than John about the cynicism, deceit, and corruption. I guess it wasn't a coincidence that John picked him as his top aide. The three of us had a couple of very frank, very pointed sessions. We finally got to the subject of what you, Richard, like to call 'drastic change.' John didn't blink, only said that he might be more helpful if he climbed in the party hierarchy—he was chairman of the Party Conference at the time—and this meant that he had to be extremely careful. We've continued to meet, but more seldom and less openly. Bates keeps him informed. Peck's never tried to talk me out of what we're doing. He knows that those who are organizing our effort are heavyweights. He's staying on the outskirts of the more detailed planning. In the Congress he continues to keep his mouth pretty much shut about his innermost beliefs, plays the game, makes the right political moves. Never did a person swallow harder."

"He's a smart guy," Pellegrini injected. "He's especially good at dealing with people and making alliances. He got the minority leader's job because he's collected so many IOUs over the years. He's had that position for two years now. Bates keeps telling us he's really on board. He maintains his distance for obvious reasons, but knows several of the people in our core group besides Gordon. Of course, Herbert knows him well."

"Tell me whom Herbert doesn't know," Bunker said. Pellegrini had stopped the car and the front windows were starting to fog up. "The best way of getting rid of the moisture is to run the air-conditioner for a while," Pellegrini said. "It's in the middle of the winter, I know, but I'll do it anyway. Sorry."

"In any case," Bunker continued, "Peck's all-important under

Plan A. Do you have any idea why, Richard?"

"I can think of one very good reason."

"Which is?"

"Peck's party is just a few seats short of a majority in the House, and they have a very good chance of becoming the majority party in the next election. The party not in the White House almost always picks up seats in midterm elections. If that happens, John Peck of Iowa will be the speaker of the House, which means" — Richard slowed down to underline the significance of what he was about to say — "*that he will be in the line of succession to the presidency, just behind the vice president.*"

Except for the droning of the radio there was silence in the car.

"By golly," Bunker finally exclaimed, "for a professor you are not all that out of it!"

Vandenhorst's smile became a quiet, mirthful laugh. He put his hand on Richard's arm.

Richard continued: "If the president and vice president should be killed — by evil terrorists — under the Constitution Peck will become president of the United States. The American people will be worried sick about what might happen next. They'll want the new president to use any methods to protect against additional evildoing. When the rest of our take-over plan is implemented the new president of the United States will be able to tell America that these drastic measures are absolutely necessary to protect the nation. He'll give a universally watched TV address to scared Americans, telling them that a dastardly, elaborate terrorist plot has been uncovered, but that he's got the situation under control. He's putting the enemies of America on notice not to mess with him. 'The American people will never be defeated.' He will do everything, *anything*, to stop them from further damaging our great country. What's in effect a purging and takeover of the government and other key institutions will be perceived by the public as necessary to securing America against ruthless terrorists who may be planning who-knows-what terrible acts. For many years the system has been scaring the American people with terrorism. Now those scare tactics will be turned against the system." Richard paused. "But there are two potential complications."

"And they are?" Pellegrini asked.

"First, the riots. They've distracted the public from the great threat of terrorism, terrorism with a capital T. Especially if the economy gets even worse and the riots spread, people's minds will be on that trouble as well. A good speech will not only refer to the evil terrorists but also to the public's concern about social turbulence.

The new president should probably speak about a more general need for order and stability."

Again only the radio could be heard. The others looked at each other. Finally Bunker started slowly clapping his hands. "Very good, Richard, very good." He looked inquiringly at Vandenhorst. "Could it be, Herbert, that you've already given our scholar-in-residence a briefing?"

Vandenhorst held up his hands, palms pointing outward, in a gesture of innocence. "Not a word—Richard's got his own mind."

"A surprisingly practical mind, isn't it?" Pellegrini mused.

"And what's the second complication?" Vandenhorst asked.

"Wait a minute," Pellegrini said. He pulled into a side street where he stopped the car, leaving the engine running. Like Bunker he turned around to face Richard.

"So Peck's become president," Richard said. He had the complete attention of the other three. "Suppose he thinks that's enough for him—to hell with some general cleansing of the System? Why risk the power he's now got? Why share it? He could use the levers at his disposal to foil the coup, capture and kill the main conspirators. The American people are not going to complain if harsh methods are used just after the president and the vice president have been killed. As Peck has not had much direct contact with you, he could feign complete ignorance of the conspiracy."

"We've thought about that possibility, of course," Vandenhorst said. "But there are several reasons why we're not worried. First of all, Peck's completely dependent on the take-over going right, at least for the first hour or so. By the time he's sworn in we have already moved into some key positions, aided in part by the assertion that we are acting on the authority of the new president. Peck's ascension to the presidency will be almost simultaneous with several other carefully planned and decisive moves. Military under the command of our people will be inside a number of key buildings and visible in the streets of Washington. All kinds of other security personnel under our control and acting in the name of President Peck will be moving in. Some National Guard troops in Virginia and Maryland will eventually move into D.C. Should Peck get cold feet and try turning on us, we would be a direct threat to him. He can't even be certain of the Secret Service. Some people there will be doing our bidding or at least not opposing us."

"Just what kind of people do we have in the Secret Service?"

"One in particular, Bob O'Brien. He is one of the top three or four in the service, and he has a couple of confidants. Others will do as he says, within limits," Bunker said. "He knows everything the presidential and vice-presidential protection units are doing. That's the reason we hope to have the president and the vice president in vulnerable positions at the same time? That's why we expect to have detailed advance inside information and access to places closed off to the general public."

"We're certain that Peck will stick to the plan," Vandenhorst said. "I, too, have talked to him at length. He's not in this for himself. He's truly revolted by the current state of affairs. He hates the people calling the shots. The economy, the protests and the riots have only made him more determined. For Peck the payoff for putting his foot right all these years will be breaking the back of the System. He knows it can't be changed without drastic measures. He's been amazingly frank with me, and Bates confirms all of our impressions. He wouldn't be associated with us in any way unless he was completely with us. It's too dangerous. Why risk wasting all those years in hiding?"

"Won't he prefer the power of the presidency to being part of some kind of collective leadership?"

"What if he did? He's not going to be president without the coup." Pellegrini was speaking emphatically. "His fate's all tied up with the take-over. He wouldn't be able to extricate himself."

Richard would not let go: "Will he not resent the fact that under Plan A, he's almost a figurehead, who will, in effect, take his orders from others?"

"Not quite," Pellegrini answered. "He knows we expect him really to *be* president, though in consultation with us as we purge and restructure the system. In some respects he will wield more power than any previous president except Lincoln, exercise extraconstitutional powers justified by the state of emergency."

"Besides," Vandenhorst said, "Peck understands that he could not possibly betray us without exposing himself."

"He may count on your not *wanting* to expose him. Exposing him would mean the end of the coup. You would rather have him as president than have the coup be an utter failure—"

"There's yet another thing for him to consider," Bunker broke in. "He knows we have assets about which he knows little or nothing. He knows we're playing for keeps and would be prepared to deal with a traitor. We're not throwing all our eggs in one basket."

"I suppose," Richard said, "that this is an example of the need to be prepared for all eventualities."

"*Exactly!*" Bunker shouted. "We have to be ready to deal with sudden problems by using overwhelming force."

"Luckily, from this point of view," Richard said, "in recent years intellectuals who are courtiers of the present system have prepared the public for this kind of action. They have put out a new conception of the presidency, the notion of an emergency presidency above the law. To protect us specifically against Islamofascists the president must have extraordinary powers, they say. They and their journalistic and political allies have been molding public opinion along these lines by writing op-ed pieces and speaking in all the usual places, the *Wall Street Journal* and so on. One Harvard professor has argued in the *Journal* that when the Constitution itself is threatened, when *America* is in jeopardy, an extraconstitutional exercise of power is justified. These people have advocated what they call a 'unitary' presidency, meaning that the president becomes preeminent, a kind of embodiment of the entire government. Many influential people have used this kind of language."

"What better proof that our leaders have been dismantling the Constitution?" Pellegrini said,

"These intellectuals are justifying and codifying a gradual coup that's been underway for a long time. The presidency broke out of its constitutional shackles long ago, but in this age of terrorism with a capital T the executive can expand its power even further, and the American public just goes along."

Bunker made the big car sway as he threw his great bulk around in the front seat to face those in the back seat. Even in the dim light of the dashboard and the streetlights agitation showed in his expression and movements.

"Those s.o.b.s have the public completely duped," Bunker said angrily. "They can do almost anything they please—those Wall Street investment bankers, the crony capitalists, the oil people, the supporters of Israel. And the public thinks it's all about fighting terrorism. The corruption, the deceit, the cynicism, the ruthlessness— it's just beyond belief! I can't wait to blow the lid off this sewer and let some fresh air in." Bunker's gesticulating arm landed on Pellegrini's shoulder.

"Hey, cool it! Sit still!" Pellegrini cried. "Do you want me to drive into a tree? That would certainly help the system."

For a moment laughter lightened the atmosphere. Nobody said anything until Pellegrini announced, "Spring Valley coming up in a minute, Herbert. This will conclude our tour of Washington neighborhoods."

Richard spoke again. "Just a final thought. There's a rather delicious irony in what we've been talking about. Some of the courtier intellectuals imagine that they are formulating timeless ideas. They are too conceited and provincial to understand that they are just pandering to the powers-that-be. They're buttressing the system, which also rewards them handsomely. They're bought and paid for, morally and financially. They assume that in advocating the emergency presidency they are advancing their own interests and those of their benefactors. They feel powerful, in charge, which is wonderful. They do not realize that by advocating the unitary presidency and a new idea of America they have prepared the ground for a presidency that will *not* serve their interests — that will serve *our* emergency presidency."

"I can't wait," Bunker said.

Only a radio commercial and the humming of the engine disturbed the silence until Pellegrini said: "Here we are, Herbert, Spring Valley! Would you like me to drop you at the house, or do you prefer to walk a few blocks?"

"I would like to walk, thank you Doug."

Pellegrini stopped the car on a dark, tree-lined street. Vandenhorst said goodnight and got out. Richard saw him press his hat down further on his head and wrap his topcoat tightly around him. He walked away in the chilly night, but not directly towards his house. Security, Richard thought, always security. For him, too, it had become a way of life.

# CHAPTER 31

"Another lead!? Another witness!?" Helen could barely contain her excitement. She withdrew her hand from Duparc's arm and forced herself to sit back in his visitor's chair.

"We spent several hours in the vicinity of that Sorbonne cafeteria asking people about that Friday morning," Duparc said. "We got the help of a couple of gendarmes from the local police station." Helen thought of the polite young policeman and the older man in civilian clothes who had assisted her in the police station near the hotel. Her next reaction was surprise that the French police were actually devoting such resources to the case. Bennini had really done his best, she said to herself, and Duparc had called in helpers. Had he then decided that this case was both urgent and important? Did he think that a life was at stake or that he was dealing with a possible murder? Helen cut her speculations short.

"At first we just found confirmation of what you had discovered. A woman who works in a university office remembered seeing the black car, and another woman, a librarian, who had just had a cup of coffee in the cafeteria, thought she remembered a tall, well-dressed, dark-haired middle-aged man heading into the cafeteria. Then we found the groundkeeper. But we also talked to a woman in her fifties who sells newspapers from a stand near the metro stop closest to the Sorbonne, the Cluny-Sorbonne."

"I know the stop," Helen said.

"One of the gendarmes found her, but my associate and I talked to her. She's what we would call a good witness. She remembered what she called"—Duparc looked in his notebook and thought of what would be the right English translation—"'a handsome middle-aged man.' He bought the *International Herald Tribune*. She thought his clothes might well have been as you described. She remembered this man because of his looks and pleasant manner and because it struck her as unusual that a man who looked American could speak French without a strong American accent."

"Richard's French is quite good."

"Yes, you mentioned that. This man also asked her if she carried the *New York Times*, which she doesn't. She had no other customers waiting, and they talked briefly about her business and the weather. The man seemed in no hurry. Then she saw him stand for perhaps ten minutes about thirty meters away near the subway stop."

"Did she know when this was?"

Duparc consulted his notebook again. "She was not sure but said it was between ten and eleven. Her business is usually slow around that time."

"Is that it?"

"No, there's more. She remembered seeing a man walk up to Mr. Bittenberg."

While Duparc looked in his notebook, Helen said, "I noticed you said Mr. *Bittenberg*."

"Yes, I did. I suppose it shows who I think it was. In any case, he talked to this other man, who seemed to be between sixty-five and seventy-five years old. He had almost white hair and a small white beard. He was thin and a little shorter than Mr. Bittenberg—yes, I'm sure it was your husband. The older man wore a gray suit with a vest, looked rather distinguished. The woman noticed them talking for a couple of minutes. She must have had some customers or was distracted by something else, because the next time she looked they were not where they'd been. They were getting into the back seat of a car that was about sixty meters away. The car drove off immediately, so somebody else must have been driving. The car was a—what is it that you call those big automobiles—SAV?"

"You mean SUV, short for Sports Utility Vehicle?"

"What a name!" Duparc smiled and shook his head. "Yes, that's the kind of car I mean. The woman could not say what brand it was. She knows little about cars, and SUVs are not as common here in France as in your country. She also wasn't looking carefully. But the SUV was probably green, and it was dirty. The wheels were caked with mud, and the sides of the car were splattered. It made her think that the car was not from Paris—where in the city would you get a car dirty in that way? Only on some kind of work site, and people in that kind of place are not dressed like the older man?"

Duparc looked again in his notebook. "The SUV had one more distinguishing characteristic. It had a roof rack, and on the rack was something like a bundle of planks. The woman wondered why somebody would be driving around Paris with something like that on the roof. She also thinks there may have been a spare tire mounted on the back of the car. That's all she could remember. She did not remember the license plate."

Helen had listened with bated breath. She noticed that her

hands were clasped tightly together and that she was leaning forward not to miss any detail of what Duparc was saying.

"Does any of this give you any ideas?" Duparc said. "Do you know a person fitting the description of the second man?"

"No, all of this has me completely puzzled. What could Richard have been up to? I suppose the white-haired man could have been a professor, an old acquaintance perhaps, perhaps an expert on whatever he was researching at the Sorbonne. Perhaps Richard had found something exciting that he wanted to discuss with him. But, to tell you the truth, I'm beginning to think that Richard's visit to the Sorbonne had nothing to do with scholarship."

Duparc offered no comment but gave an almost imperceptible nod.

"We're trying now to collect pictures of cars of the type that the woman saw so that we can show them to her. There are many brands of SUVs that answer to her general description, American, Japanese, English, German, Swedish — We're hoping that at least she will be able to narrow down the possibilities. The color, the roof rack and the spare tire, if there was one, might limit the choices."

There was a knock on the door and Duparc called out, "*Entrez!*" Léger came in. He was again clothed more informally than Duparc. He nodded in Helen's direction.

"You can speak in front of Mrs. Bittenberg," Duparc said in English. "What did you find out?"

The thin, bird-like man did not bother to sit down. Would it breach protocol in the French police for a subordinate to sit down without an explicit invitation from his superior? Léger was holding a notebook.

"The man who drove Ferguson on Friday is a man by the name of René Claire. He's a French driver for the embassy pool. He was given the assignment because Ferguson's regular driver, who's an American, had the day off." Helen noticed that Léger's English accent was more American than British. He was considerably younger than Duparc and probably more attuned to American culture. Had he perhaps received some special training in the United States?

Léger continued: "Claire did not drive the car normally reserved for Ferguson, which is a Lincoln, but a car from the embassy pool, a Crown Victoria." Crown Victoria, Helen thought. John had been right.

"Claire did take Ferguson to the Sorbonne," Léger said. Helen took a quick, sharp breath and looked at Duparc, who glanced back in her direction. "Claire knew his way to the general area of the Sorbonne but had to ask a passer-by where the cafeteria is. Ferguson asked him to wait in the car somewhere near the cafeteria. He would call Claire on the cell phone as soon as he needed the car again. After ten minutes Ferguson called. He asked Claire to bring him the briefcase that Ferguson had left in the back seat. Ferguson met Claire in the middle of the cafeteria, so Claire didn't see if Ferguson was with one or more persons. The cafeteria is large and was rather busy. But Claire got the impression that Ferguson may have come from a table with another man of middle age, who was less formally dressed. Claire returned to the car, and Ferguson followed after half an hour or so. He came back alone, and Claire took him back to the embassy. Claire noticed nothing out of the ordinary. He didn't find the trip unusual. Ferguson said nothing about what he had done at the cafeteria."

"Thank you, Léger. How did you come by this information? Léger looked at Helen and hesitated before answering. "A senior driver in the embassy pool is a former Paris police officer, and he got Claire to talk to me."

Duparc looked pleased. "Anything else?"

"We should have pictures of some of the most likely SUV models tomorrow morning to show the woman at the newsstand."

"*Excellent! Merci bien.* If that's all, you may go." Léger withdrew.

Duparc sat silently for a moment. His expression had changed. He seemed to have stuck out his jaw a little, which made him look more determined. "So there's no longer any doubt," he said. "Your intuition has been proven right again, Mrs. Bittenberg—Helen. Ferguson deliberately withheld essential information. He's been lying to us—to you and to the French police." There was irritation, a new edge, in Duparc's voice. "We will now treat him as a suspect—though of what exactly we don't know. It has to be something pretty significant. Why else would he go to such lengths to conceal having met your husband? Lying to you is bad enough in the circumstances, but to deceive the French police in an investigation requested by the American Embassy is a serious matter. I suspect now that the paper you gave him and that he's not giving up does have something to do with your husband's disappearance."

"What will you do next?"

"I'm charged with investigating your husband's disappearance. For now I will go on the assumption that there's a connection between Ferguson and the white-haired man in the SUV. It's possible, even likely, that the second man was in some way taking over for Ferguson. I wish we could impound Ferguson's cell phone or make his telephone company reveal his phone calls in the last couple of weeks, but we can't even treat him as a suspect in a criminal investigation—what's the crime? His only offense is to have lied to a police officer. Even if we had more to charge him with we could not arrest him or serve him with a warrant because of his diplomatic immunity. Only if we suspected him of a serious crime unrelated to his diplomatic duties would the U.S. State Department even consider letting us question him. But the odds are that Ferguson has been acting in a private or semiofficial capacity."

"You don't think Richard might have worked with the CIA?"

"Strange things go on all the time in the world of clandestine activities. From the outside it's often impossible to say what's what. But something tells me that we're not dealing with a government intelligence operation. It's not clean and smooth enough. If the CIA had been involved in your husband's disappearance, I would have expected him to be picked up, abducted—whatever the right word is—by nondescript American professionals of typical working age, not by an elderly man in a white beard with a dirty SUV. What would a high-ranking diplomat be doing in the middle of an intelligence operation? Ferguson's actions seem improvised. The man with the beard appears out of place."

"Perhaps he was known to Richard and trusted by him and was used as bait or to make him not suspect what was really happening."

"But his coming on the scene appears not to have been planned. Of course, your husband's meeting with white beard may have had nothing to do with his meeting with Ferguson, but the fact that he had not mentioned either meeting to you makes me think that they had something to do with each other. My guess is that Ferguson made a telephone call to white beard during his meeting with Mr. Bittenberg. Ferguson may have called his driver to ask him to bring his briefcase because it contained his telephone book. It seems significant that that he came to meet the driver rather than wait at the table. It suggests he didn't want the driver to see Mr. Bittenberg. White beard probably hadn't expected to go to the Sorbonne, but came as quickly as he could. Unless he came from something like a dirty building site, he probably came from somewhere outside of Paris, perhaps a farm. The rain the night before your husband's disappearance could help explain the car's appearance. Or it's a working vehicle that's rarely washed. Taking all of what we know into account, a rough guess would be that white beard needed about an hour to get to the Sorbonne. But a farmer doesn't show up in a suit. White beard may have come in a car that's used in muddy places by somebody else, perhaps the one who was driving."

"So you think Ferguson and the older man acted in a private capacity?"

"That's how it looks."

"But what could they be up to? Crime? Drugs? Richard would never be involved in anything like that! And he would never put me and the children in a situation like this."

"I shouldn't be speculating, but your husband may have discovered that Ferguson was involved in something compromising and given him, an old friend, a chance to stop and redeem himself. But Ferguson had no intention of stopping and had your husband abducted. Perhaps he tricked your husband into seeing the second man, who turned out to be an accomplice."

"And then they killed him, you mean?"

"Mrs. Bittenberg—Helen, please, do not let your imagination run away with you. We have no reason to believe your husband's been killed. The evidence suggests he left the Sorbonne voluntarily. He didn't seem to fear for his own safety."

"But I keep telling you that Richard would never subject us to what we've been through in the last few days."

"He could be trying to protect you in some way."

"Protect us? By letting us go through hell?"

"The alternative might seem worse. He doesn't want you to come to any harm."

"So he's dealing with people who might resort to violence against women and children. In that case, they're ruthless and capable of getting rid of Richard, too."

"You keep jumping to the most unappealing conclusions. I'm partly to blame. Instead of speculating with you, I should be getting back to work. I have your telephone number and know where to find you. As soon as we have anything new of any importance, I'll let you know."

Helen told Duparc about the procedure that she had decided to follow regarding telephone conversations. Nothing sensitive should be said on her regular telephone line at the hotel. She realized that she trusted him.

"Good, Helen," Duparc said. He seemed to appreciate her caution.

She had begun treating Duparc as an ally, she thought, but she didn't know him. What if Richard's disappearance did involve a national security operation, however far-fetched that seemed? Perhaps the operation concerned NATO interests. Was it not likely that on French soil the CIA would be cooperating with its French counterpart? The French might be conducting the operation on the ground. And then the French police would be told to cooperate by staying out of the way — .

"How long before you confront Ferguson?" she asked. "Now that we know he's been lying, I'll find it very hard not to confront him myself."

"You *must* leave this matter to us! We know what we're doing. We want the same as you do — to find your husband."

"If I'm in touch with Ferguson, you don't want me to let on that I know that he's been lying?"

"That's precisely how we want you to behave. One thing at a time. *Please*, leave this to us!"

"I'll try."

"We have to proceed with care. That the political counselor at the American Embassy is trying to deceive not just you but the French authorities indicates that what he's hiding is very important to him." Helen thought she had noticed that Duparc's tone of voice and facial expression were more than matter-of-fact; they included real curiosity, perhaps also irritation over the fact that somebody was trying to mislead him. He wanted to get to the bottom of this case, in which he had picked up a promising but disturbing scent. Duparc was squinting in an apparent act of concentration.

"*Something pretty big*," Helen said slowly and almost inaudibly. She was repeating the words that she remembered Hubert using when relating what Richard had said on that spring day back in their Washington neighborhood.

Duparc looked quizzically at her. "Yes?"

"Oh, never mind. No more idle speculation."

# CHAPTER 32

Meetings of what Richard had begun to call "the committee" were not held on a regular schedule but as the need arose, usually at least twice a month. But often just three or four of the members, in varying combinations, would meet for the discussion of topics involving their areas of responsibility or special expertise. Richard was asked to come to some of these gatherings as a counselor without portfolio in order to become more fully apprised of the specifics of the planning. Sometimes he was made a part of a team, consisting of a couple of members from the committee and one or two from a subcommittee, to screen candidates for recruitment or for some kind of adjunct status in the conspiracy. As the months passed he became increasingly aware of the indignation and passion that unified the members of the committee and the larger network, but also of disagreements and tensions regarding the form and timing of the intended coup. Some, most especially Vandenhorst, favored meticulous, broadly gauged planning and waiting for just the right circumstances. He was concerned to minimize the disruption of normal life and with saving lives. Others, including Gordon Bunker, kept hammering the point, well known in military circles, that in actual operations nothing ever goes according to plan. "The fog of war" was bound to foul things up. Instead of relying on clockwork precision, the conspirators had to be ready to break through unanticipated obstacles. The military aspect of the planned takeover had to be given preeminence. Noah Sales, a much-decorated major general in the Marines, reinforced the same point. Sales was newly stationed at the Pentagon, but had some command authority at the Quantico Marine base in Virginia some thirty-five miles south of Washington, D.C. The plan of the steering committee was that in the coup he would order troops from Quantico to Washington, command them personally, and reinforce Thomas Reed's troops, which would be the first military units on the scene in the nation's capital. These combined military forces would in a day or two be supplemented with National Guard troops from Virginia and Maryland, ordered to Washington under a claim of national emergency. If everything went according to plan, clever deceit and string pulling would then bring troops from Camp Lejeune and Fort

Bragg to Washington.

Richard met Sales for the first time on a rainy Saturday afternoon at Bunker's McLean, Virginia, home, a sizeable colonial in a rather expensive neighborhood across the Potomac River from the District of Columbia. Vandenhorst was also present. Hick had checked the Bunker home and then picked up the general, dressed in jogging clothes, outside of Fort Myer, not far from Arlington cemetery, where he resided. Sales greeted Richard with a broad smile and an iron handshake. He reminded Richard of a bull. He was of medium height but had a large, bulky torso and a square head that seemed to grow directly out of his impressive shoulders. His legs were sturdy but seemed thin under his large upper body. Sales seemed built to demolish things. He had to be over fifty years old but looked to be in excellent physical shape, muscles protruding. The jumpsuit he wore probably saw a lot a wear, not least on Saturdays, Richard thought. Sales had an intelligent face but appeared to be first of all a man of action, one ready to confront and overcome obstacles.

Sales, Bunker, Vandenhorst and Richard sat down in a room in the basement of the Bunker home, where Hick said they should be pretty safe from eavesdropping. The subject of conversation was the military assets available or potentially available to the coup. Sales was the only officer in the conspiracy so far who would be able to deploy troops on his own authority, cleverly exercised. He should be safe in his new job for two years. Richard had yet to meet Thomas Reed, a newly promoted major general of the army, who was being considered for appointment as Commanding General of the Washington military district. Several members of the steering committee were working to improve Reed's chances of getting that job. If appointed, he would be made the tenth member of the steering committee. Some of the troops under the command of the Commanding General were chiefly ceremonial, but they had other uses, and the Commanding General had additional military assets, which would be just where they were most urgently needed, right in Washington, D.C.

The meeting lasted for two hours. It exposed Richard to the details of the military plans. He felt not a little uneasy confronting the prospect of death and destruction, but he was again impressed that the conspiracy had attracted people of sophistication, competence and experience. When differences of opinion surfaced and the conversation threatened to become fractious, Vandenhorst ably defused the tension and moved the discussion forward.

Richard started to notice quirks, shortcomings, and blind spots in his co-conspirators, but none of them seemed unsuited for his intended role. During this meeting Richard realized that Sales was the only member of the steering committee who made him a little uncomfortable. Sales was clearly bright, very capable, and committed to the cause, but did he sufficiently appreciate the non-military prerequisites of a successful coup? He did not question the need for a broadly gauged assault on the existing order, but his attention seemed to dwindle whenever discussion moved from the role of military force. He appeared a little impatient with, at times disdainful even, of the details of planned non-military activities. When Vandenhorst and Richard stressed that a coup could not succeed through military force alone, Sales nodded, but seemed to want to change the subject.

After the meeting Richard drove Vandenhorst home. Hick had swept his car. Richard also turned on the car radio.

"Is Sales as preoccupied with military matters as he seems?" Richard asked."

"Not really, he's just the impatient sort, a man of action. He's a doer, and waiting frustrates him. It makes him seem less sophisticated than he is. Gordon knows him well. He's smart and he's solid. And he's the kind of person you want on your side when the going gets rough."

Richard wondered if Vandenhorst was as convinced as he sounded. His next thought was that it was unreasonable to expect every person associated with the conspiracy to be exactly what you wanted. He could hear his father expounding on "Billick's principle": "You have to make do with what you've got." Besides, who was Richard Bittenberg, professor of history, to assess who was and who was not suitable as a military commander and political conspirator? The leading members of the conspiracy might not be perfect — how could they be? — but they were impressive, considering what Richard had thought of the prospects for drastic action prior to meeting Vandenhorst.

Richard had two meetings with Charlton Stephens, the coordinator of the subgroup for academics, denizens of think tanks, and other intellectuals. Two things surprised Richard: Stephens's obvious commitment to the cause and the composition of his eight-member group. Richard knew three of them personally and the names of two of the rest, but with the possible exception of two, with whom he had had congenial discussions about the condition of the United States, he would never have guessed that any of them would commit to radical action. Here was further proof that most academics who really dissented from the reigning academic mind-set went to great lengths to conceal their true beliefs.

Richard learned that this group and a couple of subgroups

were poised to support the coup with an elaborate campaign of telephone calls, emails, letters to the editor, op-ed and other articles. They had lists of potentially receptive people in the government, think tanks, and the media.

One day the same winter Richard attended a meeting of most of the members of the steering committee in a mountain cabin in the Shenandoah Mountains of West Virginia. The cabin belonged to Douglas Pellegrini, who had a high post at the National Security Agency. Because of lack of time, Pellegrini and his wife, who worked in military intelligence, came to their vacation home only seldom. Before the gathering Stripling had swept the house and activated some strange-looking anti-listening equipment.

Vandenhorst was not present, but he and Richard had talked at length about the purpose of the meeting, which was to decide on ways of reassuring top-level government officials and bureaucrats after the coup. How to obtain their loyalty in the wake of startling, wholly unsettling events? Gordon Bunker, the steering committee's leading military authority, and Randy Gates at the CIA were especially active in the discussion. As at previous meetings, Richard argued for the importance of establishing an image of legitimacy for those taking power. This would be possible only if the events initiating the coup were perceived by the general public as earth shattering, as calling all normal expectations into question. An elaborate campaign of disinformation and rumor had to accompany the removal of key figures in the old government, including the president and the vice president, and would have to draw suspicions away from those really responsible. People already regarded by the general public as evil and dangerous — "terrorists" — had to be perceived as the culprits. Those taking the reins had to be perceived as dignified and somehow familiar and as shoring up a crumbling government and a crumbling social and economic structure. It was likely that in the American public the bad economic times and the festering social unrest would add to a willingness to accept forceful action. Richard's arguments encountered little outright opposition; they had been advanced before by Vandenhorst in somewhat different form. But a couple of those present, especially Bunker, pointed out that the new regime could not expect any spontaneous surge of support in the existing government and bureaucracy.

"Sure, establishing credibility has to be a major objective," Bunker said in a faintly irritated voice, "but we have to be ready to instill real fear in those who are uncertain of where their allegiances lie. People have to know who's in charge. They'll think those are in charge who seem to control the troops. Most government people, especially in the bureaucracy, are chronic fence sitters, and they'll jump off the fence on our side only if they think we control the situation militarily and will be the ones paying their salaries. To create that impression is central to the success of our effort. From the beginning there has to be a strong military presence here in Washington, and from the start there has to be a favorable momentum inside and outside the Pentagon. That means reassuring the brass is crucial, especially as we'll need to call out troops not just in D.C. The stated rationale will of course be that new terrorist attacks can be expected at any moment. We have to have a very plausible story to tell and tell it consistently. That story must be spread throughout the military and the government and in short order. The same information and the same commands have to go out to as many people as possible from as many points as possible and as soon as possible. Sure, it will help if the person who takes the place of the president is recognized as being in the constitutional line of succession. Plan A has great advantages, but we must not concentrate on that one plan. If the next congressional election does not turn out as we hope and the current minority leader of the House does not become speaker, we have to execute plan B or C. They're riskier, but in some ways cleaner."

"We can't avoid some shooting and loss of life under any scenario," Pellegrini said.

"That would be possible only if we were lucky and the coup worked out as planned in every detail, if we managed to create the impression that we are completely in charge and that the country's in great danger," Bunker said. "Our psychological warfare effort and our PR efforts have to work out just as we hope. But even then we're bound to have complications, mixed signals, confusion, tensions, and so on. We have to be prepared to deal with at least some determined opposition. We'll arrest and isolate many key people at the very beginning, using the ruse that we're isolating them to protect them. But it won't be long before the System figures out that it's being threatened and attempts to strike back. There'll be resistance. We're likely to have shooting and plenty of deaths even under plan A. Under plan B or C we'll have more of it. Without Peck, we'll have to force our way in where we need to be, and we'll have a much more difficult selling job. Once shooting starts, there's no holding back. It's got to be all or nothing. People in doubt about the final outcome have to learn who's in charge. We can't be squeamish."

Bunker's arguments made Richard uncomfortable. In his head he recognized their cogency—a takeover of the U.S. government couldn't very well be a cakewalk—but the prospect of death and destruction on a large scale deeply bothered him. He wanted to think of the intended coup as essentially bloodless, as a smartly and surgically executed plan A. At the same time he realized that plan A assumed very favorable circumstances and that complications and violence were inevitable even under that plan.

It was at this meeting that Richard first learned of a part of the take-over plot that made him gasp. Douglas Pellegrini outlined a plan to blow up the U.S. Supreme Court and the Senate wing of the U.S. Congress. The idea shocked Richard to the core. He was momentarily disoriented. Who were these people? He had found them intelligent and reasonable, but—he could hardly believe it— blow up the U.S. Supreme Court building and a big chunk of the U.S. Capitol? He thought at first that he had misunderstood, but Pellegrini's continued matter-of-fact briefing quickly dispelled that possibility.

"Our man in the Capitol Police is convinced that just before the coup it will be possible to bring enough explosives to a strategic point underground near the Capitol. It can be done under the guise of bringing in building material. Repairs, painting, or construction is always going on. The explosion could be similar to the destruction of the federal building in Oklahoma City. The House side would be more difficult to get to, but, if we're lucky, there may be some collateral damage to the Capitol dome."

*If we are lucky!* Richard could hardly take in what was being said.

"As for the Supreme Court," Pellegrini continued, "there's an underground parking garage and tunnel that will prove very useful. At minimum, our man will be able to park a car loaded with the explosives and a timer."

Pellegrini's presentation was followed by discussion of the practical feasibility and timing of the plan. Nobody questioned it.

Having spontaneously recoiled against what seemed to him an inconceivable idea, Richard slowly came to a realization that his first reaction had been premature. It had expressed reflexes that he shared with most of his fellow Americans. The U.S. Capitol and the U.S. Supreme Court were embodiments not only of the Constitution and government of the United States but of their history and principles. These buildings were sacrosanct, inviolable symbols of the American identity. It slowly dawned on him that, for precisely that reason, the plan under discussion was, from the point of view of advancing the coup, nothing short of brilliant. He should have thought of something similar himself! Instead of losing faith in the people planning the coup he felt a new admiration for their perspicacity and daring. The plan had such merit because it would completely unsettle the existing leadership class as well as the American people. Their world would be turned upside down! It would also greatly disrupt the normal operations of the U.S. government. It would cause deep confusion and fear in every member of the U.S. government, to say nothing of members of Congress and the Supreme Court. The most important effect would be to create dismay and anger. These attacks on major symbols of the American way of life would make it obvious to all that America was facing an utterly ruthless enemy that had to be ruthlessly combated. That America had to resort to extraordinary measures would seem plausible to all, including people in the existing government. Suspicion would be rampant. Who could be trusted? Hardly anybody would question the presence of troops in the U.S. capital. Hardly anybody would question a drastic break with accustomed routines. Disorientation would be pervasive. The images of the U.S. Capitol partly in ruins would be simply devastating to most Americans. They would cry out for revenge, ask for no mercy for those who had perpetrated this heinous deed. Americans would be receptive to the conspirators' harsh actions, disinformation, and patriotic appeals.

Just brilliant, Richard thought. Do they even understand how brilliant, he wondered. Did those of his colleagues who had conceived this part of the plot realize just how helpful it would be in creating acceptance of the new regime? The arguments he heard all dwelt on the logistical problems of preparing the explosions and the disruption of government that would result.

At this meeting of the conspirators Richard got to know Robert O'Brien of the U.S. Secret Service. He was a large man who looked just like what he was, a twenty-five year veteran of the Secret Service. According to his friend Randy Gates, the member of the steering committee from the CIA, O'Brien always wore a dark suit, some said the same suit. By long habit he also wore dark glasses, which he sometimes did not even remove indoors, and black dress shoes. O'Brien was in his middle fifties. He was considerably above medium height, muscular, and slightly overweight. He had a strong rectangular face and short graying dark hair. When on occasion he removed his sunglasses and you could see his eyes, their quick movement and squinting seemed to indicate suspicion and caution, but he also seemed guileless and straightforward. Richard liked him from the first. O'Brien was a deputy director of the Secret Service, a key figure in the administration of the agency charged with protecting the president, vice president, and foreign dignitaries. It had grown to gargantuan proportions.

In the meeting, which dealt in part with O'Brien's role in the planned takeover of the U.S. government, O'Brien gave an overview of the Secret Service and the role he could play in creating the circumstances for removing the president and vice president. He told the others that the Secret Service had made a cult out of protecting not only the president's safety but also his privacy, including sometimes very questionable conduct. A culture of secrecy had become deeply ingrained, often making Secret Service agents accomplices in dubious conduct by presidents and their entourage. Agents took great pride in revealing nothing to outsiders, which gave them a nice sense of being on the inside, the side where the power was.

During a lunch-break, Richard joined O'Brien for a stroll on the road that led down hill from the isolated Pellegrini house. For the visit to the lodge O'Brien had substituted a leather jacket for his coat jacket, which he had left in his car. But he was in his dark trousers and black dress shoes. His sunglasses were on. The air temperature was near freezing, but the sun was melting the snow and creating puddles. Richard thought it a shame that O'Brien should be walking on that wet ground in such footwear. O'Brien seemed not to care or notice. Richard saw a pager on his belt.

"You seem pretty down on your own agency," Richard said.

"It's not just the service," O'Brien answered. "It's the presidency itself and the whole damn establishment. I've seen too much, heard too much, know too much."

"I suppose you get to see a lot that nobody else sees."

"I don't want to give the impression that I or my colleagues are listening in on important conversations all the time. But you pick up pieces here and there, and they become the pieces of a puzzle. In addition to what I've observed personally over the years, I know a lot that others in the agency have told me. It doesn't make for a pretty picture, let me tell you."

"It's gotten worse?"

"Some presidents are a little better than the others, but the general trend is all in the wrong direction. It's not so much the creeps, bootlickers and hangers-on that gather around a president that bother me. I guess some of that kind of stuff is inevitable. What really troubles me is what the presidency as an institution has become. I'm not naïve. Presidents have to make compromises and deals with powerful people and interests, but some of these people are too dirty for words — my God! And ruthless! Decisions are made for all the wrong reasons. The cynicism and callousness is beyond belief. Sometimes the stated reasons for major policies, like sending in troops, have nothing whatever to do with the actual reasons. Powerful special interests often seem to be completely in the saddle.

They don't even have to be American interests. Some foreign interests and international networks wield enormous power in this country. They can launch wars. The man in the street knows nothing about it, but it's Joe Sixpack or his sons and daughters that are sent out to do the fighting and the dying. There's a lot of pretty talk about protecting America, democracy, or international order, but it's usually those hidden interests that are being served. Much of what's done is just plain sleazy and arbitrary, sometimes atrociously calculating and vicious. Sometimes the presidency is for sale to the highest bidder, not necessarily in narrowly monetary terms but in other, sometimes very personal terms, such as guarantees of financial and political support in the next election. The bartering can be so blatant and demeaning you could puke. If the American people knew even half of what I know, they would be in an uproar. And, of course, the Congress has virtually abdicated, especially in foreign policy. The president and those who have his ear or control him get what they want. The congressional leaders get their cut. They're running the same kind of sleaze factory over in their shop."

"I think you're talking about the imperial presidency," Richard said.

"Damn right, as long as you remember that the president is not always top dog but is often a kind of figurehead forced to do the will of others. This is the opposite of what the Framers wanted. I know some history. They thought a lot about how to protect the country against factions, purely partisan interests. I realize that the America of today couldn't be the sort of thing that the Framers envisioned. The world has changed, and America is different. It's bigger, it's the most powerful country in the world, and so on. You have to adapt to changing circumstances—I understand that—but you don't have to throw out the entire American tradition, do you? You don't have to sell out to the greediest, most ruthless people, do you? Those are rhetorical questions, aren't they, because the old expectations have become moot. What we have now is an imperial presidency in a system that's rotting from the inside and from the top. Not even half-decent people can make it to the top. A couple of recent presidents have been little more than criminals, packaged the way the public likes. I don't mean they're all about self-enrichment. The desire for money's usually incidental to the desire for power. Those *egos*! We keep hearing about narcissism, but the word has been cheapened by overuse. Real narcissists are not ordinary, garden-variety egotists. They have a glaring personality disorder. They are obsessively self-centered, want the entire world to cater to their every whim. Many of the really bad criminals are like that, feel themselves entitled to doing whatever satisfies their urges. The politicians are operating still under some legal and other restraints, but in our deteriorated society the people who get closest to the top are able to operate outside the rules and to adapt the system to their desires. They're good at it and are able to hide behind the usual rhetorical platitudes. The few decent people still around either withdraw in disgust or sell out their real convictions and start playing the game. The system's completely rigged against politicians of some integrity. Do you remember when the better leading politicians were called statesmen? How archaic that word sounds! In order to advance to the top these days you have to be an experienced, cunning, clever, brutal crook. And, of course, the winners are indistinguishable from the powerful, ruthless interests that financed the rise to power and gave a good push in the media. I don't need to explain how the Secret Service has gotten sucked in with everybody else. Some of the guys love the culture of secrecy, because it makes them feel special and important and gives them power. The presidential protective unit—it's big, let me tell you— has become a kind of Praetorian Guard, a state within the state. Its service to the president and its willingness to cover up questionable conduct gives it leverage with the president. The relationship has become very unhealthy."

"I hear you're up on your Roman history," Richard commented.

"How could you miss the parallels!?"

"But you are still *with* the Secret Service. You have an important post. Why, if you dislike the culture so much, haven't you left?"

"I almost did a couple of times. A part of me loved the job, especially in the beginning. But I was getting fed-up and was getting ready to bail out when I got a substantial promotion. I decided to give it another couple of years. Then, when I was again getting ready to leave, I was offered my present position. The guy they'd planned on giving it to discovered he had cancer at an advanced stage, poor bastard. I almost declined, but I thought I would try the job for a year to see if I could make a difference. Nothing doing. You can't buck the system single-handed."

"You have no allies?"

"A few. The head of the vice presidential detail is one of them. His name is Lester Andersson. He's like me. He's angry. But he feels isolated even though he's a big fish in his particular pond. He knows as much as he needs to know about our plans and will be helpful. There are another few younger guys, whose youthful ideals have been battered so much that they've thought of leaving. I was able to promote a couple of them to positions in which they can be very helpful to us without knowing exactly what they're doing. They are very loyal to me personally. They trust me. The same is true of a number of others whom I have brought along over the years. They are not clued in to what we are up to, but when I give the word they can be expected to do whatever I say, no questions asked. Unfortunately, the current head of the presidential detail and I do not get along. His name is Bart Gregory. I'm his boss in a way, but he also gets his signals from the director of the Secret Service as well as the president's chief of staff. We clash, as they say — have completely different personalities. He's like a fish in water, a real operator, thrives on the system. He panders to the president's people, manipulates, stabs people in the back. He is a suspicious s.o.b. And he's good at what he does — I have to give him that. He's got to be watched very carefully. It may be necessary to take him out together with the pres and the V.P."

"How did you become involved with our group?"

"Randy Gates and I have known each other for years. We play golf together. We'd been commiserating, and then Randy introduced me to Vandenhorst. I've been a part of the group for almost a year. If it weren't for my joining the group, I would have left the service. I would've retired to somewhere in the middle of nowhere, far away from anything that might remind me of all the disgusting stuff."

"I've been surprised to find that so many influential and intelligent people think as we do," Richard said.

"So was I, at first. But why should we be surprised? Why should we be the only ones to recognize how truly bad things are? I'm fairly smart, if I may say so myself, but there are lots of smart people, and many of them, you for example, understand a lot more than I do. So here we are, a whole bunch of us."

"You have to admit it's one thing to recognize that the U.S. is rotting and going downhill and another to be willing to risk everything to do something about it."

"Of course I agree," O'Brien said. "Moaners and big talkers are a dime a dozen."

"I kept running into them," Richard said. "When I joined this group I'd had enough of the complaining, including my own." He kicked a small stone that disappeared in a drift of snow. "I don't think I would've been able to live with myself much longer if this opportunity hadn't come along. I might have started my own conspiracy. What kept holding me back was feeling so alone, thinking that I wasn't able to accomplish very much. As soon as I became aware of this group, their smarts and influence, and their readiness to act, I was willing to take the risk. Joining the group pulled me out of the funk."

"It was the same for me, although I'll be risking less than some of the others. I lost my wife ten years ago, and I'm estranged from our only child, a daughter. I don't think my retirement years would have amounted to much. You, Dick, are risking a lot more than I am."

"Perhaps." Richard felt the familiar twinge of conscience. By jeopardizing his own future and his own life, he was exposing and endangering other, wholly innocent people. Most especially, he could not get away from the fact that he was risking the wellbeing of the family he loved. Helen might lose her husband, John and Anne their father. Even if he survived the defeat and exposure of the plan, his family would be forever tainted by his actions. The Bittenbergs in general would share in the disrepute. But he had persuaded himself that he didn't have any choice. The future of his country was at stake, and he was needed. All he said to O'Brien was, "There's no getting away from the fact that this is a high-stakes gamble, but our guys are smart, and tough, and well-placed. There aren't too many of us, but we know what we're doing and we're playing for keeps. If *we* don't act, who will?"

"That's the way I feel. I'm glad the planning stage is nearing completion. I'm getting ready to go. The sooner the better."

# CHAPTER 33

Despite having slept well the previous night, Helen was deeply asleep on top of her bed in the hotel when the telephone rang. The signal tore through the silence. She was startled and confused, had difficulty orienting herself. The room was full of daylight. Was it morning or afternoon? The telephone rang again. A glance at her watch showed that it was one o'clock. Afternoon. She remembered: She had come back from the meeting with Duparc. She had lain down to rest for a moment before lunch and had dozed off. She was fully clothed. She even had her shoes on. She reached for the receiver and mumbled a hello.

"Helen, darling, it's Hubert. How're you doing?" His voice gave no hint of whether he was calling with good or bad news.

"I was asleep."

"Sorry to wake you. I didn't expect you to be sleeping at this time of day."

"I just nodded off, didn't mean to. Must have slept for almost an hour. I must be pretty tired."

"I bet you are."

"Anything new?" Her voice was still gravelly.

"Well, I am sitting here at home on the deck with the first cup of coffee of the day. It's muggy, but not very hot yet. I thought I would call to see how you are. I talked to Anne and John and your parents last night. They're all getting along very well. You don't need to worry about them."

"I miss the kids terribly, Hubert." She was coming out of her sleep.

"Of course you miss them. But everything's fine. The kids even want to bring your dog home."

"Our dog?" Helen's grogginess and surprise gave way immediately to rapt attention. She sat up straight. They did not have a dog.

"The kids would like to fetch the dog from that kennel where you boarded it for your trip."

Helen tried to mask the tension she felt. "That should be fine," she said. "But they'd better get some more dog food. We're running low."

They talked for another minute about Helen's situation, but without her revealing any of the new information Duparc had given her.

As soon as they had said good-bye Helen ran a brush through her hair, grabbed her pocket book, and left the room. She walked briskly but not speedily in the direction of the hotel with the telephone booths, taking a couple of detours and hiding for a few moments in a store and a Metro stop. She noticed nothing unusual. Nobody seemed to be following her. The temperature had risen. It was now more obviously August in Paris. She had intended to call Hubert and the children in the early afternoon. Now the children would have to wait. At the hotel she found one booth unoccupied. She was able to reach Hubert, and within seconds he called her back.

"Helen, Dick's definitely been involved in something unusual. Reilly — that's the private investigator I told you about — has been to your house, and he's talked to a few people, including Dick's assistant. At the house he found, among other things, a rather sophisticated scrambler phone in Dick's basement study. He keeps it in one of the desk drawers. Do you know what I'm talking about? It's in addition to the regular phone that sits on the desk."

"Yes, I've seen it. He told me that it interacts better with his other electronic equipment and allows him to speak while he's using any of it. I don't understand any of that technical stuff."

"A scrambler phone makes it almost impossible for someone to listen in on a conversation. The call is scrambled at one side and unscrambled at the other end. Reilly says it's the kind of phone the president of the United States uses when he wants a secure line to a U.S. Ambassador, military commander, or foreign leader."

"Richard doesn't speak to people like that."

"Does Richard have anything to do with the CIA or one of the other intelligence agencies?"

"Not that I know."

"He's never talked to you about assisting them with anything?"

"Never. At least I can' remember his mentioning it."

"Neither can I. As far as I know, Dick doesn't have the kind of expertise that would interest the CIA. He's an historian, for goodness's sake. He doesn't even have some kind of area expertise. And he doesn't know some out-of-the-way language, the kind that might interest the CIA or the National Security Agency." Hubert's voice reflected his disbelief. "NSA's the agency that listens in on conversations all over the world. I wonder, Helen," he said, "if the universities have finally become such madhouses that the sane faculty members have to communicate by scrambler phone?"

Helen would have wanted to laugh, but couldn't. It unnerved her that she was at a loss to explain what she had heard.

"Helen, are you there?"

"Yes—yes, I'm here, but I haven't got the foggiest idea what to make of what you're telling me."

"Has Dick worked more at home than usual in the last year or so?"

"No, the opposite—he's spent more and more time at the university."

"That's not what his assistant says. Turello says that he's not been at the university as much in the last year. Some of his colleagues have commented on it. They assume that Dick's in the middle of some big writing project and that he's isolating himself in his study at home or in a library. It's even happened that Dick's missed office hours, which is apparently rare for him. And Turello's had to take over a couple of classes for him in the last few months—unusual too."

Helen was completely baffled. None of what Hubert was telling her made any sense. "Hubert, I couldn't be more surprised. Richard *hates* missing class and even missing office hours. He feels obligated to be there. I've talked to him about his being too fastidious and rigorous about it. I have the impression that other faculty members think nothing of missing classes and office hours, and I've tried to make him loosen up on that score to be able to seize various opportunities for relaxation or family travel, but he almost always reacts the same way. He's willing to accept only really professional excuses for standing up his students."

"So where's he been?"

"Hubert, I don't *know*!"

"Does the name Vandenberg or something similar mean anything to you?"

Helen thought she vaguely recognized the name, but could not place it. She searched her memory. "Let me think. Richard may have mentioned a name like that, a couple of times maybe, but I think it was pretty long ago, last year perhaps. I don't think it's one of his university colleagues." Helen didn't think that she had met the person.

"Oh, yes, it just occurred to me," she said. "It may be one of those people outside of the university who contact Richard from time to time because of something he's written—history buffs, people like that. This one may have called Richard at the house. I could have answered the phone or taken a message. And Richard may have mentioned the name. Perhaps he was going to meet the person."

"Does he often do that sort of thing—meet people who are interested in his writing?"

"It happens, but he's always trying to save time. I guess it depends on how serious or important the person is. Sometimes he hopes for contributions to his institute or for help with finding donors."

"Do you think this may have been one of those cases?"

"I simply don't remember."

"It was Ron Turello who gave Reilly the name Vandenberg. Turello was in Richard's office a couple of months ago assisting him with something when a call came in. Dick wasn't there, so Turello answered. He said "hello," and the caller assumed it was Dick and said who he was. When Turello explained that he was not Dick, the caller simply said that he would call back another time. Ron didn't quite remember the name but thinks it was something like Vandenberg. He thinks he may have been introduced to the same man once before when the man visited Dick at the university. Ron remembers a well-dressed, gray-haired man of medium height, about seventy years old."

"It doesn't ring a bell."

"Reilly has not been able to find any address book."

"Richard has one, but he always keeps it with him. He has it with him now. He's had it for twenty-five years. It's starting to fall apart."

"Reilly wasn't able to get into any of Dick's computers, the two at home and the one at the university. Did you know that he's put all kinds of passwords on them?"

"No, I have my own computer. I don't need to use his. Also, he doesn't want anybody except himself to use them. He's always afraid of losing data or something going wrong."

"Reilly got the impression from all the security that Dick's really computer savvy. He even has a couple of disks that require a password."

"No, Richard is no more than an average user, if that. He certainly isn't savvy. He's often fretting about this or that computer problem, and he sometimes asks John for help."

"Reilly says that, if Dick is not a little of a computer wiz, he must've had professional help."

"I've heard nothing about help like that. I do remember some kind of repair man working in his study—a year or two ago—or perhaps it was a telephone man."

"Well, Reilly will keep digging."

"Hubert, this really bothers me. I can't escape it any more—Richard must've had a separate life of some kind that he never told me about. But it's so unlike him to go behind my back. He must've had a very good reason to keep me in the dark. Do you suppose he's been working for the CIA after all and been sworn to absolute secrecy?"

"Surely the agency wouldn't require his keeping the association entirely secret from you, his wife. It might be different with the specifics of his work."

"Hubert, do you suppose his being so secretive could be related to that other thing you told me about, his saying to you that he was actually doing something to change America. You said he told you he was doing more than just complaining. But then he clammed up. You seemed to think that he might be involved in something pretty big."

"Darling, I have thought a lot these last few days about what he might have meant. I told Reilly about it. What's really strange is that Dick told you nothing."

"That could only mean one of two things."

"What?"

"Either that I don't know my husband at all or that he is trying to protect me and the children."

"I've thought the same."

"But if he thinks that keeping us out of what he is up to is so important, he must think that what he's doing could really damage us in some way."

"I suppose so."

Helen told Hubert all of what Duparc had discovered, and Hubert asked follow-up questions. They explored the implications of a second man being involved in Richard's disappearance. They discussed Duparc and Helen's decision to trust him. At the end, Hubert said: "Darling, I think your hunches have been pretty darn good from the beginning. If you're willing to trust Duparc, I am, too."

"I'm not sure I trust myself."

"Just get as much rest as you can. I'll be in touch. I'll be sure to have Reilly check out Ferguson. Reilly's got contacts he can use."

"Tell him to be very careful. Duparc does *not* want to alert Ferguson to the fact that we're on to him."

"And you'd better be careful yourself. Bye, darling."

"Hubert!"

"Yes?"

"If we worry about the possibility that somebody is listening in on my telephone calls at the hotel, shouldn't we also worry about our Bethesda telephone being tapped — or yours? If the government is involved, anything's possible."

"Perhaps we should worry, but since Dick seems to be the person of special interest and he's in France, you would think that your phone there is of greater interest. I'm just one of many relatives. If we're up against some giant power, the U.S government, say, we can't win, but we can at least complicate life for the bad guys. Besides, we have to communicate."

"Could that man, Reilly, do some checking of our Bethesda telephone?"

"I asked him to, and he's found nothing suspicious other than that scrambler phone."

They ended the conversation.

"Thank you for everything, Hubert. I'm so glad I have you. All the best to Dottie."

"Take good care, darling!"

Helen thought of calling the children and her parents from the telephone booth to be able to speak more openly with them, but she was worried now that their Bethesda line would not be safe. She also did not want to tip any eavesdroppers off to the fact that sometimes she made calls to the United States, and perhaps elsewhere, from places other than her hotel. She might as well return to *Vieux Logis*.

Helen left the telephone booth, which had become warm and stuffy from the long use. She exited the hotel through a different door from the one through which she had entered. She felt hot and flushed. She wanted to fill her lungs with cool air, but the air outside was warm and humid and did not refresh her. The regular Paris summer heat had returned and was apparently there to stay. The temperature had to be around eighty degrees. She walked straight back to *Vieux Logis*. Her room felt airless, and she debated whether to open the window. She kept it closed to keep what still remained of the cooler morning air in the room. She dialed the number to her Bethesda home. Her parents and the children would have had breakfast some time ago. Helen's mother answered. Anne and John were near the telephone, and Helen heard Anne fight with her brother to be the first to talk.

"Mom, why didn't you call earlier?"

"I meant to, sweetheart, I really did, but something came up."

"Any news about Dad?"

"The French police are looking for him, and they seem to be making some progress, but we have to be patient." Helen knew that

Anne was full of questions, but she had been well prepared. She did not press Helen for information.

Helen tried to boost the children's spirits while speaking in general terms. She heard the uncertainty and worry in their voices. How she longed to bring them some really good news! She felt terrible not to be able to assuage their fears. At least they seemed content to be at home with their grandparents. Sending them back had been the right decision.

Helen's mother described how they would spend the rest of the day. They planned a trip to the National Zoo. Helen's mother was telling her how much Anne was looking forward to seeing the pandas when a small but completely unexpected noise brought Helen abruptly back to her own reality. The sound startled her. There had been a knock on her hotel room door.

The knock set her imagination spinning out of control. The hotel staff never came to the room except when the key in the reception announced that her room was unoccupied. Only her children and the French police had ever knocked on that door.

She had not heard what her mother had just said, and now she interrupted her in mid-sentence. "Mother, I'm sorry, but there's somebody at the door. I'll have to answer it." She thought of saying good-bye and hanging up, but asked her mother to stay on the line. For a moment she wondered whether she should even open the door. There was another knock, a little heavier than the previous one.

Could it be Richard? Would he expect her to be still in their old room? She had a strong impulse to tear the door open but resisted it. She went to the door, paused, and said, "Who is it?"

"It's inspector Léger."

She thought she recognized his voice but opened the door only a crack with the safety chain still on. Yes, there he was, the gangly French detective who reminded her of a crane. She removed the chain and opened the door.

# CHAPTER 34

The entire committee except for Senator Pickett assembled for dinner one cold winter night in a private room at a large Italian restaurant in Bethesda. Reservations had been expressed about meeting in this rather visible place, but special precautions had been taken. Hick, the security man who had given Richard his basic education in security, secrecy, and evasive tactics, had scanned the windowless room and placed a discreetly humming and pulsating gizmo under a table that would make surreptitious electronic listening virtually impossible. He and one of his colleagues also kept a watchful eye on the surroundings. The participants arrived on a staggered schedule. A few entered the restaurant through a back door. If asked, they were all members of the George Washington Book Club. They carried copies of the book to be discussed at the meeting.

While the participants were still gathering and wine and hors d'oeuvres were served, only innocuous socializing took place. Later the waiters placed food and drink buffet style on a large table and withdrew. The doors were closed. The restaurant had been told that this was a special, yearly gathering of history buffs who did not want their discussions interrupted. The participants would serve themselves.

While eating, those present engaged in private conversations. They would get down to common business after a break, during which the waiters would bring coffee and cookies. The main topic for the meeting was the sequence of events on the day of the takeover according to each of the three possible plans.

At this gathering Richard met for the first time a ramrod-straight, obviously very fit fifty-year-old six-footer with very short gray hair. Though he did not wear a uniform, his movements and demeanor seemed to Richard almost a caricature of those of a soldier, not the modern computerized bureaucrat-soldier but the old-fashioned battlefield commander. Douglas Pellegrini introduced him to Richard as Major General Thomas Reed. He was the newly appointed Commanding General of the Washington military district. Richard knew that the steering committee had put a great deal of effort into trying to get Reed appointed to that job. Their success was a major victory. Having previously been a key member of the military subgroup for which Gordon Bunker acted as an intermediary, Reed had now joined the steering committee, which expanded the group to ten. He did not yet know Richard.

While they were still having wine before dinner Reed grabbed Richard's arm and said cordially: "Let's sit together. I've heard all these good things about you, and it's about time that we get to know each other."

They seated themselves between Douglas Pellegrini on Reed's left and Lisa DeLeon on Richard's right. The rapport between the academic and the general was virtually instantaneous. Though Richard's military background did not extend beyond his years at the Citadel, they were kindred spirits, Richard thought. They seemed to see the world in similar ways, knew before the other spoke what kind of outlook he would have, if not what he would specifically say.

"Where did you grow up, General, sir?" Richard asked in his best military voice. Reed smiled.

"Southern Indiana, professor, near a town called Marengo. My father was a farmer, but he fought in the Second World War."

"So you almost lived in the South," Richard said.

"Not almost. It *was* the South. I am just like so many others of my military colleagues. Did you know that the South is vastly overrepresented in the American officer corps?"

"Of course I do. The military profession was always admired in the South. Patriotism, gallantry, courage, and all of that. I went to the Citadel myself."

Having quickly explored their family roots and professional backgrounds, Richard and Reed plunged into conversation focused on the plans of the group. Richard was struck by the general's sharp intelligence and quick, shrewd intuition. He liked his blunt, straightforward manner. Reed's abrupt, concise way of speaking underlined an evidently highly concentrated and disciplined personality. Behind Reed's composed exterior Richard detected barely contained energy and an abundance of willpower. This was a leader, a man used to commanding and to compelling obedience. He seemed to Richard to be a resourceful, crafty and cautious military man. In this conversation he was also open and candid. Though Reed had never met Richard before, he felt no need to test how much trust he might place in him.

Richard and Reed compared notes on the progress of the planning. The general gave Richard a summary of how troops under his command would secure key points in Washington and how other military and non-military resources would eventually interact with his own.

"One of my key tasks will be to surround and occupy the White House. There could be some shooting. Some of the White House police or Secret Service may act reflexively against any intruder. But we hope that with the surge of disinformation and the assistance of O'Brien we can minimize or avoid that kind of aggravation. But we'll be prepared to shoot our way in."

"When are the explosions on Capitol Hill supposed to go off?"

"If possible, just before we reach the White House, about the same time that word is spreading on the White House staff about what's happened to the president and vice president. Everybody will be in shock. Nobody will know what to do. That's when the cavalry shows up."

Reed stressed the importance of Noah Sales moving marines in shortly thereafter to secure the periphery and key points that Reed could not hope to cover. They discussed the securing of the Capitol, congressional office buildings, several federal departments, and the four major Washington airports, including the former Andrews Air Force Base, now known as Joint Base Andrews. Reed gave his view of how the Secret Service, the FBI, and the many police forces in Washington were likely to react in what would be for them a wholly unanticipated and increasingly confusing situation. A carefully coordinated propaganda and disinformation effort was planned to make them supportive of the new Washington leadership or at least to incline them toward passive acceptance. Again, much would depend on whether the coup could achieve an air of legitimacy. Richard was impressed by the general's realism and sophistication.

"But I agree with Gordon," Reed said, turning to Richard and holding his gaze. "We can't rely on meticulous planning to carry us through. We have to be prepared to use force to beat down opposition and break through unanticipated complications." The general's eyes had become slits, and he let a light thump of his fist on the table underline his point. "Our conspiracy doesn't encompass all that many members, so we have to act all the more decisively and forcefully. My main worry, other than the great power of the people we're trying to defeat, is that when the going gets rough, as it probably will, some of our guys will be reluctant to do what must be done just *when* it has to be done, which is likely to be sooner rather than later. There won't be any time or room for handwringing."

"You mean we should shoot first and ask questions later?"

"I mean that we have to establish clearly, in the first couple of hours, who's in charge."

The general's tough talk bothered Richard in that it drew attention to the most distasteful aspect of the planned coup, but it also showed a reassuring willingness to act decisively. Much as Richard worried about a large loss of life, he realized that dealing forcefully, perhaps ruthlessly, with opposition could save lives in the long run.

The meal at an end, the conspirators took a brief break to go outside to smoke or to visit the rest room. The waiters were allowed into the room to clear the dishes and put out coffee, tea, and cookies. When the conspirators were seated again and Hick had closed the doors, Doug Pellegrini asked for attention.

"You may wonder about the choice of location for this sensitive meeting," he said. "But our technical experts tell us that the geographic spot and this room are actually good for our purpose. Besides, who would pick a restaurant for this kind of gathering?" There was laughter in the room as he continued: "Also, Hick and his colleague have swept the room for bugs and activated the electronic anti-listening device, as you can hear." Pellegrini went on to suggest that, as the meeting was to discuss operational details of the takeover and have a heavy military ingredient, Gordon Bunker should chair the meeting. There were nods and affirmative sounds. Known as Bunker was for his booming voice, it drew chuckles when he asked speakers to keep their voices down.

In the next two hours they discussed in practical detail the sequence of events and the coordination of activities under the three different plans. Gates and Vandenhorst spoke about the crucial importance of circulating to the media and parts of the government the story that the president and vicepresident had been killed in what might be only the first round in a wave of terrorist attacks on America. The early news reports had to create two impressions: that chaos and great danger threatened, but that the executive branch was functioning normally. It was in the hands of individuals who were taking every precaution against another assault on American society. The same message had to come from several authoritative, trusted sources. The few assets available to the conspirators in the national media had to be very active.

They talked at length about the timing and content of the speech that would have to be given from the White House within twelve hours of the start of the coup by Peck, the new president, or, under plans B and C, by an "acting president." Ensuring a national television and radio broadcast had to be near the top of the list of priorities. Disagreements among the conspirators led to intense discussion and raised voices, but Bunker was able throughout to forge a rough consensus on most issues.

It was as the meeting seemed to be moving to a close that Robert Bates, the chief advisor to House minority leader Peck, asked to be recognized. Bunker nodded in his direction. Unlike any of the previous speakers, Bates rose to his feet, as if wanting to draw particular attention to what he was about to say. With his gangly, slightly stooped frame, narrow face, dark combed-back black hair and strong glasses he made Richard think of a school-teacher from long before the time of teachers in jeans, pullovers, and sneakers. Bates gave his own comparative analysis of the three plans. Richard was impressed by his concise, incisive way of bringing out the strengths and weaknesses of each plan. His presentation culminated in the argument that only plan A would ensure success.

"If Peck's not the speaker of the House and in line for the presidency, we would have a hell of a time convincing Washington and the American public that we are the rightful rulers. In all three scenarios we have to declare a national emergency, but under plans B and C we would be coming out of nowhere, have no obvious source of legitimacy, however much we speak about enemies being everywhere and about our protecting the Constitution. If my party does not win the next congressional election, Peck is out of the picture. In the B and C scenario somebody has to declare himself president or acting president—no, forgot, we decided on 'interim president.' Making the claim that the national emergency necessitates ignoring the presidential line of succession—for the moment—will be a very hard sell. Americans know very little about the Constitution—they look more and more like a herd of stupid cows—but they still want to hear and think that their government is following the Constitution. That hasn't been the case for many, many years, I know, but not even a shattering event like the killing of the president and vice president will make them accept a government that has no constitutional foundation. If the people already in government fear that the new leadership will remove them and they sense widespread popular unease with the new regime, they will pull every lever at their disposal to undo the regime. If the Pentagon turns against us, we're cooked."

While Bates was making these comments several of the others tried to break in but were waved off by Bunker. When Bates finished several conspirators wanted to be recognized. Robert O'Brien, in sunglasses and a dark suit as usual, was louder and more persistent than any of the others, and Bunker recognized him.

"Listen," O'Brien said in a raised, gravelly voice, his face red with emotion, "We've been over this ground many times, *too* damned many times."

Bunker knocked hard on the table and said: "Bob, you and everybody else had better simmer down. Lower you voices!"

O'Brien raised his hands in a gesture of capitulation, drew a deep breath, and continued in a voice that was crisp but so low that it forced the others to sit very still to hear him. "We'd better get one thing clear," he almost whispered. "Either we're going ahead or we are *not*. We all agree that Plan A has the greatest chance of success, but even if Peck should become speaker before we act, all kinds of things can go wrong. Some of them *will* go wrong, it's inevitable." Richard wondered if he was thinking about his Secret Service colleague, the head of the presidential protection detail. "We have to be prepared for the worst and be ready to deal with it, and if we're willing to do that, then we are willing to do things that are not all that different from what we must do under Plans B and C. If we're not willing to go with either of those plans, we shouldn't be considering Plan A either." Noticing unrest around him he raised his voice slightly. "If there are any illusions in this room, any dreams of a perfect, bloodless coup, I would like to know about it now, because I sure as hell don't want to be a part of any half-assed, half-baked operation. I don't want to worry about anybody getting cold feet at the last moment and failing to do his part. Forget it!"

The room was filling with a mixture of assent and protest and growing tense with emotion. Gates objected to O'Brien: "C'mon, Bob, c'mon! That's not fair!" Pellegrini sharply challenged O'Brien's comments about cold feet, his dark eyes flashing. Several tried to get Bunker's attention. Bates, who had never sat down, was red in the face and obviously agitated. He and Lisa DeLeon demanded the floor. Richard noticed that diagonally across from him Noah Sales, the one Richard thought might be the most insistent on readiness to act ruthlessly, sat motionless glaring in front of him. His fellow general, Reed, also said nothing. It took the better part of a minute for Bunker to calm the group and restore order. He pleaded for quiet. He then gave the word to Vandenhorst, who seemed unruffled.

"We're dealing today with the issues that are bound to stir up the most emotion," Vandenhorst began, speaking slowly and calmly — an old hand at handling tense situations, Richard thought. "It's because we're talking about the death of fellow Americans. But there's also another reason why we may all be getting a little jumpy. It's the need for all this careful planning. It's the building frustration from having to wait."

"You can say *that* again!" O'Brien blurted out, and there were murmurs of assent.

"But that frustration must not affect our judgment or make us suspicious of each other. Let's be clear on this: there is *no* disagreement in this group about the need to act decisively when the time comes. *Nobody* here doubts that we must be ready to take lives, perhaps a lot of lives."

"Amen!" said Lisa DeLeon. Richard, who sat next to her, noticed that her fists were clenched in her lap. Others nodded.

Gates chimed in: "Anyone who's willing to knock off the president and vice president of the United States is willing to go all the way, past the point of no return."

"Exactly!" Bates exclaimed. "I resent any imputation that I'm getting cold feet."

"It's not a sign of hesitation to prefer the plan with the greatest likelihood of success," Vandenhorst continued. "To work hard to make that plan a reality and try to have the smoothest possible transition is not the same as reluctance to follow any of the other plans. And it's not a sign of squeamishness to want to limit the bloodshed as much as possible. The less bloodshed we have, the less the likelihood that opposition to the new government starts building. A reckless or indiscriminate use of violence is clearly not in our interest. I know that Bob agrees."

"Of course I do." O'Brien had relaxed a little and almost sounded apologetic.

"That we have a general consensus on everything important does not preclude particular members of our group taking a special interest in particular aspects of our effort or having their personal preferences. That's *desirable*! That we have a range of experience, expertise and perspectives in our group is a strength. It's positively *good* that we don't have a stale, passive, unquestioning consensus —"

General Sales, who ignored a sign from Bunker to wait his turn, suddenly interrupted Vandenhorst.

"That's all well and good," Sales said in a gruff manner that seemed to signal disagreement, "but I don't care for wishful thinking of any kind. We have to be prepared for the worst. Once we roll, this coup of ours is more likely to turn on brawn than brain. We have to be ready to make up for any malfunction of *any* of the three plans. That means making up for it with brute force. The one calling the shots in the takeover phase had better know how to redeploy his troops to handle contingencies. God knows that even in the best of circumstances we're not going to have that many of them. The one in charge will have to know how to make maximum use of the little firepower we have."

"That's why we're lucky to have top military talent," Vandenhorst said with a smile. "We all agree that the military men will have to play the central role in the early phase of the takeover."

Gordon Bunker used Sales's comment and Vandenhorst's rejoinder as a pretext for bringing up the chain of command during the acute operational phase, but most of the participants were tired, and what little was said merely confirmed the existing consensus that Bunker and Reed would have the command authority, the former coordinating the military part of the takeover as a whole, Reed having "battlefield" command. Comments made seemed pro forma.

Bunker mentioned what he called "the sagging energy" of the group and said, "I think it's time to conclude this meeting. Thank you all for coming. You'll be called to our next meeting in the usual way. Stay posted. Good night." Some of the conspirators looked tired. It was after 11:00 PM. They headed for their coats and hats. A couple of waiters were hovering outside the room. Hick, who had been sitting outside to discourage listening at the door, quickly disconnected the security apparatus and packed up. The rest of the rambling restaurant was virtually empty. A couple of waiters were getting the restaurant ready for the cleaners by placing chairs upside down on the tables.

The conspirators drifted out into the winter night. A blustery wind gave the cold a bite. Richard had thought he might check a few facts with Gordon Bunker, but decided to head home directly. He was exhausted, less from the lateness of the hour than from the protracted, steadily growing pressure of their work, which had been brought to a boiling point during the meeting. As he left the restaurant, he took deep breaths of the cold, fresh air. As he headed for the street where he had parked his car Thomas Reed caught up with him.

"Any impressions from the meeting?" Reed asked. They stopped.

"That all this waiting and planning is beginning to wear on the conspirators, especially the ones who have been at this the longest. They've had too much time to worry about everything that could go wrong."

"We in the military know the symptoms very well. One of the hardest things for a military unit that is expecting to go into battle is to wait. You finally almost cannot stand it. You're desperate to get on with what you've been training for."

"How well do you know Noah Sales?"

"Fairly well. Mostly by reputation, before I started meeting him in our sessions, but we've talked a good deal since then. Why do you ask?" Reed looked curious.

"I was wondering how you interpret his general attitude."

"I actually wanted to ask *you* that question."

"To be frank, Thomas, I have been wondering if he might be a little too, well—bullish. Does he fully appreciate the importance of the non-military part of our plans?"

"You have to remember that Noah is above all a military commander, and a Marine at that. He's spent his professional career securing or thinking about securing beachheads. How do you break through an enemy's defenses?"

"Does that mean that he's single-mindedly focused on achieving military objectives?"

"He's not as rough-hewn as he seems. He's smart as well as strong willed and gutsy. He reads. He even has a historical perspective on what we're trying to do. He actually knows a lot about George Washington and the War of Independence. He made some passionate comments to me a few months ago that showed that for him our work is about rescuing liberty from people who're taking it away. He thinks of himself as a Jeffersonian rebelling against corrupt government. He understands that we're hopelessly outgunned and must rely heavily on audacity, deception, foxiness, and general confusion. Hell, he won't be able to command any soldiers at all without some tricky, dangerous maneuvering ahead of time. Bunker would never have brought Noah right into the center of planning if he didn't think that he understands the larger picture."

"What if Gordon's engaging in some wishful thinking?" Richard asked. "Because Sales may be able to scrounge up some troops, perhaps Gordon wants to think the best of him."

Reed wrapped his scarf and coat more tightly around him as protection against the gusty wind.

"No, Gordon's a realist."

"Then why did you want to ask me about Sales?" Richard asked.

"I've been wondering if he thinks that only he could pull this whole operation off. It's not so much that he discounts the importance of our non-military activities as that he may suspect some of the rest of us of not quite being up to the job."

"Only he could provide the right kind of leadership?"

"That's what I suspect's on his mind." Reed stamped his feet to increase circulation.

"What you're saying, then, is that he has a big ego," Richard continued. "But he must recognize that our group includes some pretty experienced and talented leaders. Doesn't Gordon have a good reputation in the military? If Sales thinks that he's superior to him and to each of the rest of us, including you, he must be pretty full of himself."

"Don't forget the will to power. He may not like the idea of risking everything without having a chance to win the ultimate prize for himself."

"You mean that for him our plans appeal to him less because it might give our country a new lease on life than because it holds out the chance of real power for him personally?"

"No, that's not what I mean," Reed said. "It's not as simple as that. He's genuinely angry about the decline and corruption of the United States. He really wants to set things right. But human beings mix motives in subtle ways. What I'm worried about is that Noah Sales may have persuaded himself that it is he rather than any of the rest of us who's called to be the savior of our country. I can imagine his thinking of himself as a modern George Washington, as the one who might become legendary in the history books of the future. He may be concealing from himself that he's driven not just by a concern about our country but by the will to power. His blustery talk about being ready and able to act forcefully in the worst circumstances strikes me as his way of putting himself forward. I think O'Brien's tough talk, for example, is different. Bob doesn't *want* to be boss. He just wants to make sure nobody will hold back. Like the rest of us, he's also impatient. In Noah's case, I wonder if the main reason for the belligerent rhetoric may be a kind of grandiosity, his ego getting out of control. But I'm speculating, and I may be very unfair to him. What I'm saying is that I'm picking up vibes that Noah may be trouble."

Richard found Reed's words deeply disquieting. Reed had put into words an intuition that had formed in his own mind as well. "I do see what you mean," he said. The conversation had almost made Richard forget how cold he was. He was wearing only a raincoat on top of his other clothes and no hat. He was shivering.

"I'd like to get to my car," Richard said. "I'm freezing. But I think we'd better discuss this subject further as soon as possible. We'd should find out what Vandenhorst and Bunker think."

"We'd better."

# CHAPTER 35

"Would you mind coming with me for a moment? Inspector Duparc would like to talk to you." Léger's American accent struck Helen as out of place in the little French hotel. "It won't take long. He just wants to tell you something. He's waiting in the car downstairs."

"I'll be with you in a moment." Helen finished the interrupted telephone conversation with her mother, ducked into the bathroom, speedily improved her make-up, brushed her hair, and picked up her hand bag.

A gray Renault was sitting just outside the entrance to the hotel with its engine running. Duparc was in the front passenger seat reading from a stack of papers. Léger opened the back door for Helen. She slipped in, and he put himself in the driver's seat. The temperature in the car was pleasantly cool from air-conditioning. Having been cooped up in a muggy hotel room, the coolness felt to Helen like a luxury.

"How nice and cool," she said. She did not want to appear obsessed with her situation.

Duparc put down the papers and turned to face her. "*Bonjour, Madame*—Helen," he said. "Yes, detectives above a certain rank are entitled to cars with air-conditioning. You Americans are more used to it and need it more than we do."

"I've thought of moving to an air-conditioned hotel, but *Vieux Logis* now feels like my home in Paris, and people know where to find me."

"We're here to let you know about a development in the case of your husband's disappearance."

Helen could barely contain her excitement. She said nothing.

"The woman at the news stand who saw your husband at the Sorbonne took a look at pictures of a number of—SAVs?"

"S-U-V? Sports utility vehicle?"

"Yes, that's it. You Americans," he said with a smile. "The woman can't be certain, but we think we've narrowed down the possibilities considerably by considering the car's color, shape, and the likelihood that it had a spare wheel on the outside and a rack. The SUV at the Sorbonne may have been a Land Rover. Do you know that brand?"

"Yes, very well." Helen thought about the social circle she had gotten to know through her boyfriend and eventual fiancé, Burton Standish, "Stan." A number of people of her acquaintance had driven this kind of SUV. "It's British, of course," she said, "and it's quite popular among the well-to-do in America, especially people who live in the suburbs or on country estates and like to think of themselves as British gentry. Among people who know a little modern history and have some imagination, this particular SUV is associated with rugged parts of the old British Empire, with African safaris, and the like. Of course, the new models don't look so rugged. There is a more expensive model—that's the Range Rover—which is bigger and more stylized."

"Yes, we know that now. These SUVs are more common in America than in France, but there are dealers in many places here, including the Paris area."

"Did the woman say it was a Land Rover?"

"She said that it's very possible. It is one of three different SUVs that she picked out as resembling the car she remembers."

"But then it might not be a Land Rover at all," Helen said. She felt her initial excitement subside.

"We can't be certain, but we also have some new information that makes us think that this is the kind of car that she saw."

"What information?" She felt another surge of excitement.

"The day your husband disappeared there was a small accident in a village called Noisy southeast of Paris, about twenty-faive miles from the Sorbonne. The accident happened just after noon. An—S-U-V, a green one, a Land Rover, came through the village main street. In the middle of the village the street makes a rather sharp turn, and when the Land Rover made that turn several stakes fell off its roof. They were thrown into two cars that were parked in the street. The driver of the Land Rover must have noticed what happened, but he didn't stop. At least two people saw the accident. One of them, a man who happens to know a little about cars, is almost certain that it was a Land Rover—and that it was green. He says it had a spare wheel on the backdoor. He didn't look at the license plate, was watching the stakes falling on the cars, but another witness, a young woman, saw a part of the license plate. She was looking in a shop window fifty meters down the road when the SUV made the turn. She heard the stakes fall onto the other cars and when she looked in that direction she saw the SUV coming toward her. She looked for the license plate when the car drove off, but it was dirty, and she saw only a glimpse of it between parked cars. She thinks she remembers a couple of digits."

"So the SUV looked like the one near the Sorbonne?"

"Precisely."

Helen felt a burst of hope "How did you find out about this?"

"The owner of one of the damaged vehicles came out of a restaurant as passers-by were gathering around to see what damage had been done by the stakes. The two eyewitnesses gave the owner information about the green SUV, and he called the police. Today, after we issued a police bulletin regarding a green SUV of a certain description, the police in Noisy called us and told us what'd happened. Another — what is it you say in America? — *lucky break.*"

Helen was almost exhilarated.

"We think it's significant that the Land Rover didn't stop. The driver didn't want to stop or was told by someone not to stop. They had something to hide. For example, they might have had a reluctant passenger. Or they were in a great hurry. Or the people in the car didn't want to be seen together."

"Or they had a dead body in the car," Helen blurted out.

"No morbid speculation, please."

"Have you been able to find the car and the owner?"

"Not yet. We have checked for the addresses of owners of green Land Rovers within a thirty kilometer radius of Noisy."

"What did you find?"

"We've gone back ten model years and found a surprisingly high number, over two hundred in the relevant area. Three different dealerships sell and service Land Rovers in Paris and vicinity. But when we looked for a match with the two digits on the license plate, we cut the number down to about forty."

"You know where all those owners live?"

"We have the addresses of record, but we haven't put together a complete list yet. To simplify our initial search, we guessed that the owner of the Land Rover we're interested in lives no more than an hour away from the Sorbonne. So we restricted our search to a forty-five degree triangle from Noisy and 20 kilometers out. That brought the number down to eighteen. But we also thought that, to start, we might reduce the number further by concentrating on owners of Land Rovers who live on farms or estates."

"Because of the stakes and because the SUV was so dirty," Helen said.

"You should've been a detective, Helen," Duparc said with a smile. She noticed that in the front seat Léger, too, was smiling.

"Yes," Duparc went on, "it's a good guess that an owner of a

Land Rover who lives in a city or village would keep his car a little cleaner and would not drive around with stuff like that on the roof. With the help of local police we have been able to identify owners within the specified area who live on farms or estates. That leaves us with six people."

"Six! But that's really manageable! It shouldn't take very long to check them out," Helen exclaimed.

"We hope so, but, understand, we're cutting corners in this first attempt to find the owner of the Land Rover. Our assumptions may turn out to be wrong. The owner may live further away from Paris. One or both of the two digits on the license plate may be inaccurate. Or the owner of the Land Rover may have moved since he purchased the car or renewed the registration the last time. Or the owner may work or live in a place different from where the car is registered. Or the owner may be visiting friends or be at a vacation home. To mention just a few possibilities. In each case our preliminary list would be irrelevant. Our experience as policemen tells us that the easy way usually does not take you where you want to go. Do you have a saying in America that—how do I translate it?—shortcuts are not really short."

"Not that I can think of, but I understand what you're saying. At least you have a place to start."

"But I hope you'll not have unrealistic expectations. We may need a lot of time for slow, old-fashioned police work."

"I do understand." She was feigning calm.

"We'll begin by taking a look at those stakes at the police station in Noisy. Then we'll visit the owners who live the closest to Noisy and work our way outward. We're going there now. We just wanted you to know that we've made some progress and are working on promising leads."

"You're very kind." Helen's voice did not tremble, but strong emotions were welling up within her. "I so appreciate your work."

"You're—welcome. We'll spend the rest of the afternoon and at least a part of the evening in the area of Noisy. We'll return tomorrow if we have to. In fact, we should be leaving."

"I'm ready."

"Mada—Helen, that would not be a good idea. But we promise to let you know if we make any interesting discoveries."

"But I wouldn't be in the way. I wouldn't. Please, let me come."

"I'm afraid you can't. It would be against police regulations, for one thing. Just try to be patient."

Helen thanked Duparc again for coming to the hotel and

reluctantly stepped out of the car, shutting the door behind her. The gray Renault immediately pulled away.

It was almost 3:00 in the afternoon. What should she do? She could not merely sit around waiting to hear from Duparc again. It occurred to her that, if she had had a car, she could drive out to Noisy on her own. But she did not want to antagonize Duparc. What could she do to advance the search without complicating matters for the French police? She had a strong urge to contact Ferguson. How would he react if she asked again for that sheet of paper with the codes? The police were supposed to contact Ferguson when the time was right, but Duparc had now given priority to the Land Rover, a decision that seemed to her sensible. There was a good chance that they would locate the SUV. If they did, they would surely be able to find out what had happened to Richard.

When she walked back into the hotel reception the man in the moustache called out, "*Madame*, you just had phone call!"

He handed her a written note. Stephen Ferguson wanted her to call the embassy. She took the little elevator to her floor. What should she do? Duparc might have wanted her to ask his advice, but she couldn't see that, provided she was careful, returning Ferguson's call could do any harm. Back in her room, she dialed the number. Mrs. Jones, Ferguson's secretary, answered.

"Mr. Ferguson is right here, Mrs. Bittenberg. Just a moment."

Ferguson came on the line. "I'm glad you called, Helen," he said. "How're things going?"

Helen realized that if Ferguson was involved in Richard's disappearance, he would be very curious about any progress made by the French police. She decided to say as little as possible without seeming secretive.

"Oh, Stephen, everything's going so slowly. The police think they may have some leads, but it's all very vague up to this point."

"Have they told you what kind of leads they have?"

"Yes and no. I'm not really sure what to make of it."

"The reason I called you is that we haven't talked for a while. I'm wondering how you're getting along. You must be very lonely. How would you like to have dinner with me tonight?"

She was wholly unprepared for the invitation, and she hesitated. She had to be careful. She must not jeopardize the police investigation On the other hand, she hoped that in conversation Ferguson might inadvertently reveal important information. She also wanted to be available in case Duparc called. But if she had not heard from Duparc before she had to leave for dinner, she might call him on his cell phone.

"What do you say, Helen? It would be good for you to have somebody to talk to, and I have an excellent restaurant in mind."

"Would eight o'clock be too late?"

"Not at all, I'll pick you up at your hotel. Bye, Helen." He hung up. He must not have wanted to take the chance that she might change her mind. It hit her that she had not asked Ferguson to bring the sheet of paper. Just as well, she thought. That she had not asked might have put him at ease. But the last time they met he had said that he would bring it at the next opportunity. That would be this evening.

If she had not heard from Duparc by seven o'clock, she would call him from a pay phone.

She had at least three hours before she needed to get ready for dinner. She had to do something with that time. She had to leave the hotel room. If Duparc called, he would leave a message for her.

She suddenly had an idea for how she might spend a couple of hours. It was a rather strange idea, she realized, even an irrational one, but it took hold of her imagination. She would walk over to the Sorbonne library to see if she could find a detailed map of the area of Noisy. She would look in particular at the area that extended twenty kilometers outwards from Noisy in the form of a generous piece of pie. What could she possibly accomplish by doing so? She really did not know, but she didn't care. She would learn something about the area to which Richard might have been taken.

# CHAPTER 36

Richard and Thomas Reed managed to arrange a private meeting with Vandenhorst and Gordon Bunker for noon on a Saturday two weeks after the meeting at the Italian restaurant. Bunker picked up Reed and Richard in his large blue Chevrolet SUV at the Friendship Heights subway stop at Wisconsin Avenue on the Maryland-D.C. border, having already picked up Vandenhorst near his home. Richard had arrived by subway from the university, where he had worked on institute business for a couple of hours. Reed had come by subway and bus from his residence at Fort McNair at the southern tip of the District of Columbia. It was a sunny Saturday in late February. There was no snow or ice on the ground, and the temperature was in the forties. The street traffic was heavy as shoppers headed to or from stores in this upscale shopping district. As Bunker pulled away from the curb he said that Hick had swept his car just an hour earlier. But he would leave the car radio on.

Bunker steered the SUV away from D.C. into the Maryland suburbs following River Road west. They passed the road that led into Richard's neighborhood. The four men would have lunch together somewhere. Reed went almost directly to the heart of the matter that had brought them together. He looked less military sitting in the back seat in a sports jacket and khaki slacks, but his manner when spelling out his concerns about Noah Sales almost had the crispness of a military briefing. Richard made a few supplementary or qualifying observations, speaking less assertively than Reed. Except to ask for clarifications, Bunker and Vandenhorst listened in silence as the car headed in the direction of the Washington Beltway. A couple of times Bunker turned into a residential neighborhood off River Road and stopped to make sure that they were not being followed.

"I know that I may be doing Noah an injustice," Reed said, summing up, "but my worries are too serious to be kept private. The big question for me is: Can Noah be trusted to play his assigned role? Our scheme is too delicate to be disrupted by someone with ideas of his own."

Neither Vandenhorst nor Bunker seemed anxious to respond. When Bunker finally spoke he glanced back at Reed, the bald top of his head shining in the sunlight coming through the glass of the sunroof. Even in this large SUV Bunker seemed to Richard not to have enough space.

"You were right to voice your concerns, Tom." Bunker said, again facing forward. His voice was calm. "We have to be frank with each other — brutally frank, if need be, especially on important issues, though we'd better pick the right time and place."

"And what do you think about what Richard and I've said?"

"You've been forthright with us, so I'll be frank, too," Bunker said. "But give me a minute." They had passed over the Beltway and were going up a steep hill on River Road that would put them in Potomac. They were coming to what used to be the heart of horse country on the Maryland side of the Potomac River. The area called Potomac had become a ritzy suburb dominated by very expensive homes, many of them palatial. White fences on both sides of River Road, behind some of which horses grazed in the summer half of the year, helped create the illusion that here lived the descendants of British landed gentry. Bunker pulled off River Road into the Congressional Country Club, perhaps the most opulent and impressive of the Washington area country clubs. In the spring and summer time its meticulously kept grounds, two eighteen-hole golf courses, tennis courts, driving ranges, flower beds, and pools were a marvel, especially to visitors unfamiliar with the lifestyle of America's rich and powerful. The large white, multi-storeyed "club house" with spacious, high-ceilinged rooms and restaurants and terraces facing the golf courses looked more like a large Italianate European castle than a suburban club house. The premises exuded solidity and wealth. Despite its name, the Congressional Country Club had no formal connection with the U.S. Congress, but U.S. senators and representatives as well as presidents and other high federal officials could be seen there together with prominent individuals from the private sector.

"I thought we might have lunch at Congressional," Bunker said. "I've been a member since the Military-Industrial Complex paid for my membership a couple of years ago. My new bosses were able to arrange for me to jump the line. It costs well over $100,000 to join these days, if you can believe it, but the waiting list is as long as ever." Bunker pulled up under the roof at the main entrance, and an attendant rushed forward to park his car. Bunker declined the offer.

"Why don't you fellows wait for me inside? I'll be with you in a minute." Bunker drove off to park.

Richard had been to Congressional Country Club before as the guest of members. He again reflected that in America social tensions had been kept to a minimum partly because the rich and privileged had their own enclaves, geographically set apart from the world of ordinary people. Outsiders entered those enclaves only sparingly, as maids, groundskeepers, waiters, contractors, and the like. The American masses simply did not know how people of real privilege routinely live. They heard rumors perhaps and saw images in movies, but rarely did they come face to face with the concrete reality. They were not repeatedly reminded of the gulf between themselves and those others. It had also used to be that Americans were not as envious of the well-to-do as other peoples. It was a part of traditional American culture. It seemed that many Europeans were different. They were anxiously watching the economic fortunes of their fellows and having a hard time swallowing that others in their vicinity were moving ahead. But with America's chronic economic difficulties, high unemployment, and the growing number of people falling into the official poverty category, resentment over the widening gap between rich and poor was spreading. More and more people saw the really wealthy as enriching themselves at the expense of the poor. The protests and riots around the country now often involved members of the solid middle class, teachers and others who had to accept major cuts in fringe and retirement benefits. Many Americans no longer exhibited the traditional lack of envy. Class tension, previously rare in a society that prided itself on having no classes, was growing.

Bunker escorted the other three to the main dining room. The respect with which the staff treated him indicated that he was well liked and considered important. At Bunker's request, his party was seated out of the way in a corner.

As soon as the waiter had left with their drink orders, Bunker turned to Reed's question from back in the car. He spoke now in a muted, unmilitary voice. "I'll be as open and frank as I can. First of all, Herbert and I checked Noah out pretty carefully. I have my military channels. People I talked to confirmed the positive opinion I formed on my own about ten years ago. I had some contact with him when I was still on active duty—coordination work. The Marines are supposed to be a part of the navy." Bunker went on to give a general defense of Sales and summed up by saying, "He's a hell of a commander—bright, bold, and decisive but also prudent. He can be blustery and overbearing, but that's not uncommon in our business, especially not in the Marines."

"What about the possibility that he has a higher opinion of his own ability than is compatible with collegial decision making?" Richard said.

"And that he might suddenly decide that he's the one to give the orders," Reed added.

"He's got an ego. Who doesn't?" Bunker's face had gotten a little flushed. Vandenhorst sat with his hands folded against the table, betraying no emotion. "Considering what business we're in," Bunker continued, "it's better that he's got an ego than that he doesn't. Don't we all have to have a pretty high opinion of ourselves to believe that we're called to get rid of the U.S. government" — he lowered his voice even more — "to kill the president and vice president? We're even conceited enough to think that we might succeed. As for Noah I haven't seen any signs of his being a prima donna and potential troublemaker. He's used to taking orders. He's just no-nonsense, and he's uncomfortable biding his time. All commanders hate to wait."

"Even if he thinks he would be better than any of us at directing the operational phase," said Vandenhorst, "he knows that we have to rely more on coordination and the right sequencing than on sheer force. He may have some vanity, but it's not going to jeopardize our plans."

"How can you be so sure?" Reed said. Before Vandenhorst or Bunker could answer, the waiter returned with their drinks. Bunker told the waiter that they were not ready to order their food.

"What *can* we be sure of in this life?" Vandenhorst said. "Only death and taxes. And, I guess, riots. Nothing's ever just as we would like it to be. That wouldn't be real life."

*Billick's principle*, Richard thought. There was never any point in hoping that given circumstances had been more favorable. Such thinking merely led to indecision, paralysis, and inaction.

"Besides," Bunker broke in, as if he had read Richard's mind, "we have precious few military assets. Without the troops that Noah can hope to activate through some clever moves, we would have only the firepower that you, Tom, can provide, through your machinations. And that's not a whole lot. Through deceit Bob O'Brien can get us some help from the Secret Service for a while, and we have some limited assets in the FBI and in the Capitol Hill police. But to break through real opposition, occupy various government buildings, take over a couple of television and radio stations, control the airports, etc., only military force will do. The disinformation will take us only so far. And not even the troops we hope to have are any guarantee against last-minute complications. Just think about the damned traffic in this area. Unless we could move in the middle of the night or early in the morning on a weekend, Sales could have huge problems getting up to D.C."

"That's one of the reasons," Reed shot back, "why we can't

afford any last minute, unexpected, extravagant moves on Noah's part. According to the rules I'm supposed to follow as Commanding General of the Washington military district, I should coordinate much of what I do with a number of other players. Certain guys at the Pentagon, the Secret Service and Homeland Security expect to have a say. They need a very good reason to tolerate unilateral action on my part. This is where our plans — taking out Number One and Two, the distractions, deceptions, etc. — have to work pretty much as intended. One false move on Noah's part, and all of Washington will be on high alert, and then I may not be able to act as I have to."

"Or he might try to take over operational control while the initial takeover phase is still underway," Richard suggested.

"*Dick*, he's no fool!" Bunker blurted out, lowering his voice in mid-sentence. Give him some credit for smarts."

The conversation continued through lunch, hushed tones sometimes giving way to mutedly raised voices. They ate almost without noticing what they were eating. Bunker, sensing especially the depth of Reed's concern, finally said: "I'm the one who knows Noah the best. I'll make it my business to feel him out and to impress on him the importance of each of us sticking closely to our assigned roles. If I get the impression that Dick and Tom have any reason to worry, I promise we'll meet again to decide what to do. Please, gentlemen, not a word about this to anybody else in our group."

As they were getting ready to leave and Bunker left to retrieve his car, Richard looked around him once again. This was a place, he thought, where many of those who were instrumental in destroying America's constitutional structures and its corresponding ethos gathered for meals or deals or play. They were the cynical and shady politicians, lobbyists, financiers and businessmen who managed nevertheless to keep up appearances sufficiently to gain admission to the Congressional Country Club. Nothing at this club suggested that anything was amiss. The premises were painstakingly kept, even opulent. Outwardly civilized, well-dressed, well-behaved people were lunching. In a couple of months the club would look even more imposing and enticing. Its flowerbeds would be magnificent, resplendent with color, and the grass on lawns and golf courses would be greener and more perfectly manicured than anywhere else in the world. Many stood in line to pay the entrance fee for membership. The Congressional Country Club was the essence of privileged normality. Yet those average members who wanted to think of themselves as belonging to the ruling class were, for the most part, nowhere close to America's real decision makers, those shadowy individuals whose hidden influence affected everybody else in the world. Their faces were unknown to the general public. They might visit Congressional from time to time, but moved largely out of sight. Even if born in the United States, these individuals felt no deep attachment to America. They were above national allegiances and sovereignties, owned residences in different parts of the world.

Richard reflected that at the level of the Congressional Country Club the currents destroying America were still diluted or countered by other currents. There were members who were still connected, however tenuously, to America's older traditions — through manners, religious affiliations, old habits and ideas. Some of them would sympathize, he thought, with what he and his fellow conspirators were planning, though they would be careful to keep such thoughts to themselves. Most members probably preferred to think that nothing was fundamentally wrong with their country. Because things were going rather well for them personally, they could entertain the hope that all was essentially well with America. Yet other members smugly believed that, except for flaws still to be dealt with, progressive, enlightened America was a model for the rest of the world. To these people, the conspirators would be aliens, horrifying monsters.

Richard was certain that most people at the club would, despite their presumed sophistication, be utterly baffled by the news that their president and vice president were dead and that previously unknown individuals were running the country. So used were these people to the status quo that they would have great difficulty acting in the new circumstances. Richard suspected that, for all of their formal commitment to democracy, many or most might, partly out of fear, respond favorably to strong leadership.

But strong leadership in any form? The reaction of Americans to 9/11 had been one of sheer disbelief. As compared to any significant military campaign, the event had caused no huge loss of life, and it had left American institutions intact. Still, the country had been changed by it. Americans had become much more receptive to assertive presidential action and more generally to national government intruding into personal lives in the name of security. How would Americans react to a wholly unexpected assault on what had become the most cherished political institution of all, the presidency, the very embodiment of the American national identity? Nothing in American history had prepared Americans for what the conspirators were planning. Presidents had been killed before, but there had never been any great uncertainty about the aftermath.

The coup would change everything. It would unsettle deeply ingrained habits, call into question the basic terms of American political life. How would Americans behave when the president, whom they had turned into a larger-than-life figure, and his immediate constitutional successor were both gone? Would they be sufficiently disoriented and scared to accept a previously unknown person as their national leader — a "National Emergency President"? Very few Americans knew that the speaker of the House of Representatives was the next in line. Would Americans nevertheless insist on following the constitutional order of succession? Or would a crisis atmosphere, intensified by all the carefully prepared disinformation, draw attention away from the Constitution? Would the most privileged Americans, like the members of the Congressional Country Club, tolerate a supposedly temporary extra-constitutional presidency?

Richard and his colleagues knew that gaining the support of America's brightest and most successful people would be key to the long-term success of the coup, but he had long been disappointed, indeed, at times almost indignant, that in the face of American decline so many of America's privileged were either docile or too timid to protest. When Richard thought about who the people were for whom the conspirators thought they were acting, it was not the more prosperous people who came to mind. They, too, had been confused and deceived by a morally and financially corrupt system, but, except in their own imaginations, they seemed not to care very much about all those other Americans for whom life had become a struggle. Was the semi-sentient state of so many of America's brightest people as much an escape mechanism as a sign of self-indulgence and ignorance? Richard had more sympathy for the millions and millions of decent but less fortunate people, not least the young, who sensed that something was radically wrong, but had nowhere to turn. Richard hoped that, even if the conspirators were to fail, these common people would recognize that the conspirators' commitment and courage had been expended in their behalf. He hoped also that the attempt to rescue and revive the old American heritage would be an inspiration to Americans yet to be born.

As the four men were heading back towards Washington in Bunker's SUV there was at first only light and intermittent conversation. Voices and bits of music on the radio formed the background. Richard was silent, pondering a point that had begun to nag at him in recent weeks. In a lull in the conversation he decided to speak, and his tone of voice revealed that he was not about to offer more inconsequential comments.

"There's something I've been thinking about."

"More reservations?" Bunker said half-jokingly.

"I'm not sure what it is. It has to do with the way we think about the coup."

"Let's hear," Reed said.

"The more I think about it," Richard began, "the more Plan A looks like wishful thinking."

He had their full attention.

"Plan A is the Rolls Royce plan—more an abstract blueprint from the drawing boards than something made for real life." All but Bunker, the driver, turned their heads in Richard's direction.

"Whatever made you say that at this particular time?" Reed asked. Vandenhorst, who was in the front seat, turned to be able to see Richard's face.

"I think our discussion of Sales reminded me that real life is messy and full of obstacles and difficult to predict. My point's this: If success for our cause is dependent on everything going according to plan, we might just as well pack it up—we have no business even continuing to plan."

Bunker was the first to react to Richard's comment. "Dick, that doesn't sound like you at all—more like Sales or me. Or do you mean we should *scrap* our plans?"

"No, Gordon, that's not what I'm saying. I'm expressing concern about a certain mind-set or demeanor, a hidden assumption that what will make us succeed is very, very careful planning and that there could be a very clean takeover."

"You sound just like Noah," Reed said.

"Perhaps I do. The fact that I worry about him doesn't mean that I regard him as a simpleminded warrior. He keeps saying, as you do Gordon, that we must be prepared to break through obstacles by force, which sounds as if he trusts too much in his own stock-in-trade. But perhaps I'm being unfair. He may be saying something similar to what I'm now getting at. We're all agreed that we have to be prepared for less than ideal circumstances, but—here's what I'm trying to explain—it's one thing to be realistic in theory and another to be realistic in practice."

"Just what are you talking about, Dick?" Reed sounded impatient.

They were approaching Richard's neighborhood, Kenwood, which was off River Road a mile outside the District line. Bunker knew that Richard did not want to be let out at his house. To give Richard a chance to make his point, Bunker headed into another residential neighborhood. Richard continued.

"What's on my mind is not so easy to express. Machiavelli said that human beings are in charge of about half of what happens in the world and that the goddess of Fate controls the rest. She's like a woman — capricious and unpredictable. For that reason, in deciding how to act you must not rely too much on circumspection and caution. To have the best chance of getting your way, Machiavelli says, you have to try to bend Fate to your own will. You should approach her as you would a woman whom you're trying to conquer — audaciously and firmly."

"My God, Machiavelli said *that*!" Bunker exclaimed. "The feminists must hate him."

"You're giving us a philosophy lesson?" Reed asked.

"Well, Machiavelli says that Fate is more likely to favor you," Richard continued, "if you approach her with passion and daring and even try dominating her physically, than if you proceed in a deliberate, calculating manner."

"So?" Bunker asked. "Somehow I don't think you want us to throw caution to the wind."

"No, of course not. Given the scope and complexity of what we face, careful planning is essential. Anything else would be reckless and stupid."

"So why bring up Machiavelli's goddess of Fate?" Reed asked the question as Bunker pulled into a high school parking lot. He stopped the car, but let the engine idle. The sudden reduction in noise gave greater prominence to a radio commercial, but added weight to Richard's words as he continued.

"I've reached a conclusion about myself that I think may be relevant to some others in our group and probably to many people in the subgroups. It has to do with *psychological* preparedness. In *theory* I know very well that meticulous planning is not going to carry the day. There's no way of anticipating and preparing for all contingencies. If we're successful, it will probably be due most to audacity and willpower and the luck of the draw. And yet I notice that I'm thinking and acting as if not overlooking any detail is what will make the difference. The long and short of it is that *in practice* I may be ignoring what I'm affirming in theory. I don't have to swallow all of Machiavelli to regard him as an antidote to looking away from the darker aspects of politics. As an academic I may be in greater danger than others of letting abstract theorizing undermine my practical sense, but I have a feeling I'm not alone. The careful planning may be distracting some of us from — he slowed down to emphasize his words — *preparing psychologically*. We'll be taking drastic, earth-shattering action. We'll take lives, to say nothing of jeopardizing our own. And yet, are we truly preparing for practical action?"

"What else would we be doing?" Reed said. "Aren't you being a little academic? No offense meant."

"As a soldier, a true man of practice, you may have less of a problem than others," Richard said, "but I don't think that this professor of history is the only one who may have difficulty realizing that what we're planning will actually take place—in the real world. This is the United States of America, remember. Things like this just don't happen. Who can imagine it—actually happening, I mean?"

"You and Tom just raised questions about Noah Sales," said Bunker, who had turned his big bulk around to face the others. "It sounds now as if you, Dick, are defending him."

"I continue to worry about his personality—that big ego— but it may be that because he's such an action-oriented person, he's detected in some of us what I'm speaking about, a reluctance truly to prepare for action. Too much talk, too many preparations, too much living in the imagination may be symptomatic of a fear of action."

Vandenhorst, who had been quiet for the quarter of an hour since they left the country club, finally spoke:

"Richard, I think I may be hearing, even in you, the voice of impatience. The waiting is getting to all of us. And while we wait, what can we do except consider abstract possibilities and plan for them?"

"I think my point is different," Richard said. "As a relative latecomer to the cause I have less reason to complain about waiting than most of the others in the group. Sure, waiting affects our psychological orientation. At some stage it will by itself begin to turn our cause into a rather distant, abstract possibility. We may be getting close to the point when waiting starts undermining rather than boosting our readiness. All the more reason for some of us to cultivate a disposition to act without hesitation."

Vandenhorst did not respond, and Richard continued: "In the abstract getting Peck elected speaker of the House and letting him be sworn in as president after the death of the president and vice president is the superior plan. It would solve one of the biggest problems we face, perhaps the biggest of all, the problem of legitimacy. But, think about it—we have to wait for almost another year for a new House of Representatives to be seated and a new speaker to be installed. And then we have to wait for a situation in which Number One and Two are simultaneously vulnerable to attack. Any number of things could go wrong. First of all, there's only a good chance that Peck's party will win a majority in the House in the November election, and even if that happens, he might suffer some personal political setback. His own seat is safe, but political accidents do happen. Then there's the danger that Sales is transferred from his present job sooner than expected. That would leave us terribly shorthanded on the military side. I can think of a number of other drawbacks to waiting. We all know that with each passing day the danger increases that the conspiracy will be exposed or will begin to unravel."

Richard's statement was followed by a silence that was not broken until fifteen seconds later, when Bunker spoke.

"Dick's talking sense," he said. "We should fish or cut bait." His voice had an edge that took the others by surprise.

"Wait a minute, that's not what I said," Richard protested.

"That's what I *heard* you saying!"

"I was talking about being psychologically ready for action."

"Yes, and about how unrealistic it is to plan for the Cadillac scenario." Bunker's emphatic way of speaking made it clear that he wanted the subject discussed.

"Gordon," Reed said, "it sounds to me as if you are using what Dick said to push a concern of your own."

"You bet I'm concerned. I think we may be risking a good opportunity by waiting for the perfect opportunity." Bunker slapped his hand hard on the seat.

"Gordon, we're thinking about different things," Richard said.

Reed was just about to comment when Vandenhorst broke in. "Gentlemen, we can talk more in a few days."

"Herb, we can't keep pushing this issue under the carpet any longer," Bunker said sharply.

"I don't want to sidestep any issue," Vandenhorst said, "so let's have another meeting, just the four of us."

"Darn it, we have meetings coming out of our ears."

"Herbert's right, Gordon," Richard said. "We need to talk this issue through."

"Talk, talk, talk—."

In a seemingly surly and demonstrative manner Bunker threw the big SUV into gear and steered out of the high school parking lot. When they turned back onto River Road and headed east Richard said, "I would appreciate it if you would drop me off at the Kenwood Country Club. I' can walk home from there." His raising a trivial subject did not dispel the glumness that had descended over the company.

"You'll hear from me soon," Vandenhorst said, as Bunker turned into the country club. He stopped the SUV short of the clubhouse, and Richard jumped out.

"Thanks, Gordon—fellows—see you soon." The others mumbled a farewell.

As a nonmember, Richard should not be walking across the

Kenwood club grounds, but he knew a short cut to his street. The golf course was not open. He felt a need to breathe fresh air and clear his head. The sun warmed his back. He thought he felt a whiff of spring in the winter air.

The surroundings put him back in a world that seemed to have nothing in common with what had just been discussed in Bunker's SUV. What could possibly be wrong with a world that looked like this? He had been transported from one country club to the other. Here, too, everything exuded wellbeing and solidity. Luxury cars were parked everywhere. A couple of women dressed in tennis whites with short skirts walked from the parking lot towards the indoor tennis courts. At least for the people who could afford a membership, this sphere of life provided an escape from America's troubles.

Though the lovely grounds of the club almost backed up against their home, he and Helen had never thought seriously about joining it. The entrance fee at Kenwood was much lower than at Congressional, but even if they had been able to afford it, they did not think that they could justify the investment, the yearly membership dues, and the monthly minimum for meals. They did not want to be under self-imposed pressure to eat or socialize in a particular place. So far their children had been satisfied to belong to a neighborhood swim and tennis club to which they could walk and where Helen and Richard could play tennis. They rarely felt a craving to play golf, Richard because he did not want to take so much time away from his work.

Richard reflected that deciding what level of privilege and luxury to purchase was for millions of fortunate Americans a routine question. Enjoying pleasures and conveniences that were far out of the reach of most Americans had become more and more a flight from the more disturbing aspects of life. Americans seemed to have a limitless capacity for evading or hiding from festering problems.

Walking home, Richard tried to sort out what had happened in Bunker's car. What precisely had he been trying to articulate? What had made him want to air these reflections in front of his fellow conspirators? He had in a way spoken to himself, he knew, but he had had a strong feeling that others needed to hear his comments. What had made him want to speak, he thought, was that his and Thomas Reed's immediate and very concrete worries about Noah Sales had put him in a frame of mind to recognize that the conspirators were *actually*, not theoretically, going to try to overthrow the U.S. government. His country was *actually*, not theoretically, falling apart. But Richard and probably most of the other conspirators were living under the influence of a culture of distractions and escape that militated against the kind of realism and willingness to act that the situation required. The conspirators had to rid themselves of any illusions and smokescreens through which their society concealed the truth and weakened the will.

He felt a sudden need to be with Helen and the children.

# CHAPTER 37

At the Sorbonne library Helen was directed to the division devoted to maps. A librarian helped her find what she needed. She spent the better part of two hours looking closely at large scale maps of the area of Noisy and beyond. She took notes about what seemed to be estates or large farms and major roads. She did not quite know what she was doing. It was her way of handling that she had not been able to join Duparc and Léger. As her finger moved across the map and she read off the names of towns and roads and creeks, she imagined that she was somehow closer to Richard. But how could she possibly be of any help in this way? She had no idea where there might be owners of green Land Rovers. Did she think that some connection between a point on a map and Richard would suddenly jump out at her? Did she expect to have an intuition that in a particular spot they would find Richard? Did she expect a name to jog an old memory? Was she getting ready to go looking for Richard herself in case the French detectives did not succeed? Did she intend to second-guess the two Frenchmen? How could she possibly do any better than they, the professionals? What she was doing in the map room was not entirely rational, she knew. Pouring over these maps, she was administering a strange therapy. She was desperately trying to keep at bay the fear and agony that threatened to overwhelm her at every moment.

She suddenly realized that she had less than an hour to call Duparc and get ready for the dinner with Ferguson. She walked quickly back to the hotel. She was not really surprised to learn that Duparc had not called. She simply turned around and walked to a pay phone that was located in the street just a block away from the hotel. It was near a Metro station. She dialed the number to Duparc's cell phone. He answered within a couple of rings.

"*Duparc ici.*"

"It's Helen Bittenberg. I'm calling from a telephone booth. I'm sorry to bother you, but I am so eager to hear what you may have found." She realized that Duparc might find her a pest, but she had to talk to him.

"We've only visited four owners of Land Rovers, and for various reasons we don't think we've found the right SUV. We have stopped for the evening and are heading back to Paris. We'll be back out here tomorrow."

She had had no reason to expect quick results, but was deeply disappointed. She told Duparc about having accepted Ferguson's invitation to dinner, which did not please him.

"I'm not sure that seeing Ferguson is a good idea at all. Be very careful about what you tell him. It would be best if he knew nothing about what we're doing. Don't tell him about the Land Rover or the second man at the Sorbonne. Just tell him that we keep checking hospitals and local police stations. What about the paper with the codes?"

"I forgot to ask him for it. Our telephone conversation was very brief. He almost hung up on me. But he already promised to bring it the next time we meet, which is tonight."

"Again, be careful."

"I will."

"As I've said, we'll call you as soon as we have anything of consequence to tell you about the search. Good night." She heard his implicit criticism for being too nosy. But surely he would recognize the horror of what she was going through. He was a married man. When he thought about her situation again, he would regret having scolded her, however gently. She felt tears coming into her eyes. Would the feeling of terror never lift?

As she walked back to the hotel the frustration and distress that the just-concluded telephone call had generated suddenly began to give way to another kind of emotion. The feeling had made itself known before, but for some reason it was now getting stronger. She could not quite define what it was, but anger was a prominent ingredient. Anger at what precisely? Anger generally at having been placed in her current predicament, but mostly, she thought, anger at the people who had brought this nightmare on her and her children—and on Richard, if he was still alive. She realized, without having registered it fully, that she assumed that Richard had been abducted against his will. He had not become ill. He did not lie unconscious in some hospital. He could have been killed. It was all so obvious now: some utterly ruthless people had put her and her family in this hellish situation. She hated them. Her anger was turning into fury, and it mixed with a desire for retribution. She wanted the people who had done this to suffer.

This surge of feeling energized her, filled her with a desire to act. She had been far from inactive in the last several days, but she realized that she had been psychologically passive, distressed, almost paralyzed. She had acted, but in a defensive mode. She now felt an urge to act against her tormentors, to damage them. She didn't know what that might mean, but she wanted to take the initiative, take things into her own hands. Short of jeopardizing the efforts of the French police, she would break out of her paralyzing fear and trepidation.

She would start by trying to entrap Stephen Ferguson. How she did not know. She would use any means at her disposal. There really was no reasonable doubt in her mind: he was involved in the plot to abduct Richard. Why had she ever given him the benefit of her doubts?

As she stood in the shower before dressing for dinner her new attitude took more concrete shape. Starting this evening, she would try to make Ferguson lose his concentration and self-control. She would try to break through that diplomatic reserve and make him reveal more than he intended. Just what hidden truth might be revealed she had no idea, but she understood that she could not hope to achieve her objective by using blunt, heavy instruments. Ferguson was not only bright and perceptive but also experienced and used to pressure. She had to employ subtle wile and sharp tools. She must not make him suspicious—there was that caution again, damn it!— but spin a net in which she might ensnare him. She could assume that he wanted to see her to find out what the French police were up to, but she had no doubt that he was also more than mildly attracted to her as a woman. Those furtive looks and long glances suggested something like a crush.

"Bastard!" she said out loud to herself. She felt another burst of adrenalin. Indignation was welling up within her. "Be careful," she heard Duparc saying, but her immediate response was, "Caution be damned."

She considered dressing provocatively really to catch Ferguson's attention, but checked herself. He wasn't born yesterday. Besides, unless she counted her bikini, she hadn't brought any clothes that showed off her physical endowment. She didn't have many clothes of that sort even in her wardrobe at home. There was that summer evening dress that she had bought on their honeymoon, and that shiny blue formal evening dress that she had bought in a whimsical, playful moment but that she never wore because it seemed a little over-the-top. Having taken an inventory of what little was now available, she decided on a black skirt, a pair of black high heels and a red top that showed her bust line and a bit of cleavage provided she tucked it in tight under the skirt. She used just a little more make-up than for the lunch with Ferguson at *the Carousel*. She spent a little more time on her hair and put on a little more perfume.

She was finished by eight o'clock, but why not let him wait a little? When she stepped out of the elevator into the small hotel lobby about ten minutes late, she found Ferguson at the reception desk just about to call her room. He wore a light-colored suit, a blue shirt, and a red bow tie. He had probably changed at home before picking her up. She was glad to notice that his reaction upon seeing her was barely disguised delight. He seemed to take a quick breath. He kissed her cheek, and she moved a little closer to him than she had before, hoping that he would pick up her scent. "You'll have a hard time this evening, you bastard," she said to herself.

"My car's just outside."

He had come in his private car. It was parked illegally near the entrance to the hotel. As a diplomat he really didn't have to worry much about parking tickets, she knew, but he was probably the kind of person who didn't want to be known at the embassy as a scofflaw even in small matters. His car was a green BMW convertible, though with its top up. He opened the passenger side door for her. Ordinarily she would have tried while seating herself next to another person to pull her skirt down as much as possible over her thighs, but this time she did not. She did not wear any nylon stockings. Her legs had been recently shaved and had a light tan. As Ferguson sat down in the driver's seat and moved his hand towards the gearshift and air-conditioning control, she was certain that he was stealing a view of her legs. Out of the corner of his eye, he was probably also looking down her front under the guise of turning to her in conversation. She was rather pleased with her bust line. Her breasts were not large but full and shapely. The red top showed them off without baring too much skin. He might see a hint of her nipples. "I hope you will soon be as excited, tense, confused, and conflicted as you can, you son of a bitch," she thought.

# CHAPTER 38

The months had worn on, and new duties in the conspiracy had been piled on Richard Bittenberg, sometimes exhausting him and making him gasp for air. It was long ago that he had felt like the new kid on the block. He had become an experienced conspirator, a veteran who could advise and train others. He had learned with difficulty to live with chronic stress.

It was on a sunny April afternoon, over a year after he joined the conspiracy, that Richard received the call on the scrambler phone in his study that he would remember as the beginning of the period of permanent crisis. It would be a time of sharply intensified pressure, anxiety and strain. It would push him up against the limits of his endurance.

Richard had just returned home in the late afternoon after teaching one of his courses at the university. Though rushed and preoccupied, he had noticed that the weather was glorious, and on the way home he had opened the sunroof of the car. The sky was a crisp blue and the air was warm. There was almost no wind. Spring had arrived. This would have been a day for taking a long walk, for savoring the calm, beauty, and promise of nature, but he was unable to enjoy what he noticed. He had an oppressive sense of the daunting, nerve-racking task before the conspirators and of the fact that he did not have nearly enough time to live up to his many and various responsibilities. On arriving home he had found Helen starting to make preparations for dinner. She always tried hard to get the entire family together around the dinner table. Richard was well aware that he was the one who most frequently ruined her plans. He had given Helen a peck on the cheek and mumbled something about having a lot of work to do. She had smiled helplessly and squeezed his arm before he disappeared downstairs. His most urgent task was to try to make progress writing a lecture that he had been invited to give at the University of Chicago the following week. Although the invitation was honorific and his remarks would attract considerable attention, he was badly, very uncomfortably, behind in preparing the manuscript. He did not even have a rough draft, had not even started writing the most important section of the lecture. He was having difficulty concentrating. He was in a state of constant suspense, was always painfully conscious of the fact that his life and that of his family would soon, perhaps suddenly, change drastically.

The danger that the conspiracy would be discovered was never far from his mind. Though meticulous care had been taken by the chief conspirators to select only committed, dependable people for subordinate groups and to shield themselves even from the layer of individuals immediately below them, some hundred people knew quite well what sort of thing was being planned. Given the mixed motives and flawed natures of human beings, each new day increased the risk that the conspiracy would start to unravel or, worse, would suddenly be discovered by the government. Quite apart from the dangers of defection or betrayal, the government had at its disposal highly sophisticated methods for spying on its own citizens. Real privacy barely existed any more. Growing tensions within the steering committee and the need for more and increasingly dangerous planning added to the pressure. Richard found it next to impossible to find the kind of scholarly peace that the writing of a good academic paper required.

It consumed so much of his energy merely to try to hide from Helen, the rest of the family, his colleagues, students, and friends that he was almost always on tenterhooks. It pained him to see the worry on Helen's face. His words of reassurance did not have the intended effect. From her he could not really conceal his ragged emotional state. He had not even made much progress reducing his various academic commitments, as she had long urged him to do. His habits were too old and too deeply ingrained. Instead he had piled his new and increasingly demanding work as a conspirator on top of his normal academic work. He defended his choice to himself by telling himself that he must not cause speculation by markedly changing his pattern of life at the university and in his academic discipline. The result was that he had begun to cut corners. Here he was, the week before he was supposed to give a major lecture at a major academic institution, struggling to finish a rough draft of the manuscript! In normal circumstances he would have started to prepare months in advance. The week before giving the lecture he would at most be polishing an acceptable text. Taking care in writing a paper might appear a trifle compared to actions that would have large and worldwide significance, but the scholar in him was protesting loudly.

John and Anne did not even bother to ask him to do things with them. It seemed that each time he tried to make himself more available to them some pressing matter would come up. And yet, what was this delinquency compared to the danger and potential disgrace to which he was exposing his family? Sometimes he wondered how he could possibly be morally justified in associating himself with the conspiracy. His actions were at the expense of his wife and children in the present but also jeopardized their future welfare. Sometimes when doubts assailed him he almost persuaded himself to break with the conspiracy, but each time he pulled back. "No excuses. If not me, then who?"

Poor Helen, he thought. In spite of his efforts to hide it, she knew that he was under great pressure. She did not know the main reason, but he sensed her worry not just from her expressions of concern but also from her looks of empathy, even fear. At times she showed anger, but when she made a sharp remark her primary motivation usually was not personal irritation. She was trying, for his sake and that of the children, to make him change his ways. Or she spoke out of sheer frustration. She had every reason to be upset with him, and still she tried to make him reform without antagonizing him. He was very lucky, he knew, to have such a wife. Sometimes his pangs of conscience regarding Helen and the children overwhelmed him. He ached to tell her what accounted for his condition. He wanted her to comfort him and encourage him. He wanted her to confirm his assessment of his responsibility and assuage his doubts. But he knew that in order to provide her and the children some protection he must keep them wholly in the dark. He was virtually certain that, if he were to tell her about his involvement in the conspiracy, she would be incredulous, aghast. She would probably do everything to separate him from the conspiracy. But his country was in desperate trouble, and the conspirators needed him. He realized that, deep down, he was convinced of the rightness of his course. Otherwise, how could he possibly expose people he loved so much to such danger? He told himself that his involvement in the conspiracy was intended to secure a better future for Helen, John and Anne, but he recognized that he had subordinated their wellbeing to what he considered an even more important objective. Whatever he might tell himself, in practice he assumed that the cause of the conspirators mattered more than his family. He was just one of myriad people in history who had let a cause take precedence. But sometimes it troubled him that so many of those who had done so before him had been twisted, conceited, cynical manipulators of their fellow human beings. Some of them had been ruthless—monsters even. They had masked a limitless desire for power by portraying themselves as great benefactors of mankind, as people ushering in a new and vastly better age for humanity. In his darker moments he asked himself whether he might be such a person, deluded as to his real motives.

Richard neglected his physical exercise more and more, and he slept less than was normal for him. He also did not sleep well. It happened that he got up in the middle of the night and went to his study. He would rather try to get some work done than toss and turn in bed. He had started to worry about his health. His yearly physical a few months earlier had revealed no acute, serious problems, but his blood pressure had been up sufficiently for his doctor to prescribe a medicine. His doctor had also told him that unless he could lower his bad cholesterol — which would mean new eating habits and more exercise — he would need to take another medicine. Yet Richard had done little or nothing to mend his ways. He realized that he was in distress.

The conspirators used the scrambler phone only for important business that was also urgent. Richard rarely used it. He was looking blankly at the computer screen, trying to concentrate on the paper for the University of Chicago when the scrambler phone rang. It was about 6:00 PM. Helen had not yet called him to dinner. He was struggling to compose a difficult passage in the lecture while wondering how in the world he would be able to finish the manuscript in just a few days, during which he had to handle other commitments. His first reaction upon hearing the telephone signal was irritation at the interruption. As he opened the drawer in which he kept the phone he knew that the reason for the call would not be trivial.

There was no need for Vandenhorst to identify himself. He simply said: "I'm glad you were near the phone. Could you meet me in an hour at "B"? "B" was their code for a coffee shop in a Barnes & Noble bookstore in downtown Bethesda. Richard had recognized Vandenhorst's voice instantly but thought that this time he noticed something out of the ordinary about it. It seemed to have a slight tremble, a tenseness that Richard did not think that he had heard before. Was that merely because you notice more about a person's voice on the telephone? Or was Vandenhorst just a little out of breath? Richard told him that he would come to the meeting place.

Richard went upstairs to talk to Helen. They usually sat down to dinner about 6:30. She was in the middle of preparing their meal.

"Helen, I just got an urgent message. I'm sorry, but I need to go out for a couple of hours. A person's in town who wants to meet me in Bethesda. He has access to foundation money and could be a great help to my institute. I just have to seize the opportunity." Richard had become a practiced liar, and Helen did not question him about what he had just said. But she turned from the counter towards him, and he noticed immediately that strong emotions were flooding her.

"Richard, that visitor gave you awfully short notice. Pretty bad manners, if you ask me."

"I know, Helen, but he just got an unexpected opening, and I've been trying for a long time to get to see him. I really need to talk to him."

"Richard, do you know when you last had dinner with the rest of us?"

"Eh—I know, Helen—eh, it was last week sometime. But I really have to meet this person."

"You don't remember, but it was last Wednesday that you had dinner at home. And we didn't see you at all last weekend because of that conference in Atlanta."

"I'm sorry."

"What does it matter that you are sorry, when you do nothing to limit your absences or to make up for them?" Her voice was rising, and her cheeks were getting flushed. Her eyes shot arrows. She was angry, but he could see that her anger was mixed with frustration and sadness.

"I'm really sorry, Helen. I will really break free after that Chicago lecture."

"Why do you think that will happen? You keep telling me that you're going to reduce your commitments and spend more time with us, but it simply never happens." Her voice was becoming uncharacteristically loud and sharp. She usually did not speak harshly to Richard when any of the children might be within earshot. He saw tears coming into her eyes, whether of anger or of sorrow he couldn't tell.

He walked towards her, extending his arms to embrace her, but she took a step back, putting her hands up.

"No, Richard, leave me alone!" Her words had a sharp edge.

"But—"

"Just go to your meeting. First things first!" The fact that she had now lowered her voice and spoke tersely and coldly heightened the impact of her words.

"Helen, that's so unfair—"

"What's unfair about it? You can always find time for others, but never for us."

"You're exaggerating—"

"You go! We'll manage without you—we're used to it."

Suddenly Anne appeared in the kitchen door. She wore an

awkward, worried look.

"What are you two going on about?" She looked apprehensively at them.

Helen looked quickly away, but Anne had seen her flushed, upset face.

"Dad?"

"Oh, it's nothing, dear. I just need to go out for a couple of hours. An important meeting that came up suddenly."

"So, you won't have dinner with us. You haven't eaten with us since last week." Helen kept standing with her back turned to the other two, both of her hands resting on the kitchen counter.

"I'll probably be back by eight, or nine at the latest," Richard said. "I could help you with your homework, if you need it."

"At nine!?" Anne's said sarcastically. That's when mom wants me to get ready for bed." She looked in Helen's direction, then left the kitchen and ran upstairs. Helen heard her leave, turned the gas stove off, turned around and wanted to walk past Richard to follow Anne, but he blocked her path. He tried again to wrap his arms around her.

"Please, Helen, I love you."

She pushed him away, and, looking fiercely at him, said, "What makes you think so?" She walked past him.

Richard stood in the middle of the kitchen floor alone. He could not move. He felt completely empty, as if sucked into a vacuum. Then, as he became aware of his whereabouts, emotions and desires streamed over him. Anger, grief, self-pity, frustration, worry, and self-contempt battered him, paralyzing him by their intensity. For the better part of a minute he just stood there feeling utterly miserable. He finally forced himself to draw a deep breath and to take a short step, then another, pulling himself out of the crippling, painful jumble within. He knew he had to try to orient himself to that other oppressive world outside in which he was expected to act.

He realized that he had come within inches of his breaking point.

He heard Helen and Anne's muted voices upstairs. They seemed to come from Anne's room. The door was closed. Music was coming from John's room. He probably was not aware of the just-concluded scene. Richard forced himself not to go upstairs. He took a sports jacket from the downstairs closet, opened the front door, and left the house. He needed fresh air and time to settle his nerves. He would walk to the meeting place, which would take him about twenty minutes.

How long would he be able to stand the pressures? They

seemed to bear down on him from every side. It made him miserable to know that he was treating his family terribly. And yet what were his shortcomings as a husband and a father compared to the excruciating ordeal to which he might eventually subject his family! What was he doing? Would he be able to go through with it? But he was truly needed. The planned action just had to be taken. His conscience would not let him escape from doing his part. This meant that the pressures and uncertainties of the conspiracy and the strains of his family situation would intensify rather than dissipate. But how much more could he take? Helen had expressed worries about his health. She did not even know the main source of his distress.

He longed to tell her everything, but he had to bear this burden himself.

Oh, Helen.

# CHAPTER 39

Helen and Ferguson arrived at a restaurant near the Moulin Rouge. He gave the car keys to an attendant and walked around the car to open the door for her. Standing on the curb, he held out his hand to assist her in getting out of the vehicle. By not trying to catch his gaze while getting out of the car she gave him another opportunity to take her in. Once on the curb she gave him an appreciative smile.

Walking into the restaurant, he put his arm lightly around her waist. She almost whipped it away.

"It's good to see you, Helen," he said once they were seated at a table. "I've been so worried about you. You must be under such stress and feel so lonely."

You damned hypocrite, she thought.

"You're very kind," she said. "I so appreciate it. I don't know what I would do without your help."

"I want to support you in whatever way I can."

She reached across the table and put her hand on his, letting it linger for a few seconds. She squeezed his hand lightly before withdrawing hers.

"Thank you, Stephen."

When he asked whether she would like an aperitif, she said: "Yes, please, I need one. May I have a Campari and soda?"

He ordered a scotch and soda for himself. Good, she thought. This time she would try to loosen his tongue. Little alcohol for her, but as much as possible for him.

She asked him to order food for both of them. What she ate did not matter. He selected a bottle of red wine with some care. The waiter left with their order.

"How are you doing, really?" he said. How caring he sounded.

"Only marginally better than last time we met," she answered. "I suppose I've adapted more to the situation, but the uncertainty of it all is wearing me out."

"Of course it is."

"To make matters worse I blame myself for having somehow contributed to this situation—although I don't have any idea of what's happened to him. I don't believe any longer that he's trying to punish me or the children. It would be simply too cruel. Even if he had that idea to start, something else happened. I find myself thinking that he was killed in a robbery or car accident but that his body is where it won't be found for a long time."

"Your thinking seems to have turned in a gruesome direction. Wouldn't it be better not to guess at all?

"Easier said than done. My head keeps telling me not to speculate. But how do you shut down your imagination?"

"I understand."

"This waiting is frightful, Stephen. Richard and I have been gliding apart for a long time, but if he's alive I want him to be found very soon, especially for the sake of the children." She checked herself. Had she almost suggested that she wanted Richard to reappear mostly for the sake of the children? Not even an estranged wife would think like that. But surely Ferguson had not taken her to mean that as far as she was concerned Richard might just as well be dead. In conversation we often seem to say more than we mean. Probably no damage had been done, but she had to watch herself — without losing the initiative.

"I want this ordeal to be over, Stephen. If Richard's dead, I want to know it. At least the children and I would be able to get on with our lives. We're in limbo now." That's better, she thought.

She sat silently for a moment, holding her drink in her hand.

"How are the children?" he asked.

"They are brave, but they are of course worried sick. At least they are at home now, in familiar surroundings. My parents are trying to keep them distracted."

"Have the police gotten anywhere?" Here it comes, she thought. He's finally getting to what he really wants to know. First he needed to play the caring, considerate friend. Be careful now, she told herself.

"Not really, not so far as I can tell. Only a couple of people seem to be assigned to the case, and police work seems very slow and tedious. They keep checking hospitals and police records, going further and further away from Paris, but they've come up with nothing. I think they may have contacted Interpol. They don't want me to be too discouraged, so they make it appear as if no news is good news. They must be on the wrong track. But then I've no idea what the right track might be." She took another sip of her drink, masking how little of the liquid she let pass down her throat. At the same time she watched discreetly for what kind of reaction her statement had elicited. Did he look relieved?

"And you've had no further thoughts about what might be behind Richard's disappearance?" Prodding, prodding.

"I'm afraid not. The police, too, have asked me. I've kept searching my memory for clues, but I'm drawing a blank."

The bottle of wine and the appetizers arrived. Ferguson approved the wine and let the waiter serve it.

"Let's drink to better times," Ferguson said.

"I'll drink to that. In fact, let's not even talk any more about this whole situation. I need a break. Cheers!" She feigned drinking rather deeply from her wine glass. She had to seem interested in drinking. They were sitting in a line of tables that was separated from another line by a rack with plants and flowers. If Ferguson were to leave the table for a moment to go to the men's room she could pour some of her wine into a flowerpot.

He smiled, and she smiled back. She decided to rattle and test him.

"Oh, Stephen, before I forget, did you bring that paper with the strange notes?"

At first he looked blankly at her. Then he rolled his eyes and made an annoyed and exasperated face. He lifted his arms in a gesture of self-disgust.

"I'm sorry, Helen, I'm so sorry! I plain forgot. I was going to get it from the man at the embassy, but something came up in the afternoon, and I simply forgot all about it."

She almost hit him in the face. "You bastard!," she cried silently. "You lying s.o.b.!" She had to struggle to conceal her emotions. Had he detected any of her reaction?

"That's too bad," she said. Not to seem unconcerned about his delinquency, she added, "I'd hoped that the police might make something of the note." Ferguson had not contacted any expert, she knew, but he would expect her to ask, and she wanted to see how he would handle the question. He could not say that he had forgotten to talk to the expert, and a person at the embassy who had been asked for an opinion by the number two man would have offered one without delay, without being prompted. She said: "Did your expert have anything to say about those code-like notations?"

"Not much luck there, I'm afraid. He couldn't make much sense of it in terms that he recognized. It's probably just Richard's way of keeping track of something, perhaps something related to his research. A filing system?"

"But why would he be carrying the note around with him?"

"Could the notes refer to boxes or folders in a library collection that he is using in his current work? Or assignments in some research project? Or references to a book or document in some shorthand of his?"

"Perhaps so." She reached for her glass. The suggestions struck her immediately as credible, and she pondered it, forgetting for the moment her mission for the evening. She could not remember how much she had told Ferguson about Richard's intention to visit the Sorbonne library. She only knew that they had not really discussed it. That made Ferguson's last purported guess regarding the notes a particularly clever diversion. His reluctance to return the paper had made her think that it was related to Richard's disappearance, but Ferguson's guesses were more than plausible. They must have seemed to him likely to capture her imagination and steer it in the wrong direction—assuming that he had some notion of their real meaning. He must be expecting a reaction from her. After remaining silent for a while she decided to play along with him.

"Your guess about the paper containing research notes of some kind would explain why Richard brought the paper with him to Europe. He wanted to do some research at the Sorbonne library. But then the paper would interest the police only if there's some connection between his research interests and his disappearance."

Her comment should put Ferguson at ease, but even as she spoke she knew that there was at least one thing wrong with the hypothesis: When Richard went to the library he had left the paper at the hotel. But he might have forgotten that it was in his other jacket.

Ferguson had to realize that he had bought just a little more time. He would have to surrender it soon.

"There's of course another explanation for his bringing the paper with him to Europe," he said.

"What's that?"

He smiled. "He could have done it without intending to. I find old folded papers in my inside pockets all the time."

What he had said made sense, but it did not throw any light on the meaning of the notes. She was not surprised that Ferguson had been ready with a backup explanation designed to reduce interest in the paper.

She needed to regain the initiative.

"Oh, Stephen, here we go again, don't we? More idle speculation. I wish we could talk about something else. Just get that paper to me as soon as you can."

He nodded.

Their entrees were brought. To get on to non-sensitive territory she said that she had some appetite for a change—which was not true—and that she was enjoying the food. They discussed

French cooking. She took her glass and hinted at a toast. He, too, drank, though more deeply than she. He thought he had weathered the crisis, she thought.

"Stephen, when we meet we talk only about me and my troubles. We never talk about you. I would like to know more about you—about your work, your interests, your daughters."

The conversation shifted. Ferguson did not dwell on his own life but offered brief summaries. She knew enough about the Foreign Service to recognize from what he told her that he had had a stellar diplomatic career. He had had good postings in a very promising sequence. He would undoubtedly become an ambassador before long, probably in a not insignificant country. She also learned that he had generally good relations with his daughters and saw them as often as he could. He had strong cultural interests, especially in music, and had many French friends and acquaintances. He was a little of a Francophile, which was unusual for an American. He spoke good French. Helen did what she could to make her part of the conversation seem spontaneous and relaxed. From time to time she held his gaze, letting him think that she wanted to know his story but also that she was admiring him and taking a deepening interest in him as a man. She wanted to relax him and to stimulate his erotic interest so that he would lower his guard.

Helen had to drink more than she wanted not to seem to be holding back, but she kept taking small sips. She was glad to see that Ferguson was not. Towards the end of the main course he ordered a second bottle of wine for them, and the waiter topped up their glasses. He toasted her, and it seemed to Helen that he drank rather greedily. After ordering a sorbet, cheese, and coffee to follow he asked to be excused for a moment. As he left the table Helen looked around her to make sure that nobody was looking and very discreetly poured more than half of the contents of her glass into the flower pot just to her right. She would have needed to visit a restroom, but it would have to wait. She touched up her lipstick at the table.

When Ferguson returned she could tell that he had combed his hair, washed his face, and, yes, retied or adjusted his bow tie. He had barely sat down before he took another sizeable swallow from the wine glass. The waiter, who hovered attentively, soon topped it up, and Helen let him do the same for her. The waiter brought the sorbet.

Helen noticed that Ferguson was trying more and more to hold her gaze. He bent further forward in a gesture of intimacy.

"You haven't told me anything about your wife," she said.

"We met at the State Department in Washington. She was a

professional staffer. He told their story, seeming to speak fondly of his wife.

"But she got breast cancer. She received excellent care from the beginning, but it was too late. Her last year was miserable. We were posted to Geneva then. She got the very best medical care, but she kept deteriorating. It was a terrible time. Our girls were miserable." For a moment Helen did not feel merely anger and resentment towards him.

She reached across the table and put her hand over his, now giving it a sustained squeeze. He looked deeply into her eyes.

"What happened to you reminds me that I'm not the only one in the world who's had a difficult time," Helen said.

"We can perhaps understand each other," he said. You bastard, she thought. You are one of the *reasons* why I am so miserable.

"But you must have been very lonely since your wife died."

Ferguson again drank deeply from his glass. "I suppose so, yes, but my work is very demanding and time-consuming."

"Various women must have tried to get your attention. A man like you—" She gave him a glance of feigned admiration. What she had said was not implausible. Ferguson was an accomplished man, and he was handsome, if not strikingly so. His manner and conversation could be engaging, if somewhat dry.

"I suppose some women have shown an interest. I meet a lot of people socially. A diplomat has to go to many parties. But I also need to be careful and show discretion." Ferguson was speaking clearly, but it seemed to Helen that the wine was getting to him. He had almost slurred "discretion." The second bottle of wine was more than half empty.

"Any serious lady friend?"

"Not really." He looked inquiringly at her as if trying to figure out why she was asking. He offered her some more wine and filled his own glass.

"To a better future," she said, lifting her glass. She let it rest longer against her lower lip than was necessary to take a small sip.

He seemed to wonder what was on her mind. While avoiding any overt gestures, she wanted him to think that she might be sexually attracted to him. She was hoping that wine and repressed desire would undermine his accustomed self-discipline and make him confide in her.

"You must be doing something in your free time other than listening to music and going to the opera and museums. I got the impression before that you have some good male friends."

"I do. One or two of them are at the embassy, a couple are at the embassies of other countries, and I have some rather close French friends. They are usually married, though, so I'm a little of an odd man out in their homes."

"Haven't they tried to introduce you to single women?" She wanted him to think that she was particularly interested in his relations to the opposite sex and that she might even be a little jealous of any woman in his life.

"Perhaps they have, but they' haven't found me the right person. Perhaps I wasn't ready for a serious relationship."

He reached across the table for her hand, but interrupted the movement and let his hand come down on his side of the table. He gave her a hazy, bewildered look and took another swig from his glass. He changed the subject.

"But I've loved being here in Paris. This is easily my best posting to date. Despite all the work."

"You feel rather at home in France, don't you?" she said in an intimate, smiling way, as if she wanted to share his innermost thoughts. He responded by leaning even closer to her. His eyes were a little glassy, his cheeks redder than when he returned from the bathroom. The waiter brought the cheeses.

"Do you get to see anything other than Paris?" she asked.

"I have to do some traveling in my work, but French friends of mine have also invited me to their vacation homes in other parts of France. One particularly good friend has a place in Antibes, near Nice. Provence is so beautiful. That part of France is irresistible. In the summer half of the years especially, the Mediterranean is incredible."

"I know what you mean. I was there many years ago. It stayed with me."

"If I could afford it," Ferguson said, "I would buy a place there. But to be able to buy anything worth owning down there you have to be rich, like my friend." Good, Helen thought, he had become sufficiently personal not to conceal his finances from her.

"My friend's a nobleman," he added. Is he trying now to impress me with his friends, she wondered. "He inherited wealth. He's got a chateau outside of Paris. He's even got a vineyard."

He had Helen's complete attention. She had to make a special effort not to give away her intense interest. She smiled faintly.

"That sounds lovely, Stephen," she said. She tried to infuse her own voice with some of the same emotional intensity that she had noticed in his. The alcohol had clearly affected him. She wondered if he was imagining himself with her in the French countryside. She hoped that all the wine had made him less attentive and that he would not make anything of her next question.

"Where's the vineyard? Any place I might know?"

"Oh—." He hesitated. "A little village called Evremond. Just an hour or so from Paris."

Helen's heart almost stopped. Evremond—that was one of the names she had come across in her irrational exploration of the map at the Sorbonne! Near Noisy. To control her agitation she just said the first thing that came into her mind that might sound innocuous and mask her emotions.

"I've always loved vineyards. There are quite a few of them in Virginia you know, and you can visit many of them and taste their wines."

"Here, too, in many places."

Helen wondered if she was trembling. She put her hands on her lap to hide them. How could she keep him from noticing her frame of mind? She must not fidget. She thought of taking another sip of wine but thought the better of it. Her hand might quiver. And she needed to stay sober. She looked dreamily into his eyes instead.

"How did you get to know this French friend of yours?"

"He knows my father. They were both diplomats, met in Rio de Janeiro. Dad was older, but they had similar interests, and they stayed in touch. When I was assigned to Paris, my father, who's elderly now, told me to look him up. My father's friend had retired from the French diplomatic service. He was a senior ambassador and then had a high post in the French foreign office and worked in industry as well." Helen thought she detected a wish to impress her. She was also glad to notice that Ferguson had said "ambasshador." He was no longer likely to notice small changes in her demeanor. Ferguson continued: "He's generally very well-connected. He's considerably older than me, but we hit it off well, have similar views of the world." Helen noticed from both his movements and his voice that he was more than a little tipsy. A new warmth had come into his speech."

"I get the impression that you like this man very much."

"I do. He's the kind of human being you wish had some real influence in this world. He's dignified and honest, and he cares about more than himself. He's knowledgeable, experienced, cosmopolitan, and yet very French. So different from those superficial technocrats who are setting the tone in Europe these days and from those grubby, self-serving types who've taken charge of the United States." There was a new energy in Ferguson's voice. He reached for his glass, which was almost empty. The second bottle, too, was running out. He looked for the waiter.

Helen had heard opinions of this kind before. She could have said, "Stephen, you remind me of Richard," but the last thing she wanted was to disturb the growing intimacy of their conversation. Instead she said, "He sounds like a fine man."

"He is. I suppose he's become a kind of substitute father to me here in France."

"Does he have a wife?"

"She died." Finding Helen's glass almost full, Ferguson emptied the last of the wine bottle in his own glass and looked again for the waiter.

"Does this nobleman have a well-known name?" Helen tried to sound no more than casually interested.

Ferguson again seemed to hesitate. While she cut a piece of cheese on her plate she felt his eyes on her. Was he wondering why she had asked the question? She looked up, smiling as if the question barely mattered to her. His eyes were glassy and a little red. Are you having difficulty keeping your thoughts straight, you bastard, she wondered to herself.

In a half-slurred manner that was difficult for her to hear he said: "De la Broderie."

He must have decided, she thought, that she had had no other reason for asking about the name than the typical American curiosity about royalty and people with titles. She was not sure that she had caught the name, but she could not risk asking him to repeat it. To give the impression that she was not very interested, she returned to the subject of Ferguson's life in Paris, all the while trying to memorize the name. She could only guess at the spelling.

She should not openly flirt with Ferguson. Even in his present condition it might make him suspicious, but she tried without being too obvious to make herself alluring to him. Her red top had sunk a little lower in front, and she made no attempt to adjust it. She put both of her elbows on the table, letting one of her hands touch the side of her face, which made her lean forward and made her cleavage more conspicuous. She noticed that whenever she looked away from Ferguson his eyes kept returning to what had become a rather revealing décolletage. To increase his interest she occasionally drew a long and deep breath.

When the waiter returned, Ferguson indicated that he might order more wine and asked what she would like. Helen wanted to leave. She wanted to call Inspector Duparc immediately. But she also did not want Ferguson to think that she did not want to prolong her time with him, so she just said that she still had wine in her glass and was fine. The waiter asked if they would like an after-dinner drink.

Helen declined, but Ferguson ordered a cognac with his coffee. He had consumed at least two-thirds of the two bottles of wine in addition to the scotch and soda earlier in the evening. It had been a long dinner, so, though he was not really drunk, he was not sober either. He had to be in a really convoluted state, Helen thought — off balance. His memory of the evening would be foggy.

The remainder of the dinner was uneventful, but Ferguson seemed to be in a state of suppressed agitation. He got more and more careless stealing glimpses of her. He had to work at keeping his speech distinct.

When Helen glanced at her wristwatch he said, "I should be getting you home to bed, shouldn't I?," making her almost laugh out loud because of what she was certain was going on in his imagination. "It's after midnight." He waved for the waiter and requested the bill.

She asked to be excused for a moment. She had to pass him to walk in the direction of the ladies room, and she was certain that he turned around to watch her walk away. She made no effort to limit the natural swaying of her hips. When she returned she had touched up her make-up and brushed her hair. She had tucked her red top more tightly into her skirt and held out her chest. He stood up as she approached.

"This has been a wonderful dinner, Stephen. You treated me to just the kind of evening I needed."

"I'm glad you think so. I hope we can meet again very soon."

"I don't see why not." She gave him a long look and a smile intended to be at once inviting and inscrutable.

As they left the table she stepped close to him and gave him a kiss on the cheek, putting her lips near his mouth and her body closer to him than she normally would for such a gesture. She also put an arm lightly around him. She was both revolted and pleased to notice incontrovertible physical evidence of his desire for her. "Thank you, Stephen," she whispered in his ear.

"I'll take you home in a cab," he said. I've had too much to drink to drive." His speech was thick, probably from a mixture of alcohol and sexual arousal, she thought. His usually rather pale face was flushed, and there were droplets of sweat on his forehead.

Within moments they got a taxi. He held the door open for her. She made no effort when sitting down to pull down her skirt or to pull up her top. Let him stew, she thought. She gave the driver the address to her hotel. The only light in the back seat came from the dashboard of the car and the outside. She wondered if Ferguson would try to kiss her or if his self-discipline and caution would win out. He had to be a bundle of tensions, his desire fighting his caution.

"Helen," he said, in an indistinct voice.

"Yes," she answered, looking up into his face.

"I have a confession to make."

"Yes."

"I'm in a very awkward position — I —"

All of a sudden his face was close to hers, and his lips were eagerly seeking hers. One of his hands slipped behind her back and the other cupped one of her breasts. His body pressed up against her.

She was not unprepared for his sudden advance, only for the fervor of it. She forced herself not to break out of his embrace immediately or to turn her face away. She barely responded to his kiss, but let him have his way for a couple of seconds, feeling the intensity of his ardor, before she started to resist him. When she did she did not scream or slap him or violently push him away. She just turned her face and said without raising her voice: "Stephen, Stephen — no , no — wait — I don't know — It's so soon — give me some time." She pushed him away gently but firmly.

He didn't try to overpower her. He withdrew. Their being in the back seat of a taxi probably helped control him, she guessed.

"You understand, don't you, Stephen?"

"Yes, I think so. I was rash. I'm sorry."

She let her hand touch his cheek. "I'm not blaming you, Stephen — I just need time. I'm confused."

Suddenly the taxi stopped. They were at her hotel. Perfect timing, she thought. She gave Ferguson a squeeze of the hand and a peck on the cheek and got out of the car. He made no attempt to follow her. She caught a glimpse of his befuddled expression. She waved tentatively to him. The cab drove away.

She had to call Duparc right away. What time was it? The clock in the hotel lobby showed 12:30.

# CHAPTER 40

Richard was still numb and rattled from the episode in the Bittenberg kitchen. He wanted to calm himself and sort out the chaos. He walked briskly from his home and arrived at the Barnes & Noble bookstore in Bethesda with time to spare before the meeting with Vandenhorst. He bought a café latte in the upstairs coffee shop and wandered aimlessly around the store. It was a weekday, but there were plenty of customers.

This part of downtown Bethesda had become more and more ritzy over the years. Bethesda as a whole was one of America's most affluent suburbs, an entire city actually, that had grown together with the District of Columbia. Its appealing downtown featured numerous restaurants, including many noted for their cuisine, specialty stores, art galleries, a large movie theatre showing films for discriminating audiences, and a couple of upscale auto dealerships. There were office buildings and condominium high-rises to one side and residential neighborhoods, some of them rather bucolic, in the direction of the Bittenberg home. Many residents of the District of Columbia came to Bethesda for business or to shop and enjoy themselves. Parts of the area were reminiscent of central or southern Europe. Just in the middle sat the Barnes & Noble bookstore. It, the movie theatre across the street, and the many restaurants were gathering places for a rather cosmopolitan, highly educated clientele, including diplomats and denizens of Washington's international organizations. Some of the restaurants had started table service outside the week before.

Richard browsed nervously among the bookshelves. He reflected that, though the people in the store undoubtedly had personal problems and pressures of their own, they seemed to be enjoying some leisure, taking their time over books, magazines, or newspapers — as if nothing were badly wrong with their own lives. As for himself, he was fretfully preoccupied with his troubles. His walk, in wonderful weather, had taken him through pleasant residential neighborhoods with crisp green lawns where the faint colors on budding trees and bushes foreshadowed the orgy of flowering soon to come. He had been vaguely aware of the glory of nature in his surroundings, but they had done nothing to mute the pain from the scene back in the kitchen. As he knew that Vandenhorst would have important business to discuss, he had tried to distract himself, but with little success. What had happened had shaken him to the core. It had brought many months of stress and worry to the surface.

Richard saw Vandenhorst arrive through the main entrance almost exactly on time. He was well-groomed as usual, without ostentation. He wore a gray suit, a white shirt, and a discreet blue tie—looked like an old-fashioned downtown Washington lawyer, perhaps, stopping at Barnes & Noble on his way home. As Vandenhorst extended his hand in greeting, his smile and relaxed manner made Richard wonder if this meeting might have waited. His family crisis might have been avoided.

Richard asked whether Vandenhorst would like to have coffee in the Barnes & Noble coffee shop.

"No, thanks, we should be leaving in a moment. Gordon's parking his car. We're to meet him out front."

"You didn't mention that Gordon would be coming."

"No, but he's the one who alerted me to the trouble."

"What's up?"

"Something serious," Vandenhorst said in a low voice. "We'll have decisions to make."

Vandenhorst was a master at hiding his feelings in tense situations. Richard had never seen him outwardly nervous or seen him lose his temper. He had never asked for an impromptu meeting except to deal with an urgent and serious problem. Having noticed tension in Vandenhorst's voice on the telephone, Richard wondered if this time Vandenhorst's face or movements would betray real stress.

"Since it's such a nice evening, why not take a walk?" Vandenhorst said.

"Fine with me. But won't the three of us look rather conspicuous. Someone might recognize one or more of us and wonder what we're up to."

"I wouldn't worry. We all have that deep interest in history and have a little history club. But we might duck into a restaurant eventually, a noisy one. Have you had dinner?"

"No." Richard wondered what dinner had been like back home. Helen had walked away from the stove. He gulped the last of his coffee. "Is Hick around?"

"No, I didn't think I would need him or one of the others tonight."

They had no sooner walked outside when they saw Bunker's large frame approaching. He was dressed informally. His handshake was firm as always.

"Let's walk over to Wisconsin Avenue," Vandenhorst said. Wisconsin Avenue, which ran all the way from Georgetown in Washington, D.C., far into Maryland, was two blocks away. It was the most heavily trafficked and noisy street in the area, especially during rush hour. "We can return to this vicinity later and have a drink and something to eat."

"I can use the exercise," Bunker said. "Too much sitting, too much aggravation."

"What's happened?" Richard asked.

"Somebody just threw a big monkey wrench into our planning," Vandenhorst said, showing in his manner and tone of voice that lowered voices were in order. "It's about Reed."

Bunker took over, speaking in what was for him almost a whisper: "Reed just found out that he can expect to be transferred out of his present job way ahead of schedule."

"What!? Why!? He's been Commanding General of the Washington military district for less than a year!" Richard was incredulous.

"It's an unusual development," Bunker said, "but he's had unofficial word that he will be moved about six months from now. It's one of these games of musical chairs. He's in line for a top job in Europe. It will mean another star for him."

Richard said nothing, taking in the enormity of what he had just heard. The news was devastating. Reed's role in the coup attempt had been the military cornerstone of each of the three main plans on which they had concentrated their attention. Nothing could have been more unexpected than that Reed would suddenly be out of the picture. They had considered contingencies and alternatives over and over, but with regard to military matters they had always assumed that their main problem was Noah Sales, partly because his personality introduced an element of unpredictability, partly because he might be transferred not long after the new Congress would be sworn in, which did not leave the conspiracy much time. They had sometimes wondered whether the reason for Sale's growing impatience was the risk that he might miss his great opportunity. But Reed! He should have been safe for the entire relevant period.

"Couldn't Reed decline the transfer or ask to have it postponed?" Richard realized as he asked the question that it was probably naïve.

"Not in a case like this," Bunker said. "Musical chairs, as I said. Reed's replacement has probably already been picked. It would, in effect, be up or out for Reed. The top brass would really wonder about anybody resisting a move like this one."

"Do you suppose somebody over at the Pentagon has gotten wind of our plans and decided to wreck them?" Richard's question was more pro forma than real.

"Hardly," Bunker said. "What are the odds against our being found out by somebody who is also a kind of sympathizer, somebody who would not mind giving Reed a big promotion?"

"What about the possibility that the feds have discovered the conspiracy. They throw this big monkey wrench into our machinery, but do not tip us off to the fact that they know what we're up to. They wait to swoop down on us until they've mapped the whole conspiracy."

"Dick, we could speculate indefinitely about abstract, far-fetched possibilities. I say, forget it! We've just had a bad break."

"What about Sales? Could he have been trying to get rid of Reed so that he will become our main military guy?"

"Sales does not have that kind of clout. Besides, he would never jeopardize our entire operation."

They walked in silence. It was getting darker, and the air was cooling. They turned north onto Wisconsin Avenue. Traffic was still heavy. In the Washington area, a sprawling metropolis of about three million inhabitants, the rush hour got longer with each passing year.

"Gentlemen," Bunker said assertively, "the long and the short of it is that the Cadillac plan's out. It's simply out. We can no longer wait until after the November election and the swearing in of the new Congress. Peck's becoming the new speaker was never a certainty in the first place."

Again there was silence. They walked past a movie theatre. Although it was a weekday, there was a line in front of the box office.

"What do you think, Richard?" Vandenhorst asked the question in a subdued voice, signaling that Bunker had been a little too loud.

Richard's nerves, already raw because of what had happened at home, were now in another painful jumble. He did not quite know what he thought, but his spontaneous gut feeling was that the news was devastating. He gave voice to his predominant intuition:

"I've said it from the beginning—creating an image of legitimacy is indispensable for the coup. Those taking charge *must* be perceived as saviors of America, *not* as self-serving interlopers. The American people, to say nothing of the Washington bureaucracy, need a well-known, trusted face, a face like Peck's. Or they'll think they're being asked to entrust their fate to unknown outsiders."

"Peck isn't well-known outside of the Washington area and his home district," Bunker said. "And party loyalties divide this town."

"Believe me, Gordon, the order of succession will be a big issue with people in the Congress, in the departments and in the media. It will come up immediately. Our constitutional system is rotting and the rules have been corrupted, but there's some honor among the crooks. They want no interference. Within minutes it will be known to the American people that Peck's claim to the presidency is legitimate."

Bunker waved his hand dismissively. "How many Americans know that the speaker of the House is second to the vice president in the line of presidential succession. One in a thousand?"

"In the startling and almost unbelievable circumstances of the president and vice president being gone they'll be devastated, utterly disoriented, and they'll need to be reassured. They'll want to hear that America is still on the rails."

"OK, but now we'll have to do without that luxury! We can't afford to wait that long!" Bunker had raised his voice again.

"We've waited for a long time—why not a little longer?" Richard asked. "Perhaps we can find a replacement for Reed. Reed and Sales are the only ones now who could supply us with troops, but a few other generals and colonels are on board."

Even as he said it, Richard blamed himself for saying it. It was pure wishful thinking. They had long tried to think of ways of boosting their troop strength, but without success.

"Dick, you're grasping at straws!" Bunker exclaimed. "It's nothing but daydreaming to think we might replace the military resources we loose when Reed leaves."

"Then we just have to think of some new way of shoring up the appearance of legitimacy."

"How about ridding the American people of a foul, rotten leadership class and giving them some leaders who care about America? How's that for legitimacy!" Bunker underscored his point by making a fist. He again had difficulty keeping his voice down.

"The American people won't know who we are, and that's a very big problem."

"Yeah? And they know who our current president and his cronies really are?—the s.o.b.s!?"

"The president and vice president were duly elected, Gordon. They had legitimacy conferred on them by established constitutional procedures."

"What further proof can there be that the 'established procedures'"—he spoke the words in a mocking tone—"are hopelessly corrupt? They're being used by unscrupulous people to *destroy* this country."

"You don't need to tell me! I'm talking about *appearances*, Gordon. Appearances matter greatly!"

"Richard, more effort has gone into creating the right image for the coup than anything else. You've never stopped talking about it. But appearances aren't everything. What we need even more is guts and daring and firepower. I wouldn't be surprised, if after it dawns on the American people that some fresh faces have taken charge, they'll let out the biggest damned collective sigh of relief that you've ever heard."

"Oh, come off it Gordon! If the American people had such sound instincts, we wouldn't be in the present mess in the first place."

"I don't believe the American people are nearly so bad as the son's of bitches running their country." Bunker's face had a high color.

Vandenhorst, who had remained silent, raised his hands to calm emotions and lower voices. He suggested that they walk back to the area from which they had come. "We should get something to eat and drink," he said. "Richard, lead us to a large and preferably noisy restaurant in the vicinity."

"I know just the place. Right across from the Barnes & Noble."

"Let's go!"

"But you haven't given us your opinion," Richard said to Vandenhorst.

"I'm not sure, but I'm afraid Gordon may be right," he said. "Reed is essential to us. It's become more and more obvious in our planning that there may be no substitute for having troops right here in the capital. We have no idea who will replace Reed. Even if Peck becomes commander in chief, the new Commanding General might cause problems for us. To achieve our objectives we need to clean out a lot of people, and it will take a long time before new lines of authority have been established. The new Commanding General might suspect what's going on and try to block us. Sales' Marines will have a tough time as it is. They have to come up from Quantico, thirty miles or so from where they are needed. They may find themselves blocked by traffic on route 95. Suppose the Commanding General also puts up a fight."

"But Peck would be president!"

"Yes, if the November election turns out the way we hope. But by itself Peck's becoming president will not accomplish very much.

What's most important, our real objective, is the general housecleaning. You can't carry out that purge over time, step by step. That would make it possible for the bad guys to dig in, regroup, and mobilize opposition. No, it has to be done in one fell swoop during the initial state of emergency and confusion. All major figures who can be expected to resist our consolidation of power have to be gotten out of the way immediately if the coup is to succeed. No significant opposition can be left in place. We've talked about this a hundred times. Removing opposition is the really unpleasant task, but there's no avoiding it. Peck's being there would greatly facilitate the job, but we have to have plenty of people ready to carry out drastic orders. Even with the help of our friends in the FBI, the Secret Service, and the Capitol Police, you can't imagine people in those institutions making large-scale arrests and transporting those apprehended to secret locations. Can you imagine them taking over television and radio stations and the editorial offices and presses of the *Washington Post*? Only soldiers are used to acting on orders, no questions asked. Some of the soldiers and officers at our disposal will be mighty confused and surprised by the orders they receive, but we hope that in the exceptional circumstances and with the help of our propaganda and disinformation drive they can reasonably be expected to do as they are told. With Reed out of the picture, all of this would be up to Sales, who may even have a hard time getting up to D.C. That would be far too much of a gamble."

Richard said nothing in response. He needed time to digest what seemed to him disastrous news. As he walked the others towards the restaurant, his mind was running through the practical implications of the changed situation. His anxiety regarding his family problem had been pushed into his subconscious, but festered there and added to his intense discomfort. Little of any substance was said for the next few minutes.

"Here we are," Richard said as they arrived almost at their point of origin. He held open the door to a French restaurant that was well-known to him and that piped music into the street. The restaurant was only a few yards from a movie theatre, and people were milling about. There were plenty of customers in the large dining room. The music and the hum of voices would help keep their conversation private. They were able to get an out-of-the way table. When the waiter left with their drink order, Richard said:

"If the Cadillac plan is moot, what do we do with Jack Mahoney?" He was referring to the current speaker of the House of Representatives. "If we do not wait for the election and the likelihood that Peck takes over, according to the Constitution Mahoney will become president."

"We do as we have discussed," Bunker said. "We whisk him away even before the military action starts. The official line will be that Mahoney is being taken away for his own protection. O'Brien plans on using a couple of Secret Service guys. If it becomes necessary, we take Mahoney out and blame his death on the terrorists. By God, it's a good thing our rulers have made the American people see terrorists everywhere. Mahoney's one of those really shady wheeler-dealer types who's poisoned our system. If he's got to go, good riddance, as far as I'm concerned."

"And what about the next one in the line of presidential succession, the president *pro tempore* of the Senate?" Richard was referring to the longest-serving U.S. senator.

Vandenhorst answered, "There's no problem there. In, fact, the president *pro tempore*, Billy Eastman, is 89. He's so frail and so confused that nobody would dream of swearing him in as president. At the same time, while he's alive, you can't go further down the line of succession to the secretary of state. So there would be a lot of uncertainty about what to do—a constitutional impasse—and that would work in our favor. Who knows how long Eastman will survive, but he's actually worth more to us alive than dead. His condition will help justify our people holding the fort, so to speak. Eastman's age and bad health is one of the reasons why in this new situation we should act sooner rather than later."

"Eastman could die any day," Bunker said.

"We'll cross that bridge if we have to," Vandenhorst mumbled.

They spent the next hour eating and quietly discussing their options. The longer the conversation lasted and the more they considered the need to act within the next few months, the more Richard realized how wedded he had been all along to the Cadillac plan. Yet it was he who just days ago had given Vandenhorst, Bunker and Reed a little speech about psychological preparedness. He had warned of the danger that as they waited to act the conspirators might lose themselves in wishful thinking and careful planning instead of steeling themselves for acting in the real world. He cringed when he thought back to the moment. Who was he to be lecturing them, experienced, battle-scared men of practice? He had really been talking aloud to himself in their presence, making a show of his own desire for clearing away all illusions. And yet, here he was, trying to hang on to a scenario that had just slipped out of his grasp. Without Peck, how would the new regime gain sufficient credibility and support from the American people, the bureaucracy and the media establishment? Though Richard had never disputed the need for possibly harsh violence, he now had difficulty persuading himself that the conspirators would be able to make up for a perceived lack of legitimacy through disinformation, toughness and firepower. The shocking news of the deaths of the president and vice president at the hands of terrorists in combination with the elaborate disinformation and propaganda campaign might keep the new regime reasonably safe for the first forty-eight hours. Fear and confusion would be rampant. But then what? Was it perhaps too much to hope that in a frightening, precarious situation without precedent the American people would back or even tolerate the new regime?

When the waiter had brought coffee, Vandenhorst said, "We need an emergency meeting of the steering committee right away. We have hard decisions to make, and they are likely to be very controversial. One is: If Peck is not to be the president, who will be the face of the new regime?"

"Even more fundamental," Bunker said, "will all in our group be ready to go ahead in these new circumstances? Talk is one thing, action another. Now we'll find out how many in our group really live in the real world." He looked at Richard.

Richard said nothing, but it seemed to him that a person truly living in the real world would be the one having the hardest time deciding what to do. The conspirators had to contend with not very favorable odds to begin with. Indulging in wishful thinking about what might be accomplished through bold action was not realism. But hesitation and ambivalence caused by uncertainty regarding the actual situation could be just as dangerous a flight from reality. What ought to be done is rarely obvious, even in seemingly uncomplicated situations. He thought of Machavelli's idea that in troubled, unclear circumstances no amount of careful deliberation can ensure a good outcome. In the end, to be successful, the actor has to *make* his own opportunity, seize the initiative, step audaciously into the unknown and hope that the goddess of fortune will reward his daring.

# CHAPTER 41

Helen walked quickly from the hotel to the phone booth that she had used earlier that afternoon. It was after midnight, and although there were still people in the streets, some of them coming from the nearby Metro station, she felt uncomfortable. But she had no choice. She had to let Duparc know immediately what she had had discovered.

Looking back on the evening, she had to think that Ferguson was not just attracted to her but also positively smitten. He was infatuated with her. He had to be in a complete muddle. He was part of the plot to abduct Richard, and yet his concern for her was no mere act. How torn he must be between whatever had made him help kidnap Richard and wanting to be considerate of her! He was manipulating her, but also wanted her urgently. He was a leading diplomat with a promising future, and yet was pursuing the distraught wife of a missing American citizen, who was a personal friend to boot. His violating all the rules of propriety and setting normal caution aside showed the strength of his feelings for her. He obviously was not as straitlaced as he appeared. He was a passionate man hiding behind a façade of professional perfection. His wife had been dead for a long time now, and he might have not only pent-up sexual desires but also a deep longing for female companionship. Perhaps his pursuit of Helen Bittenberg was also a way of escaping from some private misery?

What was an inappropriate affair with a woman compared to being involved in the kidnapping of an American citizen on foreign soil—assuming that Ferguson was not acting in his capacity as a government official. But she was jumping to conclusions again, she realized. Why would she assume that everything was as it appeared? Ferguson might be a really good actor wooing her in pursuit of the same objective that had led to Richard's abduction. He might be trying to distract her or manipulate her in some other way.

No, she was being absurdly suspicious. In this case, surely, she could trust her female intuition. That flushed face, that wild, desperate look in his eyes—they could not have been feigned.

In any case, she wanted him off-balance. The more emotional crosscurrents he was under, the better. Because of his sexual excitement and rather heavy drinking, he would probably have a difficult time the next day sorting out just what had happened and been said between them. All to the good.

Duparc answered his cell phone on the sixth ring.

"*Oui.*" It was obvious from his one word that he had been asleep.

"This is Helen Bittenberg. I'm sorry to wake you up, but I have some important information. I'm calling from a telephone booth."

"Madame, it's almost one o'clock in the morning!" Duparc spoke quietly but with some emotion. Helen imagined that he was in bed next to a wife who was used to such calls.

"I know, and I'm sorry, but I think I know who owns the Land Rover and where he lives."

"*Quoi?*" How could you possibly know?"

"I got it out of Ferguson during dinner."

"He simply told you?"

"No, he didn't, but he told me that he has a close friend who lives in Evremond. His name is Delabordy, or something close to that. He's a retired French ambassador."

"Where's Evremond?"

"It's a village just a few kilometers from Noisy."

"So Ferguson happens to have a friend in that area. That's proof of nothing." Duparc spoke a little louder now. He had probably left his bedroom not to disturb his wife.

"The friend has a vineyard."

The line went silent for a moment.

"It's too much of a coincidence," Helen said. "Think about those stakes and the muddy SUV. Remember, last Friday it had rained heavily in the Paris area just hours before Richard was kidnapped. A car driven in a vineyard or anywhere on a farm would have gotten pretty dirty. If Delabordy owns a green Land Rover, he's the one who took Richard from the Sorbonne. I'm sure of it."

"But you don't know that he owns a green Land Rover."

"No, I don't. But Delabordy is about seventy years old."

The line was silent again before Duparc said, "Helen, I agree that this sounds like a promising lead, but we can't do anything in the middle of the night."

"Why not? Suppose Delabordy's holding Richard. Richard's life may depend on our finding him right away."

"We don't even have any strong evidence that a crime has been committed or that Richard's life is in danger, and we have no more than a strong hunch that this friend of Ferguson is involved. A magistrate would never approve our barging into a man's house at two o'clock in the morning on the basis of the evidence we have, especially not the house of a baron and retired ambassador. And it would make no sense to visit the man in the middle of the night without being able to search the property."

"But—"

Duparc cut her off. "Before taking any action with regard to this man we need to do some checking. That's elementary police procedure."

"But Richard may be alive and in danger."

"Helen, after all this time a few hours either way could hardly make much difference."

"Chief inspector, please."

"No, *Madame*. I'll get an early start tomorrow morning. Léger too. And we'll come by your hotel on our way to Noisy, probably around nine o'clock. I'll tell you if we have anything new, and you can tell me more about your dinner with Ferguson. And then, unless there are counterindications, Léger and I will go directly to Evremond."

The firmness in Duparc's voice indicated that any attempt to make him change his mind would be pointless. The conversation ended.

As she left the telephone booth her whole being told her that she had to go to Evremond. It was only as she started to think about how to arrange it practically and what she would do once she got there that she checked herself. It was unlikely that she would be able to rent a car anywhere at this hour of the night. Even at Charles De Gaulle airport, the rental companies would have closed their booths. A taxi? She didn't even know Delabordy's address. Provided she could find it in a telephone book, would she knock on his door at three or four o'clock in the morning, introduce herself, and then ask to be allowed to come into the house of the man who might have abducted her husband? Or would she go there without announcing her presence, sneak around in the darkness? How much would she be able to find in the dark in wholly unfamiliar surroundings? And she would not have much time until daybreak. She knew she was being irrational.

Her head filling with such thoughts, she walked briskly back toward the hotel. Street lamps were now almost the only source of light. As she turned into the street of her hotel a man walking in the opposite direction slowed down about thirty feet in front of her looking intently at her and holding up a hand to indicate that he would like for her to stop. She felt a rush of fear. She slowed down, too, and prepared to try to evade the man by stepping into the street.

Where could she run? She was wearing high-heeled shoes. Should she scream? The man stopped. In a gesture that would make it hard for her to pass her he spread out his arm as if preparing to embrace her. The man was of medium height, wore dark clothing, seemed to be about forty years old and to have dark hair. She could not see the expression on his face. She did not recognize him. Something terrible was about to happen. It was her turn now. There was probably another person in a car nearby.

"*Bon soir, Mademoiselle. C'est tard, mais pas trop tard.*" (Good evening, Miss. It's late, but not too late.)

She tried to walk around the man, but he moved to the same side to block her path. She started raising her arms to protect herself against a blow or to scratch the man. A scream was forming in her throat.

"*J'ai de l'argent. Une demi-heure seulement.*"

Her French was poor, but she understood. She had been propositioned. She had been offered money for half an hour of her time. Her first reaction was tremendous relief. She was not about to be abducted, beaten, or shot. What had happened was actually not so strange. What kind of a woman would walk around by herself after midnight dressed as she was? Her clothes were not provocative in the manner of streetwalkers, but had been selected to attract the attention of a male. In the very next moment she felt a new wave of anxiety. What to expect from a man looking for sex at this time of the night who thought that he had found it in a dimly lighted street?

She made an averting gesture and gave the man an emphatic but not unkind "non" and then pushed him gently out of her way. The man, who had no unusual features and looked decent enough, at first seemed about to grab hold of her to make her stop. He mumbled something in a pleading tone that she did not catch, but then his hands sank to the side, and he let her pass. The entrance to the hotel was only fifty yards away. She quickened her pace. She felt his eyes upon her back. Just before she ducked into the hotel lobby she heard him call to her, "*Dommage, vous êtes très belle.*" (Too bad, you are very beautiful.)

When he heard the clacking of her heels the doctoral student manning the counter came out of the little back room. "No messages for you," he said without her having asked him. He handed her the key to her room. "Any luck?" he asked. His solicitousness might have been perfunctory, but she appreciated it. From this young man she had nothing to fear.

"*Peut-être,*" she said. "But I still don't know where my husband is."

"I'm sorry," the young man said.

Back in her room she locked the door behind her by turning the key twice, and she put on the safety chain in addition. The air in the room felt stuffy and clammy, and she opened the window wide. It should be safe to do so on the third floor, she thought. She was exhausted, but knew that she would not be able to sleep. She was charged up. She wanted to act but was stymied. She had an impulse to call Hubert to tell him what she had discovered, but she did not want to leave the hotel in the middle of the night. She tried finally to close down her mind and imagination, starting by taking a long cool shower.

She did not fall asleep until 4:00 AM. She was awoken by the telephone and noticed that it was just past nine in the morning. She had intended to be up by eight at the latest, to do what exactly she did not know. The person calling was Duparc.

"*Madame* — Helen, we're leaving the office now to come to your hotel. Could you meet us downstairs in ten minutes?"

Helen was groggy. "I will be down as quickly as I can. I was asleep. I couldn't fall asleep last night."

She stumbled out of bed, walked into the bathroom. She splashed cold water on her face. She recoiled when she saw herself in the mirror. She was red-eyed and looked puffy. She brushed her teeth and dressed quickly in what was most handy. She did some emergency make-up, ran a brush through her hair, grabbed her handbag, and rushed downstairs. She left the key at the reception.

The gray Renault was sitting just outside the hotel. Léger was standing by the car. When he saw Helen he opened the back door for her. Duparc, who was sitting in the back seat, looked up from a pile of papers and gave her a quick smile. "Good morning," he said and removed papers next to him to make room for her. She slipped in.

She mumbled another excuse for having slept so late in the morning.

"*Pas de problème*," Duparc said. There was no hint in his voice or face that he might be irritated with her for bothering him in the middle of the night. He seemed unconcerned. Léger sat down in the driver's seat.

"We are on our way to Noisy," Duparc said, "but I wanted to let you know what we discovered this morning. I would also like to hear more about your dinner with Mr. Ferguson."

"You first," she said. "What about Delabordy?"

"There is a person just a few kilometers outside of Noisy who fits your description. He lives near the village of Evremond, as you said. His name is de la Broderie." Duparc spelt the name. "He is seventy-two years old, and he is indeed a retired ambassador. Since he retired from the Foreign Service he has had a couple of rather prominent jobs in French industry."

Helen listened intently but was also aware that Léger had not started the engine.

"Perhaps we could go through the rest on the way to Noisy," she said to Duparc.

Duparc looked straight at her as he said, "Helen, it's as before. You can't come with us. In addition to other considerations, it would violate police regulations. You are not, for example, a witness helping to identify someone."

"But, you've found the man who abducted Richard—"

Duparc held up a hand. "First of all, Helen, we do not know that your husband was kidnapped. If he was, as we suspect, de la Broderie may have had nothing to do with it."

"You must be kidding! What are the odds against—"

"De la Broderie does not own a Land Rover."

At first Helen could not speak. She was incredulous. Her surprise was mixed with dismay.

"B-b-but," she sputtered, "he may have borrowed somebody else's Land Rover, or somebody with a Land Rover drove him!" she exclaimed. She would not let go of this lead.

"That's possible, but to find out if that's the case, we have to do some basic police work. I can tell you that there is an owner of a green Land Rover in the vicinity of Noisy."

"I *knew* it!"

"Please, Helen, you are jumping to conclusions. There may be no connection between that Land Rover and de la Broderie. By the way, the Land Rover I'm talking about was not on our original list because it's more than ten years old. After receiving the information about de la Broderie from you we expanded our computer search for the area of Noisy. Léger was at work at 7:00 this morning." Helen looked in the direction of Léger, who sat impassively in the driver's seat. Duparc had to have gotten him out of bed very early. If he was annoyed with Helen or Duparc, he gave no sign of it. He was probably used to receiving sudden and inconvenient assignments.

"Who is the owner of the Land Rover?" Helen asked.

"It is registered to a Mr. Étienne Dégas, apparently a local farmer of some kind. We will visit him this morning. Then, if we think that he has any connection with de la Broderie, we will visit de la Broderie's place in Evremond."

"Perhaps Dégas works for de la Broderie."

"We'll explore all possibilities."

"Please, let me come with you."

"No, Helen. One of the reasons is that it would not help our search to let Dégas or de la Broderie know what we're really looking for. If one or both of them did in fact abduct your husband, your coming with us would make it obvious what we're after. The incident with the stakes falling off the car roof in Noisy gives us an excuse to talk to Dégas and perhaps de la Broderie without revealing our real objective."

Helen recognized the sense of what Duparc was saying, but the intensity of her desire to find Richard, be closer to him, was overpowering.

"We'll keep you informed," Duparc said.

She looked pleadingly at Duparc, but his expression did not change. She knew that she was defeated.

"Now tell me more about your dinner with Mr. Ferguson," Duparc said.

She started by conveying to Duparc her frame of mind with regard to Ferguson. She explained that it was a part of her strategy to take advantage of his interest in her as a woman. She related the main points of the previous evening, including Ferguson's amorous advance and how she had handled it. Duparc gave a faint crooked smile that was only half-amused. He asked a couple of questions for clarification.

When she had finished, Duparc said, "I can't deny that your evening with Mr. Ferguson was productive, but you probably should not be seeing him at all. We're investigating a possible serious crime, and he is a suspect. We don't know his role. You may be exposing yourself to danger. You think that you are deceiving him, but he's a senior diplomat. He wasn't born yesterday. He's bound to be perceptive as well as experienced. You're an amateur, he's a professional. You may reveal more than you realize."

"I understand. I'll be careful"

"*Bien*, it's time for us to go," Duparc said. Then, as if to compensate Helen for scolding her and for refusing to let her come along, he gave her a broad smile, and said, "You've done very well, Helen. As I've said—perhaps you should've been a detective."

She stepped out of the car. Standing on the curb watching the car disappear Helen felt deserted, disoriented, and useless. What would she do now? She could not possibly remain passive, just wait for the French police to make progress. Where could she rent a car?

# CHAPTER 42

In the afternoon of the Sunday after Vandenhorst, Bunker and Richard met in Bethesda the members of the steering committee started gathering at the Pellegrini vacation home in the West Virginia mountains. It was Richard's second visit. They came by twos from the Washington area having followed different and circuitous routes from the Washington area. They had to travel for an average of an hour and a half. A few of them had brought golfing equipment to mask the real purpose of the trip in case they were stopped.

The house was in an isolated location near the top of a heavily wooded mountain. It was a two-storey cabin built on stilts. "Hick" and a colleague had done a thorough security check and looked for any potential security problems in the vicinity. The road stopped at the Pellegrini house, and the nearest neighbor, another vacation home downhill, was a quarter of a mile away. The nearest town, a very small one, was a couple of miles distant. The Pellegrinis had not done much in recent years to clear away trees and branches to maintain the view of nearby mountains. Once the leaves were fully out the house would not be visible from a distance. Even now pine trees, tree trunks, and branches almost hid it. In Hick's view the state of the property around the house was both an advantage and a disadvantage. The less conspicuous the lights from the house, the better, but, on the other hand, an intruder might approach without being seen, especially at night. Hick or his colleague made occasional sweeps through the woods near the house. To reduce the danger that some high-tech listener might use the sound vibrations off the large windows in the family room to eavesdrop, they had covered those windows with the big sheets of plywood kept in the garage for boarding up the house. The fact that only four cars would be parked outside suggested a small party or just a family weekend get-together.

All but two members of the steering committee—O'Brien at the Secret Service and Randy Gates at the CIA—were present. As the conspirators arrived Mrs. Pellegrini offered them sandwiches, beer, and soft drinks. There was little small talk and banter. Tough decisions had to be made. Once the meeting got underway emotions were likely to run high. A decision would have to be made about whether to attempt the coup within four to five months or to postpone the plans, perhaps indefinitely, perhaps cancel them altogether. Nervousness was in the air.

Because the windows of the large room in which they would meet were boarded up, lights had to be turned on. The setting was glum.

Richard proposed that since the meeting would deal with general issues rather than a specialized topic Herbert Vandenhorst should chair it. Nobody contradicted him.

Vandenhorst accepted the assignment. He was dressed informally in a plaid shirt, a sports jacket and khaki slacks. He started by summarizing the situation they faced now that Reed's tour as Commanding General of the Washington military district would come to an end in half a year. He ended by saying: "We have to decide whether we should act before that happens. Or can we afford to wait until after the November elections and then make do with Noah's troops?"

As Vandenhorst spoke Richard looked around the room. Several of the participants seemed to be on edge. Robert Bates, Congressman Peck's chief of staff, sat with his elbows on his knees nervously squeezing his hands. Noah Sales looked surprisingly relaxed. Richard happened to be looking in Bates's direction when Bates raised his hand. He saw him draw a quick, nervous breath when Vandenhorst recognized him.

"After the attempted takeover, all Americans will want to be reassured about everything still being fine," Bates said. "They have the terrible news that the president and vice president are dead. They know that terrorist have damaged the Capitol and the Supreme Court. They'll want to hear that the government is not falling apart but functioning normally, that the person next in the line of presidential succession is taking over, which means the speaker of the House—"

"Sure," Pellegrini said, not bothering to ask to be recognized, "but your boss could not become speaker until after the next election and the swearing in of the new House of Representatives. That puts us in January, long after Tom Reed has departed Washington." Several others made assenting noises.

"Doug," Vandenhorst said, "you are speaking out of turn. Robert had the floor. Please let him finish."

"Yeah, but we don't need to hear the obvious, that it would be nice to have Peck installed when we make our move!" Pellegrini did not bother to hide his exasperation. "I don't see how we could do without Tom commanding some troops right where we need them the most."

"Who's got the floor?" Lester Pickett shouted. Several persons clamored for attention.

"Doug! Wait your turn! Robert's speaking." Vandenhorst was now using a wooden ornament to knock on a side table.

"Yeah, give him a chance," Pickett said irritably. Others grumbled. Bates started speaking, but was again interrupted by Pellegrini, who shouted: "We just can't wait until January!"

"Do you want me to chair this meeting or not?" Vandenhorst was speaking firmly, giving Pellegrini a steely look.

"Sorry, Herbert."

Bates resumed his statement, raising his voice in anticipation of further interruptions. "We've agreed that an image of legitimacy is crucial. Tom's troops are not worth as much as Peck's constitutional authority, which gives him credibility even among our worst enemies." Several people raised their hands, but Vandenhorst waved them off.

Sales did not wait to be recognized. He bellowed, "Legitimacy without force is as hollow as—"

Vandenhorst stopped Sales by loudly knocking and then holding up his hands and shouting "Wait! Wait!" Sales was visibly struggling with himself. Vandenhorst stood up.

"This discussion is getting out of hand. Either I chair the meeting and you wait for my signal, or I relinquish the chair." The room quieted. "We have to keep this orderly. You have to indicate to me that you wish to speak and let me give you the floor when it's your turn."

"Amen, brother." It was Bunker weighing in.

Vandenhorst nodded to Sales, and the latter continued.

"Nobody in this group has ever questioned the need to make the coup look legitimate. But now we must choose between a flimsy legitimacy and firepower. We've all considered the Cadillac plan the best, but it's just not available any longer. We have two possibilities. One is the chance, I repeat, the *chance*, that Peck will be the new speaker coupled with the *certainty* that then our military assets will be drastically reduced. Whatever troops I can move up from Quantico will not be enough. That's even assuming I can move them into position as early as we need them. Except for the handful of Marines I may be able to move by helicopter, they'll be well over an hour away from where they're needed. Ideally they should be on their way before we hit the pres and the veep. I would have to invent some ruse for the officers down at Quantico about an acute emergency in D.C., but then word may well leak to the Pentagon, the White House or the Secret Service, and we risk jeopardizing the assassination plot itself. Even assuming I can get an early start, traffic on 95 is usually terrible, except in the middle of the night, and we aren't likely to be able to hit the pres and the veep at that hour. If traffic's heavy, God knows when we'll be taking up position in D.C. A few helicopters with Marines will not to be enough to ensure control of the White House, especially not with confused officers and inexperienced soldiers. Coordinating with our people up in D.C. could be very messy. Besides, a lot of things have to go right in the next few months before I can expect to have any troops ready for action in the first place. To put those troops on some kind of alert for when we need them, I'll have to do a bit of fancy footwork involving some of the brass and other officers without arousing suspicion."

Sales looked around the room, squinted, and stuck his chin out in characteristic fashion as he continued. "The other option is that we act with maximum military strength. Tom's people are already near the center of action. It's not much, but it's in the right place. Even with those assets we'll have a difficult time. There are too many bases that we have to cover, the White House, the Capitol, key government buildings, Reagan National Airport, Andrews Air Force Base, perhaps Dulles Airport and the Baltimore-Washington Airport, a couple of television and radio stations, and on and on. But the odds in favor of this plan are much better. We establish a military presence in the Washington area and break through any opposition by force." Sales raised his voice: "I say we go *now*, as soon as we can make the final preparations. We have no choice!"

Vandenhorst recognized Tom Reed, who reinforced Sales's points and added: "As I think most of you know, there are some federal emergency plans for dealing with a quasi-military or terrorist attack on Washington. It involves getting some troops flown up from Fort Bragg in North Carolina. The Commanding General of the Washington military district—that's me—can request those troops, but not unilaterally. I've been looking into how I might get away with some deception."

Several hands shot into the air at the same time, one of them Richard's. Vandenhorst saw it and recognized him.

"I understand Noah's point, but we must not underestimate the advantage of having a successor to the president who will be perceived as clearly legitimate. Even those in the other party who will not like Peck will accept him as president in the new scary circumstances. Once sworn in, Peck will be able to mobilize additional troops, perhaps by ordering the new Commanding General of the military district to do some of the things Tom Reed would like to do—"

Sales, whose jaw had tightened, wanted to interrupt Richard, but Vandenhorst cried, "hold it!"

Richard continued, "Even if Peck wouldn't be able to do all the things we've planned, he would be duly sworn in, and he might do a number of them. He should have the military on his side, and in time he could make a big difference."

Sales could barely contain himself. Vandenhorst let him speak.

"Get some things done *in time*?!" Sales sneered. "There *is* no time. If there's to be any point to this coup, we have to break the back of the System in the first few hours, certainly the first day or two. It won't be long before our disinformation campaign starts to wear thin. If there's one thing we can't afford, it's to let some time go by. That's time for the system to recoup and reassert itself. We have to strike while the iron's hot. To wait is to lose."

There was again a forest of arms. For another hour discussion flowed back and forth. All of the committee members spoke. There were raised voices and red faces and anger. Vandenhorst had to struggle to keep the discussion from turning into a shouting-match. A few times he had to stand up to quell the turbulence. He finally defused rising tensions by announcing a fifteen-minute break, during which the conspirators could help themselves to coffee and cookies.

"How about some drinks?" Lester Pickett asked in his deep, mellifluous senatorial voice. Ripples of laughter lightened the atmosphere.

"No drinks," Vandenhorst responded.

As discussion resumed and positions crystallized, it became clear that a majority favored action as soon as possible. Pellegrini pronounced himself ready to go. Gordon Bunker weighed in on the same side, as did Thomas Reed and Noah Sales, all of them stressing the indispensability of having military resources right in the city. Lisa DeLeon did not say much but appeared to be on the same side. Richard spoke a few times weighing the two alternatives and elaborating on just why establishing legitimacy was crucial. Lester Pickett gave a senatorial-sounding speech considering the pros and cons of each position and coming to an ambiguous conclusion that nevertheless seemed to favor waiting for the strong possibility that Peck would become speaker. Bates argued strenuously for waiting until after the election.

Sales remarked that if O'Brien and Gates had been present, they would have been opposed to waiting. Acting the role of impartial chairman, Vandenhorst remarked that nobody should presume to represent the views of those not present.

Lisa DeLeon spoke up: "Noah's right though. Bob and Randy would be in favor of action now."

Richard said, "Although it weakens my side in the discussion, I have to agree with Lisa about Bob O'Brien. I haven't talked to Randy since the bad news about Tom."

"I have," Bunker said. "Randy is rearing to go. NOW!" He spoke the last word in a voice that reverberated in the room. Sales seized the opportunity to speak, again without permission.

"The time for talk is up, folks. Talk's cheap. What we need is action! Let's decide!" Sales's blustery, almost brutish demeanor made Richard recoil. Sales was trying to force the decision he wanted.

Vandenhorst again asserted his authority. "Hold your horses, Noah, we can't very well decide what to do without Bob and Randy. And we should check on a few practical matters before we make a definitive decision. I would like to talk to Bob O'Brien about whether the schedules of the president and vice president give us any obvious windows of opportunity in the next few months." Richard noticed that Vandenhorst's face was flushed.

Lisa DeLeon raised her hand and was recognized. She had not spoken at any length previously. She now stood up, indicating that she really wanted to be heard and noticed. She was dressed in a rather bulky and unbecoming pullover that made her look even huskier than she was. As before, Richard was struck by the contrast between her sturdy body, which seemed to exude a kind of muscular energy, and her rather pleasant, almost pretty face, which now showed intense feeling. She swept a lock of short, brown hair aside before speaking.

"Gentlemen," she said, in a strained voice that suggested her checking strong emotions. "We've talked for a very long time. In fact, we've talked and planned for a couple of years. Much of that talk was necessary, as was all the careful planning. But, gentlemen, our discussions have become repetitive. Nothing really new has been said here tonight. We have been through the possible scenarios over and over in different permutations. All that's changed is that certain practical circumstances are now *forcing* us to make a decision. What I think I've been hearing behind the reservations against action now is an unwillingness really to decide at all, to just postpone the painful moment of choice."

Bates raised an arm and opened his mouth, anger written on his face: "I must—" But DeLeon objected: "Will you let me finish? You've had your say, and I've been rather quiet this evening. Now I have the floor."

Bates looked pleadingly at Vandenhorst, then exclaimed: "I

*resent* the accusation that I'm afraid of making a decision!" When Vandenhorst motioned to him to be quiet and DeLeon tried to speak again Bates shouted, "I *do* want us to decide, but decide to *wait*." He slumped in his chair.

"To wait is the same as avoiding a real decision, frittering away the one opportunity we've got," DeLeon shot back. Bates jumped to his feet to face her, but before he had the time to say anything Vandenhorst, too, got up.

"Please, Robert," he cried, "Let Lisa finish! Let her finish."

Bates, wearing a dark, furious expression, sank back into his chair.

DeLeon continued: "Having Tom Reed's troops right in Washington is a must. We just have to have the capacity to lock the city down for a while. Noah's right about the Peck scenario. The danger is too great that without sufficient troops there'll be half-measures and dangerous delay, which will make the outcome uncertain. The bad guys will have time to figure out what's happening and to take countermeasures. Also—have you forgotten?—we actually have no guarantee that Bates will be the next speaker of the House, only a good chance. So our real opportunity is now, within the next four to five months. If we're not prepared to attack the System head-on in one fell swoop, we have no business attempting a coup in the first place. If given the opportunity, the system will reassert itself. It is so entrenched and very resilient. The people in charge can be perfectly ruthless. The system needs to be shocked to the core. So, I say, no more hand-wringing! I think Bob O'Brien should be asked right now to find a specific time when our assassination plot could be put into effect. We should put ourselves in the GO mode now! I'm very worried about detection. The system's not exactly inattentive to threats. Every week of planning and talking increases the risk that we'll be discovered and that all our work will come to nothing—that we'll all end up in the slammer."

Lisa DeLeon sat down, and Bates, Richard, and Pickett asked to be recognized. But Vandenhorst asked them to wait.

"Have you looked at your watches lately? It will be early morning before any of us are back in Washington. This session has to be concluded. We're all tired. Nerves are frayed and emotions are running high. That's not the right time to decide on anything important. I propose that we adjourn this meeting and meet again very soon to make the final decision. I'll talk to O'Brien and Gates first thing tomorrow, and—"

Sales broke in, "But we can't *afford* to wait!" Others seemed to indicate agreement.

"A couple of days either way will make no difference, and—"

"But you haven't told us what *you* think about the matter at hand, Herbert," DeLeon said. "What *do* you think?"

The room fell silent. All eyes were fixed on Vandenhorst. Like the others, Richard knew that in this group of strong-willed persons, Vandenhorst was the real, if unofficial, leader. He was highly regarded by the others and had a broader range of experience and knowledge than any of them. His personal presence, gravitas, and power of judgment commanded respect. He never lost his temper or his critical distance to the moment. Richard realized that it was to Vandenhorst more than anybody else that he would look for a sound, authoritative judgment of what should be done. Vandenhorst was the least likely to be swept up in the emotions of the moment or to be swayed by personal ambition, partisan motives, or wishful thinking.

"As you wanted me to chair this meeting, I didn't want to push a particular point of view," Vandenhorst said. "When we meet next time I will declare where I stand."

"No!" DeLeon cried. "Speak now! You owe us some sense of what you think." Several others made assenting noises.

Vandenhorst seemed to hesitate.

"OK, then, I'll tell you. I think the time for action has come."

# CHAPTER 43

After Duparc and Léger had driven off Helen stood for a long time on the sidewalk outside the hotel. She soon realized that renting a car and following the two French detectives to Noisy and Evremond was a bad idea. Inserting herself where she was not wanted might in fact damage the effort to find Richard. Duparc was right: the search would benefit from the perpetrator or perpetrators not being tipped off to what the police were really looking for. Also, if she went to the Noisy area and Duparc found out, he would be angry. She would risk his no longer taking her into his confidence. So what could she do? She simply could not be inactive.

She walked back and forth a few times outside the entrance to the hotel. Her thoughts were interrupted by the man in the hotel reception who came up behind her calling "*Madame, Madame!*" She turned.

"There is message *pour vous.*" The man smiled, as if proud to have something for her. He handed her a note and said, your brother — Hubert called."

"My brother-*in-law*," she corrected. "Did he tell you to tell me something?"

"*Non, Madame.*"

But she already knew. He would not have left any message at all unless he wanted her to call him.

"When was the message left?"

"Now, *Madame*, just a minute ago."

"*Merci, Monsieur,*" she said. Her voice did not betray how anxious his answer made him. She had just realized that, as it was around ten in the morning in Paris, Hubert had called her about four o'clock in the morning American Eastern Time. Her first thoughts were of the children. Had anything happened to them?

She needed to shower and dress more carefully for the day, but she did not go upstairs. It did not occur to her that she had not had breakfast. She headed for the hotel that had become her main place for communicating by telephone. She took a slight detour to make sure that she was not being followed.

Hubert's first words when calling her back were spoken in

a dark voice that underlined the seriousness of what he was saying: "Something very sinister is going on, darling."

"Hubert, are the children fine?" Her voice trembled.

"Yeah, no problem there. But it may be different with Reilly, the private eye. I talked to him yesterday morning. He gave me a report on the telephone. He'd been through much of Dick's papers and odds and ends at the university. He said that Dick's assistant, Turello, had been very helpful. And he spent a lot of time in Dick's study at home. With the help of a computer geek Reilly was able to get into one or two of those encrypted disks. They didn't contain much, may have been some kind of practice disks. But Reilly said that overall a pattern of some kind was emerging. Dick's been in touch with a few people who are or used to be in government or the military. He ran a few names past me. They meant nothing to me: Vandenberg or something, and Bunker."

"Hubert, I think they may be people who took an interest in Richard's writings. I remember being invited with Richard to a man called Bunker and his wife for dinner. He's a retired general or admiral who works for some big business. He had read some of Richard's work, and they talked about history and contemporary America. They seemed to hit it off well. A large, burly sort—pretty nice man. Bright. Nice wife, too. I think the name of the other man you mentioned is not Vandenberg, but something similar. I don't know if I've met him. But I think the the name's come up."

"For all I know, these people may be just history buffs, but then why would one of the names appear on an encrypted disk? Reilly seemed to think they could be more than retirees who like to read. I got the impression from him that he was going to interview them later in the day. He said he would call me in the evening with any news. But he never called. I assumed he'd discovered nothing of interest. Instead I got a call from his partner, a guy named Burt, about 10:30 last night. I was just getting ready for bed. Burt wondered if I knew where Reilly was. He'd not come home, and the wife had called Burt. It seems Reilly never comes home late without letting the wife know. All I could tell Burt was that I'd talked to Reilly earlier and that he had said he would be in touch with me after a couple of interviews. Burt knows what kind of a case Reilly is on, but he didn't know what people Reilly was going to contact."

"Aren't Burt and Reilly working together on the case?"

"Sort of, but Burt's just providing backup, devoting most of his time to another case. He knows just some of what Reilly's discovered and doesn't know what Reilly is up to at any particular time. And now I'm getting to why I called you. Burt woke me up at 3:00 in the morning to tell me that he'd just heard from the Virginia state police. He'd called them earlier to report Reilly missing. Burt used to be a county police detective in Virginia. A duty officer called him with information in the middle of the night. Last night a car had been reported abandoned off a dirt road in a forest near Harrisonburg, Virginia. I don't know where that is, but maybe you do."

"Yes, it's about two hours west of D.C."

"OK. The car had been driven in among some trees and bushes and then covered with branches and twigs. The car might not have been found for months, but in the early evening yesterday a jogger happened by and caught a glimpse of something between the trees. He stopped to have a look. There was nobody in or near the car. The jogger thought the whole thing suspicious and called the local police. They eventually sent a patrol car. The license number of the hidden car matched Reilly's car. The local sheriff contacted the state police, and they finally got around to calling Burt after midnight. Burt then talked to Reilly's wife. She says she has no idea why he would have been in that part of Virginia. Reilly is still missing."

"You think he's been abducted—killed?"

"I've no idea, but it's hardly a coincidence that a private eye investigating Richard's disappearance has himself disappeared. Somebody did not want him to sniff around. It convinces me that Richard, too, did not disappear by his own volition—as you've been saying. Burt will try to figure out who Reilly was supposed to talk to that afternoon. He will have to go over the same ground that Reilly covered in the last couple of days. It also means that he can't go anywhere alone. I've told him to hire whatever help he needs. The police are likely to do their part eventually, but in the absence of evidence of foul play they can't commit a lot of resources to a missing person's case. People go missing every day. Some *want* to disappear without a trace. Luckily, Reilly was—eh, is—a resident of Virginia. That gives the Virginia police more responsibility."

"Hubert, isn't it pretty clear?" She spoke now in a calm, controlled voice. "Whatever Richard has been up to, it's big. It involves people with clout and wide reach. They can get things done both here in France and back home. What could that be except the CIA? Or it could be organized crime. But Richard would never have anything to do with something shady—unless he was working with the police, the FBI, the CIA, or something similar." She hesitated. "But why in the world would he be doing that? Could he have stumbled onto something that poses a real threat to some criminal enterprise, say, the Mafia"? Her voice had started trembling again. "But how could that be?—Where would Ferguson fit in? Hubert, I don't understand—I don't understand anything." Her previous calm was dissolving. "I'm going crazy—" Her voice drifted off.

"I understand, darling. This is the craziest thing I've ever heard of. It makes me wonder if I'm dreaming."

"But isn't it time we woke up? I never had a nightmare last this long."

"Darling, if you want me to, I'll join you in Paris. You must be climbing the walls. You need somebody to talk to, somebody to lean on. I could be there within twenty-four hours. I think my passport's up to date."

She was silent pondering his proposal.

"Helen, are you there?"

"I'm here. Thank you, Hubert, but what could you really do, other than keep me company? You can do more good where you are. Somebody's got to stay on top of things in the U.S., make sure the police, the FBI, or *somebody* does some serious investigating. Surely, the disappearance of that private eye will lead to some action."

"But how will you manage by yourself over there? You've had a miserable time, alone in a foreign country."

"I'm getting used to it." She tried to steady her voice and give it a touch of levity. She feigned some humor: "It's gotten to be a habit."

"You're brave, I'll give you that."

"I'll manage somehow. At least I have Duparc and Léger, and they are getting somewhere."

She told Hubert about her evening with Ferguson and about the new leads.

"My goodness, darling! You're a lioness, or should I say a fox?"

They discussed the likely repercussions of the most recent developments.

Hubert finally said, "But don't stop thinking of anything in Richard's behavior back in the States that might give us a clue about his disappearance."

"I won't, but I just can't think of anything—just trivial things."

"Perhaps they aren't."

"Well, here's an example. When it happened it was actually pretty scary, but it turned out to be nothing at all. It was a couple of months ago. Richard had gotten it into his head that he would do some gardening around the house—very unlike him. When I looked into the backyard to see what he was doing I couldn't see him, so I went outside. I found him sitting in the shade in a garden chair.

He seemed to be sleeping. I worried that he might have had a heart attack and started talking to him, but he didn't react. I got frightened and started to shake him. He finally woke up, of course. He had just been very tired. The scene stuck in my mind somewhere because it was so out of the ordinary, but it was hardly significant in our present context. It tells us nothing that we haven't already talked about—that he's been overworked and so on."

"I suppose you're right. But keep thinking."

"I will, Hubert."

"Talk to you soon, darling. You'll be careful, won't you?"

After hanging up Helen just sat for a few moments in the small telephone booth, thinking back on the news Hubert had given her. She realized that she had not been afraid for her life before.

# CHAPTER 44

The conspirators left the Pellegrini cabin by car at intervals, now with different companions than on the trip to West Virginia. The drivers also returned by different routes than when they had come. During the discussions at the house Hick and his colleague had checked each car for possible microphones or tracking devices. Richard was one of the passengers. His driver this time was Lisa DeLeon. Back in Washington she would drop him off at his home on her way to her apartment in the Watergate apartment complex near the Kennedy Center in downtown Washington.

As they headed down the mountain it was almost one o'clock in the morning. Neither one said anything. The tensions and anxieties of the evening had tired them and made them subdued. They reached the highway and drove through the little town, which was in virtual darkness.

"Hick told me to go via Leesburg and Dulles Airport this time," DeLeon said."

"Let me know, if you'd like me to drive for a while."

"Thanks, I'm fine."

"If we're stopped by the police, at least we won't have any alcohol on our breath," Richard said jokingly.

"And what do we say if we're asked what we're doing out at this time of night?"

"Perhaps we try to look a little guilty and signal that we are lovers out for a drive," Richard said. She flashed a smile in his direction.

"As we are not exactly young, that might mean we're illicit lovers," she said and chuckled.

"Let them wonder."

Silence descended. Richard was weary. The stakes in the meeting could not have been higher. There seemed to be inexorable movement in the direction of early action. Vandenhorst's final comment, indicating his support for the majority position, had not surprised Richard, but it had made him realize how deeply he had wished that Vandenhorst would tilt the other way. The thought that the coup might not be more than a couple of months away made him intensely uncomfortable, and he was not exactly sure why. For years people had annoyed him who talked about America's decline but showed no willingness to do anything tangible about it. He had considered himself different from and superior to them. Now that Vandenhorst had shown himself to be on the side of early action Richard asked himself whether his own motives for holding to a different point of view were suspect. Had his spirited insistence on the importance of establishing legitimacy concealed something else? Was he having doubts about the whole undertaking? Had Lisa DeLeon and others been right that those who resisted action before the election were really afraid to decide on any real action at all? In an earlier conversation with a few of the conspirators Richard had suggested that it might be psychologically difficult for some to move from theoretical plans to action. Was he one of them? Was his hesitancy caused in part by fear of the effect of an unsuccessful coup on Helen and the children? After the scene in the Bittenberg kitchen he had felt more miserable about his family situation than ever. He yearned to tell Helen everything, but knew that he could not. He had returned home after the Bethesda meeting with Vandenhorst and Bunker in a state of acute anxiety. He had managed to collect himself and had been genuinely apologetic when talking to Helen. Sitting on his side of the bed he had pledged to Helen, who was in bed with her back to him, a new effort to reorganize his life. She had let him kiss her goodnight. The next day she had appeared on edge but not standoffish. The children had been very quiet. In spite of the pressure building within the conspiracy, he had made a great effort that day and the next to spend time with Helen and the children. He had called the University of Chicago and done the unthinkable, canceled his big invited lecture the following week. He had claimed a family emergency. He had cut his time at the university to a bare minimum, which intensified his bad conscience while mollifying it.

Lisa DeLeon interrupted his thoughts by asking if he had interpreted a road sign the same way as she had. They agreed that they were on the right road. They were on a small winding highway in rugged West Virginia terrain. There were few lights outside.

Richard was acutely aware that at the meeting his driver had spoken forcefully for the majority point of view. She was a real Amazon, physically rather imposing but at the same time sharp as a whip and highly experienced in the ways of the world. Could he claim to have better insights than she into which plan for the coup would have the greatest chance for success? Was she perhaps more attuned to actual, live politics, and better equipped to act in that world than he, a bookish academic? Vandenhorst had sided with her, not him.

After more silence, DeLeon said, "We've talked a lot this evening, I know, but it may help me stay alert at the wheel if we kept a conversation going."

"Should you turn the radio on in case we get into sensitive subjects," Richard asked.

She pushed the button for one of the pre-set stations. A Washington FM station came on. They could hear a Beethoven piano concerto, but the signal was weak and faltering. She switched to AM and found a local station offering a late night talk show. She looked over at Richard.

"That's fine with me. Just leave it. Let them jabber on."

"Do you think anybody might be listening in out here in the boonies, in the middle of the night? I haven't seen a single car since we left the cabin."

"I suppose we're safe," Richard said, "but I know nothing about electronics, so I just follow Hick's instructions regarding car conversations. Doug Pellegrini knows everything about electronic surveillance because of his job at NSA, and he tells me that anybody with real resources can listen in on almost anything. That means the federal government can do it. Maybe our conversation can be intercepted via satellite and GPS or something like that. Unlikely, I guess, but who knows?"

"You wonder if a free society is possible any longer."

The radio host, exhibiting the typical gift of gab, was responding to a listener's comment and berating the lack of patriotism in "the media." *"Those leftists really want the U.S. to lose this war in Saudi Arabia. They would like nothing better."*

"I marvel at those talk show hosts," Lisa said. "Are they really as ignorant as they seem. They seem to have made the views prescribed by the System their own."

*"Either we fight the terrorists over there, or we'll have to fight them here at home."*

"They're all using the same playbook," DeLeon commented. She was drumming her fingers impatiently on the steering wheel.

*"If the left gets its way, get ready for a nuclear cloud over Manhattan."*

"Hell!" Lisa exclaimed with a ferocity that made Richard wonder if she had encountered a sudden obstacle in the road. But he could see nothing. She was driving on as before. She had reacted to the radio program. She continued: "Does it really never occur to these radio hosts that it's the reckless, shortsighted policies of the U.S. that create all that hostility against us, all over the world. It's utterly frustrating to see the American public so ignorant. They have no idea how manipulated they are, the poor suckers. The big media have turned them into trained seals. And thousands have to die as a result."

Richard wondered why DeLeon was bothering to express these sentiments and was doing it with such intensity. The callousness of those who shaped U.S. foreign policy thinking and who kept putting American soldiers in harm's way was one of the most deeply felt grievances among the conspirators. There was no need to draw attention to this subject and make these arguments. So why was DeLeon doing so? He soon got the explanation.

"We keep dodging the issue of how to neutralize the darn media elites and the really big people in finance."

So that was it. DeLeon wanted to push an agenda item. Richard cringed.

"We're hardly avoiding that subject, Lisa! We have rather elaborate plans for handling them."

"But they're not nearly as extensive as they should be. We should be throwing far greater resources in that direction."

"Do I need to remind you that our resources are already overcommitted, that we're too thinly spread as it is?"

"I know that very well, and so what I'm saying is that we have to *reallocate* our resources."

For the next half hour Richard had to listen to the case for what DeLeon wanted. He was again impressed by her smarts and toughness. She was sophisticated but also strong-willed. She was a rock. Richard would not want her as his enemy. But, without knowing why precisely, he also felt more and more impatient and oppositional. Whatever the source of his resistance, it mingled with irritation over the distraction of the voices coming from the radio. He had never gotten used to carrying on a conversation against a background of radio noise. The main reason for his discomfort was not that he disagreed with DeLeon but that he feared the practical upshot of her argument. He strongly suspected that she would demand not only that the conspiracy expend greater effort in the area of special concern to her, but that he, Richard, should take on another assignment for which he had neither the time nor the energy. He was already staggering under his responsibilities. Craving relief from the unrelenting pressure, he was being badgered to think about the work of the steering committee and difficulties it faced. He did not want to hear DeLeon's arguments. He wanted to flee, but she had a captive audience. Her voice competing with the talk show host grated on his nerves. He was dead tired and felt bad-tempered. Richard had felt drowsiness coming on. He thought of feigning nodding off and then trying to fall asleep, but DeLeon was his chauffeur. He did not want to risk her dozing off from lack of stimulation.

He thought he might try diverting her.

"Dulles Airport coming up," Richard said, pointing to a large road-sign. The AOL campus must be somewhere around here. It's amazing that the Washington metropolitan area extends all the way out here. A neighbor tells me that in the early 1970s the only thing between the Washington Beltway and Dulles Airport was bucolic wide-open fields with cows and some horses."

But DeLeon stuck doggedly to her subject.

"So what do you think, Richard, about what I have said? It seems to me that we have no choice but to do more to deal with the media and financial bigwigs."

Richard did not answer.

In the distance they could see the dramatically lit up main terminal building of Dulles Airport. Richard would be home in about half an hour. Helen would be asleep. What was it that he had told her to explain why he would probably be late? He hated the lying.

"Well?" DeLeon said.

"To tell you the truth, Lisa, I'm rather tired."

DeLeon looked at the clock in the dashboard.

"I guess you have a right to be. It's after two in the morning. But we might as well finish our business."

"Our business?"

"A few of us on the steering committee think that we need to give much more attention to throwing these particular elites into disarray. The rest keep dancing around the subject. Without confronting this issue we might jeopardize the coup. We've talked to Vandenhorst, but he doesn't seem to see the need for any special measures beyond what we have already talked about."

"Special measures?"

"We've been focusing too much, if not exclusively, on what must be done in Washington. But some of the most important decisions are made by people who do not live there, but in New York City and other places. Some of them travel much of the time. Unless we neutralize some of them, they will be quick to mobilize public opinion and other opposition in ways that could be very dangerous to us."

"We already have plans to try to neutralize key individuals in other parts of the U.S. and even abroad. But Herbert's worried that we don't have nearly enough people to handle matters like that."

"Herbert's a good guy, but I and a couple of the others think that on this issue he just has to change his mind. He would listen to you."

"To *me*?" There it was, Richard thought—just as he had feared. He was being asked to do yet another thing. He rolled up inwardly like a hedgehog. He wanted no further discussion.

He said: "It's been a long day, Lisa."

"OK, Richard, we'll talk more later, but it has to be soon, preferably before the next meeting of the steering committee."

The West Virginia radio station had begun crackling and fading, contributing to Richard's edginess. Lisa DeLeon's virtual monologue with its implicit demand that he take on more responsibility would have been unnerving without the incessant babbling on the radio. She switched back to her Washington FM station for classical music, which helped to sooth him. They drove on in silence interrupted only by occasional small talk.

At Richard's request, DeLeon let him out a couple of blocks from his home. He walked slowly filling his lungs with fresh air. He felt depleted, and he dreaded the next few days. He went to bed in a state of complete exhaustion. Helen stirred and said something to recognize his presence, but never quite woke up, which saved him from inventing yet more excuses. He forgot to set the alarm clock. He fell into a deep sleep.

Helen woke Richard at 8:30 the next morning. The blinds had kept most of the morning light out.

"Richard, don't you have that ten o'clock class this Monday?"

Groggy and disoriented he tumbled out of bed. In the shower his head cleared slowly. He would have preferred oblivion. He shaved and dressed less carefully than usual and rushed downstairs. He needed to collect some books and notes from his basement study before leaving for the university. He smelled coffee in the kitchen and saw that Helen had put out breakfast for him. He felt a surge of tenderness for her. In the basement he found what he needed, stuffed it into a briefcase, and was just about to leave the room when the scrambler phone rang inside his desk. He thought of ignoring it. He couldn't be expected to be available all the time. But he pulled out the drawer and lifted the receiver.

"Yes."

"It's Randy, I need to see you. Can you be at "Crooked" at noon for lunch?" "Crooked" was their code name for one of several restaurants in the Washington area that the conspirators frequented. This one was in Rosslyn in Northern Virginia just across the Potomac River from Georgetown. It was Italian, and they joked that the Mafia probably owned and ran it.

"OK." Nobody used the scrambler phone except for urgent calls. Richard vaguely remembered that there was a departmental faculty meeting at the University at noon, but he would simply not attend, which would be unusual for him.

In the kitchen Helen looked quizzically at him. He walked up to her and gave her a kiss and a hug. She did not try to repel him, but neither did she reciprocate his sign of affection.

I thought you might have time for some cereal and coffee."

"Thanks, Helen." He sat down.

"You were very late last night."

"Much too late." He sighed, and started gobbling up the cereal. "The meeting place of the historical society in West Virginia was much further away than I had thought. I was told that it was a little more than an hour away, but it was more like two hours because of the winding roads. And then after my talk the discussion became very lively, and they didn't want me to leave. When I said that I simply had to get back, the person who was going to take me didn't want to leave quite yet, and when we finally hit the road he lost his way." It was easy to lie, Richard thought, but he hated it.

He poured some coffee into a plastic cup that he would bring with him into the car, picked up his briefcase, gave Helen a kiss on the cheek, and headed for the door.

"Richard, do drive carefully."

The genuine caring and protectiveness in her voice sent a sharp pain through him. He smiled back at her. What was he doing to her? How could he? Anne and John, too, were wholly innocent. Who was he to put his notion of his moral responsibility above their welfare? Were not Helen, Anne and John his chief responsibility?

In his car, nervously looking at his watch as he weaved his way in traffic towards the National University campus, he again tried to calm himself. He was no different, he told himself, from all those others in history who had felt compelled to put their own mission ahead of other considerations such as family. Many of them had been self-deluded fanatics, to be sure. Others had just been morally sloppy, frivolous, and corrupt human beings. But there were those who had done great good for their societies or humanity as a whole, good that had only become more apparent with time. Socrates, George Washington, John Adams — they were among the more outstanding examples. Who complained about the pain or worse that they had inflicted on their families? The world looked up to them as courageous and selfless men. They had been fully justified in risking their lives and the wellbeing of others. Should they have refrained from acting as they did out of concern for the suffering of those near and dear?

Richard was not so conceited as to think that he was in the same league as those historical figures, but they, too, must have struggled terribly with conscience. They had taken actions that endangered their families or subjected them to agony. In hindsight, all thought that they had done the right thing. They could be seen to have made the right choice in circumstances that were far from clear-cut. That was a part of their greatness. They had acted for the greater good of their societies. What about Richard Bittenberg? Was his judgment regarding the historical situation and what it required good enough?

He almost hit another car when, already endangering nearby pedestrians, he hunted for a parking place near the lecture hall where he was supposed to start lecturing within moments. How familiar this kind of situation had become. He was always late. Rarely, it seemed, did he go anywhere without being rushed and ill prepared.

After the class he went quickly by the office of his departmental chair and told him that he had to miss the day's faculty meeting. The chairman gave him a quizzical look. Richard almost never missed a meeting.

"A family emergency," Richard said. He did not have to play act to look worried.

"Nothing major, I hope," the chairman said.

"I hope not," Richard answered and left. He passed by the office used by his graduate assistant, Ron Turello, to let him know that he would not be back for his regular office hours in the afternoon. "A family matter. Please do what you can to cover for me. Give the ones you cannot help my regrets."

"Should I—?"

"Sorry, Ron, I'm very late."

He walked fast to the subway and took a train to Metro Center, where he had to change to go across the river. He arrived at the restaurant almost ten minutes late after jogging a part of the way from the nearest subway stop. He had started to sweat. Spring was on its way, and the temperature was in the mid sixties. He was about to enter the restaurant when he heard a voice.

"Richard, over here!" He turned and recognized Randy Gates getting out of an illegally parked car ten yards away. He was rather formally dressed in a darkish business suit. He could have been anybody, looked less like a spook—how does a spook look?— than a banker. He had a moonlike, rather pale face and a bald head, wore glasses without rims, and was a little overweight. Considering his dress, he had probably come from his place of work. The CIA headquarters in Langley was just a few miles north, off the George Washington Parkway. Richard was thinking increasingly about the intensifying pressures on himself. It could be no less uncomfortable for the other conspirators. Gates, for example, probably had a grueling schedule as one of the top people at the CIA. He was surely taking even more security precautions than Richard, and he had to take greater risks than Richard. The CIA had to keep an eye on their own, partly for the sake of their safety, partly to watch for signs of suspicious activity. How would Gates describe this outing to his secretary or any others who had to know? But Gates did not look harried. He shook Richard's hand.

"Let's take my car."

"You don't want us to have lunch here?"

"I had to meet you somewhere. I have another place in mind. Don't talk about anything sensitive while we're in the car. It's my own private car, but it hasn't been swept recently."

As they got into the car, Richard glanced in the back seat. There was a paper box with some coke cans and a stack of what looked like wrapped sandwiches.

"Who's the food for?"

"For us."

"Then you must have a great appetite. I know that one of those sandwiches will be enough for me."

"I thought I would provide some choice."

Gates turned on the radio. Rush Limbaugh was giving one of his monologues. In moments they were on the George Washington Parkway heading south along the Potomac River. Richard looked to the left towards the Lincoln Memorial and the city. He often wondered what was the first impression of Washington of the tourists who arrived at Reagan National Airport. They would be coming in the opposite direction. The parkland and the flowers along the Parkway and on the D.C. side of the river were rather attractive. The Lincoln Memorial and the Kennedy Center further up the river from Reagan National dominated the view. The official part of Washington with the monuments and the White House was rather flat and not much higher than the Potomac River. The Capitol on top of Capitol Hill stood out in the distance. But the Washington National Cathedral, north of the downtown area, was more conspicuously situated on the highest point of the city.

Just before they reached the airport exit Gates took a sudden right into a parking lot that runs parallel to the parkway and is adjacent to a small park-like area on a little lake. Richard had often thought that many people headed for National Airport must mistake this turnoff for the exit to the airport.

Gates parked and gathered up the food and drinks. Richard took one of the bags.

"Here," Gates said, "we're virtually under the takeoff or landing path for the airport, and there's lots of traffic noise from the parkway. Not exactly the best place for a picnic, but good for our purposes."

"There's a picnic table next to the water over there," Gates said and wandered off.

"It's already taken," Richard said. He saw two men sitting there.

"There's more room." Gates walked on.

Richard thought that the two persons at the table looked familiar. He realized that they were Douglas Pellegrini and Gordon Bunker. As they greeted each other and Richard sat down Gates smiled at Richard's surprise.

"In my business you get a lot of practice doing the unexpected," Gates said. "Now, who wants tuna fish, turkey, roast beef, or veggies? And you have a choice of lukewarm diet coke or lukewarm diet coke."

They were four people in business clothes eating sandwiches at a picnic table. Perhaps they were stockbrokers or lawyers trying to do something different for lunch. They were hardly conspiring to bring down the federal government of the United States.

"I suggest that though we should be safe here, we try to keep our voices down," Gates said.

Bunker said, "I picked up Doug at Union Station. But I didn't expect to meet you, Dick. Nice work, Randy." Richard thought again of the pressures and dangers to which the others were constantly subjecting themselves. How could somebody like Pellegrini, the number two or three man at the super-secret National Security Agency, take off from his job in the middle of the day? Every time a person like him or Gates did something unexpected, surely they risked arousing suspicion.

As if he had read Richard's mind, Gates said, "I'm not really here. I got somebody else's canceled appointment to see my ophthalmologist about something caught in my eye. Dr. Reece and I go back many years, and I'm actually on his schedule, if anybody should check. He knows what I need for him to say, if anybody asks."

"How do you avoid being followed?" Richard asked.

"I've been in operations for the better part of my life, Dick. I know my stuff. Shall we get down to business?"

The others nodded while munching on their sandwiches.

"First of all, let me tell you that Herbert filled me in on the meeting in West Virginia," Gates said. "You should know that I think we have to make our move while Reed is still Commanding General. Now that we have that resource I can't understand how we ever thought we might do without military support right here in Washington. I know that you, Dick, and Bates and Pickett counseled waiting, and I know your arguments, but I think the advantage of overwhelming force outweighs the advantage of a shroud of legitimacy. There's another major reason why I favor action as soon as possible. I'm really worried about the conspiracy being discovered. We're tempting fate. We've been scooting to meetings and making preparations for a very long time. It's a miracle that we haven't been discovered."

"Perhaps we have," Bunker said, "and the feds are just trying to map the conspiracy before catching us in flagrante."

"We've all had those thoughts," Gates said. "We're constantly looking over our shoulders."

"I'm sure I'm not the only one who looked for suspicious-looking cars and drivers in that parking lot," Bunker said. He nodded in the direction of his parked car. "You see all those limos? The drivers are trying to pick up passengers at National Airport, but they're not really allowed there without having an appointment with a passenger. So they have somebody with a cell phone stationed inside the airport who tries to get passengers on the hook."

"I know the scene," Pellegrini said and took another bite off his veggie sandwich.

"In any case," Gates said, "I've made up my mind. When the steering committee meets I will weigh in strongly on the side of moving as soon as possible."

Richard felt a lump in his throat. He was not surprised by what Gates had said, but now he had confirmation of his intuition that within a few days he would have to commit himself not to more discussion but to enacting a particular plan.

"As far as I'm concerned," Gates said, "all that remains is to streamline our operational plan B and put ourselves in readiness. Bob O'Brien has to find a couple of dates when the president and vice president will be sufficiently exposed at the same time. The president being at his ranch in Montana in August would be an excellent opportunity. He likes to go into that small near-by town for lunch. He won't listen to the Secret Service advising him against it. On the contrary, he tells them to be as discreet in their protection of him as possible. A nightmare for them, of course. At the same time, the place is really off the beaten path, and the Secret Service guys probably have become somewhat relaxed about this routine by now. Bob says the VP is almost certain to remain in D.C. when the president's away, and he thinks there are a couple of points in the VP's daily routine when he's vulnerable. The coordination of the assassinations has to run like clockwork."

"We need to make more detailed plans for dealing with certain persons outside of D.C.," Pellegrini said. His clipped way of speaking and his darting dark eyes undercut any impression that he might be just another charming Italian. He looked like a movie caricature of a wiry, temperamental conductor or film director. He added: "Specifically, we have to deal more effectively with the top people in the media and finance."

Richard's mind had drifted to how, concretely, enactment of plan B would affect him and his family, and he did not immediately register what Pellegrini had said. Now he came to full attention. This was obviously a continuation of DeLeon's appeal to him the night before. He and Bunker were the focus of an orchestrated lobbying effort.

"Certain key media and financial players in cooperation could create big problems for us," Pellegrini continued. "They can pull a lot of strings very quickly."

"We just *have* to beef up our efforts in that area," Gates said.

"You guys have brought up this issue before," Bunker said. "You're putting very heavy emphasis on that one aspect of our problems. Do I need to remind you that it's because of our slim resources that we'll be relying so much on smoke and mirrors and sheer determination. We have a very limited capacity outside of D.C." Bunker paused while another airliner came in for landing.

"We all agree on the need for deception and determination, Gordon," Gates said. "What Doug and I are saying is that we are underestimating the capacity of the media establishment and the finacial elite to create opposition to us."

"Herbert has to be persuaded to shift more resources in this direction," Pellegrini said.

There followed a concentrated briefing, Gates and Pellegrini taking turns advancing arguments. Richard was barely listening. The recalcitrance that he had felt in DeLeon's company the night before had returned and now intensified. Completely overwhelmed and without any hope of relief, he was being pressured to take on even greater responsibility. He was mired in his own misery. His imagination toyed with the possibility of just getting up and and walking away. Instead, he protected himself by offering pro forma arguments against Gates and Pellegrini, managing to exasperate them.

"Gentlemen," Bunker said in the manner of one chairing a meeting of bickering board members, "we have to adjourn this conversation. I'm supposed to deliver Doug back at Union Station by 2:00 PM. That gives me less than half an hour to cross the river and drive through D.C."

Bunker rose, and Richard was quick to follow his example. He wanted the discussion to end. The awareness that the conspiracy was headed in the direction of implementation of its plans was ever present and by itself agonizing. The thought of last-minute complications and facing new demands made him recoil.

Bunker declared, "I'll talk to Herbert. He already knows about your concerns. I would like to have a more specific proposal for what you think must be done. I'll call you, Randy, about a get-together. Since we live near each other it's easy for us to meet." Bunker and Pellegrini headed for the parking lot.

Richard helped Gates gather up the trash. His mood was surly. They walked together to a receptacle.

"Sorry, Richard," Gates said. "I suppose Doug and I came on a little strong."

Before they got into Gates's car Richard said, "I had the impression that you and Doug were trying to persuade me in particular."

"We were. Herbert seems to listen to you. You have to help move him."

Richard's mind shifted yet again to his own painful personal circumstances. Gates and Pellegrini, and Lisa DeLeon behind them, regarded Herbert as the key actor in the conspiracy, but they also saw him, Richard, as one who really had the ear of Vandenhorst and who could change his thinking—as if Richard were not already carrying an almost crippling burden.

He only said: "Didn't Lisa tell you that you shouldn't expect me to do your bidding?"

Gates did not respond.

An almost physical feeling of discomfort descended on Richard as he sat down in the front seat of Gates's car for the return trip to Rosslyn. The day had brought unmitigated wretchedness. The conspiracy seemed to be moving inexorably towards early practical action, and the demands on him just kept growing. More and more, *he* was being asked to play a central role. To all of these pressures were added a growing concern about his fellow conspirators. They were smart and experienced, true, but they also had their obvious weaknesses, idiosyncracies, and foibles. But then who was he, Richard Bittenberg, to find those others deficient? With his fears, apprehensions and doubts was *he* not among those whose limitations called the efficacy of the conspiracy into question?

Sitting in Gates's car, Richard felt as if somebody had left him in a straightjacket and abandoned him. He could breathe, just barely, but he couldn't move. He had a touch of nausea.

Gates asked whether he should take Richard to the Rosslyn subway station. Richard produced a weak, "yes." Luckily, Gates did not press the subject of the luncheon meeting. During the brief trip only the sound from the radio and some small talk broke the silence.

Richard struggled to overcome his paralysis. *Billick's principle*, he thought. You must live in the real world! Stop dreaming about perfect circumstances and partners! They can exist only in the imagination. In the real world you have to make do with the assets you've got. The members of the conspiracy were human beings, he told himself, and they were the only ones actually available.

Gates let Richard out at the subway station.

"Thanks for coming, Richard."

"Thanks for lunch," Richard said rather curtly, walked into the station and disappeared underground. He had been miserable since his first waking moment that morning, and he could see no reason why that would change during the rest of the day. He would pick up his car at the university and drive home. He used to look forward to heading home to Helen and his family. He still did – in a way he badly needed to go home – but after what had happened in the kitchen the other evening he also dreaded it.

Sitting in the subway train he felt completely alone. The other passengers seemed as unaware of the state of their country as of his torment. He had nobody with whom he could really discuss his situation. He had talked a great deal with Vandenhorst in recent weeks, sometimes about personal matters, but Vandenhorst was an integral part of the predicament on which he felt he needed a fresh perspective. Yet to talk to anybody outside of the conspiracy would be a terrible breach of security. Could he talk to Helen after all? No, he must not. No way. He was desperately lonely.

Several times during his association with the conspiracy Richard had taken his anxieties to church outside of regular services and at different hours of the day. Most of the time he went to his parish church. He might find the organist practicing for the Sunday service or the sexton doing some maintenance, but usually the church was empty. He prayed, though wordlessly for the most part. He asked for guidance. He asked for comfort. He asked for relief. Most often he asked for the strength to endure the unremitting strain.

It had occurred to Richard several times to ask the rector of his parish for spiritual counseling and to lay before him his situation and all his agonies. Richard liked the rector, who seemed to be an intelligent, decent, levelheaded man, though prone to sentimentality. It would be a terrible act of misconduct for a priest to violate the confidentiality of such a conversation. Still, Richard could not risk the rector being so horrified that he felt relieved of normal obligations. A Roman Catholic priest would not break the seal of the confessional under any circumstances, but what about an Episcopal clergyman, a priest in one of the most confused and decadent denominations in the United States? Might such a clergyman not become so appalled by Richard's story that he felt justified in breaking confidentiality. Yet so desperate was Richard for someone to talk to who was not involved in the conspiracy that he returned to the possibility of talking to his rector. Surely, that particular priest would be safe.

But when he had reached his university's subway stop he had again discarded the idea. He could not take the risk. He could not place such a load on the shoulders of an innocent bystander. Besides, what would be the benefit of receiving the reaction and opinion of one whose personal circumstances were very different from Richard's and who did not appear to have any special powers of discernment? Richard had to continue carrying the burden on his own.

# CHAPTER 45

Léger drove the car, and Henri Duparc sat in the back seat. They would pass through the town of Noisy, which they had visited the day before, and then head for the village of Evremond just five kilometers further on. Duparc had papers on his lap and spread out on the seat next to him, but he kept looking out the window, though without really seeing the rather pretty countryside and the small towns and villages. A tourist would have enjoyed the scenery. Duparc's mind was elsewhere. He could not remember an investigation like this one. He had great difficulty classifying it. He still had no definite hypothesis about the disappearance of the American professor. It had not taken him long to decide that Richard Bittenberg had not left his family as a result of some marital or familial quarrel. His wife, that perceptive and resourceful but also rather disturbingly attractive woman, had struck him as being truly at a loss to explain her husband's disappearance. She was clearly distraught. The two children gave the same impression. They had struck him as balanced and likeable. There had been no indication of any unusual family tensions. Deep worry had been written on their faces. He had empathized with the children as he continued to empathize with their mother. She may initially have been on her guard with the two French detectives, but that was hardly surprising. She knew nothing about them.

It was possible that Professor Bittenberg had suddenly decided that he had to disappear and that he could not afford so much as to hint to his wife at the reason for the disappearance. It could be his way of protecting his family. If so, Duparc and Léger were jeopardizing the safety of both Professor Bittenberg and his family by looking for him. But Duparc could not worry about that possibility. His assignment was to find out what had happened to the American citizen Richard Bittenberg.

"What do you think, Léger? What happened to Bittenberg?" They had already speculated, but they had never adopted a working hypothesis, only pursued the clues they had.

Léger turned his long neck to glance behind him in the direction of Duparc as if to ascertain the frame of mind of his superior.

"I'm not sure, boss. I'd say he was probably abducted, but it may have been done in such a way that first he didn't quite realize what was happening. Perhaps he fell into some sort of trap."

"Aha."

"And what do you think, boss?"

Duparc did not answer immediately. "I really don't know what to think," he said pensively. "I find the case rather puzzling."

"I know. Take the behavior of that diplomat. It's really suspicious. I doubt he was just meeting an old friend. But is the American government involved?"

"Do we agree that, if Bittenberg was abducted, it was not by professionals?"

"We do."

"And he probably wasn't snatched by seasoned criminals either."

They fell silent again. Léger concentrated on the driving.

"Do you think Helen Bittenberg's been telling the truth?" Duparc asked. Léger again looked in Duparc's direction, now in surprise.

"You don't think so?"

"Yes, I do. I haven't noticed any lies, and she's clearly very upset."

Léger nodded.

Duparc returned to his papers, checking the list of green Land Rovers and addresses that Léger had put together. But soon he was looking out the car window again. He just could not make sense of what they knew.

Another woman? The lack of evidence of marital trouble did not prove that the Bittenberg marriage was not on the rocks. But why in the world would Bittenberg elope without any warning while on a vacation trip with his family in France? What an extraordinarily cruel way of treating them! If there had been real discord in the marriage, Duparc or Léger should have picked up some signs, but Helen had given them almost the opposite impression. Richard Bittenberg had worked very hard and had been under great stress, and this had been a sore subject between them, but it had never put their basic devotion to each other in doubt. The vacation in France had been a confirmation of their love for each other and for their family. They were enjoying being in France and were looking forward to the rest of their stay in Europe. Helen had told Ferguson a tale of very strained relations between her and her husband to entice Ferguson and make him trip himself up, but it had seemed obvious to Duparc that she had invented the marital discord. She had appeared almost apologetic about drawing a wholly misleading picture of her marriage. Her willingness to feign an amorous interest in Ferguson struck Duparc as evidence of devotion to her husband.

One of the most puzzling aspects of the case was the strange conduct of this top diplomat at the American Embassy. If Ferguson's meeting with Richard at the Sorbonne had been merely a meeting of old friends, why would he conceal it from Helen, and why would Richard conceal it from her? Ferguson clearly knew something about Richard's disappearance. Was Richard Bittenberg involved in a secret diplomatic effort of some kind or in an intelligence operation on French soil? In the latter case, assuming that they were not acting in concert with the French authorities, he and Ferguson would be acting illegally. Richard would be risking arrest. If an operation sanctioned by the French government was under way or had gone wrong, why had a superior not contacted him and told him not to delve too deeply into the case? Experience had taught Duparc to be prepared for anything when it came to intelligence activities.

It was curious that Bittenberg's disappearance had been reported to the French police by the consular section at the U.S. Embassy through regular channels, but that it had been done in a manner indicating that the embassy attached great importance to the case. That was the reason why a fairly senior detective had been assigned to investigate. But Helen had told Ferguson about Richard's disappearance shortly after it happened, and she had conveyed to him how convinced she was that something was very wrong. Because of his diplomatic rank, Ferguson could have pulled some strings to initiate a search for Bittenberg immediately. He could have called a high official at the French foreign office. Instead he had held back. He had commiserated with Helen, but had done nothing to speed up the investigation; on the contrary, he had concealed what he knew. Duparc was curious to see how Ferguson would handle the next visit from the French police. This time the questions would be a great deal more pointed. Would Ferguson try to avoid answering by citing his diplomatic status? Duparc had already decided that, if he did so, Duparc would tell Ferguson that he would go to the ambassador with his request for answers to questions. If Ferguson had something compromising to hide that was also private, that threat might loosen his tongue.

What might he have overlooked in this strange case? Was there a romantic angle of some unexpected kind? According to Helen, Ferguson seemed to be quite taken with her. Could this be an old-fashioned murder case? Had Ferguson been desperately pursuing Helen and finally found a way to get rid of her husband? But then

Helen should have told him that Ferguson had shown interest in her earlier — unless *she* was involved in Richard's disappearance. Experience had taught Duparc to be suspicious of first impressions. He had learned to question his own spontaneous reactions to people. He was favorably impressed by Helen and her children, had to admit that he was even attracted to her as a woman, and so he had to watch any tendency to exempt her from suspicion. Could she be a part of a plot to do away with her husband? But then why would she be voicing suspicions of Ferguson and telling the French police about Ferguson's amorous advances? Perhaps precisely to make Duparc rule out collaboration between the two of them. You would expect one conspirator to steer suspicions away from, not towards, another conspirator. But would two romantically involved murderers let other people — the man in the gray beard, the embassy driver, and the driver of the green Land Rover — help carry out their plot?

No, for this last hypothesis Duparc's intuition and the concrete evidence provided little or no support. He considered it only because he must not be influenced by Helen's charms. Duparc smiled at his own fastidiousness. Helen's anxiety about her husband could not be more genuine. Duparc also thought that he had seen something like flashes of hatred in her eyes when talking about Ferguson. Her concern about the effect on her children was deep and palpable. She would have to be a master actress to have faked these emotions. No, Helen Bittenberg was no cold-blooded, calculating murderess. Again he smiled to himself.

Could the entire Bittenberg family be in on some elaborate scheme of deceit, perhaps a plot to convince others, including the French government, that Richard Bittenberg was probably dead? Was Bittenberg a U.S. operative of some sort who needed to disappear without a trace, perhaps to avoid retaliation from some group that he had betrayed? Was his disappearance part of an attempt to hide him and provide him with a new identity? Duparc was familiar with the American federal witness protection program. He had once assisted the FBI in a highly secretive operation involving an American who had informed on a Mafia boss and who had been put temporarily in France under a new identity. If Bittenberg's disappearance was a way of protecting him, the information that Helen had provided might be wholly misleading, and he and Léger were wasting their time. If they were really good at their jobs, they might still stumble on what had happened and upset the scheme. But no, this hypothesis assumed that Helen Bittenberg and her children were consummate actors.

Helen's only role in the case had to be that of innocent victim.

Whoever the schemers were, they were willing to put her and the Bittenberg children through hell. Duparc was an experienced policeman. He had taught himself not to become personally affected by cases that he investigated, whether it meant controlling indignation at the callousness or viciousness of criminals or sorrow over the suffering he so often encountered. But sometimes his emotions broke through his defenses, especially, he had noticed, when a case could be related to his own personal circumstances. What if his fifteen-year-old daughter had been raped, his ten-year-old son abducted to Afghanistan, or his wife brutally beaten by a mugger? Most of his cases in recent years concerned crimes with an international dimension and did not involve violence, but there were other ways of mistreating human beings that could be as devastating for those involved. The potential of the human race for sheer perversity and unscrupulousness never ceased to amaze him. Thinking about the Bittenberg case he felt resentment and anger at Ferguson and his collaborators and sadness for the torment of Helen and the two children.

"This is Evremond," Léger announced as they drove into a small village. "The Dégas place is supposed to be two kilometers beyond the town, just off this road." Étienne Dégas was one of just three persons in the area of Noisy and environs in whose name a green Land Rover was registered. The owners of the other two had been checked in the first round of interviews. Duparc had a strong hunch that this would be the car from which the bundle of stakes had tumbled onto a parked car in Noisy. That town was only five kilometers closer to Paris.

Duparc and Léger had visited the two-room prefecture in Noisy the day before. It shared a small house just off the town square with a tiny post office. Only three policemen operated out of the station. One was on patrol, one was on vacation, and one was manning the office. The heavyset policeman in his fifties who received Duparc and Léger was surprised that two detectives from Paris would take an interest in a trivial traffic accident in a provincial town. Duparc told him that he could not reveal the reason and impressed on him the importance of telling no one that they had inquired. The policeman showed them the report on the accident and a few photographs of the damaged cars.

"Ordinarily there wouldn't have been any report. We would have left the matter to the insurance companies. But the driver of the car that caused the damage didn't stop. That made us classify the accident as a hit-and-run. The driver had to have noticed that the stakes were falling off. Even if he had his windows up and the air-conditioner running, he must've heard or seen them falling from the roof or banging into the two parked cars. We also took the incident more seriously because the owner of one of the cars is a local judge. He was very upset."

"How far have you gotten in your investigation?" Duparc asked.

"We haven't gotten anywhere. After the personnel cuts in the last few years, we can barely keep our noses above water, and it's vacation time. We may never get around to it."

"Just leave it with us then. We'll let you know what we find out."

"Great! I have a few other cases I would love to hand over."

Duparc and Léger laughed dutifully.

The policeman had taken them into the backyard where about ten stakes had been put. "As you can see, they're the kind of stakes that are used to support vines."

As they drove through Evremond Duparc turned his mind from speculation to thinking about the practical matter immediately at hand. Coming out of the village they asked the driver of a tractor for directions to the Dégas's house. They were told where to turn off the main road. A small access road led up to a modest farmhouse. About a hundred yards behind it was a stable. It sat next to a large fenced field in which seven horses were grazing. In the adjoining fields they could not see any animals or crops. The fields rolled softly and were dotted with clusters of trees. Near the barn there was a pond and a couple of small outbuildings. Everything looked neat. The main house seemed to be in good repair. It was a rather inviting bucolic scene. A small blue Citroen was parked at the side of the residence, but there was no sign of a Land Rover. Perhaps it was parked out of sight.

It was time to interview Dégas.

# CHAPTER 46

The conspirators had expected that the big decision would be made almost immediately, but Vandenhorst spread the word that, much as he regretted it, a few days' delay was necessary because of complications and the need for more information. But they were told to expect to be called to a meeting of the steering committee the coming weekend at the latest and on short notice. Richard met with a few of the conspirators, and they all showed signs that the growing pressure was getting to them.

Richard had a brief conversation with Vandenhorst in which he dutifully reported on what DeLeon had said in the car returning from Pellegrini's mountain cabin and Gates and Pellegrini had said at the picnic luncheon near Reagan airport, but he did not make any recommendation. Vandenhorst showed some irritation.

"I agree with them in a way, but I can't adopt a whole new set of priorities to placate those three. We're terribly shorthanded. I would have to pull assets away from crucial tasks. There's just no way to cover all the bases. Some of the others are after me to put more people in areas of special concern to them. Sales's is always pushing. Just the other day Bates and Pickett pleaded with me to ensure that we do what *they* consider necessary on Capitol Hill."

Richard had heavy, important responsibilities, but no time. He slept badly and much too little. He could barely handle his classes and doctoral students at the university and was desperate for the semester to end. He found his situation almost unbearable. He had to marshal all his willpower to act normally in front of Helen and the children. Though he tried to spend moments with them now and then and to behave as if he were not doing anything out of the ordinary, she had to sense that he was finding it very hard to do what he did. She was undoubtedly wondering how long he would be able to keep up this struggle. She did not needle or try to unnerve him, but neither did she try to put him at ease. He was on probation. There were no open hostilities, but each felt that the other was keeping the guard up. Richard wondered what kind of excuses he would make when the conspiracy demanded even more of his time.

The second day after the luncheon meeting at National

Airport when the Bittenberg family had just finished dinner the telephone rang. Although the call came in on the family line, Richard felt his stomach tighten. Helen answered. He could soon tell that it was Robert Preston, his best friend. Dick relaxed. Helen handed him the telephone.

"Bob, how are you?

"Fine, Dick, how goes it?"

"All right. How are things on Capitol Hill?"

"Well, we're finished for the week, and most of the members are heading home to their districts."

"What about you?"

"I'll be staying in town. That's why I'm calling. You and I haven't had one of our breakfasts for a while. Are you free tomorrow?"

Richard did not think that he had any free time any longer. When he was not occupied with some particular task, he felt that he had to be near a telephone, preferably the scrambled one, in case he would be called to the pending big meeting of the conspiracy. Vandenhorst in particular knew his hours and where to reach him at different times. But Richard did want to see his old friend. He could bring his cell phone, which one of the conspirators might use in an emergency.

"It would have to be early. I have a course at the university at ten, and I have to make some preparations. Could we make it 7:30?"

"Sure thing. We could save you some time by meeting at that McDonald's near you."

"OK, Bob, let's do it. I'll see you there."

Helen did not mind Richard's getting an early start the next morning. She did not like his practice of leaving the house in a rush, too late for a leisurely drive to the university. By meeting Robert Preston for breakfast he would have already gotten together the books and materials that he needed and would be out of the house and on his way. She also thought that conversations with Robert did Richard good. He could air questions that he otherwise kept bottled up inside, where they festered.

When Richard pulled into the parking lot of the McDonald's the next morning, he noticed Bob Preston's car already there. He found his friend sitting inside at a window with a cup of coffee.

"Have you been here long?"

"Just a few minutes."

Richard did not sit down, and Robert motioned him to do so.

"Would you mind if we went to another place?"

"What's wrong with this place?"

"Nothing, but I got it into my head that I wanted to go to the Louisiana place." He and Preston had gone there many times.

"Whatever you want, but isn't that out of your way if you want a smooth run to the university?"

"I don't have to leave for the university until 9:30."

Robert Preston looked searchingly at Richard and then got up.

Richard was more acutely aware than ever of the danger to the conspiracy of security breaches and government attention. What if he was under surveillance by some government agency? Whoever was listening would have had plenty of time to make arrangements to listen in on his breakfast conversation at McDonald's. As they left he looked around the premises but saw nothing out of the ordinary. As he walked to his car he scanned the parking lot and noticed a couple of vans, each of which might conceal a few men with listening equipment, but the scene looked normal. There were always vans at McDonald's. Before he drove away he sat for half a minute to see whether anybody else would leave the restaurant. Only an old woman came out. He saw Preston's car pull away. Driving off he kept looking in the rearview mirror for signs that he might be followed. On his way to the other restaurant he made an unnecessary turn and then pulled into the parking lot of a strip mall. After a minute he drove off again, paying close attention to who might be following. A surveillance team might have picked up what he had said about "the Louisiana place," but it would not give much guidance.

Why was he being so cautious? Robert Preston was not one of the conspirators, but Richard had been strongly tempted to tell him in some oblique way about what was preoccupying him. He badly needed someone to talk to whose judgment he respected and who was not involved in the conspiracy. What was making him security conscious this morning was that he was seriously considering giving Robert Preston an idea of what was on his mind. Where else would he turn? He had not decided to take Robert into his confidence, but wanted to have that option.

Having found a parking place near the restaurant, he sat for yet another minute observing cars and people. When he finally came into the restaurant, a small place near a car dealership on the outskirts of downtown Bethesda, Robert looked at him with a mixture of amusement and concern.

"What took you so long?"

"I'm sorry, Bob, I forgot a book at the house that I have to have for my lecture. I had to go back home to pick it up. Sorry."

Robert gave Richard a curious glance. "Well, let's have

breakfast."

The usual small talk ensued. Richard did not see how anybody could have followed them, but he kept an eye on the entrance. How do you distinguish a person experienced in surveillance from a regular breakfast eater?

They got their American breakfasts and as they dug in Richard said, "So, what's been most on your mind lately?"

"I was going to ask you the same. You seem to be on edge."

"You answer first."

"I've been thinking about the same old thing, actually. More bad bills keep coming up, but they're just examples of the problem with the U.S. Congress. It's simply impossible to break out of the moral, political, and financial irresponsibility and corruption. It boggles the mind. I used to think that it should be possible in time to shake the place up. I thought that eventually some of the more sophisticated bad guys would understand that we're flirting with disaster. But they've adjusted to the circumstances and come up with new ways of enriching and advancing themselves. The state of the U.S. economy is terrible, but our leaders keep pushing the same policies, diluting the value of the dollar. I find myself sympathizing with some of the demonstrators and rioters, people who've been deceived and have to suffer the consequences of the actions of their political representatives. Demagoguery does not begin to describe how our leaders communicate with the American people. There's all this talk of change and a need for ethical standards, but they don't mean any of it. Those who are willing to face the big choices are making no headway. They're all discouraged or have given up."

"Does that mean you're thinking of leaving the House?"

"Of course I have thought about it, and so have many others. But I love the idea of my job: I'm supposed to represent the people in my district and the American people. I'm to look after them, protect them, warn them of dangers. I should help protect the Constitution. It's never needed more help. If I left the Congress, I guess I would practice law in Columbia as my father did. But I would not be able to hide. I could not get rid of my sense of impending doom."

"I tell you, Bob, I just can't see how this system could repair itself. It's too far gone."

"I'm afraid you may be right."

"Often, Bob, I feel something like despair." Richard felt that he was close to taking up the subject weighing so heavily on him.

"Perhaps some things can still be done," Preston said.

"Like what?"

"There are people who are not just upset but willing to take action."

"Organize politically? A new party? What would be the point? Didn't we just agree that the system is incapable of reforming itself?"

"Yes, but perhaps there's another way."

"What are you talking about, Bob?"

Robert seemed to hesitate. He signaled the waiter for more coffee.

"I've thought about talking to you about some things I've been involved in recently, but I haven't gotten around to it."

Robert had Richard's full attention.

"A few of us in the House have been meeting privately to discuss a new approach to the problem."

"Another discussion group?"

"Yes and no."

"What's the 'no' part?"

Robert looked around the restaurant.

"This may not be the right time and place to talk about it."

Richard was looking intently at Robert.

"You should be able to give me at least a hint. If what you have to say is sensitive in some way, just lower your voice a little."

Robert looked ill at ease and again looked around him, then behind him. He leaned forward over their almost empty plates and said quietly: "Some of us are discussing plans for a kind of action that has not been tried before."

"You mean congressional action."

"Not quite."

"That makes sense—you just told me you've given up on changing the Congress."

"This would be unconventional action."

"How many of you are involved?"

"Not many."

"Then how could anything come of what you're talking about?"

"We would not act on our own."

"You're in touch with people outside the Congress?"

"Yes, and the person organizing us is actually not a member."

"Who is he?"

"I can't tell you."

"Can't you be a little more precise?"

Again Robert hesitated. "Don't press me, Dick, I'll only tell you that he works for the minority leader of the House."

Richard looked at Robert in disbelief. Was it possible? Had his friend independently become involved in the conspiracy? Had Robert Bates, Congressman Peck's chief advisor, recruited his old friend Robert Preston? Richard had become very quiet.

"Bob," Richard suddenly said, "are you free for coffee later today? I have to leave now to teach my course, but I would like to talk more about this subject—as soon as possible. It's important. Can you meet me again?"

"I'll arrange it. Where do we meet?"

"I could pick you up at 1:00 at your house."

Richard stood up and put a twenty-dollar bill on the table. When Robert picked it up and tried to give it back to him, Richard just turned and walked towards the door.

# CHAPTER 47

Léger parked in front of the Dégas house, and the two detectives walked up to the front entrance and knocked. They heard voices inside, perhaps from a television or radio. After a few moments a woman looked out through the glass in the door, seemed to hesitate, but then opened the door. The expression on her face was one of surprise. Presumably, unannounced visitors were rare. Duparc wondered if he also detected fear.

"Yes?" She had graying blond hair and seemed to be fifty-five to sixty years old. She did not look like a farmer's wife engaged in partly physical work but more like a middle class suburbanite. She was wearing a somewhat dressy sweater and slacks and indoor shoes. Her medium-length hair was brushed, and she wore make-up. She could have been having morning coffee with a neighbor. She was of medium height and weight and had agreeable, if unexceptional, looks.

"My name is Henri Duparc and this is my colleague, Pierre Léger. We're police officers." Duparc held out his identification, but did it in such a manner as not to encourage closer examination. He did not want the woman to learn that he and Léger were stationed in Paris. "Are you Madame Dégas?" Duparc asked pleasantly.

"Yes, I am."

"We would like to have a word with Étienne Dégas. Is he at home?"

The woman looked anxiously at the two detectives. "What do you want to talk to him about?"

"Is he at home?"

"No, he isn't."

"Can you tell us where we might find him?"

"I'm not sure. What's this all about?"

"We are hoping that your husband will be able to help us with a routine investigation."

"An investigation of what?"

"We would rather talk to your husband."

"How important is it?"

"Somewhat important. It would save us time and energy if he

could answer a couple of questions."

"Well, I don't know where he is." She had started to sound a little irritated.

"Madame, we're very sorry to have to bother you. When do you expect your husband home?"

"I'm not sure. In an hour or so?"

"Where does he work?"

"My husband is semiretired. He used to be a military officer."

Duparc again tried to be disarming. "Somebody is keeping *this* place in very good shape. That must take a good bit of time."

"Yes, my husband does most of that work. I only help out."

Léger, who had been quiet, asked in a light, conversational tone: "I saw that you have horses. A pretty sight. Are they all yours?"

"No, just one. The others are boarding here."

"We've seen some vineyards in the area. Do you grow wine too?" Léger asked.

"No."

"You have no idea where we might find your husband?" Duparc tried again. "Does he have a cell phone perhaps?"

"No, well—yes, he does, but much of the time he forgets it at home, and when it's in the car he often doesn't turn it on, and sometimes it runs out of battery. He keeps it mostly for emergencies."

It was clear to Duparc that they would have to come back. Mrs. Dégas was not exactly hostile; she actually seemed careful not to irritate the two detectives and not to appear worried. But she would not facilitate their efforts. Duparc also did not want to give her the impression that their inquiry was urgent and serious.

"Thank you, Mrs. Dégas," Duparc said. "I suppose we'll just have to come back later."

As the two detectives were driving back to the main road Duparc said, "That woman's worried about something. She's probably trying to reach her husband by telephone right now."

"The question's what is she trying to hide."

"Not much we can do at the moment. It'll be lunchtime soon. Let's see if there's a restaurant or café in Evremond. Or we'll have to go back to Noisy for lunch."

Evremond was a village of perhaps twenty houses, a couple of small stores, and a church, all clustered around the main road. They drove slowly into the village looking for a place to eat.

"Doesn't look very promising," Duparc said.

"Look!" Léger cried out and pointed up the street that ran perpendicular to the main road. He stopped the car and reversed in order to be able to turn into the side street. Duparc saw immediately what had made Léger react. In the last couple of days Duparc had learned to recognize models of Land Rovers, and there, parked in front of a house a block away, was a Land Rover in faded green with its rear facing them. A spare wheel was attached to the back door. Léger pulled up behind the Land Rover. It was parked outside what appeared to be a tiny plumbing business. Inside they could see a man talking to another man behind a counter. The license plate was dirty but readable, and Duparc realized that this was almost certainly the car whose owner they wanted to interview.

"He should be out in a moment," Duparc said. They got out of their car. Léger, who was the taller of the two, looked at the roof of the Land Rover, wondering if he might find scratches. He found plenty, most of which looked old and rusty. The roof rack was only partial and seemed to have been put there by the manufacturer more for decorative than practical purposes, but it had clearly been much used. In general, the car looked decidedly like a "working" vehicle. It had a number of dents and other imperfections. It was beyond the stage when cosmetics might really improve the general impression.

The door to the plumbing shop opened and a square-faced, dark-haired man with a trimmed moustache came out. He seemed to be around sixty years old. He was carrying a small package. He headed for the Land Rover. He was tallish and erect and moved as one might expect of a former officer. He looked vigorous and purposeful. He gave the two detectives a curious glance. He was about to get into the car when Duparc addressed him.

"Monsieur Dégas?"

"Yes."

"Sorry to bother you. I'm Henri Duparc, and this is my associate Pierre Léger. We're police officers." Duparc extended his badge.

Dégas barely looked at the credentials.

"Yes."

"We just came from your house."

"I see. What can I do for you?" His manner of speaking, too, was that of a soldier — clipped, distinct, and easy to hear.

"We would appreciate your answering a few questions. We don't need to stand here. We could follow you home or to some other location."

"I don't care. Ask your questions."

"As you wish. We're investigating a traffic accident that happened a few days ago." As he spoke, Duparc was watching Dégas's expression closely. Was his question eliciting relief because it did not concern the whereabouts of a certain American?

"A traffic accident?"

"Yes, it took place last Friday just after noon. Do you remember where you were then?"

"Friday—I'm not sure. Could have been at home looking after the horses. I usually give them a good brushing before the weekend. I have a kid helping me."

"Please think, sir. Could you have been anywhere else?"

"It's possible. I just don't remember. I drive about a lot."

"When were you last in Noisy?"

"Hard to say. My wife and I go there pretty often—a part of our routine. That's where we buy most of our groceries. And there's a restaurant there that we like. We're there so often we hardly think about it."

"Do you tend to go at a particular time of day?"

"Well, if we're going to have dinner, it's in the evening." Dégas's tone was now sarcastic.

"Any other times?"

"We don't follow any set pattern."

Unexpected in an old soldier, Duparc thought.

"Could you've been in Noisy around 12:15 on Friday?"

"I don't remember. I suppose so."

"Would both you and your wife have gone to Noisy?"

"Now wait a minute!" Dégas spoke with annoyance and exasperation. "I've told you I don't remember! Suppose you told me what you're getting at. What's this accident you're talking about?"

"Are you the only person to drive this car?" Duparc used his head to indicate the Land Rover.

"Pretty much. My wife drives it only if our other car is being serviced or fixed. She doesn't like it. It's usually not very tidy."

"Monsieur Dégas, your car—"

"I'm Major Dégas."

"Major, your car was seen in Noisy on Friday." Duparc had become tired of Dégas's evasiveness and spoke affirmatively, not bothering to qualify his statement in any way. The retired officer had to be smoked out.

"I'm not the only person who has a Land Rover, am I?"

"No, but this car has certain characteristics, and at least one person saw the license plate." Again Duparc was stretching the truth. "Are you denying that you were in Noisy last Friday?"

The major opened the door to the Land Rover and threw the package on the front passenger seat in a gesture of disgust.

"Look here!" he said, turning in an almost threatening manner toward the two detectives. "I'm running about all over the place. You don't expect me to keep a record of where I am at particular times, do you?" Duparc reflected that as an officer Dégas had had much practice giving orders and intimidating people. He probably was not used to being on the defensive.

"So you're not denying that you were in Noisy?"

"Suppose I was." Dégas scoffed. "What of it?"

"You caused an accident, Major."

Dégas made a face suggesting complete puzzlement.

"An accident?"

"A bundle of stakes fell from the roof of your Land Rover and damaged two cars parked along the road."

Again Duparc closely observed Dégas, who stood silently for a moment, seemingly thinking hard. He then made a face as if a light was turning on in his head.

"The stakes—I see—So *that's* what happened!" Dégas's demeanor was that of person for whom a great mystery had suddenly been cleared up.

"I did lose some stakes. I discovered that they were gone last weekend when I was going to replace some rotten ones. I had bunched about a dozen of them together and tied them to the roof rack on the Rover. But they were gone. I had no idea what had happened to them. I guess I do now. So they fell off in Noisy?"

"You mean to say that those stakes came loose and slid off the roof and banged into two other cars without your noticing?"

"Yes, that's exactly what I mean. Otherwise I'd have stopped."

Of course you would, Duparc thought to himself, but you couldn't stop because you had a very reluctant passenger.

"Are you saying that you heard *nothing* and that you saw *nothing* in one of your rearview mirrors?" Duparc pointed to the sizeable outside driver's side mirror on the Land Rover. "Those stakes made quite a racket, and something out of the ordinary must have appeared in one or both of the mirrors."

"I didn't notice anything."

"But you weren't even going very fast. Where the accident happened there's a rather sharp bend in the road, so you must have been driving slowly. There was little or no engine noise."

"Still, I had no idea those stakes had come loose. Perhaps I had the radio on."

Léger who had been standing silently next to Duparc making notes, now said, "Leaving the scene of an accident is a serious offense."

Dégas turned to him. "Didn't you hear what I just said? I didn't know there *was* any accident!"

"That's rather hard to believe," Duparc said.

Dégas shrugged his shoulders.

Duparc then flatly asserted, "You had at least one passenger. If what you're saying is true, that person should be able to confirm that you didn't hear anything inside the car. I need a name."

Dégas hesitated. He was obviously in a quandary. He looked from Duparc to Léger. The latter demonstratively held his pen in readiness above his notebook.

"Passenger?" Dégas said, seemingly astonished by the question.

"Yes, we would like to have the name or the names. There was at least one passenger."

Duparc was certain that Dégas would have liked to deny having had any passenger, but Dégas knew by now that there were witnesses to the accident, and he realized that the two detectives would not take kindly to any further evasiveness or deception on his part. What he didn't know was that the reference to passengers was unrelated to anything reported by witnesses in Noisy.

"You don't remember who was with you in the car?"

Dégas finally said: "Just give me a moment—It's coming back to me." He paused. "Yes—I was doing some work at one of the vineyards that Friday, and I was out with the owner. We went to look at some new equipment."

"And who is that person?"

Again Dégas hesitated. Then he looked at his watch and said, "Gentlemen, I was in a bit of a hurry when you showed up. I thought this wouldn't take very long. But now I badly need to go. I have a water leak in our stable. You said earlier we might have this conversation elsewhere. I'd like to take you up on that. You can follow me back to the house. I just need to give some instructions to a farmhand, and then I can give you the time you need."

Duparc knew that Dégas needed time to think and that he might try to contact de la Broderie, but to deny his request or to ask him to let one of the detectives accompany him in his car would alert him to the fact that they were investigating more than a trivial hit-and-run accident.

So Duparc said, "Fine, Major. We'll do as you like."

Dégas jumped into the Land Rover and took off. Duparc and Léger followed him.

"That water leak must be really serious," Léger said.

Within a minute they could see that Dégas was on his cell

phone.

"Just as his wife told us," Léger said. "He uses it mostly for emergencies."

Duparc gave a small laugh.

"I would love to listen in on that phone call," Léger said.

"Do we need to? They're just getting their story straight."

# CHAPTER 48

Driving to the university after breakfasting with Robert Preston, Richard had conflicting emotions. He had been on the verge of revealing something of his trauma to his friend. The possibility that Robert, too, was involved in the conspiracy reassured him in that he knew Robert to be levelheaded and cautious as well as highly intelligent and an all-around good guy. That Robert, who never indulged in wishful thinking but always tried to be realistic and practical, might in fact be a part of the effort to overthrow the U.S. government assuaged Richard's occasional worries that he might have lost touch with reality. If Robert was involved, he was a relative newcomer to living as a conspirator; he had said something about recently joining a group of disgruntled people on Capitol Hill. He was not as close to the center of decision making as Richard, and the pressures on him could not be as intense, but he would be able to understand what Richard was going through. The two old friends would be uniquely able to empathize with and support each other. They had been close for a long time, were the same age, had similar backgrounds, were even from the same state and had similar family roots. They could commiserate as well as boost each other's confidence. Richard would not have to be so frightfully alone. Richard wanted to ask Robert how he handled the possibility that his life and that of his family might soon change drastically. Robert, too, was a family man. He must have some of Richard's anxieties. Had he confided in Jennifer, his wife? The problem was that, unless they got the approval of the steering committee, talking about the conspiracy and their respective roles would be a breach of basic security.

Richard was in a way disappointed to learn of Robert's possible involvement. What he thought he most needed was a frank assessment of his own situation by somebody who could understand it but who did not have anything to gain from Richard acting one way or another. Robert might no longer be a candidate for that role.

Arriving at his office at the university, Richard found Ron Turello sorting copies of journal articles relevant to the book Richard was supposed to be writing but that he had in effect put aside. The smell of coffee suggested that Ron had settled in for a morning of work. He gave Richard a cheerful "good morning."

"Ron, do I have any scheduled appointments for this afternoon?"

"Yes, a couple of students from the undergraduate class want to discuss their papers, and Lennie wants your advice on a dissertation topic. And I was hoping you might find a moment for me. I've hit a snag writing my chapter on British support of the South in the Civil War. It's holding up the dissertation."

"I'm sorry, Ron, but I'll have to cancel my appointments. Please reschedule them for next week. Something really important has come up."

Ron did not sigh or give any other indication of not being surprised. He merely said, "OK," but Richard knew that he was disappointed. Richard, who had been the embodiment of dependability and predictability, had become, in his own eyes at least, virtually irresponsible in his dealings with students. He knew that in this respect he was not much different from a few other faculty, but he took no solace in that fact. He used to disdain that kind of self-indulgent conduct. For him to behave in the same way took willpower. He cringed each time he cancelled office hours or other appointments—to say nothing of cancelling a class or asking Turello to take over.

Turello knew that Richard wanted to be left alone just before one of his lectures or seminars. Richard wanted to go over his notes, review sources from which he intended to quote, and generally think through what he wanted to accomplish in class that day. But Turello had noticed recently that Richard spent less and less time on these preparations. Sometimes he went directly to the lecture hall. Presumably, he had gotten ready at home. On this particular day Richard seemed to be reviewing his lecture notes, but he seemed distracted. Then the telephone rang.

Richard picked it up. He was not surprised to hear the voice of Herbert Vandenhorst.

"It's me. Please give me a call back as soon as you can. Thanks."

"All right." Richard hung up.

Vandenhorst had spoken as if leaving a message on the recording machine. This was a pre-arranged signal. Richard was supposed to call back on a more secure phone, preferably the scrambler phone in his study at home. Only a few times had Vandenhorst used this method of contacting him, each time because he had urgent business.

The time had obviously come. Vandenhorst was calling the

meeting of the steering committee that they had all been waiting for. Richard felt his whole being contract. A strange mixture of exhilaration and dread made him draw a deep breath. He was a bundle of tension. He remembered that Turello was in the room and looked in his direction to see whether he had noticed Richard's reaction. Nothing in Turello's expression indicated that anything out of the ordinary had happened. Richard's admiration for what the Brits call a "stiff upper lip" might make him conceal intense emotion even in private.

Did he have to leave for home immediately? Should he cancel the class that was just about to start or ask Ron to take it? It was an undergraduate class for juniors and seniors, and Ron could handle it by turning it into a discussion session. But no, Richard said to himself, not again. Those students had registered for a course with Richard Bittenberg, and the university was paying him to teach his classes. Also, if Vandenhorst was trying to get people together for what Richard thought it was, he would want all the members of the steering committee present. They were all waiting for word of the meeting, but it would take time to contact all of them.

Richard decided to teach his class, but he would go directly home thereafter instead of returning to his office to attend to some pressing administrative duties. He would know only after talking to Vandenhorst if he had to cancel his late lunch with Robert Preston. He glanced for another moment at his lecture notes and then packed his briefcase. Ron saw what he was doing and concluded that Richard would not be coming back. He had wanted to ask Richard about his assistantship duties, but he noticed Richard's preoccupied look and said nothing.

"Have a good weekend, Ron." Richard felt terrible.

Long experience carried Richard through his lecture, but his mind wandered. When students asked questions or made comments, he did not pay close attention. He was greatly relieved when time was up. As the class broke up he noticed that a couple of students were moving in his direction, probably to ask his advice about assignments, but he pretended not to notice them and slipped out of the classroom. He rushed to his car.

"Richard, you are home early," Helen said in surprise when he came into the kitchen from the garage. She was on her knees cleaning the floor of a kitchen cabinet, and she was wearing an old jumpsuit, but she looked lovely. He wanted to hold her and kiss her and forget his agony.

He bent down and kissed her and said, "Yes, I had forgotten a commitment I made. I have to make a call or two to see how things stand." In her ears this statement had to sound like more of his usual hectic, stressed, unpredictable ways, especially as he had said nothing about the rest of the day. It was early Friday afternoon, and he was certain that Helen had detected a threat to the Bittenberg family Friday evening.

"I'll know soon." He smiled weakly and went downstairs. He closed but did not shut the door to his study in case Helen would follow him. He opened the drawer with the scrambler phone and punched in the code for Vandenhorst.

Vandenhorst answered immediately.

"We need to meet."

"OK, when and where?"

"I'm calling the big meeting of the whole group for tomorrow afternoon, but we have to talk before then. It's very important. Could you possibly meet me at two o'clock this afternoon?" There was no mistaking the urgency in Vandenhorst's voice.

Richard looked at his watch. It was almost 1:00 PM. He sighed inwardly. His meeting with Robert had to be cancelled.

"That depends on the location."

"Sailor's Nest." That was their code for the home of Gordon Bunker, across the Potomac River, in McLean, Virginia. It would take Richard about twenty minutes to get there.

"That's pretty short notice."

"I know. I'm sorry."

"I'll see you there."

Richard hung up the scrambler phone and reached for the regular one. He dialed Robert's home telephone number, and Jennifer answered. They chatted briefly.

"I hear that you and Bob will have coffee together. Good idea. Bob's right here. Bye."

"Richard, I suppose you're calling to say that you'll be late."

"No, Bob. Something important has just come up. I can't come at all. I'm really sorry. I'll tell you about the reason later sometime."

"It's OK, pal. Don't worry. We can meet some other time. Tomorrow morning? Breakfast again?"

"Perhaps, but I'll have to let you know."

They hung up.

What lie was he going to tell Helen this time? There was at least a chance that he would be back home in time for dinner, but he probably should not make any promise. He did not know what Vandenhorst might have in store for him. And Richard would have to be away for a good part of the next day. He hated to have to disappoint Helen and the children, but what else could he do?

Upstairs Helen was cleaning and reorganizing a cupboard, performing a completely unglamorous and hardly rewarding task that nobody would ever even have noticed, had Richard not happened to come home early. She would never have been thanked for it, as she received no thanks or pay for so many other ordinary but time-consuming domestic chores. Richard had talked to Helen about their hiring a part-time housekeeper with some responsibility for looking after John and Anne so that she could get back to doctoral study or try the teaching of English in which she had sometimes expressed an interest. But although John and Anne were in school all day and demanded much less of her time than in the past, she had never taken him up on the suggestion. It would not be practical, not realistic, and too expensive, she said. But Richard had suspected that his own intense involvement in his work and his increasingly frantic pace was an important part of the reason why she was disinclined to return to her doctoral studies or explore a possible professional career. She was needed in the Bittenberg home, she felt, to provide a center of calm, permanence, and security, first of all for the children, but also for Richard, who, without her, might destroy himself and the family in the process. She saw it as a part of her role to relax and distract him, keep him on the rails.

He had not done his part to buttress family life. It was Helen who had been the anchor of the family, and how had he rewarded her? By taking advantage of her selfless efforts to spend even more time on his pursuits. He winced in self-criticism. And now he had to take yet more advantage of her. He had to deceive her, cause her and the children pain. He slumped in his chair and put his face in his hands. A feeling of deep self-loathing swept over him. He was near tears.

But his motive was not personal aggrandizement, he defended himself. He was not being selfish in the ordinary sense. He genuinely feared for his country. He thought again about all those others throughout human history who had sacrificed the wellbeing of those closest to them for what they considered a good and necessary cause, yet could not get away from one stubborn fact: that he was acting at the expense of Helen, John, and Anne. Soon they would have to suffer even greater pain. Many others, relatives, his students, Ron Turello, and his colleagues were already paying a part of the price for his commitment to a task about which they knew nothing and certainly had not approved. In historical hindsight he might turn out to be nothing but a conceited fool who thought he understood the predicament of the United Sates much better than he did. He could be serving some vain, reckless part of his ego that he had managed to conceal from himself. His conduct might be inexcusable.

Richard had to force himself to stop brooding. He collected himself by slapping his thighs hard. He had permitted himself a moment of pitiful emotional self-indulgence. There were things to do. He got up from his chair and toiled upstairs.

# CHAPTER 49

Duparc and Léger followed Dégas at a discreet distance. Back at his farm, Dégas drove up to the residence and parked the Land Rover. Without waiting for the two detectives he went into the house. They were walking slowly towards the house when Dégas reappeared through a side door.

"I'll be back in a moment," he cried and headed for the stable, where a young man peered out. Dégas was carrying the packet that he had picked up in Evremond. He walked in a brisk, military manner. Duparc could easily imagine him in his old professional setting.

Duparc and Léger made no effort to catch up with him but strolled around the yard, seeming to enjoy the warm summer day, but paying close attention to the outbuildings.

"Unless the residence has a good basement or the barn has some sturdy lockup, this does not appear to be a good place to keep a prisoner," Léger said.

"And if Dégas has anything of importance hidden here, he wouldn't have wanted us to follow him."

Dégas reappeared after a few minutes and joined the two detectives, who were leaning against a fence looking at the grazing horses.

"OK," Dégas said. "I suppose it's possible I caused that accident in Noisy."

"When you left to go home you were just about to tell us who your passenger was." Duparc said.

"Yes, but now that I've accepted responsibility, it's hardly necessary to involve another person."

"You are admitting that you *did* cause the accident?"

"If you say so."

"If we *say* so? Major Dégas, we're supposed to ascertain the facts. We're not prosecutors. To conclude our investigation we need to talk to your passenger, who may have been a witness to the accident."

"What's the point? Why the big to-do about something as trivial as this? I was the driver and I have accepted the responsibility!" Dégas said impatiently.

"Major Dégas, please, let us be the judges of what is and what is not needed in this investigation."

"I don't want anybody else to be bothered. What's the big deal? We're just talking about some property damage. Why are the police interested in the first place?"

"Hit-and-run accidents are taken seriously by the law and the prosecutors. The penalties can be substantial, not just suspension or loss of your driver's license. Some hit-and-run drivers have gone to prison." Duparc did not want Dégas to concede that he had deliberately run from the scene of an accident. A straight confession of guilt would obviate the need for witnesses. Duparc wanted a pretext for interviewing his passenger.

Dégas looked startled. For a person like him who used his car all the time being deprived of driving privileges would be devastating. He looked first to the one detective, then the other, as if wanting one of them to contradict what had been said.

"You can't be serious!?" Dégas finally said incredulously. "Not for an accident like this!"

"Knowingly leaving the scene is considered very serious," Duparc said.

"But I didn't notice that anything was falling from my roof."

"All right, major, so just give us the name of your passenger."

Dégas said nothing, only gave a surly stare. He finally said, "I don't want you to bother him. He just happened to be in the car."

"Who?"

Still, Dégas didn't speak.

"Who?"

"The baron." His voice was barely audible.

"Baron who?"

"Gustave de la Broderie."

Léger made a show of writing the name down and asked Dégas to verify the spelling: "And where can we find him?"

"Is this really necessary?"

"It is," Duparc said and added, "Don't worry, Major, we'll be discreet."

"De la Broderie has a small vineyard. The estate is less than two kilometers from here. When you leave this farm, turn left. You'll soon see an iron gate and a small gatehouse on the left."

"You work for the baron?"

"I'm a kind of overseer, help him out when he needs me."

"Thank you, Major." To make Dégas relax Duparc added, "If the baron confirms your story, the police may not need to bother you again."

The two detectives walked back to their car. They decided against breaking for lunch and headed for the de la Broderie estate. They found the iron gate, which was closed. There was a punch button lock and a microphone. A big hedge on the other side of the fence made it hard to see what lay behind the gate.

Duparc punched the button next to the microphone. After thirty seconds of silence he pushed it again. Finally a male voice said, "Yes?"

"This is Inspector Duparc from the police to see Baron de la Broderie."

"Do you have an appointment?"

"No, but I'm investigating a traffic accident and would be grateful if the baron could spare me just a couple of minutes."

"Hold on, please!"

After two minutes they saw the gate slowly open, and a voice said, "The baron will be pleased to see you."

The access road, which was paved, led through a hundred yards of forest that looked almost like parkland. They then came into an open field that turned into a park, and then a garden and forecourt behind which, on a low hill, stood a classical French three-storey chateau. It was a substantial manor house rather than a castle. Its architectural style suggested that it had been built in the mid eighteenth century. The building had stucco walls, typical white French windows with shutters, and a black slate roof, which glimmered in the sunlight. A couple of hundred yards beyond the mansion rows of vines ran along a gently rising hill. Nestled into the hillside was a sizeable brick building that looked as if it might be a winery. The road approached the mansion from the side and forked in three directions. To the left one could drive on to the winery, or up into a rather spacious stone-paved yard behind the mansion. In the backyard they could see a couple of brick buildings one of which seemed to be attached to the main house through a corridor. On the right the asphalt road turned into gravel, and the road made a circle in a forecourt.

"Stop and let me out here," Duparc said as they came to the fork in the road, "but then park the car in the back. Do it so that one side of the car faces away from the house. Then let a lot of air out of one of the tires on that side. But hide what you're doing. Make it seem as if you just discovered a leak."

"OK."

"I'll walk to the front entrance. Join me there."

While Duparc started walking towards the main entrance

Léger parked the car and got out. He knelt down and used a car key to release air from one of the back tires. While doing so he shook his head. He stood up, hands on his hips, looking annoyed.

Duparc rang the doorbell at the front door. A short, thin, gray-haired man, who appeared to be at least sixty-five years old, opened. "Baron de la Broderie is waiting for you in the library," he announced. "Thank you," Duparc said. "My associate is parking the car. Let's wait for him." Léger arrived in a minute giving Duparc a slight nod.

They were escorted through the large entrance hall, which was dominated by a curved stairway, and through a very tastefully decorated sitting room mixing antiques and stylish but discreet modern furniture. They came to a closed door, and the short man knocked before opening. He showed the detectives into a spacious library, whose walls were covered largely by old books. The bookcases and the wall paneling were in golden brown wood. Above a massive fireplace hung a large painting of a hunting scene. The room was situated in the corner of the building and was rather well lit because of two tall windows. In front of one of them stood a desk. As they entered a man got up to greet them.

"Thank you, Roland," the person said, indicating to the man in the black suit that he could retire.

Because de la Broderie's back was against the light, what he looked like was at first difficult to discern, but as he walked up to the two detectives, removed his reading glasses, and extended his hand they could see that he was probably in his early seventies. He wore a cashmere cardigan sweater and an ironed blue shirt and tan tie. His slacks were pressed and his brown shoes polished. He was above medium height. His rectangular face had sharp but not unpleasant features. He had white thinning hair and a white neatly trimmed small beard and mustache.

"Gentlemen, what can I do for you?"

"I'm inspector Duparc and this is my associate, Pierre Léger." Duparc held out his identity card, which de la Broderie took and did not immediately hand back. "We're sorry to bother you, Baron, but we would like to ask you a few questions about a traffic accident last Friday."

"Won't you sit down?" De la Broderie indicated a sofa and chairs. While the detectives seated themselves de la Broderie put on his reading glasses and took a closer look at Duparc's identity card.

"Inspector, this card seems to indicate that you're stationed in a Paris prefecture. Did this accident take place in Paris?"

Duparc had worried that the anomaly of the two detectives

being out of place would sooner or later become apparent.

"No, Baron, we're here about an accident that happened in Noisy last Friday."

De la Broderie handed back the card and seated himself in an armchair. He looked at once amused and confused when he said, "Why would an accident in Noisy interest the Paris police?"

Duparc forced a smile. "All I can say, sir, is that it's August. Vacation month. Everybody's short of personnel. One result is strange assignments."

"I see." Was there a flicker of relief in de la Broderie's face? "But how could a traffic accident be sufficient to send two Paris detectives into the countryside?"

"It seems the local police and local officials took a serious view of this accident."

"Was anybody hurt?"

De la Broderie was obviously no fool. Assuming that the baron had not already seen through their pretext for visiting, Duparc had to be careful not to blow their cover.

"No, but the case has another disturbing aspect."

"What's that?"

"We're sorry to have to bother you, Baron. We have just a couple of questions. Were you in Noisy last Friday?"

The baron seemed to search his memory. "Yes, I was. I went there with a man who helps me supervise the vineyard and the grounds, Major Étienne Dégas. He's been with me part-time for a few years. We went to look for a piece of equipment. He picked me up."

"And when you were driving through the town, did you become aware of an accident?"

De la Broderie looked puzzled. "No, I don't think I saw any accident."

"What about the car that Major Dégas was driving—was it involved in any accident?"

De la Broderie again looked quizzical. "No," he said hesitantly. "Not when I was in it. Nothing unusual happened."

"At about 12:15 a bunch of stakes came loose and fell off the roof of Major Dégas's Land Rover. They landed on two cars that were parked at the curb on the village's main street. The accident took place where the street takes that rather sharp turn."

"I know the spot."

"Did you see or hear anything?"

The baron was silent for a few seconds. "Not that I can remember."

"Did Major Dégas say anything indicating a problem of any kind?"

"No. If something fell off I may not have heard it because I was talking to Dégas and had my mind on other things. And Dégas likes to have the radio on for music."

De la Broderie's answers sounded spontaneous.

"Thank you, Baron. Then we have only one more question," Duparc said. He wanted to rattle the baron into making some mistake.

"Yes?"

"We have information that you and Major Dégas were not alone in the car." Duparc was again stretching the truth. A witness in Noisy had said that there *might* have been more than two people in the Land Rover.

Duparc and Léger studied de la Broderie's expression closely. If the question had bothered him, he did not show it. He merely shook his head and said in the same relaxed voice as before, "No, we were alone."

Duparc rose and said, "Thank you, Baron. That's all we need. I'm sorry we had to bother you." Léger also stood up.

"No bother, inspector. I was happy to assist."

"This should complete our investigation," Duparc said. "What you've told us confirms what Major Dégas had to say, so I doubt you or he will hear anything further from the police."

De la Broderie shook their hands and followed them into the hallway. Hearing them coming, the short man in the dark suit moved with all deliberate speed to hold the door open for the detectives.

"Compliments on your house and grounds, baron," Duparc said.

"Thank you."

"When we drove up we noticed you have a vineyard," Léger said. "Do you have your own brand of wine?" He tried to sound as if he were making light conversation about a subject of personal interest.

"Not really," de la Broderie said. "Our vineyard is not very large and we sell most of the grapes to a company. We produce just a thousand bottles a year. We do put our label on them, but don't make any concerted effort to sell them. A couple of local restaurants buy some. It's rather good. We drink much of it ourselves, give it to friends, and that sort of thing. It's largely a hobby."

"So you have your own press and vats and storage?"

"We do, but they don't see as much use as when my grandfather and father had the estate."

Léger smiled. "A very nice hobby!"

De la Broderie returned the smile, thought for a moment, and then turned to the man in the black suit. "Roland, would you fetch two bottles of the 2002?"

"Yes sir." The man disappeared.

"I thought you might want to try our wine," de la Broderie said. "Roland will be right back. We keep some bottles downstairs. I hope I'm not breaking any rules by offering you this small gift."

"It may be a breach of the strict letter of police regulations, but hardly of the spirit," Duparc said. "As of a minute ago, we finished our police business here. We're now on lunch break."

The baron laughed. "A rather late lunch."

"That's the life of police officers," Léger said. "No regular hours, especially not in August."

Roland returned with the bottles. De la Broderie took them from him and gave one each to the two detectives.

"Thank you, Baron. You're very kind," said Duparc.

As they stepped out on the stairs at the main entrance Duparc turned and said to the baron: "I'm afraid that before we leave we'll have to change a tire on our car. When Léger parked he noticed that one of the tires is almost flat. We shouldn't drive on it."

"Take your time," the baron said, "And let us know if you need any help." Roland closed the door.

"Nice man for a kidnapper," Léger said in a low voice as they walked back to the car.

"Or the host of an American professor trying to hide from the world? A pretty cool customer whatever he is."

They returned to the car. The paved yard where it was parked was bordered on three sides by buildings. The building that was connected to the main house looked like a small residence. A small car was parked in front of it. Probably servant quarters, Duparc thought. In the nineteenth century the owner of the estate might have employed twenty people: house servants, yard hands, laborers, and gardeners. Now the baron was probably getting by with three or four and perhaps some temporary help around harvest time.

"Take your time changing that tire," Duparc said quietly to Léger. "I'll be standing around and seem to be helping you, but I'll be trying to see as much as I can without attracting attention."

"Allright."

"I wish I had an excuse to see a little more of the premises and to talk to a servant. Is there any help we could ask for that would not sound far-fetched?"

Léger was taking the spare wheel and the jack out of the trunk when he exclaimed under his breath, "Got it! We need a couple of bricks or big stones to put behind the front wheels. The car's standing on a bit of an incline."

Duparc smiled. "Good idea, I'll go and ask."

Duparc walked up to what appeared to be a kitchen entrance and knocked on the door. He had to knock a second time before the door opened. A plump, gray-haired woman in a black dress and a white apron looked out. She was wiping her hands on a towel. She was about the same age as Roland, and Duparc guessed that she was his wife. They might be servants who came with the estate, as it were.

"Sorry to bother you, Madame. We're policemen. We just saw the baron, and have finished our business, but our car has a flat tire. Before we change it we should put some bricks or stones or logs behind the front wheels to steady the car. Would you have anything like that?"

The woman said, "I'll get Roland." After a short wait Roland appeared. He was now in his shirtsleeves, but was putting on the suit jacket. Duparc repeated his apology and his request.

Roland did not seem annoyed or defensive but pleased to help. "I'll see what I can find," Roland said, and headed in the direction of one of the buildings in the back, which had at one time probably been a stable. Duparc followed him.

"This house and estate are impressively well-kept," Duparc said. He was hoping that Roland might take some pride in this comment. Duparc threw furtive glances around the yard.

"Yes, the baron will not let anything deteriorate. He and the supervisor are on top of things."

"Is that Major Dégas?

"Yes." Roland opened one of two large doors to the stable-like building. It was indeed a former stable. The stalls and other spaces were full of miscellaneous items, ranging from farm equipment and bicycles to old furniture and gardening tools. One part of the building served as a garage. Duparc thought he saw the back of a maroon-colored Jaguar, probably the baron's car.

"If you see anything you can use, just point to it," Roland said. Duparc looked around and said, "A couple of bricks would probably be the best."

"I think there are some in the back," Roland said. He went to a back door that opened into a small grassy yard where a tractor was parked. Planks had been neatly stacked waist-high along the wall of the stable and covered with canvas. A gravel service road ran along the yard in the direction of the winery building. The road was obviously an extension of the main access to the estate.

"Is that the winery?" Duparc asked.

"Yes, it is. We'll be busy there in a few weeks. It's been a good summer for grapes."

Roland walked past the planks and pointed to a pile of bricks on the ground beyond them. "There, take whatever you need," he said. Duparc reached for two bricks. He declined Roland's offer to carry them.

"Have you worked for the baron for a long time?" Duparc asked as they walked back towards the car. "For twenty years. A fine man. Before that I worked for the baron's father for almost twenty-five years. The late baron de la Broderie took my parents in during the war. I grew up on the estate. My wife is from this area."

"How many work here now?"

"My wife and I look after the house and the garden next to the house, and Major Dégas takes care of the rest. He brings a man or two when needed."

Back at the car Duparc handed the bricks to Léger, who put them behind the front wheels.

"Many thanks, Roland," Duparc said.

"Just leave the bricks here when you're finished, Roland said. "I'll return them later." He gave a slight bow and returned inside.

As Léger finished changing the tire Duparc continued to look around, seeming to be merely killing time. When he looked up at the house he noticed somebody watching them through one of the upstairs windows, but the glare of the sun made it impossible to identify the face.

When they drove away from the de la Broderie estate it was two o'clock in the afternoon. Duparc had chosen to forget about the papers in the back seat and sat next to Léger.

"So what do you think, boss?"

"I think we should stop in Noisy for a quick bite to eat."

"Fine, but what I meant was, where are we in this investigation? What will you tell Mrs. Bittenberg? She's probably estimated when, at the earliest, we can be expected to be back in Paris. She'll be sitting in that hotel room waiting for a call or a knock on the door." Léger looked inquiringly at his superior.

"I know."

"I can't see that we've learned anything really new," Léger said. "All we've done is confirm that Dégas and de la Broderie came through Noisy last Friday and that they had a pretty strong reason not to stop after that accident. But that's not enough to get approval for searching the estate or Dégas's place. Their claims not to have noticed the stakes falling off the car are lies but not wholly implausible lies."

"Perhaps we should have confronted them with the abduction charge," Duparc said. "We could have asked de la Broderie to let us see the winery or the basement of the mansion. Their reactions would have been illuminating. But we can still do that after our follow-up meeting with Ferguson. The time's come to challenge him. Assuming they're in the same conspiracy, we may be able to unnerve them or make them fall out among each other."

"When do you want to see Ferguson?"

"As soon as we get back to Paris. We should be able to get to the American Embassy before closing time. I'll call Ferguson's office right now." Duparc took out his telephone. He finally got through to Ferguson's secretary. Léger could tell from Duparc's words and facial expression that despite the note of urgency in Duparc's voice they could not see Ferguson that afternoon or even in the evening at his home. "OK. Eight thirty tomorrow morning," Duparc said, closing his cell telephone and putting it in his pocket. Léger could tell he was irritated.

"What about Mrs. Bittenberg? She'll want to know whether we have any news." Duparc was interested to notice that Léger seemed to share his empathy for the American woman.

"All our news will do is increase her anxiety and frustration," Duparc said. "If we say that our detectives' intuition tells us that Dégas and de la Broderie did in fact abduct—or should I say transport?—Richard Bittenberg from the Sorbonne, she'll want us to raid the most likely hiding place—"

"—which no magistrate will let us do on the basis of the evidence we have," Léger said. "Especially not the estate of a former ambassador who is also a nobleman and well-connected in leading government and business circles."

"Precisely, and that leaves Ferguson."

"So what do you plan to tell Mrs. Bittenberg?"

"I'm not sure. There's one little peace of information that might cheer her up, but it would also make her sick with worry and frustration. I don't know whether to tell her."

"Tell her what?"

"When I went with Roland to pick up those bricks, we came out of a back door to the stable. Just outside there was a large bunch of long planks next to the wall. They were piled about a meter high, and a canvas had been put over them. The bricks were on the ground along the same wall."

"Sounds like supplies for building or repairs."

"But what was interesting was something that had been left on top of those planks near that door."

"What?"

"A tray. With an empty plate with some traces of food, silverware, a glass, a coffee cup, and a crumpled paper napkin."

Léger gave Duparc a surprised look, and Duparc nodded.

"My guess is," Duparc said, "that somebody had been carrying the tray back to the house but had gotten distracted. The person put the tray down to deal with the distraction and then forgot it."

"The tray would have been on its way to the kitchen," Léger said. "Where else would you bring dirty dishes?"

"And considering where I saw it," Duparc said, "it could have come from the winery. The cellar must be a good place to keep a person locked up. If Bittenberg had *asked* to be hidden, that would not be the place. Not that I understand why he should be kept as a prisoner and not be killed. The penalty for kidnapping is almost as severe as for murder. And if you keep a kidnapped person alive, the danger of discovery goes up."

"If the place where you found the tray is on the way to the winery, it may have been left earlier today. Otherwise, assuming that the prisoner is being kept in the wine cellar and is fed regularly, the tray should have been discovered today, if not sooner, when the food server handled another delivery."

The two detectives drove into Noisy. They found a restaurant in its own building just off main street. Its parking lot was almost empty. The luncheon rush was over.

"There's something rather curious about serving a prisoner food this particular way," Duparc continued as they made their way into the restaurant.

"I know what you mean," Léger said.

The patron, a rotund, genial man, who fussed over them, seated the two detectives without delay. He gave them menus and left.

Léger said, "Serving a prisoner a seemingly elaborate meal on a tray—almost hotel style—is not what you would expect."

"It's as if the jailers wanted to treat the prisoner well."

"Paradoxical."

"This case just baffles me," Duparc said.

The restaurant owner took their orders and was gone.

"There are of course other ways of explaining the tray," Léger said. "Roland or his wife may have decided that it was a nice day to have lunch picnic style in a favorite hideaway on the estate. The person was just interrupted by something on his way back to the house. Or perhaps Major Dégas or some worker got lunch from the house near where he worked. That person could have put the tray where you saw it, expecting that somebody would pick it up."

"Yes, I've thought of those possibilities, but they don't fit."

"Why not?"

"Because when we were behind the stable Roland must have seen the tray. Yet he didn't pick it up to bring it back to the house. I think he didn't want to draw my attention to it. And why? Because he knew that the tray was in some way incriminating."

Léger nodded. Silence descended.

"Roland would be working with the kidnappers," Léger said pensively.

"I got the impression he's very loyal to the baron. Roland's family seems to owe the de la Broderie family a great deal. He thinks highly of his employer and his late father. Roland may not question any of the baron's actions."

"So what will you tell Mrs. Bittenberg? She desperately wants to believe her husband's alive. The tray, which can be interpreted in many ways, will make her jump to conclusions, and she will demand action?"

Duparc nodded.

# CHAPTER 50

"This conspiracy may unravel right now!"

Vandenhorst spoke with uncharacteristic frankness and emphasis. Richard was surprised by the starkness of his words, coming as they did from a man who was legendary for his verbal and other restraint. Vandenhorst's concern was written on his face. He was addressing Richard and Gordon Bunker in a conversation at Bunker's home that had barely started. The subject was the meeting of the steering committee the next day. The committee would then decide for good whether to attempt the coup before Thomas Reed had to leave his post as Commanding General of the Washington military district. The meeting would take place in the early afternoon in the basement of a small rental property owned by Robert O'Brien in Silver Spring, Maryland, just north of the District of Columbia. The house was standing empty because O'Brien was getting it ready for new renters. Hick would spend the night there to prepare the premises and make sure that nobody attempted to install listening equipment.

The three men were sitting, fully clothed, in the nicely appointed eight by ten feet sauna in the basement of Bunker's McLean house. They had closed the door behind them. Richard and Bunker had seated themselves on the lower of two rungs of wooden benches. Vandenhorst had put himself on a stool and was facing them. Bunker's size seemed anomalous in the small space. They were nursing mugs of coffee.

The sauna did not have a window, just an air intake and a ventilation duct. The fan had been turned on to help muffle the sound of their conversation. Hick had brought electronic equipment for stifling listening devices and shown Bunker how to activate it. Richard had parked his car a couple of streets away. He had not seen Vandenhorst's car. Perhaps Bunker had brought him. The members of the conspiracy were more attentive than ever to concealing their small or large meetings.

Vandenhorst's comment about the conspiracy coming apart shocked Richard. Vandenhorst spoke slowly and deliberately. "Robert Bates has been badgering me to postpone any action until after the election and the swearing in of his boss as speaker of the House. Like you, Dick, he's arguing that the issue of legitimacy is crucial. Bates seems to be speaking for Peck. I admit to wondering whether their personal fortunes have shaped their opinion. Lester Pickett, too, has weighed in on the same side. He's virtually threatened to pull out and to bring his network with him unless we wait until the swearing in of the new Congress. That would be a terrible blow. He's our link to a few important supporters in media and government. That's not all. Gates and Pellegrini and DeLeon are talking out of both sides of their mouth. They want us to act before Reed departs, but they also don't want to go ahead unless we do more to neutralize key figures in high finance and people controlling big media." Vandenhorst shook his head. "Suppose they're right. What can I do about it at this stage? Direct personnel away from other urgent tasks? Whether we agree with them or not, I have a big political problem. We simply can't afford to lose any of those three."

"Of course not," Richard said.

"We already have a frightening shortage of people who can handle assignments like that. We just can't do all of what is truly needed. We have to swallow hard. In England and France I doubt that, when push comes to shove, we could muster more than a handful of operatives. Our contacts there are a few politicians, diplomats, journalists, and business types rather than security operatives. But I've told Randy and Douglas that I will talk to Tony Springhalter to try to make some arrangements. Tony's security firm does have a London branch, and he might detail a couple of reliable people to France. But Tony's already told me that we're relying too heavily on him. He cannot risk any further exposure, he says. He cannot use employees he does not know well and who may not be as reliable as we need them to be."

Gordon Bunker had been impatiently tapping his fingers on his lap. "I'm noticing an old pattern," he said. "When you and Richard get to talking, it's always about some shortcomings of the conspiracy. To be always dwelling on what can go wrong is to distort the picture of what can be expected. And if the others listen to you, soon we'll all be so discouraged that we'll want to cancel the whole damned show."

"The reason Richard and I tend to discuss the obstacles to success is that he's too smart not to be aware of them, and if we don't air those problems, he's bound to bring them up sooner or later. Now would be a particularly bad time to do that in front of the steering committee."

"You can say that again," Bunker said.

"You don't need to tell me how much is at stake," Richard said.

"OK, but I feel I have to repeat that I'm an old military hand," Bunker said. "For me it's simply self-evident that no military operation ever goes according to plan. If an operation depends on everything going just according to plan, you shouldn't attempt it in the first place."

"We know Gordon, we know," Vandenhorst said, "but this is so much more — or should I say much less — than a military operation. We're in a way planning to act against all odds, hoping that sheer pluck and audacity will carry the day. We're willing to take our chances, because the alternative is so odious: to let the U.S. fall apart. We have to put more emphasis on close coordination than in a strictly military operation. The disinformation campaign and the proper sequencing are crucial."

"Fine, as long as worries about things going wrong do not become an excuse for infinitely detailed planning and indefinite postponement."

Richard had heard Bunker say the same sort of thing many times before. Why was he saying it yet again?

Vandenhorst turned to Richard. "Gordon already knows some of what I'm about to tell you. Postponement is precisely what some of the members of our group are likely to demand tomorrow. The long and the short of it is that we're facing a crisis. We have a serious rupture within our ranks, and it may finish us off." His gray eyes rested on Richard.

Vandenhorst drew a deep breath before he said to Richard:

"You may be the person who decides the future of this conspiracy."

Richard first thought that he had misunderstood.

"What!?" His intonation expressed his confusion.

"Dick, everybody knows that you and I have become close and that I respect your judgment. But that's not the main reason why your opinion and your conduct may prove decisive. Our people know that you are smart and knowledgeable and realistic, not some idealistic dreamer. You want to act with your eyes wide open. A few of our people may initially have expected you to be an egghead, to have your head in the clouds, but you actually helped some of the battle-scarred veterans understand some things better than they understood them before. You've been particularly good at explaining why we had to give special attention to how the new regime will be perceived by the American public. The guys and the gal have also seen that you're a man of action as well as a scholar. You can be trusted to do your part in carrying our plans into practice. Perhaps more important than anything else, though, they know you're the opposite of rash. You're very cautious."

Richard did not understand why Vandenhorst was saying what he was, but it made him uncomfortable. He had difficulty sitting still. He stood up and moved in the small space.

"Dick," Vandenhorst said, "you have greater clout on the steering committee than you realize."

"Herb's right," Bunker said. "What you do tomorrow will make a big difference."

Ah, so that was it, Richard thought. Herbert and Gordon wanted him to speak in support of their position at the meeting.

"Your arguments *against* action before Peck becomes speaker have been pretty persuasive," Bunker said, "and you may have influenced those who are leaning most strongly against action now. But you've never committed yourself to a particular plan. You've just looked at pros and cons. Most of our colleagues probably assume you're leaning strongly in the direction of waiting, but it's not obvious where you stand. Richard, you could sway those who want to wait or who are torn. You could at least make them accept the judgment of the majority rather than pull out and go home."

Richard looked at Vandenhorst. "So you've decided that we have to go ahead now?"

"Yes," Vandenhorst said. "After much deliberation. I've thought about little else since I heard about Tom's premature new posting. I've consulted with everybody. I've thought about all the advantages and disadvantages. I've reached the conclusion that we really have no choice. The Cadillac plan is no longer an option. We have to have some honest-to-goodness troops right in D.C. I've talked to Tom in depth in the last few days, and it's possible that through some clever maneuvering he could have a battalion of airborne troops flown in rather quickly from Fort Bragg to support what he and Noah hope to do with their troops. Those forces could be in D.C. within a few hours of being alerted. Units of the National Guard can probably be deployed a day or two into the coup. There's a secret standing federal emergency plan for protecting the Washington area, and it's a part of Tom's normal duties to be in touch with commanders at Fort Bragg and in the National Guard units and to test readiness. Tom thinks that he might improve our military capabilities considerably."

The steering committee was generally aware of the possibility of military reinforcements. Reed had apparently become more affirmative about their chances.

"I know what you're thinking, Richard," Bunker said. "How

convenient that Tom, who wants us to act while he's still Commanding General, should now be optimistic about being able to call in troops from Bragg. But he claims he has reason to be optimistic. Since he found out about his early transfer he has tested the waters. Apparently he has good rapport with the relevant general and a couple of the colonels at Bragg who might command a Washington relief force. Tom says it's unlikely that they would question an emergency call from him or refuse to follow his directions."

Richard squirmed internally. He could not sit down and be still. Already when they had first entered the small space the air had felt thick with emotion. He had tried to lighten the atmosphere by smiling and saying, "Imagine, three guys plotting the overthrow of the U.S. government in a sauna." The others had barely chuckled. Now the sauna seemed to Richard more like a pressure cooker, though one without the steam. He felt a pressing need to open the door wide, breathe fresh air, see daylight — and escape. The sound of the fan helped fray his nerves.

Richard was on the spot. It was obvious what Vandenhorst was driving at.

"You want me to endorse what you have decided, help argue your case in the meeting?"

"Yes, Richard. We badly need you," Vandenhorst said.

"But you know that I have serious reservations about plan B."

"I do, and we all know your arguments. The problem is that, if you repeat them now, Bates and Pickett will be encouraged to stand their ground. If the rest of us press plan B in spite of their opposition, they may bolt."

"There's a solution to that problem," Richard said.

"What?"

"Postpone the coup in the expectation that Peck will be the next speaker of the House."

"Dick," Bunker said in an exasperated voice. "You're turning out to be an egghead after all! In spite of your warnings about wishful thinking, you're taken with a merely abstract possibility. You want just the right circumstances and the perfect plan — the Cadillac plan."

"Gordon, please!" Vandenhorst interrupted.

"Herb, he needs to hear this!" Bunker stood up to face Richard who was still standing. Bunker almost made Richard, who was over six feet, look small. But Bunker's manner was pleading rather than threatening.

"Dick, I'm an old soldier, and I know that in real life nothing's ever neat and predictable. Often you even have to act blindly, hope that circumstances will favor you. Look at our situation this way! We're all agreed that America is in a big mess that's only getting worse. Millions of people are desperate. The protests are getting bigger and more violent. Things have gotten considerably worse since this conspiracy was conceived. And in these historical circumstances terrible people are in charge. They're destroying what remains of our country. We're agreed that we can get rid of them only by extreme measures. Most of the people in the conspiracy joined not knowing whether we would ever be able to marshal the necessary resources. But so determined were we to try to make a go of this coup that we have actually made real progress, and we were willing to act against pretty high odds in the first place."

Richard nodded almost imperceptibly.

Bunker continued: "I very much doubt, Dick, that when you joined us you counted on having a person in our corner who's in the line of succession to the presidency. No, we got a couple of very lucky breaks. The luckiest of all was Tom Reed's appointment as Commanding General of the Washington military district. We knew we had to get our hands on some troops, but what were the odds against something like that!? But now, because there's a chance Peck might become president, suddenly that possibility has become for some of the guys the basic requirement for going ahead. Do you think I don't understand what's going on? Some people on the steering committee realize that the day for deciding on action has finally come, and they're getting cold feet. They've started thinking more concretely about the consequences of failure. They're afraid, and they're looking for excuses not to go ahead. They say, no, not yet, not yet. You have to ask whether the procrastinators were ever serious deep down."

"No, Gordon, you're being unfair," Vandenhorst said.

"The legitimacy problem is huge," Richard said. "Some of our people may not have understood just how big until they started thinking about Peck and realized just how important appearances are."

Gordon looked hard at Richard as he said, "Dick, not having sufficient legitimacy is *not* our main problem. It's just *one* important problem. Not having sufficient military and other operational resources would be a much bigger obstacle to success. After all, there would be little point in merely replacing one president with another. *We have to break the back of this damned system!*" Bunker said the sentence with a raised voice, moving his hands for emphasis. "We're all *agreed* on that—we say. Luckily, our military capabilities may be improving. Anyway, there were never any guarantees of success.

Whatever resources we finally muster, we're taking a big gamble."

"I realize that," Richard said. "But the legitimacy problem is on top of other problems. There are all kinds of dangers and intangibles. I'm not the only one who's worried that Noah Sales will behave like a bull in a china shop? And we have three people agitating for diverting resources to handle the media and financial elites. And—"

"Dammit, Dick! This is a coup! And this here is the real world!" Bunker had raised his voice further. His cheeks were flushed, both from emotion and the cramped quarters. Some anger—at what exactly was not clear—was also showing. Vandenhorst looked worried, but did not want to offend Bunker by interfering. "A coup," Bunker sputtered, "is by definition a risky business. But we've done *a damned good job*, if I may say so, of collecting people who're not only capable but pretty decent. But they are human beings. Hell, what did you expect? The heavenly choir?" Bunker was almost shouting.

Vandenhorst also stood up and raised his hands to calm the emotions. "Gordon, please! Let's quiet down. Let's all sit down."

Bunker plunked himself down, making the wooden bench under him creak in pain. He let out a deep sigh. Richard, too, sat down.

But Bunker was not finished. He spoke more calmly now. His tone was friendly.

"Remember, Dick, it was *you* who made a little speech—that time in the car after lunch at Congressional Country Club—about your worries that people in the conspiracy might think too theoretically about the coup and not be *psychologically* prepared for taking the necessary practical action. You were preaching to *us*, Dick! To *us*!"

Richard felt a pang of embarrassment. He remembered the moment well. He had spoken as if others in the conspiracy needed to be enlightened by him about the need to think more concretely about what was being planned. But it was *he* who had needed his own advice. The idea that you must be prepared for the real world and not entertain dreams of purely imaginary circumstances was sound enough, but it was for him still too much a *theory* of what ought to be. He, Richard, had difficulty switching from the mode of cautious, if very realistic, planner to the mode of practical actor.

"A bunch of guys decided that only a coup can head off disaster for this country," Bunker resumed, "They know they may fail but that doing nothing is unacceptable. They don't want that on their conscience. That being the case, they have to be willing to use the assets they have. To complain you can't have advantages that simply aren't on offer is nothing but a flight from reality!" Bunker let his hands fall on his lap.

Richard sat nailed to his seat. He had been struck to the core by Bunker's last comment. Richard said nothing in response. Vandenhorst, too, was quiet, probably wondering how Bunker's words had affected Richard. Nobody looked at any of the others. Each man was alone with his thoughts. Nobody moved. Except for the fan, the sauna was very quiet.

Richard almost forgot that the other two were present. *You've got to make do with what you've got,* Richard thought. Billick's principle — that powerful antidote to handwringing and wishful thinking, that bracing tonic for people who won't face up to life's real choices.

Richard realized that in his heart of hearts his choice was really different from what he had thought that it would be. It was not whether to attempt a coup later rather than sooner. It was whether to attempt a coup at all. The circumstances for attempting the overthrow of the government of the United States of America would never be favorable. The task was mind-boggling. Still he had felt compelled to work with the conspirators. They had never assumed a successful outcome. If he was honest with himself, Richard had to concede that he had always known that failure was as likely as success. The conspirators were daredevils, similar in some ways to kamikaze pilots. He had joined the steering committee out of desperation. He had found it hard to live with himself because he was not doing anything significant to change a terrible situation. He had been amazed that the chances of a coup succeeding were much better than he had ever imagined. The conspirators had far greater resources than he had thought possible. Competent people were on board and great amounts of work — very detailed and practical as well as careful and intelligent — had been done. What excuse for opposing action could he have now that he had not had when he first accepted Vandenhorst's invitation?

Vandenhorst broke the silence. "People in the group are like us. They all have their doubts. Like us, they're trying to think their way through a maze of difficulties and unpredictability. They are doing as well as they can. Some have less courage and strength of will than others. Some may be more ambitious than others. But they would not have stayed with us this long if they'd thought that in the end they would be unwilling to risk everything. They've already risked long prison terms. You, Richard, have questions about what will give the coup the best chance of success, but you decided a long time ago that drastic action was necessary. You also have too much historical knowledge and humility to think your judgment is infallible or superior to everybody else's."

Richard remained silent. A strange calm had come over him.

"Richard, you've been an invaluable member of our team. You've been very good at alerting the rest of us to things that needed more attention. You've laid out alternatives without showing too much bias. It's the historian and academic in you. But you've also shown that you don't view our meetings as seminars for talking about abstract possibilities. You've thought as a man of action, and that's why the others have listened."

"Thank you, Herbert, but I doubt the others take me as seriously as all that."

"Believe me, Dick. They do. I know what I'm talking about. What you say carries authority. And here I'm getting to what I need to get across. Because you've pointed to the issue of legitimacy for so long and our people admire your realism and smarts, you could sway the ones who are now letting their doubts paralyze them. They just *have* to be gotten off the fence! We can't afford a couple of people jumping ship and bringing others at lower levels with them. It would throw our plans into complete disarray. It would demoralize our people—this at a time when nerves are already frayed to the outmost. We could have a security breach at any time. We've already taken many risks to get ready for the final move. Several of our people are worried that their odd comings and goings have been noticed by people whose business it is to notice conduct out of the ordinary. Our intelligence guys are particularly worried. Government agents are supposed to check on them more or less discreetly, mostly to look after them and protect them. In fact, a couple of people on the steering committee have told me in no uncertain terms that they're not willing to postpone action any longer. We could have the FBI swarming over us any time. Tom's just one of those who thinks that way. He thinks it would be crazy to wait."

Vandenhorst paused. "So, Richard, I'm afraid it's now or never. And you may be the person who decides whether this coup will take place or not."

Bunker, too, was looking intently at Richard.

"Dick, you're not just another possible vote for action now," Bunker said. "Herb and I agree that you're the only one who could get us through this crisis."

# CHAPTER 51

Henri Duparc was deeply torn. He wanted to give Helen Bittenberg hope. She was going through hell. She needed cheering up. But he also did not want to risk her taking some precipitous action. She needed to be calmed, not agitated.

They drove into Quartier Latin just after 4:00 PM. They would be at Hotel Vieux Logis in a minute. Duparc dialed the number to the hotel. She answered after only one ring. Duparc guessed that she had been waiting to hear from him, hesitating even to go to the bathroom in case there should be a telephone call or a knock on the door.

"Chief Inspector, do you have any news?"

"If you can meet us outside the hotel we can talk."

"I'll be right down."

Léger did not find a place to stop just outside the hotel, so Duparc decided to get out of the car. He told Léger to stay with the car while he talked to Mrs. Bittenberg. Duparc was just about to step into the hotel foyer when she appeared. She walked so quickly that they bumped into each other. They laughed as they separated. Duparc could smell her perfume. She was wearing blue slacks, a white blouse, and a red summer jacket. She had shadows under her eyes and looked drawn and nervous. Her beauty still shone through.

"We couldn't find a convenient place to park," Duparc said. "Léger is taking care of the car. Let's take a little walk. The weather's rather pleasant. You haven't been sitting inside the whole day, I hope."

"Just the last couple of hours," she said. "Tell me what you've found."

Duparc summarized the interviews with Dégas and de la Broderie. He did not mention the tray. "We can be certain that the two drove through Noisy on Friday just after noon. That's when they would have come through town if they left the Sorbonne when we think they did. They claim not to have noticed any accident, but they had a reason not to stop. Your husband was probably in the car, whether as prisoner or passenger."

"He was abducted!"

"We're inclined to agree with you, but we have no proof."

"It's pretty clear that Richard was taken to the de la Broderie estate," Helen said "At least now you should be able to get a search warrant."

"I'm afraid we do *not* have enough evidence to get what you call a search warrant. No magistrate will give us permission, especially as de la Broderie is a former ambassador and a very prominent citizen."

"But Richard may still be alive! We have to find him right away!" Helen looked pleadingly at Duparc. He had expected just this reaction, and he sympathized with her.

"Helen, we're trying to get at this problem in more than one way. Tomorrow morning we'll confront Ferguson. We tried to get to see him today but it was not possible. We can't treat him as we would any ordinary suspect, especially without solid evidence. We have to follow certain well-established protocols to avoid provoking a diplomatic incident. Ferguson doesn't even have to see us, but he knows that refusing to talk to us would cause suspicion. He also probably prefers to see us in the embassy. It puts him at a psychological advantage. But if the U.S. government has nothing to do with your husband's disappearance, he's in a very tricky position. If he won't talk to us and we appeal to his superior, the ambassador will become curious about what he's been up to."

"He's involved in the abduction of Richard, I know it! It's no coincidence that he's a friend of de la Broderie."

"Of course it isn't, but we don't know the nature of the relationship."

Helen sighed deeply.

They had come to the park where a couple of days ago Helen had slumped down in despair on one of the benches and envied the daily routines of people leading ordinary lives. She had gone into a little church to pray.

She stopped and faced the French detective. "Henri, I'm going crazy with worry. I'm in limbo. In a way it would be easier to live with the knowledge that Richard's dead. But this uncertainty — it's unbearable. And the children — oh, I'm beyond myself." Duparc could see that her brown eyes were glistening. She was not wearing much mascara, but it was smudging.

"I do understand, Helen," he said. "We're doing everything we can, and I'll report to you as soon as there's any kind of break in the case." He indicated that they should return to the hotel. Helen nodded.

"I have a few things to tell you," she said.

He looked expectantly at her. Helen had thought about how

much to tell the French detectives of the news that Hubert Bittenberg had given her. She told Duparc about her husband's increasingly secretive behavior and the disappearance of the private detective who was trying to map Richard's activities. Duparc stopped, pulled out a notebook, and made notes. He asked some questions and asked Helen to keep him informed about any further developments in Washington.

"My brother-in-law and I have wondered if we should contact the FBI, but he says there's no clear evidence of any federal crime. The Virginia state and local police are aware of the disappearance of the private detective, and Hubert has mentioned the possible connection to Richard. What do you think? Could the French police approach the FBI to get some help? Or Interpol?"

Duparc thought for a moment. He didn't like the idea of foreign involvement in his investigation, not at the current stage. Outsiders might complicate his approach to the case. And he was still not certain about what crime, if any, had been committed.

"It seems that the FBI or Interpol would have little to contribute at this time," he said, though not in a dismissive tone. "Perhaps later."

When they returned to the hotel they found Léger standing on the sidewalk smoking a cigarette next to the Renault, which he had put in a no-parking space. He smiled and said hello when he saw Helen. She tried to smile back. Duparc recognized the despondency that he had noticed in her before when it was time to leave her. She needed company, friends who might commiserate with her, or distract her from her agony. The only American she really knew in Paris was Stephen Ferguson. It was not a part of Duparc's job to care for the victims of crime, but he had started to feel some kind of responsibility for Helen Bittenberg. Her situation was unusually unenviable. It had crossed his mind that he might invite her to his home for dinner, but his superiors would, at minimum, frown on such an invitation. His wife would certainly wonder why all of a sudden he would bring to their home the victim of a crime, one who was also rather strikingly beautiful.

Duparc reiterated that he would contact Helen as soon as he had any real news. The two detectives said goodbye and got into the car. As they drove off Léger could see her in the rearview mirror, standing outside the hotel, a lonely figure, abandoned in the middle of a large city in a foreign country.

"Did you tell her about the tray?"

"No." Duparc did not elaborate.

They returned to their home base at Îls de la Cité. Duparc

let Léger go home. He had worked long hours in the last couple of days. Duparc needed to file a report by email to the police in Noisy. Its content would probably please the gendarme in charge. Major Étienne Dégas had been the driver of the vehicle that caused the accident in Noisy, but there was no proof that he had deliberately left the scene of the accident. Duparc's recommendation: No need for any further investigation. Give Dégas's name to the insurance companies responsible for the two damaged cars. He sent the email.

Duparc also had to ask the Noisy police a favor that would not please them. He telephoned to make the request.

Duparc had decided to wait to file a report on the Bittenberg case for his immediate superior. He did not want to risk a report being transmitted to the American consulate, which might forward a copy to Ferguson.

On their way to the American Embassy the next morning, Duparc and Léger discussed how to interview Ferguson. They had a dilemma. Unless they confronted the American diplomat with what they knew or suspected, they were not likely to gain anything of substance by interviewing him, and if they did confront him he might clam up. How far should they go? Was their objective now to rattle Ferguson and also de la Broderie and Dégas into making some mistake? If Ferguson was involved in the abduction, their letting him know that he was under suspicion would certainly unnerve him. Unless his role in the abduction was somehow official, he would have to be careful not to invoke his diplomatic immunity. His reaction to provocative questioning might at least reveal whether he had been acting in his professional capacity. If the detectives revealed their suspicions, de la Broderie and Dégas would probably know very soon. They would be able to take precautions, perhaps move Bittenberg, if indeed he was still alive. On the other hand, if Ferguson was involved, it was not far-fetched to think that de la Broderie had already informed him about the visit from the police. De la Broderie was a sophisticated man and could have seen right through the ruse of investigating a hit-and-run traffic accident. They might get Ferguson to refrain from calling or emailing de la Broderie or Dégas by intimating that a wiretap or electronic surveillance was already in effect. Perhaps they could trick Ferguson into setting up a meeting with his accomplices.

"I think I want to challenge him frontally," Duparc said. "I want to see his reaction."

Léger commented: "If Ferguson alerts de la Broderie to our being on their tail, it may be bad news for Bittenberg, assuming he's still alive and on the Broderie estate. They may want to remove any trace of him, kill him, and bury him where he won't ever be found."

"Yes, but after our talking with Ferguson today, they will know that we're keeping our eyes on them."

"Perhaps they were tipped off by our visit to the baron yesterday and have already gotten rid of Bittenberg," Léger said.

"It's possible, but I don't think we made any obvious errors in Evremond. If they're holding Bittenberg prisoner, getting a visit from the police must have made them very nervous, but how, they must ask themselves, could the police possibly suspect them of keeping a prisoner or worse? If it hadn't been for Helen Bittenberg's persistence, scheming, and powers of observation we would never have suspected Ferguson, much less de la Broderie."

"Even if they thought we were looking for Bittenberg, which I doubt, they had to assume that we didn't know much," Léger said. "If we'd had any real evidence, we would've raided the estate."

"True."

"If we confront Ferguson today and he's conspired with them, will it not make them desperate?"

"Again, would they commit a murder knowing that we're zeroing in on them? Also, if they've kept Bittenberg alive this long, it must have been for a good reason. That reason might still be good."

"Our grilling Ferguson will certainly unsettle them."

"What I'm hoping is that they will make some compromising move, so we can convince a magistrate to let us search the baron's estate."

"So after interviewing Ferguson we head for Evremond to see what de la Broderie and the major get up to?"

"Not necessarily. I called the police in Noisy after you went home yesterday. I talked to that gendarme who mans the police station. I swore him to secrecy and filled him in on what's going on. He didn't like it that I asked him to put a man in plain clothes to keep an eye on the baron's estate for forty-eight hours, but he finally agreed. I gave him detailed instructions. He'll use two retired gendarmes in shifts. Of course, he'll be sending Paris the bill."

They arrived at the chancery of the American Embassy just after eight o'clock. They could not find any parking on Avenue Gabriel, the official street address, or any of the other streets bordering the embassy. Duparc finally told Léger to put the car in a no-parking zone, in the gardens of Champs-Élysées near Avenue Gabriel. They put a police emergency decal in the window.

Walking to the chancery, Léger asked: "If we tell Ferguson that we know about his connection to de la Broderie, won't we expose Helen Bittenberg? She's the one who got the name from Ferguson during that dinner."

"She wouldn't have to be the source. We can refer to the accident in Noisy. Also, I doubt Ferguson's friendship with de la Broderie is any secret. We could have learned of their relationship in other ways. Besides, Mrs. Bittenberg said Ferguson was rather inebriated when he mentioned the baron's name. But I'll be careful."

The embassy was not yet officially open, but their detective badges and the name Ferguson facilitated their entry. They passed through security and reported at the reception desk. Miss Jones, already at her post, appeared and escorted them to Ferguson's office.

# CHAPTER 52

"Congressman, are you in a conspiracy to overthrow the government of the United States?"

The question was directed point-blank at Representative Robert Preston of South Carolina.

"Yes, Richard, I am." The frankness and simplicity of the answer was in sharp contrast to the obfuscation and evasiveness with which politicians usually handle troublesome questions.

Robert and Richard were at the C & O canal, which runs parallel to the Potomac River on the Maryland side. They had just had breakfast at the McDonald's that was not far from their respective homes. It was eight o'clock in the morning on the Saturday before the meeting of the steering committee that would take place in O'Brien's rental house in Silver Spring. The canal was only a few minutes away by car from the Bittenberg and Preston homes. They had parked at one of the locks. Through woodland a hundred yards away they could see the river with its rocky and craggy banks and falls. Within a month the fresh foliage of spring would almost hide the river. The morning was cool but sunny. Later in the day the temperature would be in the low sixties. On weekends with beautiful weather the path attracted bikers, joggers, and people with dogs as well as walkers like themselves.

They had walked half a mile from the parking lot, and Richard had looked for any signs of their being followed. The rugged terrain on both sides of the canal would make it virtually impossible for people with listening equipment to keep up with them without calling attention to themselves. Still, Richard kept his voice low.

Richard had had time since their breakfast the previous day to get used to the possibility that his friend might have become a part of the conspiracy. The frankness of Robert's answer still took him by surprise.

"Do you realize what you're saying?"

"Of course I do. I've told you that the feds would be justified in arresting me on the spot, putting me in the slammer, and throwing the key away."

"Why, then, would you tell me?"

"Because I'm certain you won't turn me in and because I can think of no one else to confide in."

"Wouldn't your fellow conspirators be mighty upset by your speaking to an outsider?"

"You're hardly an outsider. You've been griping for years about the system being broken and about the need for action rather than words. You've been on my back for making too many political compromises. And you've spoken about the need for drastic change."

"But an actual plot, Bob! A coup!"

"Dick, what except a coup could *you* have been talking about?"

"But why would you, all of a sudden, tell me about such a plot?"

"C'mon, Dick, you've sounded as if you, too, might be receptive to the idea."

"Why talk to me now?"

"I've kept my mouth shut for a long time, as I was supposed to do. But I'm picking up strong vibrations that preparations are coming to an end and that the time for action will soon be here. I need someone to talk to. That's why."

"My God, Bob, you mean to say that plans for overthrowing the government of the United States will soon be put into effect?"

"That's what we've been told to get ready for."

Robert's voice was calm and matter-of-fact, almost disengaged. He might have been speaking about routine business in the House of Representatives.

"But, if you're serious, why tell me about it?"

"You're my best friend. I want to hear what you think."

Richard's reaction was a mixture of surprise that his old friend was actually involved in the conspiracy and disappointment that Robert Preston could not be the one to offer him the impartial, unbiased advice that he urgently wanted. He craved the opinion of a person of sound judgment who was also an outsider.

"Think about what?"

"To boil it down to essentials — do you think I'm crazy?"

It was just the question that Richard would have liked to ask Robert.

"It does sound a little crazy," Richard said.

"Doesn't it?"

"First of all, to become involved in a conspiracy to overthrow the government you would have to have given up completely on the American constitutional system recovering from within."

"I have given up — as have so many others on the Hill. We just go through the motions, holding our noses. The system is rotten. All the demonstrations and riots show that our society is fragmenting. As a representative of my district I feel like an impostor. I behave as if the system worked decently well, but I want to scream to high heaven. If I did, the system would find a way of purging me. I would be declared a wacko or an extremist or end up in the middle of some scandal."

"Secondly, you would have to think that the coup has a real chance of succeeding."

"When I first got involved I did it out of anger over something particularly egregious that happened on the Hill. It was seven or eight months ago. About that time I was approached by the person I mentioned to you before. We already knew each other. We met a few times and spoke more and more frankly. He finally told me that he and a few others were talking about how to break or change the system. When he realized that I was of the same mind, he became more open about what he and the others were contemplating. I was glad to hear about it and to learn that it was far more than talk. At first I assumed that I had gotten into something fairly new and that I and the others would be starting something from scratch."

Richard smiled to himself. "That was not the case?"

"No, the discussion and planning had been going on for a long time. Just how long wasn't clear. The leaders of the conspiracy are extremely cautious and secretive. They're pretty savvy from what I've been able to tell. The conspiracy has several layers and groups, and there's limited overlap. The group that I'm working with deals with the U.S. Congress and state governments. Like others in my group, I don't know much about the conspirators higher up, or lower down, or even about groups at our own level. We just know they exist and what sorts of activities are being handled. Through briefings and day-to-day activities we have a rough idea of the larger picture and of what is expected when the day comes, if it does. I don't quite know the scope of the conspiracy, but it is much more extensive than I had thought possible. I still don't know much about the top people. I know only one of them personally, and he's a heavyweight. I know of two others by reputation. Reassuring names. I have a favorable impression of what they're planning. It's a pretty sophisticated scheme to make maximum use of limited resources. The fact that the secrecy has been as tight as it's been is encouraging and has deepened my commitment."

"You must've had to follow tight security procedures."

"You bet."

"There must be an ironclad prohibition against breathing a word about the conspiracy to outsiders."

"Of course."

"But here you are talking to me."

"Dick, I don't think of you as an outsider. If you're not safe, I don't know who might be."

"Even if I'm safe, the feds could be listening in."

"Here? Not bloody likely. Nobody knew we would be going here. We never spoke about it on the telephone. I first mentioned it when we left the McDonald's, remember? And even if we'd been followed—which we weren't, by the way—there's been nothing suspicious around here. The feds wouldn't have had the time to rearrange any listening."

Richard recognized in his friend his own deeply ingrained habit of always taking security precautions.

"Did you want us to go to the canal in order to talk about the conspiracy?"

"I think so."

They walked for half a minute without saying a word.

"So, do you think I'm crazy?"

"Tell, me, what would be the crazy part?"

Robert looked quizzically at Richard. "You mean it doesn't stand out?"

A smile broke through Richard's own torment. Knowing that his best friend was in the same predicament as he and that he had the same doubts relieved some of his anxiety.

"Assuming that the facts are as you described them, you seem to have fallen in with a serious and smart bunch of traitors. If the scheme might work, it might be worth trying." Richard still wore a slight smile.

"Dick, this is no joking matter!"

"I know, and I'm not joking. I meant what I said."

"You're telling me I should go ahead?"

"I'm saying you haven't given me any grounds for calling you crazy."

"But do you realize what I'm saying? I'm talking about trying to overthrow the federal government of the United States!"

"Well, nobody has tried it yet, as far as we know. But you and I have talked often enough about the need for some kind of shock treatment. We're living under a terribly corrupt, irresponsible, lawless near-tyranny. Our freedoms are substantially eroded. The government acts for hidden interests, and no real opposition has a chance. The Constitution is followed only when it suits the powers-that-be. A coup has *already* taken place, Robert. It's happened over time. It's placed us at the mercy of scoundrels and criminals. You're really talking about trying to take this country back from usurpers and deceivers."

"You're surprisingly compliant."

"I'm the one who's badgered *you* for going along too much with the system. I've felt exasperated, not so much on account of you as on account of there being no real opposition to what's going on. You've probably done as much as a member of Congress can do without ruining yourself politically. But I've kept needling you anyway, haven't I? How, then, could I call you crazy for doing what you are doing now?"

"But this is the real thing, Dick, not just talk. It may actually happen—and soon."

"I guess you're worried that you're mixed up in a harebrained scheme. How could you and a few others be right when so many others seem to find the current state of affairs tolerable?"

"Something like that. It doesn't help to have nobody to talk to other than your fellow conspirators. You wonder at times if you need an entirely different point of view."

Richard made no immediate comment. He was deciding whether to confide in his friend.

"Bob, you're talking to the wrong person."

"Don't say that, Dick. You know and understand more than most, and you're my best friend."

"What if I am? What you want is someone who can offer a fresh perspective. You need a sane, knowledgeable outsider who can tell you whether you're doing the right thing or have crossed into cloud cuckoo-land."

"That describes you pretty well, Dick. I would really appreciate your frank opinion."

"And, I repeat, I'm not the person you want."

"Why do you think I turned to you? There's nobody whose judgment I respect more than yours, and I know I can trust you. Don't let me down, Dick."

Richard said slowly: "You didn't hear me just now, Bob. You're looking for an outsider, one who's not involved."

Robert stopped and stared at Richard.

"You mean—?"

Richard looked back at his old friend, nodding slowly.

"Yes, that's what I mean."

Robert Preston's expression was at first incredulous, then changed to one of concern. He glanced confusedly around the trail for any signs that they might be observed.

"But you've never so much as hinted at any involvement."

"Neither have you."

"How long—?"

"Depends on how you count. I haven't counted the months. It's about a year and a half."

"*A year and a half!* My God! How's it possible? How could you hide it? Why didn't I suspect it?"

"I guess we're both good actors and good at following instructions."

Robert shook his head, but his disbelief was starting to evaporate. Given the views that Richard had so often expressed in private conversation, it was not really surprising that he was one of the conspirators. In fact, Robert had often thought about whether to try to recruit him. He had been held back only by the absolute prohibition against mentioning the conspiracy to anybody without an express permission given through the line of command. He had mentioned the possibility of recruiting Richard to the person chairing his own group of conspirators, but a few days later he had been told not to proceed. He had assumed that there was no interest in recruiting an academic. He had accepted the verdict.

"But how could we not have come across each other in some way or heard our names mentioned?" Robert said. "You'd think we'd have some operational connection."

"Seems security and compartmentalization are working the way they're supposed to."

"My goodness, I can't believe it! You, Dick, my best friend. You've been involved for a long time and been able to keep it from me. That must have been difficult."

"At times *very* difficult."

Robert shook his head again. "Since you've been with the conspiracy for such a long time, I have to assume you know a good deal more about it than I do."

"I guess so, but don't ask me about it. We'll both learn a lot more in time. I won't ask you any questions about your group. I have only one question."

"What's that?"

"Does Jennifer know?" Richard was referring to Robert's wife.

Robert looked at his feet. He answered in a low voice. "Dammit, Dick, you just jumped on the most sore spot of all."

"Well, have you told her?"

"Yes, I did, and that was probably a big mistake. I just

couldn't stand the idea of lying to Jennie all the time. She noticed that I'd become preoccupied and worked longer hours, and she asked all kinds of questions. I finally told her — after getting her to swear on a stack of bibles that she could not tell another soul about what I was going to tell her. She was very upset at first. What would happen to us and the children? I might be arrested. She's a little more accepting now, in theory at least, but her resentment and worry are in the air all the time. She knows she's a kind of accomplice, but I've told her that if I'm ever arrested, she knows absolutely nothing. The kids don't know anything, but they must sense that something's amiss in the family. That's what bothers me the most — that I'm dragging the family into what I've decided I have to do. They were never consulted, and yet they have to suffer the consequences, whatever they are. If it weren't for Jennie and the kids, I wouldn't worry so much."

"I know exactly how you feel. But my problem's a little different. I never told Helen, and I don't intend to, which means lying and more lying. But it seems preferable to the alternative. All she knows is that I'm on edge somehow, and she thinks I simply can't break out of a vicious cycle of overwork. We had a terrible row a few days ago."

They walked back towards the lock where Robert's car was parked. It would be a pretty day. More people could now be seen around the canal. They were enjoying a Saturday morning break from their weekday routines. Later the same day they might do some shopping or work in their gardens at home, have dinner with their spouses or families in a restaurant, perhaps go to a movie, or watch television in their family room. It seemed to Richard that he and Robert inhabited a different dimension of existence where all the dangers and pressures had been concentrated. How long would he be able to endure? He had moments when the impulse to run away and to hide almost took control of him. Were not his occasional stops at church partly an escape from his oppressive circumstances? It comforted him now that his best friend, a practical, experienced, bright, responsible, admirable man, had taken the same extraordinary practical steps as he. He was in a sense no longer alone in his misery. Robert provided a connection to his own earlier life, to normality, to his youth, to his home state, to a private existence away from the reality that mercilessly crowded in upon him and robbed him of all peace of mind. He now had a special ally. But there was a downside to this comfort. Now the conspiracy had invaded the life of family and close friends. The sphere in which he could seek refuge from the exhausting claims upon him had shrunk to almost nothing.

They walked slowly along the canal. The sun was peeking

through the tree branches. Finally Robert spoke: "I've been thinking a lot lately about one thing."

"What's that? Tell me only if it's not about our roles in the conspiracy."

"It's a non-specific, very general question — just prompted by our involvement."

"Let's see what's on your mind."

Robert paused before speaking. "You know, Dick, you have to wonder whether people like us have any business doing what we're doing."

Richard stopped and stared at his friend. "Have any business? You mean the situation might not be so bad?"

"Hell no. The situation's bad all right and getting worse. It's so bad, in fact, you wonder if anything can be done about it. But, precisely because it's so bad and because we're up against very corrupt and very rough customers, you have to ask if we — people like you and me, Dick — have what it takes to deal with the situation. Do we have the right stuff? Look at us! Here we are bellyaching about family problems, about wives and kids. We're afflicted by doubts all the time. We're struggling with conscience. You know what that makes us?"

"What?"

"Ambivalent. Deep down we're not really certain, not really, that we're doing the right thing. Yes, yes, I know, in our heads and in our gut we know we have to try to overthrow this system. The attempt just has to be made. Sure! But we can't get rid of our doubts and reservations. That makes us squeamish and unreliable."

"No wonder, Bob. This is a big gamble. We're taking a huge risk. Our chances are probably no better than fifty-fifty. Too many things can go wrong. We're risking many lives, thousands perhaps, including our own, and we're dragging loads of innocent bystanders with us."

"That's just the sort of thing I'm talking about. We keep fretting like that. What kind of conspirators does that make us? Not very good ones. We aren't tough enough, Dick. We're too damned civilized, that's what. When you get right down to it, we aren't ruthless enough. We were well suited for action in a well-ordered, moderately flawed and corrupt society like the old America or some other decent society. There we can set a pretty good example for others. But here, in a conspiracy to overthrow a rotten regime in a deteriorated society, we're like fish out of water, likely to make problems with our doubts and cautions — with our damned civilized ambivalence. On the one hand, on the other hand. But dealing effectively with the current situation probably requires that doubts be put aside. What's needed is unyielding determination. Nothing, certainly not little family difficulties, must be allowed to stand in the way. Either you fuss and worry about everything, and then you're not really adequate for the job—you'd better call it quits, get out of the way. Or you decide that you're in, and then you give it your all— no fretting, no darn ambivalence. That's the kind of commitment that people like you and me have such difficulty making because we've lived our entire lives in a different world. Our deepest reflexes are conditioned by fairly tranquil circumstances. So the question, Dick, is whether people like us are cut out for the job. Damn it, the long and short of it is that we're probably too civilized—no, that's not quite what I mean. I mean we, too, are infected by our progressively corrupt culture. That combination makes us—*decadent*!" He gave added emphasis to the last word by pausing before saying it. "We lack imagination, lack adaptability. We think we're realistic and canny. We see better than others that our country's in danger and that radical action is necessary, but we have a very hard time breaking out of a mode of being that's inappropriate to the new circumstances. We're morally myopic, inflexible, caught in patterns that don't apply. That's *decadence*, Dick. Even the better people—people like you and me, brother, who think they're better than others—have their own version of that avoidance of tough problems that's become chronic in our society."

Richard gave no overt response, other than that he did not contradict his friend. Robert's words had gone straight to his gut. They articulated a feeling that had bothered him more and more but that had remained inchoate until that moment. Was he—Professor Richard Bittenberg, the scholar, the Harvard Ph.D., married and father of two, a creature of Charleston, the South, and Christian civilization—cut out for the task before him? Or was he, despite his presumed realism, too delicate and persnickety, likely to do as much damage as good? Robert was right. This really was not the time for hesitation and pangs of conscience, which could only distract him from what had to be done. Yet he often had to steel himself to break through his ambivalence.

When Richard finally spoke again it was to have Robert comment directly on one particular theme in his inner monologue.

"Do you ever wonder whether the current system, with all its atrocious problems, might still be preferable to the uncertainties attendant on a coup? Isn't bad political order better than no order?"

Robert looked at his friend and sighed. "Of course I sometimes ask myself that question. But I've come to recognize the question for what it is. It's the voice of *decadence*, Dick! It's the voice of that self in us that fears the unknown and shrinks from courage, the self that would rather not go through all the pain and suffering of making a change."

"But better the devil you know, than the devil you don't know, right?"

"Listen to you. Excuses, excuses. You know what's got to be done, Dick, but you can't leave well enough alone? You have to pick at the scab. Notice that you're giving yourself a false choice. The order of the current system is order only in the most perverse sense. It serves corrupt, callous, arbitrary power. In a sense that I know you understand, this order's actually disorder, quasi-organized perversity. It's unprincipled, deeply immoral. The Constitution has become only windowdressing. And the alternative to this charade is not chaos as implied in your question. The alternative is order of a different kind and at least the *chance* of returning to something like constitutional government and the rule of law."

The speaker was not a philosopher by profession but a politician, a man of practice, Richard reflected. Yet his friend had articulated for him, the full-time scholar-thinker, what had actually been the rationale for his involvement in the conspiracy.

"I agree," Richard said quietly.

As the two friends approached the parking lot their talk of the conspiracy ceased. Richard braced for returning to his anguished regular life. It cheered him that in personal matters relating to the conspiracy Robert Preston could now be his confidant. They could comfort and cheer each other. But the most important outcome of their walk along the canal was something different. What Richard would most remember were Robert's words about the condition of civilized people who found themselves in territory for which life had not prepared them. Those remarks had done more to unnerve and upset him than to reassure him.

# CHAPTER 53

When Miss Jones escorted the two French detectives into his office, Stephen Ferguson, the political counselor at the U.S. Embassy, rose from his desk to his full height. He did not move much away from the desk but waited for them to walk up to him to greet him. He wore a well-pressed gray suit, black polished shoes, a white starched shirt, and a blue bow tie. He wore an all-purpose smile when he shook their hands. He asked them to sit down in the two chairs in front of his desk rather than in the sitting group.

"May I offer you some coffee?"

The two detectives declined the offer, and Miss Jones disappeared.

"I'm very happy to see you, gentlemen. I hope that you have made some progress in the search for Professor Bittenberg." His manner was pleasant but left no doubt as to who was in charge of the just-started meeting. He was taking full advantage of his stature as a diplomat, Duparc thought. He was reminding his visitors that he was the second-most important man at the embassy of the most powerful country in the world.

"Yes, sir, we've made some progress," Duparc said. Nothing in Ferguson's expression betrayed whether he received this information with alarm or satisfaction.

"Excellent! Do let me hear, please." His attitude was that of a high-level diplomat expecting a report from professional staffers.

"We would like to ask you some questions, sir." Duparc said.

"Fine, but first give me a summary of your findings."

"How well do you know Professor Bittenberg?"

A shadow of annoyance passed over Ferguson's face. He paused briefly as if considering a curt retort to this refusal to take direction. He finally said, "You asked me that before, chief inspector."

"I know, but I thought you might want to embellish on your answer."

"I don't have anything to add. We got to know each other at Harvard when I had a State Department fellowship there. We met a few times thereafter, once at the New York City home of a mutual friend. We met the last time a few years ago in Washington.

"So you had no continuing contact with him, say, by telephone or email?"

"Really, chief inspector, why go over this same ground again? I told you last time that we haven't met for a long time."

"Have you had any professional relationship? Did you ever meet on government business or the like?"

Ferguson seemed to hesitate, then said: "The answer is no, but, really, chief inspector, what do these questions have to do with Richard's disappearance?"

"And when did you last talk to Professor Bittenberg?"

"I've already told you. He called me two or three weeks ago out of the blue from the U.S. to let me know that he would soon be in Paris. Will you get to the point!?"

"And you didn't speak with him after that?"

Ferguson let out an irritated sigh. "Chief inspector, I'm pleased to see you and want to do what I can to help, but going over the same ground again is hardly a good use of the time I can spare. I do have a rather busy day ahead of me."

"Mr. Ferguson, I'm afraid your answers are presenting us with a problem." Ferguson's face showed feigned or real surprise. "What reason do you have to give misleading information to the French police?"

Ferguson was sitting back in his brown leather armchair. He first raised his eyebrows, and then bent slowly forward putting his arms on the large desk. He looked at Duparc with a mixture of incomprehension and irritation. "Misleading information!? You'd better explain yourself!"

"Yes, sir. What would be your reason for misleading us with regard to when you last talked to Professor Bittenberg?"

"Are you accusing me of lying?" Ferguson said in an offended, angry tone of voice.

"Do you have any reason to lie?"

Ferguson shook his head in the manner of a father having to confront yet again a child's bad behavior.

"Of course not," he said with bored impatience. Léger who had been quiet and conspicuously taking notes started writing. Ferguson could have avoided answering, Léger thought, by hinting vaguely at some complex diplomatic matter that he was not at liberty to discuss, but he had foregone that opportunity.

Ferguson added, "I'm finding your allegation impertinent and offensive."

"Sir, we have witnesses that place you at the Sorbonne last Friday morning."

"It must be a case of mistaken identity."

"No sir, you were seen talking to Professor Bittenberg in the Sorbonne cafeteria near the university library. You were in the cafeteria for about an hour, starting about a quarter to nine." Duparc had somewhat overstated what they knew, turning strong suppositions into facts.

Ferguson again shook his head in apparent exasperation. "I've never been to any cafeteria at the Sorbonne, so nobody there could possibly recognize me?"

"What about Professor Bittenberg himself?"

Duparc had not planned to ask that question. It had popped into his mind just seconds before he uttered it. His intuition told him that psychologically it was just the right question to ask at that moment.

Ferguson's reaction was palpable. He didn't start or say anything, but blinked quickly several times. A crack had suddenly appeared in his polished diplomatic veneer.

"Richard—? I don't understand—Have you found him?"

"Why would that not have occurred to you?"

Ferguson winced. He was flustered but able to contain his outward reaction. He collected himself and tried to regain the initiative. "Chief inspector, what are you implying? You'd better explain yourself. Have you found Richard Bittenberg?"

"Mr. Ferguson, are you denying meeting Professor Bittenberg at the Sorbonne on Friday morning?"

"Answer my question! Have you found him?" Ferguson spoke in a firm, demanding voice. "The Embassy of the United States made a request to the French authorities to help find a prominent American citizen who had mysteriously disappeared. Now, have you located him?"

"No, sir."

If Ferguson relaxed, his outward demeanor did not change.

"So give me your report on how the investigation is going."

"Sir, do you deny meeting Professor Bittenberg at the Sorbonne?"

Ferguson glared at Duparc. He seemed to consider not responding.

"There's obviously some kind of mix-up."

"No, sir."

"Who would know me at the Sorbonne?"

Duparc again turned strong supposition into fact. "You were

seen, sir. You were wearing a dark suit, had a bow tie, and smoked a cigar."

Ferguson's hands suddenly disappeared in his lap in a jerky reflex. He said nothing.

"Why *deny* that you were at the cafeteria?"

Ferguson remained silent.

"You were brought to the Sorbonne by one of the embassy cars."

Ferguson sat back in his chair. He had to realize that he had been caught in a lie, Duparc thought. But instead of apologizing, Ferguson went on the offensive.

"The internal operations of this embassy are strictly off limits. I cannot possibly comment" — as if he had been asked to say something about embassy routines, Duparc thought.

"What reason do you have to hide that you met Professor Bittenberg last Friday?"

"I think we're finished on this subject, chief inspector. Do you have any other questions? I'm running short of time."

"Mr. Ferguson, did you place a phone call last Friday morning to a Baron Gustave de la Broderie?"

Ferguson gave Duparc a startled look, but otherwise kept his calm.

"I don't remember. I'm not sure. Gustave's an old friend, and we speak rather often."

"What about Friday morning?" Ferguson could not know whether the French police were relying on telephone records, Duparc knew. If such was the case, it might be a sign that Ferguson was under surveillance.

"Chief inspector, have you or anybody else been listening in on my telephone conversations? That would be a serious violation of the diplomatic code."

"No, sir, we're very attentive to diplomatic proprieties." On the spot Duparc decided to make a comment that did not describe their investigation but was a statement of fact: "But there is more than one party to a telephone conversation."

Ferguson seemed to gasp, but kept his face under control.

"You mean to say that you've been tapping the telephone of *Gustave de la Broderie*?"

"Mr. Ferguson, I'm not saying anything, and I can't comment on our procedures."

"Do you *know* who Broderie is?"

"A very distinguished Frenchman, sir, a former ambassador."

"How could you possibly invade the privacy of a person like that?"

"I didn't say that we have."

"What could he possibly have to do with your investigation?"

"We were hoping that you would be able to assist us with that question."

"I've no idea what you're talking about!" Ferguson's voice was tinged with disgust.

"Did you talk to him on Friday?"

"I've already answered."

"Does Professor Bittenberg know Baron de la Broderie?"

"Not that I know. You would have to ask the baron. What's he got to do with this case anyway?"

To protect Helen, Duparc wanted to distract attention from her as a possible source of information about Broderie. He said: "The baron was involved in an accident in Noisy — that's about thirty kilometers from Paris — that seems to be connected to Professor Bittenberg's disappearance."

"An accident? What's the connection to Bittenberg? Explain."

"I'm afraid that at this time I can't go into the matter."

"Not go into it? The U.S. Embassy would like a full report on what you have discovered about Professor Bittenberg's disappearance."

"In time the embassy *will* receive a report, but as of now our findings are preliminary. I can say this much: your own role in this matter appears to be different from what you have led us to believe. It would be much better for all concerned if you told us the truth."

"Chief inspector, your presence here is no longer required." Ferguson rose and indicated by moving his hand that he expected the two detectives to leave. "Good-bye, gentlemen."

As Duparc turned towards the door to walk out, Léger, who had been silent during the entire interview, said: "Mr. Ferguson, I believe you have that paper that Mrs. Bittenberg found in her husband's jacket, the sheet with those code-like notations. We would like to have it."

Ferguson said nothing and didn't move, as if he were simply ignoring Léger's request. When Duparc looked at Ferguson and nodded, Ferguson finally opened a drawer in his desk, took out a sheet of paper, and threw it on top of the desk. Léger walked up to the desk and took the paper.

The two detectives quietly withdrew. Miss Jones escorted

them down into the reception area.

On the way out the two detectives said nothing to each other, but when they reached the street Léger blurted out: "He's obviously involved."

Duparc nodded.

"And he's on his own, not on government business. He could have hidden behind some diplomatic screen or other, but he didn't want to risk our trying to go above his head to have anything he said confirmed. He's got something to hide from his colleagues."

Duparc nodded again. "He walked a tightrope. He used his diplomatic immunity but without really invoking it. Quite a performance."

"He must be in a real state now," Léger said. "I liked how you gave him the idea that his or Broderie's telephones might be tapped."

They got into the car, Léger taking the wheel.

They reviewed the paper with its code-like scribbles and agreed that it meant nothing to either of them.

"Where to?" Léger asked. "Do we head out to Evremond to boost surveillance at the Broderie estate?"

"I'm not sure. But I should probably let my wife know that we'll be working long hours for the foreseeable future."

"I can see that."

"I wonder if we might finally get a search warrant."

Léger rolled his eyes. "Not very likely. We don't have any more hard evidence, just a bunch of conjecture and suspicion. And the main suspects are, one, the most distinguished man in France and, two, the second in command at the U.S. Embassy. What magistrate is going to be willing to risk major embarrassment and political fall-out?"

"It might not hurt to ask."

"No? Do you remember the case of the Belgian princess?"

Duparc cringed. How could he not remember? On the basis of allegations and suspicions he had gotten a warrant from a very reluctant magistrate to search a princess's apartment, only to discover that they had wrongly suspected her. They had caused a diplomatic scandal. It had happened over a year ago, but they still heard about it when they made a less than compelling request for a warrant.

"Helen Bittenberg will want to hear from us," Léger said.

"You don't need to tell me. But there are at least two things I want to do right away. I want to call the gendarmerie in Noisy and ask them to put their surveillance man on special alert and out of sight. The other is to keep an eye on Ferguson. He must be nothing short of desperate to get in touch with Broderie, but he also thinks that we may have Broderie's or his own telephone bugged. He probably wouldn't dare to use his work computer. The embassy probably keeps a central record of all emails. He could try a pay phone, but he probably wouldn't call Broderie. Perhaps he knows Dégas or has some other way of contacting Broderie. There must be a back way or two out of the embassy."

"There has to be."

"Let's drive around to see." They pulled away from the illegal parking place.

"There's also the garage exit, Léger said. Ferguson may leave in his own car and drive out to Evremond to talk to the baron."

"If he suspects that we are on his tail, he may avoid making that kind of move."

"Except that he must be desperate to communicate with Broderie."

"Look, over there. That's a back exit," Duparc said. "I'll get over there and put myself where I can observe it but be out of sight. If Ferguson decides to leave the embassy to make a call, there's a good chance he will come out here. Why don't you put the car where you can see the front entrance and the garage exit. If he leaves in one of the embassy cars with those tinted windows up we'll not be able to identify him. Helen told me that his personal car is a green BMW convertible. Let's stay in touch by phone."

"There are probably other exits. The chancery building is connected to the building next door, which is probably an annex. He could slip out there."

"But we can't cover all the bases. I'm hoping that right now he's so worried that he will risk a little carelessness. But if we haven't spotted him in half an hour or so, I think we should concentrate on Evremond, perhaps confront the baron or Dégas. I'll call Noisy right now."

Duparc got out of the car on Rue Boissy d'Anglais, which borders the embassy grounds to the east. He positioned himself behind a street newsstand at a point where, less than a hundred yards away, he could see the rear exit from the main chancery building. Plenty of pedestrians and heavy street traffic provided camouflage. He dialed the police in Noisy and gave instructions.

Duparc had been watching the rear exit for a quarter of an hour when his cell phone rang.

Léger did not even take the time to identify himself. "Ferguson's leaving in his BMW. I'm in front of the main entrance."

Duparc sprinted towards their car.

# CHAPTER 54

It was late Saturday afternoon when the conspirators started gathering in the basement of Robert O'Brien's modest three-bedroom rental house. It was located just north of the District of Columbia in Maryland half a dozen blocks from downtown Silver Spring. The house was empty except for paint cans, rolls of wallpaper, a ladder, paintbrushes, and other implements. The partially finished basement contained only a battered sofa, eight steel folding chairs and two tables, one with a chair behind it, the other with bottles of soft drinks, glasses, a bucket of ice and a few bags of potato chips. The non-alcoholic offerings made it obvious that the business to be conducted required clear heads. Two old floor lamps provided the only lighting. The house's central heating unit was making noise behind a thin partition. Hick had installed the electronic anti-listening device, which emitted a low humming sound. The two small basement windows had been covered from the outside. One of Hick's colleagues sat outside in an inconspicuous car or patrolled discreetly on foot.

The conspirators arrived separately from different directions and at intervals within half an hour of each other. They followed old routines. Nobody parked near the meeting place. A few walked from the nearest, rather distant subway station. They all wore informal, weekend clothing. Each person carried a copy of a biography of President Lincoln to give credence to the ruse that here the American History Club was holding a meeting.

Douglas Pellegrini could not be present because of urgent business at the National Secuity Agency. Gordon Bunker had sprained an ankle and was able to move his large frame down the narrow staircase to the basement only with difficulty. Lester Pickett suffered from a severe cold and had a shawl wrapped around his neck and mouth. He did not remove his warm jacket. His face was red. He didn't shake anybody's hand. "I don't feel well, I'm probably running a fever, but I had to be here," Pickett muttered. He steered towards the sofa and plunked himself down in one corner.

The conversation was subdued. There was no effortless small talk. Noah Sales's attempt to relax tension by joking about the Washington Redskins fell flat. Lisa DeLeon's comical account of trying to challenge a wrongly issued parking ticket in the bureaucracy of the District of Columbia elicited only weak smiles. There was little inclination and no room in the small basement for last minute caucusing. Such coalitions, real or potential, as existed among the conspirators were already in place. All present knew the purpose of the meeting. They were going to decide on the future of the conspiracy.

At 5:00 Robert O'Brien raised his voice. "I guess I'm the host, so let me welcome you. All who will be here are here. We're ready to start. I think we're all agreed that Herbert will chair the meeting."

Vandenhorst moved to the little head table. For this meeting of the American History Book Club he wore a plaid shirt, a green sweater, khaki slacks, and loafers. Most of the conspirators arranged themselves on chairs in a semicircle around Vandenhorst. Richard took a seat to the side, from which he could comfortably observe the others. Robert Bates sat down next to him. Gordon Bunker limped over to the sofa and sunk into the corner away from Pickett.

For a moment Vandenhorst just sat at the table letting his gaze sweep slowly over the faces of the assembled group. They had already settled down and were waiting for him to speak. He looked at some point above and behind them and then into the table. His expression was hard to read. He seemed calm and collected, almost relaxed, but his chin jutted out and his lips were tightly shut, which gave him a determined look. He stayed silent so long that Richard wondered if something might be wrong. Finally Vandenhorst spoke:

"Friends, this is no ordinary meeting. As far as I am concerned, we're not here to make motions, debate, revise motions and take more votes. Some of us have thought about this coup for several years. We've been over the same ground repeatedly. We've discussed and planned for every possible contingency. Every argument and counter-argument has been heard. The subgroups have been over the details again and again. Some of you think that we have planned and talked for too long. The danger of our being discovered or betrayed grows with each passing day, and if we switch to operational mode that danger will only grow."

The room was completely still, each conspirator listening for signs of what was to come. It puzzled Richard that Vandenhorst had seemed to indicate an unwillingness to have more discussion. Had he and Gordon Bunker not told him that his arguments at this meeting might decide the outcome?

"Today we make up our minds what to do," Vandenhorst continued. "I'm not going to pretend that this is another meeting governed by Robert's Rules of Order. I'm not going to pretend that

I'm an impartial chairman, because I'm not. I've *decided* what *I* think we must do. I think it's the *only* thing we can do."

Richard noticed that Robert Bates drew a sharp breath. There was a shuffling of feet.

"I don't think there is anyone in our group who knows more about the overall planning than I do," Vandenhorst said. "I've spent most of the last four years on this effort. I've had countless meetings with you and other key players. In the last couple of weeks I've gone over all the operational plans yet again. I've talked to all of you individually or in groups. I've talked at length with Bob O'Brien about when we might be able to hit the president and vice president at the same time. I think I know what we can and cannot do. I've reached a firm conclusion. Tonight I'm going to ask you to approve it."

The tension in the room was palpable. Robert Bates was breathing quickly. Lester Pickett, who had been virtually lying down in the corner of the sofa, was sitting upright. Like the others, Bates and Pickett thought that Vandenhorst probably would not want to wait until Peck had become speaker.

"But, Herbert," Bates blurted out, "we *have* to have a chance to talk about your plan, whatever it is."

"No, Robert, no more talking." Vandenhorst's voice had a firmness and determination that Richard had not heard before. "I'm going to tell you all what conclusion I've reached, and I am then going to ask you for your unanimous consent. We're not going to have another round of debate or get hung up on any details. Details are for some other time. This, fellow conspirators, is it! Now we decide! I'm asking you to approve my conclusion. There is, as far as I'm concerned, no alternative. If you do not approve the plan, WE-ARE-DISBANDED." The last words were pronounced clearly, slowly, and emphatically.

Vandenhorst's words hung in the air. The conspirators looked at Vandenhorst and each other, some in disbelief.

Lester Pickett had removed the shawl from his mouth. "Now wait a minute, Herbert," he said in a raspy, nasal voice. "We're not well served by some kind of ultimatum. You can't expect us to decide on a matter of this magnitude simply on your say-so. We have to have a chance to discuss what you're proposing."

Robert Bates nodded vigorously.

"No, Lester," Vandenhorst said. "We're finished debating. I've carried more of the burden for this effort than anybody else, and I have thought about it more than anybody else, and I know more about the specifics than anybody else. You have all seemed to respect

my opinion so far, and if you've done it before, you have no reason
not to do it now. If you're not willing to accept what I have in mind
I'll take that as an indication that you don't respect my judgment,
in which case I will withdraw from these efforts. I will do nothing
further to assist them. In fact, I'll do what I can to subvert them" — he
smiled wryly — "short of turning you all in to the FBI. I'm not going
to be a part of a coup attempt that I think will fail."

"You're blackmailing us!" Bates cried.

"Calm down," Lisa DeLeon shouted. Richard looked over
at her, again noting the strange anomaly of her pleasant, almost
beautiful face sitting atop a large-framed, rather husky body. She
added: "I would like to know what Herbert has in mind."

"Amen," Noah Sales said in a loud voice. Gordon Bunker and
Randy Gates visibly indicated their assent. A very loud sneeze from
Pickett provided some comical relief.

"I will tell you what I have in mind," Vandenhorst said, "but
I want it understood that, as far as I'm concerned, the conclusion I've
reached is not negotiable. It's this or nothing. And we need unanimity.
We can't afford any dissension after this meeting. We badly need each
of you to play your role. We come out of this meeting unified. After
this meeting there will be no opportunity to talk the decision over
again. All that will remain will be to discuss the details of execution.
So if you have any doubts, you'll have to swallow them now."

"I protest," Bates said in a shrill voice. He tore off his black
horn-rimmed glasses and nervously started to polish them.

"Protest what?" Thomas Reed asked.

"Not to have a chance to offer a different opinion. Herbert
seems to think that his judgment is better than that of the rest of us.
We have to have a chance to debate!"

Noah Sales threw both arms into the air. "*Debate*?!" he
shouted. "I'm sick and tired of debate. *Sick* of it! You might think this
is the American History Book Club after all. Let me coin a phrase: It's
time to fish or cut bait! I don't know what Herbert's decided, but I
like the sound of 'decided.' No more dillydallying!" Sales's face had
reddened.

"How could you demand unanimity?" Pickett said. "This is a
difficult, complex situation." He fell back into the corner of the sofa as
if he had expended all his energy." He had a loud, violent coughing
spell. Several voices were heard simultaneously.

"I think Herbert's being unreasonable," Bates said.

"You don't even know yet what he wants," Reed retorted.

"I have a pretty good idea."

Vandenhorst used the spine of his Lincoln biography to tap

hard on the table. He kept tapping until the noise had completely subsided. In the ensuing quiet he said: "Intellectual unanimity is virtually impossible on any subject. Life's too complex and many-faceted for all to agree on what's the case. But in the world of practice, our world, it's possible to *silence* your doubts." His way of emphasizing "silence" made it seem as if he were issuing a command. "You can act as if you fully agree with a position that seems to you questionable. People do that in politics and elsewhere all the time without feeling that they're doing anything wrong or violating conscience. You can silence your own doubts because you're not arrogant enough to think that you have a monopoly on sound judgment. You show some humility. You go along with others, in fact, do more than that—you actively defend what's been decided—because you recognize that it's the best that you could do in the circumstances. You decide to trust others to know what they're doing. You stop your opposition and actively work for the good of the whole."

Nobody said anything, but Richard could see that Bates had difficulty containing himself.

Vandenhorst continued: "So I'll tell you what I think we have to do, and I ask you to give that plan your unanimous and wholehearted support—"

"—Wholehearted support?!" Bates could no longer be quiet. "All real consensus requires some give-and-take, some—"

"Will you shut up!" Lisa DeLeon yelled. "We've been giving and taking for months. Can we hear what Herbert's proposing?"

Vandenhorst raised his hands. "Lisa, Robert, and the rest of you," he said in a calm but very firm voice. "I'm not *proposing* anything. I'm not asking for negotiations or another round of the airing of problems. This, Lester, you old politician, is not the U.S. Senate. This is a conspiracy to overthrow the federal government of the United States, and we're beyond striking any deals. I'm asking you all to agree to a certain plan because it's good and has a very good chance of succeeding."

Richard didn't understand Vandenhorst's conduct. What had happened? Only yesterday afternoon Vandenhorst had indicated that Richard might be the key to swaying fence sitters. He needed to speak out in favor of early action. But now Vandenhorst had said "no more debate." That would mean no more arguments for Richard to make.

Vandenhorst, the deliberate, cautious Vandenhorst, had suddenly decided to take a high-risk gamble, Richard thought. Vandenhorst was behaving now not as a coordinator or chairman, but as someone with the authority to decide. The conspiracy had never, certainly not explicitly, handed Vandenhorst that kind of authority. The only authority he had was due to the respect the others had for his person. He had come to be viewed as the first among equals, but now he was, Richard thought, in effect presenting himself as the next president of the United States. Richard did not suspect him of doing so because he craved power over the others. Richard had always found him to be ultimately concerned about the success of the conspiracy. If he was now pushing the others to accept his will, Richard thought, it was because he believed that playing that role was in the circumstances the best means to the end.

By demanding the conspirators' unquestioning assent, by giving them an ultimatum, he was also risking everything, several years of effort. His conduct clearly indicated how deeply he believed in what he had decided. Because of that perception, perhaps he was risking less than it appeared.

Yet if Vandenhorst still favored action while Tom Reed was still Commanding General, there would be opposition. Bates and Pickett clearly wanted to wait, and DeLeon, Gates, and Pellegrini had insisted on a reallocation of available resources. How could Vandenhorst possibly get the unanimity upon which he insisted?

Richard had serious doubts about the plan he expected Vandenhorst to put forth. Like the others, he was being pushed right up against the wall. He would have no more time to think.

The room was abuzz with whispers and side-conversations, and Vandenhorst rapped the table again.

"Quiet, please!" He waited for the conspirators to settle down.

"Before I tell you what I think, let me mention that Doug Pellegrini simply couldn't be here today. If he had made excuses at NSA today, he would really have created suspicions. But I did fill Doug in on the plan I favor, and he's fully supportive." Vandenhorst paused. He surveyed the room. "And now, my friends, let me tell you what I want you to approve, and approve unanimously. I will not need to spell out the arguments why I think as I do. You know them inside out." He had their full attention.

"We undertake the coup before Tom leaves his post, and we do it at the earliest opportunity." He stopped to let his words sink in. "That is, we do *not* wait for the next election. We get into operational mode right now, starting after this meeting. We need about one month to get action-ready, but after that we'll be on standby, awaiting word from Bob O'Brien about when the president and vice president will be exposed at the same time. We have to have at least a couple of days' lead-time. Bob has looked very carefully at our options. He thinks that, unless we get some sudden lucky break and have enough time to move at that time, our first really good opportunity will be in the second week of August. Barring unforeseen circumstances, the president will be on vacation then, almost certainly in Montana. The vice president will be here in D.C. A person on the Secret Service presidential protection detail who Bob thinks might complicate matters for us is very likely to be on vacation at that time, and Bob should be able to create certain circumstances favorable to us. He will also have an easier time making use of persons in the Secret Service who are especially loyal to him. August will be good for other reasons. Many people in the executive branch, on the Hill, and so on, will also be out of town on vacation, which will add to the confusion and disorientation when we make our move."

Vandenhorst's gaze swept over the members of the History Book Club. "So that's it, my friends. We shift to the 'operational mode' NOW. You know what that means: tighter security than ever, but also more contact between the steering committee and the subgroups. This will be the time of maximum danger."

For five seconds nobody tried to speak. Then Vandenhorst added: "As I said, it's this plan or nothing. It's this, or we close down."

Bates's jaw was hanging open. His pale long face had lost what little color it had. He looked desperately in the direction of Pickett, who had again wrapped himself in the shawl and was staring at Vandenhorst with red watery eyes. Bates looked uncertainly at Richard and then raised his hand indicating that he wished to speak.

"No, Robert!" It was Gordon Bunker. "No more comments. We've heard all the arguments."

"But I—"

"Put a cork in it!" Noah Sales snapped under his breath. Lester Pickett broke out in another sneezing and coughing spell.

"Friends," Vandenhorst said, "this is the plan I hope you will approve unanimously. I want you to give your approval right now."

"Herbert, you're behaving like some kind of Mafia boss," Pickett growled.

"I didn't hear that," Vandenhorst said, forcing a smile. "What I would like you to do is this: When I call your name, please indicate your support for the plan by standing up. Then please remain standing. If you have doubts or reservations *we don't need to hear about them*. What we need is your assent. I will call your names in alphabetical order."

Richard could see that Bates fingers were trembling. Bates said, "Herbert, you can't expect us—"

"—Please, Robert, I'm asking you to approve the plan. In fact, you're the first person on our list."

Bates looked around himself almost wild-eyed. "This is not right!" he exclaimed. He looked pleadingly at Richard, his immediate neighbor.

"It's necessary, Robert," Vandenhorst said. All eyes were on Bates.

"Present," he said weakly.

"Robert, this is not a House vote," Vandenhorst said. You're being asked to support the coup."

"I pass."

"OK, I'll let you pass for the moment, but only to let you collect your thoughts before you affirm the plan." Bates again sent a desperate glance in the direction of Pickett.

"Richard, you're next," Vandenhorst announced. Bates turned around so quickly in his chair to look at Richard that his elbow hit the arm of Randy Gates, who sat next to him on the other side. All the others, too, were now looking at Richard.

*Of course*, Richard thought. In these circumstances especially, he did not have to say a word in order to affect the others. Whatever he did would speak loudly. If he did not stand up, he would be the reason why Vandenhorst would abandon the conspiracy.

Really smart, Richard thought to himself. The first person who rejected Vandenhorst's plan would be the one who took it upon him- or herself to destroy the conspiracy. Who would like to have that responsibility and that reputation? Herbert knew what he was doing. He had taken Richard by surprise, but he had not deceived him.

Richard realized in a flash that Vandenhorst's maneuver was cutting right to the heart of the matter. He was forcing the conspirators to recognize that the real issue was not which plan was superior. It was whether they could bring themselves to attempt a coup in the first place, not in theory but in practice. All else was secondary. Both plans were plausible. Richard had to concede that his reservations about plan B had been partly due to a fear of moving from theory to action.

"Richard, I'm waiting for you to approve the plan." Vandenhorst obviously did not take Richard's still being seated as an indication that he was rejecting it.

How does a person choose? Some say that there really is no such thing as choice. We are pushed to act by predispositions and external factors. There is no autonomous self, no free will. Richard was under great pressure, but no inexorable force was pushing him. Having been the victim recently of sometimes ferociously conflicting desires and emotions, he now felt a strange calm. He was alone with himself. He was not weighing arguments. He knew only that he was about to make the most important decision of his life. Was he praying?

"That looks like a 'no' vote," Pickett mumbled behind his shawl.

"Wait, give him some time," Bunker said.

Richard stood up.

The fan of the house heating unit happened to be off. The only sound in the basement was the pulsating humming of the electronic anti-listening device. All in the room knew that a critical event had taken place.

"I endorse the plan," Richard said, "and I call upon the rest of you to make support for it unanimous."

Bates was wide-eyed. His expression was confused and showed extreme anxiety.

"Gordon Bunker," Vandenhorst announced.

Bunker heaved himself out of the sofa and almost hit a pipe in the ceiling as he pulled himself up to his full height. "I endorse the plan."

His vote was no surprise to anybody.

"Lisa DeLeon."

She did not rise, but said quickly: "Herbert, you know that a major issue of resource allocation has not been settled."

Vandenhorst held up a hand. "Lisa, this is not the time to discuss the details of execution. You're being asked to approve the plan."

"You know I don't consider that issue a 'detail.'"

"Hell, here we go again!" It was the loud and irritated voice of Sales. "Can we get on with it?"

"Lisa!"

"I don't want there to be any doubt about how strongly I feel about that allocation of resources."

"I don't think there is," Vandenhorst said. "Now, may we have your approval?"

Lisa DeLeon rose and remained standing.

"Randy Gates."

Gates stood up. "I endorse the plan, but you know I agree with Lisa."

"Robert O'Brien."

O'Brien always wore a dark suit, white shirt and tie, and black shoes. Today, he wore a plaid red shirt, rumpled slacks and sneakers. Would any of his professional colleagues have recognized him?

O'Brien rose and said: "I'm a hundred percent behind the plan. Let's go!"

"Doug Pellegrini cannot vote," Vandenhorst said, "but, I repeat, he's behind the plan."

Richard and the others knew that the next vote, that of Lester Pickett, might decide the future of the conspiracy. His opposition to anything that did not include the Peck scenario was well known, but would he be prepared to sink the conspiracy? All who had voted had endorsed Vandenhorst's plan, and Pickett could be pretty certain that the two who remained on the alphabetical list, Thomas Reed and Noah Sales, would do the same. Bates might follow Pickett.

"Lester, it's your turn," Vandenhorst said. He smiled, "I would greatly appreciate it if you would resist the temptation to give a speech."

There was some nervous laughter as the conspirators turned to watch Pickett. Bunker was already standing in front of the sofa on which Pickett was sitting.

"Don't worry," Pickett said in a hoarse, sniffling voice very different from his normal mellifluous modulation, "I'm in no condition to give any speech. I probably shouldn't be doing anything today, especially not anything of importance." He made no sign of moving, only brought a handkerchief to his face and started to blow his nose.

Noah Sales suddenly got to his feet. "It's not my turn yet," he said, "but I'm ready. I'm in favor of the plan." His square body with its powerful, protruding chest underlined the firmness of his commitment.

Thomas Reed immediately rose and said, "I, too, endorse the plan."

"Thank you, gentlemen, but Senator Pickett has not yet declared himself," Vandenhorst said.

Six persons were standing. Only Vandenhorst at the chairman's table, Bates, and Pickett were still in their seats. Pickett coughed and wiped his nose. His face was flushed, his eyes red.

"Mr. Chairman, will you permit this old senator a very brief comment? I assure you I'll not use the privilege to argue for or against the plan." Pickett was speaking even more slowly than was his custom.

Richard could see that Vandenhorst hesitated. He had not permitted any other statements. But now he nodded to the old giant of the U.S. Senate. He might have concluded that granting the request would do less damage than denying it. He said, "In that case, Lester, go ahead!"

Pickett remained seated as he spoke.

"I just wanted to say that, as you must all understand, this is the most difficult decision of my long life. Who knows what I would've done if I'd been in better health, but for better or worse I've made up my mind." He stopped to blow and wipe his nose again. "Something unusual happened here tonight. I'm not quite sure what it was, but the long and short of it is that I did something that's unusual for me when it comes to really important issues. I changed my mind. Why? I don't quite know why, but it had something to do with finding you, Herbert, and young Bittenberg on the same side. You couldn't very well both be wrong. As for the rest of you conspirators, you just reinforced my change of heart. So, Mr. Chairman, count me in!"

Lester Pickett struggled out of the sofa and to his feat. He stood a little unsteadily, supporting himself against the wall.

"Besides, what the hell, I probably don't have long for this world anyway." There was some strained laughter around the room.

Every conspirator except one was now standing. All eyes were on Robert Bates, who was sitting, looking into his hands on his lap and slowly shaking his head.

Vandenhorst addressed him.

"Robert," he said. "We know how difficult this decision is, but, please, understand that we cannot do without you."

Bates did not move.

"Robert."

Bates looked up. His bony, long face was drawn. With his dark hair combed strictly back and put in place with gel, he looked like a movie caricature of an undertaker.

He stuttered, "I, I—I need more time. I, I—have to consult—"

"—NO, Bob!" It was Pickett giving a low, croak-like shout from the back. It was followed by coughing.

Bates looked back in the direction of Pickett.

"No, Bob," Pickett resumed with difficulty, "you don't need to consult. You're in charge. It's for you to decide!"

Again, Bates slowly shook his head.

Nobody said anything.

Then, as if mustering every ounce of willpower at his disposal, Bates rose slowly to his feet, still shaking his head. He stood. Randy Gates gave him a friendly pat on the back.

From behind came Gordon Bunker's loud voice, "Where the hell's the bourbon?"

# CHAPTER 55

By the time Duparc threw himself into the front passenger seat next to Léger in their Renault, Stephen Ferguson had put about a minute between himself and his pursuers. Léger swore as passing cars boxed them in but then made a daring, screeching turn into traffic.

"I think I saw him heading up Champs-Élysées," Léger said.

By driving audaciously they moved faster than the rest of the rather heavy traffic, and a minute or two later they caught sight of Ferguson's green BMW convertible. They were approaching Place de l'Étoile, the large traffic circle in the middle of which stands the Arc de Triomphe. They saw Ferguson exit the circle and head down the wide, imposing Avenue Foch, which runs eastward from Place de l'Étoile.

"He's probably on his way to his apartment," Duparc said. "He lives on Avenue Foch just a couple of blocks from here."

"That's where he's going," Léger said when he saw Ferguson turn right into the small parallel street that bears the same name. In the summer half of the year the trees and the wide swath of grass between the main roadway of Avenue Foch and this residential street made the latter seem adjacent to a park rather than one of the majestic avenues of Paris.

"What do you suppose it costs to buy one of these apartments?" Léger asked.

"You could probably get a small place for a couple of million Euros. Are you looking for something new, Léger?"

To their surprise Ferguson did not slow down to look for a parking spot near his street address. He went past it and then suddenly turned right and then right again into the street running behind the block in which he lived. He was now heading in the direction opposite the one from which they had come.

"Do you think he's seen us and is trying to shake us off?" Duparc asked.

"No, look, he's turning into a garage. He's entering his building from behind." They stopped.

"I'll bet he thinks he has some safe way of communicating with de la Broderie from his apartment," Duparc said. "Perhaps emailing or texting or phoning using a method we couldn't possibly monitor — perhaps his housekeeper's cell phone."

"Or he's just stopping at home to change his clothes before meeting de la Broderie somewhere," Léger said.

"Leave the car with me here. You go around to the front. We'd better watch the front entrance. But keep out of sight. Call me if you see anything!"

Léger did as he was told.

Sitting in the car watching the exit from the garage, Duparc wondered whether they should be following Ferguson or confront de la Broderie. He called the police in Noisy and was patched through to the retired police sergeant watching the de la Broderie estate.

"All's quiet, sir. An old green Land Rover arrived at 8:15 this morning. I think only the driver was in the car, but I couldn't quite see because of the glare. I've noticed nothing unusual."

"Call me directly if you notice any movement."

Duparc looked at his watch. It would have been possible for Ferguson to contact de la Broderie or Major Dégas from the embassy or from his car. Had there been a pay phone in the reception area of the American Embassy? Had Ferguson told his accomplices to move Richard Bittenberg? But no car had left the Broderie estate. Besides, a very cautious man would not want to use the telephone or email for a sensitive, incriminating conversation. Ferguson would more likely try to arrange a meeting.

"Thank you, Sergeant! Keep your eyes peeled."

Duparc settled in to wait. Without quite taking his eyes off the entrance to the garage, he started reading a newspaper. In his years as a detective he had had much experience keeping suspects under surveillance, but as a now senior detective he seldom needed to carry out such assignments. He turned on the radio to get some music.

The telephone rang. It was Léger.

"I think Ferguson just left the building through the front entrance. He wore a hat and very informal clothing, for him, so I can't be sure, but I'm almost certain. I'm following him. We're walking in the direction of Place de l'Étoile. He could be heading for the subway stop there. He's wearing some kind of wrinkly white summer jacket, a light open shirt, and light beige slacks. His hat seems to be made of straw."

"I'll follow you in the car. Stay on the phone."

Duparc moved over to the driver's seat.

"If he's going to the subway, I guess he'll be trying to shake off any followers first," Léger said. "He just stopped suddenly, to light a cigarette, or a cigar, and he looked behind him in a furtive way. I think I had the time to duck down behind a car."

"I'm just behind you now and can see you," Duparc said. "I'll stay in the car but move ahead on the assumption that he's headed for the subway."

"Wait," Léger said, "he's no longer walking towards Étoile. He just turned left. I'm following."

"Isn't the Argentine Metro station just as close or closer?" Duparc asked. You know the stop on Avenue de la grande Armée?"

"I know it. He may be headed there," Léger said. "Darn, now he's going into some kind of store. I don't want to move any closer. He'd spot me. It's going to be hard to follow him without his noticing me."

"I'll bring the car to where I can see the entrance to the Argentine station," Duparc said. He drove to Avenue de la grande Armée and found an illegal parking spot in the small eastbound lane of the avenue that runs parallel to the main roadway. He could see the entrance to the Metro station through the rear window of the Renault.

Having made another diversionary move, Ferguson did walk to the Argentine Metro stop. Duparc saw him and then Léger disappear downstairs.

"Try to keep up with him," Duparc said, "and let me know in which direction he's traveling. I'll try to catch up with you by car. I hope we don't lose the telephone connection."

"He could easily slip away from me down here," Léger said.

Duparc had just started the engine and was about to pull away from his parking place when he heard Léger's crackling voice.

"I've lost him! I have no idea where he is. We were headed down to the platform for eastbound trains when I last saw him. What should I do?"

"Get on the train and keep looking for him! If you haven't found him after a couple of stations, get out, call me, and I'll pick you up. Stay on the line."

Léger's response was not audible.

Duparc intended to drive eastward along the route of the Metro line. He was signaling to turn into traffic when, in the corner of his eye, he saw a tall dark-haired man in light clothes on the sidewalk some fifty feet behind the Renault on the same side of the street. He was walking next to the wall of the building and was partly hidden behind other pedestrians. He was going east from the Metro stop. Turning his head to look, Duparc saw immediately that it was Ferguson. He had removed his hat. "Clever fellow," Duparc said to himself as he stepped on the brake and backed back into the illegal parking spot that he was leaving.

"Léger!" he barked into the telephone. "Ferguson's got out of the station. He's walking east on Grand Armée. Get out of the Metro quickly!"

But he got no answer. He banged the wheel in frustration. Léger might already be on a train.

Duparc had to decide whether to follow Ferguson on foot or by car. Both had obvious disadvantages, especially the latter. How to drive at the same slow pace as a pedestrian in heavy Paris traffic? He would block other drivers and become the object of loud disapproval. And what to do if Ferguson walked where no car could follow? Duparc decided to get out and walk. He put up a police emergency decal. Ferguson was about sixty yards ahead. He seemed now to be walking faster. He disappeared once behind a kiosk, and Duparc, assuming that Ferguson wanted to check whether he was being followed, quickly hid behind a restaurant baldachin. Within seconds Ferguson walked on. He could have shortened the distance from his home to the present point by at least half by taking a direct route. He was obviously taking pains to evade possible followers.

Suddenly Ferguson turned north off Avenue de la Grande Armée. He was now moving so quickly that Duparc had difficulty pursuing him without revealing himself. Ferguson came to a small traffic circle, where he stepped into a restaurant. Duparc tried to conceal himself in a doorway. He feared that Ferguson might try to exit the restaurant by a back door, but he was back in the street in a minute. He studied his surroundings, but gave no sign of having seen anything suspicious. He walked around the circle to a small Hertz Rent-a-Car shop and went inside.

Duparc moved behind a street corner about fifty yards from Ferguson. He dialed Léger's telephone number. This time he got an immediate response. Léger had just come out of the Metro a couple of stations east of the Argentine station. Duparc quickly filled him in on what had happened.

"Ferguson is now at Place Saint-Ferdinand, a block or so north of Grande Armée. He's inside a Hertz rental place, presumably to get a car. That should take him several minutes. Take a taxi here, but don't stop near the circle. Hurry! I'll see you arrive. I'll look for another cab, in case you'll be too late. If you get here in time I'll let you follow Ferguson, and I'll get our car."

Duparc had just given Léger the instructions, when Ferguson appeared. He walked directly to a blue Citroen that had stopped just outside the Hertz store. How could he have gotten a rental car so quickly? Also, he got into the car on the passenger side. The car took off immediately.

Duparc cursed his own miscalculation. That Citroen was no rental car. It was not a new model, and it was not shining clean. Ferguson had been picked up at an agreed-upon spot. Because of the distance and the angle Duparc had not even been able to see the car's license plate. It disappeared. There was no taxi to be seen.

A blue Citroen! Of course, that was the other Dégas car.

Duparc called Léger again and told him to pick him up in the taxi.

"Ferguson got away. Somebody came for him in the Dégas blue Citroen. We have no chance of catching up with him. He'll be far away by the time you get here."

Duparc went into the Hertz store. He showed his police identification and asked the female attendant about Ferguson's business.

"He wanted to know about weekend specials in September, what different car models would cost, and the like. He browsed in brochures. He didn't seem to have any definite plans."

Duparc knew already. Ferguson had merely wanted to stay out of sight while waiting to be picked up. He was a smooth customer.

Léger was at the wheel when ten minutes later the two detectives drove away from the illegal parking spot on Avenue de la Grande Armée. Although Duparc was not sure what their next step should be, they headed for Evremond. If Ferguson and de la Broderie wanted to meet, they were not likely to do so at the de la Broderie estate, but if Bittenberg had been held there and was to be moved, the estate should be watched more closely.

Duparc dialed the number of the retired policeman posted outside the estate.

"Duparc here. Any movement?"

"No sir. All quiet."

Either de la Broderie had not left for a meeting yet or he had sent somebody in his place, or he would be able to communicate with Ferguson in some other way — or —Duparc hit his forehead with the palm of his hand.

"Why in the world didn't I think of it before?!" he exclaimed. "There could be a second entrance to the estate!"

Léger nodded.

"De la Broderie or anybody else would be able to slip in or out by car that way. Let's check it out."

Duparc called the retired policeman back to ask about a

second entrance, but when he hung up he was as ignorant as before. They would have to do their own checking.

They drove in silence.

"If we find de la Broderie at home, this time we'll put the screws on," Léger said.

"Certainly, but I've a feeling he won't be home."

# CHAPTER 56

In the weeks after the meeting in the basement of Robert O'Brien's rental house the members of the steering committee were thrown into a frenzy of activity to put the conspiracy in standby mode. In groups or individually they met with subgroups or parts of them to rehearse, coordinate, and operationalize existing plans. Members of the conspiracy had long taken elaborate security precautions. Now they had to be nothing less than meticulous, but at the same time a widening circle of individuals needed more and more pieces of an elaborate puzzle. They had entered a stage at which the danger of detection would increase markedly each day.

Vandenhorst had warned the steering committee that, after the decision to execute the plans, some members of the conspiracy were likely to get cold feet. The ambivalence on the steering committee itself would be repeated in some form at the lower levels. Some people might even want to withdraw. Vandenhorst asked Richard, Gordon Bunker, Randy Gates, and Lisa DeLeon to assist him in dealing with such cases. A team of at least two persons would handle any wavering or wayward conspirators. The methods had to be adjusted to the particular case, but might include cajoling, bribing, blackmailing, flattering, and threatening. In a meeting, Richard, Bunker, Gates and DeLeon discussed what to do in case a conspirator became oppositional, got angry and jumped ship.

"One thing going for us in a case like that," Gates said, "is that the person knows that if he goes to the feds, his own life is destroyed. In a national security case even a stool pigeon may have to do some jail time. At best he's placed in protective custody before any trials and eventually in the witness protection program. But he doesn't know the range of the conspiracy. If he squeals and brings many in the conspiracy down, he can be pretty certain that many others have not been apprehended. They could be in a good position to locate him. So, if he's really angry, he'll probably prefer to just cut his ties to us and go into hiding."

"But a hostile person poses a terrible problem," Bunker said.

"Yeah, we can't take a risk like that," DeLeon commented.

"What choice do we have?" Richard asked.

"We take care of the problem," Lisa DeLeon said.

"Meaning?"

"We eliminate the problem. Do I have to draw you a picture?"

Richard was startled by DeLeon's bluntness. He never liked to be reminded of the violence that might be required for the coup to succeed. "Wait a minute!" he exclaimed. "Even if we thought this was the only way to handle the problem, a murder investigation would be the last thing we want. It could put the police right on our tail."

"Give me some credit for intelligence, Richard," DeLeon muttered. "The person would obviously have to disappear."

"Disappear? And who's our expert on making people disappear?" he said sarcastically.

"I think that can be handled," Gates said matter-of-factly.

Richard didn't want to discuss any details, only said, "But a disappearance, too, might point investigators in our direction."

"Well, what do you prefer?" DeLeon asked. "A stool pigeon who sings his head off or the police issuing a missing person's advisory?"

"I hope we never have to deal with that kind of situation."

Richard had felt harried and mentally worn out for a long time. After the decision to implement the plans for the coup, the conspiratorial activities consumed even more of his time. There were frequent meetings, many with people whom he had never met before. He traveled to Chicago and Los Angeles. For a meeting with an investment banker and an industrialist in Chicago he linked up with Vandenhorst, who arrived a day earlier than Richard on a different airline and from a different Washington airport. Some meetings produced high pressure and raised voices, and the fear of detection hung over them all. Richard's already taut nerves tightened even further.

Richard had to struggle to finish his courses for the spring semester. He cut corners at the university in ways that in his earlier existence he would have considered inexcusable. He put Ron Turello to proctor the final examination in his undergraduate course and do all of the grading for its thirty students. He told Turello that he was in a real bind at the moment and would make it up to him in time. At least Turello was finished with the course work for the doctorate and did not need to finish any papers of his own for the semester. But this was time stolen from his dissertation project. In the case of his graduate seminar, Richard did something he had never done before but that he suspected some other faculty members of doing routinely: He gave the long papers that the students had submitted a merely browsing reading and submitted grades based on that reading and impressions he had of the students from class. His weak excuse was that in his experience the quality of the papers almost always confirmed the opinion he had already formed. He wrote no comments on the papers, something he had always done before. He did not attend the university commencement, sending a profuse excuse by email to a doctoral student whose dissertation he had directed.

The pressure lightened only slightly after the semester had ended. The members of the steering committee and especially Vandenhorst were used to making large claims on his time because of the assumption that he was in better control of his schedule than conspirators who had 8-6 jobs. Richard would supposedly have an easier time making unplanned trips around town or beyond. During the summer break serious scholars long to settle down to real, sustained work on their research and writing projects. Some of them work longer hours and more intensely then than during the semesters. But now Vandenhorst and the others took full advantage of his not being tied up by regular university responsibilities. Richard had let his scholarship slide for a long time, and now he rarely even picked up a book or article to read. He was dispatched, it seemed, whenever another member of the steering committee had difficulties making time. He was asked to put out fires and handle other emergencies, usually together with one or two others. He was pulled into virtually every aspect of the conspiracy, sometimes ending up in situations with which he was not well equipped to deal. He became a roving troubleshooter and learned more about the scope and details of the conspiracy than anybody except Vandenhorst.

For the sake of his sanity he had to spend time with his family. When he did, he tried to give them his undivided attention. At home he affected a demeanor of tranquility. Acting as if he were calm and collected actually helped him to relieve the terrible pressure. Helen seemed eager to help him relax. That scene in the kitchen, which was etched on his memory, might have receded in her mind. With a note of concern in her voice she did mention a couple of times that he appeared awfully busy for this time of year. He had to be unusually inventive thinking up explanations for his frequent comings and goings. His standard excuse for leaving the house was that he had reached a stage in research for his next book when he needed to spend much time at the National University Library or the Library of Congress. He hoped that these explanations made Helen think of him as being at leisure in the libraries, but he sensed her disapproval.

He feared the time when she would finally force him to face

the desirability of a family summer vacation. He could not possibly commit to an extended trip, especially not in August. How could he fend her off without bringing on another emotional eruption? His unwillingness to decide on a time and a place would annoy her greatly, because of her concern for him but, primarily, out of concern for Anne and John. His resistance would bring back all her pent-up frustration and bring it to a new pitch. He dreaded the moment.

Every year of their marriage Helen had had difficulty pinning him down on a possible vacation trip. Commitments and plans were always crowding him and backing up behind him, and he simply was not able to enjoy so-called vacations the way others did. After a couple of days at the beach or on the road, his conscience started bothering him. There was so much work to be done, and here he was doing nothing but lounging about with his family, "relaxing," perhaps doing some professional reading. He wanted to return to his writing, not just because of problems of conscience but also because he liked that work more than anything else. Writing was in a sense more tiring and painful than anything else, but when the work went well it was also highly gratifying. Vacation time had to be good for him as for everybody else. In a way he wanted more of it. He did enjoy being with Helen and the children. Helen looked good on the beach, and they liked their moments of privacy in relaxed circumstances. Still, he had to make an effort to stick the family vacation out without shows of frustration.

The question that he had feared was raised late one Saturday afternoon in the middle of June when he returned with John and Anne from their neighborhood swim and tennis club. He had played tennis with John while Anne enjoyed herself with friends in and around the pool.

When the children disappeared upstairs to shower Helen handed him a glass of beer.

"You don't want me to smell up this kitchen," he said. "I need to shower too. I'm drenched. It's ninety degrees outside, and John's getting pretty tough in tennis."

She came up to him and gave him a kiss. "There's nothing wrong with your smell, and you have plenty of time before dinner. Sit down, buddy." She pushed him playfully onto one of the chairs around the kitchen table.

"Uh-oh, what are you up to now?"

"I wanted to ask you about this year's vacation."

Here it comes, he thought. He tensed up, but tried not to let his anxiety show.

"And you have some ideas?"

"Yes, but I want to hear what you might have in mind."

In his mind diplomacy had no difficulty winning out over frankness, and he said, "Well, yes, I do have a couple of ideas." He knew that she didn't really expect much from him by way of suggestions and that she had already invested considerable time thinking about a plan. She would listen to ideas he might have, but not really so much out of interest in his opinion as because she liked talking about the topic of a vacation.

"And what thoughts have you had?" Did he detect a touch of sarcasm or irony in her voice? Did she assume that he did not really have any suggestions and would merely try to wing it now to humor her? But Richard had actually thought of what he might say when the subject came up. He had a vacation plan that was marginally compatible with remaining active in the conspiracy and that might also help isolate his family from the coup.

"Well, we haven't been back to Charleston in quite a while. My mother hasn't seen us since she was here last summer, and we haven't seen Hubert and Susan and their families for a good deal longer than that. John and Anne should get to know their cousins better. I have the idea that we might head to Hilton Head or something similar for some beach time and make a side trip to Charleston or perhaps link up with them at Hilton Head."

Helen did not evince any reaction.

"You said that you have a couple of ideas. What's the other one?"

Did she think that she was calling a bluff? Did she expect him now to flounder?

"We've thought for a long time that we should do something with the Prestons. Perhaps it's time. They may want to join us at Hilton Head or somewhere in the vicinity that strikes their fancy."

Helen looked at Richard. Was that surprise on her face? She probably hadn't expected fairly well formed ideas for the family vacation. She was probably pleased, although she was bound to have a plan of her own.

"Hmmm. Well." She looked cheerful. "That's worth thinking about."

She said nothing more for the moment but turned to some dinner preparations. Richard knew that this was the time for him to show curiosity about her thinking.

"So what's your idea?"

Darn it, he thought immediately, why had he said "idea," in the singular. That suggested that she had only one idea and that she was wedded to it. That was almost certainly the case, but she probably didn't like that he could see right through her. She didn't want to appear willful or calculating.

But she just smiled. Having put a casserole in the oven, she poured herself some wine and seated herself next to him.

"I have a wonderful idea, Richard. And as you might imagine I've thought about it quite a bit."

He smiled at her. "I could imagine. What is it?"

"You know we've talked for years about what we might do in the future. And now I think Anne is old enough really to enjoy what we had in mind. I know that John would."

"I get it," Richard said. He saw big trouble coming. This was an idea that he could not accept, or even appear to accept. To seem to go along and then to cancel the trip that Helen envisioned would cost them a lot of money. But he couldn't bring himself to prick her balloon. She was so obviously happy contemplating the trip of her dreams.

"What is it that you get?"

"Your idea. You want to go to Europe, don't you?"

"Yes, Richard, yes!" She moved closer to him. He could read the excitement on her face. "I have a travel route all figured out. We go to Paris first for a few days and then we see various places on the way to Rome."

"Ahhh!"

"What do you think?"

"It's a lovely idea, in theory, but I would need to think about it. You know how hard it can be for me to be away for a long time. I have various commitments on top of my research, and I don't quite know yet what my summer will be like."

She had probably expected his reluctance to commit himself, but she was disappointed nevertheless that he had not embraced her plan with enthusiasm.

"OK, Richard, but it's already very late to order airline tickets and make hotel reservations. If you like the idea, I should get to work on it very soon, right now as a matter of fact."

He felt all the worse because now he would have to string her along to avoid another scene. He said: "How long a trip did you figure on and when?"

She knew that one week of complete vacation was usually his limit. "I was thinking about two weeks, but I suppose we could squeeze a trip like that into ten days. And I was thinking about late July or August."

August. Of course! That was the time when the coup was most likely to be executed. A trip to Europe was simply out of the question. A trip to Hilton Head or Charleston was much preferable, if only in theory. Under that vacation plan he would at least be just a couple of hours by air from Washington. Once he knew when the coup would be attempted he could interrupt the vacation, tell Helen that it was due to an emergency, ask her not to ask any questions, and simply leave the family where they were. They would have extended family not far away. But this abstract scenario, too, was unrealistic. The conspiracy probably could not spare him in the week or so before the coup attempt. The steering committee would be spending all available time getting ready. None of the members who had regular jobs would schedule any vacation time in August.

Yet Richard would prefer to have his family out of Washington when the time came. If a vacation trip to Hilton Head and Charleston had been planned, he might at the last moment ask her to leave with the children on her own. She would be very upset, but he might tell her very obliquely about some big complication about which he simply could not say anything. He would tell her that he loved her deeply and ask her, please, to trust him.

"I have been thinking about this trip for a long time," she said, "but I hesitated to bring it up. I know what you are like when it comes to being away for more than a few days. But think about it, Richard! This could be the kind of break that you've needed for years. You would be away, out of reach of telephones and email. You could get your mind off of everything that stresses you. You could really rest. Richard, it would be so good for you. And the kids would love it."

For a moment he thought that he would not be able to stop himself from breaking down. Helen wanted only the best for him, and he kept deceiving her, now more than ever. Was there really any excuse?

He collected himself and said: "I'll think about it, but this summer may be a little too crowded for me. Next year might be better. Hilton Head or something like it might be best this time. But I'll think about it."

She turned away. He heard a muted "OK."

Just after lunch the following day Richard was in the basement trying to straighten out his study, which suffered from protracted neglect. The scrambler phone rang. He took it out of its desk drawer.

"It's Tom." It was Thomas Reed, who had become one of Richard's best friends on the steering committee. Even when on the scrambler telephone the conspirators were very restrictive about using names, and they spoke very concisely and obliquely and sometimes in code.

"Yes?"

"We have a situation. For weeks we've tried to get an important and urgent meeting to come off. We finally got everything together for this afternoon at 3:00, and now I positively cannot make it. Sailor just called to tell me that he's come down with the flu or food poisoning." He was using the code name for retired admiral Gordon Bunker. "He's puking his innards out. But we just can't postpone this meeting any longer. Richard, could you fill in for sailor and me? Very short notice, I know. Sorry. But Bob O. will be there and lead the meeting, so you won't be the only one there from central office." "Central office" was their name for the steering committee, and Bob O. was Robert O'Brien, the deputy director of the Secret Service.

"It's Sunday afternoon, Tom, and I never get to spend any time with my family."

"If it wasn't so important, I wouldn't have called you."

Richard sighed. "How long will the meeting take?"

"Difficult to say. A few hours. The meeting's had to be postponed several times, and there's a lot of ground to cover."

"OK, Tom. I'll do it."

"Great! Thanks, Richard! If you go to 'D,' Bob O. will swing by and pick you up at 2:30." "D" was their code name for a spot near the Dupont Circle subway station in central Washington, a few blocks north of the White House. Richard looked at his watch. He would have only forty-five minutes to get there. He would drive to the National University campus, park, and take the subway from there.

"And, Richard."

"Yes."

"Wear something informal."

"OK."

It was time to lie to Helen again. He found her in the garden on her knees digging in a flowerbed. She was about to plant some bushes. It was another hot day. Summer was far along.

"Helen, I need to go to the university for a while."

She looked up, surprise and disapproval in her eyes.

"Today!? Richard, it's *Sunday*!"

"I know, but I've hit this snag in what I'm writing, and it's driving me crazy. I can't move on unless I check something out in the library."

"Can't you work on something else?"

"Helen, I'm all wrapped up in this section of my manuscript. I need to get this question answered, or I won't be thinking about anything else until I do. If the answer is what I think it is, it shouldn't take all that long. Then I can relax."

The "relax" comment was a nice touch, he thought. He watched for her reaction. She simply sighed and shrugged her shoulders.

"Besides, the children are at the pool."

She got to her feet. She had some dirt on her nose, her hair was stringy and she was sweaty, but she looked beautiful. It ran through his mind that he could stay home.

She gave him a light kiss on the lips.

"Are you going to the university dressed like that? That's not like you." He was wearing a sports shirt, summer slacks and dockers."

"I don't feel like changing. What I want is an answer to my research question." Another nice touch, he thought. He had become an accomplished liar.

He drove to campus, parked and walked a block to the campus subway stop. Waiting underground for the train he heard a voice.

"Dr. Bittenberg!?" He started. He always worried about being followed. Was he about to be picked up by the FBI? But what he had heard was a youngish female voice. She would be one of at least two agents. Why would the FBI let a young woman take the lead in arresting a fairly large and somewhat athletic man?

He turned and saw a female doctoral student from his department.

"I've never seen you dressed like that!"

"Hi, Denise — oh, I'm just running an errand. What are you doing on campus? The semester's long over."

"A doctoral student never rests, don't you know?"

"Of course, I remember it very well."

The arrival of her train, which headed into Maryland, put an end to the conversation.

On the way to Dupont Circle he realized that he had forgotten his cell phone. What would he do if he needed to call Helen to tell her that he would be running late? He would have to borrow a phone.

Getting out of the subway station he was five minutes early. He strolled as if at random towards point "D," a street corner just a block away. The Dupont Circle area was popular among young professionals. It had many restaurants, coffee shops, and little stores. But it was a sunny Sunday afternoon, and few people were about. The peacefulness of this city scene did not reach him. He wondered whether he had been followed out of the subway.

He had barely arrived at the appointed street corner when he saw a gray Ford Taurus pull out of a driveway half a block away and head in his direction. Was this the FBI? Had the time now finally come for him to be arrested?

The car stopped in front of him. The driver waved. It was Robert O'Brien. Richard got in, and O'Brien drove off even before Richard had closed the passenger door. The car radio was on as was the air-conditioner. Richard didn't think that he had ever been in a car with one of the conspirators without the irritation of background noise.

Richard looked in surprise at O'Brien. This man, who seemed always to be in a suit and tie, was wearing shorts and a colorful Hawaiian shirt.

"Where are we going? To a picnic or to the beach?"

"You'll see." O'Brien headed south towards the Washington Ellipse.

"The car should be pretty safe," O'Brien said. "It's my own, and I had it swept earlier today. I'm glad you could make it, Richard. I shouldn't be the only one from central office at the meeting. It's been postponed before, and we have to have it. August is still our target date, but we have to be ready to seize any opportunity before then."

"What's the subject?"

"How to handle the people who are arrested in the first few hours of the coup."

"Oh, that." Various aspects of the topic, most especially who should be arrested and by whom, had been discussed at length in various meetings.

"This time all the key people involved outside of central office will be there. I don't think you have met Bruce Gaddy or Stanley Globowski. Bruce is an assistant director of the D.C. office of the FBI. Stanley's the head of the House division of the Capitol Hill Police. I think you know Bradley Donnelly, the D.C. police captain, and Walt Gregory, who heads the Washington office of Tony Springhalter's security firm. These guys have been making plans for a long time, coordinating with Tom Reed, Sales, and me, but so much is unpredictable, and in the first few hours of the coup we don't have many people to guard those who have been rounded up. We're hoping to be able to use some detectives and policemen and Capitol Police officers before Tom's troops can assist. It will be quite a while before National Guard troops from Maryland arrive so that more of our guys are freed up. As with everything else, a lot depends on the success of our disinformation campaign and the acting ability of our people. There have been disagreements about how to transport prisoners and where to warehouse them. But at least Tom has now decided that a section of the D.C. armory is the place for people-in-the way or who've been arrested because they happened to be in the wrong place. He has some command authority over the armory. But there are disagreements about just what to do with the key individuals who've been earmarked for pickup. They are to be taken first to that old abandoned prison in southwest D.C. Donnelly's the one who will arrange to have it available."

"I'm hardly the best man to comment on issues like that."

"Perhaps not on the details and practicalities, but you know the larger picture and you know how Hubert, Gordon, Tom, and Noah think, and you can help me listen and bring issues back to them."

As they crossed Constitution Avenue, they noticed crowds on the mall near the Washington Monument.

"Dammit!," O'Brien muttered, "another of those protests. You can never count on having a straight shot any more when driving in this town. I'm sick and tired of the demonstrations. Who is it this time?"

"Looks like state workers from around the country."

"Why the hell don't they protest in their state capitals?"

"You know why. They want the federal government to save their jobs and benefits."

They had to drive slowly because the crowds had spilled into the road. O'Brien used the horn and got glares and shouts in response. They passed the Washington Monument and the Holocaust museum, heading down Maine Avenue towards the so-called Washington Channel with its fish and seafood market, restaurants and marinas. The channel ends where the Anacostia and Potomac rivers flow together and the widening Potomac River heads south into the Chesapeake Bay.

They had almost reached Fort McNair, the site of the National Defense University and National War College, when O'Brien turned right towards the channel and into an ill-defined parking lot. Richard saw a small harbor and marina that he had never noticed. O'Brien found the parking lot full, uttered an expletive, and parked the car in an unmarked spot. "It's Sunday," he muttered. "They'd better not tow my car." The two men got out.

"Come with me," O'Brien said. Amazed at the anomaly of O'Brien's beachwear, Richard followed him as he steered towards a key where several boats were docked. One was a somewhat rundown yacht in white plastic and wood, which seemed to be about fifty feet long. A couple of men were standing on the dock next to the boat, and a couple of others were visible on board. One was Hick.

O'Brien and Richard went on board, and O'Brien introduced him to the men he didn't know. The main part of the cabin was a rather spacious and air-conditioned combined stateroom, kitchen and cockpit. Beyond it up front was a bedroom and a half bath. Behind it was an outside area and a small rear cabin with another bedroom. Somebody had put out an ice chest with soft drinks and beer.

Just after 3:00 PM, Bradley Donnelly, the police captain whom Richard had met before, came running out on the key and jumped aboard. "Hell, no parking places left, not even illegal ones," he puffed. "I had to put the car a block and a half away at one of those restaurants."

They cast off. Walt Gregory was at the wheel. O'Brien told Richard that it was Gregory's boat. Hick and a couple of the others kept the yacht from sliding into other boats as they backed out and left the marina. Soon they were out on the Potomac.

"We could wave to Tom Reed from here," O'Brien said, indicating one of the large red brick private houses reserved for military brass on the grounds of Fort McNair on the shore of the Potomac River.

There were plenty of other boats on the water. Summer had clearly come.

For a few minutes the conspirators stood in the sun looking around and drinking while Gregory headed south and into the middle of the river. They passed the Bolling Air Force base. The river was now so wide that it might have been a large lake or bay.

O'Brien clapped his hands. "OK, everybody. Let's go inside and get down to business."

Looking around the stateroom Richard was reminded how much he had always liked the seasoned, varnished wood on boats, ships and European trains.

"Please turn off your cell phones," O'Brien said. "We want to make it as hard as possible for anybody to track us. And no sensitive conversations outside, please. Hick's swept the boat carefully, and he says that with the vibrations of the engine, it would be very difficult to listen in from the outside—assuming anybody knows we're here. And as I speak Hick's keeping a lookout for any suspicious activity."

Within minutes they were deep in discussion, going down an extensive agenda. Richard was quiet and listening except when he could provide information about which O'Brien was uncertain. Richard was impressed by O'Brien's way of conducting the meeting.

It was not his first time, Richard thought. He was blunt and direct, but never unpleasant. He let the others speak but did not let anybody become long-winded. He kept the pressure on to make decisions. When arguments got intense he knew how to defuse some of the stress. He brokered compromises, put a stop to a threatening quarrel, and settled one fractious issue by decree, citing the authority of central office.

The proceedings were reassuring for what they showed of careful planning, but they also made Richard uneasy. Every time he came face to face with the need for violence, he worried not just about the coup going wrong but also about innocent people losing their lives.

Walt Gregory and Bruce Gaddy, the FBI man, took turns at the helm. After an hour and a half they were still heading south, and Richard realized that, even if they were to change course right then, they could be back at Washington harbor no sooner than 6:00 PM. And then it would be another hour before he was home in Bethesda. He was going to miss Sunday dinner with the family. More lying, more unpleasantness. He whispered a question to O'Brien about the duration of the meeting.

O'Brien looked at his watch, thought for a moment, and said to Walt Gregory: "Why don't you start thinking about turning back? We can always cruise around closer to D.C. if we need more time."

A few minutes later O'Brien called for a break. The conspirators got drinks from the ice chest. A couple lit cigarettes. They stood outside seemingly enjoying the afternoon on the water. It would not be long before the increasing humidity of the Washington summer made it less pleasant to be outside. People in other boats thought they saw some men on a relaxing Sunday outing on the water, but appearances could not be more deceiving, Richard thought. These men were wholly wrapped up in the momentous events they were planning.

Richard stood next to Bradley Donnelly, the police captain. He looked to be about fifty-five years old. He had a square, lined face and piercing blue eyes. He had graying blond hair. He was stockily built and was about the same height as Richard.

"How long have you been with the D.C. police department?" Richard asked.

"Thirty-five years, if you can believe it. I was born in D.C. I started out as a beat cop and then went back for more education. I could have retired with a full pension long ago, but what would I do? I don't want another career in 'security,' or 'protection,'" he said, marking the quotation marks with his fingers. "I don't want to babysit some company executive or some company. I'm a cop, and I'm too set in my ways."

"And you don't want to just retire, travel, take it easy."

"My wife would like that, she says, but I can't see the point of it. I'm where I belong. I'm pretty good at what I do. I run a good, pretty clean team of detectives, and I like getting the bad guys. You wouldn't believe how bad some of them are. And now I'll be able to get some of the worst ones, the big boys, the s.o.b.s who're selling out this country."

The meeting got back to order. They continued hammering out decisions. Many had to do with the danger that Noah Sales's Marines might be slow to arrive in D.C. and late to disperse in the early stages of the coup. There would then be very few people to handle tasks that would be hard to manage even without lack of personnel. They were discussing how to separate people who had been arrested when Bruce Gaddy spoke up. He was in his late fifties, had cropped gray hair, and fit the stereotype of the clean-cut FBI man.

"We keep dodging one question," he said.

"Which one?" O'Brien asked.

"What to do if we have difficulty controlling some of the people we've arrested. I'm especially worried about the transportation from the point of arrest to the prison."

"We've been over that issue."

"Not really. We need to talk about what we do if one or more of the arrested people try to make a run for it. We may be too short of people to chase after them."

"What's the problem?"

"What do we do?"

"I would like to know the same thing," Donnelly said.

"I would have thought the answer is pretty obvious," O'Brien answered.

"Oh yeah?" Gaddy said.

"You shoot. What choice have you got?"

"If there are just a couple of guards and one person tries to run, it could start a stampede," Gaddy said.

"So first you fire in the air, or, if there isn't time, you shoot to stop them."

Gaddy and Donnelly did not want to leave the subject. "You realize," Donnelly said, "that some of the people we're relying on for help don't really know what's happening. They're simply carrying out the orders of superiors they trust. If they are ordered to shoot in these circumstances, which will be very different from anything in their experience, they are likely to hesitate or even resist."

O'Brien's answer was emphatic: "That's why the people in charge have to show no hesitation whatsoever. They have to lead by example and show no tolerance of a refusal to follow orders."

"Meaning what?" Gaddy said.

"If worst comes to worst, you do what you do with soldiers who try to run away in a war."

"What if the other helpers don't like what they see?"

"That's why clear, emphatic leadership is needed. You don't for a moment leave anybody in doubt about what's expected. You show unyielding firmness. You've got several things on your side. Our disinformation campaign will be well underway, and you'll do your own part in that regard. If word hasn't reached the helpers yet, you tell them that the president and vice president have been murdered. News about the devastating explosion at the Capitol will be spreading and illustrate that you are fighting ruthless enemies who are everywhere. You impress on the helpers that the U.S. is in a state of emergency and that they must carry out your orders immediately and to the letter to avert disaster. You can also count on a maximum of confusion."

"Many of us will only have handguns—not very effective in this kind of situation," Donnelly said.

"I know," O'Brien said, "but you'll have some shotguns, and some of my guys will help you out. They'll have submachine guns. As soon as Tom's troops have deployed around town, they'll be freed up and you'll be shored up. And then Sales's Marine's will stabilize the situation further."

Stanley Globowski, a portly man with a round face and tiny eyes, spoke: "I'm worried about some U.S. Capitol Police getting into firefights with the good guys."

"You'll have to minimize that risk by issuing very firm orders to your people. Remember, Stan, *you* are the boss, and they have no idea what's happening. Some of their buddies may have died in the explosion. Some will be involved in the rescue effort. And that's where the attention of your superiors is likely to be focused. If one of those superiors seems to be getting in the way of our arrests or of anything else we are trying to do, you take care of the problem. The same for any others who make trouble. Take' em out! Again, there'll be a lot of confusion, and we'll be the only ones who know what we are doing and what's happening."

Richard had swallowed hard during earlier meetings in the conspiracy, but he had never before felt such discomfort about the concrete particulars of the coup. These discussions were bringing home not just the uncertainties that had to be faced, but also the ruthlessness that might be employed. He was taken aback by O'Brien's brutal, callous language. Had he really meant what he said, or was he indulging in bluster and bravado?

The conspirators turned to other subjects. Outside, the sun was starting to come down. The intermittent noise of airplanes above was a sign that they were returning to the D.C. area. Airplanes were coming in for landing at Reagan National Airport. They were touching down just over the horizon. In the far distance in the early evening haze Richard could make out National Cathedral on Mount St. Alban's.

O'Brien was instructing the gathering about the use of the D.C. armory during the coup when Hick suddenly stuck his head in the cabin, a worried look on his face.

"We may have trouble!" he exclaimed. "A large boat of some sort is coming up fast behind us. It's white. It may be a large yacht, but it's got all kinds of masts. It looks military to me. It may just be heading in the same general direction as us, but it could be trying to catch up with us."

"OK, guys!" O'Brien shouted, rising to his feet. "Get some drinks, mill about, admire the view! Remember, this is the spring outing of the John Wayne movie club. Don't look concerned, and don't look too much behind us."

Richard estimated that their yacht was doing about eight knots. To judge by the bow swell of the larger boat, it was doing close to twenty. It was now about six hundred feet behind them.

"Don't change your speed or course!" O'Brien said to Walt Gregory, who was at the helm.

Hick, who was sitting on the roof of the stateroom looking through a pair of binoculars but trying to seem interested in nothing in particular, said: "I see uniforms on that boat. And I can see a gun turret up front."

"Damn," O'Brien said under his breath.

"They're right in our wake," Gregory said. "Doesn't look good."

"Be cool, Walt," O'Brien said, "we're just on an outing. Relax. And you know the routine, if we're arrested." And to the others he said in a louder voice: "How about some smiles and some laughter? Have some more beer."

"I've kept the radio off the whole trip to make it harder to track us," Gregory said.

"Keep it off."

When the pursuer was only three hundred feet behind them,

a metallic voice over a loudspeaker cut through the motor noise and chilled them to their bones: "Cabin cruiser, please stop!"

"Do as they say," O'Brien commanded. Gregory followed his order. They slowed to steering speed.

"It's the Coast Guard," Hick announced. "There are several people on deck, all in uniforms."

The conspirators exchanged distraught, uncertain glances.

"Dammit!" Bradley Donnelly exclaimed. "Look ahead, at twelve o'clock, three hundred yards, right in our way. That looks like a D.C. harbor police patrol boat. The black one. It's just sitting there waiting for us."

Hick turned around and looked through his binoculars at the black boat. "You're right, it's the police."

So that is how it ends, Richard thought. He felt a deep, burning disappointment mixing with anger and frustration. The all-important cause for which he had worked so long and so hard was ruined. He and the others had wasted huge amounts of time, energy, and worry to no avail. All those security precautions had been in vain. Now would come a long period of shame and disgust and depression. Helen and the children would be devastated.

Somewhere in the midst of these dark feelings Richard also felt an odd sense of relief. At least now that old, growing, almost unbearable pressure would finally be off—no more of this terrible tension, anxiety, and exhaustion. There would come a different, less acute kind of pain, personal disgrace and a sort of numbness.

"Now look friendly!" O'Brien admonished. What's the point, Richard thought.

A Coast Guard cutter considerably larger than Gregory's yacht came up alongside, towering over the conspirators. Hick had been right. It might have been a large yacht. It was white and rather sleek. But it had lots of antennae and other gear up top. It also had that gun up front and a couple of heavy machine guns in the back. Richard was glad to see that none of them was manned. The conspirators were obviously expected to surrender without a fight. They would of course be foolish to resist. Five uniformed Guardsmen could be seen on deck. So far they were hiding their weapons. The skipper must be eager to avoid a confrontation and bloodshed. He was probably under orders to take the conspirators alive, in a condition to tell what they knew about the larger conspiracy. Perhaps the Coast Guard was supposed to escort the cabin cruiser to the police boat.

The skipper of the Coast Guard cutter—a lieutenant commander, Richard could see—had come out from the bridge and addressed them:

"Sorry to bother you," he called, "but you seem to be coming from the Chesapeake. Did you by any chance see a light blue cigar, one of those big speedboats? It was reported stolen up in D.C. a few hours ago, and it headed south."

Richard was at first incredulous. He had already begun to adapt psychologically to the failure of the conspiracy. Had his mind, refusing to accept reality, played a trick on him and changed the commander's real words into innocuous verbiage? But the demeanor of the skipper and his crew matched his words. He had actually said what Richard thought he had heard. Did the Coast Guard skipper notice any of the emotional sea change that had to have swept though the denizens of the yacht?

Walt Gregory, at the wheel of the cabin cruiser, called from the cockpit, whose side window and roof he had opened to be able to communicate with the cutter: "Sorry, we've not been that far away. We left D.C. at 3:00 today for an afternoon outing, and we're on our way back. I know what you mean by a cigar, but we haven't seen anything like that. Or have any of you?" he shouted to his passengers.

A couple of them shook their heads.

Gregory spread his hands in a gesture of regret.

The Coast Guard skipper gave a light salute and called: "Have a good evening, gentlemen." He was turning to get back to the bridge when he thought of something and shouted: "Go easy on that beer now!"

He must have found the laughter from the cabin cruiser a little heavier than expected.

The Coast Guard cutter and the D.C. police patrol boat must have been in radio communication, for within a couple of minutes they saw the black boat heading away.

Richard looked at O'Brien, who returned his gaze, shrugged his shoulders, and smiled. You had to admire his calm. This was the same man who had just ordered no mercy for people who might complicate the coup.

# CHAPTER 57

As Duparc and Léger approached the gate at the entrance to the Broderie estate they located the car of the retired police sergeant on stakeout duty. It had been pulled off the road among some bushes a hundred yards away from the gate on the opposite side of the road. It might have been missed by an inattentive passerby. The detectives stopped their car on the curb, got out and found the policeman standing with his cell phone behind some trees closer to the gate. He was a gray-haired sixty-year-old with a heavy, drooping moustache and the belly of a not very active retiree. Duparc introduced himself and his companion.

"Anything happen?"

"No, sir. I would've called you."

"And you still don't remember anything about a possible back entrance to the estate?"

"No sir. I've been thinking about your question, but I just haven't come up with anything. I worked in these parts for twenty years, but I don't remember another entrance or road."

"Do you know the baron?"

"Not really. He kept to himelf pretty much. But I saw him occasionally in the village."

"Does he have any particular reputation?"

"Well, pretty good, I guess. But he seems to be a rather private person, doesn't have much to do with local business or politics, except I heard he sells some of his wine to the local restaurants and a grocery store."

"What about his helper, Major Dégas?"

"I do know him, but not well. Moved here a few years ago. He's former French Legion. You can tell he was an officer. Speaks and moves in that military way, you know. Seems efficient. Probably a pretty tough customer after that kind of career. He's gotten involved in politics here. Wants to keep the Muslims out. I heard he plans to run for the council. He'll get my vote."

"How much work does he do for the baron?"

"Don't know."

Duparc thanked the policeman and asked him to report any

movement. The two Paris detectives returned to their car and drove up to the entrance to the Broderie estate. It took a long time before anybody answered the signal on the intercom. A female voice said: "*Oui.*"

When Duparc introduced himself and asked to see the baron, he was told that the baron was not at home. The woman claimed not to know when he would return.

"Would your husband know?" Duparc asked.

"He's not here. He's working in the garden."

"Please get him, so that I can talk to him."

"I can't leave what I'm doing."

"Then let us in, and I'll talk to your husband myself."

There was silence.

"Madame?"

"We are not allowed to admit anybody."

"Surely you admit people all the time, and you know who we are — the police."

The line went dead.

Duparc used the buzzer again.

No answer.

Duparc dialed de la Broderie's telephone number. After several rings, the woman answered.

"Madame, this is Henri Duparc, the police chief inspector, still at the gate. I need to talk to you and your husband."

A click announced that she had hung up.

"OK," Duparc said. "Let's see if there is another way into the estate by car."

They spent the next half hour trying to circle the estate and looking for other ways of leaving or entering. They found a few roadways or paths and tried them, but they either led to other farms or residences or just petered out where vehicles could move no further. They eventually found themselves back at the closed gate.

"Let's go around again," Duparc said. "Perhaps we can ask someone."

They had exited the paved local road somewhere behind the estate and were exploring a small dirt road for the second time when they met a tractor. There was not enough room for two vehicles.

Duparc asked Léger to stop and walked up to the driver of the tractor, a thin, dark-haired man of middle age wearing a dirty black beret. A cigarette was dangling from his lips.

"I'm sorry, Monsieur, we have lost our way. We're trying to get to the de la Broderie estate."

The man looked at Duparc with surprise and suspicion.

"We're supposed to see the baron," Duparc said. "We've come from Paris on important business." He did not want to pull out his identification badge. The man on the tractor might not react well to snooping detectives who were not even from the area.

The man looked at the car and Léger sitting in the driver's seat.

"What kind of business?"

Duparc now took out his identification card and handed it to the man. He squinted to read it.

"We're going to ask the count for assistance with a very important case."

The farmer looked noncommittal, but not unfriendly.

"My brother's a policeman in Lyon," he said.

"Really. That's far away from home, isn't it?" Duparc said.

"He wanted the city life."

"He probably got a rougher life, too," Duparc said.

The farmer nodded, then said, "But what are you doing here, on this road? The entrance to the Broderie grounds is way over on the other side." He made a gesture indicating the general direction of the gated entrance and the need to jump over a large territory. 'You have to get back to the main road, turn right, and then veer east for several kilometers to get to where you want to be."

"Is there no other way — a back way perhaps?"

The man on the tractor shook his head.

"You wouldn't want to try that way."

"Which way?"

"Oh, it's more like a cow path or logging road, not really for a car. I don't think it's really used."

"Where is it?"

"It branches out from the access road to the Guilliard farm next to this one. Over there." The farmer indicated by a turn of his head. "The path is easy to miss. Last time I went by, months ago, there was a pile of gravel near the entrance to the road."

"How far to the estate from that point?"

"Oh, it's probably no more than half a kilometer before you reach the first row of vines."

"And where's the road to the Guilliard farm?"

"After you get back on the main road and turn left it's about a kilometer away on your left."

The farmer again shook his head. "But I wouldn't try driving on that cow-path in that car. You might get stuck."

The two detectives backed up until they could turn around and got back to the paved country road. They found the access road to the Guilliard farm. Before they reached any building they saw the pile of gravel and a barely visible path that disappeared among trees and brush. There was enough room to drive a car, but from the start the car swayed as it passed over roots, rocks and an otherwise uneven surface. Although they moved very slowly, they kept scraping the undercarriage.

"I think we'd better stop," Duparc said after a few hundred yards. "This path is for a tractor — or for Major Dégas's Land Rover perhaps. Pull off the road somewhere, and let's walk instead."

It was a warm, sunny day, and they removed their jackets, which revealed that Léger was wearing his gun in a shoulder holster. His putting on a pair of sunglasses seemed apposite to his professional role. The moisture from the rain of a few days before was long gone, and the ground was dusty. The trees were not very high or dense. They stood in clumps and offered little shade.

They thought they could see some fairly recent tire tracks and marks in exposed roots. They walked cautiously, looking for movement. Soon a slanting field with rows of vines appeared between trees and brush. Beyond it, nestled into a hill, was the winery building that they had seen from the Broderie chateau. They could see the chateau in the far distance, largely hidden behind the winery.

They approached the winery, trying to hide behind the vines. They could not resist tasting the grapes, which appeared close to ready for harvesting. They looked to the sides for signs of possible trouble. They came up behind the short end of the building that they had guessed contained the wine press and the vats. The building was made of brick and seemed quite old. It had been constructed up against the hill, which had probably been excavated to create a cellar. On the other side of a small yard there was a small barn-style building that housed a tractor, a couple of trailers, baskets, and farming equipment. They saw no people, and they noticed no movement at the chateau, which was about two hundred yards away.

We'd better be careful," Duparc said under his breath. "Both Dégas and the baron may be on the estate, and who knows who else might be here?"

"There's no sign of the servants. Everything looks quiet," Léger said. "How about taking a look inside the winery?"

"Definitely."

Duparc was almost surprised by his immediate and clear-cut answer. He knew well that any search of the baron's estate might be called illegal. They had no judicial approval for a forced entry. A claim by Duparc that the situation constituted an emergency could easily be challenged. Duparc was generally a go-by-the book public servant, but he had mixed feelings about that side of his personality. He even felt some contempt for it at times. He thought he knew why he was like that. It was not because he thought that going by the rules would earn him quicker promotions. He was less of a careerist than most. He had had fractious run-ins with superiors over how to pursue investigations, and he had sometimes clashed with prosecutors reluctant to base a case on his evidence. So why was he, in his own estimation, too much of a rule-bound bureaucrat? It was his father's legacy. For his father, the stern country procurator, laws and regulations had been the ultimate authority. He had had no religion. The closest he had come to one was to refer all problems and dilemmas to adjudication according to existing laws and regulations. *Without law – chaos*, had been his mantra. Duparc realized that he had much of his father in himself, but his experience as a policeman and detective had made him more and more sensitive to the tension between law and regulations, on the one side, and justice, on the other. What might sound plausible and proper in the abstract often looked unjust or unreasonable in the concrete case. Too often, vicious, contemptible criminals Duparc had investigated had escaped prosecution or received a not-guilty verdict because adhering strictly to law and police regulations had made it impossible to obtain sufficient evidence. More and more often he had rebelled against the uncompromising formalism of his father's judiciousness and let his immediate sense of justice and street smarts overpower the rulebook. Some situations cried out for improvisation.

Duparc admitted to himself that the Bittenberg case had an aspect that had not appreciably affected his conduct of other investigations: an interest in, concern for, an attractive woman. Helen Bittenberg had an effect on him that made it necessary to exercise an unusual amount of self-control lest he lose his professional detachment and let his admiration become too obvious. He had become deeply involved in other cases, but this time he wanted to please and impress one of the main characters in the case. He found himself doubly resenting Mr. Stephen Ferguson, the arrogant, self-satisfied American diplomat, for causing Helen Bittenberg suffering and, he had to admit, for making lewd advances. Duparc would do everything he could to find Richard Bittenberg, but he had moments of silly daydreaming when he felt ambivalent about finding Helen's husband. Duparc was not prone to such silly frivolity. He was rather firmly planted in *terra firma*. He would never so much as hint to Helen that he was taken with her. Not only was she out of his reach; he was also rather happily married. He was fortunate compared to some of his colleagues who were separated, divorced, or in troubled marriages. Duparc found satisfaction in quiet domesticity. He and his wife would be together into their old age, he assumed. But whatever the outcome of the Bittenberg case, he was not likely ever to forget the woman who seemed to him to be at the center of it.

"We have to see if Bittenberg is being kept here," Duparc said. "After our talk with Ferguson he may be at increased risk, in immediate danger. Clearly an emergency situation, right?"

"Right."

The winery had two doors, both locked.

"I could easily pick the lock on that side door," Léger said.

"Do it!"

Duparc noticed that before they entered Léger felt under his arm to make sure his pistol was where it was supposed to be. Inside they stopped, listening for any sound. The ground floor was pretty much as they had expected. This was where the grapes were received and pressed. The space was about fifty by thirty feet. Light came in through a couple of dirty windows. They started a search, careful not to make any noise. There were two side rooms. They found nothing of interest.

"The best place to keep somebody locked up is of course the cellar," Léger said. "From there not a sound could be heard outside."

The cellar was half a storey below the ground floor. You reached it through a broad stairway.

"Make sure nobody's coming," Duparc said and headed for the cellar. Léger looked out the windows, saw nothing and followed Duparc.

"Darn it," Duparc said, "We should have brought the flashlight."

The light's being turned off in the cellar suggested that nobody was working there. Duparc found the light switch. The cellar was some sixty by fifty feet. The space had been created by excavating the soft rock of the mountainside. Two of the walls consisted mostly of exposed rock. The space was dominated by two rows of vats. At one of the short ends of the cellar was a wooden wall with two doors about ten feet apart. Léger moved in that direction. He stopped.

"Look, over here," Léger said. He was standing near one of the doors and pointed to a shelf about level with his shoulders. Over medium height, he could see on the shelf an unwashed white plate on which were a knife and fork, a glass, and an empty beer bottle. The dishes seemed to have been forgotten among some tools and debris.

Duparc had to stand on tippy-toe to take out the plate. He

held it gingerly between his hands by the outside edges. He studied what was evidently the remains of a meal.

"Somebody had something to eat down here not very long ago," he said. "A funny place for it, don't you think? Why not eat outside or at least upstairs?"

"This is the second time we've seen traces of a meal not eaten at the residence," Léger muttered.

The door next to the shelf was locked. The same was true of the second door in the same wall. Both doors were old and solid and had large keyholes.

They looked near the doors for places where keys might have been hidden but found nothing.

"Look upstairs," Duparc told Léger. "Try that office-like room. And while you're up there, check again that nobody's approaching from the chateau."

Duparc put his ear to each of the two doors. He thought of banging to see if there would be any response, but checked the impulse. He had better wait for Léger, who was armed.

Léger returned with a pleased smile on his face. He held up three large, old-fashioned keys. "They were sort of hidden, in a box upstairs, but not very hard to find. And all's quiet around the estate."

One of the keys unlocked the door nearest to the forgotten plate. Inside they found a light switch. This was a sizeable storage room, about twenty by thirty feet, with shelves for wine bottles. There was an old desk and a chair and a lamp, a place for someone to sit, perhaps while recording what was being placed in or taken from the room. The shelves were about half filled with bottles of wine. Some of them stood in very neat rows. Many others that seemed dustier and older stood in no particular order or were on the floor or in boxes as if awaiting sorting. The room was a curious blend of strict orderliness and messiness. Otherwise, nothing seemed suspicious.

One of the other keys unlocked the second storage room. Here, too, they could turn on a light. This room also had shelves for wine bottles, but here the shelves were almost empty. On the floor were boxes with new empty bottles. There was a clutter of various and sundry items. Again, nothing seemed awry.

"What about the third key?" Duparc asked. The keys were all of the same kind, but for different locks. Another search of the entire winery building turned up no matching door. The barn door was not locked.

Duparc said, "If there's not a third door, why would there be three keys? Let's start over!"

This time they searched to see if a door might have been concealed behind a shelf or cupboard. On the first floor they found and looked in a loft. But the effort was fruitless.

In the cellar Léger sat down on a box. "We've looked everywhere," he said. "The third key must be an old leftover."

Duparc was frustrated and ready to leave, but he had a stubborn streak that had made a difference in many of his investigations.

"Let's go back to the storage rooms for which we have keys."

They started with the one that appeared to be more of an overflow space than a room in need of a key. There was no additional door.

"Hey, wait a minute!" Duparc suddenly exclaimed. He excitedly unlocked the other storage room. Léger looked on curiously. Inside, Duparc asked, "Do you notice the difference between this room and the other one?"

"There's wine in here and no empty bottles."

"I'm not thinking about the contents."

"This room seems, well, more important—to be more consistently in use." Léger's eyes suddenly widened. "The FLOOR!" he exclaimed.

"Yes, not a dirt floor, a *wooden* floor!"

Without a word the two detectives went up to the desk and chair, which stood on an old torn rug—an attempt, it seemed, to create the semblance of a cosy corner. They moved the furniture and the rug.

And there it was, the third door—a lid in the wooden floor. While Léger stood aside with a hand on the butt of his revolver, Duparc unlocked the lid and lifted the rather heavy door with some effort.

# CHAPTER 58

After the incident with the Coast Guard cutter, nobody on the cabin cruiser, including Robert O'Brien, showed any inclination to resume the interrupted meeting. The conspirators were flustered. They had gotten a concrete, vivid illustration of what disaster for the conspiracy would look like. The experience had been shattering to Richard, presumably to the others, though O'Brien did not show any signs of being upset. For the rest of the trip up to D.C. and the Washington Channel the conspirators were quiet or engaged in small talk. Stanley Globowski kept shaking his round head. O'Brien put his arm around him in comradely fashion.

Richard asked Bradley Donnelly, the D.C. police captain, if he might borrow his cell phone to make a short call home. Donnelly, who was standing next to O'Brien, indicated to him by holding up the cell phone that he wondered if it might be OK to use it.

O'Brien shrugged his shoulders.

Richard went to the other side of the boat to make the call. It was almost 6:00 PM.

Helen answered.

"I'm sorry," Richard said, "I find myself in a very awkward predicament. I'll probably be home late for dinner."

"Why am I not surprised?" she said.

"Helen, please, I'm in a bind. I was leaving the library when I came upon a really embarrassing situation. I ran into a member of the English department. You don't know him. He was dead drunk, shouting and attracting a lot of attention. I had to do something. I got him to come with me to my car and got him to give me his home address, but then he passed out. I'm not sure what to do at the moment. A student lent me her cell phone to call you. I forgot mine at home. I'll have to try to bring the guy home. He lives in an apartment on Connecticut Avenue. The location is not too inconvenient for me. I'll try to get home as soon as possible."

What tangled webs we weave, he thought. One of these days all his lying would surely blow up in his face.

He would have wanted to ask O'Brien just what he had meant by his no-mercy comments to the people on the cabin cruiser, but except for some small talk he actually sat silently as O'Brien drove him back to the Dupont Circle subway stop. What had happened on the river in combination with his family difficulties had for the moment trumped his unease about O'Brien's callousness.

In the next several days other meetings took place. Richard participated in a grueling session regarding the use of media in the first phase of the take-over. It had become obvious that in the effort to put out stories favorable to the conspirators they had to concentrate on two network-affiliated Washington television stations and one large network-affiliated radio station where they had a couple of well-placed supporters. At one meeting he was surprised to see for the first time a local television newscaster of some prominence. It continued to surprise him that he had not been nearly so alone in his disgust with the destruction of America as he had thought. But now that the context was marshaling resources for a frontal attack on the existing system, what struck him most was how very limited those resources were. Richard was hoping that the conspiracy would be able to create a strong journalistic momentum based on early planted stories and that the journalists would show the usual tendency to run in a pack. But the clever and elaborate disinformation campaign had to be supplemented and backed up by force.

At seven o'clock one morning in the early summer Richard left his home by foot, walked across the outskirts of the Kenwood Country Club and up to the entrance of the sprawling clubhouse, in front of which was a circular driveway. Nobody paid him any mind. Golfers were arriving to get an early start. The weather report had spoken of another hot day with temperatures in the nineties.

Richard had observed the golfers performing their ritual of normalcy for a while when, at precisely 7:15, a gray Taurus turned into the driveway from River Road and stopped in front of Richard. He stepped into the air-conditioned coolness of Robert O'Brien's car. The radio, the infernal radio, was on. As he sat down next to O'Brien he noticed with surprise that Herbert Vandenhorst was in the back seat.

"Change of plans," Vandenhorst said. "I was going to ride with Hick, but he thought he should leave last night and spend the night at the house."

"You never told me where we're going."

"That's right, I didn't—no reason for you to know ahead of time. It's back to West Virginia, to Pellegrini's place. So settle in, we have a bit of a drive."

This would be Richard's third visit to the Pellegrini mountain cabin. It was there that he had first met and gotten to know Robert

O'Brien. Today the instructions were to be dressed informally, and O'Brien, the man known for always wearing a dark suit and sunglasses, was again wearing the shorts from the Potomac River cruise.

"Who're coming?"

"None of the Pellegrinis, only the people in charge of the early operational phase of the coup — Bob and I, Gordon, Tom, and Noah. You, Richard, the minister without portfolio, get to come along for the ride."

"I doubt I'll have anything to contribute to the plans."

"Perhaps so, but you won't be in the way either."

They headed northwest into the Maryland countryside. They did not take the most direct route to their West Virginia destination. Richard could see from the side that O'Brien often looked in the rear mirrors. Once he suddenly drove into a small dirt road and stopped for a minute among trees. "Now that we're here, anybody need a pit stop?"

They conversed about different aspects of the attempted coup. O'Brien indicated that, as he had expected, the president's planned vacation trip to Montana in August was shaping up as offering the best opportunity for the conspiracy. There were three different scenarios for how to kill the president, involving a sniper rifle, an explosion or a light, hand-held anti-tank weapon. The conspiracy would prepare for each of the three possibilities, but only two people would actually be available to execute any plan. In fact, in the best circumstances a single person would carry out the deed. The intended assassin was a former navy SEAL, who had been fired from the navy for overly aggressive behavior. He was considered borderline unstable. This man was known for his hatred of the American political "elite," but had never done anything for which he could be arrested. It was because he was on a Secret Service watch list that he had come to O'Brien's attention. Since he lived a couple of states away from Montana, the Secret Service would not be monitoring him very closely for the dates in question. Cultivating and recruiting him had been a delicate and risky business. The person mainly responsible was one of Tony Springhalter's most trusted agents, one of Hick's colleagues, though from a different city. That man, too, would be prepared to do the deed, but he was only a backup.

"I don't need to tell you that we're watching the navy guy very carefully," O'Brien said. "So far he's been very cooperative and followed orders completely, but if he should get out of line, Springhalter's man knows what to do."

Richard squirmed in his seat.

"Firing a grenade or setting off an explosion is very likely to kill innocent bystanders," Richard said.

"Of course, especially an explosion," O'Brien said. "But we have to be sure of achieving our objective. We have to have a good margin for error. That's why I don't particularly like the sniper scenario. It relies too much on perfect timing and positioning. This is one part of our plan that must not go wrong."

Richard had heard in general terms about the planned assassination, but he had never made it his business to find out about the details. It seemed a pattern with him, he thought, to look away from potentially gruesome aspects of the coup.

O'Brien went on, "Here in D.C. Hick and his buddy John will do the deed. Because I will be able to give them detailed information and can tell them just where they should be to get a clear shot they will in a way have an easier time than the navy guy. Both of them will use sniper rifles and will fire at the same time to minimize the risk of missing, but they'll have a hand-held grenade weapon ready in case the veep's plans suddenly change or he doesn't show as much of himself as we would like."

Again Richard moved uneasily in his seat. As one committed to the coup he should find O'Brien's unemotional, matter-of-fact account of the assassination plans heartening. Those involved were playing for keeps. That was how it should be. And yet he did not want to hear about it.

"The biggest problem we face remains the coordination of the two assassinations. They have to take place within two minutes of each other, at most. A foul-up there, and we're cooked. I'm very worried that one of those protests here in Washington will block downtown streets, create a huge traffic jam, and force the vice presidential Secret Service detail to change their route at the last minute."

Richard found an opportunity to bring up the handling of people arrested in the early hours of the coup, and he repeated in neutral language O'Brien's directive to the people in the cabin cruiser regarding assertive, emphatic conduct.

"You were coming on pretty strong, Robert. Shoot first, ask questions later, you seemed to say." Not to seem too confrontational he made the comment sound half-joking.

"Well, especially in the early hours it's better to have our people err on the side of decisive, clear-cut action than to have them dither and cause doubts about our determination."

"But you seemed to be saying, if in doubt, shoot the troublemaker."

"What if I did? The last thing we want is to give the impression that our orders are negotiable. What would *you* suggest?"

Before Richard had a chance to answer, Vandenhorst broke in:

"We do want to avoid unnecessary loss of life. We all agree. The question is what is unnecessary? Some situations will arise that just cannot be anticipated. Those on the spot have to decide what to do. I think what Bob means is that hesitation and squeamishness poses a greater danger to the coup than seemingly harsh action."

Richard saw O'Brien nodding at the wheel.

What Vandenhorst had said sounded plausible to Richard in theory, but he was somehow repulsed by the practical, concrete implications. He had a deep fear that the necessary violence would evolve into major bloodletting and lead to the death of many innocent bystanders. On the other hand, he had never thought that, with the exception of the assassination of the president and vice president, the coup could be bloodless. Why did he indulge in wishful thinking?

Richard sat quietly looking out the car window at the passing landscape. They were entering more mountainous terrain and had to drive more slowly on increasingly winding roads. O'Brien had to stop a couple of times to check his directions.

"This issue will come up again today, you can be sure," Vandenhorst said. "We'll be talking about military matters and about forcing our way in various parts of Washington. And we have to discuss the work of the action teams that will arrest people on our blacklist. That list has gotten longer at the insistence of Lisa, Doug, and Randy, but we don't have many more people now than before to put on those teams. They will have to do triple duty until more soldiers are available."

The final stretch of road up to the Pellegrini vacation home was not much more than a logger's trail with gravel. They passed two houses, only one of which seemed to be inhabited. The Pellegrini house was about half a mile from its closest neighbor. It looked even more isolated than before because the big trees that surrounded it were now in full foliage. The Pellegrinis still had done nothing to clear away trees and brush to restore the view from this mountaintop. The cabin did not look particularly alluring. The Pellegrinis have had other things on their minds in the last couple of years, Richard thought.

When they got out of the car Richard was surprised that he did not have the usual summertime sensation of his face breaking into an immediate sweat. The temperature up in these West Virginia mountains almost made air-conditioning unnecessary.

They could see only one car, probably Hick's. It had been

driven off the driveway behind the house and was partly hidden by bushes.

Hick had heard them coming and was standing in the doorway.

"All's ready," he said to Vandenhorst. "I turned the water back on yesterday. And the coffee's on. The admiral said he would bring doughnuts. I have cookies just in case."

"How's the situation outside?"

"Fine, sir, lots of deer. Hunting up here would be like shooting fish in a barrel. I'll be out and about later to make sure nobody sneaks up on us."

The inside of the house was not inviting. It seemed that the Pellegrinis had not been there for a long time. The house was still boarded up, as it had been on their last visit. The only light came from lamps and cracks in the big boards covering the windows. The walls had rough, darkening wood paneling that contributed to the cheerlessness of the milieu. Hick had tried to air the house out by opening doors, but a musty smell lingered. It mixed with a faint smell of food, perhaps left over from Hick's breakfast or from his dinner the previous evening.

Tom Reed, Noah Sales, and Gordon Bunker arrived in Bunker's large SUV within fifteen minutes. Bunker carried two cartons of Krispy Kreme doughnuts into the house, which he put on the kitchen counter.

"Help yourselves, gentlemen," he shouted jovially. "Doughnuts for every taste!"

The six members of the steering committee gathered around, making jokes about having to compete for their favorite kind of doughnut. This, Richard reflected, might have been a meeting of a church group, of birdwatchers, of amateur photographers, or of the board of the local Rotary club. Their real purpose would be the very last thing to occur to an outsider happening on the gathering.

It was as if the conspirators wanted to avoid the house. They all spontaneously took their coffee and doughnuts outside into the light and the fresh air. As during the prelude to the meeting in the basement of O'Brien's rental house, the small talk was strained and intermittent. Vandenhorst had to call them inside after coffee. They found seats. He signaled that it was time for business by saying, "I hope you all remembered to turn off your cell phones."

Richard was so used to taking security precautions that he did not even need to ask himself whether his cell phone was in fact turned off.

Only Tom Reed reacted: "Most of you know that I have a

special problem. I'm wearing this pager that I'm not allowed to turn off. They have to be able to reach me in case of a national emergency. I would call more attention to me if I turned it off than if I leave it on. I told my adjutant that I was planning to do some mountain hiking this weekend. If I'm tracked for some reason, my location would come as no surprise."

It was 9:30 in the morning when the conspirators started to work their way through a crowded agenda. Because most of the subjects would be military or connected to military matters, Bunker served as chairman. Hick disappeared outside.

Their subject was the hours leading up to the movement of troops and the actual takeover. They aired problems of communication, disinformation, sequencing and deployment. Sales kept returning to the danger that his troop columns from Quantico of up to 800 Marines would get caught in traffic on I-95 south of Washington. They had to be prepared to shove cars off the road to make way. He expressed concern that many of the troops from Quantico that he intended to use would still be in training. Their inexperience might cause major problems, but could be an advantage in that these youngsters would probably be more pliable and unsuspecting than more seasoned warriors. They would probably do as they were told by their officers without hesitation. The very last thing they expected was to be sent to Washington, D.C., but they would have no reason to doubt what their superiors told them. The explanation they were given would put them in a frame of mind to follow orders. It would require considerable rhetorical skill to reassure officers about a mission as unexpected as protecting the nation's capital. Only one senior officer under Sales was actually in on the coup. The others just had to follow orders for the plan to work. A special problem was ensuring that live ammunition would be available for distribution in sufficient quantities. Sales was already showing his face at Quantico more often than expected. He wanted to be familiar and known as one very tough customer who expected to be obeyed no questions asked. He was planning to call for an unusual on-the-spot training exercise just a few days before the coup. This meant risking raised eyebrows among his fellow brass at the Pentagon and at Quantico, but he had to take that risk for the troops to gain some relevant experience.

"On the day we move, I have to be at the base," Sales said. "I have to make sure everybody understands there's a huge emergency in D.C. and make sure my orders are followed. That puts me far away from the start of the main action, but in this extreme situation I'm sure I can get my hands on three, maybe four helicopters. I will fill them with Marines and fly up to D.C. ahead of the companies to follow. I'll probably land just near the White House, probably on the south lawn. All depends on what Tom has been able to do at that point. I hope he'll be set up on the White House grounds and be in general control of the premises. My Marines can strengthen the perimeter and disperse to other points. Once we've gotten that far, you Herbert and Gordon and our political people can move in and start kicking people out of their offices."

"I hope to have some guns, and a few tanks set up around the White House by the time Noah gets there," Reed said. "His people can coordinate with mine and spread out to Capitol Hill, the key federal departments, the Federal Reserve, the FBI, the selected TV and radio stations, and the airports. The Marines can beef up the action teams arresting people."

"I hope we won't have to shoot our way into the White House," Vandenhorst said. "I'm worried about that fellow Bart Gregory that Bob's been telling us about, the head of the presidential detail of the Secret Service. If he's not on vacation or out in Montana with the president and becomes any kind of a problem, Bob will simply have to take him out."

*Take him out.* Richard did not remember Vandenhorst using such language before. Richard felt the familiar twinge of discomfort whenever the risk of killing and destruction came up.

"If the Secret Service guys try to stop us," Sales said, "and if they resort to some of the heavier weapons they have stashed away, we have to handle the situation as a very tricky military operation. We want to limit damage to the White House. We need it for its communication capacity, and for its symbolic value—right Richard?"

Tomas Reed and Bob O'Brien discussed in front of the others the need for soldiers to assist in clearing key people out of their offices in the White House and the adjoining Executive Office Building. Robert O'Brien's Secret Service loyalists would have to assist in locating people on the removal list. Most of these people would have to be arrested and transported to another location, which would be another tricky maneuver. It would not be advisable to use the same soldiers or Secret Service agents for several such trips. They would become suspicious if they realized that a large number of White House staff were being whisked away to strange locations. How could they be put in such places for their own protection? Or how could a terrorist plot possibly have infiltrated the White House to such an extent?

The conspirators again discussed how frightfully short-handed they would be in the first hours of the coup and the risk that confused and scared soldiers would refuse orders.

"The key is to put the command pressure on tight," Reed said. "The soldiers must feel that they have no freedom of action—none."

"And how do you ensure that?" Richard asked. "You and Noah can't be everywhere and bear down on these youngsters and their officers. You have to delegate to people who will at some point surely wonder what in the world's going on."

"But they will have received an earful from Noah and me before being sent in. They will be told that they are the only thing standing in the way of the crumbling of the government of the United States."

"One more thing," Sales said. "We plan to have a conspirator near or in charge of as many of the action teams as possible, and that person *will* mean business. Disobedience just will not be tolerated. If there's a refusal to follow orders, you shoot to kill."

There was that kind of language again. Richard cringed.

He was just about to raise an objection when Bunker brought up the topic of arresting and warehousing people who might endanger the coup.

Reed was ready. "For people who've been in the way but are not on the blacklist it's pretty straightforward. We keep them in the D.C. armory, which is not too far from the center of town but out of the way. My people can handle that. This crowd just needs to be watched. We may be able to let most of them go once the situation has stabilized, perhaps in a couple of days. The trickier problem is dealing with the people on the blacklist. I understand it's grown to about a hundred in the last couple of weeks. That's blacklisted people here in the D.C. area. Noah and I will have nothing to do with people being grabbed in other cities or abroad. The first difficulty here in D.C. is arresting the people to begin with. We are so short of personnel. Just *finding* the people on the blacklist will be difficult—time-consuming in many cases. It may take us a couple of days to round them all up. Some will be away on vacation and will probably have to be left for another time. Another difficulty is transporting the arrested people to that abandoned city jail in southwest D.C. that Captain Donnelly will have ready for us. It's supposed to be rundown but usable. It's completely out of the way in a bad part of town. Just a few people will be able to guard the prisoners for the time they're there. Noah and Bob O'Brien are in charge."

"For how long?" Richard asked.

"Until we take care of them," Sales said.

Richard was confused: "Take care of them—?"

"Gentlemen," Vandenhorst called, "it's 12:30, and this is a

good time to break for lunch. Hick's prepared something for us."

Hick had returned to the house and had been doing something in the kitchen in the last half hour. They could smell food cooking. There was a large pot on the stove.

"Beef stew," Hick said. "Come and get it!"

Hick had obviously done the cooking the night before. The conspirators, who had envisioned another couple of doughnuts for lunch, were visibly cheered.

"I'm glad you didn't waste last night," Vandenhorst said, smiling, to Hick.

"We security people have to be prepared for all situations."

Richard appeared to be the only one not looking forward to food. He was not hungry. The discussions of the morning, perhaps in combination with the coffee and doughnuts, had made him slightly nauseous. He found the entire setting oppressive—the boarded-up house, the dreadful subject under discussion, the tense but controlled emotions. He wanted to be elsewhere. He was the last one to put some stew in one of the paper bowls supplied by Hick. He knew he needed nourishment, but he also needed air, and he went out on the deck of the house. He breathed deeply of the pleasant mountain air. It was an early afternoon in June, and yet the temperature up here was only in the mid seventies.

Sales was standing by himself on the deck, seemingly eating with a good appetite. Richard ate dutifully of the small portion on his own plate. He moved closer to Sales.

"Noah, what did you mean when you said *taking care* of the blacklisted people?"

Sales, squinting in the sunlight, gave him a surprised look. He seemed to hesitate.

"What did you mean?" Richard repeated.

Sales had another spoonful of stew, chewed, and didn't look straight at Richard. He finally said:

"I guess you were never told."

"Never *told*? Never told what?"

"Well, I suppose we're all operating on a need to know basis."

Richard put down his paper bowl on the side railing and looked quizzically at Sales.

"Noah, what *are* you talking about?"

"It's an old principle of intelligence and security work. People are told what they need to know and what you think they can handle."

"You mean to say there's something I don't need to know or

can't handle?"

Sales shrugged his shoulders and said under his breath, "I guess we all have our touchy spots."

Richard felt anger rising. Did Sales's voice have an undertone of contempt?

He wanted to press Sales, but the large frame of Gordon Bunker appeared in the doorway. He walked up to them, smiling.

"I hope you guys remember not to talk about anything sensitive outdoors," Bunker said. He could not have heard any of what they had said, Richard thought, and he appeared to have been joking, but, as if by extrasensory perception, he was in fact interrupting a breach of basic security. Richard realized that his emotional edginess had caused him to violate precautions that had become routine for him.

"Herbert wants us to get back to work as soon as possible," Bunker said. "He needs to be in D.C. for a late afternoon meeting."

When they gathered again Richard knew that he had to get to the bottom of Sales's comments, and he did not want to do it in merely private conversation. If anything of importance had been withheld from him, which he now suspected, he wanted to know just what it was and have an airing of the reason for the concealment. Who else might not know what Sales had in mind? The only question was when to raise the issue. He did not want to make too much of a vague suspicion. He might look foolish jumping to a far-fetched conclusion.

Bunker wanted to discuss how the conspirators could both confuse and reassure the Pentagon during the coup. The members of the Joint Chiefs of Staff would be among the first to figure out that something really strange was going on. Would they then sit on the sidelines waiting for the situation to get clearer, or would they start making difficulties as soon as they suspected what was happening?

"Some of the top brass are careerists and opportunists, political generals and admirals," Bunker said. "But some are almost as disgusted as we are. They're sick and tired of sending American soldiers into battle for things that have little to do with the American national interest. One thing's for sure, this president isn't highly regarded in the military."

Sales chortled.

"They sure as hell won't want a shoot-out in the nation's capital," Reed said. "That could lead to instability all over the country, what with all the demonstrations, and have dramatic international repercussions. We're at war as usual in the Middle East. The less disruption in Washington, the better for the Pentagon."

"So," Vandenhorst said, "as we've discussed, it's essential

that we establish contact with the Pentagon and send them the right message."

"The brass have to understand," Reed said, "that we're not crazies, but people they can respect and who respect the military. They have to know that you, Herbert, and you, Gordon, are among the decision makers. I, too, and Noah may have some credibility. Gordon's particularly well-known among the brass, and he's known the chairman of the Joint Chiefs for a long time and gets along well with him. A phone call from Gordon to him would be very effective."

The others nodded.

Sales wanted to discuss which key Pentagon figures might try to interfere with the coup. "I've said it before, there are a couple of guys I wouldn't want to have around when I start moving. They correspond to that Bart Gregory character in the Secret Service. It's not that they're bad people, just that they could get badly in the way because they happen to have the jobs they have. One major general especially has to disappear just before we strike, perhaps on the way to work or returning home."

"Noah, how many people do you think we have who can handle assignments like that?" It was O'Brien who introduced the note of dissent. "They'll be overworked as it is."

"And how could we start nabbing people and put them in that jail before the start of the coup?" Richard asked. "We risk detection before we have any real resources in town."

Richard had not listened much to what had been said about the Pentagon problem. This ground had been covered several times before. He had been thinking instead about the meaning of Sales's previous remarks about "taking care" of the people who had been arrested. The matter now at issue offered a connection to this subject, but before Richard had formulated his question Sales said:

"I wasn't thinking of jailing them."

"Then what did you mean?" Richard asked.

Sales looked annoyed. "I mean that they need to disappear—for *good*, if you understand my meaning." Sales threw a scornful look in Richard's direction.

"Noah! These are completely innocent bystanders! For all we know, they may even be sympathetic to what we're about."

Sales made a gesture of exasperation.

"I can't believe I'm hearing this," he said. "We're talking about a military operation here. As far as possible we have to remove likely obstacles to our success ahead of time."

"We're not exactly planning a straight military operation,"

Richard said. "We're not at war with the American people or with the Pentagon."

"You mean all the people who are likely to be touched by the coup must receive an official declaration of war?" Sales voice was now dripping with sarcasm.

As Richard showed signs of wanting to object, Sales raised his voice and continued: "We *are* at war! And we're up against very high odds. We're planning to strike against the most powerful government in the world with very limited resources. I trust you've heard of expeditionary forces striking behind enemy lines before the main assault. That's what I'm talking about—on a minuscule scale."

Richard decided that this was the time to get to the bottom of Sales's previous remarks.

"Gordon, I asked Noah before the break what he meant by 'taking care' of the arrested people kept in that old jail. I want to know what he's talking about."

Richard noticed that Bunker and Vandenhorst exchanged quick glances.

"You never told him, did you?" It was Sales who addressed the question to nobody in particular.

The room fell silent. Richard looked at the others and finally turned to Vandenhorst.

"It seems you have something to tell me."

"I don't think anything I can tell you will come as any surprise."

"OK, Herbert, spit it out!" Richard's tone showed impatience and irritation.

Vandenhorst spoke calmly: "The group here today, with you as a bit of an exception, have concentrated from the beginning on the military aspects of the coup and more generally on the necessary use of violence. At this operational stage many of the specifics of our planning have to be spread out to a growing number of people, but even now knowledge of some aspects of the takeover has to be kept within a small circle of people. It's partly for security, but also because many people who have lived their lives far from violence start getting nervous when they have to confront the possibility of bloodshed. There's no need to agitate people unnecessarily."

Out of the corner of his eye Richard could see that Sales was impatiently tapping his fingers on the wooden arms of his chair.

"So what is it I have yet to learn?" Richard made no attempt to hide that he was feeling resentful and oppositional. In the last many months Richard had become close to Herbert Vandenhorst. They had clicked as human beings, sometimes not needing to tell the other what he thought in order for the other to know. Richard had come to see Vandenhorst as somewhat of a father figure. He had trusted him to do the right thing. But now he felt that he was confronting him.

"I don't see how you could be in the dark about anything important," Vandenhorst responded. "You may not have received a formal briefing on what Noah was talking about—I don't think anybody has—but you've been in enough meetings to be able to put the pieces together. The fact that you've never asked me for details on this subject has suggested to me you think you know all you need to know. You've certainly never prodded me for more information. In fact, I got the impression you were not particularly eager to know all the details."

Vandenhorst's supposition bothered Richard all the more in that he knew that it contained an element of truth. Discussion of the violence required during the coup had always made him uncomfortable. Vandenhorst's words made him feel defensive and a little embarrassed. Still, Richard pressed on:

"I do want to know all there is to know."

"Then I can only confirm what you have surely concluded on your own. The conspiracy has to eliminate a number of people, a few just before we make our move. We have to be very careful because the disappearance of people in the hours before we strike must not arouse suspicions. There must be no obvious pattern."

"There's that ambiguous word 'eliminate' again—just like 'take care of' and 'deal with' and so on."

"Oh, c'mon!" Sales erupted. "Isn't ambiguity just what you want, Richard? "I don't think your sensitive ears want to hear the word 'kill.'"

"That's enough, Noah!" Gordon said in a loud, firm military voice.

Again anger welled up in Richard, but he was uncertain of its source and object. He realized that it was directed in part at himself—for having been insufficiently attentive to this dimension of the coup.

"So, let's finally get to it!" he exclaimed. "State it explicitly. What did Noah mean before when he said that we will 'take care' of the people who've been put in the jail?"

"Richard," Vandenhorst resumed, "I doubt there's a single person in the conspiracy who's unaware that the coup will cost some people their lives. How could it be otherwise?"

"Of course, but we've all assumed that the bloodletting will be kept to a minimum."

"There's never been any disagreement on that point," Bunker

interjected.

"But why do I get the idea that Noah and perhaps the rest of you are not thinking along those lines. Stop beating around the bush!" Richard voice was rising.

"Richard," Robert O'Brien said, "there's no disagreement on what is needed."

"Which is *what?*" Richard let his anger and vexation show.

"What I meant," Sales said very slowly as if addressing a weak-witted youngster, "was that, after we have rounded up the people on the blacklist and put them in the jail, we have to execute them. But we have to wait until the situation is under control and we have people and transportation available to dispose of the bodies without attracting attention."

Richard's jaw had literally dropped at the phrase "execute," and he gasped for air.

"*What*!? You're talking about killing perhaps over a hundred people here in D.C.!" he cried.

Richard looked around the room, wondering if the others were in fact agreeing with Sales. Nobody said anything. Nobody objected.

"I can't *believe* it!" he exclaimed. "This goes far beyond anything I've heard discussed. What's this got to do with minimizing the bloodshed?"

Tom Reed, who had been quiet during this exchange, now spoke:

"You, Richard, are the historian par excellence in this room. I don't need to tell you that in wars tens of thousands or millions of people lose their lives. We are in effect declaring war on the present U.S. government. And if you don't think that's what we're doing, think about coups, rebellions, and revolutions in human history. Most of them have been very costly. If what we intend goes according to plan, the cost in human life will be negligible by historical standards. Considering the scope of what we are attempting, it will be a marvel of humanity!"

"*Humanity!*" Richard cried disdainfully. "The humane thing to do is spare lives whenever possible. It's one thing for innocent people to die as the unintended side effect of necessary action. It's completely different to kill defenseless people in a deliberate, premeditated fashion."

"Can you think of a single rebellion anywhere, at any time, that did not kill opponents to the rebellion?" Reed spoke in a mater-of-fact, almost scholarly fashion. Richard could not respond before O'Brien spoke.

"Besides, think of who the people on our blacklist are," O'Brien said. "A few have to be eliminated not because they are terrible human beings but because not getting rid of them would jeopardize our success. But most are key figures in the present regime, collaborators in a heinous enterprise. They are rotten through and beneath contempt. Some have cost thousands of people their lives. In a way they don't deserve a punishment as painless as just being shot."

"So we assume the role of judge, jury, and executioner," Richard cried, "which makes us just the kind of people we say we despise."

"I guess you would prefer some televised show trials for the vipers," Sales said, his voice brimming with derision. "But I'm sure posterity will thank us for just ending their miserable lives, without any moralistic posturing."

Richard was so agitated and flummoxed that for a moment he was not sure what to say. He had difficulty controlling his emotions.

Robert O'Brien seized the opportunity to speak again. It occurred to Richard in the midst of his turmoil that the outward appearance of this large man, dressed in shorts and a garish summer shirt, was absurdly anomalous.

"You're overlooking something crucial, Dick," O'Brien said in a not unfriendly manner. "And that's that eliminating the people on the blacklist does not fall in the category of discretionary action. With very few exceptions these people are at the core of the system—in the executive, the Congress, the media, the foreign policy establishment, and on Wall Street. It's simply necessary to get rid of them. You don't attempt a coup and leave the enemy in place."

"Bob!" Richard cried. "You're not talking only about removing them from their positions but about *killing* them, which is *not* necessary!"

"Don't you know who these people *are*?" Sales shouted. "You're talking about human scum, people who deceive, steal, and defile our country! You, Mr. Professor," Sales said, pointing at Richard, "are bleeding all over the floor for a handful of s.o.b.s, who think nothing of sending thousands of young people to die in foreign wars to advance their own hidden interests. To say nothing about how they've destroyed the American economy and made the lives of millions miserable."

Richard, red in the face, was trying to control his emotions to speak coherently, and O'Brien again got the floor ahead of him.

"We can't leave these people around as lightning rods for opposition to the coup," O'Brien retorted.

"I've had enough of this!" Sales snarled and got out of his seat. "Do you think I don't understand what's going on here? I've been warning of it all along. This is just another Nervous Nellie who can't stand the heat in the kitchen. He wants to be morally superior to the people who *can* stand the heat and get something accomplished." Richard rose from his chair. "Hey, Professor," Sales continued, "think of it this way: If you just close your eyes to what has to be done, you'll have moral deniability. You can say you didn't know what was going on. You wouldn't have gone along with *that*! You aren't nearly so bad as those *brutes* who did all that dirty work. They told nobody about it! You were upholding moral standards all the time. Your hands were clean."

Richard almost screamed when he exclaimed:

"You're nothing but a ruthless, self-indulgent bastard! You *like* thinking about the fact that people will be killed. You look forward to it. It adds a spice to your own miserable life."

Now Vandenhorst was on his feet.

"Richard! Stop it!" he cried. "You're going too far. You're both saying things you don't really mean. And, both of you, *cool* it!"

Sales sat down, a slight, disdainful smile playing on his lips.

Richard remained standing. He said, "I mean exactly what I just said. This talk of deliberately killing more than a hundred people is satisfying a perverse desire in some of you. It sounds like revenge."

"Now wait just a minute!" O'Brien shouted, the earlier friendliness in his voice gone. "That's B.S.! You seem not to understand, Dick. The purpose of this coup is to *destroy* the system that's devastating this country — destroy it, not in theory but *actually*. And if you want the end, you have to want the means to the end. It's not a matter of wanting to kill people, but of wanting to do what's necessary to achieve the objective."

"That's just it!" Sales said. "The reason we're committed to this coup, is that — hear this, Professor! — we want to *break the back* of the system that's demolishing America. Did you hear that? *Break the back of it!* We don't want to leave the system in a condition to reconstitute itself in the near future. We're risking our lives to make a real difference, and that means that some of the disgusting people who are running the system have to be eliminated — sorry, Professor, I mean *killed*!"

Richard felt like rushing out of the room and the house, but anger and other agitation made him face Sales instead. The bull-like Marine general seemed to embody what he could not accept. Still standing, Richard said, his voice rising as he spoke: "It's people like you, Noah Sales, who make legitimate rebellions go wrong. People like you don't know where to draw the line. You poison sound motives and turn a valid challenge to authority into an indiscriminate, callous enterprise. Before you know it, you've replaced the old evil with a *new one*."

"*Richard*! You don't know what you're *saying*!" Vandenhorst exclaimed. "You should apologize!"

Sales seemed unconcerned. "I don't care," he said. "I don't need or want his apology." Sales sat calmly in his chair glaring dismissively at Richard.

Richard was trying to sort out his emotions. He felt as if he had woken up from one bad dream and ended up in the middle of an even worse one.

"Richard Bittenberg may be a pretty decent professor," he heard Sales saying, "but in the end he doesn't have what it takes. He thinks he lives in the real world. He prides himself on being more realistic than his academic colleagues, but with him it's all words and theory. The reason he doesn't live in the real world is that he just can't handle it. He just showed it!"

Richard might have given a very sharp, brutal riposte, but suddenly he was not quite present. He felt as if Sales were talking about some other person. Sales went on: "He cannot face doing what's necessary. He hides behind what he thinks of as moral conscience— behind *principles*, don't you know." Sales spit out the word. "Those principles are his pride, but they're phony—disconnected from the world we live in. They're excuses for backing out of difficult situations. They are dressed up as something very fine and noble, but they're nothing but an escape from confronting reality and doing unpleasant things that have to be done. If that's morality, I don't want any part of it. The professor can keep his sorry, half-assed, half-baked morality!"

Having realized that, yes, Sales was actually talking about him, Richard was becoming pale with rage. His hands were trembling. O'Brien seemed to think that Richard might attack Sales, for he had stood up and put himself near the two men. Only Richard's struggle to make sense of what was happening made him mute. Sales addressed himself to Vandenhorst:

"Herb, why did you bring Professor Bittenberg here today? You knew that we would be talking about blood and guts, and that's clearly not the professor's department. He's just not cut out for it. What he wants are half measures that may get us all killed."

If O'Brien had not been standing next to Richard, Richard would have flung himself at Sales, but the old Secret Service agent saw the move coming and deflected it by putting his arms around Richard and pushing him away. He muffled Richard's cry to Sales of "You son of a—"

Vandenhorst's face was flushed and troubled. "That was uncalled for, Noah!" he shouted. "Settle down both of you!" O'Brien was still blocking Richard's path. Vandenhorst came up to Richard, put a hand on one of his shoulders, and tried turning him in the direction of the door. "Please, Richard," he said quietly, "calm down, come with me outside!"

Richard could barely contain himself, but Vandenhorst's firm but gentle authority somehow made him do as he had been asked.

The world outside bore no resemblance to the twilight of the cabin. It was a beautiful summer afternoon. The high trees put the house in shade except for stray rays of sunlight coming through the branches and the foliage, but after the gloominess of the cabin, the light made Richard squint. The sky was a clear, problem-free blue.

Vandenhorst walked him slowly into the access road, keeping an arm around him.

"I'm very sorry, Richard. Noah was way out of line. I apologize on his behalf. He's on edge like the rest of us, and you did goad him. He didn't mean half of what he said. This is the sort of thing that happens before an operation. All are tightly wound up. But I'll patch things up, don't you worry! Noah's supposed to go back to D.C. with Gordon, and you can come with me and Hick."

Richard looked coldly at Vandenhorst, then nodded in the direction of the cabin: "I'm not going back in there."

"That's fine, Richard. No problem. I need to leave anyway in half an hour or so. Take a walk or something."

Vandenhorst turned to return to the house."

"Herbert, you never told me!"

Vandenhorst stopped and faced Richard.

"I don't remember giving you a special briefing, if that's what you mean, but I assumed you'd put the general picture together on your own. With you I didn't see any reason to dwell on the harsher aspect of the coup—"

Vandenhorst caught himself having spoken outside the house about a forbidden subject, but he lowered his voice further and continued. "One of the reasons is that you're not a soldier or even a detective or an FBI agent. You've lived a rather sheltered life as a scholar, far from the really dark side of life. Death, violence, and turbulence are not a part of your experience. It's abnormal, a disagreeable exception to your accustomed existence. For that reason what came up today has to bother you more than it does others.

Nothing would be gained by talking to you about every aspect of the necessary violence, especially as you seemed not to want to hear too much about those things."

"This, Herbert, is not my discovering a surprising detail about something that's generally known to me. This is a major and unexpected new revelation. I feel deceived."

"I'm sorry to hear that, Richard, but, in that case, aren't you guilty of self-deception? I don't see how all this time you could have entirely missed the implications of what was being discussed. I certainly thought you realized what was being planned. I wouldn't have brought you here today if I didn't think so."

"I didn't know. And what about those who aren't here today? What do they know?"

"We shouldn't be talking out here."

"Are there any others on the steering committee who don't know what I learned today?"

"It depends on what you mean. For security reasons we must compartmentalize our activities. We have to operate on a need-to-know basis. A few on the steering committee, two or three, perhaps, may not have all the details of what we discussed today. I'm afraid that rubbing their noses in this aspect of our plans might unsettle them at a time when they have to focus and play it cool. They are better off knowing just the general outline of the violence.

"*Details! General outline!?* My God, Herbert! What I heard today goes much beyond anything previously spelled out. It's terrible!"

"I disagree, Richard. It can't be avoided. If you're so surprised, you've indulged in wishful thinking. There's nothing nefarious about sharing information selectively. When it comes to war and intelligence, that's elementary, standard procedure. It has to be built into any planning that different people have different comfort zones."

Richard shook his head in disbelief. "Different *comfort* zones," he blurted derisively. "I can't *believe* what you are saying! What I just heard in that room puts the whole conspiracy in a new light. If this hidden plan had ever become known, some of our people would have been completely opposed to it. They might have gotten out if the plan was not scuttled. I think that's the real reason this information has been hidden. Deception has been a part of the conspiracy from the beginning."

Vandenhorst gave Richard a disconcerted look. "Please, we shouldn't be talking out here!" To respond to Richard, Vandenhorst was on the verge of violating his own counsel, but he stopped himself and merely said, "I need to get back indoors. Please, Richard, don't rush to conclusions."

He turned around and went back into the house.

Richard stood in the shadows of trees on a West Virginia mountaintop, more alone than he had ever been.

# CHAPTER 59

"A flashlight would have been good," Léger said as he looked into the newfound space. It was in darkness except for the dim light cast from the storage room in which he and Duparc were standing. A steep ladder-like staircase provided access.

"Anybody here?" Léger said into the darkness. There was no response, and he gingerly made his way down the steps. Duparc followed him.

"Very damp down here," was Léger's first comment. "The floor seems wet." They found a light switch and could survey another storage space, this one only about fifteen by twenty feet in size, and rougher in appearance. It had a dirt floor and four walls of exposed rock. The room had two rows of empty shelves. Marks in the floor suggested that there had once been furniture or equipment in the space. What most struck them was that the floor was wet and had a couple of small puddles. Léger touched the floor with his fingers and sniffed them.

"Not wine," he said, "probably just water."

Duparc felt the walls and found dampness there, too.

"Do you suppose water is seeping through the walls?"

"All of them?" Léger said skeptically. "And bubbling up through the floor too?"

"No, somebody's hosed this space down. Not long ago. The bottom shelves, too, are damp. I saw a long hose up in the main cellar."

"Look," Léger said, "the round marks in the dust on the higher shelves show that there used to be wine bottles on them. And those bottles must have stood there for quite a long time. I doubt much dust gathers down here in a year."

"My guess," Duparc said, "is that until recently this space was used to store wine. This could have been a vault for precious wine. Perhaps in an earlier era the room was intended as a hiding place in turbulent times."

"But now it's been used to keep a prisoner," Léger said. "Perfect for that purpose. Those marks on the floor could be from a cot."

"I bet all those unsorted older-looking bottles in the upstairs storage room used to be down here. They were removed before putting Bittenberg here."

Léger nodded and said: "Bittenberg was probably removed not very long ago, perhaps even earlier today, and the room was hosed down to get rid of any traces of him. We should be able to get a warrant now to search the whole estate and perhaps Dégas's place too."

"Perhaps, but now Bittenberg is not likely to be where we might be expected to search for him. There's a good chance he's been killed. The count and his helper are already guilty of kidnapping. They may think they have a better chance of getting away with it if they can dispose of Bittenberg in some safe place."

"The question is why they nabbed him to begin with," Léger said. "If they had a reason to keep him alive until just recently, perhaps that reason is still there."

"We can only hope. In any case, a forensic team could probably determine if Bittenberg's been kept here. There are probably fingerprints on that beer bottle and dirty plate. Let's bring them with us. Not exactly according to the rules, but we can claim duress. The danger that evidence might be destroyed is real and acute."

They climbed out of the hidden room, locked the door in the floor, and replaced the rug and the furniture. They locked the storage room. Léger wrapped the plate, glass, utensils, and beer bottle in an old newspaper. While Léger returned the keys to their hiding place and checked for movement outside the winery Duparc dialed the number to the administrative judge who had to approve a search warrant. Duparc paced the floor waiting to be connected to the right judge. She turned out to be woman. She listened to his account of the case and the current situation. Léger could tell that Duparc was encountering opposition. One of the sticking points was obviously that the estate to be searched belonged to a distinguished Frenchman — a man above suspicion — and that the case involved a leading American diplomat. Duparc could be heard arguing that it was no longer plausible to think that Bittenberg had disappeared voluntarily. The other main sticking point was the paucity of clear evidence. Duparc had to defend his presence in the Broderie winery as dictated by concern for the life of Professor Bittenberg. Duparc raised his voice several times. The call ended with his giving the telephone number to the police station in Noisy.

He closed the phone, motioning to Léger that they should leave. Having exited the winery and checked that they were not being observed, they snuck back through the rows of vines.

"How did it go with the magistrate?" Léger asked.

"Damned bureaucrats. No street smarts, just rules and regulations. First she said we should not be on the estate at all and should leave immediately. But she finally gave in. We're getting a warrant. They'll fax it to Noisy. Now we need to get some crime scene technicians out here, which won't be easy—vacation times and all. And unless Helen Bittenberg can produce something with her husband's fingerprints in usable form—his passport perhaps—establishing the identity of the prisoner in the winery may take a long time. We may have to get the help of the American FBI to compare Bittenberg's fingerprints to any they can obtain. They're not likely to be on file in America."

"And where's Bittenberg *now*!?" Léger said. "In a new prison—or in a grave?"

Duparc made two more calls, giving instructions, before saying, "Let's get back to Noisy. We need to pick up that warrant. And we haven't had any lunch, remember."

By the time that they got back to their car the afternoon heat had made them sweaty. "Air-conditioning!" Duparc demanded.

They had barely gotten back on the bumpy road when Léger stiffened in the driver's seat and craned his already long neck. "Somebody's coming!" he exclaimed.

And there, moving in the opposite direction but not yet facing the detectives' car, was another car, rocking and swaying among the bushes and trees. Within seconds they had identified it as the old green Land Rover. It was in its proper element, negotiating rough terrain. There were two people in the front seat. They were slow to see the oncoming Renault. The two vehicles were only fifty yards apart on the narrow path when they came head to head. The Land Rover stopped abruptly.

"Drive right up to them," Duparc said. "Don't give them room to turn around."

The Land Rover did not move, and Léger put the Renault just a couple of yards from it. Duparc noticed that Léger, who was in his shirtsleeves, felt to check that his gun was still where it was supposed to be.

Duparc got out of the Renault while putting on his jacket. Léger remained at the wheel. In the Land Rover, which was considerably higher than the detectives' car, there was no sign of movement.

# CHAPTER 60

The day after the fractious meeting at the Pellegrini mountain cabin Richard was in a state of virtual collapse. He felt drained and struggled with his bewilderment and anger. Hick had driven Vandenhorst, Reed, and him back to Washington the previous afternoon, but there had been little further talk of the conspiracy. When Richard had attempted to return to the subject that had so rattled him at the meeting, Vandenhorst had insisted that Richard should offer no more opinions before he had had time to reflect. Vandenhorst had expressed no irritation with him — had rather been solicitous of his concerns — but had refused to discuss them. Richard's disappointment and resentment had not slackened. He had spent most of the trip in sullen silence.

Richard had slept badly. He was incapable of concentrated work. For the first time in his many months in the conspiracy, he failed to show up at a scheduled morning meeting without letting anybody know in advance. He did not leave the house. He spent time in his basement office ostensibly sorting papers on his cluttered desk, but also wandered about the house and the yard doing nothing in particular: reading the newspaper, fixing a dripping faucet. For a while he even puttered about in the garden, something he had not done for months. Although, from long practice, he managed to maintain his outward composure, Helen knew that something had happened.

"What's the matter?" she said when by late morning he had shown no signs of settling down to work in his study or of intending to leave the house.

"Oh, I'm just a bit tired. I thought I would take it easy today and tie up a few loose ends. I have hundreds of old emails to go through, but I'm going slow — thought I might just take a few hours off."

Helen gave him an uncertain smile and a light hug. Was he not feeling well? She decided not to ask. He might see it as indirect nagging. He wondered whether she would leave him alone or take advantage of his not being busy to raise the issue of family plans for the rest of the summer. He wondered if he should take a long walk, drive to the hardware store, or drive over to McDonald's for lunch to protect himself a while longer from her entreaties.

But he stayed put. Other than conversing pleasantly when their paths crossed, Helen let him alone. John was at the neighborhood pool with his friends, and Anne was spending the weekend with a friend's family at Ocean City on the Atlantic coast three hours away.

Richard was alone with his thoughts and emotions.

Was there any truth to Vandenhorst's suggestion that he had not really wanted to hear about the more disturbing aspects of the plans for the coup? Had he, in general, understood what sort of thing was being planned but chosen to conceal it from himself? No, he told himself. Never had he been part of any discussion of such extreme measures. He had felt uncomfortable many times when violence and the effects on innocent bystanders had come up, but he had been truly shocked by the callous mention of a need to liquidate a large number of people. His surprise had surely been genuine, his indignation equally so. And yet, considering the scope of what the conspirators would attempt, the great scarcity of resources, and the need to make the coup stick, had he been willfully naïve in not realizing that more people would have to die than he had vaguely assumed? Sales, O'Brien, and the others were right that the conspiracy had to play for keeps. Was it, then, not better to "remove" — there was that ambiguous-sounding word again — too many people than too few?

No, Richard told himself, there was no excuse for excessive killing. There certainly was no excuse for cruelty or vengeance. In this all-important matter he had to follow his conscience. He sharply resented Sales's brutal challenge to his moral objections. Sales and anybody who agreed with him were compromising the integrity of the whole enterprise.

Vandenhorst, O'Brien, Bunker, and Reed had seemed not to oppose Sales in substance. They simply had a more polished, less abrasive style. Richard had been the only dissenter. Why? Was he the only one in the group with real moral acuity — he, the person among them with the least experience of the kind of practical matters that the coup would face? Was he being conceited?

He tried to control his emotions and achieve some critical detachment. As so often in the past when in a muddle, he called upon Billick's principle. His appreciation for the principle had only grown with his experience of life. It had given him some protection against wishful thinking and destructive indecision. He had no patience with himself or others who bemoaned missed opportunities or sad developments that might have been avoided if only something had been different, if only another course of action had been chosen. What had already happened was irrevocable. To dwell on what might have been was a self-indulgent avoidance of the need to get on with life as it had now become. The only point of thinking about missed opportunities was to learn from mistakes.

In his work with the conspirators Billick's principle had come repeatedly to Richard's mind. Most fundamentally, it was a reminder that human beings are and will remain human beings. They are imperfect or worse. Even the best have limitations and weaknesses. Looking for alliances you try to stay away from the vicious and corrupt ones, the ones with obvious and dangerous flaws, but you must at the same time be prepared for their shenanigans. Sometimes, when bad people have power to defeat your purposes and you cannot hope to overcome them, you cannot avoid dealing with them or even enlisting their support. Even the noblest purposes sometimes require making alliances with bad people. You always prefer to deal with decent people, but they, too, are flawed. To get something done, even to get something done for good, you have to make do with allies who are actually or potentially available. You cannot create better allies out of thin air.

Richard had asked himself at times if the conspiracy had attracted people of dubious character, who might taint and threaten the whole enterprise, but, for the most part, his anxieties had been alleviated as he learned more about them. The presence of people of real ability, smarts, and good sense had reassured him. Besides, he kept saying to himself, beggars can't be choosers. The coup had to be attempted. Although the conspiracy could not be careless in selecting its members, neither should it set such standards that it could never reach critical mass. That kind of conscientiousness would be inherently self-defeating, forever postponing the urgently needed challenge to a corrupt and dysfunctional system. So you made the best you could of the resources you had or might have. No others were available.

So what about Sales? No one was available to take his place. Even if morally dubious, he was indispensable to the coup.

Was it even obvious that Sales and those who agreed with him were Richard's moral inferiors? Richard sometimes asked himself whether a person with all kinds of qualms and mixed emotions might not pose a greater threat to the success of the coup than a brutally goal-oriented and practical person like Sales. It made Richard squirm to consider that Sales, the gruff, rough, tough-talking, no-nonsense warrior, might be a better representative than he of Billick's principle, if not as well equipped as Richard to explicate it philosophically. *Sales* might have the superior sense of what the success of the coup required and the superior capacity for disciplined, focused action.

Richard was the one who had warned the other conspirators of the danger that a realistic attitude might be for some in their ranks a merely theoretical stance rather than a down-to-earth psychological readiness to act. But was not the weakness about which he had worried actually his own flaw, the state of mind of a scholar who had spent his mature life *contemplating* historical events rather than living through intensely fraught and disturbing circumstances? His only preparation for dealing with such times was *imagining* what they would be like, extending his limited personal experience of tense, terrifying moments. Richard had had his share of struggles and fighting in his professional career, but the psychological pressure of those battles could not, he realized, be compared with putting your entire existence at stake. Could Sales be correct in regarding *him* as a weak link in the conspiracy? Might he, Richard, the supposedly hard-nosed realist, be a part of the defective material out of which Sales and others had to build a working alliance? Richard's moments of self-loathing, hesitation, ambivalence, squeamishness, and every other distracting feeling suggested that he, as much as anybody else, was an obstacle to effective action, a possible burden and complication. A person really cut out for what the conspirators were planning would take satisfaction, even find a kind of delight, in first contemplating and then executing the coup. What a person is really good at he finds pleasure in doing, whether it be running a grueling marathon, completing a painting, negotiating a complicated legal contract, or leading a battle. Richard told himself that he had undoubtedly been good at parts of the work of a conspirator, and he had taken a kind of satisfaction in it. But, he had to admit, the doubts and the fears and the pains had intensified and had at times almost crippled him. He kept returning to the danger in which he had placed his family.

Was he, then, simply showing himself incapable of standing the heat in the kitchen? Had he let moral qualms about the plans to eliminate opposition to the coup spin out of control in order to excuse himself from further participation?

No, he told himself emphatically. His moral indignation of the previous day had been genuine. He had felt a deep revulsion. The conspirators intended actions that his conscience simply could not accept. He could also imagine this kind of ruthlessness resulting in far more deaths than anticipated.

Did he, then, not have to withdraw from the conspiracy? Must he not even find a way to stop the coup? Was it not even his moral duty to inform on the conspirators? That would mean giving them up to the system that he had come to despise.

No, that was unthinkable. He could not turn the people in with whom he had so long cooperated and whom, in several cases, he liked and had come to regard as friends. And what could be worse than letting the system purge its enemies and retrench? This being the case, how could he even think of abandoning the conspiracy or causing problems for it? Coming as it did upon months of intensifying pressure and anxiety, his moral tribulation brought unrelieved wretchedness.

Helen put out soup and sandwiches in the kitchen for lunch. They talked briefly, but Richard was distracted. Desperate to take his mind off his predicament he had the idea of trying to prune a couple of bushes in their backyard. It was early afternoon. It was sunny, but the temperature was unseasonably pleasant. He told Helen what he was going to do and fetched the pruning scissors he needed from the garage. He started on an unwieldy rhododendron bush near the patio at the back of the house. He had made little headway when he found himself standing with the gardening tool in his outstretched hand, staring unseeingly in front of himself. He had been far away. He let the scissors drop to the ground and walked over to a garden chair in the shade. He slumped in the chair and closed his eyes. In mere moments he was asleep. He was mercifully dead to the world.

"Richard, Richard, what's the matter!?" Helen was shaking him. "Is anything wrong?"

He groggily opened his eyes. The situation was strangely unfamiliar. Where was he? He felt sweaty and queasy to his stomach. Why was Helen shaking him?

"I tried waking you by just talking to you, but you didn't respond. I thought you might have fainted. I had to make sure you were all-right."

He slowly awoke and was assaulted by the pain from which sleep had let him escape.

"Well, I just thought I would sit down for a while, and I must have fallen asleep."

"But you never sit out here by yourself."

"The weather is pretty nice."

"Are you sure you're all right?"

"Of course I am."

She looked at him, still uncertain what to think.

Richard rubbed his eyes, taking his time before rising.

"What brought you out here in the first place?" he asked.

"I hadn't seen you for a while, and when I looked into the backyard you seemed to have disappeared. I couldn't see this spot from inside."

Daylight had begun to fade. He looked at his watch and realized that he must have been asleep for the better part of an hour, though sitting in a not very comfortable position. His neck was sore. When he rose he noticed that he had better watch his step. He could understand why Helen had wanted to wake him. How could he not have responded when she started speaking to him? He was not a particularly deep sleeper. She must have feared that he had had a stroke or a heart attack—that he was dead.

Poor Helen. How badly he had treated her! And poor John and Anne. He had been a terrible husband and father for a long time.

While Helen watched he picked up the gardening tool. He brought it back to the garage, and went inside. He wanted to go upstairs to take a shower. When he passed through the kitchen he thought he heard through the open door to the basement that the scrambler phone was ringing in his study. The sound was muffled by its being kept in a desk drawer. Old reflexes made him race down the stairs to get to the telephone in time.

"Yes."

"We need to meet, right away." It was Vandenhorst. "Meet me in one hour at the embassy." The "embassy" was their code word for the parking garage under a rather ritzy shopping mall in Chevy Chase, right on the line between Maryland and D.C. The code word had been selected because the shopping complex also contained an Embassy Suites hotel. They had agreed long ago that a certain area of the lowest level of the underground parking garage would be a suitable meeting place. Because most shoppers did not want to drive all the way down to the lowest level to park, there were usually plenty of parking places there. Conversations would take place inside a car that was parked in that area. Security was generally good, although the only alternative exit was through the elevator or stairs to the upper floors.

"Park and look for me."

Richard was still woozy after his deep sleep. Reflexes rather than deliberation had decided his reaction to what Vandenhorst had asked. He merely said, "OK." Was he not the conspiracy's ultimate team player, utility in-fielder, jack-of-all-trades? He had not forgotten the eruption of the previous day, but the long nap had numbed and confused him and made him revert to form. Had he been more alert, he might have made some excuse not to come to the proposed meeting.

He went upstairs and told Helen that he needed to meet a doctoral student at the university, but that he expected to be home in time for dinner. He had expected her to protest by saying something like, "Now, on a Sunday afternoon?" or "In the middle of the summer?," but she just nodded. Perhaps finding him alive in that garden chair had made her feel more tolerant and benevolent.

Richard took his time showering, washed his hair, and let the water run. In the summer time the water in the pipes was almost lukewarm, and he turned the hot water off entirely. He stood in the shower thinking. He dried himself slowly and methodically, which was unlike him. He dressed in slacks, loafers, and a summer shirt and went out to his car. He did not have far to drive and had plenty of time, so he merely followed the light traffic in the slowest lane, which was also out of character.

His mind was clearing. He was as troubled as he had been earlier in the day. His anger at Vandenhorst had resurfaced. In one part of himself he did not really want to see him, but in another part he knew that he had to. He needed to face Vandenhorst, and it would not be a pleasant encounter. He felt himself moving towards some final resolution of his great struggle with himself.

But Vandenhorst was not likely to be alone, he realized. At least one of the others would accompany him. This was how the conspiracy handled people who had shown substantial discomfort with the plans and who might be thinking about separating themselves from the conspiracy. Richard wondered in which category of recalcitrance or unease he had been placed. Was he regarded as a nervous Nellie who had reservations and fears and who just needed to be reassured and reinspired, or had he been placed at the other extreme, as one suspected of turning against the conspiracy? If the latter, Sales and perhaps others might not let him withdraw. Because he knew so much, he might be considered an intolerable security risk. Sales and perhaps others might think it necessary to play it safe and to "neutralize" him. "Neutralize"? The right word was "kill." He would have to be eliminated immediately. The only question would be how?

No, Vandenhorst would never approve such a course. Upset and angry as Richard was with Vandenhorst, he was convinced that Vandenhorst cared about him personally. Vandenhorst had no children, and Richard had sometimes wondered if he had become something like a son to him. The fact that Vandenhorst had known and admired Richard's grandfather even gave him a kind of family connection to the Bittenbergs. Yet Vandenhorst had kept the truth about the executions from Richard. Vandenhorst had surely been disingenuous when suggesting that Richard must have figured out that executions would be necessary. Yes, Vandenhorst had deliberately deceived him.

Or—there was that disturbing thought again—had Vandenhorst been right in ascribing to Richard a subtle, almost unconscious self-deception? But that would mean—another thought hit him that had previously crossed his mind and that now acquired new prominence and poignancy: that he might actually have an inclination to conceal uncomfortable truths from himself. Had he deceived himself more generally? Whenever a question of Vandenhorst's judgment or integrity had come up, had he engaged in wishful thinking and given Vandenhorst the benefit of the doubt? The reason would be obvious: that he wanted to believe the best about the conspiracy. Unless he could think highly of Vandenhorst and his allies, how could he justify participating in their enterprise?

If he was guilty of wishful thinking, the people with whom he had associated might not be whom he had assumed. Under a veneer of urbane humanity, probity, and concern for the common good, Vandenhorst might conceal a callous ruthlessness and desire for power. He and the others might in Richard's presence have tried to appear to be what they thought that he wanted them to be. When there was no need to reassure a person like Richard they might show a different face.

Sitting at a red light near his destination he tried out the possibility that he had been naïve and that he had substantially misjudged many or most of the conspirators. What if, deep down, they were not much different from those they wanted to replace and just desired power for themselves—to say nothing of their other weaknesses? Sales vile bullying the day before had shown him to be a moral dullard and an irascible, ruthless operator. The preoccupation of a few of the conspirators with their pet concerns exemplified another type of myopia. Robert Bates, the congressional staffer, seemed not to be able to take a single step without the approval of his congressman boss. Lester Pickett was still full of senatorial oratory and posturing, but was he not a mere has-been, a tired old politician?

But who was he, Richard, to pass judgment on the conspirators? In the eyes of those who gave the conspiracy its direction, Richard perhaps appeared a woolly idealist, no matter how bright, thoughtful, well informed and useful he might have been. Now they probably viewed him as a source of trouble. After yesterday's scene, had the top conspirators concluded that he posed a great a danger to the coup?

Was he at this moment headed into a trap? Would he be found dead the same night or in a day or two, slumped in a car on the bottom level of a parking garage with a bullet in his head and a gun next to him, clearly a suicide? Helen would tell the police that, yes, Richard had been under great stress and that he may have been depressed. On the day of his death he had behaved unusually, even erratically.

But Richard again dismissed the thought. Vandenhorst apparently had a previously not obvious dark side, but his affection for Richard was real. The empathy, solicitousness, and consideration that he had long shown could not have been a mere smokescreen. Vandenhorst's apparent high regard for Richard's judgment and his having relied on Richard for many sensitive assignments could not have been a front for anything else. Unless Vandenhorst had regarded Richard as being able to contribute something important, why pull him into the very center of the conspiracy in the first place? A few in the inner circle might now see him as a liability, but Vandenhorst would be protective of him—assuming that Richard had not fundamentally misjudged him.

Richard drove into the garage and negotiated its narrow lanes and awkward turns. The architect had obviously done everything to save space. Few commercial areas in the Washington area commanded a higher price per square foot. There were plenty of free spaces throughout the garage. When, if not on a Sunday afternoon in June, would it not be easy to find parking? But Richard would have preferred to see more people. He might be putting himself in danger. Vandenhorst was not the only strong-willed person on the steering committee. For a moment, Richard thought of turning around and driving out of the garage. Why take this risk? But he drove on. He wanted to face Vandenhorst. Before reaching the bottom level of the garage he pulled into a space, locked the car, and strolled down the ramp to the lowest level. He was within a couple of minutes of the meeting time. He was used to observing his surroundings, but this time he did not worry about the FBI. He saw no people except for a woman who exited an elevator with a large shopping bag. In the general area where he had previously had meetings with conspirators he immediately recognized Vandenhorst's car. There were few other cars, and he saw no movement. As he approached Vandenhorst's car he noticed that there was only one person in it. Vandenhorst was sitting in the driver's seat with the window down. Richard slowed down. In a situation like this one, the conspiracy would employ a team of two or three. At least one more person should arrive soon, or this would be an irregular meeting. Richard looked around him. Was anything wrong? Vandenhorst waved to him.

Richard opened the passenger door. Vandenhorst said, "Come on in!" Vandenhorst was wearing a beige summer jacket over a dress shirt open at the neck. Seeing Vandenhorst at close range in the dim light of the garage, Richard got the impression that the lines in his face were more deeply etched than before. He looked tired.

"Who else's coming?" Richard's question showed how he perceived the situation and that he expected the intervention of a team from the steering committee.

"No one."

"No one?"

"I thought we should speak privately."

"I would have thought that a few of the others now see me as a big problem. Perhaps I should be *removed*," he said, sarcastically using the ambiguous word.

"I'm not here to discuss what others might think."

"So there *is* sentiment for *neutralizing* me?"

Vandenhorst ignored the barb.

"You didn't attend the meeting this morning, and you didn't let anybody know. That's not like you."

"I suppose not, but I didn't feel like going."

Vandenhorst did not press the matter. He knew that Richard's failure to attend was due to the quarrel the day before.

"Richard, I'm so sorry about yesterday and about having jumped to conclusions about you. I did think you understood what needs to be done with some of the worst and most dangerous members of the system."

"*No*, Herbert!" Richard exclaimed with passion. "You didn't think that! After hearing me worry so many times about people dying, you couldn't possibly have thought I would approve of large-scale executions, much less the killing of innocents, like that general Sales would like to get rid of."

"Please, calm down, Richard. I'm trying to explain something." Vandenhorst spoke in a soft, friendly, even apologetic tone. "First of all, you should not simply assume that that I wanted to deceive you. Don't I deserve the benefit of your doubt?"

"But there *is* no doubt," Richard said with greater emphasis than he knew to be justified. "I have reason to feel betrayed. You knew how sensitive I am on the issue of deaths and killing. You concealed the truth because you knew I would oppose this monstrous scheme."

Richard thought he saw real pain in Vandenhorst's face.

"I'll concede this much," Vandenhorst said. "I understood that this aspect of the coup would be distasteful to you, partly because in your life you have been spared experience of the darker side of politics and world affairs—everything from routine intelligence work to paramilitary special operations, to say nothing of war. To read about them in books is different from being involved in them, as I've been. I suppose I tried not to talk too much of parts of the coup that had to bother you especially." Vandenhorst gave Richard a disconcerted look mixed with tenderness. "I did try to spare you some of the more gruesome specifics."

Richard noticed the solicitousness in Vandenhorst's expression, but ignored it.

"*Specifics!*" he shouted. He lowered his voice as he said: "Those specifics had to do with ruthless killing."

"Surely you realized—we did talk about it from time to time—that we would have to get rid of some individuals who stood in the way of the success of the coup."

"C'mon, Herbert! Those were unavoidable deaths, like the need to kill that Capitol Police chief or that head of the presidential detail of the Secret Service *in case they should prove dangerous obstacles.* We never talked about lining up people in large numbers and gunning them down in cold blood. I'll say it again, that's deliberate, large-scale killing, and I have *NOT* been privy to any such discussion. You and some of the others have kept me uninformed."

"Richard, you say 'large-scale killing,' but what is your standard? Give me an example of a coup or revolution in any country that has not cost many hundreds or thousands their lives, I mean short of any civil war that may have been triggered. People are of necessity rounded up and, in some cases, executed. You, the historian, could hardly have thought that we could entirely avoid that kind of action."

Richard could not at the moment think of an historical example that contradicted Vandenhorst's assertion, and the difficulty fanned his fear that he had allowed himself to look away from one side of the coup that he would rather not think about. Had he invented an excuse for being critical of the coup?

"After all," Vandenhorst continued, "we're going to attempt a coup in the largest country in the Western world and try to dislodge a strongly entrenched leadership class. We are, in a way, attempting the impossible. It's partly because we have such limited assets that we have to eliminate so many of the key people who could organize countermeasures against us. We don't have enough personnel to do an effective job of warehousing opponents. One of the reasons why killings will be kept to a minimum is that we only have the resources for focused, surgical, *small-scale* strikes and executions."

"If we had more helpers we could kill the *entire* leadership class!" Richard said, his voice dripping with sarcasm.

"Please, Richard, you're being deliberately ornery and difficult. You know very well what I meant—I already said that we might have been able to afford fewer executions if we had had many more helpers to keep captured people securely locked up."

Richard did not respond. He knew that Vandenhorst's charge of orneriness was true. Something in Richard *wanted* to give everything said in defense of the harsher aspect of the coup the worst possible interpretation. He was positively looking for arguments to justify a new view of the conspiracy.

"There's something else you should consider, Richard," Vandenhorst said. "The people we have to get rid of are not only dangerous to us. As a result of getting us into one unnecessary military conflict after another, they are responsible for thousands of deaths. What we have to do to rid America of this scourge is trivial by comparison."

But Richard was barely listening. He sat staring in front of himself. A shopper on his way to his car reminded Richard that others were continuing their normal lives. His own situation was a strange, frightening anomaly. The old tension bore down on him with overpowering force. The reason why he staggered inwardly, he realized, was not only or even mainly all the conspiracy's demands on his time, or all the work he had done for it, or even the stress of being involved in something that could put him in jail and bring his family into disrepute. It was his relentless, almost permanent struggles with self. He was always in the middle of a battle between incompatible considerations. He was never quite certain what in his mind was conscience and what was cowardliness, arrogance, self-deception, conceit, or escapism. The newly discovered callousness of some of his fellow conspirators had turned the strain into an almost physical, piercing pain. He could not stand it. Like a person with acute nausea, he wanted to empty his system of offending content in a violent paroxysm.

Suddenly he knew what would have to be his next step. He had no choice. He unknowingly made hard fists, then let his hands fall relaxed into his lap.

"Richard, is anything the matter?"

But he just sat looking at his hands. His face was drawn.

"Richard!"

He slowly turned his face towards Vandenhorst, who looked at him with concern.

Still Richard said nothing.

"You don't look very well, Richard. Should I take you home?"

Richard shook his head. He looked again into his lap. When he finally spoke his voice was barely audible.

"Herbert, I've had enough. I'm out."

Vandenhorst turned in his seat to face Richard more fully.

"What!?" It wasn't clear whether Vandenhorst had been unable to hear or was incredulous.

"You must not say that, Richard, not even as hyperbole."

Vandenhorst's facial expression did not show whether Richard's statement had startled him. What it did reveal resembled the distress of a parent.

"I'm not posturing, Herbert," Richard said quietly. "I'm out—as of this moment."

Vandenhorst shook his head.

"Richard, you're tired. You don't know what you're saying."

Richard lifted his head and looked at Vandenhorst.

"I know perfectly well what I'm saying." He did not raise his voice. "It's very simple, and it's very straightforward: I'm out!"

"You're worn out, Richard. We're all tired. You need some rest."

"Yes, I do need rest, but it won't change my mind, believe me."

"Don't do anything on the spur of the moment that you'll regret for the rest of your life."

"Herbert, I've already done it! Don't try to change my mind. You won't be able to."

"This is the most important decision of your life."

"And I've made it."

Richard opened the passenger door to get out.

"Richard!" Vandenhorst's voice was loud and sharp, as if intended to break a spell.

But Richard got out of the car. He was just about to close the door when he leaned back into the car and said, "I won't make any difficulties for you, I promise. I'll just fade away."

As he pulled out his head to close the door he could see the face of Herbert Vandenhorst in the dim dome light. It struck him that it was the face of a distraught, grieving father.

Richard walked up the ramp to his car. He did not feel numb or confused, but a calm determination. He started the engine, backed out of his cramped parking place, and exited the labyrinthine garage with its sharp turns. He emerged into the daylight of that other, unfamiliar world, which he had left long ago.

He drove home in a strangely calm mood. He had turned his back on an enterprise that had completely absorbed him for as long as he could remember. He had cut the Gordian knot. The terrible pressure was off, he told himself. He was free. He gave no thought to the consequences of his decision, only relished the moment. He was not exhilarated, but felt infinitely relieved, almost serene. He had noticed earlier in the day that it was sunny and pleasant, but then he had been barely aware of his surroundings. Now he took in that it was a lovely late afternoon. The sun was beginning to dip out of sight, and he took in every nuance of a glorious, orange western sky. Springtime and early summer were magnificent in the Washington area. Flowers were everywhere. It was a beautiful day, and he was heading home. He would have dinner with his family.

He parked in the driveway. When he opened the front door to their house he immediately smelled cooking. Pop music coming from upstairs announced that John was in his room, but with the door open. In the kitchen he saw Helen and next to her Anne, who was assisting her with some chore. When they heard him coming, they turned, and their faces registered a mixture of surprise and delight.

"Home already?" Helen said.

He nodded, walked up to her and gave her a kiss on the neck. She smiled.

"How would you like a glass of wine?" she asked.

"I would like nothing better."

Helen took out two glasses from a cabinet and a bottle of white wine from the refrigerator. She poured two glasses and handed him one. He took it gratefully. For the first time in many months he was really home.

As he sat himself down at the kitchen table he said. "Isn't it high time we made plans for that trip to Europe?"

# CHAPTER 61

The driver's door of the green Land Rover opened. Major Dégas stepped out, glaring at Duparc with undisguised surprise that turned into disgust.

"What are you doing here? This is private property," he barked. "You're trespassing!"

Dégas stared at Duparc the way he had undoubtedly stared at numerous subordinates in his soldierly career.

"We would like to talk to Baron de la Broderie," Duparc said calmly.

Dégas's eyes were flashing, and the cheeks of his square face were turning red.

"Well, there's an entrance to the estate. You know where it is." The major made an almost violent gesture indicating the direction. "You can call there. You've no right to be here! Your superiors will certainly hear about this."

Dégas's brusque manner was again that of an irate officer.

"You'd better calm down," Duparc said, seemingly unaffected. "We're here on police business, and we're authorized to be here."

"Authorized!? What the hell are you talking about? You're *trespassing*!"

The baron was exiting the Land Rover, and Duparc saw out of the corner of his eye that Léger was getting out of their car and placing himself behind the open driver's door. His gun holster was visible before he put on his jacket.

"Either you settle down, Major," Duparc said, "or you will be taken into custody."

"What the hell—?"

"Just a moment. What's the matter?" The tranquil voice of Baron de la Broderie put a damper on what was threatening to become a scuffle. Dressed informally and discreetly in a light brown suede jacket, a white shirt open at the neck and beige dress slacks, the baron exuded authority. His lightly bearded face showed benevolence rather than anger, and his eyes even had a twinkle of humor.

A really cool customer, Duparc thought. De la Broderie was not easily ruffled.

"We need to talk to you and Major Dégas."

"But what in the world are you doing here!? This back road is rarely used."

"I might ask you the same question," Duparc said.

The baron stiffened.

"This happens to be my property, sir. *You* are the one who's out of place. You know where the entrance to the estate is."

"Your gatekeeper was not very cooperative."

"My butler and his wife act on my instructions. They're not to let people in without my approval."

"They were unusually obstreperous."

"You are still—out of place, inspector."

The baron had pushed back hard but without raising his voice and becoming caustic. He had much experience handling touchy situations, Duparc thought. He decided to change the dynamics of their encounter.

"No, I believe we're in the right place. We're investigating the disappearance of Professor Richard Bittenberg, an American," Duparc said.

The baron lifted an eyebrow. Duparc noticed that Dégas gave de la Broderie a sudden worried look.

"Bittenberg?" the baron said, but without showing any emotion other than surprise. "How interesting! That name is *familiar* to me. I used to know a man by that name. He was a senior American diplomat, a very fine man. He died many years ago. I met his grandson too. Are you talking about the same person?"

Duparc simply did not know the answer.

"Richard Bittenberg is a professor at National University in Washington, D.C."

"Yes, that's the one. How can I help you, inspector?"

"He disappeared last Friday, and we have reason to believe that he has been kept against his will at your estate."

Dégas again gave the baron a quick glance. De la Broderie said nothing, looked at his shoes while taking a slow breath, and then caught and held Duparc's gaze. The two were about the same height. Neither blinked.

"That's a very serious charge you just made, inspector."

"Also, we believe that you were not truthful when answering our questions about the accident in Noisy. We think Professor Bittenberg was in the car with you."

The baron at first did not react at all. Then he looked sternly at Duparc and held up his arms with the flat of his hands towards Duparc in a gesture saying "stop."

"I will have nothing further to say to you, inspector," the baron said in clipped tones. "Please leave my property. I deeply resent your accusation and this intrusion. I shall have to take the matter up with a friend of mine in the Ministry of the Interior, who will undoubtedly contact the head of your division of the police."

"You'll have to make any call from the police station in Noisy. You will have to come with me for a formal interrogation. The same is true of Major Dégas."

Duparc did not mention to the baron that a warrant to search the estate had been approved. He did not want the baron to gain a psychological advantage from Duparc's failure physically to produce any document.

Duparc had another practical problem. He could not leave the baron and the major at the estate, free to destroy more evidence, but, according to police regulations, he also should not transport the two suspects to Noisy in his own car, which was not a patrol car with a partitioned back seat and special locks for the back doors. He should call for another police vehicle.

"You cannot be serious, inspector," the baron said. "You could not possibly have any evidence justifying such drastic action. Furthermore, I just told you that I have nothing to say."

"Nevertheless, you and the major *will* have to come with us to the police station."

"This is most terribly inconvenient. And I have nothing to say. I protest."

"Protest noted. The only question is: Shall we wait for another police car to assist with the transportation, which would mean standing here in the heat for half an hour, or go now in our car, which is air-conditioned."

Duparc could tell by Léger's quizzical look that he had his doubts about Duparc's suggestion, which implied a plea to de la Broderie and Dégas to come along quietly.

Duparc did not want to wait. His intuition told him that the baron and the major would hardly attempt a daring escape. To try to run would confirm the suspicions against them. They were also intelligent enough to understand that they were not likely to get very far. Besides, de la Broderie was—Duparc was surprised at his own assessment—a baron, a gentleman. He would not take advantage of Duparc's giving him the benefit of the doubt and extending a courtesy. Major Dégas would not do anything not authorized by his employer, whatever his rough, soldierly inclinations. Duparc realized that his attitude was paradoxical. In spite of what they had found at the winery, Duparc had some difficulty thinking of the baron as a criminal. It was highly unlikely that the person kept in the winery had given his consent. The baron had almost certainly committed a very serious crime. He might now well have *killed* Professor Bittenberg! Still, he was not likely to try to run from the police.

Duparc nodded to Léger, who immediately understood.

"Lean up against the car," Léger said to Dégas, who looked pleadingly at the baron but got no reaction. Léger frisked the major with expert hands.

"You too, Baron," Duparc said. De la Broderie did not stand up against the car, only raised his arms. He too was searched.

"It's very hot here in the sun, inspector," the baron said, removing his jacket. Can we get underway?"

"Check the Land Rover," Duparc said to Léger, who walked over to the SUV and did a cursory search. He was finished in a minute and came back with the keys to the car in one hand and a pistol dangling from his little finger in the other.

"Found it in the glove compartment," he said.

"So what! I'm an old soldier," Dégas exclaimed. "It's fully licensed."

Léger put the pistol in a plastic bag and placed it in the trunk of their car.

Duparc walked aside to make a couple of phone calls, one to the police station in Noisy to announce their arrival.

"OK, let's go," Duparc said.

"What about the Land Rover?" Dégas said.

"Don't you worry, someone will pick that up."

"Pick it up? Are you arresting the Land Rover too?" Dégas was snarling.

Duparc did not mention that a forensic team would soon be going over the Land Rover carefully.

They left with Léger at the wheel and Dégas at his side and Duparc in the back seat with de la Broderie. Loaded down, the car hit the ground repeatedly as it rocked and bounced. During the drive to Noisy barely a word was said.

\*\*\*

Helen Bittenberg had taken a long walk in the morning to deal with her frustration at not being able to assist in finding her husband. She might hear from Duparc at any time, but had not expected any call until well after noon. After sitting on the bed with a book without being able to concentrate, she had put on comfortable shoes, left the room, handed the key to the receptionist, and set off without a plan. She had not even needed to tell the receptionist to be careful about messages. She had kept walking, dutifully taking in various sights. She had stopped for lunch in a restaurant near the Eiffel Tower, amazed at herself for having walked that far. Having thought of taking the subway back to the vicinity of the hotel, she had ended up walking all the way back. The hotel receptionist, who knew what would be on her mind, had just shaken his head when she came through the foyer. She had thought of calling Hubert to have somebody to talk to, but she knew that he would call if he had any significant news. She had showered and lain down on the bed. She always felt sleep-deprived. She had fallen asleep.

When she woke up after a quarter of an hour the room felt hot and muggy. She had closed the window in the morning to keep the heat of the day out and had forgotten to open it when she got back. Her first thought was that Duparc had not called. The detective's working day would soon be over. She opened the window and showered again to cool down and clear her mind of cobwebs. With a bath towel wrapped around her she paced the cramped space. She rehearsed yet again possible reasons for her husband's disappearance. What could she have missed?

To break out of a mixture of depression and tedium she turned on the little television set with the poor picture. Because her French was so poor and the hotel only offered French channels, she seldom had it on. The channel to which it was tuned was offering some kind of news report from America. A reporter stood outside the White House, a typical background for political news from the United States. She thought she would prefer music to French talk and switched the channel. Again, she got a news program. This time she saw a picture of the U.S. vice president and heard words that caught her attention: *mort — terrorisme — assassiné —* She caught the tone of simultaneous gravity and excitement in the reporter's voice. The broadcast was apparently live. Then she saw pictures from a Washington city street corner dominated by black SUVs, police cars and motorcycles, and blinking blue lights. She thought she recognized the location. Was that not Pennsylvania Avenue in Washington, D.C., near the Executive Office Building adjacent to the White House? Then there were pictures of the president. "*— n'a pas eté touché —.*"

Helen sat down. She tried other stations and found that several of them were bringing continuous coverage of the same story. Two of them used banner headlines American style to announce an assault on the American presidency. She pieced together that there had been a terrorist attack on the president and vice president of the United States. The vice president was dead, but the president was unhurt and in an unknown location.

Had it not been for her own situation, Helen would have been absorbed by the news and left the hotel in search of CNN or another English speaking channel. Televisions would be on in all the bigger hotels in Paris, and Americans would be flocking to them to learn the latest news.

For Helen, the extraordinary pictures and sounds from America only underlined the unreality and desperation that she had felt for almost a week. The rest of the world might be mesmerized by the startling news from America, but what did it matter to her whether the president of the United States was dead or alive? Curious, she thought, how one's personal circumstances dictated or colored one's view of the world and one's sense of proportion.

She left the television set on but lowered the sound and resumed her pacing. Why didn't Duparc call? He knew how eager she was to hear of any developments in the search.

A telephone signal made her jump. She tore the receiver from its cradle.

"Yes."

"It's Stephen."

Her surprise and disappointment at hearing the wrong voice was soon replaced by icy disgust and curiosity.

"How are you?" She tried to make her voice sound at least neutral.

"You've probably heard what happened in the U.S., about the terrorist attacks on the president and vice president."

"Yes, I did."

"As if you didn't have enough to worry about. I'd taken the day off to take care of some personal business, but I was called back to the embassy. You can imagine the situation here at the moment. But I felt I had to call you. For what it may be worth, I can tell you that the president is not in danger. A twist of fate thwarted the terrorist plot."

"I'm glad to hear that." Helen could muster little feeling on the matter and found it hard to talk to Ferguson.

"I understand that your mind is on different things, but I wanted to call."

"Thank you, Stephen. I do appreciate it." She forced herself to sound grateful.

There was a pause.

"I've been thinking," Ferguson said.

He was changing the subject, Helen thought. He was coming to the real reason for his call.

"You've had a terrible, terrible time, Helen, and I'm so sorry for you."

Helen felt a surge of disgust for this duplicitous, unctuous man, but managed to rein in her feelings.

"I'm afraid I've not behaved as I should."

You despicable hypocrite, she thought.

"I would've liked to tell you in person what I've been thinking, but I won't be able to leave the embassy for quite a while, and I didn't want to delay speaking to you."

What was the hurry? Why the need to speak just now? Had she detected a kind of uncertainty, even a trembling in the voice of this seasoned diplomat?

"I'm listening."

"Well, the main thing I wanted to say — you already know — is that my conduct towards you has been unacceptably influenced by very personal feelings."

"Yes?"

"The long and short of it is, Helen, that I'm, well — simply infatuated with you, and I haven't been able to control my feelings. My only excuse is that I've been under tremendous pressure in recent months. Then when I met you here in Paris, I simply lost my balance. I never told you, but you made quite an impression on me when I first met you in Washington. But then I had all my senses."

Ferguson seemed to have some difficulty keeping his voice clear and composed. She thought she heard something like a sob. Disgusted and angry as she was, she could not help being curious. Why, all of a sudden, this bout of maudlin self-recrimination?

"I hope you can forgive me?"

Helen had a strong intuition that he was asking forgiveness for more than his amorous advances.

She felt her anger rising and turning into fury.

"Helen, are you there?"

When she finally spoke, her voice was loud and cutting, giving vent to her pent-up rage: "Where's Richard, you son of a bitch?!"

There was silence.

"Answer me!" she cried.

Again there was silence.

"I'm very sorry," he said in a muted, muffled voice, and the line went dead.

Her emotions were now in complete turmoil. She had been unable to contain her anger. She had no longer *wanted* to. She thought of going to the U.S. Embassy to confront Ferguson and to try to extract a confession, but she realized that he would clam up, probably even refuse to see her. The embassy would be in crisis mode, giving him the perfect excuse to turn her away. She also did not want to leave the hotel. She expected to hear from Duparc at any moment. Her next thought was to telephone Duparc to let him know what she had done, but she should not have done what she had. She collapsed on the bed. She rubbed her face and took deep breaths. How *could* she have been so foolish? Now Ferguson knew that she knew. She had complicated the work of Duparc. She was falling apart.

The telephone rang again. She thought it might be Ferguson calling back, but wanted it to be Duparc with some definite news.

She lifted the receiver.

"Darling, how are you?" Hubert Bittenberg's drawl was unmistakable.

"As well as might be expected." She held back what had just happened. Anybody monitoring her telephone conversations would already know, but she needed to think about what to tell Hubert.

"I guess you heard the awful news about the attempts on the lives of the president and vice president."

"I did. I was just trying to make sense of French news reports."

"Well, the president's apparently OK. He was out in Montana. He likes to drive his own private car out there, but he happened not to be in it when the terrorists struck. The car had a Secret Service escort, but a Secret Service agent was driving. They were going to pick up the president's wife at the local airport. The president had decided to stay at home."

"I see."

"Some terrorist group has claimed responsibility. There are fears that this is just part of some larger attack on the U.S. government. Washington's on high alert. There's nothing else on television. All the networks and cable news stations are covering developments without interruption. New reports come in all the time. There have even been reports of troops being deployed to help protect government buildings."

"Hard to imagine. How are the kids — our kids I mean?"

"Fine. I'm actually calling about whether you think you'll be able to attend Donna's wedding next month."

As Helen knew nobody named Donna, she feigned a brief conversation about her imaginary wedding before hanging up. Because Duparc was likely to call at any moment, she thought of asking Hubert to say right away what was on his mind, but she decided to stick to their usual routine. She dressed quickly and within minutes was talking to Hubert in one of the telephone booths in the nearby hotel.

"Reilly, the private eye, is still missing. The Virginia state police have initiated an inquiry. They're exploring whether his disappearance might be related to the investigation I hired him for, but he was working on four different cases, and there are other possible angles. His sidekick is tracing some of Reilly's steps in investigating Richard, but he was just generally aware of what Reilly was doing, and he's not gotten very far. He was at your house this morning. Now I expect he won't be getting anywhere for a while because of the mess in Washington. Everybody's mind is on what just happened and on possible additional attacks. Who will have any time for Reilly's disappearance?"

"There are still no clues about Richard being mixed up in anything?"

"I'm sorry, darling. There's very little to go on, just some puzzling facts, like that scrambler telephone. The PI's assistant will need help to make any sense of what he's finding. I've told him to get whatever backing he needs. I'm thinking seriously about contacting the FBI, but now they'll be fully occupied with other things. I also don't know what to tell them. There's no real evidence of a crime, and the Virginia police are already investigating the disappearance of the PI. What about you, Helen? Do you have anything for me?"

Helen did not quite have the energy to tell Hubert about her outburst in the conversation with Ferguson. Instead she summarized what she knew about Duparc's investigation and expressed her certitude that Ferguson and de la Broderie were involved in Richard's disappearance. She had a strong feeling that there would be some kind of revelation very soon. She did not tell her brother-in-law that she was dejected, that in her rational self she no longer believed that Richard would be found alive. Yet in another part of herself, she refused to accept the idea that Richard was gone.

"OK, baby, let me know if there's anything I can do. And call me the minute you hear anything that might help the investigation here in the U.S."

Their call ended after some talk about the children.

She half ran back to the hotel.

As soon as the receptionist saw her he held up a note for her with a kind of triumph.

"Inspector Duparc telephoned."

"When?"

"About twenty minutes since."

She snatched the piece of paper and rushed upstairs.

# CHAPTER 62

The day after talking with Vandenhorst in the parking garage Richard tried hard to put all thoughts of the conspiracy out of his mind. He knew himself to be indulging in daydreaming, but could not face his real situation. He tried to be with his family and even made an effort, amounting to little more than browsing, to do some reading for a long-postponed research project. But in a part of himself he was wholly aware that his predicament was deeply vexed, morally and otherwise. It might also be very dangerous. The conspiracy was undoubtedly moving forward. At least some of its leaders now had to regard Richard Bittenberg as a threat. Nobody so close to the heart of the conspiracy had jumped ship before. Might he go to the FBI? He had promised Vandenhorst that he would do no such thing; he would simply disappear. Vandenhorst probably believed him and would assure the others that they had nothing to fear, but Noah Sales in particular, the no-nonsense, take-no-chances general, was likely to regard Richard as a loose cannon. He would want to "neutralize" him without delay. Sales would be less likely than others in the conspiracy to trust Vandenhorst's judgment on this matter. He would give less weight than others to the fact that Richard had sympathized deeply with the conspiracy and that he would risk prison and shame if he went to the FBI. Sales would not want to gamble. Or did Sales regard Richard merely as a weakling who had no other motive for leaving than to escape the heat in the kitchen? Such a person would just want to hide and might be left alone. It bothered Richard that in some moments that view resembled his picture of himself.

It seemed that in every corner of his soul he found ambivalence, ambiguity, and hesitation. A disturbing intuition kept telling him that he was dodging his moral responsibility. He had withdrawn from the conspiracy because he found the planned killings inexcusable. Was he then not morally obligated to try to sabotage the conspiracy? But he was too tired and confused to face the question. He distracted himself by attempting to return to normal life.

On the morning of the day after breaking with Vandenhorst and the conspiracy he agreed to go with Helen to a shopping mall to select a new refrigerator. He wondered whether the conspiracy now had him under surveillance and whether he might be endangering Helen in a new way. He reflected that, if the conspirators wanted to get rid of him, they would need to find some inconspicuous way of doing so, which would take planning. On the other hand, if the conspirators feared that Richard might go to the FBI, immediate action would be necessary. Or perhaps Sales considered Richard to be the type that would fret and fuss for a long time before actually turning in his old colleagues. Richard winced at the thought.

It bothered as much as soothed him that the shopping mall was crowded with people and that ordinary life was still going on. How unconcerned these Americans seemed that their society was being destroyed. How willing they were to escape from reality. But he tried now to appreciate the small pleasures of everyday life. The crowds also provided protection. He doubted that, if an attempt were to be made on his life, it would take place in public. It was deeply ingrained in him to keep his eyes open for possible unwanted attention, but now he looked not for unfamiliar faces, but for former fellow conspirators who might wish him ill.

After selecting a refrigerator he and Helen had lunch together. He could not remember when they had done so the last time in a restaurant. They talked about the arrangements she was making for the trip to Europe. He noticed that she was careful not to let her joy and triumph show too much. From time to time she shot him an anxious glance. She could not quite believe that, at long last, he was trying to change his life. Was he not feeling well? Had anything happened? Would he suddenly relapse into his old ways?

As they drove back home and entered their neighborhood he thought about what a lucky person he had been. People on the outside had to envy him his family and general circumstances. He had been a truly privileged person. All this he had placed in jeopardy.

An unexceptional American car that he did not recognize but that was parked diagonally across from their house put him on alert. As he pulled into their driveway and he and Helen walked to the front door he scanned as much of the neighborhood as he could. Was Hick now watching him or making preparations for snatching him away or getting rid of him in some other way? Richard was relieved to see a man with a clipboard in his hand, perhaps a contractor, leave a neighbor's house across the street. The man walked to the mystery car and drove away.

Protecting himself and his family looked to Richard like a strong argument for going to the feds. Another reason to do so was that, should the coup attempt fail, his involvement would be discovered sooner or later. Other than the feeble defense that he had left the conspiracy in disgust, there would be no ameliorating factors. "If you were so disgusted and really opposed to the coup, why did you not go to the authorities?" He could hear a prosecutor demolishing him before a jury. He would not have a leg to stand on. He would be almost as culpable as the other conspirators, an accessory at minimum.

And yet the idea of going to the authorities seemed not just far-fetched. It struck him as inconceivable. *Those* authorities? They were a part of a perverse, corrupt system. Would *he* be the one to come to the defense of a system that had lost its legitimacy and was abhorrent to every morally and intellectually sentient human being? It was out of the question.

So why, he asked himself, was he now sitting on the sidelines? Why had the planned killing of perhaps a hundred odious representatives of this contemptible system made him withdraw from the conspiracy?

Richard gratefully responded to his son's question whether he might play some tennis with him. "Sure, John."

His son's look of surprise was another painful reminder of how he had neglected his family.

Richard's first two days away from his grueling existence as a conspirator went by in a daze. He tried to get used to a normal life, and yet he could not assume that such a life was really in his future. The great relief that he had felt immediately upon removing himself from the conspiracy had been followed by bouts of disappointment, resentment, confusion, and fear. What would happen to him and his family and to the conspiracy? On the plausible assumption that the conspirators would leave him alone and the wholly unlikely assumption that he would not go to jail after a failed coup attempt, he vaguely envisioned himself as leading a very private existence, spending much time with his family. He would become more detached from the world around him, isolate himself as much as possible, and bury himself in research and writing. He would attend to history and his own little corner of the world. For the time being, all he felt was a profound uncertainty.

On the third day of his self-imposed excommunication, at 8:30 in the morning, Richard was in his basement discarding papers and deleting computer files that might inadvertently reveal his connection to the conspiracy. He had kept very little sensitive information to begin with, and Hick had taught him how to protect it. When the scrambler phone suddenly rang Richard reached by reflex to open the desk drawer in which it was kept. The call had to be about another urgent meeting. Then he caught himself. Why had he not disconnected that telephone and gotten rid of it? Had he not wanted to cut off communication with the conspiracy completely? He looked at the drawer. He let the telephone ring twice more. The caller must be getting ready to hang up. Why would he answer? But he activated the telephone and lifted the receiver.

It was Vandenhorst.

As soon as Richard heard who it was, he said calmly but firmly, "I'm well and truly out. I won't come back."

"Please, Richard, listen! We have to talk. We *have* to meet! For your sake."

Richard resisted at first, but the urgency in Vandenhorst's voice persuaded him."

"OK."

"Meet me at 10:30 in the cave." The "cave" was what the conspirators called the platform of the Bethesda subway station on the Red Line, which connects Maryland and D.C. Those who met there would take a train either northbound or southbound or get out of the station and go somewhere above ground. Evasive tactics had become so routine that the conspirators did not give them a second thought.

What was he doing accepting a meeting with Vandenhorst? He had broken with the conspiracy. He might be walking into a trap. Why take such a risk? He knew why. It was because Vandenhorst had made the call. Responding affirmatively to Vandenhorst was a deeply ingrained habit, but Richard was angry with him. The reason he had agreed to the meeting was that he could not believe that Vandenhorst would be part of a plot to kill him. There was also something hard to define between them that almost made Richard *want* to see Vandenhorst, even as he told himself that he did not want to have anything to do with him ever again. It was not so much that Richard wanted to rebuke Vandenhorst once more or further justify his decision to leave the conspiracy. Rather, beyond the revelation and deceit that had so disturbed Richard and made him reassess who Vandenhorst was, there remained a special bond between them, even an element of trust. Vandenhorst had been for Richard a good deal more than a fellow conspirator. Without thinking much about it, Richard had regarded Vandenhorst as his senior, not merely in age and administrative rank, but also by virtue of experience and wisdom. Vandenhorst had become a mentor, an authority, something like a father figure. They had had an increasingly intimate friendship. Richard had often thought about how much Vandenhorst resembled his grandfather. For all these reasons, Richard could not quite believe that Vandenhorst had deceived him as he had. The revelations had badly shaken his confidence in Vandenhorst, but they had not extinguished his admiration for this strong-willed and yet sophisticated and dignified representative of old America. Richard had great difficulty reconciling his sense of aversion and betrayal with the affinity, trust, and respect that he still felt.

Richard put on more presentable clothes. He told Helen that he needed to go to his office at the university, but that he would probably be back in the early afternoon. She looked a little worried, but her searching gaze found no obvious sign that her husband was falling back into his old ways. When she gave him a kiss, he returned it with unexpected tenderness and fervor. He had entertained but dismissed the thought that this might be the last time he saw her. Walking to his car, which was parked in the driveway, he noticed that it was going to be another sweltering June day with temperatures near a hundred degrees.

Although it was more time-consuming, Richard drove to the university, parked his car there, and walked to the nearby subway station, which was located a few stations southeast of the Bethesda station. Taking security precautions did not even require special thought.

He arrived at the Bethesda station almost exactly at the appointed hour. Rush hour was at an end and the passenger volume low. Exiting the train, Richard walked slowly along the platform, wondering if Vandenhorst might already be there. He could not see him. A slight tap at his elbow revealed that Vandenhorst had happened to arrive on the same train, just a car or two behind Richard.

"Let's get back on," Vandenhorst whispered, putting an arm around Richard and ushering him onto the train just before the doors closed.

"Over there!" Vandenhorst said, pointing to the very back of the car, which was empty. They seated themselves side by side, facing forward. Nobody had entered the train after they did.

Vandenhorst was wearing a light summer suit and a dress shirt and tie. Richard was probably just one of his assignments that day. Richard noticed that, while most other Washingtonians had some of the healthy-looking tan of the season, Vandenhorst's face almost had the pallor of winter, as if he had not set foot outside during the spring and early summer. His face looked more lined and drawn than Richard had seen it before. Vandenhorst usually did not look his age, but today was different. And were his fingers trembling slightly? He had his normal calm and composure, but he might be struggling to maintain them.

"Let's just stay on the train for a while," Vandenhorst said in a low voice. For the next few moments nobody spoke.

Richard felt the old tension return. Now what would he be asked to do for the conspiracy? His remembering that he had cut his ties to it and no longer had any obligations brought no relaxation. Now he had other reasons to be intensely uncomfortable and on edge. His life might even be in jeopardy. But he had willingly put himself in this subway car with Vandenhorst. Why had he agreed to meet him again?

The train slowed down and stopped. A pair of women in white naval uniforms entered the car—this was the stop for the Bethesda Naval Hospital—but they sat down in the middle of the car.

When the train started moving again, Vandenhorst said in a muted voice: "Richard, I have to tell you that you will regret your decision for the rest of your life."

Richard was not unprepared for some such comment, and he responded in the matter-of-fact tone of voice that he had practiced in the imagination: "Herbert, there's no point in your trying to change my mind. I just won't. There's no chance."

Vandenhorst nodded almost imperceptibly to himself as he said, "But when you've had time to reflect on your stated reason for abandoning us you will, I'm sure, recognize that you made a mistake. And I think you'll judge yourself severely. You will think that, when you had to make the most important decision of your life, you made the wrong one."

Richard felt anger rising within him, and he forgot at first to keep his voice down when he said, "Herbert, how dare you second-guess my moral conscience"—he remembered to lower his voice—"you who are planning cold-blooded murder." Richard stared at Vandenhorst.

Vandenhorst did not respond, only sat quietly as the train emerged from the underground into the sunlight of a typical Washington early summer morning. The train passed over the Washington Beltway. While it slowed down for the next stop Vandenhorst said calmly: "I'm saying what I'm saying not as a fellow conspirator but as a friend who wishes you well and who knows you perhaps better than you do yourself. I know what you will think of yourself in the future whether we succeed or fail. You will think that, in the crunch, you got the shakes and sat on the sidelines."

Blood rushed to Richard's head. The train was rattling to a stop, and he prepared to rise from his seat and to exit the train. Vandenhorst detected his intention and put a hand on his arm, gently motioning him to stay. Richard tensed at his touch but remained in his seat. A couple of passengers left the car. Hot air from the outside invaded the car. An elderly lady entered and seated herself next to the door.

The train moved and again disappeared underground.

"Don't be angry Richard, I'm not telling you what *I* think about your decision. I'm talking about how I think *you* will judge yourself. I've thought about your decision, and I can't say that I blame you. A person like you probably has to have the kind of reservations you have. You have a conscience, and it's been operating in the circumstances of a normal life. You've lived an essentially ordered, predictable, even sheltered life. You've been one of the pillars of a deteriorating society, helping to enforce its highest standards and setting a good example for others. What's important in the present context is that you've never had to ask yourself what conscience might demand in very different, previously unknown circumstances. You've had no practice handling situations in which the world is being turned upside down, where dangers are everywhere you look, and where nothing is predictable or certain. What you've experienced in the conspiracy has been mostly planning, not the actual thing. The really rough stuff's in the future. You've not had to experience the battlefield and ask what conscience demands of you there. You've been spared all but modest deviations from the routines of ordinary life. The long and short of it is that the conspiracy forced you into progressively unfamiliar, rather strange territory. It's not surprising if you had difficulty finding your bearings. Only a person with a lot of relevant experience can be comfortable facing situations like that."

Vandenhorst looked kindly and benignly at Richard, but Richard was peering vaguely out the window as the train was coming to another stop. A few more passengers exited. Some boisterous teenagers rushed in before the doors closed. They remained standing, seemingly in anticipation of getting off the train soon.

"I'm the one to blame for pulling you into the conspiracy," Vandenhorst continued. "I knew something about your family background, and I had read much of your writing. When we met I became more and more impressed by your knowledge and realism and your willingness to work towards real change. I and a couple of the others checked you out carefully, and we agreed that you would be a real asset. We were proved right. You adapted surprisingly well to a new kind of life. You even taught some of us old warhorses a thing or two about what might and might not work."

Vandenhorst smiled as he resumed. "Sales was the only one who worried about you, and I kept reassuring him. In his rough warrior gut he suspected what I did not, that we would be asking you to act too much out of character. How could we expect you to translate your sense of morality, which has been honed in orderly, decent, civilized life into attitudes appropriate to a dangerous, precarious operation in which everything is at stake? Some things you understand better than I do. You can diagnose the illness of our society. But there's little in your experience to prepare you for something as stark as radical surgery on a leg that's eaten away by gangrene and threatening the entire body. That operation takes an experienced, unsentimental, ruthless surgeon."

"You're talking about our people turning into the kind of people we say we despise."

"*No*, Richard, I'm *not!*," Vandenhorst said in vigorous protest. "With all due respect, I think you're letting moral laziness conceal that sometimes there's no choice but do deal harshly with an enemy. If you want the end of defeating the enemy, you have to will the means to the end."

"You're talking about *murder!*"

"No, I'm *not!* Murder is wanton killing to advance a selfish objective. What we're talking about is killing without which a great and urgently needed goal cannot be accomplished. We simply cannot take the risk that the people on the list will stage a comeback. It would be morally indefensible!"

"*Morally indefensible!* Don't make me laugh!"

"Please lower your voice," Vandenhorst said, "the train's stopping."

The youngsters left the train laughing and jostling. No one walked into the car. There was only a couple of stations left before the end of the line.

"I meant what I said," Vandenhorst continued, demonstratively keeping his voice low. "In the circumstances, it would be *wrong* not to eliminate the ones we have in mind. In fact, it's possible that we're *underestimating* how many people we must get rid of, but we don't have much choice, because we don't have the resources to go any further."

"Listen to you!" Richard exclaimed. "And you're speaking in the name of morality." Disgust reeked from his words.

"Get off your high horse, Richard!" Vandenhorst said, his voice strong but still under control. "You're not usually so pompous. I don't think you're nearly so offended as you make it seem. I think in a part of yourself you understand pretty well what I'm saying and know that I may be right."

"No point in my speaking for myself, then, is there?" Richard said sarcastically.

"Richard, I'm not lecturing you. I'm not trying to persuade you. I'm just trying to make you see that you may not be giving me and the others the benefit of the doubt. You're bringing to the conspiracy a moral sensibility that developed in a different context. You can't assume that it is working as well now as in those familiar circumstances. A man like Sales, who strikes you as a moral simpleton, may well be, in his no-nonsense, practical, soldierly way, the one who saves the day. He sizes up the situation and takes charge. He acts. He may make mistakes, but he's not going to be sidetracked or paralyzed by qualms about doing what's necessary. He may save decent, morally scrupulous people from themselves."

"Ah, I see. So *that's* why you wanted to meet! To give me a lecture. To tell me that I'm a weakling, and that you and the others are made of sterner stuff? That's not exactly urgent business."

"No, Richard, that's not why I wanted to see you. What I thought you needed to hear, for your own sake, is that you and I are *not* very different. Not even Noah Sales may be all that different from you. We've just lived different lives, had different experiences, gotten used to different possibilities. Because of my career I've been involved in things that would make the hairs on your head stand on end. Believe me! I have *lived* the sort of things you've only read about in books. Every society has people assigned to that kind of work. I have had to learn how to make my way in terrible situations while trying to follow my moral compass. One can try to do the right thing even in terrible circumstances, work up a sense of how to set the bad guys back and advance the good you want. Sometimes you can afford to be soft and lenient dealing with opposition, sometimes you have to be hard as steel. All I'm saying, Richard — and that's what I think you need to hear — is that I'm no monster. I'm just one who's learned from sometimes bitter experience what will and will not work in a good cause. I don't claim to have an unerring moral sense, but I've got a lot of practice looking for the best way forward in tough situations. All I ask, Richard, is that you give me some credit for integrity. I'm not in this conspiracy to indulge a streak of cruelty. I'm merely trying to be realistic."

"You've got your conscience, and I've got mine. Don't get them mixed up!" Richard said sharply and rose. The train was coming into a station again, and this time he was determined to exit.

"I'll be returning home now," he said, and now Vandenhorst did not try to stop him. He just followed Richard out on the platform, which was above ground. They stood there together in shade from a hot, glaring sun, waiting for a southbound train.

"I'm very sorry, Richard," Vandenhorst said after a minute of uncomfortable silence. "I wish you would stay with us. I truly think that in time you will regret having left us. I should not conceal that your departure is having repercussions, none of them good. This is happening at the worst possible moment. Replacing you is proving difficult, and there are all kinds of ripple effects. Speculation about your status has become a major problem. We're having to resort to duplicity to conceal what's happened."

"Deceit! How out of character!"

Vandenhorst sighed. "Richard, that's unworthy of you. A conspiracy is indistinguishable from deceit. It's in the very nature of what we're doing. Because of our limited resources smoke and mirrors has to be a central feature of our actions."

"But you're talking now about deceiving even your own people, just as you deceived me."

"Oh, Richard! You're being unreasonable. You're letting personal pique cloud your judgment. Some dissembling and concealment is inevitable in a situation like ours. We're operating somewhere in the shadows between an intelligence operation and a war. For heaven's sake, there's an element of deceit in *all* of human life, as when a woman touches herself up with make-up or when a parent who's sick with worry tells a child that all will be fine. The greater the hazard and the greater the task, the greater the need to obfuscate. In war, deceit becomes all-important. Sometimes it's needed to trick the enemy, sometimes to boost the morale of your own troops. Your departure at this time is undermining the morale of the conspiracy, to say nothing of the operational complications. The alternative to deceit regarding your status could be the unraveling of the conspiracy, the crumbling of years of preparations."

"That sounds like putting pressure on me to reconsider. I doubt my comings and goings matter very much one way or another."

"Richard, I wish you wouldn't be so ornery and argumentative. You're denying even what I think you understand quite well. I've already told you that some of our people pay much more attention to your opinion than you think. Your abandoning us is a serious problem, quite apart from the hole you're leaving in the operational chart."

"I've said it before, and I'll say it again, Herbert: I will not return. That's *definite*. You'll just have to do without me."

Vandenhorst looked at his shoes. A distant rumbling announced an incoming southbound train.

"I'm very, very sorry, Vandenhorst said. "I'm afraid I came to take you for granted. I've come to depend on your counsel. Without you, I'll feel much more alone."

*More alone*. This rang true. Richard couldn't help sympathizing with Vandenhorst. Vandenhorst had obviously become attached to his younger colleague. Vandenhorst had lived for a long time with great risks, and an enormous responsibility rested on his shoulders. Richard had often wondered how Vandenhorst could stand the pressure. Now he was in the middle of yet another emergency. But, Richard told himself, Vandenhorst had only himself to blame.

"But you'll have to do without me."

Vandenhorst looked sadly at Richard. Richard wondered whether it was desperation that he saw mixing with sorrow in Vandenhorst's eyes.

"I understand, Richard. Asking you to change your mind would be asking too much."

Vandenhorst paused before adding: "I appreciate all of what you've done for us. You've carried a heavy load, and it kept getting heavier. You were asked to do too much. That's my fault."

Vandenhorst looked down and seemed to slump, as if the air had gone out of him. But then he rallied, looked at Richard, and said, "You can be certain that I'll never do anything to hurt you. If I have anything to do with it, neither will anybody else. I don't need to tell you that there are different opinions about how to deal with you, but I've said I'm absolutely certain that you will do nothing to betray us. Sales and one or two others might prefer to take no chances, but I've been very clear with them, and they *will* follow my direction."

"How nice of them."

# CHAPTER 63

Helen dialed the number to Inspector Duparc. He answered on the second ring.

"Inspector, it's Helen Bittenberg, you called. Do you have any news?"

"Can you meet us outside the hotel in about ten minutes?"

"I'll be there."

Helen was outside within five minutes. Duparc had not sounded excited, so she prepared herself for more disappointment. When the Renault drove up, she saw Duparc sitting in the back seat and quickly got into the car next to him. Duparc said, "*Bonjour, Helen,*" and Léger gave a nod and smile from the driver's seat.

"We heard about the big news from the United States, that terrorists tried to kill your president. We're sorry."

"Yes, I know about it, thank you." she said. That the detectives bothered with preliminary small talk, seemed not very encouraging. "What about Richard? Is there any news?"

"We think so," Duparc said. "We're now convinced that he was held at the Broderie estate, in a secret room in the winery."

"I knew it!" Helen exclaimed. "He had to be at that baron's place!"

"But he was moved."

"You have any idea where?"

"No, but we've brought Baron de la Broderie and his assistant, Major Dégas, in for questioning. We just came from the Noisy police station. Right now they're being transferred to Paris. They refuse to talk. They claim to be victims of some terrible misunderstanding, and they demand legal representation. The baron has threatened us with all of his influential friends in the government. Police technicians are at the Broderie estate now, going through the building where we think your husband was kept. Later today we hope to know whether we can arrest Broderie and Dégas on suspicion of having abducted your husband."

Duparc gave a five-minute summary of the days events. At the end, Helen asked the question that wholly dominated her mind:

"Do you think he's still alive?"

"We believe he was alive as late as last evening or this morning."

"But not now?" Helen's voice almost broke with emotion.

"We simply don't know, but we're going on the assumption that he's alive. The fact that he's been kept alive for several days may mean there was never any intention to kill him. The baron and his helper now have an intricate problem. If they've hidden your husband in a new location, and if they've acted alone, they may not be able to attend to his need for food, water, etc. If the baron's servants are involved, as we suspect, they won't know what to do. A moron might decide to let your husband die in the hope of avoiding a kidnapping charge, but the baron is certainly no moron. He realizes that in time we're likely to find out where your husband is being kept, and, if too much time goes by, he and the major will face a murder charge. We're hoping that when they've added everything up, including the position of the servants, they—or at least one of them—will simply give up and tell us where Professor Bittenberg is."

"But you're not telling me about the most likely possibility."

"What do you mean?"

"You know very well what I mean, inspector. The baron has suspected for the last day or so that sooner or later you would come looking for Richard on his estate. The only thing he could do to stay out of jail would be to get rid of any evidence that he had had any contact with Richard. Most of all he would have to get rid of Richard, get rid of the body. He would kill him and dump his body in some remote place where the police could never find it—at the bottom of an abandoned mineshaft or well or at the bottom of a ravine or something like that."

"For obvious reasons I didn't want to throw that possibility in your face."

"You don't need to hold anything back, Henri. Forget about sparing my feelings. I need straight talk, whatever's on your mind. I've gotten almost numb. I just want all of this to be over, one way or another."

Duparc nodded slowly to himself and glanced at his colleague in the front seat, who had said nothing.

"In that case I'll tell you that when we stopped the baron and the major on that back road, we found a pistol in the glove compartment of the major's Land Rover."

Helen drew a sharp breath.

"The major claims that keeping it with him is just an old habit from his Foreign Legion days. It's licensed. We're bringing the pistol with us for analysis. We'll find out if it was recently fired."

Léger turned around in his seat to face Helen, and said, "I sniffed that pistol pretty carefully, but I couldn't be sure. We don't have as much experience with guns as detectives in the U.S."

Duparc said, "It may have been used merely to get your husband to do as he was told when he was taken away from the estate. That would leave other ways to kill him."

"I can think of one argument against the hypothesis that Richard's dead," Helen said.

"Tell me," Duparc said.

"The people just around the baron — Dégas and the servants — seem to be extremely loyal to him, but the baron must understand that, once the police start putting on real pressure and talk about a charge of murder or being an accessory to murder, that loyalty might crumble. That knowledge might hold him back."

"Good, Helen." Duparc smiled, "That *is* a very plausible point against the worst-case scenario. On the other hand, a similar argument could be made about a charge of kidnapping, which is almost as serious. Assisting in and then staying silent about kidnapping would also require exceptional loyalty. It makes you wonder whether there are some ties between these people other than personal or family ties, something like membership in organized crime or an extreme political movement. But we have no evidence pointing in that direction. And how would Professor Bittenberg relate to that kind of organization?"

Léger again turned to face Helen. "All we know is that Major Dégas is interested in local politics and has plans to become a candidate for the National Front, the anti-immigration party."

"This is a strange case," Duparc said. He looked at his watch and asked whether Helen had any questions.

"Are the police looking for Richard now?"

"We have nothing to go on yet. The servants won't say anything. We hope something will come out of interrogating the baron and Dégas. We can only estimate that your husband is somewhere within a two-hour radius of the Broderie estate, which is a huge area. But a general police advisory, which includes a picture of your husband, is going out, asking about any sightings yesterday or today involving an old green Land Rover. The police in Noisy and neighboring towns will be asking around. Unfortunately we have very limited resources. This is vacation month. But now that we have evidence of a serious crime and have reason to believe that a life may be at stake we expect another couple of detectives to be assigned to the case. Tomorrow we'll make another attempt to interrogate de la Broderie and Dégas."

"Why not today?"

"The lawyer the baron's demanded is not available. Also the baron and Dégas won't say anything. But a night in jail often makes people more talkative. Anything else?"

"I have to tell you about Ferguson."

Léger and Duparc looked at her in surprise.

"He called me at the hotel. He said first that he was calling to tell me about the killing of the vice president and the attempt on the president's life. He told me that the embassy was in emergency mode. But then he became more personal. He apologized for his behavior towards me, for his advances. He said he had been under great stress. I'm afraid I got so upset listening to his self-centered moaning that I lost my temper. I lashed out against him and asked what he'd done to Richard."

Duparc and Léger looked at each other.

"How did he react?"

"He didn't ask what in the world I meant, only repeated that he was sorry. Then he hung up."

"He's clearly involved. We intend to question him again as soon as possible. This time we'll tell him that, unless he cooperates, we'll turn to his diplomatic superiors. His diplomatic status is a complicating factor, and now he'll be able to fend us off for a while by citing what's happening in America."

"Thanks for the information," Helen said. "Call whenever you have any news about Richard."

"*Au revoir.*"

Léger was out of the car and held the door open for her. He gave her a friendly smile and a slight bow.

Back in the hotel room Helen was in the bathroom when the telephone rang. She scrambled to reach the telephone in time and dropped the receiver on the floor before saying a flustered "yes."

"Darling, I don't know how much you know about what's happening over here in the U.S. of A."

"Not much. I have access only to French TV, and I didn't listen for the last half hour. I was talking to the police." She hesitated, but decided that after the arrest of de la Broderie, she could hardly jeopardize the investigation if she gave Hubert a brief summary of the most recent developments. She did so, leaving out information about what the police would be doing next.

Hubert seemed to recognize that he should not prod while on this telephone line. Instead he said, "OK, dear. But you may want to turn on that television set. Really big things have been happening over here. The president has undoubtedly been taken to a safe location.

There's an eerie feeling up in D.C. There's a lot of worry that there will be more attacks. There's something like martial law up there. People in the metropolitan area, except for essential government employees and other workers, have been told to stay in their homes until further notice. Everybody's waiting for the other shoe to drop. All kinds of rumors are flying. The situation's very confused. It seems government officials have gotten their wires really mixed up. There's one story that some cowboy general got it into his head to bring troops from a base south of D.C. to protect the government. Another general up there mobilized troops for deployment around Washington to do the same thing. It seems the federal government has produced another big fat mess."

Helen would ordinarily have wanted to learn more about these events, which were taking place in her home town, but she found them merely a distraction from digesting what she had just learned from Duparc. The situation in Washington seemed to belong to that other universe, the normal universe, but she did wonder how it might be affecting her parents and her children.

"Did you call our house recently?"

"I did. This morning. Your parents are following the news. The children had to be ordered to go to bed last night. At first your parents hoped that all the excitement would be a kind of diversion for the children, especially John, but I think your parents worry now that what's happening may be too scary for them, making them feel even more insecure. But John won't leave the television set or his computer. He's following everything."

Helen sighed. "I'll call them again tomorrow."

"That's all for now. Take care, Helen!"

"Thanks, Hubert, my best to Dottie."

Helen distractedly turned on the television set. The first picture on the screen was the face of the U.S. secretary of State who was standing at a podium with the presidential seal, apparently at the press briefing room in the White House. She reflected that with the death of the vice president, the secretary of State was next in the line of succession to the president in the executive branch. She could hear him in English reading a prepared text. Helen could tell by the subtitles in French that it was not a live broadcast.

"The President is safe and fully in charge," the secretary of State said. "He will be addressing the American people tomorrow evening. The government of the United States is functioning normally. It will be in no way disrupted by these vicious acts. The perpetrators will be hunted down and brought to justice. To any others who might wish America ill, let me say that—" A voice-over in French interrupted the words of the secretary of State, and then a French reporter standing outside the White House gave the latest news about the American crisis.

It seemed somehow apposite, Helen thought, that the language difficulty was placing a kind of screen between her and the newscast. The latter involved the biggest story in the world, but it was far from the forefront of her mind. When the chips are down, she thought, not even great events of history matter as much to people as the fate of those who are near and dear.

Helen again went over all that she knew about Richard's disappearance. She weighed the most recent developments in the search. She paced the room, sat on the bed, went into the little bathroom, lay on the bed, brushed her hair, hand washed or ironed clothes, browsed distractedly in brochures, tried reading a page in a book. Several times she was on the verge of calling Duparc to ask him questions and make suggestions, but she held back, afraid as always of jeopardizing the good will that she obviously enjoyed. She paid intermittent attention to the television, which she left on with the sound volume low, mostly for company. The occasional words of English reminded her that she had once had a different life in a different part of the world. Now and then she switched channels. She found that two of the few channels available on her television set were providing continuous coverage from the United States. If the French were as focused on the American story as all this, some other European countries were probably paying attention to nothing else.

It suddenly occurred to her that she had given no thought to dinner. She had almost lost interest in food. She had to force herself to eat with some regularity to have the energy to continue. She was certain that she had lost weight since Richard's disappearance.

She should eat dinner, but she kept postponing the moment. She did not want to leave her room with the telephone that was her contact with the outside world. She expected that her ordeal was coming to a head. She felt at times as if the walls in the room were closing in on her. Often the gnawing, dull pain of dread and uncertainty mixed with sheer boredom.

It was almost 8:00 PM when she decided that she had to break away and eat something. She should have a glass of wine or two. She should not buy food and bring it back to her room. She needed a complete change of scenery. It was not likely, she said to herself, that Duparc or anybody else would call her at this hour. She should eat a full, cooked meal in a restaurant. There were several of them in the vicinity, including a couple of inviting ones on the nearby *"Boul'Mich."* She might seat herself outside and observe human beings living normal lives.

Helen picked up a summer jacket and her handbag. She left the TV on, locked the door behind her and descended the stairs. As she passed by the small reception desk, the doctoral student at the Sorbonne peeked out of the side room. She smiled at him and said, "*Bon nuit, Monsieur.* I should be back within an hour or so. If anybody should call, be sure to take a careful message."

"*Certainement!*" said the young man and smiled back.

Helen stopped for a moment just outside the hotel and thought about where to go. The air was pleasantly warm. Under different circumstances, she would have enjoyed a leisurely stroll, looking at different restaurants before selecting one. She was in one of the more popular parts of Paris. *Boul'Mich* would be full of people, although most students at the Sorbonne were not in town. Tourists more than replaced them.

She had walked less than fifty yards when through the slight street noise she thought she heard a cry somewhere behind her. She thought a father was trying to get the attention of a child or that a workman was shouting instructions to a helper.

"*Madame!*"

Some woman was being called.

"*Madame!*"

She turned around out of curiosity and discovered that the man in the hotel reception was running in her direction waiving a raised arm.

"*Madame!*" Telephone!"

She turned around and ran back towards the hotel together with the doctoral student.

"An important call from a Mr., ah, Beni—." The receptionist hesitated. "He's waiting."

When they returned to the reception Helen said, "I'll be in my room in a moment. Please transfer the call."

"Of course."

She ran up the stairs and rushed through the corridor. Back in her room she tore the telephone off its cradle."

"Hello!"

"Mrs. Bittenberg?"

"Yes. This is Helen Bittenberg." Helen was winded, but held her breath to hear the response."

"This is Daniel Bennini, at the American Consulate."

Helen took several quick breaths to steady herself before answering.

"Mrs. Bittenberg?"

Her emotions were a jumble of excitement and fear. Why would a consular officer at the American Embassy call her—she looked at her wristwatch—so long after business hours?

"Yes, I'm here. And I remember you well!" Helen exclaimed. She braced herself.

"I'm calling because I need to see you."

"Just tell me when and where." Helen could not understand why Bennini would call her at this hour. He must have bad news. Or perhaps, she told herself, he had been working late at the consulate, catching up on routine work, and he had just come to the Bittenberg folder and needed some information. But it was a strange time to make a routine call.

"What I mean is that I need to see you as soon as possible."

"Fine, when do you want me to come? I'll be there."

"Could you come to the consulate? You remember the location."

"Of course. When?"

"As soon as you can."

"First thing in the morning?"

"It's rather urgent. You should come right away."

"Now? This evening?!" Helen was stunned.

"You can use the call button at the main entrance to the consulate. Ask for me in the reception, and I'll come and get you."

Helen felt her chest tighten. For the American consulate to contact her in this manner had to mean that there was some major development. Why would Bennini even be at the consulate at this time of the day? The last time she had talked to him on the telephone after hours he seemed to be on call at home. She could not hold back a surge of panic. What other reason could he possibly have to ask her to come to the consulate than to break bad news and be in a position to comfort and assist?

"What's happened? Tell me!"

"I'll tell you when you get here." Bennini's tone of voice showed that he would not answer her question on the telephone. Helen was terrified.

"I can be there in twenty minutes."

She left the hotel room within moments and was in a cab a few minutes later. She sat upright in the back seat, wringing her hands and rocking back and forth.

# CHAPTER 64

In the week after the final conversation with Vandenhorst, Richard Bittenberg had great difficulty adapting to his changed circumstances. Reflexes from his involvement in the conspiracy continued to shape his reactions to whatever happened. Although he had cut his ties to the conspirators, he could not help wondering about their activities. Vandenhorst had given Richard to understand that his departure was causing practical difficulties as well as morale problems. Had he not done so mostly to make Richard reconsider his decision? If not, what were the concrete difficulties? How might they be remedied? Richard did not envy Vandenhorst or the other members of the steering committee having to resolve a major complication while the conspiracy was moving into the final, active phase. He had to force himself to ignore what was no longer his concern.

His repeatedly returning to what might be happening in the conspiracy showed not only how deeply his life had become entangled in the conspiracy, but also that, in a part of himself, he was still identifying with the conspirators. He was like a person watching the *Godfather* movies who takes the side of the protagonist Mafia leaders against rival families and the police. Was he, then, in that part of himself even wishing the conspirators well? If so, why was he no longer one of them?

He reminded himself that he could not possibly go along with deliberate, cold-blooded killing. That Vandenhorst and a few of the others had concealed that part of the plan confirmed that everything was wrong with it: it was too callous and brutal to be openly discussed even within the steering committee.

When he had met Vandenhorst the last time Vandenhorst had given not the slightest hint that the plan might be cancelled. Short of becoming an informant for the FBI, did not Richard then have a moral obligation to spread the word to as many of his former colleagues as he could? To do so would break an ironclad rule of the conspiracy, but so what? He was no longer bound by that rule. Spreading the information would shake up the conspiracy. He imagined that controversy over the executions might cause it to unravel from within. Was that not precisely what he wanted? He found it difficult to answer the question, but why? If he really did not want the conspiracy to crumble, how could he justify sitting on the sidelines?

He realized that he did not want to be responsible for ruining the coup attempt. But did that mean that in his heart of hearts he might not be quite so horrified by the planned killings as he had been telling himself and conveyed to Vandenhorst and the others? Was he leaving room for the possibility that the evil of the killing did not outweigh the good that might be accomplished by the coup? At bottom, he must not be certain that he had sized up the whole situation properly. Though he was extremely reluctant to admit it, it did carry weight with him that Vandenhorst considered the planned executions necessary. Yet how could Vandenhorst possibly be right? In any case, Richard told himself, he had to follow his own conscience. He could not simply give Vandenhorst the benefit of the doubt. His decision to withdraw from the conspiracy assumed that Vandenhorst's leadership was morally unacceptable, but on that assumption Richard should be trying to derail the conspiracy. He was doing nothing of the sort.

Richard kept fending off a painful thought: that without realizing it, he had invented a reason to relieve the terrible pressure that was making his life unbearable.

No, he told himself, that was being unfair to himself. He had been able to stand the pressure for a very long time. Why, when the goal of the entire effort was finally within reach, would he suddenly want to run away? No, he had separated himself from the conspiracy for the best of reasons: His conscience would not permit him to stay.

Did he, then, not at least have an obligation to alert close friends, persons who would expect him to warn them of danger, as they would warn him? Others were likely to share his reactions to the plan for executions, but as long as they were unaware of the plan, they would not have any opportunity to decide for themselves what to think or do. Like Richard until a few days ago, they would be unwitting collaborators in something they might find abominable.

There was one obvious argument for remaining silent. Vandenhorst had seemed to offer a guarantee that the conspirators would leave him alone. This was clearly on the understanding that Richard would do nothing to damage the conspiracy. Even as he continued to keep quiet, he went nowhere without worrying about his safety. His worst nightmare was that the conspirators would try to ensure his silence by threatening or even kidnapping somebody in his family, but that would be a dangerous game of blackmail and would be a big drain on the conspiracy's scarce resources. Yet, should it come to the attention of the leadership that Richard might be talking to others in the conspiracy, Sales, in particular, would have no patience whatever.

But, Richard thought, his best and oldest friend just had to be told. With all the facts at his disposal, surely Robert Preston would agree with Richard's decision.

It was a Thursday evening after dinner. Richard was in his study, but had told Helen that he would watch a movie with her, which had delighted her. In the last two years he had rarely sat down with her or the children except for a few minutes at a time. He had a quarter of an hour to spare and decided to call Robert Preston.

His friend answered.

"Dick, how *are* you? We haven't talked for a while." Robert sounded cheerful, and Richard wondered whether he was hearing his friend or the South Carolina congressman, practiced at feigning the expected response.

"I'm fine, thank you. I was wondering whether you might be in town this weekend. It would be good to see you."

"I won't go back to my home district this week."

"How about breakfast tomorrow morning?"

"Tomorrow? Well, yes, I suppose I could do breakfast, but I don't have a lot of time. I have to be on the Hill midday at the latest—a group of businessmen from Columbia."

"So let me pick you up at 7:30. I'll bring you back to the house."

"Pick me up?—Well , I suppose—that would be fine."

Richard hung up and walked upstairs to join Helen. She was half-surprised to see him keep his promise to her.

The next morning Richard was at the Preston house as agreed. Robert came out as soon as Richard drove up. Jennifer, his wife, waved from the doorway.

"Why did you want to pick me up? I could have met you at one of our regular places."

"I know, but why come in separate cars?"

Robert looked curiously at his friend.

"I'm in your hands."

Richard put his index finger on his lips to indicate caution and then started some small talk about Robert's family.

Richard surprised Robert by driving to the National University campus.

"Are we headed for the subway?"

"Wait and see."

Richard parked, and they walked to the nearby Metro stop

on Wisconsin Avenue. They descended the escalator on the west side of the street, but Richard steered Robert underground to the up escalator on the other side. Back above ground Richard almost immediately ducked into a doorway from which stairs led down again. Robert could see from posters and pictures on the walls that they were entering some kind of eatery or bar offering a selection of European beers. At the bottom of the stairs they walked into a surprisingly cheerful-looking, medium-sized restaurant and bar with predominantly German decorations. Some daylight came in from windows at street level. German oompha music flowed through loudspeakers. The tables had checkered tablecloths. There were booths separated by partitions, small tables and places to sit around a bar. The restaurant was about half full.

"May we have that corner booth?" Richard asked a waitress, pointing in the direction of the most distant corner, and got a nod and smile in response.

"This is 'The Munich,'" Richard said. "I doubt you've been here before. It's a popular watering hole for faculty and students and residents of the area, but they also serve breakfast. They have anything you might want."

The waitress served them coffee and left them to examine the menu.

"And I have a feeling you didn't bring me here to discuss the next election or the causes of the Second World War."

"How did you guess?"

Richard sought and held the gaze of his friend.

"Bob, I'm out."

Robert said nothing, but his eyes widened.

"You're *out*!? What do you mean? What's happened?"

"I've left the network. I'm out for good."

Robert stared at him in disbelief.

"Dick, you've been in the network for over a year and a half! Why now, just as the real action is about to start? What's the matter? Are you leaving on your own accord, or are you being forced out?"

"It was my decision."

"I don't understand."

"I'll explain."

"You'd better."

"To let you have the truth will be to violate the secrecy code that I have followed scrupulously — with one exception, that conversation we had down at the canal. But I no longer feel bound by the secrecy."

"Dick, what *are* you talking about? You don't mean to turn us all in, do you?"

"Of course not. But I can't keep the reason for leaving from my best friend. You'll understand why when I tell you about it. Perhaps I should inform some others too. I just don't know what to do. I'm in a real quandary."

"Dick, I'm flabbergasted. You've been talking forever about the need for drastic action, and you've been a part of the leadership for all this time. What in the world's happened?"

Richard placed his arms on the table and folded his hands. He was seated against the back wall facing the entrance and could see almost the whole restaurant. By deep-seated habit he glanced around the premises for anything suspicious. The only table near them was behind the partition between their booth and the next one. As long as they spoke in a normal tone of voice, nobody could hear them through the background music.

"First of all, Bob, you need to know that I was a member of the group that coordinated and directed all the others."

"*You*! A professor?"

"Believe it or not. I've been a kind of odd man out, rather different from the others."

"So you know who the real leader is?"

"I think I do."

"You *think* you do?"

"Well, the lead group has been operating as a collective, but with one person acting as a kind of chairman. That person has emerged more and more as the real leader. The network is so compartmentalized that it occurred to me early on that there might be another group that really calls the shots, but no, that's not the case."

"So you've helped make the key decisions. Then why would you suddenly leave? Have you lost confidence in the leadership? Or are you just worn out?"

The last few words felt like a stab in Richard's gut.

"Well, it's nothing so simple."

The waitress brought their food, full American breakfasts. Richard had always enjoyed the first meal of the day more than any other. He particularly liked bacon, eggs sunny side up, home fries, and toast with jam. Now he stared at the plate in front of him, wondering how much he could eat. The waitress poured more coffee and left.

Feeling a little sick to his stomach Richard forced himself to put some food in his mouth, chewed, and swallowed before launching his explanation.

"I'll leave out names and details and concentrate on the main reason for my decision," he said.

In the next five minutes, Richard set the stage for making his key point. He interrupted his summary only to answer occasional questions and to try to eat of his breakfast.

He finally got to when he discovered the planned executions. As he spoke he wondered whether he might be exaggerating how startled and surprised he had been. He was not entirely sure just how much Vandenhorst and the others had told him, but he was almost certain that there had never been any discussion in his presence of the need for outright executions, much less executions on the contemplated scale.

"So there it is!" Richard said. "I simply couldn't accept what I had learned. This would be cold-blooded murder. This would make us as bad as the crooks and schemers who are running the country now. I felt deceived. Since my resignation I've been wondering what else may have been kept from me and others. I understand the need for secrecy and compartmentalization, but you can't withhold major, basic facts. People have to know what they're involved in. That's why I felt I had to tell you."

Robert, who had eaten more than Richard, had no immediate reaction. He looked at his friend, but continued to chew on a piece of toast and jelly. He sipped his coffee.

"Well?" Richard was getting impatient.

"I have a question."

"Yes?"

"What's your opinion of your fellow conspirators? Are they capable, are they smart, are they experienced, are they decent — do they know what they're doing? Do they have the right motive?"

Richard hesitated.

"They're a mixed bag, I suppose. A few of them have hang-ups and hobbyhorses, and I'm asking myself if one of them might have a screw loose. But, yes, on the whole I guess they're a fairly savvy, level headed bunch."

"Do they strike you as power hungry, more concerned about their own glory or power than the good of this country?"

Richard found himself looking for reasons to answer in the affirmative, but he had to say, "I guess not."

"So you're describing people way above average for the U.S. Congress. But then I would like to know something very important, whether you think these people can make a go of this coup — *succeed!*"

"The point of what I've been telling you is that I'm not sure

I *want* it to succeed. It would mean the deliberate killing of a lot of people."

"Dick, answer my question! Do we have a real chance of success?"

Richard flinched.

"The question is," he said, "whether they will get us out of the frying pan and into the fire."

"*Dick!* Answer my damned question!" Irritation colored Robert's banter.

Richard sighed and leaned back in his seat. He pushed his half-eaten breakfast to the side.

"Yes, I think they have a chance. They're well organized and determined. When I first got involved I was mighty surprised that so many able and influential people were already in the network. The planning has been very careful and, I have to admit, sophisticated. I can claim some of the credit. They're making maximum use of scant resources. Because of all of this, the planned executions bother me all the more."

Robert sat silently looking at his almost empty plate. The waitress appeared and asked whether they wanted anything else.

"Just the check," Richard said. The waitress put the check on the table, collected the debris, topped up their cups of coffee, said a sunny "Have a nice day" and left.

The two friends looked at each other across the table. Robert's face was expressionless.

"Well?"

"You've told me that the leadership is pretty damned competent. For what it may be worth, I've gotten the same impression. And if you've been able to get along with them reasonably well for all this time, they're hardly a bunch of ogres. How could they have deceived you for so long about who they really are?"

"But some of them *did*."

"C'mon, Dick, nothing of great consequence could have been hidden that long."

"Those executions are no big deal? They might involve a hundred people or more."

"To tell you the truth, I don't know what to think, except that some real s.o.b.s will have to be gotten out of the way. Sometimes I wonder if you know how atrocious some of the people are who are running the system. You understand it, sort of, because you talk about it. But perhaps your way of thinking about them is too abstract. I've had to deal with some of them, and I hear from others about them. But never mind that. Are you sure you didn't know more about those executions than you are letting on?"

"Bob, I resent that! Are you accusing me of lying?"

"No, not really. I'm thinking that we all tune out at times. You may have tuned out when the subject was getting painful or gruesome. Perhaps you didn't *want* to hear too much about that stuff."

"*Tuned out*!? Certainly not! If I'd heard anything about executions, I would certainly have objected." Richard found it disturbing and uncanny that Robert, who knew him so well, would raise the same possibility as Vandenhorst. But, no, he could not have been made privy to those brute facts.

"Perhaps then it was a part of an intentional compartmentalization—to avoid offending your moral sensibilities and the moral sensibilities of some others. Perhaps you were kept out of discussions that might have bothered you, given you pause."

"That's it! That's indefensible! I was *deceived*. I told you."

"Hmmm."

"A few members of the leading group decided to keep this information to themselves. It's as simple as that. It's unforgivable!"

Robert did not speak, and Richard was puzzled by his reaction. He had not detected any outrage, rather a strangely passive, standoffish attitude. It troubled him.

When Robert did not spontaneously offer any opinion, and the silence at the table just got deeper, Richard finally said: "So what do you think of what I've told you?"

Robert Preston took his time.

"Well, Dick, I think I understand why you pulled out."

"Yes, because I found the callous killing of a large number of people and the deceit morally unacceptable."

"Perhaps you did."

Richard felt anger stirring.

"What do you *mean*—*perhaps* I did?"

"Human motives are complex, Dick. Sometimes not even we ourselves know why we act as we do. Sometimes it takes us a long time to figure out why we did what we did, and much of the time we can't figure it out at all. Life's too damned—well, too damned complex."

"You're saying I'm confused, even deluded?"

"Not the way you mean it. You're more well put-together than most. You try to do the right thing. You're deliberate. If you have time, you think everything through before you act. And your profession has given you a lot of time to reflect on what life's all about. So, you're in the habit of thinking things through. You may even have had too much time to think about everything."

"What do you mean by that—that I'm an egghead intellectual who's got a difficult time living in the real world?"

"Not exactly. I'm back to what I told you once before: That people like you and me may be too soft, too deeply affected both by civilization and our morally corrupt society to be able to find our way when everything's falling apart, when life's up for grabs. The danger is that we are affected by reflexes that really belong in that other, civilized life. We apply them to situations where they simply do not fit."

Richard felt as if he had been hit in the solar plexus. He realized that without being fully conscious of what he was doing he had long tried hard to protect that area from blows. He had heard similar remarks before, but had sensed their potential for inflicting real pain and had deflected them by not quite listening. Now his self-defense had failed him. Robert's point had landed like a hard blow. There was no missing its merciless poignancy.

Richard cringed physically.

"You're saying I'm a sissy."

"Dick, *please*, I'm not accusing you of anything. I'm not trying to judge your conscience or your toughness. All I'm saying is that it's possible that you've lived a more protected life than I have. I'm sure that some of those academics you've told me about can be pretty ruthless in their own way as well as plenty neurotic. The bad side of humanity must be as much on display in universities as elsewhere. But I imagine that I've come closer to observing and dealing with a more thoroughgoing, expert ruthlessness than you have, the kind of egotism that thinks nothing of hurting or killing thousands of people to get its way. Some of what I know takes your breath away. I've told you about some of it, but it's one thing to hear stories, experience something viscerally, registering it intellectually—that's what you specialize in, my friend—and quite another to have to confront it in practice, come face to face with it. My God! A few people in our network have probably seen worse than I. They're in the network precisely because they couldn't stand the ruthlessness, and the greed, and the irresponsibility any longer. They know we're up against nothing better than criminals, but gifted criminals who have risen so high that they can instrumentalize the presidency, the Congress, the military, the FBI, and the police."

"So, I'm a sissy?"

"I didn't say that, Richard. You've shown that you're not. You've stood the heat in the kitchen for a very long time. You've risked everything. Considering your background, I'd say you're pretty damned tough."

"Why, then, do I get the impression that you disagree with my reaction to the executions?"

"I've already told you, Dick. I really don't know what to think. The thought of lining people up and gunning them down does not appeal to me, it goes without saying, but, considering what we're trying to accomplish, some drastic actions like those probably can't be avoided."

"My God, Bob, you're talking about cold-bloodedly taking the lives of well over a hundred people! If we're prepared to go that far, what separates us from the bad guys?"

"I'm surprised to hear you ask that question. I doubt you mean it quite the way you sound. You're usually more down to earth about that kind of thing. Aren't you the professor who's always complaining about moral idealists who refuse to live in the real world? Obviously the motive makes all the difference in the world. We're trying to give America a second chance, to get rid of a tyranny that's getting worse every day. The only question that should be asked about those killings is whether they are necessary to achieving the objective."

"And you're convinced that they are, are you? On what grounds?"

"Again, I'm not certain, but I know enough about history to know that a coup cannot be bloodless."

"Don't be absurd! Nobody's insisting on a bloodless coup. There are bound to be deaths and plenty of collateral damage. Of course! What I'm objecting to is deliberate killing."

"But it's hardly wanton killing. If you've described the leadership of the network correctly, they must have decided that not eliminating certain people would be dangerous to the coup."

Richard was incensed. "Where's your *conscience*, Bob?"

"I hope I have one, but I also haven't thought through all the ins and outs of the coup the way the people in the leadership must have done. Some of them are better equipped than I am to assess what's required. I guess what I'm saying is that I'm willing to let them make some decisions for me. I can't assume that, with all the facts at my disposal, I would reach a very different conclusion."

"I think I have virtually all the facts they have, and I strongly disagree with them."

"What about the possibility that they have a better gut feeling than you for what the success of the coup requires. They're after all, as I understand it, men with a lot of relevant training and experience."

"Did I just hear a bit of anti-intellectualism?"

"No, you didn't, and I wonder if you thought you did. I'm getting at the fact that as an historian you, Dick, are used to mulling over moral questions at length and taking as many historical circumstances as possible into account. Doing that you have the benefit of hindsight. You may not be as well equipped to pass judgment in the here and now when the circumstances are unclear and several courses of action may look plausible. You're not really satisfied until you have scrutinized every conceivable angle and think you have come up with just the right course of action. But rarely, if ever, does this world offer clear-cut choices. We know only a part of what we should know to make truly well-informed choices. You, Dick, may not be as willing as politicians and men of practice to admit that most of the time it's darn hard even to know your actual circumstances. Situations are usually rather confused. Even if you have the best of motives you have to act a little bit in the dark, take a risk. To choose is morally dangerous, but there's no alternative — other than passivity, which is really a choice too, but the coward's way out."

Richard felt another painful spasm.

Robert continued: "Decent and intelligent men of practice may in their way know this better than the philosophers. They realize that often they can't afford to wait. And they usually can't afford to waffle and wring their hands. They have to cut though the fog and hope that their intuition is steering them right. If the leaders of the conspiracy now seem to you to be overdoing something, the reason may be that they're erring on the side of caution."

"And lots of people have to die unnecessarily."

"That's possible. But have you considered the possibility that what the leaders of the coup are planning may not be enough?"

"One of them actually hinted that this might be the case."

"And you assume you're better equipped to judge."

"But what about the deceit, Bob, that disgusting *deceit*!? It seems a few people in the leadership have kept an important part of the plan hidden. Everybody else is in the dark."

"Nobody likes being deceived. I can understand that you're upset. But deceit is often necessary, isn't it? Those few leaders you're so angry at decided at some point that the executions had to be carried out. Perhaps they also sensed that you and others would resist those plans. If they'd been able to square the plans with their conscience, were they obligated to throw the matter open for discussion? They might then have had to enact revised plans about which they had very strong reservations — this to accommodate people whose conscience or judgment seemed to them defective."

"Who are they to assume that they're better able to judge than all the rest and are entitled to deceiving them?"

"It's not as if they were tricking everybody into participating in a coup attempt. No, they were merely acting as the representatives of the other participants. That's what leaders are for. They make particularly difficult decision *for* others."

"A decision nobody had any reason to expect."

"How can you be so certain about that? I wouldn't be surprised if some in the network are expecting, and hoping for, some very rough vengeance."

"So much the worse."

"You may be right. But there's some deep resentment, even hatred of the powers-that-be in our ranks. Understandably so. All I mean to say is that I'm not so sure as you seem to be that there would be general outrage if the planned executions became more widely known. There might be cheering. This regime has a lot to answer for — my God! Can you really get rid of it without getting rid of the ringleaders? In any case, it may have been prudent to keep those plans within a very small circle."

Richard swallowed hard. He wanted to contradict Robert, but was temporarily speechless. How could his friend be tolerant of the plans that had so upset him?

The waitress returned to top off their coffee cups yet again. She had recognized the signs of breakfast eaters who cared more for the conversation than the food.

"I have what I think is an important point," Robert continued. "But it assumes that the people you're so upset with are not really bad people, but truly trying to do their best. Have you thought about the fact that they may be performing a great service for the rest? They've put all of that weight on *their* shoulders. They're taking on *all* that moral responsibility. It is they who must take the blame if they turn out to have been wrong in their assessment of reality, if, for example, they have wasted human life. This is the sort of thing that all leaders must do. Their acting for the rest of us in terribly difficult circumstances is a great gift to the rest of us. Their souls are on the line in a way that ours are not. Assuming again that they are not obviously bad people, we may owe them some trust and loyalty."

"The problem with your reasoning, Bob, is that *my* soul is on the line. I was very much a part of the group in which the key decisions were being made, and I had access to pretty much the same facts as the rest. The moral responsibility was on *my* shoulders. I could not turn a blind eye to what I discovered. I felt I had no choice but to drop out."

"I think I understand, Dick. I guess I'm just not as scrupulous as you are. Considering how difficult it sometimes is to know what to do, I'm more willing to give the people in charge of the coup some leeway, trust that they know what they're doing. Perhaps that means I'm more fed up than you are about the state of America."

"Not bloody likely."

"I find it pretty significant that, although you have severed your ties to the network, you're not now on a rampage against it. You behaved this morning as if you were still a part of the operation. You don't want it to be discovered by the authorities."

"I admit to feeling some ambivalence. I can no longer be a part of the network, but I don't quite want it to fail either. I think I'm hoping that my withdrawing will cause the leaders to exercise more restraint and rethink some things."

Robert sat quietly looking at his hands and sipping his coffee. Then, as if he had just had a new thought, he looked up into Richard's face.

"In the last few days we've received some rather surprising signals from the leadership. Some kind of reorganization is apparently underway. There have been some musical chairs. I'm sure most people in the conspiracy assumed, as I did, that the changes had to do with our moving into the final operational phase, but now I wonder if these are repercussions from your leaving."

Robert fell silent again before asking: "How's Helen and the kids?"

"I've been spending more time with them, and I think they're happy about that."

"I can imagine."

"How's Jennifer?"

"Not very well. She worries about me, the kids, everything, and sometimes she's angry. I've not been in the network nearly so long as you, and still I've thought many a time about doing what you did. The pressure and the uncertainty are hard to take. I often feel like withdrawing from everything — the Congress, the law, everything — and just fading into the woodwork. Sometimes this country seems beyond repair. But somehow I get up in the morning, and I do what I can to get through the day. There's a lot to do. Now at least we're very close to the final action."

Robert looked at his watch and put thirty dollars on the table for the bill and a generous tip. They got up and headed for the daylight.

On the stairs to the street, Robert said, "I'll feel a lot more alone knowing you're not on the team."

Richard tried to hide a stifled sob.

# CHAPTER 65

Helen pushed the button on the intercom outside the American consulate.

"American consulate, reception," a male voice said.

"This is Helen Bittenberg. I'm here to see Mr. Daniel Bennini." She could barely control her voice.

"Please come in," said the voice, and she heard a buzz and a click, which indicated that the heavy door had been unlocked. She opened it and found herself in a glassed doorway with a second door. The glass door too buzzed open. Beyond it in a dimly lit hall a young man in a Marine dress uniform rose behind a reception desk and approached her. He put her metal objects in a plastic bowl and directed her to walk through a metal detector.

"You can wait here at the reception desk." The Marine indicated a small bench. "Mr. Bennini will be here shortly," he said.

"Thank you," she said. She tried to make her voice normal. She was too nervous to sit down.

She looked over at the entrance marked "Passports and Visas" through which she had passed on her previous visit to the consulate. That large room with glassed stalls for the consular staff and rows of chairs for visitors was now deserted and in virtual darkness. Helen remembered the anxiety she had felt on her previous visit to this building. Only the thought of young Mr. Bennini lightened the memory. She felt even worse now. Her apprehensions tore at her viscera.

"I'm surprised anybody is here at this time of the day," she said.

"Much of the time nobody is. Just me or somebody like me," the young man said. He seemed glad to have somebody to talk to. A small TV stood behind the counter next to two security screens. To judge by the barely audible American voices it emitted, it seemed to be set to a channel covering events in the U.S. "But sometimes one or two of the consular officers work late, and when we're in high season or expect urgent business a consular officer is on duty here at the consulate until midnight. Sometimes the consular officer on call has to come to the office to handle an emergency."

"Of course, tonight is kind of unusual — with what's happening back home, you know. Another guard will be added tonight."

She nodded.

He smiled. "If you you're wondering what's going on in the U.S. of A., feel free to look over my shoulder. What a mess that is! Seems those terrorists have the government all tied up in knots. They're worried about more attacks."

Helen was just about to sit down on a bench near the reception counter when she heard footsteps and saw Daniel Bennini approach from the passport and visa office.

She half-ran to meet him. Undoubtedly he could read the dread on her face. She didn't even try to hide it.

"What's happened, Mr. Bennini?" She could not hold back her fear. "Tell me!"

Bennini took her hand and gave her a reassuring, kindly smile. You're a nice man, Mr. Bennini, she thought, but don't torture me any longer.

"Please, Mrs. Bittenberg, let's go back to my office." He walked her back through the passport and visa office waiting area, unlocked the side entrance to the innards of the consulate, and walked her down the corridor she remembered from her previous visit. Few lights were on. She heard sounds as from a radio or television set, and behind a glass partition in a poorly lit area she thought she saw the back of a man's head. The person seemed to be watching television in what might be a coffee lounge. She could hear that the broadcast was in English and remembered that she was back on American territory. She realized that what was happening back in America was now everywhere in the center of media attention. Wherever Americans were not asleep their television sets would be on. Those startling terrorist attacks eclipsed all other news.

To her surprise, Bennini slowed down in the corridor and seemed about to stop. Helen looked at him in puzzlement. They were still a couple of doors away from his office. He stopped and held out his arm in front of her, guiding her into the TV room that they were about to pass. She felt annoyed that at a moment like this he would want to check the latest news or thought that she was as absorbed by the events in America as everybody else. Or had he called her to the consulate only because he thought that she might need some company on this awful night? Did he think that being on American soil with a fellow American would give her a feeling of comfort and security? A nice thought, but he should at least have asked her what she wanted.

She reluctantly stepped into the lounge. It was lit only by the television screen and the light that came in from the corridor through the glass partition. She glanced at the TV and recognized a CNN reporter holding a microphone. The lit dome of the U.S. Capitol formed the backdrop.

Out of the corner of her eye she noticed that the man watching TV was rising from his seat. When she shifted her attention in that direction she realized how distraught she was. At first she thought that the shadowy person looked like Richard. She was becoming hysterical, and her imagination was projecting her subconscious wishes into what she couldn't clearly see.

"Helen."

She stared in complete bewilderment at the figure whose outstretched arms seemed to motion her to come closer. She took a step back to clear her mind, looked at the figure in disbelief, and then felt her knees buckle. The figure caught her and half lifted her to a small sofa.

She did not lose consciousness, but for a moment she was so disoriented that she could make no sense of the scene.

"Richard?"

The man was kneeling in front of the sofa holding her hands.

"Yes, it's me."

"But—"

"I'll be in my office." It was Bennini's voice. He discreetly left his place in the doorway.

Helen looked after him as he disappeared down the corridor and then looked back at the man. Reality finally began to sink in. The person kneeling before her on the floor was not a creature of her imagination. It was Richard. She straightened herself out from her crumbled position and flung her arms around his neck, nearly knocking them both to the floor. They held each other without a word for the better part of a minute. As her embrace relaxed, Richard moved to sit down on the sofa next to her. As he did she embraced him again, kissed, and held on to him. She would not let go.

"Richard, Richard, I've been *so* worried," she whispered into his ear. "What happened to you?"

"Helen, darling, I'll tell you everything. It's a very long story."

"You were abducted, weren't you?"

"Yes, Helen, I was, but there's so much to explain. First, tell me, how're the kids?"

"They're fine. They're back at our house in Bethesda. My parents are looking after them. We've talked every day on the telephone. We've got to call them right away. They've been so worried."

"Of course, we'll call as soon as we can. But you, Helen, you stayed in Paris," he said in a soft, quiet voice and gave her another prolonged hug.

When he let her go she drew away a little.

"Let me look at you," she said. She rose, pulling him toward the better light in the corridor. She studied his face and clothing.

"I don't think you shaved this morning," she said, smiling.

"No, I didn't."

"And your clothes look a little rumpled."

"They probably don't smell too good either."

"Whose shirt is that? I don't recognize it."

"Somebody gave it to me."

"*Gave* it to you?"

"Yes, my own had gotten rather soiled."

"You've been locked up?"

"Yes, I'll tell you all about it later."

"Where was it?"

"Somewhere east of Paris."

"Were you fed?"

"Yes, pretty well."

"Are you hungry now?"

"Mr. Bennini, this young consular officer, gave me a yogurt, some crackers and coffee."

"You look a little pale."

"Well, I haven't been out in the sun for a while."

"When did you escape?"

"I didn't escape. I was set free, just a few hours ago."

"Set free!? A few hours ago? Why didn't I hear about it sooner?"

"I'll explain as soon as I can."

"How long have you been here at the consulate?"

"About two hours. I had to wait for Bennini to arrive. He was at home."

All kinds of questions crowded into Helen's mind, and she had difficulty digesting his first answers to her questions.

"*Who* set you free? Broderie, Dégas?"

Richard looked at her in startled surprise. "How in the world did you come up with those names?"

"The French police have been looking for you."

"I expected that, and Bennini confirmed it, but how could the police have come up with those names?"

"I'll tell you. I've helped them in various ways."

Richard looked incredulous. "*You* have helped them?"

"I have quite a bit to tell you as well."

"I'm afraid I understand nothing."

"Then you know how I've felt this last week." She smiled at Richard. "How and why did you end up here, in the consulate?"

"I thought quite a bit about it and concluded that in the circumstances it was the best place."

"Did you know that I was still in Paris?"

"No, but I heard that from Bennini. I first went to the U.S. Embassy building, thinking that the consulate was there and found out about this location. It was after normal office hours, but I figured there might be some kind of emergency procedures. It took some time, but I was finally put in touch with this Mr. Bennini. He seems to be a nice person. He told me he knows you and is familiar with my case, and, as I said, he's the one who told me you were still in Paris."

"Bennini's been very good to me. In fact, he deserves a medal."

"Well, he must like you. I asked him not to contact the French police until I had had a chance to talk to you. That seems to have bothered him a little. I think it meant bending the rules. But he went along when I said that there were some very special circumstances and that it was out of concern for you that I had to see you before talking to the police. He wanted to know what had happened to me, but I haven't told him yet. He agreed to let me rest for a while and to talk to you before contacting the police."

"Why didn't you just take a cab to the hotel? Bennini must have told you that I was still staying there."

"He did, but I had my reasons not to go there."

"What reasons?"

"For one thing, I didn't have much money."

"Surely, the consulate would have lent you some."

"But I also didn't want to run into the police, and I didn't know how safe it would be to go to the hotel."

"*Safe?*"

"It has to do with the circumstances of my abduction. You'll understand when I've told you the whole story. The consulate was the best place I could think of, especially as I didn't have my passport."

"Why didn't you contact your friend at the embassy?"

"You'll understand that too when I've told you everything."

"I know the reason. Stephen Ferguson was a part of the abduction, wasn't he?"

Richard stared in disbelief at his wife.

"Helen, I'm *amazed*! How could you *possibly* know that?"

"As I said, I have a lot to tell you." She embraced him again and kissed him on the cheek. They had been moving about in or near the lounge. The television set was still on, but Richard had turned down the sound volume. Now he said, "Let's sit down!"

He nodded over in the direction of the television screen.

"Have you followed what's happened at home?"

"A little, but my mind's been elsewhere."

"Of course." Richard put an arm around her and pulled her to him.

"I've been watching quite a bit of TV since I got to the consulate, and Bennini has told me more about what's happened. The embassy's in crisis mode."

But she was barely listening. She looked smilingly at him. Then her expression turned serious.

"I thought I was never going to see you again."

"I'm *so* sorry."

"Sorry? It wasn't your fault, Richard!"

He drew a deep breath.

"Helen."

"Yes."

"I don't have the time now to tell you the reason, but it's absolutely necessary that we agree on a plausible explanation for why I disappeared."

At first she thought that she had misunderstood him, but he continued, "We simply have to get together on one explanation and stick to it—it can't be the truth—for your sake, the children's sake, the rest of the family's sake, and for the sake of our friends. You will know why when you've heard the whole story. It's quite a story."

"Richard! What *are* you talking about?"

"It will take you some time to get used to."

"What have you been involved in, Richard? It must be something big that you never told me about."

"It is. I probably should have told you. The reason I didn't was that I wanted to protect you and the children and others."

"Tell me now, Richard, what is it?"

"There simply isn't time. There is too much to explain. I just have to ask you to trust me that what I'm suggesting is for the best. We have to tell the consulate and the police a plausible story that makes them see no further need to investigate my disappearance."

"*What!?*"

"Yes, Helen, that's what I mean. It's necessary. It's *absolutely* necessary."

"You' were kidnapped, and you're telling me the police should not be trying to catch the people who did it."

"That's exactly what I mean."

She stared at him, her jaw dropping. "Richard, those people put me and the children through hell. I hate them. They should be punished. That Stephen Ferguson belongs in jail."

"I understand what you must feel like, Helen. I do. But there are things you don't know, big things, and you have to think about the children, yourself, and a lot of other people."

"I don't understand, Richard."

"There's no way you could. You just have to trust me on this. Please! We don't have much time before Bennini comes back."

She shook her head.

"To be able to tell a believable story I have to know how much the police or the embassy already know. Bennini didn't have much to tell me, only that the police had some leads and some suspects. Before we leave here tonight we need to tell him something that he can transmit to the French police. He must be able to say that as far as he can tell no crime's been committed. The French police must lose interest."

Helen sunk down on the sofa, and Richard sat down beside her, taking her hands.

"I'm so confused," she said.

"Of course you are, but tell me briefly what the police know."

Helen gave Richard an almost despairing look.

"The police know that Broderie and his helper, Major Dégas, and Ferguson were involved."

"I still can't understand how they could know that, but you'll have to tell me later. Go on."

"They know you were kept in the winery at the baron's estate." Again Richard lifted his eyebrows. "The two detectives in charge of the case have seen the underground room. In fact they confronted the baron on the estate earlier today, and they have taken him and the major in for questioning. But, as far as I know, the two won't talk. The police technicians are going over the winery and the major's car, perhaps other parts of the estate. More policemen were going to be assigned to trying to find you. The police know you met Ferguson at the Sorbonne cafeteria before the kidnapping and that you were abducted by the baron in the vicinity of the university." As Helen talked the expression of astonishment on Richard's face only became more pronounced.

"This is amazing! I didn't think anybody would ever be able

to find out what happened to me."

"They also know that on the way to the Broderie estate, the Rover you were traveling in had a mishap in Noisy. Some stakes fell off."

"I *can't* believe it."

Helen continued for another couple of minutes to summarize what she knew about the police investigation, and Richard got answers to a few questions. He sat quietly for a moment, thinking intensely, before saying.

"The police know far more than I thought, which makes it all the more difficult to explain away my disappearance."

"Explain it *away*!? Richard, I don't like this at all."

"I know you don't, but we don't have any choice. You'll agree when I have had a chance to explain. Just give me some time—"

They heard a door opening and then footsteps. Bennini was returning.

"Helen, look angry!"

She gave him a bewildered look.

"*Just do it!*" he whispered.

A smiling Daniel Bennini entered the coffee room. Noticing that he had walked into an awkward situation, he assumed a more neutral expression. He noticed that Helen Bittenberg did not look very happy.

"I'm sorry to intrude," Bennini said, "but I was thinking that you two probably want to get out of here as soon as possible." He smiled again. "But before you leave I need to know what to tell the French police. I should have called them already, and I can't wait any longer."

"I understand," Richard said. "I'm afraid that my wife and I have had a rather emotional and difficult reunion. Would you mind terribly giving me just five minutes to clear my head?"

Bennini looked a little nonplussed, but simply nodded, turned around and disappeared in the direction of his office.

"Helen, Bennini can't keep us here. We are free to leave. But I must tell him something that will begin to defuse this whole affair."

"*Defuse* it!?"

"Yes, the important thing is for me to say that nothing illegal happened."

"Like what?"

"That we have been through a very bad patch in our marriage and that I cracked. We had a terrible row, and I walked out in a state of fury and confusion."

Helen was already well familiar with this scenario. She had

invented it and used it herself with Stephen Ferguson. Although a brazen lie, it would, she had thought, strike a person who knew nothing about the Bittenberg marriage as at least plausible. But she exclaimed:

"Richard! That's the very opposite of what I've told the police. I have assured them there were no problems like that in our marriage and that we hadn't quarreled. That story would make a complete liar out of me, and you would of course look terrible. Who would abandon his family like that?"

"I'm quite willing to look bad, Helen. I'm afraid I have other things to answer for that are far worse by comparison."

Helen looked at him in dismay. "Richard, what *are* you talking about?"

He lowered his gaze and looked at his hands, as if they might provide the answer.

"Helen, I'm sorry. I'm so very sorry. I'm talking about something that must not get out—for your sake and the sake of the children first of all."

"But for us to say that this is what happened would mean that I've deliberately misled the police. I wouldn't be surprised if they could accuse me of breaking some law."

"I very much doubt it. It depends on how it's said. You can claim that you really underestimated what had happened between us. In your view there simply had to be some other explanation for my disappearance. Only now that I've returned and we've had a chance to talk have you realized that I was much more vulnerable, more fragile, than you knew at the time and that I had given the worst possible interpretation to something you had said during the quarrel. What seemed to you to be nothing more than a garden-variety spat had made me, who was already on edge, go to pieces."

The little lounge was silent except for the low-volume voices from the CNN broadcast. *"Washington is quiet at this hour. Police and troops are patrolling the city, and—"*

"Richard, I don't like your story."

"Of course you don't. But it *would* explain my sudden disappearance and that I didn't even bother to collect my stuff from the hotel. The point of the story is that I flipped, but that nothing illegal happened. I left in fury, deeply wounded, in a neurotic state. I was able to get an acquaintance outside of Paris to put me up for a few days. I stayed with him while I licked my wounds, managing to conceal my brittle condition. When I finally cooled down and came to my senses, I realized that I had overreacted and was treating you and the kids terribly. I decided to come back. I'm now very apologetic about what I did and recognize that I need help."

"This all assumes *you* are some kind of a psychological basket case and that *I'm* some kind of insensitive, thick-skulled battle-ax. I doubt Inspector Duparc would believe a word. I know he thinks I'm bright and have good intuitions about things. He even thinks I'd have made a good detective. If we tell him your story, he would either despise me as a liar or think I'm some kind of neurotic masquerading as a sane person."

Richard spread his hands in a gesture of capitulation.

"Helen, then what do you want me to say? I can't think of any other story that would be halfway plausible and explain all the facts. What choice do we have? Should I say that I had a bout of disgust with you and the children and that I suddenly, unexpectedly ran away to spend some time with a mistress? That would make me look even more mixed-up, and turn you into an even more unsuspecting, or, as you said, 'thick-skulled' woman. Or should I claim that I had some more basic mental breakdown, wandering off to who knows where? How would I explain that Broderie put up this deeply disturbed person for several days? Why did he not take me to a hospital or bring me to a psychiatrist?"

"But why would he have denied to the police that you were at his estate?"

"At my urgent request. I had fed him some line about needing absolute privacy."

"And that's why he would have put you in that underground room in the winery?" Helen asked sarcastically.

"I could say that after the police started to nose around the estate I asked the baron really to hide me. I simply could not face going back and needed more time to sort myself out."

"You would have wanted to hide in an underground cellar? Hardly credible."

"I'm supposed to have been quite messed up, perhaps in need of treatment. Besides, I'm under no obligation to offer an elaborate explanation, and neither is the baron."

"And why would a person you hardly knew take this interest in you and go to such lengths to follow your wishes, even deceive the police?"

"I can exaggerate how close we are and how close he was to my grandfather."

"What about telling the truth, Richard?"

"Helen, that's the one thing we simply cannot do. Believe me! I'm sorry." He gave her a pleading look.

Again they heard footsteps in the corridor and Bennini

appeared in the doorway with an unreadable expression. He said nothing, only looked at Richard.

Richard got up from the sofa and placed himself between Helen and the young consular officer.

"I'm afraid I've behaved rather irresponsibly, Mr. Bennini. I've been very foolish and caused a lot of worry as well as unnecessary work for you and the French police."

Bennini raised an eyebrow. "Unnecessary, Professor Bittenberg? You suddenly disappeared. Indications were you'd been abducted."

Richard gave a deep, prolonged sigh, as if he had just made a decision to come clean and tell all.

"Mr. Bennini, I've been under a great deal of stress for a long time. My professional responsibilities and commitments have just kept accumulating. I was unable to say no to anyone. Because the pressure built only gradually, I was able to hide from others and even myself that I was simply overwhelmed. I became a rather practiced deceiver and self-deceiver, couldn't understand myself how bad the situation had become. I didn't dare to check my blood pressure, so to speak. The truth is that as we left for this vacation in France — which took almost superhuman willpower on my part, let me tell you — my life had become unbearable. I had been pushing myself so hard for so long that I was coming apart at the seams. Now the vacation was taking me away from all of my commitments and put me all the more on edge. My life just came apart. Don't ask me to explain what happened. All I can say is that I had some kind of breakdown. I just couldn't take it any longer. I went into hiding. I fled. From my own life."

Bennini glanced in the direction of Helen, who was seated and staring into her lap.

"Professor Bittenberg, the French police have been going on the assumption that you were abducted, and your wife seemed to be under the same impression."

Richard shook his head slowly.

"I'm terribly sorry. Now that I'm getting back to my senses I can't understand how I could have done what I did."

"Were you abducted?"

"No, Mr. Bennini, I just ran away. Don't ask me to explain. I didn't quite know what I was doing. I just knew I had to get away, very far away. I couldn't stay anywhere close to my regular life, not even near my family. I'm not sure what triggered my running, but it had to do with my suddenly realizing that in my research I had badly misinterpreted some historical evidence. I had published an article with a very dubious thesis, and I would have to start a book of mine over — a professional disaster. My emotional state also had to do with something my wife said to me before I ran. To her it probably was little more than a passing comment in a trivial quarrel, but to me in my fragile condition that comment together with the scholarly catastrophe became the straw that broke the camel's back. I just couldn't stand my life anymore. I ran. I didn't see how I could ever come back. I didn't end up in a corner somewhere curled up in a fetal position, but a psychiatrist would probably call what happened a mental breakdown."

"So where did you go?"

"I had enough contact with reality to get in touch with a couple of friends, one at the U.S. Embassy. The other is an old friend of my grandfather's who lives outside of Paris. I told them some story and asked one of them to put me up for a few days. They weren't exactly happy to do as I asked, but they went along."

"But your family, Professor Bittenberg! Why didn't you let them know that you were all right? You must have understood how worried they were."

Richard shook his head again. It was not clear whether he did so to indicate that he had not understood the effect on his family or that he was now disgusted with himself. He started to pace the floor. As if talking to himself, he said, "I think contacting the family was a no-go zone. I couldn't bring myself to think of anything that reminded me of that unbearable life of mine. I guess I'd escaped, taken some sort of vacation from reality. I could barely function and this only in a separate world that had nothing whatever to do with my old life."

Helen observed Bennini. Did he believe what he was being told? Could he reconcile Richard's picture of what had happened with what she had told him? He looked skeptical, confused at minimum.

"Then what made you come back?"

"I guess it finally dawned on me what I'd done, that I'd gone off my rocker. I realized I had to reestablish contact with reality, however painful it might be."

"You didn't know your wife was still in Paris?"

Richard glanced at Helen and said, "No, and I was not ready to face her in any case. I thought I had better go to the American consulate. For one thing, I didn't have my passport."

Helen had listened to his every word, and she had found herself almost believing what she had heard. There was enough truth mixed into Richard's account to make it sound plausible to an outsider. But would Henri Duparc, who had confronted the baron and his helper, dismiss this story as a fabrication?

"Mr. Bennini," Helen suddenly broke in, "I can tell that my husband's not himself. I think he's very tired, and it's getting late. He needs rest."

"Of course, Mrs. Bittenberg. But I have to inform the French police."

"Yes, I understand."

"They will undoubtedly want to talk to your husband."

"Of course."

"Will you be able to manage, Mrs. Bittenberg?" Bennini looked at her with apparent concern and empathy. He seemed to be examining her face to ascertain her reaction to what Richard had said.

"I'm sure I can manage." She rose from the sofa. "I'm very grateful to you, Mr. Bennini. You've been wonderful throughout this dreadful period."

She walked up to him and without warning gave him a prolonged hug and then a kiss on the cheek. "Thank you!" she whispered in his ear before letting him go.

"I will escort you to the reception area."

Helen and Richard held hands as Bennini guided them out of the consular offices. When the three of them walked into the reception area and headed for the exit the Marine waved cheerfully in their direction.

"Good-night," Bennini said as he held open the door to the street for them. "Will you need a cab?"

"Don't worry. We'll be fine," Helen said. The door closed behind them. It was almost eleven o'clock, but the street was not quite deserted. There was light traffic. The temperature was pleasant. It was August, and tourists were still drifting about all over Paris. Shop windows and streetlights helped keep darkness at bay.

Richard and Helen faced each other.

"I'm not sure Bennini believed you," she said.

"He doesn't have to. He only needs to think that probably nothing criminal happened. Since I'm obviously not pressing any charges, that should be it, as far as the consulate and the embassy are concerned."

"Except that I may be accused of having misled the police. Chief Inspector Duparc, the French detective in charge of the case, is going to be very suspicious—no, incredulous. I never gave him any reason to believe that you might have been on edge and had some kind of breakdown."

"OK, but it wouldn't be far-fetched for you to have downplayed my delicate condition with the police. You didn't want them to treat my disappearance as perhaps due to a touch of neurosis. That would have made the case less urgent in their eyes."

"But what I told them made them suspect rather the opposite. And my hunches proved right. They got more concerned each day. When I talked to Duparc this afternoon Broderie and Dégas were being brought to the police station in Paris, and I think he was very worried about you. He wanted more police to help in the search. He was even afraid that you'd been murdered and your body dumped somewhere."

"But here I am, alive and well. It's understandable that you jumped to disturbing conclusions, and some of the evidence could be interpreted along those lines, but now everything gets cleared up. I'm pretty certain that most missing persons cases end up having fairly innocuous explanations. Here's one such case."

"Duparc won't buy it."

"So let him speculate. Broderie and Dégas will not contradict my story."

"How do you know?"

"I just do. We've talked."

Helen looked at him in bewilderment.

"And I won't tell the police very much. I don't have to. I'm not even a French citizen. I'll plead psychological exhaustion. I'll say I don't feel up to talking, will feign some mild confusion."

They were walking slowly past the chancery of the U.S. Embassy and in the direction of Place de la Concorde.

"How tired are you?" she asked.

"We badly need to talk."

"Don't you need to rest?"

"Not yet. I've probably slept too much in the last few days. You need to hear my story. Tonight. Now. If you're up to it."

She looked searchingly into his face. Her feelings were a blend of tenderness and dread.

Richard flagged down a taxi. In the cab they sat close together, but did not quite know how to relate to each other. They were at *Le Vieux Logis* in moments. The night porter at the hotel, the doctoral student in anthropology, showed delight at seeing them and greeted them in an exuberant manner, which forced them to smile and hold each other.

"What happened, Monsieur Bittenberg?" he asked.

"I'm afraid that's a very long story," Richard answered. "But I'm very glad to be back." He forced another smile.

Helen tried to do the same.

They took the tiny old elevator to their floor.

Despite the hour of the day, very early in the morning on the East Coast of the United States, they called their Washington home to break the news to the children and Helen's parents. Helen's father was already awake, and within moments John, Anne, and Helen's mother were also up and on the line. Helen and Richard became teary-eyed and hugged each other as they heard the joy in the children's voices. They said as little as they could about the reason for Richard's disappearance. More than once Helen said to the children, "Your father has been under a lot of stress. We'll tell you more when we get back."

Helen asked her father to call Hubert with the news.

They hung up. The time had come for their conversation.

# CHAPTER 66

Within minutes of finishing the phone call to Bethesda Richard and Helen found an open brasserie just a couple of blocks from the hotel. There were plenty of young people at the tables outside, but few inside. They seated themselves at a corner table indoors. They ordered soup and sandwiches from a bar menu. Helen realized that she had had nothing to eat since lunch, which had been about twelve hours ago.

Richard took her hands and looked into her eyes. "Helen, how're you feeling?"

"Much better now than a couple of hours ago." She smiled at him. For a moment she indulged the fantasy that they had just resumed their interrupted vacation.

"I think you've lost weight," he said.

"I'm sure I have."

"I'm so terribly sorry about all this, Helen."

Her expression turned serious.

"And there's more to come?"

"I'm afraid there is. I realize I can't hold anything back any longer. And what I'm about to tell you will be another hard blow. I'm very sorry. But we've got to have something to eat first."

For the next several minutes they sipped wine and ate pieces of baguette while talking aimlessly about the children, Helen's parents, Hubert, and Helen's time in Paris after Richard's disappearance.

When the food arrived Helen found that she could eat—if not with a good appetite, at least without having to force herself. Her trepidation about the truth to be revealed could not obviate her immense relief that Richard was alive and had come back to her. The terrible hard knot in the middle of her stomach was dissolving. They did not say much. They were together and did not need to speak for the other to know how precious the moment was. Whatever the future, they had each other. As long as they kept the rest of the world at bay, the present was just as it should be.

"You say you have a lot to tell me, but I have a lot to tell you, too," she said.

Richard looked at her full of curiosity.

They ordered coffee and pastries. Again they tried merely to enjoy the moment.

Richard took her hands. "You have to promise me that you will never tell a soul any of what I'm about to tell you—unless we agree otherwise. We're going to have to get together on how much we can tell the children and the family. It's quite possible that the police here in France or in America will interrogate you thoroughly. I'm not just thinking about the French detectives coming to see us tomorrow. When and if they do press you, you must always say the same thing: You had no idea about what I will now tell you about the reasons behind my disappearance."

"But I *didn't* know!"

"No, you didn't, but before we go to sleep tonight you will. And once you know my story, you might be legally obligated to go to the FBI and turn me in—except that we're married. I'm not sure about the legalities. At least in a court of law you may not need to be a witness against me."

"Richard! Have you committed some crime!?"

"If you go strictly by the law books, yes, I have. I've committed a very serious crime. How guilty I am morally is quite a different matter."

In a part of herself Helen did not want to hear another word— she wanted to shut herself off from any further threat to her peace of mind—but what she exclaimed in an urgent tone of voice was, "Tell me!"

"First you have to promise me that everything I'm about to say will stay between us, except if we agree on something different later. Can you promise that?"

She looked at him in bewilderment. She had lived for almost a week in a world turned upside down. Just as her existence seemed about to return to some semblance of normality it threatened to spin out of control again. Was she about to jump from the frying pan into the fire?

"Helen?"

"Yes," she said weakly.

"Can you promise?"

She gave him a despairing look that sent a wave of reproach and self-disgust through the very core of his being. She looked down at their intertwined hands, and then she nodded.

"Yes," she said in a barely audible voice.

"How much have you heard about what's just happened in the United States?"

She looked up at him. "Why are you asking me about that?

Please, Richard, let's get back to your story."

"Helen." He looked intently at her and squeezed her hands and asked again, "How much do you know?"

"I haven't been paying close attention. Terrorists killed the vice president, but the president is OK. D.C. is in some kind of turmoil. There are police, perhaps troops too, all over the city. Some general behaved stupidly. They're afraid of more attacks."

He nodded.

The waiter returned with their coffee and pastries. As he left Helen noticed that they were now alone in the inside part of the café. Outside young people were still engaged in conversation.

"Richard, must we talk about this terrorism? We need to talk about your disappearance."

"There was no terrorist attack, Helen. There was a failed coup attempt."

"*What!?*" She stared at her husband in utter disbelief.

"Yes, it was an attempt to overthrow the federal government of the United States, and until a couple of months ago I was a part of that conspiracy."

His words simply did not register in Helen's mind. The idea was so far-fetched that she could not accommodate it in the region of human existence to which she belonged. What Richard said simply made no sense. It was some kind of preposterous fantasy. Why would he say such a thing? This was no time to play with her imagination.

"Richard, what are you *talking* about? Don't confuse me. You're saying that you've been collaborating with terrorists?"

"No, Helen. The terrorism is merely a ruse, a cover story for something else — an attempt to take over the federal government of the United States. It was an attempt by regular Americans, from the inside."

"That's not what I've heard on television."

"Which is another reason why you should never trust anything you hear in the media. They're so easily manipulated, and sometimes they're complicit in deliberate deceit. Anyway, the reason I was abducted is that I had left the conspiracy to overthrow the government. Some people here in France and probably in Washington thought I posed a threat to the coup, and they kidnapped me."

Helen was incredulous. She shook her head. "Richard, I don't understand a word of what you are saying. First you tell me that there was supposed to be a coup in the United States, and then you tell me that you were abducted here in Paris. It makes no sense!"

"I can't blame you for being puzzled. The short and simple explanation is that the conspiracy in America had some supporters abroad, some of them here in Paris."

"De la Broderie?"

"Yes, he got word just as the coup was about to start that I was a security risk."

"And what about Ferguson?"

"Ferguson was the one who alerted him. I met Ferguson at the Sorbonne in the morning the day I disappeared. Since we left the U.S. for our European vacation I had been thinking about whether I should see him and at least tell him that I had left the conspiracy. It was as if our leaving for France and coming to Paris changed my perspective, gave me some distance to what was happening back home. I'd promised the leader of the conspiracy that I'd stay silent about leaving, and I meant it, but my conscience kept bothering me. I'd had strong reasons to leave the conspiracy, and I asked myself whether I had an obligation to tell others about my reasons. I think the fact that Ferguson was here at the embassy rather than close to the center of the conspiracy made me think of him as more of an innocent bystander than some of the others. He's not a really close friend, but I've known him for a long time. I arranged the meeting with him on the spur of the moment. When I told him I was no longer involved, which meant I'd broken my promise to the leader of the conspiracy, he pressed me to tell him the reason. I don't know what got into me, but I finally told him. The reason had to do with plans for really brutal action. He seemed upset. He then asked me to talk immediately to de la Broderie, who is one of the French conspirators. The count happens to have known my grandfather well, which is one of the reasons I agreed to meet with him. Ferguson called him from the Sorbonne, and 45 minutes later de la Broderie showed up."

"At that newsstand near the Sorbonne subway stop."

Richard looked at her in astonishment and was about to ask her how she could possibly know, but she said, "I'll explain later. Go on."

He shrugged his shoulders and continued: "I expected to have a fairly brief conversation with Broderie. I got into his vehicle, an old SUV. The driver was that Major Dégas you've mentioned. But once I was inside the count pulled out a gun, and they drove away. They took me to the Broderie estate, and they kept me there until this morning."

"But if you left the conspiracy a couple of months ago, why would you be kidnapped here in *France*? Why not back home, long before we left on our trip?"

"I had assurances that I would be left alone, but it seems that when we arrived in Paris the decision had been made to start the coup within a few days. I did not know it then, but things were really heating up. The final preparations were being made. There was probably a good deal of confusion and perhaps some tensions within the leadership. In any case, it's not hard to understand why Ferguson and Broderie would perceive me as an acute security risk. Broderie probably talked to Washington. I know of at least one person in the leadership who would have wanted to take no chances on me whatever. I'm not quite sure whether the count acted on his own or on orders from Washington or against orders. At first I thought I would be killed, but I think the count himself was uncertain about what to do. I'm the grandson of a person he really liked. Because he had a good place to hide me, he probably thought he could afford to wait and see. I was kept in a terrible place underground, in a winery, but I was pretty well treated. Major Dégas and two servants attended to my basic needs. I even had a couple of conversations with the count. He's a rather close friend of the person in the coup whose protégé I used to be."

"How did you escape?"

"I didn't. Last night, as soon as it was clear that the coup had failed, that it had never been fully executed, the count decided to let me go the next morning. He told me the French police had gotten rather nosy. This morning after breakfast I helped the count and the major to remove traces of me in the winery. I was able to clean myself up. I got this shirt, some clean underwear and socks. The baron could be certain that I would not go to the police. If I did, I would have to tell the truth about myself, which meant that I would have to go to jail as a coconspirator, accessory, or whatever, and that my family would be disgraced. We agreed on a story in case it became necessary to answer questions from the police: that I had sought refuge at the home of de la Broderie because of serious personal problems, that I had stayed at the estate on my own volition. Broderie had every reason to believe that I would stick to my part of the bargain."

"During all this time, why did you not try to get word to me that you were alive?"

"I did try. I pleaded with de la Broderie, but he would not hear of it, wouldn't do anything that might complicate the situation. He was in crisis mode, and the major did as he was told. From the beginning they seemed not to know what to do with me. While hiding me the count was acting his part in the larger conspiratorial scheme. I gathered his role had to do with spreading the word about terrorism to top French government officials and, when the time came—as it never did—to reassure the French government about the members of the new U.S. government. Ferguson was probably supposed to play a similar role in the State Department."

"When were you released?"

"Midmorning today I was driven from the estate by a strange, bumpy back road. They must have thought that the front entrance to the estate was being watched. I was driven to the subway station at the end of the line of one of the Paris Metro lines. The count gave me fifty Euros to supplement what I had in my wallet. I promised not to use any cash machine for a while. I agreed to go into Paris but to wait until the evening before contacting the American Embassy or the police. The count needed more time, wanted to meet someone—it could've been Ferguson—and needed to remove all traces of me in the winery. He also wanted to give further instructions to the servant couple on the estate. I was supposed to tell the embassy and the police that I'd been a guest at the estate. The baron and the major would say nothing in case the police asked questions. We were hoping never to have to spell out just where I'd been kept or why. My having had a psychological breakdown and getting a place to hide from the world was to be the explanation only if one positively had to be produced. I said what I said to Bennini only because the police already knew so much more than I thought, which came as a great surprise. I still can't understand how the police could have learned so much so soon. In the circumstances, I gave Bennini the agreed-upon line. Refusing to say anything would have looked much more suspicious, and it would not have made the police relax."

"I had something to do with the police suspecting de la Broderie."

"You!?"

"Soon after you'd disappeared I talked to Ferguson"— Richard gave her another surprised look—"and he told me that without evidence of a crime or a mishap the embassy and the police could not start a search for a missing person until after a few days. Of course, Ferguson had every reason to delay an investigation. It was actually young Mr. Bennini at the consulate who got the French police involved fairly soon and he who got them to make an extra effort. But before then I'd started my own search. I began by trying to find out what you'd been doing at the Sorbonne. The children were still here then."

"You were able to pick up some kind of trace?"

"Yes, and before long I started to suspect that Ferguson had something to hide."

"How in the world—?"

"It's a long story that I'll have to tell you some other time. You have to finish your story first. I'll just say that I've never been angrier with a person in my life than with Ferguson. He deceived me from the first moment and then at every turn. But once I caught on I started to deceive *him* to get information out of him. I could tell that he was infatuated with me, so I vamped him a little, got him drunk."

Richard's brow wrinkled. He looked searchingly at his wife.

"I actually got him to open up a little. He became very badly conflicted. He was besotted with the wife of a friend he had helped to abduct. I think he's in a very bad way right now. I last talked to him after the news from America. He told me he's been under a lot of stress recently. Poor baby. He deserves anything he gets."

"This is remarkable, Helen. How — ?"

"*Continue your story*, Richard!"

"All right." He sat forward on his chair and folded his arms on the table in front of him. "It all began when I was contacted by a man named Herbert Vandenhorst."

Richard had spoken for only five minutes when Helen, who had interrupted him only briefly to ask questions, suddenly rose. She was pale and looked disconcerted.

"I have to go to the bathroom," she said.

Richard started to get up. "Are you all right, Helen? Shall I come with you?"

She put up her hands as if to keep him at bay. "No, I'll be fine. Stay here! I'll be back in a minute."

She disappeared. Richard wanted to follow her, but he had a strong intuition that she did not want him to. He stayed at their table. When the waiter came by he ordered two cappuccinos. She still had not come back when the waiter brought the two cups. Richard was just about to go looking for her when she reappeared. He could tell that she had brushed her hair and improved her makeup, but she was still pale. She sat down expressionless and without a word.

"Did you feel sick to your stomach?"

"It doesn't matter. I think you'd better tell me the rest."

"But are you all-right?"

"Not really, how could I be? Now let's get this over with, Richard. Go on."

He gave her a concerned look and hesitated, but then slowly resumed his narrative. For the better part of an hour he spoke, in a low voice, interrupted only by Helen's questions. He summarized much but held back none of the more disturbing parts of his story.

They heard occasional laughter from that other universe outside. The customers were slowly thinning out.

"Richard," she said suddenly, "how *could* you go behind my

back this way?"

"I felt I *had* to, but it was for me the worst part of the whole thing. I *hated* the lying. But I couldn't involve you. You had to be completely ignorant of what I was up to in case I got caught."

"But we *were* involved. You dragged us in without giving us any say in the matter."

"Don't I know it? I'm sorry, Helen. I didn't know what else I could do. I felt compelled to take part in the conspiracy, but you shouldn't have to take any of the blame if the FBI nabbed me."

She gave him an angry look. "You don't think you kept this from me because you thought I would never let you do what you did?"

"I'm not sure, but I knew I had to be involved. I could not have lived with myself if I'd stayed out."

"And *we* didn't matter?"

"Of course you mattered. Don't be argumentative, Helen. You mattered so much that my going behind your back and endangering you was the greatest burden I had to carry. That deceit took a very heavy toll on me."

She stared at him. "It *should* have. And you *should* have told me what you were thinking of doing."

"You would have forbidden me to become involved in the conspiracy."

"Perhaps I would, but I'm your wife, and I had a right to know about and have an opinion about something that would affect me and the children so much."

"But then you would have been an accessory."

"If you felt you *had* to go forward, why did you finally drop out?"

"I've *told* you! I found out about the executions."

"Yes, yes, you've told me you consider a few of the conspirators too ruthless, but your conscience could hardly have been as clear as you are telling me. If you could be so easily dissuaded, you must have had some doubts from the beginning, or you were getting cold feet."

"*Easily dissuaded*? Helen, the ruthlessness I discovered was very bad. It deeply bothered me."

"Richard, you must have realized that some deliberate killing would take place. The coup was supposed to get rid of a whole power-structure, wasn't it? Why only the president and vice president? I think I understand what happened. You'd lived under a lot of pressure for a long time. Then the pressure got really bad, and when you found out that some people were to be executed, that became your pretext for pulling out."

"Helen, it was no *pretext!*" Richard raised his voice, but quickly lowered it again. "I couldn't be a party to murder."

"You're kidding yourself." Her voice had no empathy. It was sharp and dismissive. Richard flinched.

"*No*, Helen, you are just angry at me!"

"Believe whatever you want."

"Helen, you weren't *there!* You don't know what it was like."

"Let me tell you what I'm thinking. I find it difficult to understand how you could have gotten mixed up in something like this in the first place, but I'm not second-guessing your involvement. I know you didn't join the conspiracy for some flimsy reason. I'm certain the opposite was the case. You had thought forever about the sad state of our country—don't I know it?—and I think you had decided that nothing but shock therapy could work. You were probably also convinced that the coup had a good chance of success."

"That's all true."

"Now I'm not qualified to pass judgment on what America's current situation requires. Perhaps you are. I'm even prepared to assume the possibility that you people were justified in doing what you did."

"Thank God for that!"

"But if you've decided that a cause is right, you give it your all, don't you? You don't hold back!"

"Those *executions*, Helen!"

"You keep bringing them up. But what's so special about those particular deaths? If you were determined to topple the U.S. federal government and dismantle the entire power apparatus connected to it, how could you avoid getting rid of key figures? I'm no historian or political scientist, but what kind of an air-conditioned coup would that have been?"

The harshness of her words cut him deeply. He wanted to defend himself but did not have the energy.

"I'll be back in a moment," he said. It was his turn to have to go to the bathroom. He needed to empty his bladder, but his innards were also stirring uncomfortably. His discomfort was made all the worse by the realization that Helen's hostility might make it difficult for them to present a unified front. They could not afford to be alienated from each other. He and Helen would soon be interrogated, first by the French police and then by the American authorities. For the moment attention in America was focused on a hunt for terrorists, but it would be only a matter of time before the FBI found their way to his door. Life would eventually come crashing down around him and his family. They would be devastated. A wave of nausea swept through him, but nothing came up. He drank some water, splashed his face, and steadied himself. He returned to the table on shaky legs.

She didn't look up and didn't see the pallor on his face. When he was seated she kept staring into the table and merely said, "It will take me a long time to adjust to what you've told me."

"I understand."

They sat silently for a long time barely looking at each other, plunged deep in their own thoughts. She finally said in an expressionless voice: "What about that paper in your sports jacket, the one with letters and numbers?"

At first he didn't grasp her meaning. He was about to ask her when he realized what she was talking about.

"Oh *that*! I didn't even know I had it with me. I shouldn't have brought it. Those are numbers for that special telephone I have in my study. It's a secure connection. I used those numbers to dial members of the conspiracy."

She didn't bother to ask any follow-up questions. What did the details matter? She was overwhelmed by the magnitude and dreadful implications of the revelations.

When they left the restaurant the waiters had started cleaning the premises, signaling to the few remaining guests that it was closing time. Richard and Helen walked slowly the few blocks to *Le Vieux Logis* barely talking. They were together but alone.

# CHAPTER 67

Richard and Helen found themselves in a daze of conflicting emotions. Their pleasure at being together again was almost obviated by disorientation, fear, and the awareness that their lives would never be the same. They realized that from now on their marriage would be divided into the period before and after the Great Revelation. Their relationship would have to be reconstituted in ways that they could not foresee. Their interactions in their little Paris hotel room were a curious blend of mutual compassion, closeness, and distance. They were solicitous of each other but tentative and awkward. The more Richard realized what his wife had been through and what she had done to find him, the more his sense of gratitude and tenderness grew, but so did his shame. It was his unilateral decision to take part in the conspiracy that had caused her all this agony. In a part of herself Helen was grateful and happy that Richard had been restored to her and their children, but she was also full of anger, confusion, and dread. What would happen to their family? Would anything ever get back to normal? Would she ever be able to accept or forgive what Richard had done?

Helen was somehow less inclined to condemn Richard for the enormity of having participated in a conspiracy against the government of the United States than for having concealed it so completely from her and for having jeopardized her and their family's future. She was deeply resentful. She tried to comprehend how Richard could have acted as he did. She recognized that she had not understood the depth of his concerns about his country, though he had kept returning to it. Because *she* had not seen the situation of the United States as being quite so desperate as Richard did, she had not been able to imagine what his frame of mind was really like. She had stuck rather inflexibly to her own interpretation of his conduct. Was it then partly her fault that he had not wanted to confide in her? In defense of herself, she told herself that she had always tried not to nag and needle him about being so preoccupied with his work. Surely, her efforts to make him reduce his commitments had come out of a genuinely loving concern for his well-being, not just a concern for the family, and surely she had been perceived that way. But how could she have failed to notice that he was involved in something so large and important? How could she not have suspected that his tenseness had been due to more than "overwork"? She had to admire Richard's ability to hide his emotions and to dissemble. He had to have been a good conspirator. But what kind of wife would not have been able, after so many years of marriage and so many months of rising pressure, to see through appearances? She was not without blame.

Yet her moments of self-doubt and self-reproach were no more frequent than her moments of bitterness and anger. It would take a long time for her to get used to her new picture of her husband. She was married to a man who had been willing to risk the future of his family, who had committed treason, who would be arrested, and who would probably spend years in prison.

Richard's predominant feeling was a general numbness interspersed with pangs of shame, grief, and despair. During his imprisonment he had thought a great deal about the conspiracy, about possible final outcomes, and about his own situation, but it was only now that he had come face to face with the prospect of disaster for himself and his family.

Neither Richard nor Helen slept much the night after their reunion. They embraced, but half-heartedly. They talked intermittently and in whispering voices until very late and then slept sporadically.

It was not yet 6:00 AM when Helen and Richard walked to the nearby hotel in whose telephone booths Helen had spent so much time in the last week. Richard reached his brother on his cell phone and asked him to go immediately to a pay phone and call back. He told his brother to stop all investigations into his disappearance. There were no sinister aspects to his disappearance, he said. He had had a breakdown. "Don't ask me about it now. I'm too tired. I'll tell you all about it later." Hubert sounded skeptical and started grumbling, but understood from Richard's voice that he must not make any difficulties.

"If you're asked by the police about me, you don't know anything, Hubert, other than that I seem to have had some sort of collapse. You say nothing!"

"OK, Dick, but you've got some explaining to do."

Back at their hotel they showered and were getting ready to go downstairs for breakfast when the telephone rang. Helen looked at her watch before answering. It was only 7:45. The caller was Inspector Duparc, who announced that he and his assistant were just about to arrive at *Le Vieux Logis*. They would like to see Richard and Helen without delay. Helen hesitated for a moment, looked at Richard, and then told them to come up to the room. She didn't need to explain to Richard who had called.

"They don't want us to slip away this morning before they've had a chance to talk to us," he commented.

From the beginning, the interview with the police was intensely awkward and uncomfortable. Richard and Helen had talked more about what to say to the French police, and Richard had reiterated how important it was that they stick to the made-up story of why he had disappeared. The rather intimate setting of the small hotel room only made the discomfort and embarrassment of talking to the detectives worse. There were four adults in the cramped space. Richard and Helen sat on the unmade bed. The two detectives sat on the chairs by the small table.

Richard told his fabricated story. Though it made Helen squirm inwardly, she thought he made it sound rather believable. He gave a good imitation of suffering from badly frayed nerves. He stuttered slightly, made his voice weak, made his fingers tremble, and kept wringing his hands. Sometimes he made long pauses, staring into space. When Duparc pressed him on a few key points he kept saying as little as possible. He repeated that he was tired, exhausted, signaling to the two detectives that being interviewed by them was an ordeal. His performance was probably helped, Helen thought, by his lack of sleep the previous night. He indicated that Baron de la Broderie had merely tried to help an old family friend in distress. Richard managed to give plausible answers even to questions about Ferguson. Ferguson too was an old friend who had tried to assist. It was a good act, Helen thought, but she saw the doubt in Duparc's face. He frequently looked in her direction to assess her reactions. She had to assume that he suspected Richard of lying. Some of his questions suggested as much. "Why would the baron and the major rather spend the night in jail than tell us the truth?" Helen did not have to feign embarrassment. She had never felt more ashamed in her life. This nice, dedicated French detective and his associate had worked hard to help her find Richard. He had genuinely cared about her situation and made a special effort. Now she was complicit in trying to deceive him.

When Duparc finally turned to Helen, she thought she detected a touch of disgust in his voice. Had he now reached the conclusion that she had deliberately misled him about what might have caused Richard's disappearance? Did he think that she had done so in order to make him investigate the case more diligently, or did he suspect a more sinister motive?

"Do you have anything to add, Mrs. Bittenberg?" Duparc asked. He had said "Mrs. Bittenberg," not "Helen." He added, "This does not sound at all like what you thought had happened."

She looked into the carpet.

When she finally answered, she didn't look into Duparc's eyes: "I'm very sorry, Inspector. I simply didn't realize how stressed my husband was. I just didn't see the signs. I guess he was too good at hiding them from me. I'm really sorry." She raised her eyes and looked pleadingly at him. She looked next at Léger, who had sat there impassively. His expression was hard to read, but he seemed to close his notebook demonstratively and with irritation.

Duparc stood up, and Léger followed his example.

"Professor Bittenberg, I would like for you to come to my office to make a statement. I will need a formal, written declaration of what happened."

"May I have breakfast before I come?"

"Fine, but we can't wait here for you," Duparc said. "Come on your own after breakfast." He handed Richard a calling card. "This is the address. Your wife knows where it is." Helen winced.

Duparc moved towards the door, and Léger followed. Before they left, Duparc looked back at Helen. Neither detective said "good-bye."

When the door had closed Helen buried her face in her hands.

"I'm *so* sorry," Richard said.

She did not respond.

After breakfast Helen accompanied Richard to the building on Ils de la Cité. They announced their arrival in the ground floor reception and were sent to the small reception area on Duparc's floor. When Duparc came to fetch Richard he said nothing except that Helen should remain where she was. Duparc and Richard disappeared into the corridor she remembered.

Richard spent a very uncomfortable half hour with the two French detectives. He was asked again about weak points in his story, but he merely repeated what he had said before. He resisted providing more details by claiming poor memory or by calling the questions an invasion of privacy. Why this interrogation? He had done nothing wrong, certainly nothing illegal, had just had a breakdown. He slumped in his chair. He gave the impression of being nervous and having difficulty concentrating. He let his eyes wander erratically and aimlessly. Once he feigned being close to tears.

"Why would de la Broderie and Dégas refuse to say that you had been a guest at the estate?"

"The baron promised me not to tell anyone."

"He would rather be arrested than answer the questions of the police?"

"Perhaps he believes in a right to privacy," Richard muttered in an almost inaudible voice and closed his eyes as if nodding off to sleep.

Duparc finally said, "OK, Professor Bittenberg. I'm going to ask you tell your story one more time, this time for the tape recorder. What you say will be typed up, and you'll be asked to sign the statement."

Richard nodded weakly.

In another half hour it was all over. Duparc escorted Richard back into the reception area where Helen was waiting. When she saw them she rose abruptly from her seat, looking anxiously at Duparc. The French detective did not betray any emotion and did not say anything. He did not move towards Helen, just let Richard join her. But this time, before he turned around and disappeared behind the security door, he gave a slight bow in Helen's direction and said a curt "good-bye."

Richard and Helen were able to book seats on a flight back to the United States the following day. They called home with the news. The excitement in the children's voices both cheered and disconcerted them. Would Richard actually get home to Bethesda before the FBI arrested him? For what remained of their last full day in Paris they moved around the city without purpose, talking quietly. They returned to the hotel a couple of times to try to catch up on their sleep, but found it hard to settle down. The weather was pleasant, and it might have been a wonderful part of their vacation, Helen thought. Passing television screens, they saw more images from the United States. They spent an hour watching a CNN broadcast in a Marriott hotel lobby. According to one newscast, a massive search for the terrorist perpetrators of the assassination of the vice president and the attempted murder of the president was underway, but Richard assumed that the FBI was also pursuing other leads that would soon disclose the true perpetrators. As they spent their last hours in Paris he was prepared for the French police suddenly showing up and arresting him at the behest of the American authorities.

But nothing happened.

At the airport the next morning, they saw excerpts of a nationally televised speech given by the American president. The president looked determined. He promised "a relentless war on the enemies of the United States." Seeing the face of a man who presided over a rotted, perverse regime and who cared very little about the well-being of his fellow Americans sent a wave of utter despair through Richard. Whatever his own personal fate or the fate of his family, his country was headed for disaster. Only the particular forms of the suffering in store for the American people were yet to be revealed. The just-discovered new threat to the regime would certainly result in an expansion of the burgeoning police state.

They arrived at Dulles Airport in Washington in the afternoon. As their plane was taxiing towards the gate Richard braced for his imminent arrest. He pictured two or three FBI agents waiting to escort him off the plane. But their arrival at the gate proved uneventful. They could move routinely through passport control and customs and into the arrival hall, where their jubilant children and Helen's parents met them. While Richard hugged them his eyes swept the crowd for signs of what was to happen. Still nothing. The heat and humidity that hit them outside as they walked into the short-term parking lot confirmed that they were really back home. Richard was puzzled. When would his time be up?

Richard and Helen spent the first evening at their Kenwood home with the children. The scene might have looked to an outsider like a typical family reunion. Richard and Helen had agreed on what they could tell the children about Richard's disappearance, and despite John's and Anne's frustrated sighs they would not tell them any more. There were no knocks on the door.

Once the children had gone to bed, Richard—though exhausted from his imprisonment, the ordeal of his rejoining Helen in Paris, the transatlantic trip, and the time change—spent a couple of hours going through his study again for possibly incriminating evidence. He had done so before leaving for France, but he thought now about what he might have missed. He could see that the two private eyes had rifled through his papers and computer disks. He looked through his computer again, tore up some more papers before flushing them down the toilet, and broke a couple of innocuous computer disks that he had used when learning the encryption method. He had already disconnected and reset the scrambler phone, but it was still sitting in the same old drawer. Why had he not gotten rid of it? He had told himself that it was not illegal or even suspicious to own a scrambler phone. In view of all the electronic threats to privacy, there really was nothing strange about a person wishing to protect privacy. But who except a person with something to hide would have such a telephone? Why had he kept it? Had he not wanted to sever his last direct contact with the conspiracy? Was it yet another sign of his infernal ambivalence?

At one o'clock in the morning Helen was asleep in their

upstairs bedroom. Richard left a note on the kitchen table that he had gone for a drive, quietly went into the garage, backed out his car, and drove away. He took some strange turns to make sure he wasn't followed and finally drove to one of the canal locks near the Potomac River. It was a dark August night. The only light came from a hazy moon. He parked the car and walked across the bridge at the lock and walked in the direction of the Potomac River. He took his time to get used to the darkness. Not to fall he walked slowly and carefully among rocks, branches, and brushes. Between the trees and through the foliage the river glimmered from the moonlight and a few weak lights in the distance. He found a small strip of land and rocks that jutted out into the swirling waters of the river. He walked out on it, steadied himself, and flung the scrambler telephone as far away as he could into the river.

# CHAPTER 68

In the days after Helen and Richard's return to their Bethesda home, the Bittenberg family seemed to live a normal life, but appearances could not be more deceiving. The dread of things to come put a pall over all that Helen and Richard did to get on with life. They interacted in a provisional, almost formal manner. Helen's attitude towards Richard went back and forth between empathy, anger, and tenderness. For Richard, shame and sorrow colored his every action. The children worried that their parents seemed different, less spontaneous towards each other than in the past. What had really happened in Paris? Their parents would only say vaguely that their father had collapsed from overwork.

Immediately upon returning to America Richard made a reservation to fly down to Charleston, primarily to talk to his brother. He badly needed legal advice. It was just a matter of time before the FBI showed up. He had rehearsed possible evasive answers to questions. It would not be long before they knew enough about the conspiracy to want to question him, if not necessarily arrest him right away. The delay was in a way not surprising. The FBI might need more time to gather evidence before striking against any of the key suspects. This would make sense. Any arrests would come at the end of a full investigation. Richard thought of contacting one of the members of the steering committee to get some idea of what might be expected, but he realized that doing so would be too risky. He might also be shunned. He did not even want to contact Robert Preston. Many or most of the leading conspirators were probably under surveillance. He read the newspapers and various Internet sources closely for any information that might give him a clue about the general direction of investigations and any progress made. It surprised him that in the big media the recurring theme remained the same as before. Terrorism was a greater threat than ever, various officials and politicians said, and the FBI and other organizations were pursuing possible connections between the assassination attempts and the Taliban and Al-Qaeda. At a left-wing web site he read allegations that what was really behind what had happened was a sinister conspiracy centered in the Pentagon and the CIA.

Early in the morning two days after returning to the United States Richard flew to Charleston for a two-day visit. He went to see his mother and took her out to lunch. She had been told that he had suffered a breakdown, and she was deeply concerned about his health. Richard did his best to reassure her. She was cheered by his general appearance and decently good mood, which Richard was able to produce only through great effort.

At Richard's request he and Hubert then met at Hubert's law office. If the feds were on his tail, Richard reasoned, there should be little danger of their trying to listen in at a law office. Confidentiality rules would make that highly illegal. Traditional rights and protections of that kind had become less and less dependable in America's expanding national security regime, but rights associated with lawyering, America's most favored and privileged profession, had suffered the least. At minimum, evidence gathered through eavesdropping on a lawyer's office would be inadmissible in a court of law.

Before telling Hubert his story Richard surprised him by saying that he would like to speak with him in his capacity as a lawyer. That would mean that anything he said would be strictly confidential. Hubert said: "You don't think it's enough that you're my kid brother? What in the world have you been up to?"

Richard told Hubert everything, which made Hubert's eyes widen and his jaw drop. Richard answered many questions. At the end, Hubert just shook his head. "Dick, this is the damndest story I've ever heard, and I've heard a few in my day. This calls for bourbon." He left the office, and when he returned with a bottle he said, "Dammit, Dick, this puts me in a big bind. I'm not even sure where I stand legally. I hired that private eye to help find you, and he's disappeared. Who knows what's happened to him. His assistant stepped in, but he hadn't gotten very far when you reappeared, and I told him I no longer needed his services. Especially if the missing private eye turns up dead—murdered?—the police will soon be in touch with me. Now that you've in effect made me your lawyer, I can't tell them very much, which will make them mighty suspicious, especially if I have to invoke the lawyer-client privilege. Hell, Dick, a lot of different roads can lead the feds to your door."

"Don't I know it?"

Hubert broached the possibility of Richard giving himself up and turning state's witness. "Imagine, Dick, you could become the biggest media darling ever, the man of conscience who exposed the foulest crime in American history. You'd get off lightly, and you'd be a great hero to many." Richard had already considered this course of action, and he would not hear of it. Hubert did not press the matter.

"Damn it, Richard, you're in one tough spot. When the FBI asks you questions, you must have nothing to say. You just call me!"

Richard returned to Washington. Life went on. The children returned to school. He realized that he should get ready for his fall semester courses at the university, but was there any point? He would not be able to teach for long. Richard was barely functioning, moving, he thought, in slow motion. Sadness and dejection infected all that he did. His courses started. He had to force himself to seem engaged and cheerful. He picked up some of his old habits, but he no longer found it difficult to decline proposed new commitments. He could, after all, be arrested at any time.

Life acquired a kind of abnormal normalcy. Nowhere did he pick up any signs that the FBI was on his tail, and yet his head told him that the authorities had to be encircling him and the other conspirators. Strangely, none of the names of conspirators he knew surfaced in news programs or newspaper stories. The FBI obviously did not want to risk any premature interrogations or arrests. The FBI would act when they were good and ready. In months past Richard had lived in constant fear that the conspiracy would be detected, but the worries and premonitions then had been rather vague. He had been too busy and tired to dwell on the dangers. Now his imagination regarding his arrest was pointed and concrete. Images took turns in his mind. Men in suits would show up. They would pick him up outside a classroom in full view of exiting students. Or they would even arrest him during a lecture. Or they would come to his university office and pick him up in front of a befuddled Ron Turello. Amazed colleagues would see him being taken away. Or agents would come to the house, two knocking on the front door, one watching the kitchen door. Anne and John would be terrified.

His relationship to Helen slowly improved. He spent virtually all the time away from the university at home, much of it with her and the children. He did so partly because he was painfully aware that he could be separated from them at any moment. He and Helen did not talk at length about the Big Subject. He had warned her that the FBI might have him under surveillance and be listening in. Only now and then, with music or radio noise in the background, did they have whispered conversations about the topic.

Helen continued to have difficulty accepting that in becoming a member of the conspiracy Richard had risked everything, pulling her, the children, the family, and their friends with him. But she started to think that at least she had to allow for the possibility that he had been right in his assessment of what America needed.

Nobody had to prove to her that her country was in deep trouble and that the political system seemed incapable of reforming. Perhaps she owed her husband more trust and loyalty. She wondered if his feeling the need to take action was the result of some specifically male compulsion that she could not fully understand, but should try to tolerate. She had also begun to feel a grudging admiration for his courage and perseverance. He had carried a great burden for a long time. Her Paris nightmare had taxed her to the utmost, but it had lasted for only a few days. Richard's ordeal had dragged out over many months, and it was far from over.

Though she worried greatly about their family's future, she smiled more often, sometimes even at Richard. They both sensed that a new intimacy was forming between them. It had to do with their shared suffering, which would continue for the foreseeable future, but also with his spending more time with the family and being less distracted than in the last few years.

Richard often thought back to Helen's way of handling his disappearance in Paris. He marveled at what she had done. He had always known her to be bright and strong-willed, but during this period she had exhibited extraordinary persistence, smarts, resourcefulness, and guile. It was she who had made it possible for the French police to track down de la Broderie. She had seen through Ferguson and then trapped him into spilling information. What a performance! She had truly been "Miss Ironpants." He had told Helen more than once how impressed he was. Her reaction had been to embrace and hold him.

Richard found himself wondering how she would have reacted if he had taken her into his confidence before joining the conspiracy. Why had he assumed that she would oppose him? Because she would be so protective of their family. She was also rather apolitical. She did not so much disagree with his views of America as have her mind on other things. After hearing him out, might she have supported him, however reluctantly? If so, he would not have had to be so frightfully lonely. She might have become his best advisor. She could have helped him through the grueling times. He knew now that she had a great reservoir of toughness.

Richard had the impression that Jennifer, Robert Preston's wife, had at times been a thorn in her husband's side, but Robert had not had to keep up an exhausting, demoralizing campaign of lies and deception. Richard had never gotten to know Celeste Vandenhorst well, but it appeared that she and her husband had no secrets from each other. They were a team. Had she known about the executions? If so, had she approved of them? Or—a strangely comforting thought — had she urged them on him? No, he reflected, how could a woman do such a thing?

How would Helen have reacted during his great crisis in the conspiracy? He flinched when he thought back to the dismissive comments on his moral qualms about the executions that she had flung in his face in that Paris brasserie. Surely those were not her final words. They had to have been triggered by her anger at the Great Revelation and by his having hidden everything from her. In typical female fashion she had sensed where he felt the most vulnerable and had challenged him mercilessly in that very area to punish him. A part of him wanted to ask her what she really thought, but another part feared to do so.

Surprisingly, Helen now seemed less despondent than he was. It was she who tried to encourage and cheer him rather than the other way around. It was he rather than she who brooded. While he was prone to passivity and despair, she was adapting to the new situation. He noticed that as soon as they returned home she started to make plans for how to handle the family upheaval to come. She wanted to work out with Richard what they should say to John and Anne, her parents, his mother, other family members, and friends once he was interrogated or arrested. They would tell different people different things while making it all compatible with his legal defense. She asked Richard to sit down with her to review the family finances. She was the one who paid their monthly bills, and she already had the general picture, but now she wanted to be prepared to take charge of the family assets. Because of the inheritance from Richard's father, the Bittenbergs were financially more comfortable than most academic families at a comparable stage of life, but now their financial future was very uncertain. Her frame of mind was practical and attentive to detail. If it became necessary to post bail to have Richard released from custody pending a trial, how much could they hope to raise? She wanted to know how much was in their bank accounts, their brokerage account, and in their retirement accounts. Could they withdraw money from the latter if they needed it? How much equity did they have in their house? What was the credit limit on their credit cards? Hubert would probably donate his legal services, but other legal expenses were likely to become a heavy burden. In a crunch, how much help might they expect from Richard's mother and siblings and from Helen's parents? They were in no immediate danger of financial hardship, but Richard was the only wage earner in the family. Once National University stopped payment of his salary because he could not perform his academic duties, the Bittenbergs would soon find themselves in an economically precarious situation. If he were to be convicted of a felony, his tenure as a professor would almost certainly be revoked. Thinking through these matters with Helen brought home to Richard in excruciating detail the consequences of his actions as a conspirator. He had knowingly exposed his family to the danger of financial ruin as well as ignominy. He would have preferred not to sharpen his misery by discussing these issues, but Helen left no doubt that she wanted them fully aired. At one point in this protracted conversation she said: "If worst comes to worst I should be able to find a teaching job. Most women have to work outside the home, don't they? Mom may help out with the kids."

His conscience gave another twinge, and he said: "I'm so sorry, Helen — about everything."

"I know, Richard, but what's done is done."

She had the attitude of a "survivor," he thought to himself. Where did she find the strength?

Long experience had taught Richard how to stay outwardly composed while being inwardly in anguish or turmoil. He was still able to do so, but he had to struggle to stay fully functional. In some moments he was racked by self-recrimination, which included doubts about the fundamental assessment of reality that had pushed him into the conspiracy. Had he been too rigidly attached to certain traditional values and beliefs and too unwilling to concede that the new America was offering a different but in many respects acceptable way of life? Had he been too inflexible, narrow-minded, and unimaginative? In other moments he wondered whether he had been a fool to think that anything like a coup might halt America's decline. The problems were gargantuan. He himself had always questioned the efficacy of political action in trying to change the fundamental direction of society. So why had he gone against his own best judgment and enrolled in a virtually hopeless cause? In yet other moments, he was as convinced as ever that his decision to join the conspiracy had been justified, a moral obligation even. But in that mood it bothered him that Vandenhorst and the others should have tarnished the whole enterprise and retroactively sullied his involvement. Although worries about his own and his family's future were now taking precedence, awareness that his country was headed for catastrophe formed the backdrop for his thoughts.

When would his time be up? The uncertainty was in a way harder to handle than an arrest. The electronic media and the newspapers provided no clue of where the investigations might be leading. They explored one tantalizing theory after another about who might have tried to kill the president and vice president, but with amazing persistence speculation returned to Islamic terrorism. Spokesmen for the FBI and the Department of Homeland Security had no definite hypotheses. Richard wondered whether the permanent government of the United States might be afraid that raising the possibility of a homegrown, elaborate conspiracy might undermine the government's credibility. The president and his spokesmen contributed to the terrorism theme by often referring to the need for vigilance against terrorism and for defeating America's enemies in the Middle East. But there were no reports of a breakthrough or major lead in the investigation.

In the week just after the "Day of Outrage," as it had become known, much attention was paid to examples of the confusion and mix-ups in Washington that had resulted from garbled reports that the president and vice president had been attacked. Government institutions had gotten their wires crossed, and the media had contributed to the general turmoil. It had taken a couple of weeks just to sort out what had and had not happened. In the early days the media covered the curious story of a Marine general, one Noah Sales, who had taken it upon himself to improvise a Marine mission to the U.S. capital to protect against suspected attacks on Washington. He had acted just as the first reports of the attempted killings and of other possible deeds of terrorism were starting to spread. The general had taken charge of troops at the Quantico training base and tried to move them fully armed to Washington. This was apparently not a part of any pre-existing government plans to protect Washington in case of attack, but who could tell for certain? The general had become known as "The Cowboy" or "Rambo." He had aborted the mission once he realized that the president was alive and safe and that the situation in Washington was less fragile than he had thought. According to the Pentagon, the general had breached regulations and would be disciplined. But Sales's curious enterprise had been just one of several peculiar incidents covered by the media in the first few days, and it had faded away. It had been eclipsed by the discovery in a Capitol Hill underground parking garage of a stolen contractor's van that was a rolling fertilizer bomb. The explosive device had been prepared for detonation, but the van had been abandoned near some construction materials and equipment. Workers making repairs to the underground train line between the Capitol and the Russell Senate Office Building had discovered it. The confusion on the "Day of Outrage" had caused so much and such extravagant speculation that no particular episodes had etched themselves in the media mind. Then, just over a week after "the Day of Outrage," other major news had started to compete for media attention. Another large demonstration had turned very violent, this one in Rochester, N.Y., where unemployment had reached twenty percent and state and local governments were simultaneously trying to make emergency cuts in social benefits. Because fifteen people died and the damage to the city was extensive, this story replaced the "Day of Outrage" as the main news for a few days. Shortly thereafter "sympathy riots" broke out in several places, the biggest in Albany, New York, the state capital. The media and the public having been sufficiently distracted, life returned to normal.

The uncertainty robbed Richard of all real concentration. He attempted to return to his research, but his imagination would not stay focused. When he was at the house every unfamiliar sound made him think that the FBI had finally arrived. When at the university or elsewhere, he frequently thought that particular people might be agents keeping track of his movements.

# CHAPTER 69

Almost two months passed that seemed to Richard an eternity of apprehension and anxiety. The threat of imminent arrest hung over all that he did. He often felt like a convalescent who is trying to regain his strength after a major operation but who knows that he will soon have to undergo an even bigger one. He wondered what he would have done without Helen. She kept encouraging him to do things that would take his mind off his wretchedness. She got him to do more exercise. It boosted his spirits even more that her own activities signaled faith in the future. The Bittenberg family would pull through somehow.

Richard and Helen spent more time together. They even started to go to the movies and had an occasional dinner in a restaurant. They were careful not to talk of sensitive subjects when they might be overheard. They got used to conversing in an intimate, almost whispering manner. They no longer needed to talk about the torments of the past. All important questions had been answered. Helen's anger had subsided. She understood why Richard had kept his involvement in the conspiracy from her. His main reason, she had decided, was not an unwillingness to face her opposition but a wish to protect her and the family. She blamed herself for not having been sufficiently sensitive to his frequently expressed concerns about America and to his frustration that so little was being done to address them. She had observed many of the symptoms of the decay of American society, but had directed her attention elsewhere. She and her family and their friends could have a rather satisfying life despite America's troubles. She could get on with life without worrying about them. She had, in other words, left it to others to do the worrying. She had, in effect, depended on those others to take on the responsibility for dealing with the problems. She still was not certain that Richard had been right to join the conspiracy, but he had done what he truly thought he had an obligation to do. She knew him to be a man of conscience, and he had spent most of his life thinking about the state of America and the Western world. If he was not the kind of person who should decide what needed to be done, who was? He clearly had not been acting out some scheme of self-glorification. Who was she to question his judgment?

But what about his risking his family's future? Was it not always a father's primary responsibility to protect his family? Whenever she asked that question she felt a pang of resentment against Richard, but the resentment had weakened with time. Richard was but one of countless people in history who had put their families in jeopardy, some of them for the best of reasons. And Richard had taken precautions to shield his family.

She might have regarded Richard's leaving the conspiracy as an act favorable to his family, and yet her reaction when first learning of it had been negative. She did not quite know why. It had something to do with his abandoning ship at a critical juncture and with his giving up at the last moment after expending such tremendous effort. But the issue had faded in her consciousness. How could she presume to know better than her husband what the situation required? She did not know all the circumstances.

A new closeness was emerging between them. They knew and understood each other better than before. Much, if not all, of what Helen had learnt about her husband had increased her respect for him. She had to admire his daring and bravery as a conspirator. His having lived for so long with intense and sometimes horrendous pressures seemed to her an extraordinary feat. That he had risen to a central position in a conspiracy of so many able and experienced people had to mean that he had practical and political skills as well as a first-rate mind. She had had a hard time coming to terms with another of his newly-revealed strengths, his capacity for deceit and concealment. It kept bothering her that he had employed it against her. But she realized that developing this skill had been a necessity in the conspiracy, and she had to admit that his acting had been exceptionally good. It had never so much as occurred to her — his wife! — that he might have been involved in something like intelligence or undercover work, to say nothing of a conspiracy to overthrow the government.

Richard for his part remained in awe of Helen's determined and clever machinations in Paris. In potentially paralyzing circumstances she had acted. She had shown great perspicacity, cunning, and energy. She had gone to great lengths to find him. The esteem in which he had always held her had deepened. Her inability to understand the depth of his worries about America he excused as the weakness of one whose life had never been focused, the way his had been, on assessing the moral and cultural condition of their country.

Despite lingering grievances, unresolved questions, and

hesitations, Helen felt that she and Richard belonged together. She could not embrace him unreservedly, but she owed him her support as he owed her his. Their life settled into a fragile routine of preparedness out of which love drained some of the pain. They could read in the faces of John and Anne that they detected this bond between their parents. Whatever their father had been through, they did not need to worry about him.

One Friday morning Richard was in the kitchen of their home sipping his morning coffee and reading the *Washington Post*. Helen had gone with Anne to her school to assist on a field trip. Flipping through the Metro section and the obituaries his eyes fell upon a rather large article whose headline read, "Statesman, Advisor to Presidents." At first Richard did not recognized the picture of a clean-cut man in his fifties. Then, as he turned to the text of the article, the identity of the dead man forced itself through his own incredulity and resistance. The person in the picture was Herbert M. Vandenhorst. Richard's head registered the information, but his heart refused to believe it. Vandenhorst! Richard had always thought of him as destined for a very long life. He would be ramrod straight into his nineties. The article gave the cause of death as a stroke. Herbert Vandenhorst had died at home without any forewarning.

Richard's dominant feeling was searing grief mixed with complete surprise. Vandenhorst had become an important part of his life. Only after the revelation of the plans for executions had Richard begun to reassess his admiring and friendly attitude to this man. He wanted to show the article to Helen immediately. She knew about his deeply ambivalent feelings for Vandenhorst. Richard needed her comfort. He wanted her to take some of the edge off his pain, which involved more than sorrow at the death of Vandenhorst. It included a more pervasive sense of loss, regret that all the struggle and pain connected to this man had come to nothing except ignominious defeat. Richard forced himself to read the article line by line. Vandenhorst's career had been even more varied and distinguished than Richard knew.

Richard had long known and now realized with full force that he had come to regard Vandenhorst as a substitute father. He had gotten to know him very well. Although they had never quite developed a family-like relationship—Herbert and Celeste did not even know Helen—he had gotten close to Vandenhorst. He had deeply admired his judgment, self-control, administrative skill, leadership ability, prudence, guts, and perseverance. Yet Richard had broken with the conspiracy because of Vandenhorst's deceit. He realized now that he had always assumed that one day he and

Vandenhorst would be able to settle their accounts, compare notes, assess who had been in the right. That would never happen. Richard was on his own again.

Grief and practical questions dominated the next several hours. Could he contact Vandenhorst's wife to offer condolences? Could he attend the funeral? The FBI would of course be in attendance, videotaping everything. On the other hand, it was likely to be a very large funeral. Richard could disappear in the crowd. He could be there to honor his friend the student of history. But running into former colleagues in the conspiracy might become very tricky and awkward. He took a long walk to sort out his conflicting impulses.

When Helen and Anne returned in the early afternoon Richard signaled to Helen that he wanted to talk to her. She gave him a worried look. When Anne had disappeared upstairs and they heard music they went into the family room, which looked out on the garden.

"This is in today's paper," Richard said, almost whispering as was their custom when conversation turned to the Big Subject. He handed her the article. Helen sat down. She had only glanced at the article when she looked up at Richard.

"Oh, Richard, I'm so sorry," she said in a low voice. She started to rise, but he motioned to her to stay seated.

"Please, finish the article."

She read quietly without stopping while Richard stood looking out into the garden. Then she got up and walked over to him. She embraced him and whispered in his ear, "I'm so very sorry, Richard." A few moments later, still holding him, she added: "I know how much you liked him—in spite of everything." She noticed that he was shaking from sobbing, and she held him for a long time. She understood that he was crying not merely for Vandenhorst but for himself, for all that he had been through, for the suffering to which he had exposed his family, and for a painful, degrading, and uncertain future.

"I'll be back," she finally said and disappeared into the kitchen.

He heard noises that made him think that she was emptying the dishwasher, but she returned with two glasses of white wine, holding one of them out to him.

"Helen, it's not even three o'clock in the afternoon—on a weekday!"

She smiled at his surprise and gave him a kiss on the cheek.

"I thought this would be just the right time for a drink. It might get some of the sting out."

How lucky he was. Helen had gone through hell in Paris. Then she had learnt that her life was not what she had thought and that she and her family were facing disaster. She was in danger of losing as much as he. Still, she was propping him up, offering him solace. He was often mired in discouragement, feeling drained of all energy. She was not only kind and considerate but prone to act.

They sat down, and Richard gratefully drank of the wine. She turned on some music, and they had a whispered conversation about Herbert Vandenhorst and the practical issues now on Richard's mind. She refilled his glass. After a while he began to feel drowsy and rested his head against the back of the sofa. In moments he was asleep. When he awoke half an hour later the first thing he saw was her smiling face.

In the late afternoon Richard turned on the television set in the family room, which merged with the kitchen. Helen was starting to make preparations for dinner. Anne and John were upstairs, and music came from both of their rooms. Richard had just started to open a bottle of wine when suddenly there were two solid knocks on the front door that sounded almost like bangs.

Richard realized immediately that the moment had finally come. Their extended reprieve had come to an end. The FBI were finally swooping down on the conspirators. He and Helen exchanged knowing glances. He put down the wine bottle, walked up to her, embraced her tenderly and kissed her.

There were two more bangs on the door. As he went to the door to open another insistent two knocks indicated the urgency of the caller's business. Anne appeared on the landing, asking, "What's going on?" Music kept John isolated from the world.

"Oh, it's nothing," Richard said. "Go back to your room." She stayed where she was.

He opened the door.

He had expected two men in suits, at least one in dark glasses, but he saw only one. He was hard to see clearly against the setting sun. Squinting against the light, Richard noticed that the man's hair needed combing. He was big and burly and unexpectedly old. He looked somehow familiar. The figure was dressed not in a suit but in a bomber jacket and slacks.

It was Gordon Bunker. It was Richard's old fellow conspirator, the retired admiral who had been a heavyweight in the conspiracy both in bulk and influence. His face seemed flushed.

"I have to talk to you!" Bunker said.

Richard thought that Bunker's words had sounded somewhat slurred. Did he not look a little unsteady on his feet? Was he drunk?

Richard knew that he shouldn't be talking to Bunker. He didn't want to invite him into the house. Yet this was a person to whom he had been close for a long time.

"We were just about to have dinner — and I don't think — "

"That's not important. That can wait, Dick. Let's go!" Bunker swayed as he motioned to Richard to come with him.

"What's the matter, Gordon? Have you been hitting the bottle?"

"What if I did? Why shouldn't I? Stop being so ornery. I have to talk to you."

"I don't think that's a good idea," Richard protested.

"It's a *very* good idea! And we must talk *now!*"

Helen appeared in the doorway, and Richard could see Anne a couple of steps behind her.

"Helen, everything's fine," Richard said. "This is an old friend of mine who's been interested in my writing. He seems to need some help."

"Good evening, Mrs. Bittenberg," Bunker said in an almost normal voice. He attempted a small bow and had to take a side step to recover his balance. "We met at our house."

"Yes, I remember," she said with a hesitant smile.

"I may have to go out for a while," Richard said.

Relieved not to be confronting FBI agents, Helen made no objection. She nodded to Bunker and returned inside.

"How did you get here?" Richard asked Bunker.

"By car, how else?"

"You *drove* here?" Richard saw a beige Toyota Camry parked in the street near their driveway.

"Why not? Who cares?"

"You should not be driving."

"Stop blabbering and let's go!"

Richard quickly calculated his options. He decided that he should not talk to Bunker and that he risked becoming an accessory after the fact if he did. If he left his house in Bunker's company, he would have a hard time arguing that he had fully and definitively broken with the conspiracy. What he actually said was:

"Wait here. I'll get my wallet and a jacket." He told Helen not to worry. He would try not to be late. He put his jacket over his shoulder and his cell phone in his pocket, being careful first to turn it off.

Richard knew that he was letting the impulse of the moment overpower his better judgment. But, he told himself, he could not let Bunker drive away in his present condition. In fact, the law would not permit him to do so. But most of all Richard's head was full of questions about the failed coup and what the feds might be up to. Bunker would be able to answer some of them.

"Give me those car keys, Gordon. I'll drive you home."

"No, that's *not* where we're going. I need another drink."

"It seems you've had one too many already."

"Who cares?" Bunker threw the keys to Richard but almost missed.

Richard didn't remember seeing the beige Camry that Bunker had come in. He took the wheel. On wobbly legs Bunker moved around to the passenger side, opened the door, and almost fell into the passenger seat, making the car rock. From old habit Richard turned on the radio as they drove off.

"Shut that damned radio off!" Bunker growled.

Richard did not do as he was told. Keeping his voice low he said, "It's a bad idea for us to meet in the first place, and it's an even worse idea for us to talk about anything sensitive. Especially with you in this condition."

"I already told you, I *have* to talk to you!"

"Is this car even clean?"

"Clean enough," Bunker muttered.

"What do you mean? Has it been swept for bugs or not?"

"Oh, c'mon, there's no need for that."

"Of course there is. We have to assume FBI surveillance."

"Dick, you're the most uptight, fastidious person I ever met. OK, so I used that little bug detector Hick gave me. I did it this morning, although this is my wife's car. But I'm telling you the FBI hasn't caught on yet. Turn the damned radio off, or do I have to do it?" Bunker reached for the button, but seemed uncertain of where it was. Richard deflected his hand and just lowered the volume. Bunker fell back in his seat.

As Richard steered in the general direction of Bunker's home in northern Virginia, he did a couple of sudden turns and then stopped the car to make sure they were not being followed.

"Really, Dick, stop it! And drive us to your favorite watering hole."

"I don't think any self-respecting bar would let you in, Gordon. And how would you know the FBI is not on your tail, or mine for that matter?"

"Because I pay attention, Dick, that's why, and because I've lots of friends in high places." Again he slightly slurred his words. "The feds are still investigating those Islamic terrorists. Perhaps that's all they'll ever do. They aren't stupid exactly, but for years the system's been geared to watch and hunt for Islamic extremists, and our disinformation campaign pointed them in the same direction. And, of course, their resources are stretched very thin because of all the investigations related to the protests and riots. Counties, cities, and states have been clamoring for federal assistance. To get federal help they point to the interstate dimension of so many of the demonstrations, the involvement of national unions, for example. Or take that walkout of flight controllers in New York, Atlanta, L.A., and Chicago just a couple of days before the coup attempt. I guess you were in France by then. The feds are way behind in their routine work. On top of their lack of resources, there's the general disorder and disruption in the country. When the FBI don't get anywhere in their search for the assassins or don't come up with some Islamic scapegoats, perhaps they'll begin looking for a connection between the perpetrators and the riots and demonstrations. There's a lot of anger out there. Some fanatics among the protesters, some skinheads, or survivalists, or anarchist kooks may have turned against the presidency. Where to start looking? And then, after a good long while of fruitless investigations, the president appoints a commission to figure out what really happened, like that Warren Commission that never got to the bottom of the Kennedy assassination."

"But how in the world could the FBI not get to the bottom of what happened? For example, how could they miss the clue in what Noah did."

"Poor Noah," Bunker sighed. "He got a garbled message about the assassinations, and he didn't think there was time to double-check. He just decided to act. You've got to admire his guts."

"But that gave the FBI a big fat angle to work on."

"Not really. As soon as Noah realized the president was alive he interrupted his operation. The Marines had barely taken off in those helicopters when he aborted the mission. No Marines were ever seen in D.C. So the whole thing never showed up on TV. It remained a kind of internal military matter. Noah was severely reprimanded. He was demoted to colonel and forced to retire. His stunt was just one weird event on a very confused day. And everybody thinks they know about gun-happy generals. *Cowboys*, aren't they? Just as we know who the really bad guys are—those terrorists and Islamic fascists. They're everywhere, aren't they? Besides we'd been pretty darn clever masking our moves, and the coup never got off the ground. Herbert shut it down the minute we knew the president was alive. Reed even got some kudos for acting so quickly to mobilize troops to protect Washington."

"But what about the killing of the vice president?"

"That was an incredibly clean operation. Bob had provided first-rate information and then created a diversion that widened the window of opportunity. The timing was just perfect. The coordination with the other operation was a marvel to behold. The guy shooting the missile at the president's car even managed to slip away. Beautiful! The Secret Service reprimanded Bob for violating some procedure, and he decided to retire."

Richard had been driving aimlessly. For lack of a goal he got back on River Road and headed in the direction of the Washington Beltway further west in Maryland. Rush hour traffic was rather heavy, and they got caught in lines at traffic lights. It was a rather warm, sunny fall evening, and many drivers had the tops down on their cars.

Bunker fell silent. Richard wondered whether he might be nodding off. But soon Bunker spoke again.

"What I wanted to talk to you about, Dick, is not any of that. What I need to talk to you about is Herbert."

The shock and the tension of seeing Bunker had pushed Vandenhorst's death into the back of Richard's mind.

"Herb was the best friend I ever had," Bunker said. Richard thought he detected something other than the effect of drink in Bunker's voice and glanced over at him. Tears were running down the cheeks of the tough, big retired admiral.

"I never knew a better man." Bunker made no effort to hide that he was crying. "Now what do you" — his question was interrupted by a sob — "say to *that*?"

Richard didn't know what to say. "I think I understand. I was very sad to read the article in the *Post*."

"You *understand*! You're very *sad*! Is that all you have to say?"

"What do you *expect* me to say?"

"Hell, I expect you to say what you really *think*!" Bunker was shouting through his tears.

"Then I'll tell you that I got a very bad shock this morning, and that I'm really grieving Herbert's passing."

"Oh, yeah? Didn't you think that he was a bad guy and that he *deceived* you?" Bunker said in a voice full of sarcasm.

"Well, I do think he kept some important things from me."

"And you thought that was enough for you to turn your back on him?"

"I had to follow my conscience."

"Your *conscience*, that precious *conscience*!" Bunker was no longer sobbing. "And what made you think that your conscience was so superior to Herb's?"

"I didn't assume that. But my conscience is the only one I've got."

"Hell, Dick, have you ever heard of humility?"

"Why ask rhetorical questions?"

"Has it ever occurred to you that we owe our elders some deference and respect?"

"Of course. And I did respect Herbert."

"But not enough to trust him. You, the bookish professor, had to second-guess this very experienced, knowledgeable man who knew a lot — from practice, not theory — about how the world works. You had to sit in moral judgment of *him*! You, who have only the intellectual's detached point of view — you had to lecture *him*!"

"I don't think being an intellectual has to make you a poorer judge of the world."

"I need a *drink*!" Bunker shouted — whether out of disgust with Richard's remark, out of sorrow, or out of thirst, Richard could not tell. Bunker looked outside and said, "The Beltway's coming up. We're almost at Congressional, my club, remember — just across the Beltway and up the hill! They won't turn me away there, certainly not after I've straightened myself out." Bunker tried to turn the visor to look at himself in the mirror. His reaching into a pocket of his slacks for a comb made the car sway.

Richard reluctantly followed Bunker's directions. They turned left off River Road into the Congressional Country Club access road with its guard booth. The meticulously kept grounds and impressive white buildings of Washington's most exclusive country club would again provide the background for a secretive conversation. Richard told Bunker to adjust his clothes.

"Will they let you in dressed like that this time of day?"

"In the sports bar, yes."

"Can you order a meal there?"

"Yes."

They drove to the main entrance to let the valet parkers take care of the car. Richard discreetly helped Bunker out of the car and to walk steadily through the building. They made it to the sports bar without incident. The bartender recognized Bunker and smiled in recognition. Because the evening sun did not reach the terrace and the temperature was now borderline for sitting outside, all tables there were empty except for two golfers who seemed to be finishing their beers. Richard steered Bunker to the table furthest away from the golfers.

"We should still keep our voices down," Richard said.

The outward setting could hardly be more pleasant. They were in a fairly high location and could look out over the gently rolling hills of one of the golf courses. The sun was disappearing behind distant trees and threw long furrows of golden light on the grass, trees, and brush. Flowers closer to the building completed the picture of countrified perfection.

A male waiter appeared with menus, and he too recognized Bunker.

"Good evening, Admiral. Anything to drink?"

"A double scotch on the rocks."

"A Heineken," Richard said.

The waiter disappeared.

"You'd better have something to eat," Richard said.

"I'm not hungry."

But when the waiter returned with the drinks and asked if they wanted to order any food, Richard immediately ordered a hamburger each. Bunker shrugged and gave a noncommittal wave of his hand. The waiter left.

Bunker reached for his drink and took a substantial sip. He put the glass down carelessly and spilled a little when the glass hit the table. He leaned forward in his chair, fixing Richard in his sight.

"I tell you, Herb was like a brother to me. My only brother."

Richard did not say anything. Bunker kept looking at Richard.

"He loved you, y'know."

Richard looked at Bunker, whose eyes were again getting misty.

"He and Celeste never had any children, and you became like a son to him. He never said so, but he didn't have to. He talked about you a lot. He had a very high opinion of you, and he really cared about you, and he worried about you."

"Worried about me?"

"Yes, he understood what it cost you to be a part of the conspiracy, how hard it was for you, with your family and all. You were surprisingly tough, but you were not an old hand at dealing with politics and conflict. You knew about it in theory, sure, but you had little direct experience of the rough stuff. Herb worried that you would have difficulty with the parts of the coup that took you too far from your normal territory. He worried that you might crack. But he loved you, Dick, and because he loved you, he took a chance on you. He looked out for you. After you left, he protected you. A couple of days before the coup we received some unnerving information — from Paris, don't you know — that you might be creating trouble for us there. There was disagreement about how to deal with you. I was not directly involved, but I heard that Noah didn't want to take any chances, if you know what I mean. But Herb was very clear. He protected you."

Richard swallowed. He was at once embarrassed, touched, and distressed by what Bunker had said.

"But he was right to worry about you," Bunker went on. "He shouldn't have brought you into the very heart of the conspiracy. A few of us wondered about it, but we trusted him. We thought he knew what he was doing. We could see with our own eyes that he was right to respect you. But he was taking too much of a risk. Herb didn't make many mistakes, but this was one of them. And why did he make it? Because of love, that's why. Because he liked you so much. He wanted to keep his picture of you. He indulged in a bit of wishful thinking." Bunker had been sipping his scotch, but it was now as if the drink was oiling his tongue rather than interfering with his articulation. The drink also made him more emotional.

"The grief you gave him over the plans to get rid of some of the bad guys bothered him a lot. He realized you were looking for a way out, and I think he also realized he'd concealed from himself the danger that one day you would do precisely that."

"No, Bob, I wasn't looking for a way out," Richard exclaimed. "I had deep moral misgivings, and I had to follow my conscience."

"It doesn't matter now what *you* thought you were doing. I'm talking about Herb and what *he* thought. He didn't think your reservations were as strong as you made them sound. You were too smart to mean what you said. He thought that our focusing on the execution plans simply deepened your general hesitation. The plans rattled you and became your excuse for withdrawing. The real reason was that you simply couldn't take the pressure any longer."

"That's simply wrong!" Richard almost shouted.

"*I'm telling you what Herb thought.*" Bunker had raised his voice and was speaking slowly. "And a few of the rest of us thought the same. I think your attitude regarding the executions bothered Herb all the more because in a way he'd known from the beginning that he was asking a little too much of you."

The waiter, who brought their food, interrupted Bunker.

"Bring me one more of these," Bunker said to the waiter, raising his almost empty glass. The waiter seemed to hesitate, but disappeared without a word.

Richard looked at his food, including a mountain of French fries, which would normally have made his mouth water. But he was now like Bunker. He had no appetite. He poked in the food with his fork, munched on a French fry and then put the fork down again.

"Did Herbert actually tell you he thought I was running away?" Richard finally said.

"Not in so many words. He didn't have to. I could tell he was very disappointed, and I think he blamed himself rather than you for what'd happened."

"There's another possible explanation for what you call his disappointment?"

"What would that be?"

"That my challenge disturbed him. That the executions bothered his conscience, too. After seeing my reaction he may have reconsidered his position and started to have doubts of his own."

Bunker rolled his eyes and was about to respond when the waiter placed his second double scotch in front of him. Bunker quickly drained the first drink and handed the glass to the waiter, who left.

"You should be eating something, Gordon, or those drinks will finish you off."

"You handle your own eating," Bunker said gruffly. "As far as I can see, you haven't touched your food, either."

Richard took a bite out of his hamburger and chewed dutifully. But he could not work up any appetite. Bunker's words were agitating the deepest reaches of his soul. In the corner of his eye he noticed that the two golfers were leaving. Richard and Bunker were alone on the terrace. It was dusk and getting cooler.

"I can tell you this," Bunker said, "that if Herb had any moral qualms about those executions, he didn't say peep about it to anybody else. If you think that, after you had left, there was discussion of changing the plans, you're mistaken. Nobody gave it a thought!"

"So Herbert and I had a simple disagreement."

"No, not simple, not simple at all! Not for Herb. Your making that big fuss and then bailing out really affected him. The others may not have noticed it, but I did. There was a kind of sadness about him after you left. Quite apart from that effect on him, your departure had — what's that word? — I think I may've had too much to drink — well — *ramifications*! That you left made a few others wobbly. It had an unsettling effect. You did have a special credibility with some of our people. We had to put out a couple of fires. A number of practical complications had to be handled in a hurry. There were all kinds of administrative ripple effects because Herb had involved you in so much. Your leaving was a big nuisance, let me tell you!"

Bunker stared at Richard.

"The musical chairs after you left was a part of the reason

for the communications slipup between central office and Montana on the day of the assassination attempts. If it hadn't been for that confusion, we might have gotten the president after all, and the coup would have come off."

Bunker fell silent, but kept looking at his companion. Richard averted his gaze. He had been deeply affected by Bunker's words — but he did not quite know why. If Bunker thought he could get Richard to take some of the responsibility for the failure of the coup, he was badly mistaken. Those planning cold-blooded murder had only themselves to blame, Richard said to himself, and they deserved to fail. How was it, then, that in a part of himself he seemed to be reproaching himself? For what?

For lack of anything else to do, he reached for his hamburger and tried to eat some of it. He chewed, but had difficulty swallowing.

To Richard's surprise, Bunker let his second drink just sit on the table. Instead he started fingering his French fries and put a few of them in his mouth. Bunker munched pensively. Suddenly he stopped eating and stared at Richard.

"Do you know what just sticks in my craw?" Bunker asked.

"No, do tell me."

"Your damned arrogance."

"*Arrogance!?*"

"Yes, *arrogance*, as in pride and as in being just *too damned full of yourself.*"

"You mean my paying any heed to conscience?"

"There it is again, that precious, fine conscience of yours! I do wonder about that. What is it really? Have you ever asked yourself if it might not be all that it's cracked up to be, that it's not working too well in unfamiliar circumstances?"

"Then there isn't much that I can do about it, is there? I still have to follow the one conscience I've got."

"*Listen* to you! Can't you hear the sanctimoniousness? If you weren't so damned conceited, it might have occurred to you to rely on the judgment of someone who really does know the real world, someone like Herb. But you assumed that you knew best, didn't you? You saw more deeply than anybody else, didn't you? You had a much finer conscience. You had no reason to give Herb the benefit of the doubt. No, in the end you treated him with the same moral condescension as you treated Noah, only a little more subtly, a little less confrontationally. You, Vandenhorst, are not at my moral level, you announced. And because you're not on my level, I can't associate with you any longer."

Richard felt both humiliated and indignant. He wanted to protest, but could not find the right words.

Bunker looked from Richard to his waiting fresh drink, but continued: "You worked with Herb for a very long time, following his directives, and you must have trusted him. I never heard you fight seriously with him before. But then, at the very end, at a very difficult time, when we could least afford it, you had to put your foot down—hard. Herb gets one little thing wrong—no, don't interrupt, I'm talking—and you think you must come down on him like a ton of bricks, just like that! Until then, Herb's conscience had apparently matched yours, but all of a sudden you realized you were the much better man. And if you couldn't have it your way, you wouldn't play anymore."

"Those killings were no *little thing*! For me they were a *big* thing."

"For you, you, and you. Herb had far greater experience of conflict and war than you, but you wouldn't give him the benefit of the doubt? Oh, no. And when—"

"All those *killings*, Bob—!"

"—were quite necessary *to make the coup stick*! We weren't undertaking a scouting project, were we? Herb wasn't organizing an afternoon tea party, was he? We were planning to overthrow the damned government of the United States, and we weren't performing an experiment. *We were playing for keeps*! Can you *understand* that? No, it had to be just he way the conscientious professor wanted, or nothing. You had such a concern for the sanctity of human life, didn't you?" Bunker made a grimace of disgust before continuing. "*Bullshit!* You were a bleeding heart about some of the most disgusting specimens of the human race, people who sold America down the river. They've not one iota of concern for anything other than their own personal advantage. They're criminals, big-time criminals! They exploit, they plunder, they kill, and they're ruthless. Government exists to *protect* us from people like that, not to facilitate their schemes. But to you, Dick, it was more important to keep those people alive than to ensure the success of the coup. How perverse is that!? And that's what your *conscience* demanded? I don't give a rat's ass for your conscience."

Richard wanted to lash out verbally at Bunker, but all he could produce was a meek, "Those people were human beings, Bob."

"Well, weren't you nice to look out for them! Human beings, indeed. No, those people are scum, and the worst of it is you *knew* it! Do I need to remind you of some of their names?"

"Don't bother."

"No, you know who they are. Still, instead of trusting Herb to know what he was doing, you spoke out for those people and turned your back on him. You *betrayed* him!"

"I *didn't* betray him. He deceived *me*!"

"C'mon. You're fooling yourself. Herb got you right. You were looking for a way out—a pretext. You just couldn't hack it any longer."

Richard half rose from his chair in anger and protest. He pointed to Bunker and said loudly, "What makes you think you know better than I what was on my mind!? How *dare* you!?" Anger rising in his chest, Richard wanted to make a devastating comment and walk away. But he could barely think straight. He finally sank back in his chair. He wanted to leave but could not move.

Silence descended over the scene. Bunker looked at his drink without seeing or touching it.

"You may not know yourself as well as you think," Bunker said in a tone of voice that had now lost its edge and belligerence. "Think about this," he said pensively. "Even if Herb had withheld some information from you—to protect your tender feelings perhaps—why would you be so unwilling to believe that he was acting for the good of the cause, that he might actually understand the needs of the situation better than you did? Had he struck you as an unreliable, shifty, dirty double-dealer?" Some sarcasm crept back into Bunker's voice.

"We all have our weaknesses and blind spots."

"Except *you*, you mean? What if in this instance the weakness and the blindness were all on *your* side?"

Bunker's words cut deeply, but his tone of voice was no longer provocative or hostile. His earlier feistiness had dissipated. It sounded more as if he were helping Richard to analyze what was actually the case. He spoke without apparent emotion, almost as if making philosophical points. What he had just said disturbed Richard, but he no longer felt the same urge to punish his tormentor.

"Perhaps I've been a little too hard on you, Richard. I've had too much to drink. Considering your background, you did pretty well. You were surprisingly tough for a long time, lived up to Herb's expectations. And you may have been the one who carried the day for Herbert that day in O'Brien's basement, the time when Herb forced the issue and insisted that we all get behind plan B. You were able then to take the pressure and to put any doubts aside for the good of the whole. Herb admired that. He mentioned it several times later. But there were limits to what you could handle. There are limits to what any of us can handle. You'd lived your life in protected, cushioned surroundings. Your imagination failed when you had to size up a very unusual situation — unusual for you. Because your imagination could not adapt, all that ambivalence in you overwhelmed you."

Richard wanted to contradict Bunker, but he did not respond immediately. The old admiral's words had a strange and disturbing incisiveness that made Richard unsure of what to think or say. He just looked at Bunker, whose great bulk filled to overflowing the garden chair in which he was sitting. Bunker had become more and more contemplative. Was he turning morose? Was he finally going to pass out from all the drinking? But his gaze appeared clearer and sharper than at any time during the evening.

Richard finally spoke. "Why are you so preoccupied with me, Gordon? So I left the conspiracy. I fell short in your eyes. So what? Why beat me over the head? I couldn't have been all that important. You failed all on your own. It sounds, Gordon, as if you are looking for someone to blame, somebody other than the ones who actually attempted the coup."

"No, Dick, it's not that. I'm grieving." Bunker wiped his nose with the back of his hand. "I'm grieving 'cause I lost my brother. I'm grieving 'cause my country is going to the dogs. And I'm grieving 'cause human beings are so damned pitiful."

"I suppose you mean me in particular."

Bunker struggled to sit up straight in his chair. Richard wondered if he was finally going to down his untouched drink. Bunker put his hands on the table, but left the drink where it was. He leaned closer to Richard.

"Dick, Herb really liked you and cared about you. Your leaving was a hard blow at a time when he didn't need one. He carried a tremendous weight on his shoulders. He thought that he had lost you, a virtual son. The debacle of the coup finished him off, Richard. He was a broken man after that. He knew that all of his work, all of our work, had been for naught. The old-timers will be fading from the scene, and the younger generation have been too affected and infected by this disgusting, corrupt regime and culture. They don't really know what they're doing. They have no real, historical memory of what America was and could be, have only some very abstract notions. The ones who speak about defending American principles today are just a bunch of superficial ideologues and yahoos. Herb's losing you was the personal side of his great failure. That the coup didn't come off was to him a sign that it's all over for America. We're going the way of all other empires in history. All that remains is for Americans and others to suffer through the rest of the great disintegration. It won't be pretty. My God, people have no idea."

Bunker sank deeper into his chair. Richard could see that

his eyes were once more glistening. The drink just sat there. Bunker did not bother to hide another sob. Soon tears were rolling down his cheeks again. He was lost in his own thoughts.

But suddenly Bunker reached for the napkin and wiped his eyes and nose. He bent forward and caught Richard's gaze.

"Let me ask you a question, Dick."

"Go ahead."

When Bunker spoke he did so in a slow, deep voice made gravelly by his tears:

"Are you happy now?"

The question hung between them in the autumn air at the Congressional Country Club, where, to judge by appearances, everything was always right with the world. Richard did not quite know how to respond, and he took his time.

So Bunker spoke again:

"The choice for you, Dick, was between an imperfect coup and no coup. You didn't want an imperfect coup, so what you got, the status quo, must be what you wanted. Right?"

## ACKNOWLEDGMENTS

A number of people commented on the manuscript for this novel in whole or in part at one stage or another or assisted me in other ways. Because it might seem to imply that I did not value all the help I received, I will not single out particular persons for their interest and kindness. But you know who you are, and I greatly appreciate your help. Special thanks go to my friend and colleague Joseph Baldacchino, whose assistance extended beyond literary matters to editorial and technical support.

                     —C.G.R.

## ABOUT THE AUTHOR

CLAES G. RYN has lived for most of his adult life in Washington, D.C., where he is Professor of Politics at the Catholic University of America. He and his wife reside outside the District line in Potomac, Maryland. His teaching and research have focused on politics as it relates to philosophy, history, culture, and ethics. Ryn has taught also at Georgetown University, the University of Virginia, and Louisiana State University. He has lectured widely in the United States, Europe, and China. A frequent visitor to China, he gave the Distinguished Foreign Scholar Lectures at Peking University in 2000 and was named Honorary Professor at Beijing Normal University in 2012. He is the author of many scholarly books. In addition to numerous scholarly articles, he has published much writing in newspapers and magazines. He appears with some frequency on radio and television.

www.ingramcontent.com/pod-product-compliance
Lightning Source LLC
Chambersburg PA
CBHW032250020726
47495CB00001B/36